FIRE SEEING . . .

Sioned knelt in the goddess' grove, gazing into the still pool where her future waited. She summoned Fire, and tiny flames burned at her call atop the rock cairn. The Air of her own breath fanned them higher, brighter, until they were clearly reflected in the Water. She plucked a single hair from her head to represent the special portions of the Earth from which she had been made, and floated the strand on the still water.

The Fire leaped higher on the rocks, startling her. And in the Water, the reflection of her face transformed into the face of the woman she would become. The Fire flared again. Another face was next to hers now, burning with a light of its own through the mirrored flames. It was a man's face, fair hair sweeping across a wide brow to shade river-blue eyes, a face with strong bones, yet with a gentleness to balance the stubborn line of the jaw.

Fire slid down the rocks, igniting the pool, and Sioned drew back with a cry of fright. The single red-gold hair floating on the water writhed, became a thin rivulet of flame that crossed the man's forehead like the circlets worn by princes—and then extended to form the same royal crown for her. . . .

*　　*　　*

"I thoroughly and completely enjoyed DRAGON PRINCE— and you know my long-standing involvement with dragons. These are quite different and rather marvelous. . . . Impressive: good detail, good plotline (several of them), and the fascinating use of light to communicate. Laser beams, move over!"
　　　　　　　　　　　—Anne McCaffrey,
　　　　　　　　author of *Dragonriders of Pern* novels

DRAGON PRINCE

BOOK I

MELANIE RAWN

DAW BOOKS, INC.

DONALD A. WOLLHEIM, FOUNDER

375 Hudson Street, New York, NY 10014

ELIZABETH R. WOLLHEIM
SHEILA E. GILBERT
PUBLISHERS

http://www.dawbooks.com

Cover art by Michael Whelan.

For color prints of Michael Whelan paintings,
please contact:

Glass Onion Graphics
P.O. Box 88
Brookfield, CT 06804

Maps by Marty Siegrist

DAW Book Collectors No. 764.

First Printing, December 1988
35 34 33 32 31

DAW TRADEMARK REGISTERED
U.S. PAT. OFF. AND FOREIGN COUNTRIES
—MARCA REGISTRADA
HECHO EN U.S.A.

PRINTED IN THE U.S.A.

to my mother
Alma Lucile Rawn

and to the memory of my father
Robert Dawson Rawn

DRAGON PRINCE

PART ONE

Faces in Fire

Chapter One

Prince Zehava squinted into the sunlight and smiled his satisfaction. All the signs were good for the hunt today: claw marks on the cliffs, wing marks on the sand, and the close cropping of bittersweet plants along the canyon ridges. But the prince's perceptions were more subtle and had no need of these obvious signs. He could feel the presence of his prey all along his skin, scent it in the air, sense it in every nerve. His admirers said he could tell when the time was ripe for the hunt simply by glancing at the sky. His enemies said it was not surprising that he could sense such things, for he himself had been dragon-spawned.

In truth, he seemed a human version of the dragon he hunted today. A long, proud nose reared out of a lean and predatory face, saved from ruthlessness by the humor lurking at the corners of his mouth. Nearly sixty winters had framed his eyes with deep lines, but his body was still tough and supple, his pose in the saddle easy, his back straight as his sword. The proudest of old dragons was Zehava, a cloak as black as his eyes billowing out behind him like wings as he rode a tall black war-horse into the Desert he had ruled for thirty-four winters.

"We advance, my prince?"

Zehava glanced at his son-by-marriage. "We advance," he replied in the time-honored formula, then grinned. "We most certainly advance, Chay, unless your sword arm is already growing tired."

The young man grinned back. "The only time it ever did was when we fought the Merida, and then only a little, and only because you kept tossing so many in my direction!"

"Tobin wanted to boast of your prowess, and I've never been able to deny my daughter anything." He pressed his heels to the horse's ribs and the troop advanced into the Desert behind him, bridles muffled and saddles devoid of the usual trappings that might clatter a warning to the dragon.

"Another ten measures, I make it," Chaynal said.

"Five."

"Ten! That son of the Storm Devil will be holed up in the hills and strike from there."

"Five," Zehava said again. "And he'll be at the mouth of Rivenrock like High Prince Roelstra at Castle Crag."

Chaynal's handsome face pulled into a grimace. "And here I was enjoying myself. Why did you have to mention *him*?"

Zehava laughed. Inwardly, however, he was wishing that this fine young man was truly the son of his body, his heir. He felt much closer to Chay than he did to his blood son, Prince Rohan—a slight, quiet youth given to study and thoughtfulness rather than devotion to the manly arts. Rohan was a credible swordsman, an excellent hunter of everything but dragons, and a cunning whirlwind in a knife fight, but Zehava found his son incomprehensible in that these things were not the end and aim of life to him. Rohan's taste for books and learned discussion was utterly beyond Zehava's understanding. Honesty compelled him to admit that Chaynal had interests other than the hunt and the skirmish, but at least he did not prefer those other things to all else. Yet when Zehava attempted to press Rohan into other activities, his own wife and daughter flew at him like furious she-dragons.

Zehava grinned to himself as he rode through the scorching heat toward Rivenrock Canyon. Tobin should have been born the male child. As a young girl she had been able to out-ride and out-knife any boy her age. Marriage and motherhood had calmed her, but she was still capable of black-eyed rages to match Zehava's own. Part of Chaynal's marriage contract stipulated that she was forbidden to bring a dagger into their bedchamber. Chay's idea of a joke, of course, which had brought

howls of laughter from everyone—including Tobin—but
it added to the family legend, which was something Zehava
despaired of·Rohan ever doing.

Not that Tobin was lacking in femininity, he mused,
glancing at Chaynal again. Only a completely enchanting
woman could have captured and held the fiery young
Lord of Radzyn Keep. After six years of marriage and
the birth of twin sons, the princess and her lord were as
besotted with each other as ever. A pity Rohan hadn't
yet found himself a girl to stiffen his spine and his manhood. There was nothing like the desire to impress a
pretty girl to turn boy into man.

Zehava's prediction proved accurate: the dragon had
chosen the lookout spire at the canyon mouth for his
perch. The hunt paused a full measure away to admire
the beast, dark gold as the sands that had hatched him,
with a wingspan greater than the height of three tall men.
His malignant glare could be felt even at this distance.

"A real grandsire of a beast," Chay murmured appreciatively. "Have a care, my prince."

Zehava took the caution as it had been intended, not
as a warning that he might lose this contest, but as a
reminder not to damage himself during it. If he came
home with more than a few scratches, his wife would
alternately coddle his injuries and rage at his clumsiness
in acquiring them. Princess Milar was as legendary for
her temper as for the golden looks, so rare here in the
Desert, that she had passed on to her son.

The twenty riders fanned out, taking up positions according to the etiquette of the game, and Zehava rode
forward alone. The dragon eyed him balefully, and the
prince smiled. This was a profoundly angry beast. The
stench of oil was rank in the hot air, oozing from glands
at the base of the long, spiked tail. He was ready to mate
the females hidden in their caves, and anyone who distracted him from his purpose was marked for a painful
death.

"Hot for it, aren't you, Devil-jaws?" Zehava crooned
low in his throat. He rode at a steady pace, his cloak
blowing back from his shoulders, and stopped half a
measure in front of the rocky spire. Striated sandstone in

a dozen shades of amber and garnet rose like the Flametower at Zehava's castle of Stronghold. The dragon clung to the stone with claws thick as a man's wrist, balance easily kept despite the repeated lashings of the gold-and-black patterned tail. The two rulers of the Desert sized each other up. On the surface it was a ludicrously unequal contest: the massive, dagger-toothed dragon against one man on horseback. But Zehava had an advantage that had made him the champion in such encounters nine times before, more than any man living and part of the family legend. Zehava understood dragons.

This one burned to fill his dozen or more females, but he was growing old and knew it. There were battle scars on the dark golden hide, and one talon hung at an unnatural angle, damaged in some earlier combat. As the great wings unfurled threateningly, showing the velvety black undersides, badly healed tears were visible as well as crooked wingbones that had not remeshed properly after breaking. This might be the dragon's last mating, and Zehava suspected that the beast knew it.

Nevertheless, he was capable of giving the prince a good long battle. But Zehava understood something else about dragons. Though notoriously cunning, they were entirely single-minded. This one wanted to mate. His fighting style would thus be direct and unsubtle, without the tricks a dragon used once mating was over for another three years. He had already been inhaling the stench of his own sexuality for days during the preliminaries— the sand-dance and the cliff-dance that had attracted his females to him. His brain was drugged now and his fighting wits would be dulled, for his one purpose was to seed his females and this made him at once more vicious and more vulnerable. Though Zehava had a healthy respect for those talons and teeth, he could also grin in his anticipation of a tenth triumph. He was going to outthink this grandsire dragon, and have a rousing good time doing it.

Fifty measures distant, in a fortress that had been carved out of solid rock by successive generations of Zehava's family, Princess Milar sat with her sister Lady

Andrade. The two were silent for the present; the entrance of a servant into the solar with cool drinks and fruit had interrupted a stormy passage between the twin sisters on the subject of Prince Rohan.

When the servant had bowed and departed, Lady Andrade flicked her long blonde braid back over her shoulder and glared at her sister. "Stop fussing the boy! Things are brewing in Roelstra's court that Zehava can't hope to understand, but Rohan will!"

"Are you calling my husband a fool?" Milar snapped.

"Save your theatrics, Mila. He's a brilliant soldier and a fine man, but if you think the coming conflict will be one of arms, think again. The Storm God alone knows what Roelstra's planning, but it won't be something to march an army against." She reached over and plucked a bunch of grapes from a bowl, subjecting their ruby gloss to a critical inspection. "You may think your princedom too rich and powerful to be threatened. But the High Prince is constitutionally incapable of abiding anyone richer than he. And Zehava hasn't been exactly subtle about his wealth. I heard about the birthday present he sent Roelstra."

"It was entirely in keeping with—"

"With Zehava's conceit! Two horses or even four, nicely caparisoned, would have been fine. But twenty! And all in silver! He's flaunting his riches, Mila, and that's dangerous—like this imbecile dragon hunt today. He's killed nine of the monsters, why does he need a tenth?"

Princess Milar wore an expression before which scores of highborns had quailed; her face was none the less lovely for its icy hauteur. "It's his duty to rid the Desert of dragons. It also demonstrates the cunning and strength which are so important in war. That's politics."

"That's stupidity. Better he should have sent Rohan out to kill this dragon, so his *heir's* cunning and strength are made clear." Andrade popped a grape into her mouth and split the skin with her teeth, drawing off the sweet juices before spitting out the remains into a silver bowl provided for the purpose.

"Rohan has no heart for fighting dragons," Milar admitted unhappily.

"But he's warrior enough with heart enough," Andrade pointed out. "Dressing in common trooper's uniform that last campaign against the Merida when you'd forbidden him to leave Stronghold—"

"We've never worried about his spirit. But you know he spends too much time at his books and talking with the most unlikely people. I've defended him in the past, but now I'm beginning to agree with Zehava. Rohan ought to learn how to be the kind of prince his forefathers were."

"That's precisely what he doesn't need to learn! Building a princedom is fine work for a soldier, and Zehava's done very well. He consolidated what his grandfather began, strengthened his hold on what his father grabbed from the Merida, and enlarged the whole through his own efforts. Actually," Andrade said in thoughtful tones, "one can't blame him for wanting to show off. He's worked wonders, especially against the Merida."

"If I required a history lesson, I would send for my bard," Milar snapped.

Andrade ignored her remark. "Zehava's problem is that he's run out of things to do. All he can think of is to spend money on you and Tobin and this pile of rock we're sitting in—and to waste his time killing dragons. Believe me, sister dear, Roelstra can think of many occupations for his own time, and none of them healthy as far as you're concerned."

"I fail to see—"

"You usually do," Andrade interrupted. "Let Rohan read his books and talk with the ambassadors—yes, and even with the servants of the ambassadors! He'll learn things that Zehava could never teach him."

"Why don't you go back to your duties in that moldy old keep of yours, and leave the work of the world to the people who can do it?"

"What do you think I do in my moldy old keep—knit?" Andrade snorted and picked out another fat grape. "While I'm training silly boys and girls to be good *faradh'im*, I listen to them. And what I hear these days isn't pleasant, Mila." She began ticking off points on her long, slender fingers, each one circled by a gold or silver ring with a different gemstone. The rings were linked by tiny chains across the backs of her palms to the bracelets of her office as Lady of Goddess Keep. "One, Roelstra doesn't plan to make war against anyone, so Zehava's show of strength and skill in hunting dragons counts for nothing. Two, the High Prince has agents in every court—including yours."

"Impossible!" Milar scoffed.

"Your wine steward has a nasty look about him, and I wouldn't vouch for your assistant stablemaster, either. Three, the High Prince has seventeen daughters, some of them legitimate off poor, dead Lallante. All of them need husbands. Where will Roelstra find eligible men for them? I'll tell you where: from the most important courts, even for the bastard girls."

The princess sat up straight on the blue velvet lounge. "Do you mean an offer might come for Rohan?"

"Good for you!" Andrade exclaimed in a voice that dripped sarcasm. "Yes, an offer will be made. Can you think of a more eligible young man than your son? He's rich, of the noblest blood, he'll rule this wasteland someday—which, though not a recommendation in itself, does imply a certain amount of power. And he's not all that difficult to look at."

"My son is the handsomest young man on the continent!" Milar defended. "He's perfectly beautiful and I—"

"And a perfect virgin?"

Milar shrugged. "Zehava says you can tell a woman from a maiden just by the way she walks, but I've never heard of a similar test for boys. But what does it matter? It's the prince's bride who should come virgin to the marriage bed, not the prince himself."

"I only wanted to know if he's heart-whole. He's not the type to spread every pair of female thighs he can find just for the fun of it. Rohan's the romantic kind, poor thing." She mused on this for a moment, then sighed. "In any case, an offer will be made regarding one of the legitimate princesses, because a bastard would be an insult to your house, and—"

"But that's wonderful!" Milar's blue eyes shone beneath the sunsilk of her hair. "The honor of it—and the dowry! We must be sure to ask for Feruche Castle. Rohan couldn't do better than a daughter of the High Prince!"

"Mila, think. You'll be allied to Roelstra by marriage—"

"I *have* thought! He would hardly attack his daughter's husband!"

"Listen to me! Rohan and his princess will have sons who will one day rule the Desert. What would be more natural than for the grandson of the High Prince to annex his holdings to his beloved grandsire's?"

"Never! The Treaty of Linse gives the Desert to Zehava's family for as long as the sands spawn fire."

"Very pretty. A direct quote, I take it? But the Desert will continue to belong to Zehava's family through Rohan. It will also belong to Roelstra's, through the daughter he sends as Rohan's bride. The High Prince is only forty-five this year, Mila. Let me conjure a vision for you."

The princess' eyes went wide. "No! Andrade, you mustn't! Not here!"

"With words only, sister. Say Rohan marries this girl, whichever one it is. I can never keep them all straight. Say they have a child within two years. Roelstra will be forty-seven. Say he lives to be eighty. It's not unlikely. His grandfather was ninety-three when he died—"

"And his father barely twenty-eight."

"Pathetic age. I've always had my suspicions about that bottle of bad brandy said to have caused his death. But where was I? Ah, yes. Zehava is sixty this year and doesn't come of a long-lived clan. Oh, don't go all teary-eyed on me, Mila. He'll probably prove me a liar just for spite and live to be a hundred and thirty-five. But say something happens to him before the grandsons are grown. Rohan becomes prince. Say further that something happens to Rohan—and believe me, my dear, when his sons are past the usual childhood illnesses, Rohan will be expendable. This leaves us the widowed princess, her sons of ten or twelve winters—and Roelstra hale and hearty, not even the age Zehava is right now."

"A ridiculous fantasy!" Milar exclaimed, but shadows were in her eyes.

"If you like. Another conjuring with words. Rohan really becomes unnecessary once he's fathered a son or two on this girl. With him out of the way and Zehava as caretaker for the boys until they come of age, Roelstra could let your husband die in his bed and *still* do anything he likes once the grandson inherits."

Lady Andrade applied herself to the grapes and waited for her twin to absorb the implications. Truly, Andrade had no idea why she bothered with this lovely lackwit sister of hers. Milar had inherited all the looks in the family, leaving Andrade to get by on the brains and energy. What was delicate gold in Milar was ruddy in Andrade; the temper for which both women were well-known was a flashfire rage in Milar, but carefully calculated in Andrade. Milar was perfectly happy being wife to a rather remarkable man (Andrade could admit Zehava's virtues in private), mother to his children, and running his fortress. Andrade would never have been content with that life. She might have married a man through whom she could have controlled vast stretches of the continent, but as Lady of Goddess Keep she ruled more lands indirectly than even Roelstra. Her *faradh'im*, commonly called Sunrunners, were everywhere, and through them she influenced or downright controlled every prince and lord between the Dark and Sunrise Waters.

She supposed she bothered with Milar because of Rohan. He took after neither of his parents in personality—nor did he resemble Andrade, so it was not herself in masculine guise she saw in him. He was unique, and she valued him for that. Milar loved the boy devotedly, and Zehava was just as fond of Rohan, though puzzled by him. Andrade alone understood him and had glimpsed what he might become.

"I see your point, Andri," Milar was saying slowly. "I wish you had explained it all clearly to begin with. We'll simply have to reject the High Prince's offer when it comes."

Lady Andrade sighed. "How?" she asked succinctly,

wondering if her sister was entirely the fool she sometimes acted.

The princess' face, scarcely lined even after nearly thirty years in the harshness of the Desert, wrinkled now in alarm. "An open refusal would be a horrible insult! Roelstra would be down on us like a dragon on a yearling!" She fretted silently for a moment, then smiled. "Zehava can win any battle. If Roelstra dares attack, he'll slink back to Castle Crag in total defeat!"

"You *idiot*!" Andrade snarled, totally out of patience. "Have you heard nothing of what I've said? Didn't you listen to points four, five, and six?"

"I didn't listen because you didn't tell me!" Milar flared. "How can you expect me to make a decision when you withhold information?"

"Sorry," Andrade muttered. "Very well then, point four—Prince Chale of Ossetia is in Roelstra's camp with a trade agreement they will make public at the Rialla this year. Five, Lord Daar of Gilad Seahold needs a wife and wants a princess. Point six—and for the same reasons— that piece of offal, Prince Vissarion of Grib, is also on Roelstra's side. Do you seriously think Zehava can stand against all of them in addition to the allies Roelstra openly admits to? They've all seen what you and Zehava have built here. The Desert will never be a garden, but you've made parts of it into nearly that. This keep, Chaynal's Radzyn, Tiglath and Tuath and Whitecliff Manor—all the work done by Zehava's ancestors is finally bearing fruit. Don't you think they'd all love an excuse to pluck the tree bare? An insult to a High Prince's daughter would give them a fine reason to avenge her honor, especially if some of them are married or betrothed to her sisters." She stopped, seeing by her twin's stricken face that Milar at last understood the gravity of her position—or, more to the point, Rohan's.

"Andri," she breathed, "if all this is as you say, then what can we do? I can't let Rohan marry one of Roelstra's daughters—I'd be lighting his pyre! And if we refuse—"

"Oh, Rohan will be married, and soon," Andrade said, having worked her sister around to exactly where she wanted her. "I have just the girl for him. Roelstra can't propose a marriage to a man who's already wed, now can he?"

The princess sagged back in her chair. "Is she pretty?" she asked forlornly. "What's her family like?"

"Very pretty," Andrade soothed, "and very well-born. But even if she was ugly as a she-dragon and born of a whore, she'd still be perfect for Rohan." Andrade tossed the stripped grapestem into a bowl and smiled. "My dear Mila, the girl has a *brain*."

The midday heat was suffocating. Lord Chaynal watched his father-by-marriage battle it out with the dragon, wiped sweat from his forehead, and wondered how long this was going to take. Blood oozed from nicks in the dragon's golden hide, and a long slash had been cut into one wing; by its twitchings, a nerve had been hit as well. The dragon snarled his fury as Zehava toyed with him. But it was taking a long time to subdue the beast, and Chay was getting worried.

The other riders were restless, too. They were still in semicircular formation, having moved back only a little when the dragon leaped off his perch to attack Zehava from the sand at the canyon mouth. The decision of whether or not to charge was Chaynal's, and he was under orders not to do so unless there was no other choice. All those men and women present had had practice with lesser dragons, for Zehava was a generous prince and liked everyone to come away with a tooth or talon as a souvenir of between-years hunts. But the prince himself was the only one allowed to kill mating sires like this one, and nobody interfered without excellent reason.

Chay began to fret, wishing for the cool sea winds of Radzyn Keep. The air swirled around him with every angry beat of dragon wings, but the heat sucked sweat out of him and dried it instantly on his skin, giving the air no chance to cool the perspiration. He squinted into the canyon where merciless sunlight reflected off the rocks, then looked away, closing his eyes for a few heartbeats to ease the ache of glare. Shifting in his saddle, he sensed his unease being communicated to his horse. Silver-tufted

ears flattened back and quivers chased each other through
silken muscles beneath a glossy black hide.

"Patience, Akkal," Chay murmured. "He knows what
he's doing." Chay hoped so, anyway. Much time had
passed since the dragon had chosen his ground and Zehava
had drawn first blood. The prince's movements were
slower and the curvettes of his great war-stallion were
growing sluggish. It appeared to Chay that the two old
warriors, dragon and prince, were evenly matched now.

The dragon roared and snapped at Zehava, whose
horse barely got him out of the way in time. Rocks
clattered in the caves within the canyon, and the whimpers of waiting females rose to a whine. Each of them
was safe and nervous and anxious to be alone with her
chosen mate, calling out to him in plaintive demand for
his presence.

Akkal trembled again and Chay calmed the horse. To
distract himself from growing concern as Zehava narrowly avoided talons and teeth, Chay began to calculate
how many females would die unmated in the caves and
how many eggs would lie unfertilized once this dragon
was dead. Fifteen females, perhaps, with twenty or so
eggs each, of which five or six at most might survive to
fly. Multiply this number by the nine other sires Zehava
had killed in mating years, plus their females, and the
total was staggering. Yet there were always more dragons. The Desert gave forth hundreds of hatchlings every
three summers that roamed over the princedoms ravaging
crops and herds. Killing the mating sires was the most
efficient way of cutting down the population, for the
unmated females and their unfertilized eggs were lost,
too. But even this was a losing proposition in the end.
There were always more dragons.

Chaynal sighed and stroked Akkal's neck. Zehava's
power rested in part on his ability to cut down the dragon
population. Would Rohan be able to do as much when
his turn came? It was not a happy thought. Fond as he
was of his wife's brother, and much as he sincerely respected Rohan's gifts, he knew the young prince hadn't
the stomach for killing dragons. Strength in battle as
demonstrated by these hunts was an integral part of the

Desert's power. What other basis for rule was there than military victory?

Chay's own family had guarded the Desert's one safe port for generations, their prestige firmly based on providing and protecting trade. He was honest enough—and had enough of a sense of humor—to acknowledge that his forebears' original power had come from baldfaced piracy; the money to build Radzyn Keep had not come from port fees legitimately gathered. In these civilized days, fast ships bearing the red-and-white Radzyn banner no longer roamed the Small Islands or hid in coves waiting for rich merchantmen. Nowadays his ships patrolled the waters to keep them safe. But war and thievery endured in his family line, he reminded himself with a whimsical smile. He had fought with great enjoyment as Zehava's battle commander, and every three years at the Rialla he entertained himself with legal robbery when he sold his horses. Fighting battles and outsmarting one's trading partners: these were excellent bases for power. Rohan had shown himself a capable warrior that memorable day against the Merida—though he'd nearly given his parents apoplexy when they had discovered his unauthorized presence—and he was clever enough when he chose to be. But Rohan was not a warrior by choice, nor an instinctive bargainer.

Chay's attention was pulled back to the battle before him as the dragon's wings spread and cast a shadow across the sun. He circled upward on thermals and bellowed his fury, then hurtled down with claws extended toward Zehava. The prince calculated the leap to a hair's breadth, waiting until the last instant before hauling his outraged stallion around out of range. As he did so, his sword slashed a bloody rent in the dragon's hide. The beast screamed in agony and a muted cheer went up from the other riders as the dragon's hind legs sank into soft sand, wings flapping as he struggled for purchase. Zehava swung his horse around and stabbed the dragon's flank just behind the left wing. The females in their caves howled in response to their mate's shriek.

Chay began to feel better. Zehava was still every bit the prince he had always been, skills and cunning intact.

The dragon was bleeding now, his movements and breathing labored. But the fire in his eyes was unquenched, and as he regained his footing he swerved around with death in his hot gaze.

Princess Tobin loved her children dearly, but did not feel compelled to spend her time looking after them. At her husband's keep there were servants enough to make sure the twin boys were fed, taught, and kept out of serious mischief while their parents ran the vast estates. Here at Stronghold on their annual visit there were yet more servants happy to attend the young lords. So when she heard laughter from the main courtyard outside her windows, she assumed the boys were being entertained by one or another of the grooms. She glanced outside to find Jahni astride a dappled pony and Maarken riding a bay, each child brandishing a wooden sword at a young man who flourished a crimson cloak like dragon wings. But the twins' playmate was definitely not one of the grooms.

"Rohan!" she called down to the courtyard. "Whatever are you doing?"

"Dragon, Mama!" Jahni shouted, waving his sword. "Watch me!"

As the twins attempted to ride down the heir to the Desert Princedom, Tobin shook her head in fond exasperation. She dismissed her secretary and hurried to the staircase, muttering to herself. "Honestly! Wrapped around their fingers! A prince in *his* position, playing dragon for a couple of five-year-olds!" But there was affection in her voice and as she emerged from the foyer into the courtyard she laughed as Rohan, dealt a glancing blow on his "wing" by Maarken's sword, fluttered the cloak and sank to the ground like a dying dragon.

Tobin regarded her loudly triumphant offspring with a sigh, then turned to her brother. "Do get up from there and stop playing the fool," she scolded. He peeked up at her, bright-eyed, from under the cloak. "And as for you," she said to her sons, "take those ponies back to their stalls and don't come back until you've seen to their comfort. Your grandsire didn't give them to you to have you neglect them."

"I killed the dragon, Mama, did you see?" Maarken exulted.

"Yes, darling, I saw, and a very good warrior you are, too. Now, you'll excuse the dragon while he talks with me for a while, won't you?"

The dragon stood up and brushed courtyard dirt from his clothes. "I've heard it said that dragons have a taste for gobbling up princesses—the prettier the better."

"Not *this* princess," Tobin said firmly, then laughed as Rohan began to stalk her, cloak flapping. "You wouldn't dare!"

The twins squealed with glee as he rushed forward and folded her in his cloak. Ignoring her cries of protest, he dumped her unceremoniously into the horse trough. Tobin spluttered, spat water, and glared at her brother.

"Hot as a hatching cave today," he observed casually, and climbed in beside her.

She swept his feet out from under him with a well-placed kick. He collapsed in the knee-deep water, yelling his outrage. "Ever seen a drowned dragon?" she asked sweetly, and hastily backed off as he made a grab for her.

"You've just about drowned a prince!" he grinned, slicking back wet hair.

Tobin gathered up her sopping skirts and climbed out of the trough. "If you two don't want to share a similar fate . . ." she warned her sons playfully.

It was invitation enough. They bounced off their ponies and jumped into the trough for a water fight. She gleefully joined in, helping the boys dunk Rohan thoroughly. At last—breathless, soaked, and victorious—the boys went off to tend their ponies. Rohan picked himself up and climbed out of the trough and grinned at Tobin.

"There! You've been looking entirely too regal and serious the last few days. Now you look human again."

She batted at his wet blond head. "Imbecile! Come on, let's go dry off in the garden where no one will see us. Mother will have us skinned if we drip all over her new Cunaxan rugs."

Rohan slung a companionable arm around her shoulders as they walked through the courtyard to the garden gates. The flowers were in their best late-spring bloom and once again Tobin marveled at the miracle that had brought roses to the Desert. The transformation had begun when she was a child, and by now she could barely remember a time when Stronghold had not been as gracious and comfortable as it was now. Radzyn's luxuries she took for granted, but her soul still belonged to the Stronghold of her ancestors, and she gloried in the beauty her mother had brought to this place.

She chose a stone bench in full sunlight and spread her skirts out to dry. Rohan obliged her by unplaiting her long black braids and helping her finger-comb her hair.

"Remember when Father used to play dragon for us?" he asked.

"And you always let me have the best chance at him," she replied fondly. "He didn't have quite your flair with a cloak, though. You're a born actor."

"I hope so," he answered a bit grimly.

"Jahni and Maarken adore you," Tobin went on, pretending not to have noticed his tone of voice. "You'll make a wonderful father to your own boys."

"Not you, too," he muttered. "Mother's been talking of nothing else all spring. At the *Rialla* she'll find me some fecund, bovine fool of a noblewoman to make babies with."

"Nobody will force you to marry a girl you can't love. You'll have your pick of women."

"I'm twenty-one and I haven't found a single girl I'd spend two days with, let alone my life. You and Chay were lucky to find each other so young."

"Goddess blessing," Tobin said. "And you really haven't gone out looking yet, you know."

"Mother and Father intend to do it for me," he sighed. "And that's the problem. Mother's looking for someone so highborn she probably won't know how to get dressed without the help of three maids. And Father wants somebody pretty and fertile—says he wants handsome grandsons." Rohan laughed ruefully. "And as for what *I* want—"

"Don't you dare pay meek and obedient with me," she told him severely. 'I know you, little brother. If you don't want to marry a particular girl, you won't, no matter what Father and Mother have to say."

"But sooner or later I'll have to play stud to some girl or other. Are your clothes dry yet? Father will be back with his dragon."

"This one should have been yours."

"No, thank you. I'd rather watch them than kill them. There's something about their flying, Tobin, and listening to them roar when they're hunting. . . ." He shrugged. "Oh, I know they're a nuisance. But the Desert would be poorer without them."

Tobin frowned. Everyone knew the dragons had to be killed off. They were more than a nuisance; they were a threat. Radzyn had lost six good mares and eight promising yearlings this spring to dragons, and caravans crossing the Desert were never safe. Dragonwings had swept destructive winds from Gilad to the Veresch Mountains for centuries, dining off livestock and crops.

"I know you don't agree with me," Rohan said with a smile, correctly reading her expression. "But you've never been interested in watching their dances or finding out about them. They're so beautiful, Tobin—proud and strong and free—"

"You're a romantic," she said, and brushed the drying hair from his eyes. "The dragons have to be killed off, and we both know it. Chay says that once they get down past a certain number, nature will do the rest of the work for us. There won't be enough dragons to repopulate the flights."

"I hope that never happens." He got to his feet and patted the damp material of his shirt. "I don't think we'll drip too much. We should get back inside and get ready for the come-home feast."

"And to sew up the rents in Chay's hide." Tobin grimaced.

"He only takes a few scratches so you'll have something to yell at him about. I never saw a man more willing to accommodate his wife's temper!"

"I have a very sweet, docile, placid nature," she protested sententiously.

He nodded, blue eyes dancing. "Just like the rest of the family."

Right on cue, the twins came squabbling through the garden gates, calling for their mother to settle an argument. Tobin sighed, Rohan winked at her, and they went to bring some order to her unruly offspring.

Lady Andrade, having soothed her sister's fears after purposely provoking them, had suggested a game of chess to while away the time until Zehava's return. The two women left the solar for the family's large, private chamber, elegantly furnished and currently decorated with Jahni and Maarken's toys. For all that the fortress was said to have been carved out by dragons in ages past, Stronghold was remarkably civilized, even beautiful. Andrade knew this to be Milar's doing. Windows that had once been set with crude, smoky glass were now filled with fine, clear, beveled panes. Floors that had been either bare or awash in frayed carpets now boasted rugs thick enough to sleep on. Carved wood was everywhere, its natural fragrance enhanced by the oils used to keep it shining and protected from the ravages of the climate. Decorations of gold, crystal, and ceramic abounded, the more precious items displayed in glass-fronted cases. Milar enjoyed free run of Zehava's wealth and was forever receiving merchants eager to sell her even more luxuries; these merchants carried away with them tales of the magnificence of a once comfortless keep. Certainly it would be no hardship for Rohan's future wife to live here.

Andrade was engaged in a tactful loss to her sister at chess when shouts outside turned their attention from the game. "What's all that racket?"

"Zehava is back with his dragon," Milar replied excitedly, rising to her feet, her cheeks flushed and eyes sparkling like a young girl's.

"He made short work of the beast. I didn't expect him back until nightfall." Andrade joined her twin at the windows.

"If he drags the thing into the main courtyard like he did last time, the stink will invade the halls for weeks,"

Milar complained. "But I don't see any dragon—or Zehava, either."

Stronghold was built in a hollow of the hills, reached by a long tunnel through the cliffs. Riders were emerging from the passage into the outer court, and the gates had been flung open in the wall guarding the main yard. Spotting Chaynal's dark head and red tunic, Andrade wondered whether Zehava and his dragon were following more slowly. "Let's go down and greet them," she said.

"Highness! Highness!" Milar's chamberlain accosted them on the stairs, his shrill voice grating on Andrade's nerves. "Oh, come at once, please, please!"

"Did the prince take hurt while slaying his dragon?" Milar asked. She hurried her steps a bit but was not overly alarmed. It would have been miraculous if Zehava had escaped without a scratch.

"I think so, your grace, I—"

"Andrade!" Chay's voice bellowed from the foyer below. "Damn it all, find her at once!"

Milar pushed the chamberlain out of her way and flew down the stairs. Andrade was right behind her. She caught at Chay's arm while Milar raced outside into the courtyard. "How bad?" she asked tersely.

"Bad enough." He would not meet her gaze.

Andrade sucked in a breath. "Bring him upstairs, then. Gently. Then find Tobin and Rohan."

She hurried back to Zehava's suite and busied herself making the bed ready to receive him. He would die in it, she told herself sadly. Chay was no fool; he had been in battles enough to know a mortal wound when he saw one. But perhaps with careful attention, Zehava might survive. Andrade tried to hope, but when they brought the prince up and placed him on the white silk sheets, she knew Chay was right. She stripped the clothes and makeshift bandages from the big frame, unable to hold back a gasp at the hideous wound in Zehava's belly. She was barely aware of Tobin beside her, Milar standing silent and stricken at the foot of the bed. She worked furiously with water, clean towels, pain-killing salves, and needles threaded with silk. But she knew it was all in vain.

"We thought the dragon nearly defeated," Chay was

saying in a hoarse voice. "He'd scored it many times—
there was blood everywhere. He came at it for the killing
stroke and we thought—but between the teeth that got
his horse and the talons that ripped him open—" Chay
stopped and there was the sound of liquid being gulped.
Andrade hoped the wine was strong. "It was all we could
do to beat the dragon away from him. We got him onto
my horse and—after three measures we had to stop.
He'd been holding his guts in with his hands, pretending
he wasn't too badly hurt."

Andrade cleaned and stitched the wound, knowing her
actions to be useless. Now that the blood had been washed
away, she could see the fearful work of the dragon's
claws: through skin and flesh right down into muscle and
the thick looping strands of the guts themselves, which
were not only exposed but sliced clean through in places.
She could make Zehava comfortable and free him of
most of the pain, but Rohan would become ruling prince
in a few days at the most. She glanced around at the
thought of him, noting that he had not yet arrived.

"We cleaned him up and bound him as best we could,"
Chaynal went on. "Then we came back as fast as we
dared. He hasn't spoken or opened his eyes once." At
last the young lord's voice cracked with grief. "Tobin—
forgive me—"

The princess looked around briefly from her work at
Andrade's side. "You did everything you could, beloved."
She knuckled her eyes with one bloodstained hand.

Andrade was nearly finished sewing the skin together.
She did so very quickly, without thought to how it would
heal, for she knew it would not matter to Zehava how it
healed. Dressings soaking in a pain-numbing solution
were applied, and at last she wrapped clean bandages
around the prince's midsection. Her back ached and her
eyes stung with the strain of so much fine work done so
fast. Straightening up, she turned to her sister. The blue
eyes saw nothing but Zehava's ashen face. Andrade washed
her hands in a basin of blood-clouded water, dried them,
and flung her long braid back over her shoulder. "Mila,"
she began.

"No," her twin whispered. "Just leave me alone with him."

Andrade nodded and ordered everyone out with a glance. In the antechamber, she closed the door and gestured to the frightened servants, who scurried away.

"He's going to die, isn't he?" Tobin asked softly, tears rolling slowly down her cheeks. She wiped them away, leaving thin stains on her face.

Chaynal made a strangled sound low in his throat and strode off down the hall. Andrade said, "Yes."

"Poor Mother. And poor Rohan."

"I need your help, Tobin. Grief must wait. You know that what I possess, your mother does not. These things sometimes skip generations, the same way you bore twins but Mila did not. What is within me is also within you."

The princess' eyes went wide with shock. "You mean I'm—"

"Yes. I'm tired, and I need the strength you have but were never trained to use." She led Tobin down the long hallway to the rooms kept for her, and locked the door behind them. Sunlight sloped in, gilding the furniture and bed hangings. Andrade stood with her niece at the windows that faced the slowly dying sun. "Perhaps I ought to have told you, shown you how to use what the Goddess gave you. But you were content as you were, and *faradhi* powers are not taught to those who have no need of them."

"You're going to use me, the way you use everyone," Tobin said, but without resentment. "What do you want me to do?"

"Listen to me. Don't stare directly into the sun, girl, you'll burn your eyes. Look instead at what it does to the land—the hollows filled by light, as Water fills hollow stones and Air fills the hollow dragon caves and Fire fills the hollow hearth. The light moves," she whispered, "caresses the Earth like a lover, warms the Air, sparkles across the Water, finds its mate in the Fire. Of these four things, all is made. Touch the sunlight with me, Tobin— feel its strands weaving between your fingers, its colors like silk threads made of jewels . . . yes, that's it. Now follow it with me. Become sunlight, flung out across the land. . . ."

Chapter Two

When Sioned was three years old, the death of her parents left her brother Davvi, her elder by twelve winters, Lord of River Run. Within a few years he married. His bride was a girl whose father had no other heirs, and when the man died, everything that was his became his daughter's. Davvi found himself the *athri* of two fine keeps and lands that stretched for twenty measures along the Catha River. But the new Lady of River Run was the possessive sort, begrudging Sioned not only the share of wealth that would have been her dowry but even the fondness between brother and sister. Thus she purchased—at a price far less than marriage to a suitable lord—Sioned's entry into Goddess Keep. Unhappy at home, twelve-year-old Sioned had gone gladly to the great castle on the cliff's edge in Ossetia. There she found companionship among the other students and knowledge enough to feed her ravenous appetite for learning. The small oddities that her sister-by-marriage derided as "fey" turned out to be indications that she had the *faradhi* gift and could become a Sunrunner.

Not everyone who went to Goddess Keep became *faradhi*, and Lady Andrade did not tolerate arrogance among those who could or envy among those who could not. But there were certain distinctions involved in becoming a Sunrunner: the rings of earned rank and periodic visits to the grove of pines near the keep. In the year 693, when Sioned was sixteen and had earned the first silver circle on her right middle finger, she went to this place where, if her talents were strong and the Goddess was disposed to revelations, she might glimpse her future.

After a long walk through the woods, she emerged into

brilliant sunlight that warmed her body and danced over the waves far below. Towering coastal pines formed a ring around a small rock cairn from which water bubbled up and splashed its way down to the sea. Sioned paused outside the circle, removed all her clothes, and stepped lightly across the carpet of blue and purple flowers to the spring.

Each of the five pines had a name: Childtree, Maidentree, Womantree, Mothertree, and Hagtree. Clad only in the cloak of her long red-gold hair, Sioned knelt beside the cairn and caught water in her hands, spilling a few drops for the first two trees before turning to the Womantree. She had come here twice before—first as a little girl to offer some water and a lock of her hair, then a year later when her first bleeding meant she was no longer a child. Now she was ready for the next step: declaring herself a woman. For the previous night she had known the embrace of a man for the first time.

She returned to the spring and knelt, facing the Womantree. The sea whispered against the cliffs at low tide, reminding her of the soft sounds of flesh against flesh last night. There had been no words spoken and in the total darkness she had not known who the man was, nor did it matter. No girl ever knew, for the spell woven was a powerful one. Care was also taken that no children would come of the woman-making night; when Sioned chose her husband, then she would come to the grove and ask the Mothertree for a glimpse of the children she might bear.

She could wait for that. It was some years off, and she was barely sixteen, after all. A smile crossed her face as she thought about the silent encounter, all warmth and excitement and potency in the darkness. But she also knew that something had been missing. There had been affection, learning, and joy, but it had lacked the communion her friend Camigwen told her she'd found with her Chosen, Ostvel. Sioned wanted the same thing for herself. Perhaps the Womantree would show her the man with whom she would find it.

Tossing her hair back, she gazed at the tree and wondered what the boys and young men of the Keep felt during their own rituals here. For them, the trees had different names: Child, Youth, Man, Father, and Graybeard. No one ever spoke of what occurred at such times, but she hoped that others heard the water singing and their names sighing through the pines. She smiled as she listened, then lifted both hands.

Her first ring had been given the previous day, when she had formally proved her ability to summon Fire, and tiny flames burned at her call atop the rock cairn. The Air of her own breath fanned them higher, brighter, until they were clearly reflected in the Water. She plucked a single hair from her head to represent the special portions of the Earth from which she had been made, and floated the strand on the still water. Her own face was mirrored there—pale, big-eyed, soft with girlhood and framed in a tumble of bright hair. She slid her hands into the water and gazed at the Womantree, holding her breath.

The Fire leaped higher on the rocks, startling her, and her fingers clenched around silky water. Her face had changed: her cheeks were thinner, the high bones and delicate jawline in proud relief. The green eyes were darker, their expression more serious, and her mouth had lost its childish curve. This was the woman she would become, and her vanity was pleased even as she chided herself for the conceit.

Sioned memorized the face she would one day wear, eager to become this woman with her confident eyes and composed features. But while she gazed into the reflection of her future, the Fire flared again. Another face was next to hers in the water now, burning with a light of its own through the mirrored flames. It was a man's face, fair hair sweeping across a wide brow to shade river-blue eyes, a face with strong bones and an unsmiling mouth. Yet there was tenderness in the curve of the lips, gentleness to balance the stubborn line of the jaw.

Fire slid down the rocks then, igniting the pool, and Sioned drew back her hands with a cry of fright. The single red-gold hair floating on the water writhed, became a thin rivulet of flame that crossed the man's forehead like the circlets worn by princes—and then extended to form the same royal crown for her.

It was a very long time before Sioned rose from her knees. Even after the Fire died away and the picture in the Water vanished, after the Air had ceased to sing in the pines and the Earth was calm beneath the pool, she stared wide-eyed at the cairn and the spring. At last the chill of oncoming night wrapped around her naked body and she shivered, the spell finally broken.

The next day she sought out Lady Andrade, troubled by what she had seen. "Was it true?" she asked urgently. "What I saw yesterday—will it come true?"

"Perhaps. If the vision disturbed you, it can be changed. Nothing is written in stone, child. Even if it were, the stones can be shattered." The Lady gazed musingly at the brilliant sunlight outside. "When I was about your age, I looked into the Water and saw the face of my husband. He was not the man I would have Chosen for myself, so I did everything I could to make the vision change. I know now that what the Goddess showed me was a warning, not a promise. Perhaps she did the same for you."

"No," Sioned murmured. "This time, it was a promise."

A wry smile played over the Lady's mouth. "Just so. But remember that a man is more than a face and a body and a name. Sometimes he's a whole world within himself, even if he isn't a great lord or a prince."

"I think I saw the whole world in his eyes," Sioned admitted, frowning. "Is that what you mean?"

"How young you are!" Lady Andrade said indulgently, and the girl blushed.

Now, five years later, Sioned knew her own face had changed until it was very nearly the version of herself she had seen that day. Only the royal circlet was missing, and her first real sight of the man. She had spent the last years looking carefully at every blond, blue-eyed man who came to Goddess Keep, but had not found anyone like him. Who was he?

The answer had come to her very suddenly as she'd helped Lady Andrade pack for her journey to Stronghold. Fair hair, blue eyes, certain angles of bone—Sioned had been amazed and appalled that she'd never seen it before. Then she had realized that "before" had not been the right time, not for knowledge like this. She saw at last the echoes of that masculine face in Lady Andrade's, remembering the royal circlet and the fact that the Lady's nephew was a prince. Though she had said nothing, Andrade had seen the shock in her eyes and nodded silent acknowledgment of the truth.

One thing still puzzled Sioned. The circlet had been formed of herself, the hair floating on the Water. Yet he was already royal, already the heir; how could his becoming Prince of the Desert have anything to do with her? She was thinking about it as she walked the sunswept battlements of Goddess Keep one afternoon. The sea was a placid blue beneath a cloudless sky, sunlight reaching deep into the water to warm the new life there, and around the cliffs otters laughed uproariously as they played with their young. Sioned was fascinated by water, whether it was the ocean below Goddess Keep or the Catha River where she had spent her childhood. But she had a Sunrunner's wariness of it as well, for few *faradh'im* were able to set foot on anything that floated without becoming sick as a gorged dragon.

Sioned unplaited her hair and ran her fingers through it, feeling the sunlight warm each strand. Soon she would have to go back inside and help with the evening meal— not that anyone ever let her near the cookpots except to taste their contents. She was hopelessly inept at the skills Camigwen practiced with a decided flair, and had never even learned how to blend herbs and cloves for a decent cup of taze. Sioned laughed ruefully to herself with the whimsical hope she would indeed marry the prince—for then she would never have to worry about her total lack of practical skills. His servants would take care of everything, and—

Sioned.

She whirled around, looking to the east from whence the call had come. She automatically opened herself to the colors brushing against her mind. There was always a Sunrunner on duty to receive messages sent on the light, but it was not Sioned's turn today. Someone was calling specifically for her.

She wove rays of light back across fields and valleys,

over rivers and the vast grassy sea of Meadowlord. The threads met and her own colors tangled with those of Lady Andrade. There was a second presence, like yet unalike, oddly familiar in some of its shadings and strong in ways very different from Andrade. Sometimes when the light was chancy—at sunset or sunrise especially— *faradh'im* worked together. But Sioned was certain that the person with Andrade was not trained, though there were unmistakable gifts in the bright colors of amber and amethyst and sapphire swirling with the pattern of a powerful mind.

Thank you for coming to meet me, child. But I need you to come even farther, in person. Arrange an escort of twenty, Sioned. This will be no pleasure trip. You must be here within six days. But before you enter Stronghold, make yourself stately and beautiful. You come here as a bride.

Though she had been waiting for this for five years, the shock was still profound. All she could think to ask was, *Does he know?*

Not yet—but he will, the instant he sees you. Hurry here to me, Sioned. To him.

Andrade and the mysterious other withdrew down the faltering rays of sunlight, and Sioned raced along her own weaving back to Goddess Keep, not pausing as she usually did to appreciate the beauty of the lands below her. She found herself almost too abruptly back on the battlements, and caught her balance mentally and physically. Below in the fields, wide-shouldered elk were being unharnessed from the plows and the sun had nearly disappeared into the sea. Sioned trembled, knowing that had she delayed her return, she might have become shadow-lost, falling into the Dark Water along with the sun.

"Sioned? What are you doing way up here? And whatever's the matter?"

Camigwen approached from the stairwell, scowling in response to what Sioned knew must be in her face. They had come to Goddess Keep at the same time, were only a year apart in age, and had become fast friends their first day here. Camigwen was the only one besides Andrade who knew what Sioned had seen in the Water and Fire, and so the explanation Sioned gave was a simple one.

"It's time, Cami. I'm to go to him."

A flush darkened the older girl's taze-brown skin. Her eyes, large and dark and slightly tip-tilted in her pretty face, held a hundred questions. But all she did was grasp Sioned's hands.

"Will you come with me, you and Ostvel?" Sioned pleaded. "I need you both—I don't know what I'm to do or say—"

"You couldn't keep me from a sight of this man if there were a thousand dragons in my way!"

Sioned gave a nervous laugh. "Well, you have the dragon part of it right."

"The *Desert*? But who—?"

"The young prince," Sioned replied, strangely unable to say his name.

Camigwen stared at her for some time, unable to speak a single word. But when she finally recovered her voice, it was to give a moan of dismay. "Oh, Goddess—and there's not a single stitch sewn on a bride-gown!"

Tension dissolved into laughter and Sioned hugged her friend. "Only you could be so practical at a time like this!"

"Somebody has to be, with you standing there like a scattershell! Oh, Sioned! It's wonderful!" Camigwen drew back and regarded her friend narrowly. "You *do* think it's wonderful, don't you?"

"Yes," Sioned whispered. "Oh, yes."

Camigwen nodded, satisfied. "I'll tell Ostvel at once to arrange the escort. How many do you think we'll need?"

"Lady Andrade said twenty. And we have to be there within six days."

"Six?" She groaned and shook her head. "We'll never make it. But we *must*, and on time, too, or I'll never get my sixth ring and Ostvel will be demoted back to stable-boy instead of Second Steward of the Keep! We'll leave tomorrow at first light. I can cut cloth tonight and sew along the way!"

Between Camigwen's efficiency and Ostvel's authority, all was arranged so quickly that Sioned's head spun. She found herself on horseback before dawn the next morning, riding east toward the Desert. She turned only once to look back at the castle on the cliffs. Blue-gray veils of mist swirled around it, and the sky beyond was still night-dark over the sea. She knew she should have taken time to ask her future of the Mothertree, but there had been no chance. She felt only mild regret, however; the things of Goddess Keep were past now, and she was riding to her future.

A future with a man she didn't even know.

The first night they stopped before dusk beside a branch of the Kadar River, having made excellent progress during a hard day's riding. With Sioned were lifelong friends—Antoun, Meath, Mardeem, Palevna, Hildreth, all around her own age and with whom she had gone through *faradhi* training—as well as several others with relatives along the way who would be glad of a sight of their *faradhi* kin and would provide shelter for a night. There were younger men and girls who were responsible for the horses and provisions, making the ordered total of twenty. Sioned was amazed that so many people had been willing to ride so far for her sake on such ridiculous notice.

Most of them sat around the fire after their meal, Mardeem idly singing a love song and glancing slyly at Sioned whenever he reached a particularly suggestive lyric. Camigwen sat within the secure circle of Ostvel's arm and fretted that there wasn't light enough left to continue sewing the bride-gown. Sioned joined in the laughter as Ostvel teased her, wondering if the same kind of loving, playful relationship waited for her with *him*. She didn't know him, had only seen his face years ago in the Fire. She was still a girl enchanted by blue eyes and her own fantasies of what she thought was in them. Why was she riding so many hundreds of measures to marry a man she didn't know?

"Are you tired or just thinking?" Ostvel asked with a kind smile.

"A little of both," Sioned replied. "And dreading the idea of crossing the Faolain in a few days."

"It's the last river you'll have to cross for a good long while," he reminded her, amusement making his gray eyes sparkle in the firelight. "The Desert is just the place for you Sunrunner types. Tell me, Sioned, are you like Camigwen, who gets queasy looking at a bathtub?"

Cami fisted him in the ribs. "Watch what you say or I'll be sure to get sick all over *you* when we cross!"

Grunting, Ostvel gathered long legs under him and stood. "Come on, Meath, Antoun—let's go check the horses before my dainty and gentle beloved decides to break my arm."

Mardeem, unable to cause more than a blush in Sioned with his songs, declared himself out of voice and in need of sleep. Most of the others followed his example and rolled themselves in blankets on the ground nearby, tactfully out of earshot of the fire where Sioned and Camigwen lingered. It was too quiet without music. Sioned reached for a twig, pulling it from the fire, moodily watching the little flame.

"Cami—will you and Ostvel stay with me there for a little while? After I'm—" She couldn't bring herself to say *married*, and the word *princess* was for the woman she'd seen in the Fire years ago. "I think I'm going to need somebody to talk to," she finished lamely.

"We'll stay as long as you like. But you won't need us, Sioned. You'll have him."

"That's what I'm afraid of," she muttered.

"What's the matter? You've hoped for years that this would happen, and you've been so happy all day today."

"What if we can't *talk* to each other?" Sioned burst out. "What if we find we have nothing to say? Cami, look at me. I'm nothing. A six-ring Sunrunner who barely knows her craft, born in a holding nobody's ever heard of! Can you seriously see *me* as a princess?"

"You're shadow-fearing, Sunrunner," Camigwen said briskly. "Stop being so silly. Of course you're going to love each other."

"But what if we can't? I don't know him, and he certainly doesn't know me. I don't want to tie myself to a man I can't love."

"Listen to me, Sioned. Look into the Fire. There aren't any shadows to lose yourself in and never come out. There's only the light."

At her friend's coaxing, Sioned dropped the twig back into the fire and faced the flames, and within them was his face. She flinched at the grief that clouded his eyes and scarred his sensitive mouth. Her hands reached involuntarily and she cried out as Fire seared her fingers and her mind.

"Sioned!"

She was scarcely aware of the cold water Camigwen poured over her burned fingers or of the worried voices around her. The pain had raced up her hands and arms to her heart, and deep into that portion of her brain that knew how to ride the woven threads of sunlight. She rocked back and forth, gasping around the agony until it gradually began to fade and she could see clearly once more.

Her friends had gathered in a circle of concern. "I'm sorry," she murmured, ashamed, and bent her head, cradling her burned fingers in her lap.

"The fire blew sparks, that's all," Camigwen told the others.

"Be more careful, Sioned," Meath cautioned, patting her shoulder with rough affection. She nodded wordlessly, unable to look at any of her friends.

"Yes," Ostvel drawled. "We owe the prince a bride who doesn't wince with pain when he kisses her hands. Everybody get some sleep. We've got a long way to ride tomorrow." When they had gone, he crouched down beside Sioned, tilting her face up to his with an insistent finger beneath her chin.

"I'm sorry," she repeated.

"No, *I'm* the one who's sorry," Camigwen said. "I only wanted you to look at him again and realize you don't have to be afraid."

"You lost control of a Fire-conjure?" Ostvel asked, and when Sioned nodded miserably, he whistled. "I can hardly wait to meet this prince of yours. Any man who causes a Sunrunner of your rank to make a mistake like that—"

"It wasn't him, it was me," Sioned told him, then burst out, "and Cami tells me I have nothing to fear!"

"If you do," Ostvel murmured, "it's fear of too much

brightness. Too much Fire. Not the shadows, Sioned—
never those."

"I could get as easily lost in the one as in the other,"
she whispered, staring down at her hands.

Rohan managed to elude his aunt successfully until the
evening after the dragon hunt. Andrade, after sending
Tobin to rest and recover from the drain on her energies,
had sought the young prince but had not found him. Her
dignity forbade asking anyone for his whereabouts. She
had a reputation to maintain, after all, and refused to
admit that she was unable to find one man in a finite
area. Irked at his ability to vanish when he wished—and
entirely familiar with it from his childhood—she decided
to stubborn him out, knowing full well that *he* would
choose the time and place of their meeting.

She spent part of the day with Tobin, giving her niece
a deserved explanation. Chay was sleeping off physical
and emotional exhaustion—and all the wine he'd drunk
on an empty stomach, trying to forget the sight of Zehava
being gored by the dragon—when Andrade appeared at
the door of Tobin's chambers late in the morning. The
two women went down into the gardens for a private talk.

"It was very strange," Tobin admitted when Andrade
asked her reaction to what they had done the previous
evening. "I always wondered how *faradh'im* worked with
the sunlight."

"Don't think that because you helped me once you'll
be able to do it on your own," Andrade warned. "The
balance is a delicate one, and control of it takes a good
deal of training." She paused as a groundskeeper bowed
his way out of their presence near the roses. "But I think
I'll have Sioned teach you something about it when she
arrives."

"Is that her name? Sioned?"

"Yes, but accent the second syllable more. 'Sh-*ned*,' "
she repeated.

"It's a lovely name," Tobin mused. "Does Rohan know
yet that he's expected to add 'princess' to it?"

"I thought you'd figure that out. Yes, she's going to be
his wife. He doesn't know it yet, but he soon will."

"I liked her. It's as if I touched her somehow. There were—colors, almost as if I could hold them in my hands. Beautiful colors."

"I don't think this kind of touching is completely new to you." She cocked an eyebrow at the princess.

"Sometimes with Chay I feel something of the same thing," Tobin said slowly. "Almost as if I'm looking into him and he's all sorts of colors. Does that mean I can learn to be *faradhi*?"

"Sioned can teach you a little—but no more than that. It's dangerous."

"I remember when Kessel got shadow-lost," she replied quietly. "Mother and I took care of him until he died."

Andrade glanced away, remembering the handsome young Sunrunner who had been posted here for a time. He had misjudged the light late in the day. Shadow-lost was the most fearful risk *faradh'im* could run, for thoughts unraveled in darkness never rewove, and colors forgotten in the night never knew sunlight again. The mindless body soon died, its essence having following the sun into the Dark Water.

"Then you know the consequences of overconfidence," Andrade said. "And speaking of arrogance, Rohan seems to be making quite a game of avoiding me."

"Mother says he was in Father's room late last night for a little while. But I don't know where he is this morning." She sank down on a bench in the shade. "And before you ask—yes, I know most of his places, and I'm not going to tell you. He'll appear when he's ready. Don't push him, Aunt. Not now. I'm worried about him."

Andrade sat beside her, shrugging irritably. It was probable that Rohan was in no state to talk to anyone, not even his family, and especially not Andrade. "He'll have to face me sometime."

"How dare you imply that he's a coward!"

"I didn't. But why isn't he with Zehava?"

Tobin sighed. "I suppose he's like me, and can't believe Father's dying—not so quickly, or so slowly. Does that make any sense?"

Andrade understood. A strong and vigorous man one day, Zehava was dying the next. Yet life lingered painfully in the ravaged body, refusing to relinquish its hold on flesh.

"In any case, it's forbidden for the next prince to watch his father die," Tobin went on.

"That's a very bad idea. Rohan must watch or all his life Zehava's image will be in front of him, never really dead and burned."

Tobin's black eyes sheened silver with tears, like rain at midnight. "You are the cruelest woman I ever knew," she whispered.

Andrade bit her lip, then grasped her niece's hand. "Never think I don't grieve for your father. Zehava is a good man. He gave me you and Rohan to love as I would have loved children of my own. But I am what I am, Tobin. And you and I are both women of consequence with responsibilities. When we have time for it, we feel. But there is no time. Rohan must be told."

Yet he eluded her for the rest of the morning and afternoon. Andrade grew furious at the dance he was leading her and was reduced to the humiliation of setting one of her Sunrunners outside his chamber door, with orders to report instantly if and when the young prince appeared. Her other *faradh'im* she posted at various places around the keep with identical instructions. But none of them came with news during the whole day.

With the evening, Andrade was exhausted. She had attended Zehava twice, hoping but not really expecting him to awaken, and had sat vigil with Milar for several hours in the suffocating heat. At dusk she decided to go up to the Flametower, where there might be a breath of air to cool her. She opened the door of the uppermost chamber, panting after the climb, and cursed viciously— for Rohan was in the huge circular chamber, alone.

The light from the small fire in the center of the room turned his hair fiery gold and glistened on the sweat that beaded his forehead and the hollow of his throat. As Andrade entered, he glanced up without curiosity from his seat before the little blaze.

"It took you a long time to find me," he observed.

She resisted the impulse to blister his ears with her reply. Choosing a chair from the few stacked against the far wall, she placed it opposite his at the fire and stared into the flames. "Gracious of you to wish at long last to be found," she told him in a rigidly controlled voice. "Although this isn't the most agreeable place for a talk—or the most comfortable." She gestured to the fire that was kept burning year round.

"Comfortable?" Rohan shrugged. "Perhaps not. I keep seeing Father in the flames."

"A trifle premature. He's not dead yet."

"No. But when I don't see Father, I see myself." He rose and paced to the windows, pointing arches left open to whatever wind chose to blow. They circled the room at regular intervals, each one surmounted by a sleeping dragon carved into the stone. Rohan made the circuit slowly, stray gouts of fire-sent breeze ruffling his sweat-damp hair.

"They'll signal his death from here," he said musingly. "Build up the fire so high and hot that this room will turn to flames. You can still see the soot from when my grandfather died, and all the other princes of our line, back three hundred years or so. . . ." He swept his fingertips along the walls. "And then I'll take the spark from here that will light his pyre, and this fire that was his will be put out. Mother and Tobin will clean the floor themselves—did you know that? It should be my wife, but I have no wife. I'll come up here and light new flames that will eventually become *my* pyre."

The shadows licked at his face as he talked, a proud and elusive face, not easy to know. But Andrade knew him, and kept silent.

"Someday my son will do for me what I'll do for Father in a few days. And on it will go, for more generations. All that's ever left is this." He held up his blackened fingertips with an unpleasant smile. "Goddess, what a morbid thought!" The smile crumpled as he whispered, "Why does he have to die?"

It was the cry of a boy for the loss of a beloved father, but it was also a moan of dread. There had been a time like this for Andrade, too, over twenty years ago, when the Lord of Goddess Keep had died and she had been chosen to wear the rings in his place. She had been alone.

But there was someone for Rohan to turn to in his need. She caught his gaze and drew it to the flames by the force of her powerful will. Stretching forth one hand to the fire, she whispered Sioned's name.

Rohan tensed, the pulse beating faster in the hollow of his throat. A face coalesced in the glowing flames, a pale oval of fine bones and green eyes framed in red-gold hair. Andrade held the conjure for a few moments, allowed it to fade, and sank wearily back into her chair.

"Who is she?" the young man breathed.

Andrade said nothing, almost too tired to care if he had any instinct for seeing into his own heart. It was a long while before he spoke again, and when he did his tone was deliberately casual.

"I haven't seen you do a conjuring since I was eleven years old. You did it then to please a child. I think you did it now to promise me something. What will she be to me, Andrade?"

How odd that he had used Sioned's word: *promise*. "You already know."

"You want me to marry a Sunrunner witch?"

"Does the thought of a Sunrunner witch like me frighten you, boy?" she snapped.

"You don't frighten me, and neither do your kind. But I can't marry a *faradhi* woman."

"Isn't her blood pure enough for you, princeling?"

Rohan's lips curved in a feral smile she had never seen before. "First let us clarify something. I am neither a 'boy' nor a 'princeling.' I honor you as my aunt and for your position, but you will remember who I am."

She gave him an ironic little bow. "And forget whose nose I wiped and whose skinned knees I bandaged."

All at once he laughed. "Oh, Goddess—I deserved that, didn't I?" He sat and put his elbows on his knees, hands clasped between them. "Very well, Andrade, let's talk things over like rational people instead of arrogant prince and Lady of Goddess Keep. I need an alliance as well as a wife when I marry. What do I gain by taking one of your *faradh'im*?"

"You could do worse. Much worse." She hid her pleasure at what had just passed between them. Never having suspected him capable of such hauteur, she was glad he could not only use it but laugh at it. Arrogance—or its appearance—would help him rule, but laughter would keep him sane while he did it. "You don't have any other women in mind, do you?"

"I was bemoaning their lack only yesterday." He shrugged again. "You know, I'm not quite sure what to feel. I don't want my father to die. I know I should be terrified of becoming ruling prince—but I'm not. Goddess help me, Andrade, I want the power of it. There's so much I want to accomplish. But why does Father have to die in order for me to do it?"

"You're tired of being one step away from the power that is your right. It's only natural, Rohan, especially when you have dreams. One fire goes out and a different one is lit. You're eager to try your wings and that's a very fine trait—"

"In the son of a dragon?" he interrupted.

She grunted her appreciation of the remark. "Let's leave them out of this for now, shall we? What I meant was that caution in flight is also a good idea." She paused a moment, then rapped out, "Does the girl repel you?"

"No!" was his quick response. "She's beautiful!" Then he blushed. "Any fool could see that. Men my age are usually fools about women."

"So she doesn't disgust you physically. That's a start," Andrade said wryly. "Now that we've established her as a woman and not a witch—"

"Have we?" He gave her a tiny smile. "I have your word for it, but the face in the flames said otherwise. If not a witch, then certainly something enchanted. What comes from Goddess Keep that is not?"

"Oh, very pretty," she mocked, restraining laughter with difficulty, more and more pleased with him. "Have you studied charming phrases, or do they come naturally? As for the girl—she's a fit mate for a dragon's son. Your children should be the wonders of the world."

The hot color came back to his cheeks, the sight an education to Andrade. He rose and went to the windows again, saying with an attempt at nonchalance, "We'll tithe one of them to you for playing matchmaker."

"Don't be facetious." Waiting until he faced her again, she went on, "Your mention of an alliance is something I'd expect. But you're so rich that very few could aspire to your hand and your bed." He did not blush at this reference to sex, and Andrade rightly concluded that the prince could consider such things but the man was shy about them. "Of the great lords and princes, only a few of them have daughters of marriageable age. Most of these are out of the question, being either promised or too ugly or stupid for consideration. None of us wants you tied to a fool."

"Is that a polite way of saying I'm going to need all the help I can get?"

"You were lonely as a little boy," she said with a gentleness that surprised her. "I don't want you to live your manhood lonely as well." To cover the emotion she continued more briskly, "Of the few eligible ladies, most of them are the High Prince's daughters."

Rohan's face pulled into a grimace. "Thank you, no. The son of the dragon has no wish to marry a daughter of the lizard. I would gladly live my manhood lonely, as you put it, in exchange for the assurance of living it at all."

"And what do you mean by that?" she asked, wondering if he had figured it out for himself.

He gave her much the same reasoning she had given Milar, and Andrade sent heartfelt thanks to the Goddess. Rohan would not have an easy time of it as ruling prince, but neither would he be the victim of those more clever than he. There would not be many. When he had finished a succinct summation of why his life would be worth less than nothing after he had gotten an heir on one of Roelstra's daughters, Andrade smiled her approval.

"Your wits are in working order, at any rate," was all the verbal praise she gave him. "Now that you've had a chance to think about it, tell me why you should marry my *faradhi* witch."

Rohan took several moments to answer, but when he

did it was with growing enthusiasm. "Information, for one thing. A network of *faradh'im* all over the princedoms would be very useful."

"And what makes you think I'd allow you to use them?"

"The same thing that makes me think you've got some grander plan for me that doesn't preclude using anyone or anything you can get your hands on. I know why you pushed your sister into marrying my father, and I know all about your spies—I'm not talking about the *official* Sunrunners, Andrade." The line of his jaw hardened. "What is it you really want? Why show me that face, knowing I'd find her beautiful? How do you plan to use *us?*"

"If I live long enough—if *you* live long enough—we may all find out. I do only what the Goddess bids me."

"Dragon shit," Rohan said in a pleasant tone, his eyes blue ice. "She tells you what you feel like hearing. You're setting me up in direct opposition to Roelstra. Why?"

"You mean that with all your studies and all your deep thoughts, you haven't yet seen it?" she taunted, angry and a little frightened by his perceptions.

He took a step toward her, the fire between them, and there was nothing boyish or gentle about him now. "What do you plan for me, Andrade?"

Years and responsibilities, old hates and hopes and even a few dreams settled on her like a cloak of iron. "Rohan—it's all as you've said about Roelstra's daughters. I was afraid the offer would come before I could speak to you. Your father would never listen to a word I said. He doesn't entirely trust me."

"Should I?" he asked, his voice cold.

"If not me, then Sioned."

"So she has a name. I'd wondered."

"She's very dear to me, Rohan. What I want doesn't matter. She was the one who saw you years ago in the Fire."

"Did she?"

"Couldn't you feel anything when you looked at her tonight?"

"What I feel isn't your concern. Have you sent for her?"

"She'll be here soon."

"And you call *me* arrogant! It runs in the blood—like the *faradhi* gifts that Tobin has and I don't. That's what you wanted from my parents, wasn't it? A *faradhi* prince. Sorry to have disappointed you. But now you're about to try the same thing, aren't you? Does Sioned know it, I wonder?"

Andrade met his gaze stoically, not reacting to his sarcasm—for she heard how he tasted the girl's name as if schooling his tongue to its syllables and his ears to its sound. "You need not marry her if she doesn't please you. When she arrives, you'll both know one way or the other."

"Haven't you planned it all out?" But in the next moment his expression changed and he murmured, "I'm sorry."

She watched him, this manchild with the deceptively gentle eyes, this princeling who would soon rule over the vastness of the Desert—and perhaps one day, if her misted visions were accurate and the Goddess had not teased her with lies. . . . It would be enough if Rohan and Sioned could be together. They were right for each other; she knew it. "I apologize for my sharpness," she said. "You're right—I really ought to keep in mind who you are."

"No, it was the right way to do it. I can't sit up here feeling sorry for myself. But it's awkward, you see. Waiting for Father to die. Being afraid and having to hide it. Being—alone. I can't really admit things to anyone but you. Do you understand?"

She nodded, thinking that the day he could admit everything to Sioned would be the day he was no longer alone. "Go downstairs and get some sleep. Zehava will live for some days yet. He's too stubborn to let death have him quickly. Your mother will need you to be strong."

Rohan smiled sadly. "No one will need me for anything until it comes time to acknowledge me as prince. And then they'll need even more than I can give. What I have to offer won't seem like much to them—not compared to my father."

Chapter Three

The higher peaks of the Veresch were smothered in white and would remain so well into summer, crowning the heights above Castle Crag. The keep itself was lower down in the hills, perched on the side of a terrifying gorge like a dragon with its claws sunk deep into the cliffs. Land on either side of a canyon carved out by the Faolain River was summer-green, thick with trees and bright with flowers below a sky pierced in the distance by the highest range of snow-capped mountains.

Lady Palila had absolutely no interest in any beauty but her own. She stood on the steps above the thick lawns of the trellis garden, frowning in annoyance because the groundskeepers had shorn her favorite rosebush, the one that produced blossoms exactly the pink of her cheeks. Instantly she reminded herself that wrinkles resulted from unpleasant emotions, and smoothed her face. Her power for the present lay in her looks, and these she had in abundance, starting with but not limited to the wealth of auburn hair that was held back by a thin gold chain studded with brown agates that matched her eyes. Skin the color of pale honey; a bone structure that sculptors dreamed of and had paid homage to in silver, bronze, marble, and even gold; delicate arched brows and a finely carved, passionate mouth—Palila was the most beautiful woman of her generation, and it was only fitting that the High Prince had chosen her as his mistress. She had been careful not to allow her four pregnancies to mar the perfection of her body, and intended that this fifth child—*A boy, a boy at last*, she chanted silently—would leave no mark on her, either. The cut of her dark violet gown concealed her thickening waist for the time being. As ardently as Roelstra desired a son, pregnancy repelled him. But Palila knew she would have to go on getting pregnant until she presented him with a male heir. And then she would be mistress no longer, but wife. Princess. *High* Princess.

There were princesses scattered all over the gardens this afternoon. Four of them, plus thirteen other daughters dignified by the title of "Lady"—seventeen girls, she thought in disgust. By six different women, all that Roelstra had managed were girls and yet more girls. His only legal wife, Lallante, had birthed three boys who had all died within a few days. After his wife's death, the High Prince's search for a single male offspring had taken him through five mistresses—all nobly born and all dead now, with the exception of Palila. She had gone to a lot of trouble to make sure that she was indeed the exception. Castle Crag positively seethed with women, and the oversufficiency frayed her nerves. She loathed her own sex on principle, seeing all women as rivals for Roelstra's attention. She was fond enough of her own daughters, but not even they escaped this basic suspicion. Palila rested one hand on her belly and vowed that *this* time there would be a son.

She descended the short steps, irritated anew that Roelstra was busy elsewhere in the keep, for the gardens were a charming context for her beauty—and for the little play she had perfected over the last few years. The place was a great bowl sunk into the rock, filled with flowering vines and daughters in bright summer silks. Palila visited each little group, pausing to smile and chat, keeping up her role of solicitous foster-mother to them all. Her position as their father's sole mistress for the last four years had gained her their respect, if not their liking. She cared little whether they liked her or not, so long as everyone behaved as if terribly attached to everyone else—no matter how much they all hated each other.

The four princesses were seated beneath a trellis, playing cards. Tall, dark, well-built girls; of the four, Ianthe alone had inherited their father's shrewd brain. Naydra was placid and biddable, Lenala was simply stupid, and Pandsala had a sidelong way of glancing at people which Palila thought might be a sign of slyness or intelligence or both. But Ianthe, at twenty-two the youngest of the four, was sharp and never bothered to hide it.

Lady Vamana's four girls were plain and boring. Their mother's looks had been lost somewhere; Vamana had lost them, as well, to a disease that might have been cured had Palila not switched medicine bottles. She hadn't meant for Vamana to die—but she hadn't wept at her pyre, either. Lady Karayan's daughters stood by the rose wall solemnly tossing a ball back and forth. Palila dismissed little Kiele and Lamia with a shrug, much as she had dismissed their mother from Roelstra's service with a drop of poison in her breakfast wine.

Lady Surya's girls, Moria and Cipris, were near in age to Palila's elder daughters and competed with them for Roelstra's attention, just as Palila had with their mother until a slip on wet tiles by the bathing pool had cracked open Surya's blonde head. Palila hadn't even had to push her very hard.

Yet having rid herself of three rivals, she had soon been presented with a fourth. Roelstra's infatuation with charming, empty-headed Lady Aladra had lasted for two miserable years. She had been genuinely liked by all the daughters; Palila's stomach curdled whenever the pretty idiot opened her mouth. Her death in childbed, giving birth to another daughter, had sunk the castle into honest mourning. Palila, though innocent in this case, had made a substantial donation of wine to Goddess Keep—supposedly in Aladra's memory, but really in thanks for her deliverance.

There had been no new mistresses since. Palila reigned supreme. Even though she was no novelty to him, her hold on Roelstra was still strong and the baby on the way had increased it. Yet fond as he was of the daughters she had given him—his "little flowers," he called them—and showing no signs of becoming bored with Palila, she knew that neither sentimentality about his children nor sensuality in her bed would be proof against a woman who could give him a son. Thus she intended to provide the long-awaited male heir herself, become his legitimate wife, and preside over the marriages of his seventeen daughters.

Their marketability was the one good thing about them.

For the foreseeable future they could be parceled out like gold coins to reward useful men. Roelstra would be pleased to have tedious negotiations taken care of by Palila, and even more pleased when her arrangements increased his power. She would make herself essential to him politically and gain a tidy profit for herself into the bargain through bribes exacted from princes and lords wishing to marry the High Prince's otherwise useless daughters.

She went to her own girls and hugged them, laughing aloud in anticipation of the time when she would find for them the richest and most important men in all the princedoms. But they were very young and she need not worry about their futures yet. Currently she was shopping for men to marry the legitimate daughters, and her primary prey was Prince Rohan. He was rumored to be studious, so Naydra's quietness might attract him; he was also said to be rather blank of eye on occasion, so perhaps Lenala's stupidity would suit him. Palila promised herself that neither clever Ianthe nor sly Pandsala would have him, for the idea of either married to such power was intolerable.

"Just look at her," Pandsala whispered to Ianthe. "That bitch!"

Ianthe smiled sweetly. "Lenala, you cannot play the horse atop the rider, dear. Naydra, explain the rules to her again, won't you? Sala and I are going for a stroll."

The younger pair left the elder and wandered across the lawns. Vines spread splashes of color across rough-hewn stone walls that rose to twice the princesses' height and sealed in the trellis garden, just as the rest of Castle Crag and, therefore, their world was sealed. But they could feel the sheer drop of the cliffs beyond the wall, and the free, swift rush of the Faolain far below, just as without looking at it they could sense the silent, spired bulk of the castle behind them. Generations of their forebears had made it the most imposing keep in all the princedoms. The maze of rooms and corridors, antechambers and staircases was punctuated with turrets and towers jutting out wherever builders had found breathing space—with the result that there *was* no breathing space anywhere in the piles of gray and black stone. It was said that long ago the dragons had favored the cliffs here as a summer home during non-mating years, and had flown across the sky in so many hundreds that they blocked out the sun. It was from this place that Ianthe and Pandsala wanted desperately to flee, as the dragons had done long ago.

Pandsala plucked a rose from the wall and put it in her hair. "When are we going to do something about Palila?"

"I've been thinking about it." Ianthe's dark eyes sparkled gleefully. "Have you ever noticed how many women there are at Castle Crag, and how many of them are pregnant at any given time?"

"It must be in the air," Pandsala replied, making a face. "Women breed, and they breed daughters."

"Not all of them."

Pandsala frowned, then stared. Ianthe laughed.

"If Palila has a son—which isn't likely, but all things are possible—I have my eye on several girls right now who are just as far along as she is."

"Why not do to her what she did to poor Surya?"

"I've considered it," Ianthe admitted. "But her personal servants are absolutely loyal—Goddess alone knows why! She sleeps either with Father or with guards outside her door and two women on the floor of her chamber. She doesn't go out riding, she doesn't leave the grounds, she doesn't bathe with the rest of us and she *never* eats anything her own servants haven't prepared. If you can find opportunity in those things, be my guest!"

"I always did think her 'delicate stomach' was a flimsy excuse."

"She doesn't trust us any more than we trust her. Oh, she makes sweet eyes at us and pretends we're all the closest of friends. I don't know who she thinks she's fooling—certainly not Father!"

"He doesn't give a damn about any of us, except when we can amuse him. Ianthe, I'm so tired of amusing him! Tell me what you have planned."

"If we're to be rid of her, we'll have to be even more devious than she. You know she's planning to sell us to the highest bidder."

"I could do with a husband. It would get me out of this

nursery!" She gestured to the lawns where their half-sisters played in the sunshine.

Ianthe paced along the garden wall until she found a perfect violet rose. She plucked it and ran the soft petals across her cheeks and lips. "There's nothing wrong with a husband of one's own choosing. But remember who's sent emissaries recently? Prince Vissarion—now, there's a fine specimen, if you like lechers. And then there was that lisping idiot sent by Prince Ajit. How would you like to join the list of wives he's buried? Four now, isn't it?"

"Five—no worse than Father," Pandsala retorted, but there was fear in her dark eyes now. "Very well. So the idea is that if Palila manages a son, we'll find some way to switch the child for a girl."

"If Father gets an heir, we'll count for less than nothing."

"I know." Pandsala scuffed the toe of her slipper against a clod of newly turned earth. "But Ianthe—this is our *brother* we're talking about."

"And if he grows up a servant's son instead of a prince, what of it? It's *our* future we're concerned with, Sala! Father's wealth split seventeen ways is bad enough—but if there's a son, instead of a seventeenth part we'd be lucky to get a hundredth. You and I and Naydra and that imbecile Lenala will get larger shares, of course, being princesses. But five hundredths is still nothing multiplied five times." She crushed the rose in her palm. "If there's no son, Father will have to choose the next High Prince from among *our* sons."

Pandsala's eyes narrowed for an instant, but then she hastily smoothed her expression. "Some other woman than Palila might give him a boy. You know, Ianthe, we'd do better to have him gelded."

The younger girl burst out laughing. "And you call *me* foul-minded!"

Pandsala laughed with her. "I'd call us both practical, wouldn't you?"

But as they walked on, conversing in perfect accord, neither spoke of the sons they hoped *they* would have—or the husband each hoped would father them.

*   *   *

The High Prince—who was not as unaware of his daughters as they believed him to be—sat behind the desk of his private study high above the gardens. Roelstra's forty-five winters showed in a thread or two of white in his dark hair, a line or two around his pale green eyes, a notch or two let out in his belt. He had been a remarkably beautiful youth and had matured into a handsome man; oncoming age only added to his looks. But many years of absolute rule had set certain things into his eyes—arrogance, cynicism, contempt. All of these were in evidence as he looked at his most valued, though not most trusted servant.

"So. The old dragon is dying. It's certain, Crigo?"

"Yes, your grace. He was gored most horribly and now lies in his bed, from which he will not rise."

"Hmm." Roelstra tapped his index finger against his lips and regarded Crigo. "You seem tired. Have you been indulging too much or too little?"

The man's fair head bent. "I . . . apologize for my condition, your grace."

"Sleep it off. Come back to me at moonrise, for I wish to send a message to our contact at Stronghold. And you must take better care of yourself, Crigo," he cautioned, smiling without humor. "It's not every prince who has his very own renegade Sunrunner."

Crigo's lean shoulders flinched at the reminder of what he was. Roelstra studied him for a few more moments, thinking that it might become necessary to acquire a new *faradhi* soon. Crigo was beginning to look used up.

"Leave me," he ordered, and rose to look out the windows. The door latch clicked softly, and Roelstra was alone. He gazed at his daughters, saw Palila's auburn hair gleaming in the sunlight, and wondered what plots were whirling around in their heads today. The princesses were getting to a dangerous age, he reflected—too old to be placated with toys and games, old enough to want more of the silks and jewels that were an idle woman's playthings. Ianthe and Pandsala in particular would bear watching, for they were intelligent. A woman with a brain was not a thing to be relished.

He wondered if the young princeling had a brain. Son

of the old dragon and nephew of the redoubtable Lady Andrade; perhaps he *could* think. Roelstra hoped so. It would make life much more interesting.

He wondered, too, if Andrade knew about Crigo or the *dranath*. Such a humble little plant, growing only in the highest reaches of the Veresch, but incredibly potent when boiled, dried, and refined to powder. Crigo was its slave, and because Roelstra was master of his *dranath* supply, the Sunrunner was Roelstra's slave as well. It was a pity so useful a tool was wearing out.

Inhaling deeply of the moist breeze off the river, he thought of the dry heat of the Desert and grinned. One of his daughters would soon find out how people survived there. The Goddess had not cursed him with so many female offspring for nothing. Prince Zehava would be dead soon; by late summer when the Hatching Hunt was over, the new prince would be seen for the weakling he was. At the *Rialla* in autumn, Rohan would find himself matched to one of the princesses and overmatched in his dealings with their father.

Roelstra stretched his powerful shoulders and smiled, thoughts of the *Rialla* bringing to mind the beach at Brochwel Bay and making love to Palila there. But he reminded himself that pregnancy would have swollen her to grotesque proportions by then. Roelstra preferred very slender women. But if her looks were lost for the sake of bearing a son— He bit his lip against a hope that surely ought to have died after seventeen daughters.

Which one should be Rohan's bride? Naydra might do; Lenala was impossible. Pandsala or Ianthe—now, there was a thought. Beautiful, brilliant Ianthe. But would she come to relish power and forget who had given it to her by making her Rohan's wife? He tried to identify the faces and characteristics of his other girls, and could not; there were so damned many of them. Still, the fact that they had rarely been called to his notice led him to believe that they might be more trustworthy than Ianthe. Women who wanted his attention inevitably wanted something more—gowns, jewelry, trinkets to keep them content for a while before they desired more. Those things were easy compared to doling out power. No true child of his would ever be content with anything less.

Which of them would understand his goals and play the game with relish to match his own? Which of them could be used best and trusted most? It was a pretty problem, and he mulled it over as he gazed down at his girls. A pity Kiele was too young; aside from Ianthe and Pandsala, she showed the most spirit. But perhaps one of the others would surprise him. He would have to keep an eye on them over the rest of the summer.

Whichever one it turned out to be, he would have to provide handsomely for her. A nice, fat dowry, and the border castle of Feruche thrown in, none of it very hard to part with because within ten years he would have it all back, and the Desert itself besides. All the wealth of mines and salt, horses and silk trade would be his. He would have everything.

Except a son.

Crigo shivered in the day's warmth as he crept between the bedsheets. His head ached abominably, his tongue was thick in his mouth with the wanting of *dranath*, and his fingers shook as he clenched blankets in his fists. But he was used to the physical discomfort and knew how much of it he could take. What he had never grown used to was the betrayal of everything he was.

Five years ago he had been on his way north to Fessenden, assigned by Lady Andrade to replace a *faradhi* killed in a climbing accident. Crigo had been thrilled by the honor and enchanted by the long journey overland, for aside from Goddess Keep and his home farm in Grib, he had never been anywhere in his life. He'd sent his impressions back on the sunlight to his friends at Goddess Keep, keeping them amused and envious for many days. But just inside Princemarch it had been necessary to cross a branch of the Faolain River, and even that short row over placid water had left him insensible. And that was when the High Prince's men had taken him.

Crigo had not been bound; there had been no need. All they had had to do was keep him on the river. Technically he was free to leave at any time—but sick,

shaking, unable to think past his physical misery, he had
barely been aware of the journey upriver to Castle Crag.
When he finally was in possession of his faculties again,
he found himself lying in a soft bed within a luxurious
room. This chamber, with its brocade hangings and its view
of the mountains, had become his prison—for this chamber
had contained a pitcher of wine laced with *dranath*.

At first he hadn't known. Lady Palila herself had brought
him the wine, and the honor of having her serve him had
not seemed unusual to a Sunrunner accustomed to instant respect and hospitality wherever he went. She had
told him word had been sent to Goddess Keep that he
was safe, and he need not worry. She had been all smiles
and solicitude. He had suspected nothing.

But the wine had changed. Crossing water had been
nothing compared to the loss of *dranath* during those
rainy days of late autumn when the sun denied itself to
him and the moons vanished behind clouds. His physical
agony was made all the worse by the fact that this time
he had all his wits about him. At last the High Prince
himself had come to him late one night after some sort of
celebration, wrapped in a cloth-of-gold cloak that shone
in the firelight. Its brightness seared Crigo's eyes and
sent swords of cold fire into his brain. After drinking the
wine Roelstra offered, he had listened in mounting horror as the High Prince explained exactly why Crigo felt
better now.

A thousand times since that night he'd asked himself
why he hadn't chosen to die. There were easy answers:
he was young, he loved life, he had thought to wean
himself from the drug, he had intended to report back to
Lady Andrade in secret. He had long ago recognized all
these answers as lies. Shuddering into his blankets, he
wondered bitterly why he could still feel such shame, and
closed his eyes to the cool silver pitcher on the table. He
hated it, craved it, blessed it, cursed it. It owned him as
surely as Roelstra did. And that was the only answer that
counted.

A thousand times since that night he had ridden the
light for the High Prince, using his *faradhi* skills to communicate with Roelstra's spies in major courts. Today he

had made his regular contact with Stronghold's wine steward, bracing himself against the bite of that rapacious mind in order to glean the information the High Prince wanted. Tonight he would use the moonlight to contact the steward again, this time to convey whatever message Roelstra wished. Crigo nearly sobbed aloud as his aching body crying out for the drug. Lady Andrade had special ties to those at Stronghold, ties of kinship and affection. To betray the young prince was to doubly and triply damn himself. Worthless in his own eyes, he was worth a very great deal to Roelstra. It was the difference in the price they each set on his soul.

Slowly, painfully, Crigo sat up. He raked the thin blond hair back from his eyes, drew in a long breath— and poured himself a measure of drugged wine.

Palila was in Roelstra's chambers when the renegade Sunrunner was admitted. She was always nervous in Crigo's presence, for he was a reminder of the bizarre old crone who had provided her with the *dranath* years ago. She had heard of a sorceress in the mountains who guaranteed all sorts of charms and spells. Desperate for a son— and needing something to put in Lady Surya's wine that could not be traced or suspected—Palila had summoned the old woman secretly to Castle Crag. No son had come of it, though Palila had done everything required. But Surya had died of something the crone claimed was dragon's blood, and in addition Palila had learned the secret of *dranath*. She would much rather have had the son than the presence of this pallid, drawn Sunrunner at Castle Crag. Roelstra had been forbidden an official *faradhi* by Lady Andrade for offenses not even rumor could guess at, and Palila did not mind the lack. Sunrunners did things she feared, and in the five years Roelstra had been using Crigo she had never gotten over the suspicion that one day he would reach his limit. Who knew what somebody trained by that witch Andrade might do? But Palila was wise enough to sit quietly on her couch and hide her wariness, for Roelstra wanted her to witness what happened this night.

"Come in, Crigo," the High Prince said. "Be seated."

A chair had been placed in the full moonlight. He huddled into it, wrapped in a thick cloak though the room was still warm with the day's sunlight, shivering, his eyes slightly glazed with the effects of the drug. The three small moons were far apart in the sky, casting a blurred series of shadows and making Crigo's usual pallor almost greenish.

"Before the message is sent, you'll do something for me, Crigo," Roelstra said. He withdrew a candle from a pocket of his tunic and Crigo flinched. "I have a whim to see this young princeling. Conjure him for me."

Palila caught her breath and Roelstra glanced at her over his shoulder. Quickly she said, "Forgive me, my lord, but I've never seen—"

"I'm sure you'll find it interesting." He held out the candle to the *faradhi*. "Light it," he commanded softly. "Show me the princeling, Crigo. I want to see what manner of foolish child I'll encounter at the *Rialla*."

Crigo lifted both thin hands, the six rings of his earned rank glimmering in the moonlight. The wick sprang to life. Crigo looked up at Roelstra dully, his eyes reflecting the tiny flame. Palila held herself from shrinking back as the Sunrunner stared into the Fire of his calling.

The flame grew and a face began to form. Palila was drawn forward despite herself, fascinated. First the vague oval of the face, crowned by fair hair; then the lines of jaw, brow, nose; at last the features resolved and the curve of the mouth and the color of the eyes were clearly seen. A proud face, and very young; untested, unripe, and unaware of Roelstra's fine manipulations of power.

"Well?" the High Prince asked suddenly. "Which of my girls will do for him, Palila? I value your advice."

She stared at him in shock, distracted from the face in the flame. So this was why he had spoken with his elder daughters tonight at dinner, she thought. He usually ignored them, preferring to concentrate on the little ones and their amusing chatter. But tonight he had tested each of them, and now he was testing her. Mind working furiously, she tried to outguess him. He had already decided which daughter would marry Rohan, of course. She would have to anticipate that decision. His green eyes were coldly amused as they watched her during the few seconds she had in which to think.

"Ianthe," she said.

He frowned and she knew it was the wrong answer. "Why her?"

"She's the prettiest of your legitimate daughters, and close to this boy in age. She's sensuous, and this man-child is obviously a virgin. Anyone looking at him could see it. Ianthe will be able to rule him through his senses if she's clever enough. And Goddess knows the girl *is* clever." She paused and made herself look at the flame again.

"Why should I give him one of my legitimate daughters?"

"Would a man of his wealth, family, and position accept a bastard?" she asked bluntly.

"Any daughter of mine would be an honor, but I suppose you're right. There's great pride in that face—and his mother is even worse. Go on."

"Ianthe is also intelligent. She'll understand where her advantage lies. I assume I'm correct in that this advantage will not be with her new husband?" She smiled, more confident as ideas came to her. "And she is ambitious."

"How would that serve me, if she's wed to this power-ful young prince?"

"How long would he be able to keep that power on his own?" she countered. "I've never heard anything of him except that he's quiet and studious. You'd never waste a daughter on a man who lets power dribble through his fingers. Ianthe will keep it for him—and for you. The Merida still sit in Cunaxa, north of the Desert border. Would Ianthe allow them to put so much as a boot heel on anything she owned?"

"She does have rather acquisitive instincts. But I fail to see how I may be assured of keeping her in line."

"She is ambitious and intelligent—but she is also not stupid in any way that I've ever seen. Of course you can't trust her. But at least you know her qualities. Can you say the same of Naydra, who can barely string two sentences together, or Pandsala, who never says what she thinks—if she thinks anything at all? As for Lenala—we all know very well that she *cannot* think. But you know Ianthe. And Ianthe knows it." And apart from all that,

she thought silently, how wonderful it would be to get rid
of the girl, who was the main reason Palila lived so
cautiously.

As if Roelstra had heard the thought, he smiled and
said, "The advantage to *you* being her removal from
Castle Crag."

Palila smiled back, inwardly cursing his perceptiveness.
"Her elevation will increase your power and honors."

"Then it may be Ianthe," he mused.

Crigo made a soft sound and the face of the young
prince vanished from the flame, Roelstra turned, scowling. "Control yourself, Sunrunner. You're not finished
for the night."

"I—I'm sorry, your grace—" he mumbled, gripping
the candle now with both hands.

"Ianthe is indeed a clever girl," Roelstra said to Palila.
"But I worry that perhaps she's *too* clever."

"She will rule her husband, and you will rule her."
Palila shrugged. "You have spies enough at Stronghold,
my lord, to keep her effectively under your eye at all
times. All she really needs to do is have a couple of
sons—grandchildren for you to protect."

Roelstra laughed. "We must make sure this thought
does not occur to her—or that she knows anything of her
future honors until the *Rialla* at Waes. I will need you
there, my dear."

"I am yours to command," she said formally, but with
a smile that invited commands pertaining to the bedroom. Her expression hid relief at having talked her way
out of potential danger.

Roelstra laughed again and placed his hands on Crigo's
shoulder. "You may douse the Fire now and make ready
to ride the moonlight to Stronghold."

But Crigo cried out in sudden agony and the candleflame
surged upward, becoming a pillar of writhing Fire that
grew talons and teeth and dragon wings. Palila screamed
as faces formed and vanished in the brilliance: Roelstra,
Ianthe, Pandsala, herself, Prince Rohan, Zehava, and a
girl's face surrounded by a cloud of hair that seemed
made of fire. The dragon reared up, snarling, and the
flames caught on Crigo's sleeves. He toppled to the floor,

hands clawing the air, visions spitting into the wildfire light.

Roelstra tore the curtains from the window and smothered the *faradhi* in it, cursing. Dragon and Fire vanished. The High Prince lifted Crigo's limp form and went to kick open the door. Flinging the unconscious Sunrunner into the antechamber, he roared to the servants, "Get him out of here!" He slammed the door shut and wiped sweat from his forehead.

Palila closed her eyes and trembled. She feared little in life beyond the loss of her beauty, but she was utterly paralyzed by fire. Her mind ignited with pictures of the whole room in flames that licked up the tapestries and wooden paneling, eating at her hair and consuming her flesh and bones while she still lived. She whimpered and wrapped her arms around herself, feeling the baby in her womb jerk and quiver in response to her terror.

"You were in no danger," Roelstra said above her. "Palila, stop this. You might harm the child."

She looked up at him, so tall and powerful. Her fingers dug into his tunic and she moaned as he gathered her in his arms to carry her to the bed.

"Palila, calm yourself," he said.

She raked her nails across his chest, ripping the silk tunic, and he looked astonished for an instant before he burst out laughing. The flames still burned in her imagination—inside her body now, consuming her from within. Roelstra twisted a handful of her long hair into a rope and wrapped it around her neck as he undressed her.

"So your fear of fire makes you burn, does it? Remind me to change my method of execution," he crooned. "I can hardly wait to find out what watching someone being burned alive will do to you. Would you like to see that, my pet? Just imagine the flames as they devour some helpless man or woman. How hot the fire can be, my darling," he whispered as he bent her head back and tightened the rope around her throat. His lips brushed her mouth, fiery moist, and she used up the last air in her lungs on a scream that made him laugh with delight. "Think about the flames, Palila—"

Chapter Four

Prince Zehava regained consciousness on the morning of the third day. He was too experienced a warrior not to know within moments of waking that his wounds were mortal. Andrade, seated at his bedside while Milar closed her eyes for some needed rest, saw in the black eyes that he knew was dying.

"So," he breathed, one eyebrow cocked almost rakishly. "The dragon-slayer has been dragon-slain. Better this way, Andrade, than of a sickness or by an enemy's sword."

"As you say, Zehava. If there's pain, tell me. I can ease it."

"No, no pain. Not for me, at least." He closed his eyes again and nodded. "It's a good potion that numbs the wounds while leaving the mind clear. My thanks, Andrade. But I doubt you have anything to ease Mila's pain."

"Not even time heals a woman who loses a man like you, Zehava."

He looked up, surprised. A smile danced across his face for an instant. But what he said was, "I want to see my son."

"I'll send for him."

"Alone. Do you hear me, Andrade? *Alone.*"

Rohan was there quickly, dark circles beneath his eyes and strain tightening his features. Andrade lingered long enough to see him sit and take his father's hand, then left them alone.

Rohan pressed the cold fingers between his own. "I'm here, Father."

Zehava's hand curled around his. "There are things I must tell you. Will you listen to me at last?"

"I've always listened."

"And then gone your own way. Well, I won't be here to listen to much longer, so pay attention." Zehava licked his lips and made a face. "It won't be the dragon claws through my guts that will kill me. I'll die of thirst and starvation. Get me something to drink."

Rohan took a square of white silk soaked in water and pressed it to his father's lips. It was all that was allowed; anything Zehava swallowed would only make the pain worse. Andrade had ordered that nothing be given the prince but her own concoctions, which would kill the pain before they caused it.

Zehava sucked at the moisture, grimaced again, and closed his eyes. "Never trust anyone, Rohan. Especially not the Merida, and most especially not the High Prince. The first will slink into the Desert to attack when you least expect it—and the second would like to."

"Actually," Rohan replied, "the Merida will probably try to test me next spring. I thought it might be interesting to fight them for a while, then buy them off. Oh, I know it's risky," he admitted, seeing his father's eyes widen in outrage. "They'll purchase weapons and support that won't make it any easier to crush them when they grow arrogant enough to attack in full force. But if they can't defeat us after I hand them the money to do it with—and they won't, I promise—their sources will dry up. Still, I'm afraid that I'll have to spend a great deal of money to lure them into doing what I want them to."

"Buy them off! Of all the—!" But then he gave a short cough of laughter. "As if I have anything to say about it now! My pride would never have permitted it. But I have to trust you, don't I, Rohan? Laugh for me when they're beaten back."

"I will."

Zehava nodded and changed the subject. "You'll need a wife soon."

Rohan smiled slightly. "I promise she'll be pretty, and you'll have handsome grandchildren."

Zehava grinned his appreciation, teeth flashing whitely in his black beard that seemed to have acquired gray streaks very suddenly. "Pretty or not, treat your wife as you would a dragon. Prepare yourself carefully to meet her, and approach with respect and admiration. Always preserve her pride by letting her show her strength—and then educate her as to exactly who her master is."

Rohan thought of the face in the flames and said nothing.

"The promises of a prince die with him," Zehava went on, shifting slightly in the bed. "You'll have to see to the holdings soon. Send Chay to the lesser ones as your deputy, but go yourself to the greater. They must feel your hand as they have felt mine. Don't try to buy *them* off."

"No. I won't."

"I wish I could have seen your wife," he fretted. "Make sure she's not *too* beautiful. A beautiful woman is her own temptation. She'll think more of herself than of you. The only exception I ever met was your mother."

"Yes, Father."

"Your real wealth is in your children, Rohan." The fierce black gaze slid away to a corner of the room. "Mine has been."

Rohan's eyes stung at the rare words of tenderness. "Is it?" he asked, his throat tight. "I'm not the son you wanted. You would have done better with someone like Chay."

"I would have known him better," Zehava acknowledged. "I don't know you very well, do I? And I fear for you because of it. I'm leaving you a strong princedom built by four generations. Hold onto it, Rohan."

"My ways aren't yours, Father. But I promise I'll keep what's ours."

"*Yours* now," Zehava said gruffly. "I give all to you alone. Remember that. Not a grain of sand or a breath of wind over the dunes is anyone's but yours. You'll have your battles to keep them. I wish I could see those, too." He paused, looked up, and gave his son a tiny smile. "I never told you how proud I was, did I? My scholarly fool of a son in common trooper's harness, covered in Merida blood. . . ."

"You didn't tell me, but I knew."

"You'll have to become a better liar," Zehava observed wryly.

"Not with those I love," Rohan replied firmly.

"Do you?"

He held tighter to his father's hand. "Yes. I never really knew you, either. And I'm sorry for it. But I do love you."

Sunlight crept a finger's width across the bed before the old prince spoke again. "A pity we never really talked before now."

"But we *are* talking, and that's what's important." Rohan tried to believe it, tried to forget all the years when one approached the other and found only incomprehension.

"If you have daughters—and I hope you will, for there's no delight in a man's life like a daughter—" He coughed and again Rohan gave him the square of damp silk. Zehava nodded his thanks and continued, "Indulge your daughters as shamefully as I've done with Tobin. It's a husband's duty to tame a woman, not her father's."

Rohan chuckled. "Chay hasn't had much luck that I can see!"

Zehava grinned at him. "Remember that with your own wife! Don't break her spirit, but let her know who's master in your bed. Have you ever had a woman?"

Rohan cursed himself for blushing. "I'm not entirely ignorant."

"A nice, evasive answer. You've a talent for them. I wish I could meet the girl who'll make a man of you. But remember to make a woman of her at the same time. *Your* woman."

Again he thought of the grave, earnest face framed in fire-gold hair, and said nothing.

"Be tender of your mother's feelings, but don't let her meddle. Your wife will be princess here, and you mustn't let Milar trod the girl underfoot."

"I'm sure Mother will understand."

"Your mother understands nothing except that I'm dying."

"She loves you so much," Rohan whispered. "I hope I'm as lucky in my wife."

Zehava sighed quietly. "Take my ashes to Rivenrock

and blow them in the face of that damned grandsire who killed me."

"I'll do better than that," Rohan promised. "I'll mingle his ashes with yours and let the winds take them the length and breadth of the Desert."

The black eyes gleamed. "If you aren't the most perverse son a man ever had! Yes, do that. I'd like that. Two old dragons."

"Exactly," Rohan replied with a smile, amazed and grateful that his father had not questioned his ability to kill the dragon.

"Let me sleep for a while, and then send your mother to me. She'll need you, Rohan. Tobin has Chay, and you'll have your duties. But Mila won't have anyone." He sank deeper into the pillows. "Poor Mila. My poor darling . . ." He paused for a moment, then repeated, "You'll have your duties. It's good that you'll go through them alone. That's a cruel thing, but necessary. You'll have to stand alone, my son. Do it proudly. Not even your wife can share it all. Find someone who understands that."

Rohan hesitated, then decided to tell him. "I've already found a wife."

Zehava struggled for a moment to sit up, eyes blazing, then collapsed back into the pillows with a grunt. Rohan didn't fuss over him, knowing it would only irritate him. "Who is she?" the old prince demanded. "What's her name?"

"Sioned," he murmured.

"Does your mother know?"

"No one knows except Andrade."

Another short laugh escaped his lips. "Andrade, eh? Well. The family witch. Don't let her trap you. She's sly and does as she pleases for her own reasons."

"I know. I've learned a few things from her over the years." He grinned down at his father.

Zehava choked again on laughter, forcing himself to calm down as a spasm of pain hit him. "Oh, by the Storm Devil, I wish I could see the prince you'll make! I never knew you before, Rohan. Promise me you'll talk to your own sons more than I talked to you."

He could think of no reply, so he merely nodded. Then he bent and pressed his lips to his father's hand in token of homage and love. Before the stinging in his eyes could become tears, he said, "Rest now. I'll send Mother to you in a little while." Then he left the chamber.

At his own suite he dismissed his squire and stood before the open windows, looking down at his mother's gardens below. He'd done what he'd promised himself he'd do: ease his father's worries so he could die in peace. Zehava no longer feared for his son or his lands. It would be a long time before his son stopped fearing for himself.

Stronghold was hushed, and would remain so until Zehava was dead and his pyre extinguished. Rohan felt he was living in a silent shadow-world, alone and not quite real. The only reality was in fire—the dying blaze of his father's life, the flames that would engulf Zehava's remains, the light in the Flametower that would be quenched and then relit, and the face he had seen framed in burning red-gold hair. Himself a wraith wrapped in shadows, he could think of those fires but not be lit by them. Flames would make him prince, husband, and—he hoped—lover. But right now they had no power to illumine those future selves.

He listened to the quiet and watched the patterns of shadow play over the trees below. He should be thinking of the time when his own light would kindle and spread across the Desert with a very different blaze than his father's. He should be thinking about his bride's arrival, his mother's anguish, his sister's and nephews' inheritances from Zehava. The hundred details of death and the million more of life ongoing should be occupying his mind. But Rohan inhabited the shadows of Stronghold, waiting for the fire.

Legend had it that long ago when the world was very young, the first Sunrunners had learned from the Goddess how to weave light. Fire, pleased to be the source of their weavings, struck bargains with her brothers Earth and Air so that *faradh'im* might work their magic unmolested. But their sister Water proved recalcitrant, being

Fire's natural enemy; though she could not interfere with
Sunrunners gliding over her on light, she proved remarkably resourceful when they attempted to cross her in
person. Placid Earth did not much care what happened
above her, being constantly busy with his own concerns,
but whimsical Air sometimes gave Water a little help,
blowing up fearful gusts whenever a *faradhi* was foolish
enough to sail on the open sea. Help or not, Water
enjoyed herself every time a Sunrunner so much as rowed
across a stream.

Thus the ten Sunrunners in Sioned's bridal party looked
in dismay at the wide expanse of the Faolain River and
gulped. Camigwen reined in her horse, staring at the
rushing river. "I am *not* looking forward to this," she
stated.

Ostvel laughed at her. "It's only one little river."

"Little?"

"We went a hundred measures out of our way to avoid
the wider crossings," he reminded her.

Sioned sighed. "A good thing, too, or I'd arrived at
Stronghold not fit to speak with."

When Ostvel laughed again, Cami chided, "Oh, stop
it! You don't know what it's like to look at that river and
know you're going to be deathly ill!"

"Ah, but *you* don't know what it's like to set sail to
Kierst-Isel, the sun overhead and the wind at your back,
sails tight and deck swaying beneath your feet—"

"Ostvel, *please*!" Sioned begged.

He winked at her. "You're definitely going to the right
country," he teased, then tossed his reins to Cami and
swung down off his horse. "Here, hold onto these while I
bargain with the riverman for a decent passage fee."

Camigwen gave the water another nervous glance and
muttered, "Why don't they just build a bridge?"

"Too easy," Sioned answered with another sigh. "Ostvel
says he'll send us across first and leave the baggage for
last. Nice of him to give us some time to recover."

"And there's this monster to cross again on the way
back," Cami moaned. "I might stay with you in the
Desert forever! Just look at that flimsy raft!"

"It doesn't look so bad," Sioned replied, trying to

sound confident but not at all sure herself about the manner of their crossing. She dismounted, wanting nice, firm ground beneath her feet for as long as possible, and helped Meath organize the line of horses to be loaded. All the *faradh'im* were already green beneath their tans.

When Ostvel returned with the riverman, Cami demanded of the latter, "Why isn't there a bridge?"

"Across this water, lady? How do you propose we span *that?*" He pointed proudly to the river. "She swells up in the spring like a pregnant doe to the very walls of my house. My grandsir, now, he lashed together a bridge one autumn, and it worked fine until the spring when the Lady River decided she didn't like it and swept the bridge away—and my grandsir with it."

"Oh," Cami said, peering at the deceptively smooth surface of the water. "Well, she doesn't look too angry now," she added.

"See that little ripple halfway across?" He indicated a spot where sunlight glanced off a pulsing bulge in the water. "The current there runs faster than the best-blooded horses Lord Chaynal of Radzyn Keep ever bred. I took his lordship across some years ago and he told me that himself!"

Sioned ached to ask questions about Lord Chaynal, whom she knew to be the prince's brother-by-marriage. But she held her tongue, for it would not be seemly for a future princess to be caught gossiping.

"Never fear, ladies," the riverman finished cheerfully. "Eldskon is what my mother named me, the way all good folk have names that mean something in the old way of speaking, and it's a good name in my trade for it means 'soft passage.' And that's what I promise you," he ended with a flourish.

"Goddess, I hope so," Camigwen muttered.

The raft was big enough to hold twelve loosely hobbled horses tethered to its railing, stout tree trunks lashed together with wrist-thick ropes. But the instant Sioned set foot onto the flat wooden planks, her stomach fluttered and her eyes ached with the beginnings of the usual *faradhi* reaction to water. She swallowed hard. This was only the shallows, where the raft floated gently in calm

water without any currents. Reminding herself that she
had her dignity to maintain, she vowed to stay stone-
faced and in possession of her breakfast.

It was problematic whether the horses or the Sunrunners
regarded the river ahead with greater trepidation. The
raft surged forward, guided by two huge cables anchored
on the opposite shore. Ostvel kept his eyes on the horses,
Eldskon on the heavy iron rings through which the cables
were threaded. The raft used the river's own speed for
the crossing, the cables angled downriver to take full
advantage of the currents. There was a similar crossing
upstream angled for east-west travelers. Sioned had carefully examined the arrangements and while her rational
mind told her the system was sound, her senses froze as
the raft bumped into a current and she realized she was
entrusting her life to a few planks, some rails, and a
couple of woven cables. The notion was not reassuring to
her stomach.

Camigwen was huddled on her knees, grasping the
lower rails with both hands. Sioned was the only other
faradhi still upright. The horses shifted nervously and
whinnied to their fellows back on the western shore as
the raft swayed and bumped as the main current caught
it. Sioned managed to keep her feet, but as they hit the
bulge of fast water in midriver she could no longer keep
her breakfast. Clinging to the rails, she bent over and
was inelegantly sick.

A little while later she was vaguely aware of someone
carrying her onto dry land. She was placed on a warm,
sunny patch of grass and heard someone say in an amused
voice that she would feel better soon. She wanted to tell
him he was a damned liar, but hadn't the strength. It was
a mistake to open her eyes; the sunlight hit her like a
sword to the skull. Croaking out a feeble curse, she
fainted.

Shouts roused her. Sitting up blearily, she clutched at
her head with both hands and gulped down nausea, wondering dully why her stomach thought there was anything
left to rid itself of. The sunlight stabbed into her eyes
again, but at least that was bearable. What was not was
the confusion of her vision. The horses tied up nearby

were very big, then very small, then fogged as if the winter mists of Goddess Keep had descended around them. The riverbank receded into the far distance, then snapped back so suddenly she put her hands to ward it off. Sioned was vastly tempted to lie back and be miserable for a few days, as it appeared she was actually going to live through this. She hoped the prince would appreciate it.

But someone was still shouting, and despite the confounding of her senses she forced herself to rise to her knees. She squinted, trying to bring the raft into focus. Halfway across the river, it seemed halfway across the world.

And the horses that should have been on it were gone.

"Sweet Goddess," she breathed. Downstream she glimpsed the terrified animals trying hopelessly to fight the current. Her own cream-colored mare submerged and did not reappear. Sioned unwisely attempted to stand, failed, and furiously tried again. This time she gained her feet and dug her nails into her palms. Staggering to the riverbank, she fell; the icy shock of the water and cut of stones into her knees and hands combined to clear her head. She gulped down water, choked, and lifted her head to the river.

She saw at once what had happened. The cables on the opposite shore had broken, and upon their snapping the raft was at the river's mercy. The lurch had sent the horses against the rails, their weight breaking the wood. The cables on this side were the only reason the raft had not hurtled downstream, for those on board hung on tight, trying to pull the raft to safety. Sioned cried out as she looked around to the moorings. The cables, straining against the four massive posts that anchored them, had began to fray.

Sioned pushed herself upright and stumbled over to where Mardeem lay face down on the grass. She rolled him over and slapped him, yelling his name, then hauled him by the ankles down to the river. She repeated this treatment on Meath and Antoun, and the snow-cold water did its work.

"Mardeem!" Sioned cried, and he winced at the sound of her voice. "Wake the others, quickly! Antoun, Meath, get up and come with me. Hurry!"

She tugged the two men to their feet and led them to the cables, where they wrapped their hands around the taut cords and began to pull. The work of three people against the surging river was hopeless, and Sioned knew it. Pain tore through her shoulder muscles and she grunted with effort, hearing Mardeem's chanted curses just behind her. Part of her wanted to laugh hysterically, for he was as poetic in his oaths as he was in his songs.

Eldskon and Ostvel lashed the cables around the iron ring, for to pull would be to negate Sioned's plan. More hands were helping now. She looked around and saw Camigwen bringing two horses. Ostvel yelled encouragement as the ropes were secured on saddles, and with the added power the raft began to move more surely to the bank. But as the distance narrowed, Sioned saw that the ring was pulling free of the splintering boards around it. Those on board grabbed hold of the cables to ease the strain.

At last the river let go of the raft and it was hauled into the shallows. Its shaken occupants leaped off as *faradh'im* collapsed like felled trees. Sioned had no memory of toppling over into the sand, nor of being carried once more to soft, warm grass. It was past midday before she knew anything at all, and her first sensations were decidedly pleasant. She lay wrapped in a blanket of shadows and sunlight, and there was a taste of fresh mossberries on her lips, sweet and spicy. She sighed luxuriously, turning her head to look at the smiling blue eyes she knew would be watching her, framed in sunsilk hair.

"Well," said a voice nearby. "It's nice of you to wake up so we can thank you, Sioned."

Disappointment pierced her. This was not the voice she had thought to hear. Memory rushed back and she opened her eyes, propping herself on her elbows to peer up at Ostvel. In the next instant every muscle in her body seemed to twist, and she sank back onto the grass with her lower lip caught between her teeth. The prince would *not* appreciate giving welcome to a cripple.

"Stay there. Everything's all right now—or at least mostly all right." Ostvel held a cup to her lips. "Have some water. It's a thimbleful compared to what I would have swallowed if you and Cami hadn't thought so fast. I'm in your debt, Sioned."

The water tasted of mossberries, and regret sliced through her again. "What happened?" she mumbled.

"Nothing that makes tragic hearing, except for the loss of the horses. The twenty of us are all safe on this side. But we only have twelve mounts left. A somewhat unequal balance, one might say."

She sat up again, stretched carefully, and winced. "So twelve of us will have to go on. The rest can stay here with our friend of the 'soft crossing,' " she said with a faint smile. "I hope he thinks seriously about building a bridge."

"I doubt he can think at all just now. He's incoherent with terror of what Andrade would have done to him if he'd lost us—or what he believes the almighty Lady would do." Ostvel sat back on his heels and shrugged. "He's not our problem though. *You* are."

"Me?"

"Sioned, I can't take you to Stronghold with only eleven in attendance. You're going to be a princess!"

"A princess without a wedding dress," she reminded him. "All my things were on the other horses. Ostvel, we have to go on as we are. She told me to be there in six days."

"You're supposed to arrive in a state befitting the bride of a prince," he said stubbornly, his kind, rugged face furrowed with concern.

She smiled fondly. "I'll be lucky to arrive at all, at this rate. How's Cami doing?"

"Still insensible, poor darling. I'm amazed she was able to get up, let alone think of the horses. I'm amazed *any* of you moved as fast as you did. We owe you Sunrunners our lives."

"Remember that the next time you tease us about crossing water." Sioned ran her hands back through her damp hair. "We're losing the day, Ostvel. Prop Cami on her horse. Tie her to the saddle if you must, but we have to get moving."

Camigwen recovered enough to sit her horse without the measures Sioned suggested, and fretted for the rest of the afternoon about the loss of Sioned's clothes and consequence. No amount of reassurance could convince her that Sioned did not much care. In truth, she was relieved to be going to Stronghold in simplicity rather than in state. She wasn't a princess yet, and still couldn't quite make herself believe she would be.

By the time they stopped for the night, everyone was exhausted. Muscles accustomed to riding were not used to hauling on cables, and muffled groans were heard as the twelve dismounted. They spent the night on a farm belonging to Palevna's maternal uncle, but the *faradh'im* were unable to do full justice to his wife's splendid cooking and after dinner dragged themselves out to the barn to collapse onto blankets in the soft hay.

"Just think," Ostvel said brightly, gray eyes dancing, "we'll have to go back across the Faolain on our way home again!"

Camigwen glared at him. "Think again," she said darkly. "I'll have Mardeem *sing* a bridge into being if I must, but I'm not going to cross that water on anything but my own two feet." She threw her arms around her Chosen and buried her face in the curve of his neck. "I almost lost you to that damned river!"

Sioned watched him soothe her, and smiled. Goddess blessing was surely on this pair. Her smile faded as she realized that when they married, she herself would be far away, unable to join in the celebrations.

And her own wedding? She could neither visualize it nor believe in it. The man, yes—she could see him in every color of the sky and every gleam of sunlight. But the prince was a stranger. Who was he? Was there a mind to match those beautiful, brilliant eyes?

She lay awake long after the others slept, and stared up at the stars through loft doors left open to the soft night. Such clear, sweet light; to ride that would be feat indeed. If it could be done, then even on nights when the moons did not rise one could still go where there was need by dancing down those pale, fiery trails of light. But it was forbidden to Sunrunners, the glow of the stars. Perhaps the protection of the Goddess did not extend to those faraway pinpoints of light. The Fire of sun and moons was under her blessing, but what of the stars? They threw whispery shadows over the meadows and mountains, mysterious and dreamy. What colors were hidden within them? Sioned, with six rings circling her fingers, was capable of riding both sun and moons. She counted those rings in the starlight, four gold and two silver, plain circles that at Goddess Keep did not set her apart but which out in the world marked as her different. She remembered what it had been like at River Run during her childhood, when her sister-by-marriage had eyed her askance and whispered about her to her brother Davvi. In her maturity, Sioned could think of Lady Wisla with something approaching gratitude, for if she had not been so eager to be sole mistress of the Holdings and their wealth, Sioned would never have been sent to Goddess Keep.

And she would not be riding now to become the wife of a prince.

Why was Andrade doing this? she wondered. The last trained *faradhi* to marry into the important nobility had been Sioned's grandmother, who, though not a highborn herself, had married a prince of Kierst. Their daughter had married Sioned and Davvi's father, having shown no signs of the gifts. Younger sons and daughters of highborns sometimes become Sunrunners, but usually they stayed untrained despite evidence of talent, marrying rather than coming to Goddess Keep for instruction. A prince or lord wearing *faradhi* rings was unheard of. Sioned did not interest herself overmuch in the affairs of the princedoms, but she knew enough to understand that a Sunrunner prince would be perceived as a threat. But there was a very good chance that one of her children would be just that. Though Princess Milar did not possess the gifts, they had been known to skip several generations before showing up again.

All at once Sioned realized that the son she bore to the prince would rule after him. She cursed her stupidity in not having considered it earlier, for being so wrapped up in her thoughts of him that she had not thought about children at all. And she knew what Andrade wanted of her at last: a *faradhi* prince ruling the Desert, using all the power of his position and his gifts to—to do what? That was what she could not understand. Or, rather, she hoped she did not understand.

Chapter Five

Prince Zehava died before dawn on the sixth day, his family attending him. He had drifted in and out of awareness all the previous day and night, oncoming death dulling his mind and slurring his speech. But he died without pain, and without fear for the future of the son who became ruling prince when Zehava breathed his last. Ignoring the tradition that forbade him the death chamber, Rohan was with his father when he died. Milar closed her husband's eyes; Tobin ran her fingers gently over his forehead to smooth out the lines of stress. Rohan bent and kissed his father, then turned and left the death chamber.

Andrade waited a little while, then went after him. He was where she knew he'd be: in the Flametower, helping the servants build the fire high enough to shine out over the Desert and inform Zehava's people of his passing. The blaze would be seen from distant hills where other fires would be lit in a chain of light that by nightfall would extend the length and breadth of the princedom.

Moisture had become an unpleasant trickle down her spine and between her breasts before Rohan had satisfied himself that the fire was sufficiently bright. She was not in the best of moods anyway, and the heat worsened her temper. Though never deeply attached to Zehava, she had appreciated him and knew the world to be poorer for his death. But now she had a new prince to deal with, and as they left the inferno behind, her voice was perhaps sharper than it should have been.

"Not a single preparation has been made for Sioned's arrival. Why are you denying your bride her proper honors? I refuse to have the girl slink in here like a common guest, and not a very important one at that!"

"Peace, Andrade," Rohan said tiredly. "It's been a long night, and I have a longer day ahead of me."

"You'll answer me before it grows any longer, boy!"

A glittering gaze met hers, fierce as a dragon on the hunt. "The girl is coming to *my* keep. Andrade, not yours. Her welcome or lack of it will be arranged as *I* dictate."

"Rohan!"

But he was off down the stairs, supple limbs setting a pace her older bones could not match. She spat a series of oaths that would have shocked even those who knew her best, then went to her rooms for a fruitless try at sleep.

The signal fire burned throughout the day, but Rohan was not at Stronghold to feel the heat melt slowly down through the keep. At daybreak he rode from the courtyards through the tunnel cut into solid rock down to the desert. With Chaynal at his side and his guards commander Maeta supervising nine more soldiers, he rode toward Rivenrock Canyon.

The sun rose, broiling the air, small updrafts brushing at his clothes and his horse's mane. Rohan's fair hair soon darkened with sweat and the thin gray silk of his tunic clung in damp patches to his chest and back. He told himself the salt sting in his eyes was sweat and that the hollow in his body was only the growling of an empty stomach. Over forty measures passed in silence. The sweltering air kept all animals in their shelters with barely enough energy to whimper their complaints to each other. A few birds were aloft on their way somewhere else, as birds always were in the Desert. Sometimes there came the soft shussh of shifting sand or a snort as one of the horses cleared its nostrils. But none of the men or women spoke for a long, tense time.

Finally Chay, who had let his horse lag behind Rohan's to give the young man some privacy, caught up to him again. They rode ahead of the troops, out of earshot even in the profuund stillness. Rohan glanced around at him. "Yes?" he prompted.

"You've never hunted a dragon before. It's past mating now, and he'll be even more vicious."

"I promised Father."

"Rohan, I wish you'd let me—"

"No. This dragon is mine."

Chay glanced away. "As you wish, my prince," he said stiffly.

"No! Chay, don't—I never want that from you!"

The cry from the heart softened Chaynal. "I'll have to call you that around the others, you know. But we'll stay to each other as we've always been, if that's what you want."

Rohan nodded his gratitude. "I need that, Chay. I'm going to need your help."

"You have it. You don't need to ask." Chay shrugged his shoulders against the heat. "I can almost hear the Merida getting ready. They'll have seen the fires by evening and know Zehava's dead. There'll be trouble, Rohan."

"I have a few ideas," the young prince responded. "And not just for them."

"Roelstra?" Chay guessed, and saw confirmation in the set of Rohan's jaw. "You'd better be in one hell of a secure position before the *Rialla*."

"I'll be in what he'll think is an untenable position. He'll like that. He'll think I'm ready to grab whatever support I can get, even from him. And support will come in the form of one of his doubtlessly charming daughters as my wife."

"But Tobin said that Andrade—"

"Don't believe everything you hear."

"You're going to disobey the Lady of Goddess Keep?" Chay whistled softly between his teeth.

"I'm scared to death, if you must know," he confessed. "She loomed over Tobin and me like a she-dragon when we were little, and the feeling lingers a bit. But I'm going to live my own life, not her version of it. And that's why I'm going to need your support, especially at the *Rialla*."

"I'll do whatever you want, of course. But do you know what you're doing?"

"Yes," Rohan said flatly. "I'm going to build a princedom that doesn't depend on my sword. Father said the promises of a prince die with him. Not *this* prince, Chay!

When I die, my sons will inherit peace, not just the absence of war for a few seasons or years while enemies think up new ways to attack." He paused for Chay's reaction, and when none was forthcoming remarked, "You're not being very enthusiastic."

"It's a fine idea," Chaynal said carefully. "But I don't think it's very practical."

"I'll make it work. You'll see."

Rivenrock rose up before them. The reddish striations in the stone might have been dried blood, dragon or human. Rohan drew rein, contemplating the mouth of the canyon with its great spire.

"He's still here." Rohan pointed to dark patches of plants. "See the bittersweet along the cliff? He's been cropping it to keep up his strength, because he's not done mating. Usually it grows back almost overnight, but this is eaten right down to the ground."

"It doesn't take a dragon six days to mate his females," Chay protested.

"Father wounded him badly. Can't you sense that he's still back there in the canyon?"

Chay saw and heard nothing, and said so. Rohan only smiled. All at once a shriek echoed off the canyon walls, its force clattering loose stones down to the gully. "He's here," Rohan repeated, and rode forward. Half a measure into the canyon he dismounted and unsheathed his sword, gesturing for Chaynal to do the same. "Maeta," he said to the commander, "Keep everyone else back. You're here to help me drag this monster home, and that's all. Chay, come with me."

"Your grace," Maeta began, her eyes narrowing with worry—black eyes like Zehava's, whose kinswoman she may or may not have been depending on which family rumor one believed. Rohan gave her a long look and she subsided with an obedient nod.

Rohan and Chaynal climbed the narrow shelf that passed for a trail along the canyon wall. The acrid odor of dragon mating was in the air. Caves lined the cliffs, many of them walled up by females who had already laid their eggs within. Eight caves on the opposite side of the canyon were sealed, and Rohan wondered how many

dragons curled within shells there, baking in ovenlike
heat to maturity. Dragons, with broad and graceful wings
for flight, long throats for calling to each other on the
wind—and deadly talons that ripped flesh to shreds. Rohan
had to think of the dragons as killers today, not as the
soaring, beautiful creatures that had enchanted him from
childhood.

He had been certain that the grandsire would still be
here. Zehava had crippled the dragon and slowed him up
in attending to his females. Two caves were still open on
the opposite wall, and the shifting of pebbles within told
him there were she-dragons inside, waiting impatiently
for their lord. An unmated female, too heavy with eggs
to fly, died quickly; crumbled skeletons of those who had
attempted flight littered the gully below. Rohan had ridden out here often, collecting talons, teeth, and the odd
wing- or thigh-bone for study. He knew how the skeletons fit together and how the muscles lay along them,
and how the whole became an animal of rare beauty—at
least to him. But now he was going to kill a dragon,
finish the work his father had begun before he started
work of his own.

He climbed faster. It was not recommended to scram-
ble up a cliffside with a naked sword in one's hand, but
he didn't dare sheathe it in case the dragon surprised
him. Even the instant or two it would take to draw his
sword might mean his life or Chay's. Risky enough to
send rocks clattering down the walls as they climbed, but
he hoped the dragon would think it only the sound of the
stone ovens settling into place for the summer.

At last they reached the cavern he'd spotted from
below. After catching his breath, he told Chay to find a
good place to hide.

"Rohan, will you forgive me if I tell you you're out of
your mind? This is all very good sport, but I'd feel much
better if I knew what we were doing."

"Take a look at this cave. It's walled up, the eggs laid
and the she-dragon gone. Now, if you were the sire and
you'd been through hell to mate this year, and you saw
two puny creatures about to attack the fruits of your
labors—"

Chay snorted with laughter. "You *are* out of your mind. All right, what do you want me to do?"

"Nothing much, unless I'm killed. If I am—run like hell. And tell Mother to forgive me."

"If she knew about this, she'd kill you herself and save the dragon the trouble." Chay shook his head, then went to the far end of the ledge where a sizable pile of rocks provided adequate cover.

Rohan wiped sweat from his forehead and turned to study the opposite wall where empty caves gaped tauntingly. From which would the dragon emerge? Or was he in a cave on this side? Instinct said not. Rohan refused to contemplate the insanity of this undertaking and slid behind an outcropping of rock to wait. The ledge was about a man-height wide and about twice that long—plenty of room for him to maneuver, but difficult for a dragon. Rohan hoped so, anyway.

The shadows were shortening toward noon when the dragon limped out of a cave opposite Rohan's perch. Replete after a morning of wholehearted attention to one of his ladies, he yawned widely and stretched first one hind leg, then the other. Rohan heard Chay's muffled laughter nearby. It really was rather funny to see this randy old grandsire of a beast grown sleepy with his sexual exertions. But Rohan lost all impulse toward mirth when he noted the many rents in the dragon's hide that still oozed blood. As the great wings unfolded to prepare for flight, Rohan also saw how stiffly the dragon moved. There was a large splotch of congealed blood on the underside of one wing, and a smaller patch on a flank. Rohan gathered himself and stepped out into the sunlight, calling a derisive challenge to the dragon that had killed his father.

Because the sun was over Rohan's shoulder and his position was higher up this side of the canyon, the dragon had to squint to see him. In other circumstances that would have been funny, too, watching the great baleful eyes narrow as they sought out the call's source. Rohan sent a prayer of thanks to the Goddess for arranging things thus; the dragon would have to beat his injured wings strongly to bring himself up to Rohan's position.

Between his wounds and his excesses of mating, the dragon was so exhausted that the effort would be immense.

Exhilaration flushed through him as the wings stroked once, twice, unsure of their strength. The dragon grunted in annoyance and pain, then lurched into the air. For an instant his ability to fly was in doubt. But with three powerful beats of his wings he was airborne—and heading straight for Rohan.

The prince gulped down terror, brought up his sword, and held his ground. The dragon loomed over him, sunlight glaring off his golden hide. Jaws parted, revealing broken teeth, and Rohan felt the heat of the dragon's breath in his face. He had a sudden mental image of his own head being swallowed into that gaping throat. He had never been so close to a dragon before, and what he wanted most of all was to hide until the terrible beast flew away.

Instead he leaped to one side, slashing his sword down with all his strength. By the span of his own fingers he missed getting sliced in half by dragon jaws. The beast howled as he slammed into the ledge, one wing bent up against his body and blood welling where Rohan had chopped at it. As he tried to extend the wing again, bones cracked like blasts of lightning across the sky. Balance and flight gone, the dragon clawed at the cliff's edge with his hind legs, forelegs scrabbling the air in an attempt to gain purchase—preferably around Rohan.

Looking into those reddened, infuriated eyes, Rohan felt his own blood boil. This was the enemy. Something very old and fierce welled up in him and he hacked at the nearest foreleg, laughing as the dragon screamed. One wing stroked frantically, the other useless. Rohan plunged his blade into the long, writhing neck. Gore spurted out as he withdrew the sword and he stabbed it in again. The dragon's head lashed back with an agonized bellow, then fell forward. Rohan hefted his sword a last time and sank it into the dragon's eye.

There was a hot, ripping sensation down his arm as he lunged out of the way. The sword that had been so light only an instant before now seemed impossibly heavy as he tried to pull it from the eye socket, where it had caught against the jutting browbone. Rohan cried aloud with the effort and the sudden burning in his shoulder. The dragon's head was flung toward the sky, the sword still protruding from the bloody hole that had been his eye. He clawed at the rocks, found no hold. His wing swept back and forth, instinct demanding flight, tail thrashing against the canyon wall. The dying dragon gave a last terrible shriek and slid down the cliff, his great frame crashing onto the ragged stones below.

Rohan glanced down at his arm, where a talon had scored flesh and muscle. He judged it a minor wound as he wiped it clean, not knowing which was his own blood and which was the dragon's. He wondered with vague interest if the tales about dragon's blood being poisonous were true.

All at once there was no warmth. The sun had no heat, the air turned to frigid water through which he moved with painful slowness. The searing breeze froze sweat on his body and congealed smears of blood into ice. He looked over the ledge at the dragon he had killed. Sick, swaying, he staggered back from the brink, fell to his knees, and vomited.

Canyon and sky were still spinning around him when he felt cool water dribbling onto his face. He shook his head irritably and groaned. "Bite down on this," Chay's voice instructed, and Rohan gagged on something bitterly salty that made him want to retch again. He swallowed convulsively and made himself sit up. "Give it a moment to work," Chay said. The small wafer of herbs and salt reached his stomach like a goblet of strong wine before breakfast. His arm began to hurt in earnest, and he winced.

Chay sat back on his heels. "For a while there I thought I'd have to sail for the Far Islands and never come back. Tobin wouldn't have let me live past telling her you were dead. But you killed him, Rohan—Goddess, how you killed him! It was beautiful! Everyone saw it, too. Your first dragon."

"First and last. Never again, Chay. I don't want to do that ever again."

He accepted his friend's help in getting to his feet.

They started slowly down the rocky path, sliding uncertainly on loose rocks. Rohan's knees worked, just barely. Maeta had their horses ready when they reached bottom, and Chay spent some moments calming the frantic Akkal, who had never been riderless at a dragon hunt before. Then he joined Rohan and the others beside the massive corpse.

It took all Rohan's remaining strength to yank his sword from the dragon's eye. He took off his tunic and used it to wipe the blade clean, instructing Maeta to take just the talons and teeth for now. "We'll send someone out for the rest of him tomorrow."

"Yes, my lord." Maeta bowed low. She had taught him archery, horsemanship, played with him during his childhood, concealed his escapades from his parents. And now she bowed to him.

Rohan drained half a waterskin down his throat, wishing it was brandy. Chay helped him wash some of the blood from his face and chest, exclaiming in surprise at the long talon mark from right shoulder to to elbow. The wound was cleansed, bound with the remains of Rohan's tunic, and the prince held himself from flinching at his brother-by-marriage's rough, expert handling.

All at once there was a low rumble in the canyon: sinister, terrifying. He whirled around, one hand on his sword. The others stopped their work and froze, staring into the empty gorge. The sound thickened, intensified, a dozen different notes and all eerie enough to set the hair rising on Rohan's nape.

"They're mourning him," Chay said, breaking the terrible thrall of dragon voices. "Hurry it up and let's go home."

The wailing rose and fell as they worked. The she-dragons grieved for their dead just as Rohan and his family would grieve tomorrow night when they set the torch to Zehava's pyre. At last the talons and teeth were all in large velvet pouches, clattering soft percussion to the requiem music that followed Rohan and his people out into the Desert. He shivered in the blazing sunlight and silently repeated his vow. *Never again.*

*   *   *

Sioned drew and stood in her stirrups as she caught sight of the riders. Their goal was the same as hers: the cleft in the Vere Hills where Stronghold crouched between the cliffs. She glimpsed the sheen of afternoon sunlight off fair hair and felt all the color drain from her face.

"Him?" Ostvel murmured at her side.

She nodded, unable to speak.

"Oh, Goddess!" Camigwen exclaimed. "Be quick, Sioned—wash your face, and here's my comb—hurry!"

"Leave her be, Cami," Ostvel said. "What man can expect a woman to come through the Desert looking as if she'd just stepped from her own chambers?"

Sioned told himself the world was full of fair-haired men. She sat down in her saddle and tightened her grip on the reins, trying to calm her ragged breathing. The party's sober gray mourning clothes told her that someone had died, someone important. But the prince wore no shirt or tunic at all. A swath of silk was wound around his right arm, and as the riders neared Sioned saw it was a hastily made bandage, soaked in blood.

"I hope we won't have to wait long. It's damned hot out here," Ostvel remarked with casual understatement. "Arrange yourselves around Lady Sioned."

The title made her start in surprise, but Ostvel had achieved the desired effect. The others formed a semicircle around her as if they were a guard of honor and she already a princess. Sunlight wavered across the sand as the riders approached, and Sioned wished futilely she had followed Cami's advice. She glanced down at her brown riding clothes, thought of the untidy knot of the braid at her nape, regretted her lack of a wash. At least he would see the worst of her first, she thought, resigned. After this, she could only improve.

The riders paused atop a dune and the blond man rode ahead, a taller, darker figure at his side. The face of her Fire-conjure appeared before Sioned in the flesh. As for the rest of him—of middle height but in elegant proportion that made him seem taller, with shoulders pulled straight despite his obvious exhaustion. They were good shoulders, strong and broad. His chest was smooth, lean muscles under golden skin shining with sweat and streaked with dried blood.

He reined in and nodded greeting. "Welcome, my lady."

She inclined her head. "Thank you, my lord." Her voice worked. Amazing.

"May I have the honor of presenting my sister's husband? Lord Chaynal of Radzyn Keep."

She looked into a pair of compelling gray eyes set deep into a tanned face. "My lord," she acknowledged with a slightly less formal nod. He was, she supposed, quite devastatingly handsome. His intense interest in her was just this side of embarrassing, and a corner of his mouth curved in a small, wry smile.

"I am indeed honored, my lady," he said, and bent his head to her.

Sioned remembered civility and gestured to the friends flanking her on either side. "My lord, may I make my companions known to you? Ostvel, Second Steward of Goddess Keep, and the Sunrunner Camigwen. These others are my friends as well."

"You are all most welcome to my lands," the prince said, and Sioned's body went nerveless. *His* lands, not his father's. They were in mourning gray for the old prince, and that meant that she would be marrying not an heir but a ruler in his own right. He was still speaking, and she attended desperately to his words. "It's fortunate that my business concluded in time for me escort you to Stronghold. Lady Andrade will be pleased to see you safely arrived."

"I look forward to talking with her," Sioned heard herself say.

Lord Chaynal's eyes said, *I'll just bet you do,* and the corner of his mouth lifted a little higher. But the prince's face was perfectly calm as he said, "My lady, will you do me the favor of a few moments' private conversation?"

Before she could answer he swung down off his horse and she remembered at the last instant to let him lift her from her saddle. His fingers closed around her waist and she blushed, hoping her sunburn would hide the rush of color. If it was this way with layers of clothes between

them, how would it be when skin touched skin? Sioned
stared at the toes of her boots as she walked, struggling
for control, and as they moved away from the others she
risked a glance at him. Her eyes were on a level with his
lips. She wondered what his smile was like and let her
gaze travel down to where a pulse beat rapidly in his
throat. Realizing he was as tense as she, Sioned relaxed a
little.

"Your business looks to have been dangerous," she
said in an astonishingly composed voice. "It's not your
own blood, I trust?"

"No. A dragon's. He drew only a little of mine." He
spoke almost absently, his gaze fixed on the hills.

Sioned resolved to keep her mouth shut unless he
asked her a direct question. Many more strides were
paced off across the white-gold sand before he stopped,
faced her, and spoke in a rush. "You know why you're
here, and so do I. Andrade expects us to marry."

"Andrade expects many things," Sioned answered.

"Further," he went on as if she hadn't spoken, "she
expects it to happen soon. But it can't. Not yet." He
looked into her eyes. His were very blue, with circles of
black around the outside of the irises. "Please believe me
when I tell you that I will marry you and no other
woman. I knew it from the moment Andrade conjured
your face in the Fire. But there are things I must do
before we can marry. Some of them may hurt you, and
for that I'm sorry—but my father is dead, I'm ruling
prince, and what a prince must do a man often regrets."

Sioned was deprived of the powers of speech by this
extraordinary recital. She simply stared at him.

"I must show everyone what manner of prince I intend
to be," he went on. "I'll explain it all to you once there's
time, and I'm hoping you're the kind of woman who can
understand such things. If not, you'll have to learn," he
said bluntly. "But I wouldn't do them if they weren't
necessary for our life together. I want to live in peace,
not at the point of a sword. Do you understand?"

She was still incapable of speaking, but for a different
reason now.

"It'll start for us when we arrive at Stronghold. I've

killed the dragon that killed my father, you see." A thin flush mounted his cheeks. "None of them thought I could."

"Whyever not?" The words popped out of her mouth before she could think, but she found them entirely natural. Who would believe this man incapable of doing whatever he chose to do?

The blue eyes narrowed with suspicion, but then a smile stole across his face and transformed it. She nearly caught her breath. "Thank you," he said. "You're not flattering me, I can tell that. You must always speak the truth to me, Sioned."

The sound of her name on his lips was her undoing, but she had no intention of allowing him to know it. Instead she hung onto her pride, made an effort, and smiled back. "I will, if you promise me the same." So much depended on his answer and his ability to keep that promise.

"I will my lady. My word on it." He touched her arm and quickly let go, startled. Touched by Fire, she thought, seeing it at last in his eyes.

"Tell me how I am to behave," she said. "We should go back to the others and we won't have the chance to talk until later, if at all."

"You know castle life, I see," he observed. "We won't have time for ourselves unless we arrange it—and I *will* arrange it. But I can't give any definite sign that I intend to marry you, and you'll find no bridal welcome at Stronghold. I'm sorry. If it was only the two of us, I'd give you—" He broke off and color again stained his cheeks. "But we're not private people and we never can be. Are you sure you want that kind of life?"

She hesitated, then shrugged and decided to tell the truth as she had promised. "When I was sixteen years old, I saw your face in the Fire. Lady Andrade told me then that I could change the vision if I wished. I never wanted to change it—and I never will."

He seemed caught between a dozen conflicting emotions, as speechless now as she had been earlier. She smiled at him.

"Silly, isn't it?" she said with another little shrug.

He swallowed, cleared his throat, and managed, "No

sillier than what happened to me when Andrade showed me *your* face in the flames."

To cover the emotion, she asked again, "How should I behave? Shall I pout, bear it bravely, or act as if I haven't a thought in my head about anything at all, let alone marrying you?"

"You'd never be able to sustain *that* role for long," he said with a sudden grin, then sobered. "But have you thought about it? Marrying me, I mean."

Impulsively she dared the Fire by touching his cheek. The shock of it went through them both and she snatched her fingers away. Yet burned into her fingertips was the feel of his skin, the moistness of his sweat, the faint stubble of unshaven beard. "Answer enough?" she whispered.

"You feel it, too," he whispered, shaken. "I couldn't believe it when I saw you—that it could happen for me the way it did for my sister and Chay. I have to marry, I've always known that, and I was hoping for a pretty enough woman with at least half a brain—but looking at you—" He drew in a breath and shook his head. "I can't expect you to understand what I'm trying to say when I'm not sure I understand it myself."

"Oh, I understand," she said almost ruefully. "It's a shock to find your emotions can tell your mind to go rot, isn't it?"

He smiled again. "Exactly. But that's how I have to behave, as if I haven't made up my mind about you." He touched her shoulder and they stared at each other in silence before he removed his hand. "That kind of thing can't happen too often, especially not in public. I'll never be able to play my part, otherwise."

"Perhaps I should pretend to be unsure, as well. Would that fit your plan?"

"Yes," he decided at once. "Perfectly. Act as if you're uncertain about marriage to me as both a man and a prince. It'll leave you some pride, at least," he added with a grimace. "I'll make it up to you, Sioned, once we're married. But that can't happen until after the *Rialla* at Waes. I'll explain everything when we can talk alone. But we have to go back now."

"I can feel them watching us," she agreed. As they started back, she said, "I was frightened on the journey here. I'm not anymore."

"I was scared, too, that Andrade's Fire had lied. I've been in the shadows these last days—all my life, it seems now. But I thank the Goddess she's sent me a Sunrunner."

"I think we'd do better to thank Andrade," Sioned replied mischievously.

"Stop looking at me like that or we'll never be able to pull this off!"

She schooled her face into solemn lines. "Better?"

"Much. But I can still see things in your eyes. Are they in mine, too?"

Casting him a sidelong glance, she said, "If they weren't, I'd do everything in my powers to put them there, Rohan."

It was the first time she had ever spoken his name aloud, to anyone. He looked away and muttered, "This isn't going to be easy."

"No."

"I'll send word by my squire—he's twelve, with black hair and freckles, and his name's Walvis. You'll like him." He paused. "Sioned?"

"Yes, my lord?"

"The dragon today—that was nothing. *You* are everything."

She did not dare reply. But as he lifted her into her saddle and the Fire sped through her again, she looked into his eyes and felt all apprehension vanish. She rode to Stronghold between Ostvel and Camigwen, dazed and happy and not minding at all that no welcome had been prepared for her, that her position was very nearly impossible, and that a difficult role had been assigned her with only the sketchiest of explanations from a man she didn't even know, a dangerous man who could do such things to her. As he rode home with his tokens of a dragon slain he did not look at her, not even after they were in the huge inner courtyard of the keep. There was no sign from him that he was aware of her existence. But she knew. She knew. They both did.

Chapter Six

It took all afternoon, a cool bath, and a visit from Lady Andrade to restore Sioned to sanity.

She effaced herself during the welcome given Rohan, standing apart with Camigwen and Ostvel. The latter had sent her escort to find the Sunrunners already at Stronghold and ask them what was going on. Sioned heard him give the order and was vaguely annoyed; Rohan would let everyone know what they ought to know. They ought to trust him, as she did.

His people not only trusted him, they obviously adored him. Their fondness he would have won as a child, and she suspected he had confirmed their respect today by killing the dragon. Of wariness or strict formality in his royal presence, there was no sign. Sioned was grateful for that. A court strangled by etiquette or silent through terror of the master's wrath would have indicated very unpleasant things about its ruler.

"Do you have any idea who these people are?" Cami whispered at last.

"I think so," Sioned answered. "The blonde lady who's been crying must be Princess Milar."

"Oh, wonderful—what powers of observation!" Cami said impatiently. "Anyone with eyes could see she's twin to Andrade—speaking of whom, she didn't look very happy when she went by us just now."

Sioned pretended she hadn't heard the remark. "The black-haired woman must be Lord Chaynal's wife."

"Who else but a wife would scold a husband so?" Ostvel asked wryly, but beneath his light tone was a nervousness Camigwen shared and Sioned did not.

Princess Tobin was indeed giving her husband the rough

95

side of her tongue. She had not been told about the hunt and was raging at him in full view of everyone. The servants unsuccessfully hid smiles and winks at some of the language that passed her lovely lips; her temper seemed to be a known commodity and when it was not directed at any of them they could enjoy it. Lord Chaynal endured his wife's blistering comments about his probable lifespan and undoubted ancestry while he uncinched his saddle and checked his stallion's hooves for stray stones. Then, having discharged his duties to his horse, he turned his full attention on his wife. Taking one long braid in each hand, he pulled her to him and shut her up with a kiss.

Two small boys came running into the courtyard, dodging horses, grooms, and castle servants. They clamored to be shown the spoils of the dragon hunt immediately. Their gray eyes proclaimed them to be Lord Chaynal's sons, and Sioned smiled as he released his breathless wife and swept the twins up for a fond hug.

Rohan was the center of his mother's and aunt's attention, bearing patiently with the former's anxious inquiries about his well-being and the latter's glowering countenance. When the family began to move toward the stairs leading up to the main hall of the keep, Ostvel looked around in complete bewilderment. "Sioned—nobody's even welcomed you!"

"There won't be a welcome for me, not in the way you're thinking," she said, following the prince with her gaze.

Camigwen stared. "What? How dare he!"

"Please, Cami! His father is dead. We can't expect—"

"I can and do expect!" she retorted.

"Cami—not now," Sioned told her.

Lady Andrade separated from the others at the foot of the steps and approached Sioned, grim-faced. "You made decent time getting here."

"We came as quickly as we could," Sioned answered.

After a withering glance up and down her travel-stained clothing, Andrade said, "So I see. Go upstairs. Urival will see to your comfort, since no one else has any time for you. I'll expect you ready to receive me before nightfall, Sioned." And with that she stalked away.

"Why is she so angry?" Camigwen complained as they crossed the courtyard. "We haven't done anything wrong!"

"If anyone's in the wrong, it's the prince," Ostvel said. "What sort of welcome is this for his bride?"

"I don't want to hear anything more about it!" Sioned exclaimed. "And don't talk about me as if I'm his betrothed, because I'm not—and I don't even know if I want to be!"

She regretted the shock and hurt in their faces. They cared only for her honor and happiness; they loved her. She hoped Rohan would give her leave to tell them why this charade was necessary—and she began her journey back to rationality with the thought that he had better provide *her* with an adequate explanation first.

Urival, Chief Steward of Goddess Keep, was in the banner-hung foyer, and called Sioned's name as the three tried not to gape at the display of carpets, fine furniture, and carved wood around them. His smile was sympathetic as he came forward to greet them.

"You must have expected better greeting than this, but what with the old prince's death before dawn this morning and this crazy dragon hunt of Rohan's to kill the beast that killed his father. . . ." He shrugged. "You couldn't have chosen a worse time to arrive, Sioned."

"It doesn't matter." She knew it had been the best possible time. No one would notice her in the press of events and she would be able to get a feel for the place and personalities of Stronghold.

"I've arranged for rooms, baths, and fresh clothes. Mourning gray," he reminded them. "I had to guess at the sizes."

Camigwen sighed. "That means I'll be tripping over my hem and Sioned's ankles will be showing. If only we hadn't lost all our baggage in the river!"

"Now, that's a story I want to hear," Urival commented. "But for now I'd better tell you something about this place so you don't get lost." They started up the main staircase, a wonder of silky wooden banisters and thick blue carpeting. "To begin with, it's huge. Five floors about the ground, one below for cold storage—or as cold as anything ever gets here—and the Flametower is so high it's said that some days you can see to the Sunrise Water. The fires are burning there now for Prince Zehava's passing."

"We saw as we rode in," Ostvel said. "When is his ritual?"

"Tomorrow night. I don't know if you'll be expected to attend."

"Of course Sioned will attend!" Camigwen bristled.

"As one of the *faradh'im*, nothing more," Sioned told her firmly.

"But you're going to be—"

"No!" She glared at her friend for the first time in their lives, and Cami's dark skin flushed with the shock. "I'm *not sure*, I tell you. It may be I'll accept him, and it may be that I won't." And after only a brief talk with Rohan she was ready to behave this way to friends of a lifetime. What had he done to her? She began to realize that he was a dangerous man indeed.

She tried to smile, to make amends. "Come, we're all tired, and I didn't mean to be so sharp with you. Urival, tell us more about Stronghold, please?"

His eyes were an unusual shade of golden brown, huge and beautiful below thick brows in a thin, angular face. She had never been able to hide anything successfully from those eyes before, and the expression in them now made her nervous. But he chose to oblige her with a recital of the rooms and wonders of the keep. They reached the second floor, turned down several long hallways, and entered what Urival described as the north wing. Windows were open along the gallery from floor to ceiling, and a riot of scents from the garden below filled the sun-heated corridor.

"This is all Princess Milar's doing," Urival explained. "The gardens used to be nothing but bare rock and sand. She planned the gardens, laid out the walks, and put that little stream in. There's even a fountain on the family's side of the building."

Sioned looked down at the neat flowerbeds and trees through which a stream and paths of silvery gravel wove like threads in a tapestry. Stone benches were set here and there, and little arched bridges painted blue and white spanned the thin trickle of water. Water was the most precious of elements here in the Desert. It was real wealth to have enough for the pleasant folly of a stream and fountain. Folly? Where she had grown up, they worried about floods. It occurred to her that she was already beginning to think like one born to this land, and was troubled anew by Rohan's influence over her.

"It's beautiful," Camigwen said. "Like a giant's hand with a little garden in its hollow. But what do they do when they want to see the sky?"

"Oh, it's not like Goddess Keep, where we're fog-bound so much of the winter," Urival said. "If there was nothing but an open sky between you and the sea and barely a tall rock in all the Long Sand, you'd feel very secure in these cliffs." He raked back his graying dark hair and smiled wryly. "Hurry along, children. Your baths are getting warm."

"Warm?" Ostvel asked blankly.

"Only a fool would take a hot bath in an oven like this."

Sioned was left alone in a chamber off her main room that, though small, was entirely adequate to her needs. The bath was ready, but for a time she was more interested in the tiny room that contained the tub. Cheerful blue and green tiles lined the floor, repeating the colors of the bedchamber. A large iron tub painted white rested in a carved wooden frame. Sink, shelving, towel racks—even the privy—were as dainty and elegant as the roses in a ceramic vase from Kierst beside the tub. Evidently Princess Milar had strong ideas about private comforts as well as public ones.

If this was the sort of room given an unimportant guest like herself, what must the rest of the keep be like? Sioned undressed and sank into the cool water, deciding Urival must have commanded one of the grander rooms for her. Luxuriating in the bath that soaked her tired body clean, she was glad he'd taken the trouble. But was she truly to become lady of this strange place?

She washed her hair and watched the strands float on the water, remembering something she knew and Rohan did not. From her would come his crown, the Fire of

Sioned herself becoming the golden circlet across his brow. Yet it was he who would make *her* royal when he made her his wife. She recalled the dirty, exhausted young man she had met that afternoon, his quiet voice and his ability to ignite her senses, his mysterious plan that she had agreed to without thinking twice. He intended to use her, she thought suddenly. What kind of man used people so easily?

The answer came from a ruthlessly practical portion of her mind, the part untouched by Fire. He was a prince. She would be marrying power and lands and ambitions, not just a man. If he truly intended to marry her at all.

She rose from her bath and pulled the plug, noting how swiftly the water was sucked down—probably to flush out the middens, she thought, approving of the efficiency and cleanliness. During her childhood at River Run they had removed to a nearby manor for a time every summer so the filth could be cleaned from the garderobes. Again she realized how much water must be here, to waste it in keeping not just bodies but the castle clean.

After toweling dry, she went to the bedroom and dressed in the things left for her. The gown was a good fit, despite Cami's apprehensions, and by far the prettiest thing she had ever worn. Sioned brushed and braided her hair, then draped a thin veil of silvery gray silk over her head, securing the material with a few plain pins. There was a full-length mirror set into one tiled wall, and as she considered herself in it she smiled. Rohan had seen the worst of her, but would never do so again if she could help it.

Sunset approached, but no knock sounded at her door. Sioned toyed with the idea of investigating the keep on her own, but chose to stay within her room and enjoy its comforts. River Run had been a pleasant enough place, and Goddess Keep was in some chambers the epitome of elegant living. But the rooms given those who lived there were not half so large or lovely as the one Sioned was in now, and she explored it with interest. The bed was big enough for four people, decorated with a pile of plump pillows covered in blue and green silk. The hangings were not the thick wool from Gilad or Cunaxa usual in colder climates, but sewn of silk fine enough to see through and embroidered with tiny white flowers. The object was, of course, to keep insects out, not to keep warmth in. The floors were polished hardwood and bare but for a few rugs scattered casually around, and Sioned realized that never again would she wake in the morning and put her feet to a frozen stone floor. The same tiles used in the bathroom framed the mirror, the windows, and the doorways. The rest was white plaster over smoothed stone.

The outer door opened and Sioned jumped. But it was Camigwen, not Andrade, who looked around and nodded her satisfaction. "I knew it! This *is* grander than mine or Ostvel's. I was sure Urival would give you something befitting your coming rank."

Sioned let the reference pass. "It's lovely, isn't it? What's yours like?"

"More or less the same, only not so large and with less furniture. And I have to share a bathroom. Now, when you meet Princess Milar, be sure to get her to offer you some silk for new gowns. She'll probably mention it herself, but in case she doesn't—"

"Cami, I won't go begging—"

"You idiot, you're going to *own* all this soon, and don't start denying it again, either! I saw your eyes—and his!"

"You didn't see anything."

"And you made sure I didn't hear anything, didn't you? What went on out there between you?"

"That's precisely what I'd like to know." Lady Andrade's voice from the doorway made both girls jump. "Camigwen, you will excuse us, I'm sure."

Reluctance in every line of her, Cami left the room and closed the door behind her. Andrade was more stately than ever in the dark gray silk, her bright hair concealed by a matching veil. She looked Sioned over coolly as she sat down in a blue-cushioned chair by the windows.

"What do you think of the face in the Fire now?"

"I'm not sure I understand you, my Lady." Sioned

took the other chair without asking permission to sit in Andrade's presence.

"My dear child, we both know you have an adequate supply of wits and a more than adequate portion of pride. Let's have done with the usual and be honest with each other. Will you have him?"

"I don't know."

"He's young, rich, reasonably handsome, intelligent, and a prince. What do you find lacking? You told me once that you saw what he was by looking into his eyes."

"They're interesting eyes," Sioned admitted. "But I think they hide a great many things."

"What in the name of the Goddess did you two say to each other?" Andrade exclaimed.

Sioned discovered a perverse pleasure in frustrating the powerful Lady of Goddess Keep. "We agreed to wait," she said quite truthfully.

"For how long?"

"He mentioned something about the *Rialla*."

"What? He won't have any time for that sort of thing at Waes! Every prince watching, Roelstra ready to—" She burst out laughing. "*Roelstra!* Why, that miserable, cunning son of a dragon!"

Sioned stared, mystified. Her mind worked furiously as she thought of everything she had ever heard about the High Prince. Ruthless, sly, and manipulative—qualities Andrade possessed in abundance—Roelstra was Andrade's enemy for reasons no one had ever been very clear about. He ruled Princemarch from Castle Crag, meddled in the affairs of most other princedoms—and was possessed of an embarrassment of daughters.

She sucked in a breath between clenched teeth. So *that* was what Rohan was about, was it?

"Good. You understand," Andrade said, correctly reading Sioned's grim little smile. "Do you trust him?"

After a brief hesitation, Sioned answered with complete honesty this time. "I'm not sure. When I'm with him, it doesn't matter. Nothing matters but him. I'll trust him if he gives me reason to."

"Make him take you into his confidence, Sioned. Force his truth if you have to, then show yourself worthy of it—and make him do the same. Suspicion is all very well to whet a lover's appetite, but it's fatal between husband and wife."

"We need to believe in each other," Sioned murmured. She rose, giving Andrade a look of appeal. "Tell me it will come out all right. Please."

"Oh, Sioned." Andrade rose and framed the girl's face with her fingers. "May you kindle Fire and never be burned by it. May the Air never send storms across your path. May that path across the Earth be a soft one, and the Water of your tears always taste sweet with joy." Sioned's eyes filled with tears as she received the ancient blessing, and the Lady smoothed the drops from her cheeks. "Only let him love you, and love him in return."

Chaynal had swallowed a bellyful of questions all the way back to Stronghold. Rohan had been in no mood for conversation. When Tobin followed him into the bathroom demanding to be told everything, Chay could only shrug.

"If I knew anything, I'd share it. Wash my back?"

She stripped down to her undershift as he got into the tub, and wielded a scrub brush with such energy that he yelped. "Oh, don't be such a baby. You're as filthy as the boys after a day with the horses at home, and you smell worse. At least *I* know the girl's name."

"Which is?"

"Sioned. She's going to marry Rohan."

"Oh, I *never* would have guessed, not from the look on his face!"

"But he didn't look at her once in the courtyard, and there's no welcome for her. Chay, he didn't even introduce her to Mother!" She started soaping his arm. "Tell me about the dragon."

His brief synopsis was frequently interrupted by her exclamations. Chay finished with, "Don't tell anybody he got sick afterward. It's not exactly heroic, and won't listen well in bardsong."

She grinned back at him. "We'll make sure it doesn't get into the official version. Oh, Chay, how proud Father would have been!"

"It's the last dragon he'll ever kill, you know. Even if he hadn't said as much out there, I saw it in his face."

"I suspected as much. Turn around, love."

He obliged, scooting around in the rub to face her. "Anyway, we rode back and damned if the girl didn't show up like a shimmer-vision in the sand! He took her off for a talk. I couldn't watch as much as I wanted because the dark girl—Cami-something, the one with the eyes—kept asking questions. I rather liked her young man. Good seat on a horse, and an air of authority, for all that he's not *faradhi*." Chay closed his eyes as his wife rubbed soap across his chest, her fingers more caressing than efficient. "Oh, that's good," he murmured.

"Keep talking," Tobin ordered.

"Well, it seems they lost some of the horses and all their baggage crossing the Faolain. I know that fording. It's dangerous enough for most people, and I can imagine what those poor Sunrunners went through. The girl kept apologizing for their appearance. I think she expected them to make a grand entrance into Stronghold."

"So did Andrade, and she's not happy about it at all. Why won't Rohan acknowledge Sioned?"

"I watched him with that dragon today," Chay said slowly. "We've always known he's clever, but I never saw anything like the way he tricked that dragon. He knew all its weaknesses and played them to his own advantage. I have the feeling it's going to be like that from now on, Tobin. And none of us is going to be able to figure him out in advance."

"He's going to tell me everything I want to know," she said firmly.

"I'd walk carefully if I were you. He's not your little brother anymore."

"He'll always be my little brother, and Goddess help him if he forgets it!" She lathered his hair. "What happened next?"

Chay squeezed his eyes shut as soap dripped down his face. "Nobody said a word the whole way back. But Rohan wasn't thinking about dragons, believe me."

"Hmm." Tobin dumped a pitcher of clean water over

his head. "Finish it yourself. You know what happens every time I wash the rest of you."

He smiled at her over his shoulder. "And things were getting interesting, too!"

Rohan's bath was much less interesting, and much delayed. His mother stayed with him for quite some time. making him tell the entire story of the dragon-slaying twice while she ruthlessly cleansed and bound his wound. She then let him know precisely what variety of fool he was to do such a dangerous thing—before she suddenly started to cry.

Andrade appeared at last, ordered the princess to her own chambers, and wordlessly pointed to the bathroom door. Rohan balked.

"I washed you the morning you were born," she reminded him tartly. "You put your fist in my eye then. Once is all you're allowed, prince or no prince, so stop looking murderous. I want to talk to you in private." She eyed the young squire, Walvis, who had attended her into the chamber. "Go on, child. I'm perfectly capable of handing him soap and towels."

Walvis glanced uncertainly at Rohan, who nodded and told him, "Come back later. I have work for you." The boy bowed and fled.

Rohan went into the bathroom, stripped—blushing as his aunt's critical gaze ran over him—and slid into the cool water. The lecture began at once, as he had expected.

"I don't know what game you think you're playing, but I'm not overly fond of intrigues not my own. Especially when the master of the plan is my own kinsman who won't tell me what he's up to."

"Why do you think I'm up to anything?"

"Sweet innocence! You do it very well, Rohan, but don't try it with me! Why didn't you give that girl her proper welcome? Oh, not as your future princess, I'll admit to a marginal understanding of that. But if Urival hadn't seen to her comfort, she'd still be standing out in the courtyard!"

"I knew I could count on him." Rohan scrubbed determinedly at a dirty foot.

"You did, eh? And are you counting on Sioned as well? She says very little—your instructions, I assume—just that you both agreed to wait until the *Rialla*." She snorted. "As if you needed all that time before you know each other, when you've already felt the Fire!"

"Have you ever felt it?" he asked suddenly.

"None of your damned concern," she snapped.

Unsuccessful in his attempt to take the skirmish onto enemy ground, he decided to return to a subject that concerned him profoundly. "What else did she say?" he asked, his nerves tightening. If he could not trust her, then everything would be ruined.

"That you have interesting eyes," Andrade replied in disgust.

Rohan hid a smile. "You haven't really told me much about her family."

"I thought genealogy was Mila's hobby, not yours. On her father's side, Sioned descends from a prince of Syr whose younger son inherited the lands at River Run. Her maternal grandmother was a Sunrunner before Prince Sinar of Kierst winked at her and carried her away to his island. Her ancestry's quite good enough for you."

"You chose her for me, so I never doubted it," Rohan said with deliberate sweetness. "What is it you think I'm planning?"

"Learn to be more subtle," she said scornfully and he felt color sting his cheeks. "The part about the *Rialla* tells me a great deal, you know. I'm looking forward to watching you blink those big eyes of yours at Roelstra as you trick him into thinking you're an imbecile."

He laughed. "Slightly foolish and very young, but not a complete idiot, please!" He rose from the bath and wrapped a towel around his hips.

"Sioned also had things to say about parts of you other than your eyes," Andrade drawled maliciously.

If she intended to make him blush, she succeeded admirably. He damned the curse of a fair complexion and glared at her. "I assume you'll tell me what she said after you've finished embarrassing me."

"Oh, no," she chuckled. "You'll have to find out for yourself." She draped a towel around his head and rubbed his hair dry. "Make your plans as you wish. I'll help, if you'll trust me enough to let me. But you must promise me . . ."

"What?" he asked warily, peering at her from under the towel.

"Marry her, Rohan. You're both very dear to me," she said, looking anywhere but at him. "And you'll never find any woman more suited to you than Sioned."

"And if I don't promise?"

She laughed again. "Your body already has, at the very mention of her name."

Rohan thought she hadn't noticed, and was humiliated. But his sense of humor was still in working order, and he grinned. "What do you suggest? A longer tunic?"

"Or a nice, concealing cloak," she answered wickedly.

Rohan waited, hidden among the trees near the grotto his mother had designed to be a refuge during the worst of the summer heat. Fruit trees had been brought at outrageous expense from Ossetia, Meadowlord, and Syr, transplanted with such loving care to Desert soil that not a single one had been lost in the shock. For ten years they had been pampered into lush maturity near the rock grotto where the spring that fed Stronghold splashed down into a small pool. He had loved playing here as a child, and had always found it a good place to sit and dream and listen to the water. He wanted to be the first to show it to Sioned.

Walvis had arranged everything. The squire had sidled up to him just after dinner with the breathless information, "My lord, your lady will attend you at midnight." The boy's term made Rohan smile; Walvis was no fool. He was of an age where romance between a prince and a pretty lady caught his imagination, and secret meetings late at night were exactly to his taste. Rohan knew what it was like to be Walvis' age and a go-between, for he had been just eleven the year Chaynal had inherited Radzyn and arrived to pay homage to Zehava. Though he'd teased his sister mercilessly, he'd been thrilled to arrange encounters between her and the handsome young lord. He had liked and admired Chay at once; despite the ten years' difference in their ages, Chay had never treated him like a child. Politic of him, Rohan thought now with fond amusement. One did not antagonize one's future prince, let alone the brother of the woman one hoped to marry. But their friendship was based on more than canny self-interest, he knew. It had grown stronger over the years until Chay was one of the few people Rohan really trusted.

Much depended on whether he could trust Sioned. Much depended on Roelstra, too, whom he knew very well he could not trust. His whole scheme rested on the beliefs of two people—or, rather, on his ability to make two very different people believe two very different things.

Prince Zehava had ruled by his sword, demonstrating strength through victories over dragons and the Merida. High Prince Roelstra ruled by his wits, demonstrating strength through political and personal humiliation. Rohan intended to base his power on a little of both for the present—victory over the Merida after humiliating Roelstra at the *Rialla*—and eventually to work his way around to leadership through law. Sioned would bring him no alliance and no lands, but she brought something much more useful: the *faradh'im*. The Desert's resident Sunrunner, Anthoula, was growing old, and Rohan intended to send her back to Goddess Keep with Andrade so she could live her remaining years untroubled by the Desert's searing heat. Anthoula had taught him how the network of *faradh'im* worked and where their loyalties lay—not with the courts they served, but with Goddess Keep. They were forbidden to do battle except to protect their own lives, forbidden to take sides in any dispute, and most especially forbidden to use their powers to kill. With Andrade as Lady, however, the distinctions of nonpartisanship had grown a little blurred, though she had thus far behaved with scrupulous impartility. She had been waiting for him to grow up so he could marry a Sunrunner.

But Sioned's loyalty must be to him, not to Andrade. He refused to torment himself with doubts of his ability to win her mind as it seemed he had already won her body and, perhaps, her heart. A rueful laugh escaped him as he realized they had *both* been scorched by Fire. But he needed a princess, not just a wife.

He had long since surmised that Andrade had purposefully arranged the match between his parents. Milar had used Zehava's wealth to embellish his home and their lives, adding to his prestige and his power by impressive display of its rewards. This, Rohan saw now, was the foundation for his own coming power. He was grateful for the benefits of his mother's tireless work. But he needed more of a woman than someone to run his castle, bear his children, and order tapestries. He needed what Chay had found in Tobin: a woman to trust in and work with, who understood him and his ambitions. A *faradhi* princess would make him a very powerful man indeed. Andrade's design, of course—but to what end?

Rohan had to admit that his actions in pursuit of his own ends would be incomprehensible to most. He would play the indecisive prince when the vassals arrived to do him homage, then next spring fight the Merida for a time before buying them off and sending them home rich and smug to plot his destruction. He wished them pleasant dreams of retaking Stronghold, for two or three springs hence he would show himself the true son of the dragon.

As for the *Rialla*—he smiled tightly and rubbed his fingers against the smooth silver bark of a tree. Roelstra would offer a daughter. Rohan would pretend to consider. The High Prince would sweeten things with treaties, and Rohan would make certain they were binding, not like the promises that had died with his father. He would lead Roelstra a wonderful dance, make him sign wonderful parchments, and all the while have a wonderful time pretending to decide between princesses. And then he would marry Sioned.

Rohan coolly reviewed possible reactions to his marriage, specifically to his *not* marrying one of Roelstra's daughters. Prince Clutha of Meadowlord would probably have an apoplexy; his country was the traditional battleground between Princemarch and the Desert. The last war had been in the reign of Rohan's grandfather Zagroy, who had wrested the Treaty of Linse from Roelstra's ancestor, the agreement giving the Desert to his line for

as long as the sands spawned fire. If Roelstra was angry
enough—or could drum up support enough to "avenge"
his rejected daughters—Clutha would be frantic to prevent another war across his landscape. He would, in
brief, do Rohan's work for him. But there was another
place from which Roelstra might attack with the help of
the Cunaxans and the Merida they sheltered. Rohan
thought hungrily of Feruche Castle, set into the mountain
pass just above the desert. Long a Merida holding, in
exchange for assistance several years ago Zehava had
promised the keep to Roelstra. It had been to the High
Prince's advantage to support Zehava in that final campaign against the Merida, for Feruche guarded the major
trade route across the north. Fees for caravans' safe
passage were lucrative.

Rohan had seen Feruche at his one and only battle.
Disguised as a common soldier, he had fought alongside
the vassals' recruits while his parents thought him snug at
Stronghold. Afterward he had camped in the sand below
the castle with his new companions, for to enter the keep
with his father and Chay would have necessitated revealing his true identity. Feruche nestled into the mountains
like a gemstone between a woman's breasts. It would
make a perfect summer residence, with its cool spires of
pink and golden stone. He decided he'd give it to Sioned
as a wedding present. If she fulfilled her part in his plans
as well as he hoped, she would deserve the extravagant
gift.

All thoughts of her usefulness fled when he saw her
coming toward him. Moonglow turned her to dark silver
from the veil over her hair to the hem of her gown. He
had seen her shape more clearly when she'd worn her
riding leathers, of course, but there was something about
the allure of shadows shifting down long thighs that made
the breath catch in his throat. He told his body to leave
him alone and called her name softly. Turning, not quite
startled, she approached him with a shy smile.

"I've never met a man in secret in the middle of the
night before. I could learn to like this!"

Rohan blessed her for saying the perfect thing. "I'll
arrange it every so often once we're married. Although I

don't know what people would say if they knew their prince had to sneak around in the dark to spend a few private moments with his own wife!" He paused an instant, then went on, "After the way I behaved today, I'm surprised you're even speaking to me. Sioned, have you thought about this?"

"I need to hear what it is, first," she replied, not looking at him.

Rohan nodded, approving her caution. But part of him was disappointed that she was no longer so blindly trusting. Knowing this to be absurd—for it was reassuring proof that she could think as well as feel—he coaxed her over to a bench and when they were seated, side by side but not touching, he began.

"You know what happens at the *Rialla*. Everyone comes to arrange the next three years' trade, settle disputes, and so on. There's a huge fair as well, and races—Chay usually wins most of them and makes pots of money selling his horses."

"The High Prince will be there, too—with his daughters," Sioned purred.

"The eligible ones," Rohan said, hiding a grin. "And that's why you're so important. When they think I'm indifferent to you and you to me—but with wounded pride on your part—they'll talk. My sister picks up all sorts of useful information talking to the other women at the *Rialla*. And she's an expert at passing along information my father and Chay want circulated. You'll like Tobin," he added.

"I like the way she treats her husband," Sioned answered mischievously.

Rohan had a sudden vision of his bedroom turned into the kind of verbal battlefield he knew Chay's sometimes became—and lost the image of an infuriated Sioned in the even more compelling picture of her between the sheets of his bed. He pulled in a long breath, managed a smile, and told her, "She'll probably give you lessons, if I know her."

"Oh, I didn't say I wanted to emulate her," Sioned answered earnestly. "I'd never yell at you in public, Rohan."

He regarded her with a whimsical smile. "Don't go making any hasty promises, my lady. You don't know me all that well yet."

"But we can talk to each other and find out. I was afraid we wouldn't have anything to say, that you'd be too serious or too proud to speak what was on your mind. Or that you wouldn't have a mind to speak of."

He nearly took her hand, but remembered what had happened earlier in the day. "I was worried about the same thing. You don't know how glad I am to find you're as clever as you are beautiful."

"You still haven't told me what you're planning," she reminded him.

"Oh." She was the first woman he had ever met who didn't preen or at least smile after a compliment. "Well, I'm not quite sure of all of it yet myself. Roelstra will be looking for a naive princeling and that's just what I'll present him with, while I pretend to look his daughters over."

"To bait the hook," she replied, nodding. "But I don't suppose you do any fishing in the Desert!"

"Chay and I go sailing when I visit Radzyn. I'd offer you the same, but I'm told you *faradh'im* have a slight problem with water."

She grimaced. "I've never been so sick in my life as when we crossed the Faolain. And now I'll have to cross it twice more to get to Waes and back. Rohan, you had better be worth it!"

It was a challenge no man could let pass. His arm slid around her waist before he could consider the danger, and he drew her toward him. "I hope you'll find reward enough, my lady," he murmured. And, because a glimmer of caution remained, he pressed his lips to her temple rather than her mouth.

Touching her at all was a mistake. Her body was warm and slim and supple, seemingly lit from within by the same Fire that flashed along his own nerves. Her arms locked around him, her fingers tangling in his hair, and he felt her thigh trembling against his own, muscles leaping as his hand slid of its own will from her knee to her hip. Her fingers followed a similar path toward his groin and she turned her face to his, eyes and lips inviting more.

Rohan caught his breath and shuddered, and it nearly killed him to let her go. He got to his feet quickly, fists clenched. Sioned gave a little gasp of mingled surprise and dismay as he stared down at her.

"I've never touched a woman like that in my life," he said roughly. "Sioned—it isn't just being near you—hearing your name is enough!"

"Is it that way for you, too?" she breathed in wonder, then shook her head. "Rohan, how are we going to manage? It's not even a day old between us. We don't even know each other! I've never felt like this with any other man."

In that instant he learned what jealousy was. He wanted to know the name of every man she had ever even looked at, whether they had touched her—and most especially where to find these men so he could kill them. What was the matter with him? She wasn't his wife yet; he hadn't even kissed her lips, let alone made love to her. But because he, too, could think as well as feel, he realized that if she was prey to the same jealousy that gripped him, he would have to be very careful during his charade with Roelstra's daughters or there would be bruised princesses. He considered the brilliant green eyes and amended that; she would not be so gentle, would his Sioned.

"We knew from the first that this wouldn't be easy," he told her with a rueful smile. "I promise to keep my hands and my eyes to myself."

"Ah, now there *you* are, making hasty promises," she teased.

"Everyone will think you have some sort of disease if I never get within arm's length of you!"

"I get hives when I eat marsh apples," she said gravely, her dancing eyes belying the tone. "Shall I eat a few and turn lumpy and splotched? Would that make things easier?"

"Splotched if you must, Sioned, but *not* lumpy." They laughed together and he exclaimed, "Do you know, I feel as if I've been married to you forever!"

"You don't know me, either, Rohan," she reminded him. "Maybe you'll find out I'm a—"

"Witch," he finished for her. "I decided that when I saw you in the Fire. But I have a little magic of my own, you know. Come with me, I want to show you something."

She walked with him deeper into the grotto toward the cliff walls. Giving him a sidelong glance, she said cautiously, "You must have something of the gift, you know. Your mother is Andrade's sister."

"What of it?" he asked in casual tones.

"Nothing."

Rohan hid a frown. She knew as well as he did that Andrade wanted *faradhi* children from their marriage. Why couldn't she trust him enough to tell him? He decided to talk more about his own plans—as much as he dared right now—and acknowledged that he didn't yet entirely trust her, either.

"Roelstra will tempt me with treaties and agreements that I intend to make him sign before we get around to discussing his daughters. But I swear to you, Sioned, that after I'm through with the game, I'll claim you in front of everyone." He stopped walking and said, "Here—this is what I wanted to show you, before anyone else could."

Trees parted around a silent pool for the long, pale waterfall that appeared from nowhere high above their heads. Flowering mosses and ferns softened the ragged rock, and moonlight turned the water to a ribbon of silver. This was the life of the castle, this precious water from the north. It ran underground, protected from the heat, then tumbled down to nourish this one hollow in the rock. Rohan glanced at Sioned's eyes and suddenly knew what his ancestors must have felt when they had first discovered this gift of cool, sweet water in the Desert.

But when she spoke, it was not about the miracle before them. "Does my being *faradhi* make you uneasy?" she asked softly.

"No," he answered honestly. "Why should it?"

"It will give your people pause, you know. A Sunrunner witch married to their prince, mistress of all this wealth, helping you rule the Desert."

"You'll win them as quickly as you've won me," he said quietly.

She glanced at him, then turned to the water. Lifting her hands, moonlight sparkling off her rings, she wove the silver moonrays into a conjuring over the pool. He saw his own face and hers, and a single burning red-gold strand that formed the circlets that were their crowns. After a moment the conjure faded and Sioned met his gaze once more.

"I had to do that to prove something to myself. I lost control of a Fire-conjure on the way here, and I've been afraid to try again. But I'm not afraid anymore, Rohan. It's too soon for me to trust you. My brain keeps saying that, and I have to listen. But in every way that counts, I *do* trust you." She shrugged slightly. "I probably shouldn't have said that, and I know I shouldn't be doing this, but—"

Her kiss on his mouth was as swift and startling as heat lightning across the Desert sky. But before he could reach for her, she was gone.

Chapter Seven

News of Prince Zehava's death reached Castle Crag on the morning sunlight. Crigo's contact with the wine steward at Stronghold incapacitated the already over-wrought Sunrunner, who took to his bed after downing a large cup of wine laced with *dranath*. Roelstra celebrated the news with a good long laugh and a lavish breakfast, then closeted himself with his ministers for the rest of the day. It was left to Palila to arrange the evening's ritual and make sure all the daughters dressed in mourning gray to honor their royal "cousin." A piece of nonsense as far as Palila was concerned, and doubly irritating because gray was not her color. But grief must be shown, and she comforted herself with the knowledge that at least the slate-colored gown hid her pregnancy.

Roelstra led the procession into the oratory of Castle Crag as soon as the first evening stars appeared. The chamber was a wide half-circle of Fironese crystal jutting out from the cliff like a giant soap bubble. During the day, sunlight streamed in to bathe everything in gold, dazzling from the ornaments and plate. Chairs of white wood cushioned in white silk were arrayed on a thick, snowy wool carpet that swallowed up all sound in its depths. Onto this background the faceted windows poured rainbow sparks that slurred down the walls and decorated the floor with brilliant color. But at night only the cold, pale moons shone, and the oratory was a place of silvered shadows where colorless faces showed eyes and mouths sunk into dark hollows, eerily emphasized by the white candles carried by each mourner.

They filed in according to strict rules of precedence and took their seats. Palila sat with bowed head and folded hands in the front row, the daughters all around her. Ambassadors, ministers, officials, and the minor nobility of Princemarch sat behind her—an assembly of men and women who thoroughly loathed her, she thought with a tiny smile. Nearly all of them had come to her at one time or another, hoping to influence Roelstra through her. She took what they offered and promised nothing— for they could scarcely run to the High Prince with complaints when their bribes to his mistress failed. Roelstra laughed whenever Palila showed him some new jewel or gown presented in hopes of a word whispered when his head was on her pillows. He encouraged her to keep the bribes that satisfied her acquisitive instincts without his having to spend a thing, for the splendor of the gift was an indication of how badly the giver wished his favor. He was never influenced by presents to his mistress, but he pretended sometimes that he was, to keep the expensive trinkets coming.

They hated Palila for another reason. She was a noble-woman who had besmirched the dignity of her class, even though the position of mistress to the High Prince held a certain honor. She had betrayed them by not working actively in their behalf, instead seeking to increase Roelstra's power at their expense. Worse, she had not produced a son. And, even more damning, she kept Roelstra from seeking out another woman who might give him a male heir. They all had candidates for Roelstra's next mistress, but Palila had not lost her hold on him. The thought of her as his legal wife horrified them.

The nobles, ministers, and ambassadors would also have candidates to put forth as possible brides for young Prince Rohan. No one knew much about him except that he was quiet and studious, and at the last *Rialla* had effaced himself to such effect that few even remembered what he looked like. Palila could sense them judging the daughters and wondering which of them would catch his fancy at the *Rialla*.

The daughters were wondering the same thing. Palila was sure that Ianthe at least knew the direction of her father's thoughts, for the girl showed signs of hurrying to catch up. Neither was Pandsala a fool; she had insinuated herself into mealtime conversations these last days, making remarks designed to show her loyalty and intelligence. Gevina and Rusalka, the eldest of the illegitimate girls, could hardly have missed noting that their wardrobes and jewel cases had improved in content recently. Let them fret, Palila thought complacently. Let jealousy spread like wildfire among them—and let the nobles place their bets on the most likely bride for the princeling. She alone knew what Roelstra had in mind, and would share that knowledge with no one.

After a period of silence to show respect for the dead, Roelstra stood before the assembly's flickering candles. He had a fine voice meant for ceremonies and for murmuring in bed, and he knew how to use the resonance of his tones to excellent advantage. He gave a little speech of regret that the great and noble Prince Zehava had been taken so untimely from the world, and entreated the Goddess to allow Zehava's spirit to find her loving embrace. That he meant not a word of it was not lost on anyone present. Everyone attended not to make sure the proper forms were observed but to enjoy Roelstra's irony and contemplate the delicious prospects before them. Hardly a mind in the oratory was not making some plot toward Rohan's disadvantage.

When Roelstra fell silent, Palila glanced up at him. His dark hair was crowned by silvery light, his eyes nearly colorless, the candle in his hand giving off a thin yellowish glow that picked out the strong bones of his face and the sardonic line of his mouth. His gaze met hers and she smiled slightly. How fortunate it was that they understood each other, she told herself. Her position would be a precarious one until she gave him a son, but because she comprehended her lord, she could follow his thoughts and, sometimes, outguess him.

One by one in ascending order of importance, the gathering rose and filed out. They left their candles on shelves to either side of the arching doorway. Palila had the honor of immediately preceding the High Prince and placing her candle next to the place where his would be. It was a privilege no one but his legal wife should have had, but she enjoyed many similar privileges at Castle

Crag and guarded them jealously. One day they would be hers by right.

She was tired, and the ornate silver pins holding her veil in place were giving her a headache. Yet when everyone went down to the copious supper laid out in the main hall, Palila did not join them. Neither did she seek her bed. She returned to the oratory and picked her way carefully through the moonlit chamber to the outer curve of crystal. Crigo would be here soon, to ride the moonlight to Stronghold. He often performed such small services for her without Roelstra's knowledge, for it was Palila from whom Roelstra got the supply of *dranath*.

The muted whisper of the opening door made her turn, the Sunrunner's name hovering on her lips. But it was not Crigo who entered. It was Pandsala.

Palila covered her startlement and hoped Crigo had the sense to listen outside before opening the door. She smiled sweetly at the princess and asked, "Why, whatever are you doing here?"

"I might ask the same thing of you." A little smile played about Pandsala's mouth, visible even in the dimness. It made Palila nervous. The princess walked forward with stately grace along the white carpet, almost as if she came here in her wedding procession. "It certainly isn't grief for the old prince that brought us back. Actually, I don't know why you came and I don't care, except for the fact that we're alone. A rare circumstance, isn't it?"

"Yes. But why do you want to talk to me alone, Pandsala?" Her mind seethed and she raked the girl's gown with her gaze. Knife? Vial of poison? Who would suspect a princess of murder? The son Palila was sure she carried was a threat to all the daughters. Perhaps Pandsala had been delegated to remove the threat. There were enough strangers at Castle Crag to blame it on, enough people who hated her to make the list of suspects practically endless.

"Won't you sit down?" Palila invited, reasoning that a seated enemy would be easier to outrun than a standing one.

"Stop playing lady of the castle, Palila," the other

woman snapped. "I am the princess here, not you—no matter what state my father keeps you in. I don't like you any more than you like me, but we can be of use to each other."

"In what way, my dear?" She put amusement into her voice, but sensed that control of this had gone beyond her grasp, and was frightened.

Pandsala's long fingers trailed over the chairbacks as she approached, the smile pale on her face. "First let us discuss how you may help me," she suggested. "I'm not a fool, as you well know. I have ears and a brain. And my ears have heard interesting things which my brain tells me can be worked to my advantage."

Palila began to understand, and relaxed slightly. "Prince Rohan requires a wife, and you intend to be the chosen lady."

"Make Father *see* me," the princess urged. "You can do it, Palila."

"Why should I?" she responded with a carelessness she was far from feeling. "Ianthe would be the best choice."

"Could Father be certain of controlling her? Ianthe cares only for Ianthe."

"While you are the perfect, loving, loyal daughter," Palila sneered.

"Gently, gently," Pandsala murmured, her smile gone and her dark eyes sunk in shadows. "Begin thinking of me fondly, I warn you."

"Why should I?" Palila was beginning to enjoy this.

"Because I can save your life."

She burst out laughing, but inside she fought sudden fear. Had Pandsala come here to kill her? She cursed herself for all the years she had thought the princess less dangerous than Ianthe.

"You believe you carry my father's heir," Pandsala went on. "Perhaps you do. But if you do not—must I give the details? Another mistress, younger and more beautiful, will supplant you. A woman who might give him a son. You've had four chances, Palila. This one is your last, and you know it."

She gave up all pretenses and sank into a chair, gesturing wordlessly for Pandsala to continue. The princess sat just across the aisle, smiling again.

"If you have a son, there's nothing for you to worry about. Father will marry you and your position will be secure. But if you have another girl, one might say it would be the end of your life, don't you agree?"

Palila rallied enough for an answering smile. "No, my dear. He is not what one would call indifferent to my bed."

"But when that younger, more beautiful girl comes along—how do you know she won't be just like you, and get rid of you the way you disposed of Surya?"

She betrayed herself with a gasp, and cursed. The princess laughed and stretched her arms wide as if to gather in the moment of triumph.

"Not even Ianthe knows that I know about it. I was only fifteen, but I remember every detail—how you stood in the trellis garden one morning and paid off the servant who'd helped you. Lucky for you, Father was so furious that he had the woman executed before she could accuse you."

"Roelstra would never believe this ridiculous story!"

"Perhaps not. But all he'll want is an excuse to get rid of you if you have another girl. He's not unkind, when it suits him. He might just send you away. But when I tell him about Lady Surya, I'll add the name of the man who put the poison in Lady Karayan's wine."

"Father of Storms!" Palila cried. "You bitch!" The penalty for murder was execution—and she had a sudden, terrifying memory of Roelstra's words about changing his methods to fire.

"How nice that you've stopped pretending," the princess observed. "Now we may do business. I want Prince Rohan. I'm sick of living in this nursery and I want a rich, powerful husband. I'm told he's quite good-looking as well. He'll do very nicely for me. And now that you know what I know, you'd love to see me gone, wouldn't you? What better place for me than far away in the Desert?"

Palila gathered herself. "How do you know I won't do to you what I did to them?" she hissed.

"Because I know something else, Palila, which really could mean your life. Well? What do you say? Shall we make a bargain of it?"

Palila pushed herself to her feet and went to the long table where silver candle-branches winked in the dim moonlight. Between them was an intricately etched gold plate. She tilted it up and saw her own reflection crossed with tiny lines—a vision of old age when her looks and her power would vanish and she would have only her son to keep her in luxury. It must be a son. Roelstra must make her his wife. She must do whatever Pandsala asked.

"I will promote you as Prince Rohan's bride," she said tonelessly, still staring at herself in the flat golden plate. "I'll do everything I can to ruin Ianthe's chances. But I can't promise, Pandsala. You know your father."

"All I ask is your influence—subtly, if you please. For my side of the bargain, I won't tell Father what I know. Nor will I run to Ianthe with tales. I knew you'd be nervous about that," the princess added slyly, and Palila hated her. "She's attempted your life, you know."

"More than once," Palila said, and put the plate down. She turned. "My servants are loyal."

"I'm counting on it. Will they say what you tell them to say, even if they find iron burning in front of their eyes?"

Fire—Palila repressed a shudder. "They know I will do worse to them if they disobey me."

"Excellent. Now listen to me, Palila. Ianthe's plan is complex, and you must understand completely if we're to turn it to our advantage." Pandsala laughed suddenly, a sound that frayed Palila's nerves. "You're going to have a son, Palila—one way or another!"

Crigo paused outside the entrance to the oratory—not from any caution, but because his heart was always caught by the beauty of the wooden doors. Panels of equal size spread vertically below the stone arch, showing in sequence the Water of the sea, whitecaps picked out in silver; Air rippling across a golden wheat field; the majestic Earth of the Veresch Mountains topped in silver snow; and the Fire of a sunburst carved deep into the wood and lavishly gilded. Yet even as his spirit sang with the beauty, he cringed inside at knowing how little he deserved entry into this place.

He sneered at his own scruples. The Goddess had surely abandoned this oratory long ago in disgust at the man who had ordered it built. He would not feel her presence within, disapproving and perhaps a little sorrowful. No, not that; the only sadness was his own self-pity. His lip curled and he reached out to push the doors open. But then he heard the faint sound of laughter from within. Not Lady Palila's voice, though it held much of her malicious amusement. This laughter was deeper, more full-throated. Crigo cracked the door open just wide enough to see, and peered into the dimness.

Two women were seated on either side of the aisle in the first row of chairs. He recognized Palila from the silver pins that held her veil at the crown of her head, but had trouble identifying the taller woman. Yet a turn of her head showed him the profile that boasted the High Prince's fine, proud nose and brow. Crigo swallowed a gasp of shock. Princess Pandsala loathed her father's mistress as much as the rest of the daughters did. What was she doing here having a private talk with Palila?

He did not want to know. He knew too many secrets already, things that would mean his death if Roelstra ever lost faith in the powers of *dranath*. Yet the temptation was almost overwhelming. He owed Palila for the "gift" of *dranath*; should he overhear something useful, he might have his vengeance on her at last. He opened the door a little wider and strained to listen.

Pandsala spoke in a low, earnest voice, leaning forward in her chair. ". . . make the change . . . four of them . . . surely a boy in the lot . . ." Crigo heard only a few words, none of which made sense to him. But Palila suddenly sat bolt upright, her posture one of rapt attention and no small amount of fear.

"But the risk!" she gasped out. "It's insane!"

"Be quiet!" the princess exclaimed. "Do you want the whole castle to hear?" Her tone dropped again and Crigo frowned in concentration. "Ianthe plans very well . . . should work . . . but fool my clever sister . . . save your neck . . . Father gets his son at last . . . trust your servants with this?''

Crigo bit down hard on his lower lip as the meaning of the princess' words nearly shattered his composure. He shut the door soundlessly and crept back down the hall, barely breathing until he had reached his own chamber and the door was firmly locked behind him. He turned at once to the drugged wine.

Goblet in hand, he lay back in a soft chair and drank deeply, gulping down the liquid as much for liquor's customary effect as to get the *dranath* quickly into his system. The first sign of its presence was a headache that made him grit his teeth. It soon vanished, as he had known it would, replaced by a delicate haze that lasted little longer than it took to identify its warmth floating through his arms and legs. During the first year or so of his addiction, this feeling had been superceded by a strong need for a woman, but for a very long time now his only lover had been the *dranath*. He waited for the real effect of the drug, the one he wanted tonight, and eventually felt his senses sharpen to almost painful clarity. He had left almost half the wine for later, when he would need the blessed unconsciousness of a large dose.

Opening his eyes, he stared up at the carved beams of the ceiling and assessed what he had seen and heard in the oratory. He thought he understood what Pandsala was offering Palila—and wished he did not—but what could the princess hope to gain in return?

The answer was so obvious that he choked on laughter, not knowing if he was more amused or appalled. The daughters had been fluttering for days, ever since realizing that some of them were likely candidates to be Prince Rohan's bride. He wished he could attend the *Rialla* this year and be entertained by their graceless maneuverings—especially the little dance Ianthe and Pandsala would do. Crigo had so few diversions; this was one Lady Andrade would appreciate, he told himself, wishing he had the courage to inform her on the moonlight. Palila would be just as amusing to observe, especially if she and Pandsala really thought she could influence Roelstra's decisions. Her role would evidently be to aid Pandsala's cause in payment for the plot outlined tonight, but Crigo did not underestimate Ianthe's powers of scheming—not with such a prize at stake. That was the appalling part of it, the thought of the young prince wedded to any of Roelstra's spawn. Crigo knew the High Prince's daughters. As the spring was poisoned, so flowed its streams.

He turned his winecup around and around in his hands. He wondered whether or not he would tell Roelstra about what he had heard. A thin smile stretched his mouth. It might be difficult to choose between ruining Palila and cherishing the secret knowledge that Roelstra's son was not in fact his own. Both offered satisfactions.

Crigo set the goblet aside and rose, slightly unsteady on his feet. He went to the windows that had been left open to the moonlight. The rocks opposite Castle Crag were stark and cold, the river invisible far below. But he could hear its muted thunder from the north, where it crashed over a cliff and foamed into rapids before settling into a smoother flow past the keep. Closing his eyes, he listened and shivered. He could never escape that sound, and longed for an absolute silence he found only in *dranath*-induced sleep.

It would be silent now in the Desert as they watched Prince Zehava's corpse burn. Lady Andrade would be there, with many *faradh'im* to attend her. The old prince had chosen a fine time to die, with so many there to do him honor. Crigo would receive a full account tomorrow from the spies at Stronghold, but they would have watched the ritual through cynical eyes. He felt the whispery chill of moonlight on his face, the spurious strength of the drug in his veins, and decided that he dared look with his own eyes. He longed to commune with his own kind again, to belong again. He could not, and knew it—but neither could he resist this chance to watch their work, even if he could not join with them on the clean, pale light.

He lifted his face to the three glowing circles rising in the night sky, and wove the thin light into a fabric of delicate beauty. He flung it like an unrolling carpet to the east and south, exhilarated as he sped along it to the sands outside Stronghold. So free, this feeling, and so

much like flying that his shoulders shifted as if he possessed dragon wings. There was a pinpoint of light below
him, like a golden star earthbound, and as he descended
toward it he saw the gray figures standing nearby. Crigo
yearned to call out to them, to feel the brilliant colors of
their minds. But he held himself back, the shame burning
anew as he watched them honor the dead prince with
Sunrunner's Fire that freed Zehava's spirit to ride the
Desert winds.

Tobin held her sons' hands as the moons rose above
her. Jahni and Maarken were exhausted, having gone
with their father and Maeta to assist in moving the dragon's carcass from Rivenrock. Their faces were hidden by
gray hoods and despite their weariness they carried themselves like the young lords they were, but their palms
were moist and they shifted restlessly as the assembly
waited for Rohan to begin the ritual.

Along with the family and more than two hundred
others, they had followed him in silence the three measures to the Goddess' Apronful, a scattering of huge
boulders that took on strange, fearsome shapes in the
moonlight shadows. Legend had it that the stones had
dropped from the sky when the mountains had been
built, to lie here forgotten in the sand. Maarken and
Jahni had active imaginations even for five-year-olds, and
Tobin knew they would be seeing monsters lurking behind every stone. She wished she could whisper a few
soothing words to them, but silence was the rule.

Rohan stood apart and alone, holding a torch in his
hand. The flame turned his hair to molten gold and sank
his eyes into darkness. He was a stranger tonight. For
almost the first time, Tobin could see their father in him;
the Desert had claimed him for its prince. Zehava, too,
had had this look about him, for despite the comforts
Milar had brought to Stronghold, the sand and the wind
had been bred into him. The dragon that had killed the
old prince sprawled between the largest boulders. There
was a long, hollow wound in the sand, the path made as
the great corpse was dragged to this place. Nearby on a
flat stone that had been the final bed of fifteen genera-

tions of princes, Zehava lay beneath a silvery cloak that
concealed his body from neck to feet. Torchlight picked
out the sharp profile and black beard, so different from
his son's finely drawn features and clean-shaven cheeks.
Yet they were alike, Desert-bred and dragon-born.

Rohan turned at last to Princess Milar, who walked
forward to the funeral stone with the steps of an old
woman. The shining scars of tears were on her cheeks,
and she stood for a long time at her husband's side,
stroking back his hair and letting the Water of her grief
fall onto his face. Andrade came forward to trickle a
handful of sand onto Zehava's motionless chest, the Earth
from which he had been made. Anthoula, *faradhi* to the
dead prince for many years, limped to his bier and spread
her hands wide. The cloak's hem stirred as she called Air
to touch him lightly in farewell. Then she bent her head
in homage for a moment, and returned with Andrade to
the place where the other Sunrunners stood cloaked,
hooded, apart.

At last Rohan approached his father, carrying Fire. He
lifted it high, his right arm a little stiff from his wound.
The light was painted over Zehava's body and on the
great bulk of the dragon behind him, dripping down to
the sand. Rohan touched the flame to the four corners of
the cloak. The material caught and flared, beginning the
blaze that would liberate Zehava's spirit from the elements of which his physical form had been made.

Then Rohan did a shocking thing. He went to the
dragon and took a small waterskin from his belt, pouring
the contents over the beast's wing. A handful of sand was
scooped up and flung atop the water, and a fiery breeze
created with a sweep of the torch over the dragon's head.
At last he set fire to the carcass and stepped back, his
shoulders set defiantly.

Tobin was stunned. She had known he intended to
burn the dragon, but honoring the creature as Zehava
had been honored was unthinkable. Yet as she looked at
her brother's face, she thought she understood. Enemies
killed in battle were accorded decent burning; so, too,
the dragon.

Sweat began to bead on Tobin's forehead as the flames

rose higher and hotter, augmented now by the silent efforts of the *faradh'im* standing nearby. Piles of sweet herbs and incense had been placed around both corpses, but they could not mask the smell of charring flesh. She glanced at the faces around her, seeing that Stronghold's people wept unashamedly for their prince. Various foreigners who happened to be at the keep stood in little groups, wearing conventional masks of solemnity. Tobin resented their presence, but they had to witness the ceremony and Rohan's conduct during it. He had undoubtedly shocked them all by honoring the dragon, but they would learn by it that he was not to be predicted.

As the first waiting time ended, the outsiders filed toward Rohan, bowed, and started back to Stronghold. The servants and soldiers followed after they, too, had acknowledged their new prince. Before too much longer only the family and the *faradh'im* would remain here. Tobin tried to pick out Sioned in the cluster of anonymous gray-clad Sunrunners. At last Tobin saw the ends of the long fire-gold hair that hung loose down Sioned's back below her veil. There were so many things Tobin wanted to know about this woman whose colors she had touched so briefly, but there had been no chance to talk. What did Sioned think of Rohan, of Stronghold, of the Desert—of becoming a princess?

Rohan accepted the homage of the last of the squires, then went to Anthoula and touched her arm, nodding toward Tobin and the twins. The *faradhi*'s limp was even more pronounced as she approached and held out her hands to Maarken and Jahni. She led them forward to pay their last respects to their grandsire. They turned then to bow to Rohan, and started back to the keep. Tobin was grateful for her brother's kindness—Anthoula was too old to endure the entire night here, and the boys were too young. She pressed his hand in silent thanks and stood beside him, watching the flames.

Scenes from their childhood seemed to flicker in the fire, and a smile came to her face beneath her veil. Their father had been so good to them, loving them with a vast, gruff, indulgent affection even when he did not entirely understand them. As the hours wore on, she relived the past in the flames, glimpsing Zehava playing dragons with them, teaching them how to survive in the Desert, taking them along as he rode his lands—Radzyn, Tiglath, Tuath Castle, Skybowl, Remagev, Faolain Lowland, and a dozen smaller keeps where she and Rohan learned what it was to be ruler of the Desert. Tobin felt her grief burn away as the memories lit her heart.

Thank you for my life, Father. You never had much use for rituals, did you? But this one reminds me of all the things you gave me by giving me life. I love you as I love the Water I drink and the Air I breathe, the Earth's bounty that feeds me and the Fire that's between Chay and me. You gave me all those things. Thank you for my life.

When the three silent silver-cloaked moons were at their highest and their light very pure, the *faradh'im* formed a semicircle as close to the death stone as the Fire would allow. Smoke and bits of ash rose up to form a gray-black background as they linked hands, twenty-five slate-colored figures with Lady Andrade in their center. At any other time, Anthoula would have performed this ritual alone. Tobin was glad the old woman would be spared this strain—and that so many had gathered to give power to this ritual. She felt the flare of energy around her and swayed slightly. Chaynal, standing at her side, put his arm around her waist. She was aware of the exchange of frowns between him and Rohan over her head, but could not seem to look at either of them. Power was being woven nearby, and she sensed it along every nerve.

The *faradh'im* were stitching the moonlight into a silklike covering that reached the length and breadth of the land from the Sunrise Water to the island of Kierst-Isel, sending word to every other *faradh'im* that the old prince was dead. Tobin's eyes were dazzled by the multiple prisms of color, each one different, all woven together in a loose, complex fabric flung out in all directions. And she was part of it—gliding with them down the skeins over moonswept meadows and mountains, across forests and lakes and deep gorges, skimming snowcaps and broad plains rich with wheat. She was a silver-winged bird gazing down at the whole of the continent, sending feathers of light drifting down to be caught by *faradh'im* in a hundred keeps. She was herself, and she was all the Sunrunners standing with their faces to the flames.

How beautiful it was, this landscape of an improbable dream. She flew with them, within them, colors shifting and dancing around her. Without any training and without any control but the general guidance of Andrade's skill, Tobin was part of the gleaming fabric of moonlight across the land; was a bird flying free; was a dragon soaring and gliding through the night sky. She lost herself in image and color, dancing through light and shadow, enchanted.

"Tobin!"

She felt a vague disapproval as someone broke tradition by breaking the silence. Her name sounded again and something wrenched inside her. Too abruptly she returned, and was standing in the Desert near her father's pyre. Chay's arms were around her, his face stark with terror. A stabbing pain went through her skull and she whimpered, groping for that part of her that still winged over the moonlight. But she was alone, earthbound, and cried out in anguish for the loss of that incredible beauty. From somewhere there came an answering cry, as despairing as her own, the voice of some unknown *faradhi* who understood her pain as none of the others could. She had a swift image of bright colors gone dark, and wanted to weep.

"Sioned!" called out another voice, and with faint surprise she realized it was the first time she had heard her brother speak the girl's name. She shook like wind chimes in a storm, her bones clashing wild chords as each heartbeat brought new pain lancing through her head. "Sioned!" Rohan called again.

But it was Andrade who answered. "Urival—keep her breathing! Sioned, help me!"

The colors intensified, needles of reds and blues and greens slicing deep into her flesh and bone. Some of them hurt as they were torn away, but others melted into her body and she recognized these as her own.

Tobin became aware that she was propped against someone's chest and there were hands around her ribs, squeezing rhythmically to keep her breathing. Urival, she thought, not even wondering how she knew. Someone else knelt at her left side, holding her hands, and without opening her eyes she knew it was Sioned. She could sense Andrade just as easily on her right. She sagged back, unutterably weary and desperately glad to be alive.

"Tobin?" Chay whispered, and at last she opened her eyes. He was kneeling by Sioned, the flames shivering along the lines of his face and shoulder. She shifted away from Urival's support and toward her husband. Freeing her hands, she touched his cheek and smiled slightly.

"Stay right where you are," Andrade ordered sharply. "I'm not going to tell you twice, so listen carefully. You were nearly shadow-lost tonight, Tobin, and if Sioned and I hadn't known your colors, you would have died. Don't you ever attempt to follow a Sunrunner again!"

Milar gave a soft gasp. "Is that what happened? But how could she do it?"

"Isn't it obvious?" Andrade shrugged. "She has the gifts, Mila."

"From me." The princess turned her head away.

"But it was beautiful!" Tobin protested. "It's nothing to be ashamed of!"

"Of course it isn't," Andrade said, casting an annoyed look at her twin. "Just the same, you shouldn't have been able to do it."

"It wasn't her highness' doing, my Lady," Sioned whispered, her head bent. "I was the one who caused it. Forgive me. It's because I'd touched her before, you see. I—I'm not fit to wear my rings. . . ."

Andrade rocked back on her heels, scowling. But it was Urival who spoke in deliberately mild tones, saying, "I thought I taught you better than that."

"It would seem she was not paying sufficient attention," Rohan said coldly.

Sioned flinched. But though they all stared at him in shock, no one dared make the retort such arrogant rudeness deserved. He was not brother or son or friend tonight; he was the prince.

Andrade finally broke the silence. "Chay, take her

back to the keep and make her rest. She needs time to heal."

"But she'll be all right," he said, not quite a question.

Tobin pushed herself to a sitting position, hiding sudden dizziness. "I wish you'd stop talking about me as if I weren't here. I'm fine."

"We'll see," Andrade said. "Chay, get her into bed." Rising to her feet, she took Milar's arm and returned to Zehava's pyre.

Tobin submitted meekly as Urival helped her to stand and gave her into Chay's worried keeping. After assuring himself that she could walk, he didn't let her; he picked her up and carried her the whole three measures, telling her to keep her mouth shut when she began a protest. She looked back once over her shoulder at her brother, who stood alone and rigid and staring at Sioned's bowed head.

Tobin managed to stay awake until Chay had tucked her into their bed and made her swallow a cup of wine. After the day's fasting and the events of the night, the wine hit her like a fist to the jaw. The next she knew, it was morning and he was still at her side. The dark stubble of his beard scratched her cheek as he caught her fiercely against him.

"You scared me to death, you silly bitch," he growled.

She snuggled into his arms, rightly interpreting this as proof of his love, then kissed his neck and pulled away. "I'm quite all right now. Have you been awake all night?"

He placed her back on the pillows as if she was made of Fironese crystal. "You stopped breathing out there, you know. So I kept count while you were sleeping."

She bit her lip, then managed, "I'm sorry, love."

"You ought to be. Turn over and go back to sleep."

"I can't. I have to talk to Sioned before Rohan does— and especially before Andrade gets the chance to shout at her. It really wasn't her fault, you know."

"I don't know anything of the kind." He was frowning.

"Chay." Tobin sighed impatiently. "Does she seem like the kind of person who'd be so careless? Or, to put it another way, would Andrade have chosen her for Rohan if she was? I know what I experienced last night. I want her to explain exactly what happened, that's all. We both have to know."

"I can't argue about that."

She hesitated, then plucked at his sleeve. "Does it matter to you? That I've turned out to be—"

"What matters to me is that you're still safe. And it hasn't been proven that you're *faradhi*. I'll get a servant to go find the girl." He rose and went to the door, then turned. "But if anything like this ever happens again—"

"It won't," she promised but did not think it wise to tell him just yet that it would be because Sioned was to teach her the uses of her gifts.

The Sunrunner arrived within moments of the summons, as if she had been waiting for it—or fearing it. She wore the same gray gown of the previous night, though the veil was gone; by the sand clinging to the material below the knees and the harsh circles beneath her eyes, Tobin knew she had not slept and probably had not even lain down on her bed. Sioned bowed deeply, sat down in a chair near the bed when invited to, but would not look at either of them.

"There's nothing to forgive," Tobin began. "It was an accident, if I understand correctly what happened."

"I wish somebody'd explain it to *me*," Chay muttered.

Sioned stared at her tightly laced fingers. "Some days ago Lady Andrade communicated with me on the sunlight back at Goddess Keep, my lord. Princess Tobin was part of that sunrunning, and I learned her highness' colors."

"My wife is not a *faradhi*," Chay said.

Tobin shrugged. "Do you remember the only time you ever took me sailing? I was sick the instant I stepped into the skiff."

"That was because you were pregnant and we didn't know it yet," he replied stubbornly.

"No, love," she said gently. "That wasn't the reason."

He glared at her, then at Sioned's bowed head. "All right," he said at length. "Tell me what happened."

"I'm unfit to wear my rings," Sioned murmured. "The prince was right."

"It was *not* your fault, and my brother is a fool,"

Tobin said. "And Andrade should have known I'd be caught up in it."

"Not even she knows everything," Chay observed.

"But she's always known I have the gifts." Tobin watched his eyes for a moment, then turned to Sioned again. "It was indescribable, Sioned. I've never seen or felt such beauty in my life."

"You sensed what we were doing and wanted to be part of it, your highness. But you were never trained. Because we'd touched each other before, you recognized my colors and I yours. It's very hard to explain, my lord," she went on, finally looking at Chay. "Think of it like a Fironese crystal window, with sunlight and moonlight shining through it. Every person is made of a unique pattern of colors that *faradh'im* can touch. I know it sounds odd—like being able to touch a scent. *Faradh'im* learn their own colors very early, and keep the patterns in their minds so they can return to their own light."

"And because you and Andrade knew Tobin's colors, you could bring her back. Otherwise, we would have lost her."

"It shouldn't have happened, my lord. I'm sorry." She paused, twisting her hands together in her lap. "I'm sorry," she repeated.

"It was beautiful," Tobin said wistfully. "So much light, threading all through itself like a great tapestry of jewels."

"And the shadows they cast," Sioned added quietly. "We're all made up of shadows, too."

Chay shook his head. "I'm not sure I understand it, but. . . ." He met Tobin's gaze and she glanced to the door. "I don't want any more apologies from you, my lady," he told Sioned as he got to his feet. "It happened, and it's over. And now I think I'll go check on the boys." He bent over to kiss Tobin, and left.

Tobin sat up straighter in bed, wishing Sioned would look at her. "Subtle, isn't he?" she said by way of easing the tension.

The Sunrunner finally met her gaze, a little smile teasing one corner of her mouth. Tobin took a quick survey of her features, seeing passion and stubbornness, intelli-

gence and pride. Rohan just might have met his match as
well as his mate, she told herself whimsically.

"I'll have to learn some things about being *faradhi*.
Will you teach me, Sioned?"

"If Lady Andrade says I may—"

"I think she will. She never lets anyone or anything of
potential use get away from her. I know my aunt very
well. I want to ask you about another thing that happened last night. I sensed someone calling out, someone
who wasn't a part of the group here."

The Sunrunner frowned. "Calling out how?"

She thought for a moment. "It was terrible to be torn
away from the weaving," she said slowly. "He seemed to
understand that. There was such despair in his voice."

"His?"

"I don't know how I could tell, but I'm almost positive
it was a man."

Sioned rose and walked over to the windows that overlooked the fountain down below in the gardens. "You're
more gifted than Lady Andrade suspects. It's not easy to
tell sex from a person's colors. Which did you sense?"

"Sapphire, mostly—and something that felt like a black
diamond, if such a thing can exist. Why?"

"You think in gem tints," Sioned commented, turning
to face her. "That's a very ancient way of identifying
faradh'im. Color patterns stay the same, but the shadings
can change sometimes. Urival has a theory that when
paler colors grow dark, like this black diamond you sensed,
then something has happened to alter a Sunrunner's personality. Sometimes it's a reflection of mood."

"Do you know who this man might be?"

"No, your highness. But I'll tell Urival about it, if you
like."

"It was probably just an echo of my own loss. It really
was an incredible experience. One I'd like to repeat,
after you've taught me a few things. Now, before Chay
gets back, and speaking as woman to woman—what do
you think of my brother?"

The unexpected query brought a crimson flush to
Sioned's cheeks. "You know the colors of my thoughts,

your highness," she said with admirable control. "You should know that, too."

"I'm afraid you found out more about me than I did about you. You're sapphires and emeralds and something else besides, but that's not what I'm interested in right now. What do you think of Rohan?"

Her spine stiffened and her green eyes shifted to the open windows again. Before Tobin could think up a way to put the girl at ease and coax the information out of her—and had she just accused Chay of being unsubtle?—the door burst open and her sons ran into the bedchamber. She pulled them close for a hug, and when she had settled them beside her on the bed, she saw that Sioned had slipped silently out of the room.

Chapter Eight

Lady Andrade lingered at Stronghold long past the date when she had intended to return to Goddess Keep. Some of her reasons were personal, others political. Her duty to her bereaved sister demanded her prolonged stay, and keeping Milar from succumbing to her grief became her chief occupation. She wanted to lend the weight of her presence to the assembly of Rohan's vassals when they arrived for the Hatching Hunt—and, not incidentally, amuse herself by watching him deal with them. She allowed it to be hinted, rumored, and then reported as fact that she would be honoring the *Rialla* this year by attending, a piece of news sure to irritate Roelstra no end and have the other princes on their best behavior. But personal and political aims were combined in her intention not to go home until Rohan and Sioned were firmly married. This had been her goal for years now, and she would see it through. Besides, Sioned's white silences and withdrawal from the daily life of the castle worried her.

Rohan was far too busy to worry about Sioned. This was just as well; Sioned worried enough for both of them. The near disaster of the moonrunning had shaken her badly. She had lost confidence in her abilities as a *faradhi*, and if she was to be of any use to Rohan in that capacity she would have to regain her faith in her own powers. To this end she asked his permission to study in Stronghold's small but impressive library. The vast majority of the books had been collected by the young prince himself, and the breadth of his interests astounded Sioned. History, geography, agriculture, geology, metallurgy, botany, animal husbandry—he owned at least three and often a dozen volumes concerning each, and on many other subjects besides. Sioned spent a long time going through the collection, gaining a feel for the tenor of his mind. But after satisfying herself that he had more formal education than any prince had ever had before him, she ignored the books and used the library instead as a private study. Seated with Urival at Rohan's long fruitwood desk, she relentlessly questioned, practiced, and reviewed with the older Sunrunner those things she had learned at Goddess Keep. Apart from his position as Andrade's chief steward, he was a teacher of note and had more than earned his nine rings. He understood her need. He took Sioned through the most basic lessons, guiding her, refining her technique, showing her subtle variations that most *faradh'im* were not taught until they wore at least seven rings.

She called Fire, lighting candle after candle until the study was ablaze, then snuffed the wicks out with a single thought. She wove her own complex pattern of colors into the sunlight streaming through the open windows, called Air to cool the room during hot afternoons. She reviewed everything taught her over several years of training until she had once again reached the third ring, the level of apprentice Sunrunner. But the next step, a Fire-conjure, proved difficult. The only vision she could produce in the candleflame was Rohan's face. Urival made no comment on her choice of subject that was not really a choice, and urged her on to the next level.

She rode the sunlight as far as her childhood home of River Run and returned with perfect control. The same night she wove the thin moonlight into a path leading as far as Goddess Keep, and when she came back she found Urival looking at her with a sour smile.

"I don't know what you're so worried about," he grumbled. "How many times do I have to tell you that you weren't to blame for what happened to Princess Tobin? Everybody knows that except you."

"I have to be sure of myself," she replied stubbornly. "I have to know exactly what I'm doing."

He leaned back in his chair, light from a single candle flickering over his craggy face with its large, beautiful, golden-brown eyes. "Why don't you stay on at Goddess Keep if Sunrunner's rings are what you truly want? You've always been mind-hungry, Sioned, ever since you first came to us. What are you after?"

"If I decide to marry Rohan, I won't bring him land or gold or anything else a prince usually marries for. His vassals will be unhappy about that. I have to show them I'm worth their trust and their loyalty. And if it happens that I don't marry him, then I'll have to know how to practice my craft at another court." She shrugged. "I don't belong at Goddess Keep anymore, Urival."

"So what you're really after is a seventh ring, and an eighth."

"Yes. Will you teach me?"

He spread his hands flat on the table. All but his left ring-finger wore gold or silver, most of the circles set with tiny gemstones. "You want dangerous things. Tell me why—and no more stories about marriage, either. You may be able to fool Cami and Ostvel, and perhaps even Andrade, with this nonsense about not being sure. But not me."

Sioned took a long time about replying. "When I first came to Goddess Keep, all that mattered was that I wasn't thought of as a freak, or fey, or an outsider in what should have been my own home. My brother's wife made me feel that way, and her servants followed her example. I don't blame her for thinking as she did, Urival. To her, I *was* strange. And through her I was sent where I belonged. Where I could learn. Once I found out what I could become if I worked hard enough, the thought of *not* learning all I could hurt more than the lessons ever could."

"So you want your rings for yourself alone?"

"Not completely. For myself, and for Rohan. It's not just that I have to make up for my lack of lands and wealth. I have to protect him, and all the Desert. I owe it to his people if he takes me to wife."

Urival said nothing for some moments. Then, quietly, he told her, "I will teach you nothing more."

Sioned jumped up from her chair and cried out, "But why? What have I done wrong?"

"You want your rings for the wrong reasons. Had you considered that a *faradhi* who is also a princess is another kind of freak, Sioned? Do you think more rings will give you power enough to ignore those who, like your brother's wife, will think you strange—even dangerous? Peace between the princedoms depends on the balance of power between rulers. The *faradh'im* thread that web of power together, hold it steady."

"Andrade's web!" she said furiously. "Andrade, who ordered me to leave Goddess Keep and be Rohan's wife!"

"Andrade," he agreed calmly, "whose reasons are many and perhaps not the same as yours."

"Then what does she want? Explain it to me!"

He got to his feet. There was pity in his eyes but his voice was cold as he said, "Do not order me, Sunrunner. You are not a ruling princess yet."

She watched him go, rigid with fury. What did they want from her? Rohan had commanded her to play a role that hurt her; his cruel remark about her training could still make her flinch, for it implied a lack of trust in the only advantage she could bring him as his wife. Andrade was set on the marriage for reasons she did not trust Sioned to know. Urival refused to teach her things he did not trust her to use wisely. None of them believed in her except insofar as she could be useful to them.

She ran down the hallways to Urival's chamber and demanded to be let in. Urival sat by the windows, gazing at her with quiet compassion. All her anger drained away, and she whispered his name, humiliated when her voice trembled with threatening tears.

"Ah, Sioned," he murmured, and held open his arms to her. She knelt beside him and buried her face against his knee, shaking. Urival smoothed her hair, saying nothing until she was calm again and lifted her face to his. "Do you understand now? Do you see how difficult it will be for you?"

"I—I see Andrade on one side, and the *faradhi* traditions of the past. And Rohan is on the other, with my future and my heart. But if she doesn't want me to use my gifts on his behalf, why did she command me to come here and be his wife? I don't understand any of this, Urival! Help me!"

"I think she has faith that you'll use your gifts wisely, and for everyone's good—not just Rohan's."

"But they'll both use me. I'm not a rope, tied one end to an ox and the other to a stallion, trying to make them pull in harness together!"

"I can guess who you cast in the role of ox," he said, and she couldn't hold back a smile. "There, that's better," he approved. "I'll admit I've likened our dear Lady to less flattering animals, myself. Sioned, I'd rather see you as leading both those stubborn beasts along, your abilities as the link between them. They can only use you if you allow it, child. You're free to choose."

"Am I? I was born with the *faradhi* talents, and what I saw in the Fire gave me no choice at all." She sighed and shook her head. "I'm sorry I yelled at you."

"You should be. Now go to bed and sleep, and tomorrow night I'll teach you what you want to know."

She gave a start. "But—you said—"

"Yes, and I made you think about a few things, didn't I?"

Sioned got to her feet. "You're a crafty, stubborn old beast yourself, Urival. Why do we all let you get away with it?"

"Goddess blessing," he said, smiling. "Off you go now, princess."

She stared at him as he gave her the title, the first person ever to do so. He winked at her and made a shooing motion with his hands.

"You will be, you know. You'd be utterly wasted as anything else."

As the days were measured off before the Hatching Hunt, neither Sioned nor Urival was much in evidence around Stronghold. Rohan knew it must be wrong to be so grateful she was busy elsewhere, but in truth he had too much to do to concern himself with her. But each night when he slid into bed he dreamed of her beside him, and each morning when the sun touched his face he thought, half-waking, that it was the caress of her lips.

His occasional glimpses of her were always a shock; he
had to remind himself that he could not yet call out to
her, smile, go to her for a touch or a kiss, behave as if
they belonged to each other. He could not even be caught
looking at her. He prided himself on control of his expression, but he knew that any glance at Sioned lasting
more than an instant or two would have his feelings
scrawled all over his face. Part of him resented the charade, and part of him resented that she could do this to
him. Worse, she was not even aware that she could do it.
She seemed as completely unaware of him as he was
painfully aware of her. It was maddening—and an excellent lesson in patience.

The vassals began to arrive. Instead of spending his
days studying prior agreements, his time was taken up
with maneuvering them into changes he wanted to make.
He had met with all of them before, of course, but those
times had seen him at his father's side, recipient of respectful bows but no words of real substance. Now all the
honors were his, and all the responsibilities. He had
never realized the scope of their demands on Zehava's
time. Each manor and keep had its own problems, each
lord his own ambitions. Rohan was glad of Tobin's unob-
trusive presence during some of the meetings, for her
special knowledge as Lady of Radzyn Keep gave him
subtle guidance regarding some of her husband's fellow
athr'im. Chay sat in at other times; as Zehava's field
commander, he had fought beside all these men and his
knowledge of them was essential. Andrade never attended, but her very absence was surety that all the
vassals thought of her. Rohan wondered in amazement
how she did it.

He listened dutifully to the various wants and needs
presented for his consideration. He would be his vassals'
representative at the *Rialla*, and what he won for them
there would decide their wealth or poverty in the coming
three years. Their lists included everything from timber
for houses and ships to Fironese crystal birthing goblets.
One lord requested a score of short-bearded sheep from
Gilad to improve his herds; another wanted a necklace of
silver and agates—jewel of seduction—to appease his

jealous wife. Rohan listened to them all without smiling or frowning; not only was this how his father had always heard their demands, but it was also good practice for his pretense of borderline imbecility at the *Rialla*. Some would think him too foolish to understand what they were saying; others would believe him imitating his father while thinking up ways to avoid his obligations; still more would consider him too frightened to show any expression at all. Those reactions suited Rohan perfectly . . . for now.

Privately, for Chay's and Tobin's ears alone, he sometimes exploded with mirth at some of the things his vassals said they could not live without. But he knew the extent of their requests was in no way amusing; he had long, hard bargaining sessions ahead of him in Waes, and had no intention of wearing himself out now in dickering with his vassals.

"Father always let them stew while he pretended to consider," Tobin reminisced one evening as they sat up late over cool wine and a plate of cheese and bread. "They did most of the give and take among themselves."

"Zehava had an economical mind," Chaynal added, grinning. "If two lords with adjacent holdings each wanted a new stud for his mares, he let them argue between themselves who'd get the horse and who'd get free stud service."

"I can't let them do that anymore," Rohan told them. "They don't think I'll get much for them this year, anyway, and that's why their demands are so outrageous. If I go asking for a lot, they figure they might get what they really need—if the other princes are kind to the idiot child." He grimaced. "What my vassals are offering won't pay for a third of what they're asking, and I'd have to make up the difference." He took a sip of wine, then snorted with laughter. "Imagine, Lord Baisal wants enough Syrene stone to build a new keep! The giving he proposes from his holding won't pay for the cellars!"

"Isn't there a Prince of Syr among Sioned's ancestors? That might be of some help, you know," Chay murmured wickedly, and was ignored.

"The only thing I can do for now is listen and not

make any decisions. That way there won't be any bargains to go back on once I have what I want."

"Without settled agreements, they'll get restless," Tobin warned.

"They're already restless. They don't think I have two wits to rub together. Besides, they're going to like it even less when they learn I'm going to do away with this triennial song and dance." He laughed as they stared at him. "Think about it for a minute. I'll set up standard agreements with them all—a set amount of their production every year, and no more trying to wheedle extras out of their prince. They tell me what they need, and if I in my wisdom decide they really deserve it, they'll get it. This bartering back and forth is damned undignified and I won't stand for it."

He drained his winecup and held it out to Tobin. She obliged him by pouring more, but her attention was on her husband. Rohan grinned.

"Ah, I see my chief vassal is getting nervous," he teased.

"Damned right," Chay agreed. "You're not making sense. The way things are now, when they want something special—stone for a new keep, for instance—they offer more of their own produce to pay for it."

"Have you ever noticed how often they fail to deliver? Father would get them what they swore they couldn't live without, and then their mines would produce less than anticipated, or their crops would mysteriously fail, or any number of other things would happen to get them out of having to pay up. Father never worried about it because he was building a princedom and had more important things to do. But it's my job to hold onto what he built and make it prosperous. Chay, what I'm proposing is that everyone gives me a fixed amount every year—or I'll send my stewards to find out why. But in return I'll give them more than Father ever did, and on a regular basis."

"And if you can't give what you've pledged?" Tobin asked.

"Then I'll make up the difference from my own pocket. I want everyone to know exactly where he stands. No more of this bargaining over how many goats or carpets or winecasks.''

"And if *they* can't meet their obligations?" she went on warily.

"Then add the delinquent amount to next year." He rolled his glass between his hands. "I'm only interested in a steady supply of what I'll need. Tobin, you know how often we've ended up with more of one particular thing than we can use, just because a vassal paid for something with it and Father couldn't trade away the excess at the *Rialla.*"

She made a face. "I remember the year we ate Lord Baisal's blushberries in every conceivable form for an entire summer! I've never been able to look at one since!"

"That's the kind of thing I want to avoid. I decide what I need here at Stronghold per year, and arrange with the vassals to supply it. In return, I give them their basic needs that only I can arrange for them—wool, foodstuffs, building stone, things from the other princedoms. I'll get the precise amounts of what I require, and so will they."

"They're likely to get rich, you know," Chay commented.

"Don't quote Father at me, that a rich man is a danger to his overlord. Father was wrong. A rich vassal is a loyal one because he needs to protect those riches, and I'm the one who has that responsibility. That's why he keeps me in food and wine—and horses," he added, grinning.

"The *finest* horses, if you please!" Chay retorted, and laughed back.

"Oh, of course," Rohan agreed. "Your pardon, my lord of Radzyn. But you see that my way, everybody wins. We all get what we need, and they get used to the idea that what they receive comes from *me.* I'm the only one who can represent them at Waes, and I'm also the only one who can protect their lands."

"Does the agreement stay the same during war?"

"I'll pay for what I take, Chay, and that's the difference between Father and me. He was busy securing the borders and he had the right to demand what he needed to do it. But I want to build a different kind of security, and I can't do it the way Father did."

"Are you calling Zehava a thief?" Chay asked, gray eyes dancing.

"The *finest* kind of thief," Rohan said, straight-faced.

"Rohan!" Tobin's fist connected with his arm and he winced. "Oh, stop it. You've long since healed—and it was the other arm, in any case. How dare you say Father stole from the vassals?"

"Well, he did. In a good cause, naturally, but what else do you call taking without paying?"

"He repaid them in security, as you yourself pointed out."

"But they were poorer in the only ways they understand: money, horses, and food."

She scowled at him. "So you don't like haggling, and this is why. I think you're going to change too much too quickly, but I have another question. What about Sioned?"

Chay gave a soft whistle and sat back, hands lifted in surrender. "Leave me out of this one!"

By some miracle, Rohan kept his color and met his sister's gaze levelly. "She fits in where and if it pleases me."

"Don't you dare," she warned. "You've avoided the subject—not to mention her!—for half the summer and I'm tired of it! The poor girl hasn't been seen by anyone for more then a moment since she got here. She won't talk to anybody and she looks dreadfully unhappy. She's too fine for whatever game you're playing, Rohan."

"If she's so fine a lady, then she's wrong for me," he said bluntly. "I'm not looking for a victim, Tobin. I need a wife and a princess. I want what you and Chay have. How could I watch you for all these years and not want the same thing for myself? But if we can't trust each other the way you and Chay do, then I'll have to find someone else. She hasn't decided about me, either, now that you mention it."

"Have you even talked with her? Sweet Goddess, Rohan, do you know what she thinks or how she feels?"

"Tobin," Chay said softly, "leave be."

"She's probably terrified of coming into the Hall for fear you'll snub her again! She has her pride, Rohan—"

"And so do I!" he reminded her pointedly. "I'm not

going to be seen running after some fool of a woman who can't make up her mind about me!" He set his wine-glass aside and rose. "It's late, and I've got a lot to do tomorrow."

"This discussion is nowhere near finished!" his sister raged.

"Let be," Chay said, more firmly this time.

She glared at them both. "Oh, get out, then! If you're not going to tell me anything, then I refuse to let you stay here and enjoy it!"

"But it's more fun than I've had all summer," he replied innocently, then backed off. "Chay! Grab her before she murders me!"

"Grab her? I'll help her!"

Rohan beat a hasty retreat from their chambers, laughing. But he did not seek his bed. He ran quickly down the privy stairs to the gardens and strode the gravel paths to the pond. The fountain had not played since his father's death; Milar could not bear to look out from her rooms onto the sparkling display she had created for her husband's pleasure. Rohan bent, scooped up water to splash on his face, then sat on a bench to wait for Sioned.

It had been quite a while since they had met like this. Walvis had brought back replies that the lady was too tired, too busy, or unable to get away in secret. A respectful apology was always appended to these refusals, but Rohan had had enough. That afternoon he had sent Walvis to her chamber during the worst of the heat, when anyone with any sense simply collapsed in private to endure somehow until evening. The message had been brief and specific: His Grace the Prince Rohan required Lady Sioned to attend him at midnight near the pond. Rohan had wondered if she'd dare refuse this time, too, but she had not. And he had been in a slow fever of impatience all day, longing to see her alone again.

He looked around him at the signs of aging summer— grass that had put up a brave fight but was now dry and yellowing, ripening fruit on nearby trees. The Hatching Hunt neared as summer wore on, and Rohan had no need to play the indecisive prince on that score. He really had no idea what he would do when the day came. He had been on one such foray and been sickened by the slaughter of hatchling dragons as they emerged from caves into the sunlight. But it was expected that he attend and applaud the carnage—and do a great deal of the killing himself. His father always had, and his father before him.

He turned his face up to the star-dappled sky, wondering how soon it would be before the she-dragons left their sentinel posts at Rivenrock. They were the reason no one could approach the caves and break through the walls to get at the eggs. But once the females were gone, it would be only a few days before the eggs hatched, and everyone considered killing dragons a wonderful sport. Rohan got to his feet and began to pace restlessly, helpless to find his way out of countenancing the slaughter for another year.

"You *require* me to attend you?" a furious voice hissed in the darkness, and he jumped. Sioned appeared out of nowhere, quivering with anger. "I had not been informed that I was to be numbered among your servants, my lord prince!"

Well-used to the rages of the other two women in his life, he was able to meet Sioned's fury calmly, even with a certain amusement. "I asked politely and you never came. I thought an order would bring you out of hiding—if only to shout at me."

"How dare you command me as if you owned me! If you ever send words like that to me again, I'll make sure you're unable to be a husband to *any* woman, let alone me!"

She looked as if she really meant it, something he had never encountered in his mother's or sister's explosions of temper. Evidently there was fury and fury, he mused. He would not make the mistake of judging Sioned by other women again. Still, his own pride demanded a certain kind of response, which he gave in sharp tones. "When I want to see you, my lady, you'll come no matter what the method of the summons!"

"Well, *I* don't want to see *you*!"

"Then why did you come?"

Contrary to all his expectations of infuriated females,

she neither shouted at him, slapped his face, nor stormed off. Instead she gave a little gasp and a muffled giggle. "You've got me there," she admitted ruefully. "So much for a good rousing fight!"

Rohan stared in total bewilderment that intensified as she shrugged and sighed.

"I needed to see you, Rohan. I keep catching glimpses of you in the halls, and you're always so busy and out of reach. I refused before because I didn't want to add to what you're already carrying, with the vassals here and planning for the *Rialla* and all."

He discovered then that the Fire could also be sweet as a hearthflame on a chill winter evening. "Sioned, you're no burden to me. You're the only promise I have for the future." He slipped his arms loosely around her waist and she leaned comfortably against him. He smiled as he rubbed his cheek against her hair.

"Thank you. I almost forgive you for what you said about my training. And speaking of that, I've been studying with Urival. There's so much I need to know, and there's not much time before we leave for Waes."

He was annoyed that his own sense of romance had not been communicated to her. He had no desire to discuss schemes and problems tonight. He wanted to try out all the phrases he'd practiced alone in bed.

"I've been watching what goes on at Stronghold, too," she went on. "I'm not sure I'm going to be any good at being a princess. Cami's always told me I'm as disorganized as a winter storm. So I've had her give me some lessons, too. Except I'm afraid I'm pretty hopeless."

"Cami? Oh—the dark-faced girl with the gorgeous eyes."

She drew back and made a face at him. "The lesson I *don't* need, thank you very much, is how to be jealous!"

He grinned, realizing he'd found his path to romance—of a sort. "I don't think you'll need any training in that at all."

"If you look too long at any of those princesses, you'll find out how much I know about it," she warned playfully.

"Sioned, even if I'd never met you, there's nothing under the sun or moons that would make me wed one of Roelstra's daughters. I want to live to a decrepit old age, and the day I fathered a son on one of them would be the day I could start counting every breath. There wouldn't be many."

Her eyes went wide. "But—oh, Goddess, I hadn't thought of that! Rohan, they might attempt your life. You mustn't go."

He laughed, delighted by her worry. "Nobody's going to try to kill me, and I have to go. Besides, I'll have my Sunrunner witch there to protect me."

"Don't make fun of me!" she snapped. "Once they find out it's me you've Chosen, neither of us will be safe."

"Don't see shadows where there aren't any. And just think of the fun we'll have shocking them! The last night of the *Rialla* you're going to enter the banquet on my arm, dripping in emeralds. The women will all want to murder you for being so beautiful, and the men will want to have me gelded, and . . ."

She gave a snort of mingled laughter and irritation. "All right, then. If it'll make you happy, I'll wear something cut from here to there and back again, and try not to fall out of it. But had you seriously considered how many enemies you'll make with this game? When those princesses *do* marry, they'll remember the insult and try to turn their husbands against you."

"My position will be strong and the advantages many for those who cooperate with me, so the influence of their wives will count for nothing."

"And *my* influence as a wife?"

He smiled. "Can't you answer that question for yourself yet? Or won't you believe me until you're standing by my side in your shocking dress and emeralds?"

"You have an answer for everything, don't you? But you know what I meant. Am I going to be a part of your life outside your bedroom?" she asked bluntly.

"I'm going to work you like a slave," he promised, smiling. "Stronghold runs itself, so don't bother with learning that kind of thing. What I'll need you for is to help me with running a whole princedom. My father *let* things happen. I intend for us to *make* things happen."

Sioned nodded thoughtfully. "You're serious about that, aren't you? I've read through your books, you know.

And all the little notations you put in the margins." She laughed up at him suddenly. "And the rude comments about your tutors, as well!"

"I was very young," he began.

"And shouldn't have known such words at that tender age," she interrupted. "I must say, though, some of it was very creative. . . ."

"If you quote me an example, I'll—"

"Threats?"

He tightened his embrace. "A prince never threatens. He just . . . promises."

"Ah." She nodded sagely. "Promise away, my prince. I'm terrified."

Rohan gave up and laughed. "I can tell." He paused, then, more gravely. "Will you come with me on the Hatching Hunt? Not openly, of course, but we can arrange some time alone. I want to show you Rivenrock."

"Where you killed your one and only and ever dragon. Yes, I'd like that."

"I think I'll need you to be there," he said slowly, and bent his head. "The slaughter is horrible, Sioned. I'll spare you the sight of that, but I do want to show you the caves. I've always had an odd feeling about the dragons, as if they're more important than anyone realizes. I can't really explain it."

"I've seen them in flight. They used to travel over River Run north to the Veresch. But they were too high in the sky for me to hear them."

"This year we'll listen to their songs together. I—" He broke off and glanced over her shoulder. "Someone's coming."

They parted as a slight shape appeared in the shadows. Rohan sighed with relief as Walvis, every line of his expressive face showing his embarrassment, slunk forward and bowed deeply.

"Your lady mother is asking for you, my lord," the boy murmured. "I'm sorry."

"It's all right, Walvis. Thank you for the warning. I'll be up directly."

The squire nodded and melted away into the night. Sioned touched Rohan's arm and said, "I'll see you next at the Hatching Hunt." She leaned up to kiss his lips lightly, then hurried away. Rohan left in the opposite direction, his body tingling and his thoughts centered around those hours he would spend alone with her in the Desert. So rapt was he in the pleasure of contemplation that he bumped right into his sister.

"Well, now," Tobin said very sweetly. "And here I thought you were so tired, and gone to bed."

He wondered wildly how much she had seen or heard. "No—I—Mother's waiting for me, Tobin." He started past her, but she put a hand on his arm.

"No, she isn't. That's only what I told Walvis."

"You did *what*?"

"I followed him," she explained with a shrug. "Rohan, I told you I wanted some answers, and you're going to give them to me. Why were you out here alone with Sioned?" As he scowled down at her, the fingers on his arm tightened and he was reminded that she was much stronger than her delicate looks indicated. "Tell me! She's in love with you, don't you realize that? What are you using her for?"

"What makes you think she's not using *me*?"

"Don't start lying to me. You're not very good at it. If she'd wanted to seduce you and force you into marriage, she could have done that a long while ago. Andrade trains her *faradh'im* quite thoroughly!"

The breath left his body in a rush. "What?" he whispered with no voice at all.

Tobin let go of him, gasping softly. "You didn't know?"

"Tell me. Now." He grabbed her arms, both of them, and held tight.

Tobin stared up at him wide-eyed and apprehensive. "Before I married Chay she teased me about not knowing how to best please a man, and offered to lend me one of her *faradh'im* to give me the same sort of lessons they receive at Goddess Keep."

She explained haltingly that upon receipt of the first ring, Sunrunners spent a night with an unknown lover so that when they went to the grove the next day, they would no longer be children. "A girl can't see what the

Womantree must show her unless she *is* a woman," Tobin finished. "Rohan, I thought you knew."

"So. Our dear aunt runs a whorehouse. How many men do the teaching, sister dear?" Had touched Sioned, tasted her mouth, held her supple body close and discovered her secrets—

"Don't be a fool! It's only the once, only one night—"

"Once? You expect me to believe that?"

"You're only angry because you've never—" She broke off and took a step back from him, frightened now.

"How little you know about me, Tobin," he said smoothly. There had been a girl—once, after the victory over the Merida, when he'd been incredibly drunk. She had been an archer from one of the smallest keeps along the coast and had not known who he was. He'd awakened the next day with a ravaging headache and the panicky realization that he had to leave before she found out his identity. The real trouble had been that he had very little clear memory of exactly what had happened between them. He was not entirely ignorant of sexual matters, but he lacked real knowledge, and it galled him.

"Rohan—"

"What else did Andrade forget to mention? Does she honestly believe I'll take used goods to my bed?"

"Rohan! How can you think of Sioned and say such a thing?"

He ignored her and strode off, wondering how he could still breathe with dragon claws gripping his chest. Inexperienced, was he? He stifled the impulse to kick something and told himself savagely that there were methods of remedying that situation—and the sooner the better.

Chapter Nine

R ohan could not have chosen a worse time for it if he'd tried. With family, servants, and vassals watching every move he made, he could not have snuck a mouse into his chambers, let alone a girl. Having worked himself around to the point where he almost didn't care if everyone lined up in the Hall to observe his choice of a bedmate, he ran into an unexpected difficulty. Not a single female in Stronghold—with one obvious exception—appealed to him.

The pretty ones were too young, married, or betrothed, and therefore unapproachable. He was, after all, an honorable man. Besides, the picture of himself as infamous seducer was ludicrous. After rejecting the pretty ones, he tried to interest himself in the plain. At this juncture his pride rebelled. Why should a prince of his wealth and importance have to settle for some long-nosed, pillow-hipped girl who reeked of onions? Working up enthusiasm for the task would have been impossible. So back to the pretty ones his gaze went, and they lost any charms they might otherwise have held for him when he contrasted them with Sioned.

Unsurprisingly in a man so young, he directed his anger at her. His masculine pride had taken a severe blow and his sense of humor was incapable of restoring his balance. Rohan cursed his position and his character for landing him in this mess. Production of royal bastards was never a good idea, and he had long ago decided he would never complicate the succession by siring any. Fastidious as well, he had never distributed his favors among the girls at Stronghold, much to their chagrin. To do so now, when everyone knew he would be choosing a wife at the *Rialla*, would be a revolution of character that would make him ridiculous. So, compelled to anticipate a marriage bed where his lack of practical experience would be only too evident to a woman of Sioned's undoubted accomplishments, his temper grew increasingly foul.

It did not improve on the late summer afternoon when, moodily staring down at a stack of parchments waiting for his immediate attention, he sensed a strangeness in the air and knew, without knowing how he knew, that the she-dragons had taken flight. He leaned out the window of his private study—Sioned and Urival were still in possession of the library, and he avoided her like poison—and saw the dark shapes rising in the sky. His heart soared with them, air filling his lungs as if he could call out to them and be heard. But in the next instant he remembered what their flight meant.

The vassals were jubilant that night in the Hall. Rohan watched them from the high table, drinking too much wine and pushing his food around on his plate. This would be the last Hatching Hunt, he vowed. What good was being a prince if one couldn't issue an arbitrary order now and then? He listened to his vassals betting on who would kill the most hatchling dragons, and felt physically ill. Couldn't they understand that something as beautiful as a dragon should be allowed to fly free as the Goddess had obviously intended?

The next day dawned cool and splendid. Rohan greeted it with a frown and reluctantly took his position at the head of the hunting party. He could feel stares like thin knives pricking into his back. His vassals were uneasy about him, and his obvious disapproval of their sport made them even more uncomfortable. That he had worked hard to gain their doubts was no comfort; that he had been trapped by tradition into this triennial slaughter infuriated him. The fierce blue of the sky and the dazzling sunlit sand was an insult to his black mood, and he further disgusted himself when he realized his feelings were being communicated to his horse. The stallion shifted restlessly between his thighs, and it took all Rohan's skill to keep the horse calmed down.

Jahni and Maarken had the honor of riding between

their father and their prince at the head of the hunt. The two boys chattered constantly with the excitement of the grown-up game, bouncing in their saddles and driving their ponies to distraction. Jahni pestered Rohan about how many talons and teeth they might collect from the sand, and Maarken complained for the hundredth time that morning about his father's edict prohibiting them from entering the canyon with the rest of the hunt. Chay bore his sons' entreaties with the patience of long practice until they spoke just once too often.

"If you won't listen to your father, then take heed of your prince," he snapped. "Don't you remember what he told you last evening?"

Correctly assuming he was being called on to repeat his warning, Rohan said, "I don't need to remind you, do I, how dangerous this will be? If you two don't mind your horses and hold your tongues, I might begin to regret allowing you to come along at all."

This unexpected sternness from the indulgent uncle they adored silenced both boys for the better part of a measure. At last Maarken slanted a look at Rohan and muttered, "You were much more fun *before*."

Life had been much more fun before, Rohan told himself sourly. He had thought himself fully aware of the problems he would face as a ruling prince. But there were so many others for which he was unprepared and inexperienced—that damned word again, he thought in disgust, and turned in his saddle as one of the vassals called out the sighting of a she-dragon in the sky. Rohan did not look up with the others, though, for his gaze abruptly found Sioned. He felt the muscles of his jaw tighten and faced forward again. But the image of her straight-backed form in brown riding clothes, the coil of bright hair at her nape, and the delicate lines of her cheeks and brow stayed with him as if burned into his eyes. She would expect him to arrange some time alone for them, and all he could think about was avoiding her.

The hunt paused to watch the greenish bronze dragon float lazily on thermals, wings spread to reveal shining black undersides. Chay squinted into the glare and mur-

mured, "Oh, but she's a beauty, isn't she? I don't think
I've seen that color more than two or three times before."

"Will she attack us?" Jahni asked, both fearing and
eager for a fight.

"No, she's not interested in us," Rohan replied. The
dragon beat powerful wings, changing direction. "There,
you see? She's heading for the Veresch. Come on, let's
get moving again. I want to reach Rivenrock by noon."

But just what he would do when he got there, he had
no idea. He only knew he would not kill another dragon.
It was obscene, this murder of hatchlings as they emerged
into the sunlight for the first time, wings barely dry as
they staggered about on unsteady legs. He glanced at
Chay over the boys' heads. Neither did his brother-by-
marriage have much liking for this unequal contest. But
Chay had no doubts about the necessity of eradicating
the dragons, either. Rohan asked himself yet again why
he wanted so much to protect these creatures that ravaged lands and herds. He could never come up with a
better answer than that they were beautiful and free, and
a part of the Desert. But what better answer was there?
he argued with himself. Something within him cried out
against their destruction. The vassals would find excellent
sport today and brag about the hunt for the next three
years. Rohan could do nothing but watch in bitter silence
and refuse to join in.

At the mouth of the canyon, beneath its rocky spire,
the hunt paused. Skins of water and wine were broached
and food was brought from saddlebags, guards demoted
willy-nilly to squires as they served luncheon. Rohan ate
nothing. The holiday atmosphere nauseated him. As the
company refreshed itself, Maeta and two other riders
ventured into the canyon and returned to make their
report to Rohan.

"The she-dragons are indeed gone, my lord," Maeta
told him. "Three cave walls have been battered down
and the hatchlings are flown, but there are twelve more
by my count that are in various stages of being demol-
ished." She glanced at the vassals who had crowded close
to hear the news. "Good sport to you, my lords."

Rohan's face set in stone and he gestured wordlessly

for Maeta to help Chay organize the hunt. He would witness this if he must, but he was damned if he'd participate in it.

The hunters rode into the canyon laughing, shouting jests and challenges back and forth. Soon they abandoned their mounts to take the slippery, narrow paths on foot, and Maeta waited with her detachment of guards in the bright sun, holding the horses. None of the hunters was so foolish as to break down the remaining layers of wall in any of the caves, for beyond was an unknown number of hatching dragons. Though small and unsteady on their feet, they could nevertheless exhale a searing fire. The flames dried and toughened their wings—and could crisp human skin right through leather clothes. The trick was to wait until the dragons had torn down most of the wall themselves and then, when they staggered out into the dazzling sunlight, kill them.

Rohan shut his eyes. *Goddess, what do I allow here? They attack our herds, so we kill them. But what about wolves, birds of prey, the monsters in the sea? Aren't dragons part of our world, too? How do I justify this? How do I stop it?*

"It seems we're alone, my lord," said a soft voice at his side.

He flinched. His stallion reacted to the movement and danced delicately over the rocky soil. He reined in and patted the horse's neck soothingly.

"Rohan, what's the matter?" Sioned went on.

"I hate this," he whispered, staring at the canyon walls so he would not be tempted to look at her. "I've always hated this. But I can't stop it."

"If you were any other man I'll tell you that as their prince, you could order them as you like."

"But I'm too much of a coward to use my power, is that it?"

"No. I wasn't going to say that, and you know it. Rohan, look at me, please."

He did so because he could not help doing so. There was nothing but tender concern in her eyes. She loved him; he felt the emotion reaching out to wrap him in strength and light like a Sunrunner's weaving.

"What's wrong?" she whispered.

"The day." He dug his heels into his horse's sides and cantered into Rivenrock, unable to bear the look in Sioned's eyes. He heard another horse following and reined in. But it was Andrade, not Sioned, who rode to his side.

"What have you been telling Sioned?" she demanded.

"Leave me alone."

"Stop behaving like a child. I know how much you hate what's happening here today, but directing your anger at her won't cure anything. Being a prince isn't all it's rumored to be, is it?"

"No." He could stop the hunt with a single command. No one would disobey him. He was their prince. The knowledge that he could order anything he pleased frightened him for no good reason he could think of. "What right do I have?" he burst out suddenly. "Why give me all this power, instead of someone else? What makes me so special? Don't tell me it was an accident of birth. It was no accident and we both know it."

"I've wondered how much you knew about that," she responded calmly. "It wasn't entirely my doing. Oh, I might have pushed Milar toward Zehava, but neither of them needed much pushing."

The first high-pitched screams came from the hatchlings as they emerged from the caves and died. There was the smell of blood on the warming breeze.

"My father had a man in mind for me," Andrade went on. "I refused. So it was up to Milar. She had the spark, but never used it. She passed it to Tobin, and I suspect you'll pass it to your children, strengthened through Sioned. If you're looking for a grander design, Rohan, there isn't one. My father and I wanted the same thing: to see our family powerful."

There *was* more, and he knew it, but something else was of deeper concern to him right now. "At least you sent my father a maiden, not a *faradhi* whore," he said bitterly.

Andrade sucked in a breath. "You young fool," she breathed. "If that's how you view Sioned, then I wish you much joy of your life with her. She's in your blood now, Rohan. You've made Fire between you, and whether you warm yourself at it or let it sear your soul is up to you."

He kicked his horse forward again, and she did not follow. The morning wore on and the slaughter continued. Sometimes a small frantic shape would take wing through the canyon, and he rejoiced that at least a few dragons would fly free. There were long periods of near silence as the hunters waited for the dragons to break down the walls, but as more caves opened the air grew thick with screams and death. One of Rohan's elderly vassals, Abidias of Tuath Castle, climbed down to his horse, the heat too much for him. From his saddle was hung a limp-winged corpse the size of a four-year-old child.

"Here's one who won't be gobbling down my sheep!" He patted the little body almost fondly. It was a reddish dragon with black underwings. "I'll cure his hide for my favorite chair, and string his claws and teeth from my war standard."

An agony of hate throbbed in Rohan's skull, hate for this spectacle and for himself in being ultimately responsible for it. He felt every death cry like a sword in his heart. He could do nothing.

"Rohan!"

He swung around, furious as he recognized Sioned's voice. How long had she been watching him—and how dared she intrude? But the terror on her face swept away his anger. She pointed at the canyon wall, where far above them was a small cave, the ledge narrower than most. Shadows dripped from overhanging rocks so he could not see whether there were dragon-made walls, but he saw very clearly two small figures clinging to the ledge. Jahni and Maarken hauled themselves up and stood looking down into Rivenrock.

Rohan yelled to the boys as he jumped down from his stallion, but dragon screams and human shouts echoed too loudly through the canyon for him to be heard. He started climbing, scrabbling for footing in the loose stones, and heard Sioned follow. His gaze on the cavern ledge, he gasped aloud as a flash of light came from the

shadows. Sioned's harsh breathing sounded behind him,
in time with his own. As they scrambled upward, the boys
cried out in fright. He shouted an order for them to find
shelter, but the ledge was neither deep nor wide, without
large rocks for them to hide behind. If anything happened to the twins, Tobin would murder him—and he
would want her to.

Rohan struggled to the ledge on all fours. Heaving
himself up, he saw Jahni huddled against the face of the
cliff, trembling head to foot, as far away from the cave's
mouth as it was possible to get without falling into the
gorge. Maarken was frozen on the stony shelf, staring at
a hatchling dragon as small and terrified as he. Rohan
knew he would never be able to draw his sword in time
to kill the hatchling. The little creature's eyes had kindled and his lungs expanded in a deep inhalation, teeth
gleaming like fine white needles as his jaws opened for a
burst of flame that would mean Maarken's death.

"Maarken!" Sioned screamed from behind Rohan. "Get
down!" In the next instant a thin, broad sheet of Sunrunner's Fire flared up from the rocks to hover between
the dragon and the boy, touching neither.

The hatchling reared back, a squeal of alarm leaving
his throat along with a blast of fire directed up at the sky.
Rohan found purchase on the ledge and hauled himself
upright. Ignoring the uncertain footing, he sidestepped
Sioned's Fire, drew his sword, and slapped the dragon on
the backside with the flat of the blade. The hatchling
howled with the bruising pain, flapped his wings, and
jumped to one side. Too frightened to defend himself
against the sword-wielding prince, the dragon scrambled
around the flames, beat his small wings with desperate
strength, and flew.

The Fire vanished, and Rohan glanced over his shoulder to find Sioned clambering up onto the ledge, shaking
with relief. Maarken was trembling, too, as Rohan scooped
him up into a fierce hug.

"Are you all right? Not burned anywhere? Maarken,
talk to me!"

The child shook until Rohan thought his slight bones

would shatter. His arms went around Rohan's neck and he stammered out, "I'm all r-right—"

From the corner of his eye he saw Sioned rocking the terrified Jahni in her arms. Holding Maarken tighter, he said, "You scared me half to death! Do you know you could have been killed?"

"We only wanted to s-see the dragons! I'm sorry!" Maarken sniffled. "Mother's going to be mad at us."

"And then some."

"Did you kill the dragon?"

"No. He flew off."

"Good. I'm glad." The boy drew away and knuckled his eyes. "He was just a baby. He didn't know we didn't want to hurt him."

Rohan nodded. "Are your legs working now?" He set Maarken down. "We'd better get out of here before your dragon's brothers and sisters come to find out what all the fuss is about." He glanced over at Sioned and Jahni. "Everything all right?"

"Fine," she replied, setting the boy on his feet. He clung to her wrist with both hands, but his tears had dried. "A bump or two, I think. But it could have been much worse, couldn't it? I hope this teaches you both not to disobey your prince." She arched a brow at each child in turn, and Rohan hid a smile as they looked away, shamefaced.

"Lesson learned, I think," Rohan said. "Come on, let's go back down."

They slid down the loose rocks much faster than they'd climbed up, and by the time they reached bottom Chaynal was there to meet them. He grabbed one son in each arm, hugged the breath out of them, told them they were ungovernable little terrors who ought to be horsewhipped— then clasped them to his chest again, eyes closed, lips moving in a soundless prayer of thanks.

Rohan watched for a moment, then glanced around for Sioned. She had started back up the path and he ran to catch up with her. "What are you doing?"

"You dropped your sword. I was going back up to get it for you."

He put a hand to his empty scabbard. "I'll be damned.

I didn't even notice. But I'll go, Sioned. You're *not* numbered among my servants," he added, a tiny smile touching his mouth.

Her eyes regained their sparkle. "You promised me some time alone with you—but I didn't know it would take so much effort!"

Rohan chuckled. "All right, but let me go first. There may be a hatchling or two left up there."

He led the way, muscles protesting this second slippery climb, and when they reached the ledge he poked his head cautiously over, watching for telltale signs of dragons. There were none. He pulled himself up and turned to help Sioned. But she was already beside him, brushing dirt from her hands as she looked around.

"It's a miracle none of us fell off," she commented, shaking her head. "Do you want some light?"

Without waiting for his answer, she conjured a small flame just inside the mouth of the cave. Rohan smiled, knowing she had guessed his real motive in wanting to come back up here. Maybe she even shared the desire to investigate. He peered into the dimness, but other than shell shards, there was no further evidence of dragons.

"Was there only the one?" she asked. "What about all these other eggs?"

"Come inside and I'll show you." The little flame lit their way inside, and soon they were standing in the center of the cave. Walls rose in ragged curves to meet high overhead. "There must've been about twelve eggs. But only one of this group was strong enough to survive."

"But—*oh!*" She swallowed hard as the light picked out several withered wings and blots of dried blood. "You mean the one we saw lived because he—"

"Exactly. It's unusual for only one of a clutch to survive, but I suppose this one was pretty ruthless." He shrugged and poked at a shard with the toe of his boot. "They're not so different from us, you know," he mused. "We just wait until we're grown to kill each other off. And it might be said that we consume each other, too, if you think about it."

"I'd rather not, thank you. Will we need more light?"

"Please."

The flame brightened and now they could see the jagged stones of the walls and the high ceiling, a cave large enough for a she-dragon and her mate. Rohan ran his fingers over the stone. "A river flowed through here once, ages ago. It carved out the soft stone. But the dragons hollowed out a lot of it, too. See where they've been at work with their claws?" He pointed out the marks that had deepened the cave. "They use the debris to make the hatching walls."

"And then the little ones break them down. Those that hatch first do the bulk of the work and exhaust themselves, so they're fairly easy prey for the later ones."

"Very good. We'll make a Desert dragon out of you yet." He crouched down in the sand, scooping up a handful to sift through his fingers. It glistened in the light of Sunrunner's Fire.

"It's beautiful, isn't it?" Sioned murmured.

"Give me your waterskin," he said abruptly. She did so, and he pulled the cork out with his teeth. Pouring the contents over his hand, he rubbed the fine sand with his fingers. Shining grains remained in his palm. With a soft exclamation, he emptied his waterskin and poured sand into its narrow neck.

"What are you doing?" Sioned asked, mystified.

"It's not obvious?"

"Rohan, more sand is the very last thing you need!"

"Look at it, Sioned. And at the shells."

With a lift of her finger she conjured the Fire higher. By its light the whole cave sparkled. She picked up a stray shard and examined it. "It's ragged where the dragon poked through it with his claws," she said slowly. "But on this side it's smoother, almost as if it had been—melted?"

"To dry and toughen their wings after they're born, they breathe fire. They also breathe it at each other. Roast dragon meat is their first dinner."

She gulped. "Go on."

"They lose the capability by winter. But look what happens when they breathe fire on their own shells." He plugged the waterskin and stirred the shining sand with his fingers.

"Rohan," she whispered. "This can't be real gold."

He hefted the waterskin full of sand. "I'll take this home and do a few experiments, find out for sure. But do you know what it means if I'm right?"

"You can't let the dragons be killed off—and you certainly can't tell anyone else about this! Every other prince would be marching across your borders within days!"

"Do I look that stupid?" He rose to his feet, grinning.

Sioned laughed. "You look like someone who's just found his heart's desire. I had no idea you were so greedy!"

"Oh, but I am!" Light-headed with his discovery and its possibilities, he laughed back. "And I found my heart's desire at the beginning of summer, as filthy and sweaty as she is right now."

"The things you'll say to seduce me," she chided playfully.

All the effervescent excitement died. "And you know all about seductions, don't you? Who was it for you, Sioned?"

She blinked. "What?"

"Who was it?" he demanded. "The man who taught you—"

"I don't know. I never wanted to know. What difference does it make?"

"What did he do, wear a robe and a mask to bed? Never say a word so you wouldn't recognize his voice? Did you expect me to welcome the idea that you've been with other men?"

Her green eyes lit with fury and her conjured Fire leaped in response. "Do you expect me to be ashamed? It's something that happened and doesn't have anything to do with us!"

"How many, Sioned?"

She gasped. "How dare you! You have no right to ask me that, as if every man at Goddess Keep had been through my bed! I never asked you about your women, did I?"

He was so startled he almost forgot to be angry. "What are you talking about?"

"Don't you think I've wondered 'how many' of the

women at Stronghold have been in your bed?" she spat. "Neither your hands nor your mouth are exactly virginal! It was one night, part of my training as a Sunrunner that happened before I'd ever seen you in the Fire!" She took a step closer, glaring at him. "Did you think I'd try to father another man's child on you? Is that the real reason you're waiting so long before marrying me? How dare you ask 'how many?' How many has it been for you? But I promise you now, my lord prince—there'll be no other women once you become mine! I may have no right to question you about the past—but your future is *mine*."

She stalked out of the cave and the Fire vanished with her, leaving Rohan alone and speechless in the dark. He stayed there for some minutes, his adult brain telling him he'd made a fool of himself. But something wiser chuckled softly with satisfaction. The inner laughter continued as he picked his way carefully out into the sunlight. He found his sword, the thing he'd ostensibly come for, and sheathed it before pausing at the ledge to watch Sioned's swift descent. A little of the laughter escaped. His smile did not fade all during the long ride back to Stronghold.

Sioned flung herself across the blue-green bedcover, having just slammed her door in Camigwen's startled face. She had no desire to attempt an explanation of her refusal to attend the evening's banquet, nor to hear reasons why she should change her mind. Punching an inoffensive pillow into lumps, she spent a great deal of creative energy cursing men in general and Rohan in particular. Stupid, arrogant, thick-skulled, jealous, possessive—

A knock on the door interrupted the muttered invectives. "Go away!" she shouted, and punched the pillows again.

The door opened and a soft voice that was not Cami's said, "Perhaps I can help, my dear."

Sioned leaped to her feet, crimson as she made her bow to Princess Milar. She had spoken only once to Rohan's mother, formal words in company with the other recently arrived *faradh'im*, and there could be no reason for this visit that Sioned could think of—unless Andrade had been talking. She gulped as the princess smiled and seated herself in a chair.

"I'm glad we're going to have this little talk," the princess said with a disarming smile. "I've been waiting for the right moment, but we've all been so busy." She gestured to the other chair. "Please. Unless you'd prefer I came back another time."

Sioned sat down, unable to say a word.

"Now we can be comfortable while we discuss things. I was about your age when I came here to marry Rohan's father, you know. What a difficult man he was! Nearly as bad as his son, if you want the truth. It's a strange place, the Desert, and its rulers take as much adjusting to as its climate. When I arrived here, Stronghold was in a terrible state, without a comfort to be had. Can you imagine, the only table in the Great Hall was Zehava's and everyone else had to stand while they ate! But I changed all that, and I changed Zehava, as well."

She went on in this vein for some time while Sioned wondered wildly what she was leading up to. But during the princess' seemingly aimless chatter, the tension gradually seeped from her. Milar was as crafty as Andrade in her own way. Sioned smiled.

The princess noticed at once and interrupted herself in the middle of a sentence about the gardens. "That's better. You see, you needn't be frightened of anything here, especially not of me. Certainly not of tonight's banquet."

"I'm not frightened, your highness," Sioned told her. "Only a fool."

"That makes you a perfect match for my son," Milar said dryly. "But we're all a little foolish at times, aren't we? My sister seems to think I've made a career of it. You mustn't worry about any little misunderstandings between you and Rohan. I had plenty with his father! Oh, the names we used to call each other! You really must appear tonight, you know. We want to thank you in public for saving Jahni and Maarken. Don't worry about what to wear, I've taken care of that. You'll come and enjoy yourself, won't you? Please say you will!"

The blue eyes were so artlessly appealing that it was impossible to refuse. If Rohan ever looked at her this way, she'd be helpless. And she told herself with a twinge of annoyance that she already was, like it or not. At the moment she liked it not at all. She nodded slowly, and Princess Milar clapped her hands together in delight.

"Oh, splendid! I'll send the dress to you at once, and one of my maids will do your hair. I think you'll approve of the gown," she finished with a happy smile, rising with a rustle of gray skirts and a wash of rose scent. "I'm positive my son will!"

"Your highness, it's very kind of you to go to so much trouble for me, but I think I should tell you something about myself and your son and—"

"Oh, my dear!" Princess Milar laughed. "There isn't anything important you can tell me that I don't already know! And it's no trouble at all to arrange suitable clothes for you. When you return from Waes, I'll have filled a whole wardrobe. Women in our position have certain obligations, you know. Your friend Camigwen understands them quite well. I do like her very much, Sioned. But as I was saying about obligations—I hope you won't find them too tedious. There are compensations, even when our men are being difficult."

Sioned watched the door close behind the princess, dazedly wondering if there was anyone left at Stronghold who did not believe Rohan would marry her. Was the "secret" such common knowledge that they would never be able to pull off his plan?

The maid arrived some time later, bowed low enough to indicate that she considered Sioned a princess already, and said, "Good evening, my lady. I'll just spread the gown on the bed and we'll take care of your bath before we start on your hair. Her highness says not to worry if you're a little late, because it's the perfect night for making an entrance. If you're ready, my lady, then we can begin."

Sioned began to suspect that Andrade—and Camigwen—had a hand in influencing the prevailing attitude here. They probably felt that if everyone behaved as if Sioned was Rohan's acknowledged bride, he would be pushed into an admission of it in public. She doubted they fully understood his stubbornness.

Sioned herself was of two—perhaps three—minds about

the future. She wanted Rohan. She wanted his schemes to succeed, for she knew that their life together in peace might depend on concessions he could gain from the High Prince at the *Rialla*; the charade was necessary. But she also resented Andrade's meddling in her fate, and her encounter with Rohan had given her some angry second thoughts about him.

The maid gossiped away, and Sioned learned something interesting: mindless chatter was a very good thing when one wanted to avoid listening to one's own thoughts.

"Where is he?" Milar pleated her napkin atop her plate and glanced yet again down the length of the Great Hall.

"If I knew, I'd find him and drag him here by his nose," Andrade snapped. She was tired after the long ride in the heat, and wanted nothing so much as her dinner. But the vassals and guests would touch neither a morsel of food nor a drop of wine until their prince finally decided to grace the high table with his presence. He was not fool enough to be hiding, although from the expression in Sioned's eyes during the ride back from Rivenrock, hiding would seem the wisest course until her temper cooled. Andrade could make a shrewd guess about the words that had passed between them.

She shifted in her chair, the cushion beneath her doing little to ease the soreness of too many hours in the saddle. The rest of the company was growing nervous, eyeing the main doors. Andrade took mental inventory, matching each vassal to his battle flag draped high above the torches, which were themselves set high enough to give off light but not too much heat in this perpetually warm room. At the end of the Hall huge double doors stood wide open, as did the windows on either side of them and along the outer wall, to admit any breeze that might stray in to cool the diners. But the banners moved only fitfully and the torchflames were steady and smokeless. Andrade licked her dry lips and pushed a lock of hair from her neck, cursing her nephew's lateness.

All at once her eyes popped as Rohan strode through into the Hall. He walked the long aisle between the tables with the ease and authority of absolute ownership, dressed in black and silver, his golden hair gleaming as if it had been polished. Andrade choked on a giggle completely unsuited to her age and rank. The entrance was pure Zehava, son of the dragon, and she forgave him her discomfort for the amusement of seeing him dazzle everyone in the room.

An open-necked shirt that clung to his body was tucked into snug black trousers. Silver embroidery winked from his throat, wrists, and the tops of his high black boots. Two rings—one topaz, one emerald—shone from his fingers, and a single fat onyx swung near the angle of his jaw from a silver clasp that circled his ear. The effect was perfect—and not intended solely to impress his vassals.

Rohan paused to make his bow to his mother. The two halves of the high table had been pushed apart so that Milar sat on one side of the division and Rohan on the other. He took his seat next to Andrade, and as Walvis came forward to pour his wine the feast began at last. Andrade looked him over and murmured. "Now, what is all this in aid of, I wonder?"

Tobin was frankly staring. "You look wonderful!"

"Thank you," he said airily. "But Tobin, I'm surprised at you! Your hands aren't red from spanking your two hellions."

"Chay did it for me—and they won't be able to sit down for two days. But where's Sioned? I want to thank her."

"Isn't she here yet?" he asked with a casual glance around the Hall.

"She will be," Milar said. "Now, don't embarrass her, Rohan. She's really rather shy, you know. How handsome you look, darling! I'm glad I haven't been sewing my eyes blind to no avail."

"You should've had your women do it," he scolded fondly.

"Don't be silly. It gave me something to do while Andrade bored me with her stories. Besides, my women are planning how to change the prince's suite for you when you get back."

"It sounds as if you're not coming with us," Chay said.

"I've too much to do here." She dipped delicate fingers into a bowl of scented water held by her squire. "Rohan will want to bring his bride home to rooms suitable for her. And that reminds me—go upstairs and find her, Jary."

The squire hurried off. Conversation stopped for a few moments while everyone pretended not to notice Rohan's blush. Andrade crooked a finger at Walvis. "Set a place at the high table for Lady Sioned, and don't be subtle about it."

The boy bowed, his usual wariness of her dissolving into a pert grin. "My lord ordered it earlier, my lady."

Andrade winked at him. "Very thoughtful. I approve." She turned to her nephew. "She'll murder you for it, you know."

"She should have thought of the official consequences before she saved Jahni and Maarken today." His eyes lit with wicked anticipation. "It wouldn't be princely of me not to thank her in public."

"I still say she'll murder you."

"That egg hasn't hatched yet. But what do you think of my first portrayal of ruling prince?" He picked up his goblet and struck a pose.

She laughed. "Very impressive. I like the jewelry. Don't ever wear more than that, Rohan. Your hair and eyes do it all. There's not a woman in this room who's not drooling over you. But I suspect it's the woman who's not here yet whose eye you want to catch."

"Dearest aunt, *that* egg hasn't even been cracked, so don't anticipate its dragon's flight."

Her brows arched. "My, how poetical we've become with our phrasing, my lord prince! Practicing for Roelstra —or for Sioned?"

"The former, of course. Better high-flying phrases than what I'd really like to say to him."

"Spent days thinking them up, have you?"

"Years." He grimaced, lifted his winecup to his lips, and stopped in mid-motion. Andrade followed the direction of his gaze and in the abrupt hush heard Chay give a low whistle of admiration. There was much to admire as Sioned made her way across the flagstones to the high table.

Quietly attired, without jewels, and with her hair in a simple braid threaded with thin gold ribbons, still she was as regal as a princess dressed in dark green silk just the color of mossberries in shadow. She looked neither to right nor left and her movements were a little rigid as she paced up the center aisle, all eyes on her. Walvis started forward to her rescue, but Rohan put a restraining hand on the boy's arm. Andrade nodded to herself; Sioned would have to get used to being stared at, for once she was Rohan's wife she would often be on public display.

The prince got to his feet as the Sunrunner made her bow to him. As she bent her head and her knees, gaze stubbornly directed on the floor, Rohan stepped between the tables and stood at the dais before her.

"A moment, my lady," he said as she rose, his voice carrying admirably to the far ends of the Hall. The girl's cheeks were crimson as she glanced up wildly, eyes like a startled bird's. Rohan continued, "We wish to thank you formally for your courage today on the hunt. For our sister and her lord, for our lady mother and our aunt, but most especially for ourselves we thank you. You have kept safe the two young lords who are our heirs—until we can get one of our own."

Andrade settled back to enjoy the show, fully approving Rohan's words and the furious flash in Sioned's green eyes. Naughty boy, to use the royal "we" to imply their mutual children!

Rohan held out one hand to her. Helplessly, she put her fingers in his, and a moment later was wearing the emerald ring. Andrade nearly choked. He had placed it on her left third finger, the one reserved for a tenth Sunrunner's ring and which for a *faradhi* was never circled by any other.

"It is our desire that you wear this as a reminder of the debt we owe you," he said. Pulling Sioned firmly up beside him on the dais, he gave her over to Walvis' escort and as the squire took her to her place at the high table, Rohan lifted his winecup. "The Lady Sioned," he called out.

The assembly roared out her name and drank to her health. Sioned looked like someone whose health was in need of a few toasts. Andrade grinned behind her goblet and mused on what methods the girl would use to make Rohan pay for this.

He waited until the Hall was quiet, then spoke again. "My lords, I've listened carefully to your wants and needs for the lands you hold of me. Your desires are many and varied. But I have never negotiated at a *Rialla* before, and I am reluctant to commit myself to promises I may not be able to keep. Therefore I ask that before I leave for Waes in three days' time, you choose from among yourselves three to accompany and advise me."

Andrade stared. Chay would be going to the *Rialla* as usual, of course, but for lesser lords to accompany their prince was not done. What scheme was the boy hatching now?

"My father Prince Zehava once told me that the promises of a prince die with him. I do not intend that this shall be the case with me. The vows he made to you in former years are unknown to me, but I do know that he concerned himself first and foremost with the wealth and happiness of his lands. If we are to keep the Desert strong and prosperous, we must work together. But it has occurred to me that—" He paused and took a deep breath, not entirely for effect, Andrade saw with narrowed eyes. "You and your families have served me and mine long and well. Yet with the exception of my lord of Radzyn Keep, who received the grant on his marriage to my sister, none of you truly own the lands and keeps you administer. Upon my return from the *Rialla*, what I propose is this. In autumn I will travel to each of my holdings, inspect it, allow you to show me its strengths and weaknesses. If all is to satisfaction, I will invest those who show themselves worthy with the privilege Lord Chaynal alone now enjoys."

Pandemonium.

"I hope you know what you're doing!" Chay shouted to Rohan over the racket.

"Darling," Milar said worriedly, "do you think this is wise? Zehava broke all precedent by gifting Chay with Radzyn, and it was for the best, of course, but—"

"You're out of your mind!" Tobin exclaimed.

But Andrade understood. The vassals would be kept busy readying their keeps for Rohan's inspection—and when he returned with whatever he decided they deserved from the *Rialla* negotiations, they would agree to anything in order to have true ownership of their lands. Moreover, Sioned would be accompanying Rohan on this progress, which would afford everyone the chance to get to know her. Lastly—if she read him right, which she believed she did—a war with the Merida was in the offing next spring. People who fought loyally for the prince who ruled them would fight ferociously to protect lands deeded to them by written law in a promise that would not die with this prince.

She touched Rohan's arm, and he turned to look at her. "Make them pay for it," she advised.

"With enough to support Stronghold every year from now on," he agreed.

Andrade nodded her approval. "You give them what they already have, and they pay for the privilege. Very economical, Rohan."

He sat down and took a long swallow of wine. "Being a prince is thirsty work," he commented.

As the moons rose, wine flowed in torrents and conversation in the Hall never let up for an instant. Andrade relaxed happily into the tumult, appreciating the quality of the entertainment Rohan had given her. It had been years since she'd been in the midst of doings like these, and if he was capable of a show like this at Stronghold, his performance at the *Rialla* would be something prodigious. She could hardly wait.

The night was not yet finished with surprises, however. Andrade kept an eye on Sioned, noting that the girl ate and drank almost nothing. Rigidly controlled, she sat with her hands folded in her lap, her lips compressed, her whole demeanor ice in contrast to the fire of her hair. As the dishes were cleared away and steaming pitchers of taze were placed along the tables, Andrade saw that Sioned no longer stared at her hands, but down the long aisle between tables to the main doors. Curious, Andrade glanced that way. Moonlight made hazy rectangles of the tall windows on either side of the entry, cool silvery light competing with the warmer glow of the torches. But Sioned was not watching the light. Her attention was on someone down at the bottom of the Hall. She rose slowly to her feet and glided along the outer aisle next to the window wall behind the diners' backs. Andrade anticipated her course and stiffened as she saw the object of Sioned's stare.

The wine steward Andrade had warned Milar about stood in one of the patches of moonlight beside the doors. His pale eyes were glazed over, his face blank, his body frozen in place. She recognized the look of someone being used by a Sunrunner as distant eyes and ears.

Sioned stood now before the second window, her slender body limned in quicksilver shadows. Andrade got to her feet, but knew it was too late to stop the *faradhi*. Coldly, politically, she knew there was no better time for Sioned to demonstrate her usefulness as Rohan's princess.

Silence flowed in a slow wave up the Hall as people noticed Sioned. She lifted both hands; the emerald spat fire from her finger and her other rings took on a strange glow. As light gathered between her hands, Andrade shared a gasp with the rest of the Hall. But only she and the other *faradh'im* knew that this was a skill Sioned should not have had. In the unlit space before the open doors a form coalesced, called up by the Fire Sioned had woven into the moonlight. The image wavered, steadied, became recognizable. Andrade's fists clenched as she recognized Roelstra. Someone screamed.

"Who are you?" Sioned raged at the wine steward, speaking not to him but to the unknown *faradhi* who controlled him. "What else have you seen for your master, the High Prince? Tell me what you plot against my lord, or I'll follow you all the way back to Castle Crag and wrap you in your own shadows!"

The High Prince's specter moved. His lips formed words unheard, his hands coming up to grip invisible shoulders. The steward's head lolled back and forth in time to Roelstra's movements as he shook the distant *faradhi*.

"Tell me!"

The steward's face was a mask of terror now. "I swear on my soul—"

"You have none! Were you planning to kill him? Tell me!"

"No! No, I swear to you—"

"Hear me, Roelstra! Tell him my words, traitor! Tell him I'll see him and his dead if he harms my lord!"

Andrade grabbed Rohan's arm to prevent him from running to Sioned. He swung on her in a black rage. "No!" she hissed. "Let her be!"

Sioned's eyes were wild as she proved herself worthy of her rings—and more—by tangling the other *faradhi* in light, threatening him with limitless shadows. But it had gone on too long; Andrade sensed the strain of the conjure and the moonweave drag at her own perceptions, and knew Sioned had not the strength to continue much longer. With the skills possessed only by a Lady or Lord of Goddess Keep, Andrade quickly gathered strands of light; sorting, separating. It was as if she unraveled a fine silk veil made of a thousand colors, each painted in silver and Fire, then rewove them into the unique pattern that was Sioned. Yet the girl fought her off, her strength still formidable as she struggled to keep the link between herself and the *faradhi* at Castle Crag. It took almost everything Andrade could call up to bend Sioned to her will.

All at once the steward's face turned, and even over the distance between them Andrade saw someone else looking out of his eyes. Hopeless, desperate, the man cried out in a voice not his own: "My Lady—forgive me!"

She cringed back from that terrible plea and tried to find the pattern of colors that would identify the Sunrunner. But the steward's body arched in a spine-cracking spasm and he slid to the floor even as Roelstra's ghostly fingers let go of the unseen traitor. Skeins of light tightened around Andrade, then shattered into fragmented colors behind her eyes. She moaned, pressing her aching skull between her hands. A mist of whirling hues concealed Roelstra's image. Then all was gone.

"Why did you stop me?" Sioned's voice rang out in furious accusation. Then she swayed, the emerald's fire dying at last as she sank to the floor in a graceless heap.

As Rohan ran to gather her in his arms, Andrade

heard someone calling her own name in frantic tones. "Andrade! Andri, look at me, please!"

Eyes aching, she turned to her sister, aware that despite Milar's lack of training she had felt the backlash of Sioned's power. She clung to her twin's arm. "Mila—get me out of here. I mustn't show weakness!"

"Urival!" Milar cried out.

Somehow she stayed upright and in control of herself as she left the Hall at Urival's side. Once beyond the doors, however, she sagged against him. Without ceremony he lifted her in his arms and carried her upstairs to her chambers. She was marginally aware of being propped in bed amid soft pillows.

After a long time she opened her eyes. Urival sat beside her, waiting, and when she frowned at him, he said, "How much have I taught her? Enough, obviously. I knew you'd be wondering."

"How much does she know?" Andrade winced as she sat up.

"Not everything. Yet. I assume you're not speaking of her *faradhi* skills."

She grunted and sank down again. "You taught her too much." When he only shrugged in reply, she accused. "You always favored her—helped her, taught her, looked after her—"

"And you have not?"

"I should never have sent you to her. You should not have been the one to make her a woman."

"Perhaps the same thing could be said of your coming to me the night I became a man. She knows you're using her, just as I knew you'd use me. I was willing to play along, but I don't think Sioned will be as biddable. You heard her tonight."

"She'll lose sight of her rings, become Rohan's princess first and a Sunrunner second. That's not what I wanted, Urival!"

"We always knew there was a risk. But to be fair, I don't think either of us ever suspected her strength."

"You taught her too much," she grumbled again. "You care too much about her."

"And you care too much about power!" Urival rose

and went to pour wine. More calmly, he went on, "She's recovering, as is Tobin. I've got Camigwen with her and Sioned, and Ostvel soothing Chay and Rohan. Milar ordered the steward's corpse decently taken care of."

She sat up again, finding it more agreeable this time as she sipped from the winecup he handed her. "How long have you known it was me that night?"

"The Goddess' spell can reveal as well as conceal," he answered with a small shrug. "What do you plan to do about Sioned?"

"Give her a seventh ring, of course. A pity the coffer isn't here, but I'm sure my sister will part with something of her own to mark the occasion."

"Sioned already received her seventh ring tonight—and somewhat in advance of demonstrating her skills," he reminded her.

"Damn Rohan." She finished the wine.

"It's not just the ring that's wrapped around her finger. It's his vassals. I was watching their faces."

"What you mean is they're frightened of her power lest it be turned against them. Damn them all!" She threw the empty cup across the room. It clattered against the dressing table before rolling on the floor.

"Lie back and be still," Urival ordered. "If you were fully recovered, it would have hit the wall."

"What has Roelstra done?" she demanded of him. "The usual spies didn't content him—he took one of our own, a Sunrunner—"

"But against that Sunrunner's will, Andrade. That was a cry from the heart."

"What difference does that make? He's a traitor, whoever he is." She gazed up at Urival for a long moment. "Perhaps it's just as well you taught Sioned so much. She may need it."

PART TWO

The Rialla

Chapter Ten

Rohan had decided to travel in much less state than his father had always done. He felt uncomfortable with the ceremony Zehava had delighted in, and ceremony translated into people who arranged it. Thus the column of attendants and baggage wains stretched a mere half-measure behind him on the road to Waes, and camp was blessedly quick to set up in the evenings. Not that this sped their progress much, but at least he could see the end of the column when he looked back over his shoulder.

The dry scrub of the Vere Hills gave way to the summer green of lowlands watered by the Faolain River, and they crossed into Meadowlord. The pace slowed as eyes bred to stark sand feasted on trees and grass and grain. The people were different here than in the Desert, too— plump and rosy-faced, lacking sun-wrinkles and browned skin. No riders hurried ahead of Rohan with announcements that his royal highness would soon grace their humble earth by riding over it, or with commands to clear sheep and cattle out of the way. Rohan enjoyed the delays that gave him a chance to talk with the herdsmen and villagers, who more often than not were unaware that the unprepossessing young man they greeted owned the passing line of horses and wains. He was offered bowls of fresh milk and tree-ripened peaches, shown smiling babies and given glimpses of blushing maidens whose admiring glances did a great deal for his self-esteem.

The group had sorted itself into three sections that first day out: Rohan in the lead with his family and their personal retainers, then the Sunrunners, and lastly the baggage carts with servants and guards to protect them.

Not that they needed protection in peaceful Meadowlord.
If a soldier drew his or her bow, it was to take down a
choice bit of game for the night's cookpots.

Rohan found the simple pleasure of a long ride in open
country a blissful relief from the tensions left behind him
at Stronghold and those waiting ahead of him at Waes.
No one approached with any problem more serious than
where to make camp for the night, and usually one of his
family rode at his side. Tobin in particular was excellent
company—when she could be parted from her lord. There
were always flowers in her hair, picked by Chay every
morning, and he saved a sprig of whatever he found to
wear in his swordbelt. With their children at Stronghold
in the care of an adoring grandmother, the Lord and
Lady of Radzyn behaved like young lovers again. Rohan
smiled indulgently and imagined himself and Sioned in
similar circumstances.

She rode with the others of Goddess Keep and he saw
very little of her. Rohan had accomplished his purpose in
making sure his vassals knew who she was, but he had
not counted on her graphic demonstration of her advantages as a wife. To have singled her out during the
journey would have been foolish, even though he knew
none of his people would gossip at the *Rialla* about his
probable choice of a bride. He watched her from a distance, aching with worry, for her eyes were lackluster
and she rode round-shouldered, seeming not to notice
the beauty of the country at all.

The vassals picked to accompany him also rode with
him sometimes. He had been pleased with the results of
his maneuver and could not have chosen better himself.
Farid of Skybowl was a dry-humored man of middle
years who had been selected because he had an uncanny
ability to wring profit out of a holding that consisted of
rock, water, and nothing else. High in the Vere Hills,
Skybowl sat on the slopes of an ancient lake that resem-
bled a round cupful of sky. The keep had been built
handspan by slow handspan out of gray stone brought up
the sides of the crater, where terraced fields yielded
enough to feed a small herd of sheep and not much
more. But somehow Lord Farid endured and even prof-

ited from his herd and his small quarry, and rarely asked anything of his prince other than wine or a little food to tide him through an unusually long winter.

Rohan had visited Skybowl as a child, and the sight of so much water in one place had astonished him. Wonder had given way to terror when his father had picked him up and tossed him into the shallows. Zehava had jumped in a few moments later to make sure his heir did not drown while he learned perforce to swim. Lord Farid, however, had taken Zehava to task for scaring Rohan, and in the days that followed had taken the boy out to demonstrate the finer points of the art of staying afloat. Rohan had overcome his fear of water and even regretted leaving Skybowl—and had never forgotten Farid's defense of him.

The second vassal chosen was Eltanin, who ruled Tiglath, a walled northern city formerly held by the Merida. Eltanin was a young man and had inherited from his father only a few years earlier, and his eagerness to attend the *Rialla* was augmented by his hopes of finding a wife there. Rohan liked him, and in their conversations Eltanin shyly admitted that he could understand exactly how Rohan felt about being an inexperienced young man in an important position.

Rohan was not completely happy about the third choice, but he hoped to use Baisal of Faolain Lowland to advantage. The *athri*'s new keep was his sole concern, which in some ways made him the perfect advocate for the other lords. Stone for his castle was far down on everyone's list of priorities, so he would fight tooth and claw for the other lords' wants in the hope that Rohan would eventually get around to haggling for his Syrene stone. The young prince marveled at the odd logic of his vassals in sending Baisal, but it made sense of a sort. At least they hadn't saddled him with Abidias of Tuath Castle.

The journey was a miracle of organization, especially as there were nearly a hundred people to oversee. Princess Milar's chamberlain had stayed at Stronghold to help with remodeling chambers for Rohan's use, and the loss of his nervous fluttering was a blessing. Rohan had expected Urival, as Andrade's chief steward, to take offi-

cial charge, but instead the duty had fallen to Ostvel and
Camigwen. The young woman was a wellspring of capability and firmness, and her Chosen was a man of tact
and good humor. Between them they provided meals
that were both delicious and on time, efficient organization of the camp, and strict supervision of everything.
Rohan mused about persuading Andrade to part with
them. His mother's chamberlain would drive him utterly
mad if they dealt with each other on a daily basis, and
Sioned had admitted a total lack of the talents Camigwen
had long since mastered. Besides, she would like having
her friends with her at Stronghold.

Accordingly, on the fourth afternoon of the journey
Rohan instructed Walvis to bring Ostvel up from his
usual place with the *faradh'im*. Respectful but not obse-
quious in manner, with an open, cheerful smile, Ostvel
spoke to him not as underling to prince—which would
have made Rohan uneasy—but as knight to lord. The
difference was one Rohan appreciated more and more as
time went by and his new power set him apart.

"I wanted to thank you for keeping this menagerie in
line on the trip," Rohan began.

"Thank you, my lord, but it's not really so difficult.
Not with my Camigwen ordering everyone around!"

"Please compliment your lady for me. Do you plan to
marry soon?"

"Well, my lord, she comes of a very good family up in
Firon—as you can tell by the color of her skin and those
eyes of hers—"

"Mmm, yes. Those eyes," Rohan murmured, and Ostvel
smiled at the compliment.

"I'll confess, my lord, the minute I saw them—" He
shrugged and gave a comical wince. "And we weren't
more than fifteen, either of us! Her people aren't as
highborn as some of Sioned's, but certainly they're more
exalted than my family. I told her long ago that until I
could offer her the chief steward of Goddess Keep for
her husband, I wouldn't offer her anything."

"I'm sure it wouldn't matter to her. But pride makes
us do odd things, doesn't it?" he added with a rueful
smile.

"Doesn't it just," Ostvel agreed, sighing. "But I expect I'll give in soon. She's persuasive, is my Cami—and I get persuaded nightly."

Rohan blinked at this casual reference to their intimate life. Chay and Tobin had never made any secret that they expressed their love for each other frequently in bed, but they were married people, not just betrothed.

"I'm not *faradhi*-trained," Ostvel went on. "But that makes me even luckier that she chose me, my lord. Sunrunners know what's what when it comes to that sort of thing."

"So I've been told," Rohan murmured.

"Lust she could have had with a dozen other men, but for her, love comes only with me," Ostvel said with shy pride. "And it's no timid, frightened girl I find waiting for me, either." He laughed. "That's what makes her so damned persuasive!"

Rohan chuckled. "It doesn't seem so terrible a problem, you know!"

"That's the beauty of a woman, my lord. The predicaments they land you in are always the most exquisite ones."

"Of all the predicaments waiting for me at the *Rialla*, the women will provide the most interesting ones— although I'd hardly call them 'exquisite,' " Rohan admitted.

Ostvel's smile vanished. "Just so, my lord," he said colorlessly. "If you'll excuse me, I should be seeing to the baggage train. They're falling a little behind." He gave a brief nod and wheeled his horse around.

Rohan regretted the loss of easy warmth with a man he was sure could become a good friend in time. But having begun the charade, he had to keep on with it.

On the eighth day they crossed the Faolain—by bridge, to the profound relief of the *faradh'im*. They bore the teasing of their less vulnerable companions with good grace, caring for nothing so long as they were allowed to ride over the bridge instead of rafting the river. Rohan called a halt early that day and had Ostvel set up the tents for the first time on the journey. Carpets and furnishings were not brought out, for it was only necessary to find out what sort of arrangements would work best at the *Rialla*.

The size of the encampment proved formidable. Rohan's tent was the largest, a silken thing of blue, silver, and gold that Zehava had ordered for this *Rialla*. The pavilion would be useless in the Desert itself, where shelters had to blend into the colors of the sand. But Rohan had to admire the proportions of it as he wandered around inside, finding that his father had provided for a private area as well as a public one. Rohan and Ostvel toured the encampment, plotting out the exact location of each tent at Waes, and despaired of arranging things to the convenience and satisfaction of all until Camigwen arrived and had all settled in the time it took her to draw a map in the dirt.

Rohan kept the pair with him for a time, asking questions about the horses, the food, and the furniture. Although interested in their answers, he was more concerned with observing them. Cami was brisk and decisive, remembered every detail, and kept a mental inventory of everything. She was in her element, and Rohan knew she was the very person to free Sioned of the running of Stronghold. Ostvel was her match in logistics when it came to the horses and guards. Rohan resolved to put his proposal to them once the *Rialla* was over—though at the moment it was nearly impossible to believe that in another ten or twelve days, all this would be finished and Sioned would be his.

He wandered slowly among the tents after they left him, thinking about the future. If only it could all be over *now*, and he and Sioned could ride back to Stronghold in perfect understanding, handfasted and sure of each other. Plans that had seemed so clever and exciting now only irked him. He kicked at a tent stake, telling himself he was testing its security in the ground. But he had never been very good at lying to himself.

"Well, nephew," Andrade said at his side, startling him. "Your little entertainment will begin soon. I'm looking forward to it."

By the early evening light she looked tired, her bright hair dusty and the lines of her face dragging downward. "I hope you sleep better tonight, beneath a tent," he said, concerned for her.

"I'll not sleep well until you and Sioned—" She broke off with a shrug. "But I suppose that will have to wait until you're through scheming."

"Does it ever stop?"

"Not for a prince. I've been waiting for you to ask me what I know about Roelstra. He probably knows everything about you, through his spies." Her eyes looked haunted, but before he could say anything she went on coolly, "Although I hope they're only the things you want him to know."

Rohan took her arm and they walked through the encampment. "I'm more interested in his daughters."

"I'll just bet you are. He's kept them tight in Castle Crag, so I'd judge them anxious for freedom. Only the legitimate ones will be proposed to you, so you needn't worry about the others."

"I'm going to look them all over. The more the merrier."

"The dragon among the herd, you mean," she countered with a smile. "I see more and more of your father in you, Rohan—in your own sweet, ruthless way. Since those girls probably don't have hearts, you won't be breaking anything. But you'll wound their pride, which is more dangerous."

"You've taken a hurt to your pride, too," he commented gently. "Have you found out anything about this *faradhi*?"

"No, but I will," she replied in a grim voice. "Roelstra will answer for this. I'll wait until you're through with him, but leave me some pieces."

"He used *your* Sunrunner to spy on *me*—he owes us both. But tell me about his daughters."

She did, as much as she knew, and Rohan listened attentively. Naydra was pretty, placid, and malleable; Lenala was stupid, end of report. Ianthe and Pandsala were the ones to be wary of.

"Ianthe is the most beautiful and seems to be the most intelligent, so she'll long since have figured out the advantages of marrying you. I'd be surprised if she doesn't slip into your tent some night. As for Pandsala, she's nearly as beautiful and almost as smart as Ianthe, or so I'm told."

"By whom?" he asked, knowing she wouldn't answer.

"Never you mind. Just have a care to Sioned's feelings. Tobin and I will do what we can to protect her from their spite. Have you decided just how and when you'll end your little comedy?"

"I thought I'd see what develops," he answered. "Is that dinner I smell?"

"One day soon you're going to have to give me a straight answer, you know. Yes, that's dinner, and I'm starving. Chay and Tobin are coming to my tent for family dinner tonight. You'll do me a favor by joining us to provide some intelligent conversation. I don't know how long I'll be able to stand watching them watch each other."

A long time later, as Rohan left his aunt's tent in the dark, he tried to recapture the feeling of freedom he'd had on the journey. Impossible now. Conversation at dinner had revolved around the *Rialla*. Tomorrow they would reach Waes, and the next day the princes would begin their talks. Rohan walked slowly to his own tent and stood outside it for a time, staring moodily at the gilt poles with their stylized dragon heads on top. Ostvel had ordered guards set around the royal tent tonight, good practice for the *Rialla* when such would be necessary, and one of them paused in his measured pacing to salute Rohan.

"Will you be retiring now, my lord?"

"No. Not yet."

"Very good, my lord." After saluting again, the man continued his rounds.

Rohan remembered the last *Rialla*, when he'd been watched far less formally and all the real attention had been on his father. No longer could he go where he pleased; he would be the cynosure of all eyes from now on, his movements watched, his words analyzed, his every gesture commented on. Feeling suddenly stifled, he turned and headed down toward the river.

He stood on the shoreline and watched the black water. The moons had not yet risen, and the starlight was feeble between wispy clouds. Up the opposite shore trees splayed darker shadows, a breeze whispering through them in answer to the low, insistent murmur of the river. Rohan shivered, reacting to the hint of autumn in the air, and rubbed his hands together to warm them. He was not meant for such places, he told himself, places with a careless abundance of water and effortlessly thriving crops and herds. He had been bred to the bone-burning heat of the Desert, the harsh winter wind off the Long Sand that could strip away a man's flesh and bury his skeleton without trace. Yet even dragons sought out softer lands—to pick them clean. Rohan shivered again, and not from the chill, before turning to walk back to his tent.

The simple shift in position saved his life. A finger's breadth from his ribs the air suddenly hissed with the sound of a passing knife. He dropped instantly into a crouch, boot-knife in his hand, eyes scanning the darkness. A second blade whisked past him, missing his head by a handspan, and he cursed his fair hair that shone even in the moonless night. The nearest cover was twenty paces up the slope. All he could do was become a shadow like any other.

A bird sang out and small animals chittered furiously as a nest was disturbed. Rohan stayed frozen, listening. When the night settled back to silence and there was nothing to be heard but the river, he blinked the cold sweat of tension from his eyes and got slowly to his feet.

Though he presented an easy target now, the night was free of more knives. He waited a moment, then searched the riverbank. A thin hilt was embedded in the mud, angled down as the assassin anticipated Rohan's defensive crouch. He pulled the knife out and ran his fingers down the fine, smooth blade, catching his breath. It was not made of Cunaxan steel, but of glass.

He hid the knife with his own inside the top of his boot, and returned to his tent. Walvis drowsed in a corner near the lamp. Rohan held the glass knife to the light, unsurprised to see the characteristic notch in the blade that was meant to catch in the victim's flesh when he tried to remove it. The hilt was wrapped in thin strips of brown leather, the blade made of green glass. A tight smile stole across Rohan's face and he hid the knife deep in his saddlebags where his squire would not find it.

So the Merida wished to warn him, he thought as he gathered a blanket around him and settled down to sleep. "Merida" meant "gentle knife" in the old language—gentle because the sharp glass blades were as quick and deadly as steel, and the Merida had come to power as a guild of assassins renowned for their silence and skill. Rohan's death would have been nice for them, but failing that, the knife had put him on notice that they were near. They wanted him nervous and suspicious, hoping he would make mistakes. Rohan smiled again and stretched beneath the blanket. This new problem added to all the others set excitement welling in his blood, eagerness for the coming battles of wits and nerve. If the Merida had meant to frighten him, they had failed.

Sioned reined in her horse at the top of the hill, looking down in wonder at the vast encampment. Other princes had arrived early and set up their tents, and Sioned identified them for Cami and Ostvel, who had come to inspect the area before the main column of Rohan's suite arrived.

"That yellow group over by the woods, that's Prince Saumer of Isel. He's as far away from Prince Volog as he can get—they share their island very unhappily, so they stay away from each other at the *Rialla*. The orange tents are Prince Durriken's. He's going to bake down there, so far from any trees."

"Who's been drilling you in this information?" Cami asked. "Urival?"

"Princess Milar. Let's see—red is Prince Vissarion of Grib, that silly pink for Seldeen of Gilad, and green for Chale of Ossetia—that one's easy, Cami, you remember when he came to visit at Goddess Keep and the whole place was awash in green uniforms." She identified the colors and their owners effortlessly, glad now of the princess' instruction. Scarlet, black, leaf-green, the turquoise of her own native Syr—she knew them all. Conspicuously absent were the High Prince's violet tents, and when his name was left out of her inventory Ostvel gave her a curious glance.

"He makes an entrance?"

"He makes an entrance," she confirmed. "He'll sail down the Faolain tomorrow morning with all due ceremony. Looks like a carnival, doesn't it, with all those colors clashing against each other?"

"And people doing the same," Camigwen observed. "Especially princesses. No, I will *not* be quiet, Sioned! Two gowns were all you'd allow Princess Milar's women to sew for you—two, when you'll have to appear at five times that many functions!" She turned in her saddle, eyes flashing. "How long have we been friends? Don't you know how much I want your happiness? Why won't you do anything to secure it?"

"After he's had a good look at the princesses, I'll know that if he chooses me it'll be because he really wants me."

"To hell with the princesses!" Camigwen exploded.

"The others are almost here," Ostvel interrupted. "We'll have to find a good place to set up camp. Fight with her later, Cami, we've got work to do."

"How can I fight with her when she doesn't care?" But she followed Ostvel down the hill, leaving Sioned to stare down at the gaudy camp, biting her lip.

By evening the Desert contingent was established in blue tents. Having done her part at Camigwen's direction, Sioned slipped away to explore. The *Rialla* would officially begin tomorrow with the High Prince's arrival, and she would have to become Rohan's extra eyes, ears, and tongue. She must behave as if she did not want him, conduct herself with silent modesty in public and private—and try to ignore a growing desire to flay the royal daughters until their skin was in ribbons.

But something more serious worried her, and that was the Sunrunner Roelstra had somehow corrupted. Andrade had questioned her during the journey, but Sioned had been unable to supply many details. She was certain, however, that whoever it was had also been there the night Princess Tobin had been ensnared in the moonrunning. It was a pity she did not know how to identify and seek out this renegade *faradhi* and help him. Sioned's heart cringed every time she recalled his despairing plea to be forgiven.

As the sun went down, lights were lit within the tents, making huge colored lanterns of them. Sioned paused in her walk through the camps—unchallenged because of her rings—and watched the shadow-shows given by people unaware that their movements could be seen against the light. One expanse of scarlet silk showed her a man and woman locked in an embrace; laughter sounded and the light was abruptly extinguished. Farther along, a turquoise tent showed one man gesturing angrily at another. The latter's defiant posture slowly wore down until he fell to his knees with head bowed. Sioned wondered what might be seen on other nights, especially against the blue walls of Rohan's tent.

She returned to the Desert camp and sat down on a small stool outside the tent she would share with Camigwen and three other *faradhi* women. A brazier filled with glowing coals was before her and she gestured them into flame with a wave of her hand. The motion brought a quick spark from the emerald on her finger. Both hands out in front of her, she stared at her rings. Eight of them now, but only seven earned in the *faradhi* manner. She still did not know why she had done so dangerous a thing as to weave herself into the distant *faradhi*'s working—or, rather, she knew why and feared to admit it. What would she not do for Rohan? she wondered, troubled anew by her response to him. Urival was right to be wary. She would use her gifts and her skills on Rohan's behalf, no matter what his intentions. Her power with sun- and moonlight was nothing compared to his power over her.

Rebellion stirred, and she told herself she would not become one such as the other *faradhi* obviously was to Roelstra. Yet the man hated his enslavement; Sioned knew that her own would be welcome. Goddess, what a fool her heart had made of her. She glared down at the emerald, which Tobin had informed her had been in the family for nobody knew how long. It was said to be possessed of a magic all its own. Green for her eyes, she thought, damning Rohan again for putting her through the public display.

The gold rings caught her attention and her thoughts turned to the discovery in the hatching cave. If Rohan was correct, then life would change drastically in the Desert. With unlimited wealth, he could buy whatever he wanted for himself and his people. He could purchase whole princedoms and their princes—or princesses, she added with a grimace. Everyone had a price.

She tried to believe that she did not, that nothing could induce her to betray her training as the other *faradhi* had done—but the living refutation suddenly walked into view, arms wide as he stretched. Hot color rose in her cheeks and she turned her face to the fire. For him, anything; it frightened her. He would never ask—or so she had to believe—but it was bitter to know she would betray anything and anyone for him.

"Sioned?"

His footsteps whispered in the damp grass. She held out her hands to the brazier again, gaze fixed on her rings as he crouched beside her.

"You're up late. You must be tired—it was a long ride, and I'm sure Camigwen didn't spare you a share of the work."

"I'm not sleepy."

"Nor I. Roelstra's arriving tomorrow, and I'm worried."

"Surely you know what you're going to do." Her gaze strayed to his fine, sun-browned hands, held near hers as he warmed them at the fire.

"More or less. But it all may change when I meet him face to face, one prince to another. What if he sees through me?"

"If those who love you have their doubts, why worry about a stranger?"

"Oh, I've been fooling my family for years," he replied, and she knew he had not heard her implication. "Sioned, what if I fail? I must have those treaties. Only then can I begin to build a life for us."

"If it's what you truly want, you'll find a way to succeed." She heard the platitude and loathed herself for it.

"Sioned, please look at me."

Unwillingly, she did so. His face was all gold and Fire, his eyes reflecting the flames.

"I need you to want this, too. Before, it was for myself and the lands my father gave me. But now it's for you as well. The private reasons are just as important as the public ones."

She hesitated, then shrugged. "It's been difficult, and it's going to get worse for both of us before it gets any better. What you said to me on the Hatching Hunt, for instance. I can pretend to be what I'm not, but I can't and wouldn't change the past even if I could. You have to trust me."

He held her gaze in silence for so long that she began to tremble inside with nerves. "Tell me one thing," he said at last.

"Yes?" she asked, wary.

"Tell me you love me."

Sioned looked away from those impossible eyes, unable to speak.

"You do, and I know it. But I need to hear you say it, Sioned. And that should tell you everything you need to know about me. Maybe the next days are going to cost us more than we're willing to pay, but I've got to believe it'll be worth it in the end. When it's all finished here, we can go home and love each other in peace. This isn't our beginning yet. That has to wait until we're safely in our own country again. But the life we'll have, Sioned—when I'm able to put my sword away for good, between us we can—"

"Your highness?" someone ventured from beyond the firelight, and Rohan cursed under his breath. He got to his feet and brushed his fingertips over Sioned's hair as he left her.

"Yes, Lord Eltanin. Forgive me, I'd forgotten we were to talk. Shall we go to my tent and be comfortable?"

The firelight reached for him, unable to give up the touching of his body and hair. Sioned went into her tent, huddled on the bed, and did not sleep.

At dawn she rose and dressed in her riding clothes, careful not to awaken the other *faradh'im*. But as she was pulling on her boots, the encampment roused with noises a warrior would have associated with imminent attack. Swords clanged, boots and hooves pounded in the dirt, guards shouted orders. Sioned leaped up and pulled the tent flap aside, astonished by the frantic activity.

"What in the name of—?" Camigwen, long hair streaming down her back, pressed to Sioned's side. "Why are they all running around, shouting at each other?"

The other Sunrunners, startled from sleep, crowded around and speculated among themselves, but no one had any answers until Ostvel strode past the tent and called out, "Get dressed, all of you! Hurry!"

"Is something wrong?" Cami asked, bewildered.

"That's one way of looking at it," he tossed back, leaving them more confused than before.

Cami pulled on her clothes and followed Sioned outside. They spotted Ostvel in the crowd that flowed down to the river. As they reached him, they heard him give a sharp order for the guards to form ranks.

"Fasten your tunic, woman! Straight lines, now! Look alive, even if you're not awake!" When they were arranged to his satisfaction, he turned, caught sight of the *faradh'im*, and gave an ironic salute. "Good morning, ladies. You're just in time to line the riverbank with the rest of us poor mortals. The High Prince has arrived."

"All this, for him?" Cami marveled, gesturing to the bustle around them that was repeated in every other prince's camp.

"All this and more. But the Desert is *not* going to present him with the very picture of a rabble in arms," he added sternly to the troops. He snapped out an order and they marched down the slope to the river. Sioned and Camigwen followed in their wake, grateful for the path they carved out of the crowd.

Upriver, Sioned could see violet sails limp in the motionless morning sunlight. Roelstra had not been scheduled to arrive until later, and Sioned suspected he had come early on purpose. Keeping people off balance seemed to be a favorite ploy of princes, to judge the breed by her own. The barge rounded a slight bend in the Faolain and drifted majestically toward the dock. Immense, painted white and gold and violet, it could easily hold over a hundred people in luxurious comfort.

"Will you look at that!" Camigwen whispered.

A man standing nearly snorted. "Aye, and look at the wary watcher on the prow! Some use dragons, some use monsters horrible as the sea creatures they're put up to scare—but Himself's ship changes guardian ladies the way Himself changes mistresses. It's said the latest is with him, big belly and all."

Though Sioned's interest was not in Roelstra's mistress but his daughters, she inspected the magnificent carving. She gave the craftsman full credit for incredible skill and, if the image was accurate, the High Prince's mistress full credit for surpassing beauty. As the barge floated past, figures and then faces were visible on the upper deck. Most of them were women, and the face matching the wary watcher belonged to a lady who was indeed heavily pregnant. The other women were slim and elegant, high-piled hair glittering with jewels, white dresses accented with violet trim. Four were dark, one was blonde, and the sixth had hair the color of tarnishing copper. All of them were beautiful.

Roelstra himself was even more impressive than his ship. Tall, clad in a white cloak and a violet tunic, he stood at the rails of the upper deck with one hand lifted to greet the crowd. But Sioned, watching closely, saw that his gaze lingered on no one; he seemed to be looking for someone, and Sioned knew who it must be.

"And there's Himself," the man beside her said, "all dressed up to dine off my own lord and all the rest. His whore looks ready to whelp—may it be yet another girl! The princesses are a fine lot—lovely as Lord Chaynal's purest bred fillies, and kicking down their stalls to get at the best stallion, the young Prince Rohan—beggin' your pardon, ladies, but what I think, I say out plain. Seventeen daughters, would you believe it? You'd think that with as many women as Himself has bedded, there'd be at least one boy in the litter. But no, the Goddess gives as she sees fit, and there's justice in her giving. My own lord, now, I'm glad he's happily wed. I wouldn't want one of the royal bitches as my lady, and that's the honest truth—beggin' your pardon again for my unseemly talk, and in the presence of gentle-bred *faradhi* ladies like yourselves, as well! Come along with me if you want a good view of the show. I'll escort you close and you'll see my lord and all the others come down to greet Himself."

"That's very kind of you," Camigwen told him with her dazzling smile. "Our own escort seems to have abandoned us. Lead on, sir!"

"Care of a Sunrunner brings Goddess blessing," he replied with a wink and a gap-toothed grin. "But the truth is I like being seen in company with pretty women!"

He made a path for them by shoving others roughly out the way, and to any protests growled only, "*Faradh'im!*" Sioned bit back a smile as she realized that while giving them protection and a good vantage point, he was also using them as the perfect means of getting close to the action himself. They neared the dock and she searched the throng of highborns for Rohan. The short pier was crammed with nobility—even Lady Andrade was there, along with Tobin and Chay. But of Rohan's blond head she saw nothing.

High Prince Roelstra and his mistress had descended from the upper deck, his daughters trailing along behind. The barge slid smoothly into dock and trumpeters blew out a fanfare, answered by a stately drumbeat from eight young men wearing the Waes city lord's garish red and yellow. Sioned's escort pushed through to the very front of the crowd onshore, and she scanned the assembly once again. There was still no sign of Rohan. Surely it was unwise to be late for the High Prince's arrival—and even worse to miss it altogether. She began to be afraid, for there was no conceivable reason for him to insult Roelstra in this fashion.

With the first step Roelstra took onto the wooden planks, every highborn sank to one knee—everyone except Lady Andrade, who only bent her head. He gestured graciously for them to rise. Some of them wore respectful faces, others looked guardedly resentful of the act of homage. Lord Chaynal's bright gray eyes were without emotion, but Princess Tobin looked carved of ice in her gown of white and red, her husband's colors. Roelstra distributed smiles all around, then turned to Andrade.

She smiled with poisonous sweetness visible even at a distance when Roelstra presented his mistress to her. Sioned shared a grin with Cami. "I'd give a lot to listen in," she whispered, and their escort chuckled.

A commotion at the steps to the pier turned all heads. " 'Way! Make *way*!" a man bellowed. "Move aside for His Royal Highness Prince Rohan!"

Sioned clapped a hand over her mouth to stifle giggles— not that anyone would have heard her in the sudden buzz of speculation and outrage that followed close on this arrogant proclamation of Rohan's presence. He strode up the steps two at a time, tugging at the cuffs of his shirt and running a hand through his hair as if he had dressed in such hurry that he hadn't had time to comb it. A masterpiece of effect, Sioned noted gleefully. He had arrived late on purpose so he would not have to bend his knee to the High Prince.

Andrade had come to the same conclusion, though she was more successful in hiding her amusement. She slanted a look at Tobin, who was red-cheeked and tight-lipped, black eyes snapping with mirth. Chaynal prudently hid his grin with a fit of coughing that made it necessary for his hand to cover his lower half of his face. His quicksilver eyes danced merrily as Rohan gave Roelstra a short bow that was perfunctory courtesy between princes.

In a breathless voice the young man said, "Pardon, cousin! Today of all days I overslept! I didn't hear a single murmur of all the fuss, can you credit it? Why didn't you warn me, Aunt?" he asked plaintively of Andrade, his eyes little-boy wide. "High Prince Roelstra must think me the worst kind of scattershell!"

"Not at all, cousin," Roelstra responded smoothly. "I understand that the demands of fatigue on healthy youth are answered only by enough sleep."

Rohan bestowed on him his most endearing smile. "My father always said you were a generous to a fault— and I'm glad you're generous with *my* fault!" His gaze went to the woman behind Roelstra and his eyes rounded to their largest. Andrade nearly choked. The effort not to laugh brought tears to her eyes.

"Are you all right, Aunt?" Rohan asked solicitously, without a hint of wicked enjoyment in his eyes. When she nodded helplessly, he turned again to Roelstra. "I know it's not polite to stare, but—" He shrugged, sighed, and stared anyway.

"It is I who have not been polite. I have failed to introduce you to my daughters. Come forward," Roelstra snapped at them over his shoulder.

They were presented: Naydra, Lenala, Pandsala, and Ianthe as princesses, Gevina and Rusalka by the title of Lady. Rohan bent over six slender hands and pressed his lips to the insides of six braceleted wrists. Naydra openly looked her appreciation of Rohan's golden looks; Lenala simpered; Pandsala turned crimson. Ianthe looked Rohan straight in the eye, holding his gaze for a long bold moment before glancing away. Gevina giggled and protested that he tickled her skin, and Rusalka snatched her fingers away as quickly as she could.

"My daughters," Roelstra said casually when Rohan had finished saluting them. "The ones old enough to make the journey with me this year."

"And with even more at home!" Rohan exclaimed admiringly. "What luck for you, cousin, to live in so fair a garden! My father always said that his daughter was his greatest treasure—and you have seventeen of them! Oh—do you know my sister, Princess Tobin? And her lord, Chaynal of Radzyn Keep?"

They were introduced. Andrade promised herself a good long laugh when she had time and privacy to enjoy it.

"But you must be weary," Rohan went on to the High Prince with the sweet solicitude of a young man for one nearing his dotage. "I shouldn't keep you standing here in the hot sun. I look forward to talking with you very soon, cousin—and, may I hope, your charming daughters?"

The High Prince and his entourage returned to their barge until their tents could be raised and furnished. The other princes and highborns left for their own camps, the welcoming farce over, all points going to Rohan in a game few were yet aware was being played. As Andrade descended the steps of the pier, she caught sight of a pale, intense face crowned by untidy red-gold hair, and lost all amusement at Rohan's performance. Sioned had eyes only for him, and in those eyes was her heart.

Chapter Eleven

A violet sky loomed close and dark, dripped a stinging crystal rain that needled into his flesh. He moaned, covering his face with hands frozen into brittle carved ice, and sucked a deep breath of water-thick air. It hurt going into his lungs, hurt even more when it choked out of him in a sob. So it had finally happened, one part of his mind observed; he had taken too much *dranath* and was dead. There was a certain peace in the idea, although death was even more painful than life. Perhaps that served him right.

He peered through his parted fingers at the sky to see that it formed distinct segments, rising on either side of him, angling up to a point over his head. Not sky at all, only one of Roelstra's violet tents. No freezing needles of rain, either, merely the lack of *dranath* turning his nerves to pinpoints of agony.

Crigo sat up, throbbing head gripped between his hands. Near his bed was a table with a silver wine pitcher. He gulped half the drugged wine directly from the chill container, then fell back with a long shudder of anticipated relief.

He had no memory of a journey, but there was only one place he could be: Waes. The tent around him, the voices outside, the scents of crushed grass and the river all confirmed the location. But he ought to have remembered sailing down the Faolain from Castle Crag—unless the drug-hunger meant he had been deliberately deprived of *dranath* so that the trip over water would incapacitate him. Either that, or he had indeed come close to killing himself on that night he had woven a moonlit path to Stronghold.

The last thing he truly remembered was that night, and he wished he did not. Especially did he recall the colors of the *faradhi*'s mind, lucent and distinctly feminine—fire-gold to burn him, river-blue to drown him, summer-green to seduce his arid mind into the richness of her, and the black anger of fierce protectiveness, implacable condemnation. Forcing himself to reconstruct the scene, he saw again through the wine steward's eyes the assembly of vassals at Stronghold. He had done it before, using the man's eyes and ears to observe for Roelstra. But she had caught him at it. He gasped as he looked on her face in memory—proud features too strong for conventional beauty, raging green eyes, red-gold hair. But more than the sight of her, the memory of her mind's grasp terrified him. How skillfully she had woven the moonlight into a trap, until he had cried out to Lady Andrade and lost control.

He paused to calm his racing heartbeats, sank deeper into the drug. He knew the girl's colors now; she might be able to identify his. But who was she? The wine steward had been about his kitchen duties earlier, so Crigo had not seen why she had been placed at the high table. Other *faradh'im* had been seated elsewhere in the Great Hall. Why had she been singled out?

"Awake at last, I see."

The sound of Roelstra's voice spasmed Crigo to a sitting position. The High Prince stood in the center of the carpet, magnificent in a violet silk tunic, dominating and angry. Crigo stammered out, "My l-lord—"

"You were unconscious for two days, and even when you woke you made no sense before falling back into your stupor. Tell me what happened that night."

"I don't know." He drew bony knees to his chin and wrapped his arm around his legs. "I watched as you bid me. There was a girl—"

"What girl? What did she look like?"

"Green eyes, red hair. A *faradhi*." He frowned, bringing the picture into focus again. "Seven rings—no, six, and an emerald not given by Andrade. We—they—don't use jewels much. She was powerful, my lord, she caught me—"

"Her name?"

Crigo shook his head. "I don't know."

"You've not been gone from Goddess Keep for that many years. She must have been in training before you left. Think, damn you! Tell me her name!"

Unbidden, there came to mind the image of a red-haired girl, one of the scores of girls at Goddess Keep and beneath the notice of an arrogant young Sunrunner like himself. Yet he remembered her. "Sioned," he whispered.

"Sioned," Roelstra repeated. "A *faradhi* named Sioned. . . . If I can detach her from Andrade—"

"The *Lady* is here?" Crigo gasped.

"That doesn't concern you." The High Prince approached and glanced down into the half-empty pitcher. "Drink up, Crigo," he said with a cold smile. "After all this time, you need it."

The Sunrunner obeyed as Roelstra strode from the tent. Andrade was here. Terror griped him, suddenly and paradoxically replaced by joy. He could ruin the High Prince by revealing that the *faradhi* she had thought dead these many years was still alive. The power of it made him laugh softly and he clutched the knowledge to him like a long-sought lover. But in the next instant he trembled, empty once again of all but the drug. Roelstra would never have brought him here if he feared betrayal. Crigo had no power at all over anyone, much less the High Prince. The game, as always, belonged only to Roelstra.

Tobin kissed her husband good morning to such effect that he tried to pull her back down into their bed with him. When she resisted, laughing, Chay opened his eyes, then opened them wider. She was fully dressed, her hair in a cool twist atop her head, and at her belt was a fat leather purse. Chay groaned.

"Oh, Goddess! You're off to make me a pauper again!"

"And I'll have a splendid time doing it, too," she teased. "Come on, move your lazy bones. It's well past sunup. And you know that anything I spend at the Fair, you'll only win back when you and Akkal come in first at the races."

"You spend so much to give me an incentive to win," he glowered.

"How well you know me! Anyway, it's not all ours. Mother sent some for me to spend on Rohan, and *he* gave me quite a bit—to spend as I like, or so he said, but what he really meant is that I'm to buy things for Sioned."

"She's going with you?"

"Of course." Tobin kissed him again. "It seems I'm getting predictable. You're going to get bored with me."

She threw his clothes at him on her way out of the tent. Outside in the warm sunlight, she stretched widely, sneezed away the tickle of unaccustomed scents, and walked over to the Sunrunners' tent where Sioned and Camigwen were waiting for her. With them was a young *faradhi* introduced as Meath.

"If it pleases your highness, I'll escort you today," he said giving her a bow as elegant as her husband's.

"That's very kind of you," Tobin replied sweetly. "You can carry the packages."

Meath sighed. "That's exactly what Cami has in mind, your grace."

"I'd like it very much if you'd all call me by my name, and forget this nonsense of titles," Tobin said as they started off.

"Thank you," Camigwen said shyly. "I'm Cami to my friends, and if Sioned doesn't promise to buy something pretty for herself, I'll tell you what her nickname was as a child!"

"You wouldn't!" Sioned protested, her eyes dancing. "Besides, remember all the things I know about *you*! And stop worrying, Cami—I'm going to spend every copper I have. I've never been to a *Rialla* Fair. Will it have everything we're told it will, y— Tobin?" she corrected herself with a smile.

"And more," Tobin promised. They joined the line of people waiting to cross the bridge over to the fairground. Just upriver at the dock, the High Prince's barge bobbed gently on the water, violet sails wrapped tight around the masts. Tobin averted her eyes, determined that political

thoughts would not spoil this, the first day of the *Rialla*.
"If you would, please keep an eye out for things my sons
would like. We have a thriving trade through Radzyn
port, but I want to find something special for them today."

Meath was all for shouldering a path through the crowd
to the front of the line, but Tobin explained that today
everyone was of a rank with everyone else to prevent
wasting time over silly questions of honor and prestige.
Enough of that sort of thing went on at the more formal
functions, and it certainly did not belong on a holiday at
the Fair. As they crossed the bridge, Camigwen gazed
straight ahead, her expression grim. Tobin noticed, and
smiled.

"Even the sight of water gets to you, doesn't it?"

"I can't watch the waves break on the cliffs without
getting sick."

"What about you, Sioned?"

"You'd never get her to admit it," Meath chuckled.

"I was used to it before I left home," she explained.
"My father's keep is called River Run, so I've lived
waterside all my life."

Tobin's brows arched fractionally. River Run was a
holding kept in the family of the Princes of Syr; Sioned's
blood was better than Tobin had thought. Not that it
mattered to her, but a bride with noble connections was
better than one without insofar as the vassals were concerned. She reminded herself to spread the story and
wondered why Rohan or Andrade had not already done so.

Meath was indeed cast in the role of pack horse. The
Fair was a treasure house of goods from all over the
continent, and Tobin couldn't buy things fast enough.
Camigwen added even more to the load. Needles, embroidery thread, candles, pottery, carved boxes, Fironese
crystal, painted tin boxes filled with spices for taze—the
two women spent recklessly, their packages wrapped and
handed to Meath. At first he stowed them away about his
person, but soon ran out of pockets. He then acquired a
sack with a drawstring top. It quickly filled; he bought
another. Whenever Tobin directed a merchant to send a
made-to-order item to Prince Rohan's tents, Meath's eyes
gleamed with gratitude.

Sioned picked over the offered merchandise but purchased nothing. Toward noon she treated the others to a delicious snack of fresh spicebread, fruit, cheese, and a small bottle of mossberry wine each. They sat beneath one of the trellises along the river to eat, laughing as Meath speculated whether it was the wooden beams or the flowering vines that held the ancient arches up.

Sioned opened the wine, saying, "We make this in my part of Syr. I haven't tasted any of this holding's vintages since I was a little girl." She took a healthy swig, closed her eyes, then swallowed and smiled happily. "Perfect!"

"Then open mine, quick," Meath implored. "My throat thinks it's back in the Desert."

They lingered after the meal, enjoying the cool breeze off the river scented with the crimson and blue flowers overhead. Other fairgoers strolled past, and as Tobin returned their greetings she kept up a running commentary so Sioned could learn about the people she would deal with as Rohan's princess. Not many of the *athr'im* attended, only the most important ones or those in high favor with their princes—or the young ones who needed brides, like the Desert's own Lord Eltanin. Tobin asked Sioned why her brother was not here, considering his close connection with the Syrene royal house.

The *faradhi* snorted. "Davvi leaves River Run once a year, to pay his duty to Prince Haldor at High Kirat. I think his wife's afraid someone will make off with a grain or two if he's gone more often. She's rather tight-fisted."

"Lady Wisla," Cami said acidly, "is miserly. You know it's true, Sioned. She begrudged you a dowry and that's why you were sent to Goddess Keep. And not a single invitation since to visit home," she added to Tobin.

"I've heard that River Run is a beautiful holding," the princess said, while thinking that it really was a very good thing that Sioned had no more ties with Syr. Denied her own home, she would more readily embrace Stronghold and the Desert. She rose and brushed off her skirts. "I still have to find something for the boys. And Sioned hasn't bought anything except our lunch."

Camigwen poked the prone Meath in the shoulder. "Wake up, we're going."

"Huh?" He straightened up from his nap in the grass. "Oh—sorry. Lead on, ladies. The old horse has a few good measures left in him yet, but will need to be fed and watered well tonight."

"Perhaps you can persuade Hildreth to brush you down," Sioned teased, and Meath glowered to cover his blush at the mention of the pretty *faradhi*.

On their return to the Fair, Camigwen gave a delighted cry at a display of lutes and settled down to bargain for one decorated with white elkhoof inlay. Tobin wandered over to the next stall to admire a rainbow of silk ribbons, but was distracted by Sioned's excited call from a booth crammed with toys. She held up a pair of carved wooden knights on horseback, one dressed in a red tunic with a white cloak, the other in the opposite combination of colors.

"The saddles are real leather," Sioned told her. "And look—the cinches really work, and the swords come out of the scabbards, and the knights' heads and arms move! Aren't they wonderful?"

Each was a full two handspans high, the workmanship exquisite. Tobin knew the twins would be wild to own them. "And in Chay's colors, too! Thank you for finding them, Sioned!" Then, eyeing the toymaker, who was preening himself at the praise, she asked, "How much are you going to claim they're worth?"

While they bargained, Sioned picked up another toy. Tobin watched from a corner of her eye as the girl admired a glazed pottery doll dressed in the height of fashion. Big blue eyes winked from a lovely little face crowned by hair made of fine silk threads arranged in golden braids.

"I wish I knew someone who had a little girl," Sioned murmured wistfully.

"*You* might," Tobin said just as softly.

"A very reasonable price, my lady," the toymaker said, scenting another sale. "The delight of any child—and another dress comes with her, too. See?" He brought out a box and revealed a gown of pink silk set with chips of crystal. "Look how it matches her necklace," he urged. "What little lady wouldn't adore a doll like this? If there's no small darling in her cradle now at your keep, look to the time when there will be—imagine her playing with this little charmer!"

A smile touched the corners of Sioned's mouth. But before she could speak, she was jostled from behind and nearly dropped the doll. She gave a little gasp and turned, brows slanting down angrily.

"How clumsy!" a sharp voice exclaimed. As Tobin looked around icily, the tone became all oil and honey. "Forgive me, cousin! Someone stumbled into us."

"No damage done," Tobin replied, looking Princess Pandsala straight in her wide brown eyes. "Cousins," she added as an insulting afterthought to Pandsala and her sister Ianthe. She had met both yesterday on the pier, and had disliked them instantly. Either of them married to Rohan was unthinkable.

"How clever of you to bring your waiting-woman to assist you," Ianthe said with a quick glance at Sioned. "Sala and I thought only to browse, but we've seen so many lovely things and we're having to carry our packages ourselves."

Tobin's spine became a sword blade, but she made her voice as sweet as Ianthe's. "I know how isolated you've been at Castle Crag all these years, but surely you recognize the rings of a *faradhi*. Allow me to make Lady Sioned known to you."

"Oh, I beg your pardon," Ianthe said. "Her fingers were lost in the doll's clothes."

This was not true, Tobin noted as she made the introductions; the emerald was certainly visible enough, gleaming from Sioned's finger. The Sunrunner had recovered her aplomb and there was a little smile on her lips, but there was also a dangerous light in her green eyes.

Tobin went on, "We were just choosing gifts for some children. Perhaps you could advise us, being surrounded by so many little sisters. Undoubtedly you're quite used to playing with their toys—to amuse them, of course."

The barb hit with obvious impact, but Ianthe made short work of a tactical maneuver. "Sioned?" she asked. "Oh, of course—the Sunrunner proposed by Lady Andrade as Prince Rohan's bride. It's the talk of the *Rialla*."

Pandsala nudged her sister. "Ianthe, you're embarrassing her."

"Not at all," Sioned replied coolly. "Some may have matched us, but I have not. Princess Tobin has been an excellent advocate for her brother, but I find him a trifle. . . ." She finished with a delicate shrug that could imply anything.

Tobin admired her survival instincts, but decided she'd better help anyway. "Men are like that! It takes a woman to teach wisdom—and you're just the one to do it, Sioned. But I really shouldn't gossip about my brother's private concerns," she added, hinting with her eyes that she would like nothing better.

"It seems Prince Rohan is the concern of the whole *Rialla*," Ianthe observed coyly. "I hope you find the toys to your satisfaction, Lady Sioned—even if Prince Rohan is not. Come along, Sala."

The pair moved off and disappeared in the crowd. Tobin counted to thirty under her breath before whispering a particularly obscene oath that would have shocked her husband—even though she'd learned it from him. Sioned's smile lingered, her heavy lashes drooping slightly over fierce eyes.

"Bitches, both of them," Tobin said. "Pay them no mind."

"No? He can't marry any of them and expect to live long past the birth of his first son. But—Goddess, Tobin, they are both so beautiful—"

"And you're not?"

Camigwen came up, triumphantly carrying the lute. Sioned busied herself admiring the instrument, almost feverish in her praise. Tobin, deciding she would not allow the royal bitches to spoil the day's pleasure, formed her plans quickly. She paid for the two knights, ordering them wrapped and sent to her tent.

"Wrap the doll as well," she instructed. "Sioned, Cami, we're going to a jeweler's next, and then—"

"No," Sioned murmured, placing the doll back on the counter. "Thank you for showing her to me. I'm sure she'll be greatly loved by some lucky little girl. I'm older, and my toys are different. Cami, you're about to get your wish."

Tobin's plans sailed away on the afternoon breeze as she and Cami followed Sioned through the Fair, Meath in silent attendance. Past booths filled with rugs, copperware, blankets, saddles, and parchment books they walked, purpose in Sioned's every stride. She paused to buy a single blue candle, then continued on, ignoring the displays of furniture, leather goods, and stained glass. Finally she stopped at a silk merchant's and after a moment spent scrutinizing the wares, pointed imperiously to a bolt nearly hidden in the back of the booth.

"I want to see that one," she informed the merchant.

He looked her up and down, obviously discouraged by her plain clothing. Tobin, standing beside and slightly behind Sioned, signaled with a lifted finger and a nod. The merchant shrugged and the silk was produced.

Thick, heavy, nubby stuff it was, the color of pale cream and made even stiffer by silver traceries of flowers and leaves wandering all over it. By sunlight it was dazzling; by torchlight, it would blaze as if made of stars.

"Yes," Sioned affirmed. "Have it ready for me by the Lastday banqueting."

"Impossible!" the man wailed.

"All things are possible. I'll send someone with the design, and Goddess help you if it's not followed exactly." She held out her hand silently, and Camigwen gave her a purse. Sioned counted out gold coins, weighing them in her hand. "The rest when I see the finished gown. And for this price, I expect stitches so fine I won't be able to see them."

"Yes, my lady," he breathed as she spilled coins into his waiting palm.

"I thought so." She headed for the next booth, where she bought a white linen shift as plain as the silk had been ornate. It was wrapped and given to Meath, who accepted it philosophically and added it to his bags. The next stop was a display of Fironese crystal that shot sparks for ten paces around. Cami, native of Firon, bartered with expert knowledge, and Sioned came away with a pair of intricately etched blue goblets. At another merchant's, slippers were bought to match the gown, and when Sioned had chosen a bottle of fine Syrene wine she was satisfied at last. They returned across the bridge, Meath pretending to stagger under the weight of his burdens.

"I may take up a new profession: hermit! Away from all women and especially away from all merchants! But it's been a real pleasure, ladies, watching you spend money that isn't mine."

He went to deposit their purchases in Tobin's tent, and the women continued along the river to find an isolated spot beneath a tree. Camigwen sat down with her back resolutely to the water, her arms wrapped around the lute.

"I suppose you forgot that Ostvel doesn't know a note," Sioned remarked.

"But he has a wonderful singing voice, and he said once that he always wanted to learn how to play. This will be my wedding gift to him." She winked. "He doesn't know it yet, but the Lastday ceremonies will include us!"

"I'm glad," Tobin said warmly. "Chay and I will drink to you both. Now, would either of you care to enlighten me about Sioned's purchases?"

The *faradh'im* shared a grin, and Camigwen said, "She has an advantage over those princesses, you know. They're virgins."

"Down to their toenails," Sioned agreed.

"Isolated at Castle Crag all their lives—"

Tobin joined in, laughing. "Precious flowers without even a brother to show them the difference between boys and girls—"

"And probably not knowing what to do about it even if they're aware of the difference!" Camigwen concluded with a sly smile.

"My father always said you could tell a woman from a maiden by the way she swung her hips," Tobin mused. "I could swear he knew the very next morning after Chay and I first—" She broke off, blushing.

"I assume this was somewhat in advance of the wedding?" Sioned teased.

"A little," Tobin admitted. "But what this means you're

going to seduce my brother, which means you intend to marry him. Oh, Sioned, I'm so relieved!"

"I knew it all along," Camigwen scoffed, and nudged her friend playfully.

"You did not! Not for certain, anyway. *Please* tell me I'm a better actress than that or I won't have a hope of fooling anyone."

"You know you had me doubting," Cami soothed. Then she addressed the princess. "But it's no simple seduction we're planning here. There are certain spells no one's supposed to teach us until we have at least eight rings, and Andrade doesn't know that we know them." She sighed. "I never had reason to use them on Ostvel. It would've been fun to try!"

"It's nothing dangerous, Tobin. Just a little Fire woven here and there—that's what the candle's for—and nothing you can use on a man against his will. Actually, I think it's mostly the wine." She winked at Camigwen.

"Tell me how I can help," Tobin said.

"Does anyone sleep in his tent but him?"

"His squire, Walvis."

"Oh, he'll be in on things. He's on my side anyway. If you can arrange to have the guards look the other way, I'll do the rest."

"It's already arranged." The princess glanced around to make sure they would not be overheard, then leaned forward and said, "You'll have my help and my blessing, but I want to know a few things."

Camigwen laughed. "But how will you explain to Lord Chaynal where you learned them?"

"He won't have strength or breath to ask," Tobin purred.

After a private dinner with Prince Clutha of Meadowland and Lord Jervis of Waes, his hosts here, Roelstra repaired to his barge and spent a little time with his mistress and his daughters. The first day of the *Rialla* was always dull, for no real business was done while everyone swarmed over the Fair. Roelstra had stayed in his tent and the princes had come to pay their respects. The only advantage to being bored by them was that occasionally one would let a hint drop about some matter, giving Roelstra something to think about. Still, his spies were efficient and he had heard nothing new today.

But as he sat with his female possessions over wine and sweet cakes, he reflected that there had been rewards to this day after all. Pandsala and Ianthe had gone to the Fair as ordered, and had returned to the barge with their impressions of Lady Sioned.

"Scrawny," Ianthe sniffed when Palila asked what the girl looked like. "Bones and skin—freckled and tanned from being in the Desert all summer."

"I thought her rather pretty," Pandsala said unwillingly. "And there weren't any freckles."

"Dirt-specks, then."

Naydra glanced up from her embroidery. "What can one expect from a Sunrunner drudge?"

"Is it true she's to marry Rohan?" Palila asked on cue as Roelstra signaled her with a glance.

"I had my maid talk to one of their grooms last night," Gevina said. "They're confused about it. She arrived on Lady Andrade's order to become his bride, but he wouldn't have her. And what's more, they also say that *she* won't have *him*!"

Lenala cleared her throat. "He's very handsome, though."

Roelstra favored her with a patient gaze. "How observant of you, my dear."

"Gevina's right," Pandsala put in. "The girl said herself this afternoon that she's not sure she'll have him. What a fool!"

"He is *very* handsome," Lenala said, emboldened by her father's approval.

Ianthe rose and tucked a pillow behind Palila's back where she lounged on a velvet chaise. "Is that better?" she asked solicitously as Palila stiffened.

"I'm quite all right," the mistress snapped, and Roelstra hid a grin. He sometimes missed the stimulation of several mistresses who all loathed each other, but the clashes between his daughters and Palila were nearly as amusing. Aladra had been the first truly nice woman he had been attracted to since the death of his wife, but he knew himself well enough to realize he would have grown bored with her eventually. It was better that she had died and left him with fond memories. Had she established peace and sweetness in his household, he would have expired of nausea and boredom.

"Princess Tobin is on her side, it seems," Ianthe said after she had reseated herself near the windows. "Sioned made a point of saying that."

"She also said she didn't find Rohan much to her tastes," Pandsala added. "I think that's much more important. She doesn't seem the type to bow to Lady Andrade's wishes if they went opposite to her own. Frankly, she strikes me as being incredibly stubborn."

"I like her more and more," Roelstra drawled, just to see them react. A smile teased Ianthe's lips, Palila's eyes narrowed, and the others began a chorus of protest about the foolishness of disobedient women. Roelstra lifted a hand for silence. "No reflection on any of you, my dutiful darlings. Her headstrong nature will only make it easier for you to contrast yourselves to her in front of the prince—to your advantage."

Palila gestured languidly with one hand, and Roelstra noted how thick and puffy her fingers had become. "Your interest in him will be a soothing pleasure after her indifference," she told the girls. "You must remember to be soothing, my dears. Men do not like contention. And Rohan is very young. He will want to be admired and fussed over, made to feel important as a man."

"I liked his looks," Lenala said wistfully.

"Everyone is aware of that, my treasure," Roelstra said.

The daughters returned to shore and their tents, but Roelstra lingered in Palila's room for a time. The sight of her disgusted him, but there was nothing wrong with her instincts.

"And so?" he asked, arching a brow at her.

"Pandsala wants him. Ianthe seems not to care, but she wants him just as much. I would wager on Sala, however."

"She may overplay it."

"She's not a fool, my lord. And Ianthe looks her wits

too much—Rohan is too young to appreciate intelligence in a wife." An elaborate bedrobe concealed most of her bulk, but her fingers were bare of rings she could no longer slip on, and bracelets around her wrists bit into swollen flesh. She gave him an alluring smile in a face still beautiful, and he toyed for a moment with the idea of the pleasures to be had from her even in this state. But he found himself thinking instead of a slim girl with red hair and tanned skin, a girl he had not yet seen but intended to, very soon. "Will you stay here with me tonight, my lord?" Palila invited.

"I have other things to attend to, or I would stay all night," he lied, smiling. He started for the door, then turned. "Why Pandsala?"

"Why not?"

"You championed Ianthe before."

"I've changed my mind after seeing Rohan."

"You may be right, my dear. Sleep well."

Chapter Twelve

By the next day Rohan was already monumentally weary of playing naive prince for Roelstra's benefit. He chafed against the role, and the fact that it was self-imposed did not improve his temper. The plan that had seemed so clever at the beginning of summer was more of a strain than he had ever imagined it would be—and not all of it was due to the unexpected addition of Sioned to his plans. The scheme had been hatched by a prince-in-waiting, a boy who had spent his life effacing himself (never very difficult in his father's overpowering presence), listening, learning everything he could from everyone who crossed his path. Fooling the High Prince had seemed only a briefly necessary extension of those years of deception.

But between the hatching and this time of flight, he had known power. Killing the dragon that had killed his father had shown him his skill and wits in a deadly fight. Meeting Sioned had shown him another kind of power— the Fire that bound them together and was capable of burning his soul. Presiding over his father's pyre, over his vassals, over the banquet in the Great Hall, had given him a heady taste of being master of the Desert. And he admitted to himself that the journey from Stronghold had brought a freedom he had never known before. Out from under the eyes of his parents, commanding the entire company, all the decisions his—no, it was not easy to play the idiot's role when he knew himself worthy of the position he could not yet claim.

He pretended to be guided by the advice of his vassals, and it was a good thing their suggestions were wise ones; he was prevented from having to overrule them, which would ruin the impression he struggled so hard to create. The other princes were firmly convinced he could be led like a lamb. But the tension was fraying his nerves.

Roelstra hinted constantly about his daughters, which added to Rohan's discomfort. Lenala and Naydra had been present when Rohan had arrived for the morning session at Roelstra's tent, and served him wine while eyeing him in the most embarrassing fashion. The other princes winked and nudged each other. At the midmorning break, Ianthe and Gevina had shown up to bring refreshments; more grins and elbow-poking had made Rohan blush to his earlobes. At least, he told himself ruefully, it added to his guise of fool.

He had the daughters sorted out by now. If he had looked over the women at Stronghold and found them lacking, then these princesses fell even farther short of the perfection he associated with Sioned. Gevina had a tendency to giggle; Rusalka behaved as if Rohan was of an entirely different species from herself and invariably looked surprised, as if she had doubted that he ate, drink, and scratched his nose like other men. He thanked the Goddess for Sioned, whose laughter was honest and who met him on human terms as well as man to woman.

Naydra was very lovely if one appreciated the type. But Rohan's tastes had been formed by his mother's golden beauty and his sister's vivid dark looks, so Naydra seemed to him simply brownish. She also had a certain covetousness in her eyes and tended to look at his lap as if to measure him. He was equally thankful for Sioned's frank sensuality; Naydra's furtiveness was disgusting.

Lenala stared at him outright, and he supposed it might have been flattering to have his looks so openly admired if there had been the faintest spark of wit in her eyes. Grateful for Sioned's intelligence, he pitied the man who married this empty-headed princess.

As for the other two—they were undeniably beautiful. Richly colored, graceful, they behaved like women and not girls. Pandsala affected a slightly distant manner which Rohan assumed she thought would intrigue him. Ianthe, on the other hand, issued an open invitation with her eyes every time she looked at him. Rohan was honest enough to admit that if not for Sioned, Pandsala would indeed have been tempting and Ianthe well-nigh irresistible. He was finding that to be a young, wealthy, good-looking prince could be very enjoyable indeed.

It ceased to be pleasant when Roelstra got him alone after the day's session was over. "My girls can't keep their eyes to themselves," the High Prince chuckled. "I've kept them at Castle Crag too long, without many young men to look at. I shall hate to part with them, you know."

Did he think Rohan would take the whole lot off his hands? Rohan made his expression bashful and mumbled something about their being very nice girls.

"Cousin, you might assist me with a small matter having to do with them. I can never decide which is the prettiest. I'd value your opinion of my girls—your mother was one of the great beauties of her day, and your sister is the most exquisite woman I've ever seen."

Rohan fended off making this impossible judgment with another mumble and a question about the output of Cunaxan wool, information that might allow them both to wring another concession out of tight-fisted Prince Durriken. Rohan had become an expert at the art of blushing evasion, as if the very thought of Roelstra's daughters flustered him so completely that he had to take refuge in practical matters. And all the while he coaxed the High Prince into signing more and more documents.

He had managed several of them that day: a renewal of the agreement that Feruche belonged to Roelstra but all lands below it were Rohan's; a pact of mutual assistance should the Merida attack and interrupt trade; and, foolish enough to Roelstra but important to Rohan, an agreement that Princemarch would conduct a census of dragons when they flew north to summer in the Veresch Mountains next year.

"I heard about your first dragon," Roelstra said. "Valorous work! And to burn him along with your father, their ashes scattered by *faradh'im* on the morning winds—I know Zehava would have approved."

"I don't mind confessing that I was scared half out of my wits when I saw that dragon coming at me," Rohan replied.

"Only a fool isn't frightened when there's danger. But only brave men do what must be done despite their fear."

Rohan heartily agreed. He anticipated a nasty test of his courage when Pandsala or Ianthe maneuvered to be alone with him. But it was nice to be wanted, if only for his money and power. The thought teased his mind that perhaps he might give into their maneuverings—just once— and see what sort of experience he could acquire. But he banished the notion instantly. One did not do such things to princesses, and especially not when one was in love with another woman who was a Sunrunner into the bargain. Being an honorable man was a bother.

Prince Clutha gave an outdoor dinner for his fellow princes and a select group of *athr'im* that second night, and Rohan was profoundly grateful that all the talk was of the next day's races, not of politics, trade, and defense. *Almost* all the talk.

"—and the river of fire-gold hair down her back? Incredible!" Lord Ajit of the five wives smacked his lips and grinned at Lord Bethoc beside him, directly across the table from Rohan. "You're a young man, Bethoc, and wifeless—but I tell you from experience that redheads are fire inside and out!"

"She's a Sunrunner," Bethoc sniffed, thereby ending any doubts Rohan might have entertained about which lady they were discussing. The Lord of Catha Heights selected a ripe plum from the fruit tray, squeezed it to pulp the innards, and slit the skin with his knife. "The *faradhi* bitch assigned to my keep—fah!" He sucked at the plum and discarded the emptied skin on the grass. "I asked her to conjure me a little Fire on a cold night, and she told me I could strike steel to flint as well as any man and had an army of servants to do it for me if I was getting feeble!"

Ajit grinned wider, his dark eyes gleaming in the torchlight. "So you tried to seduce her, eh? A mistake, my friend. Try it again and you'll have Andrade looming over you like a she-dragon."

"I note that doesn't keep you from lusting after this fire-haired girl."

"Lust is one thing, prudence quite another. Not even Roelstra dares anger Andrade. There are times when I believe she truly *is* a witch."

"You just noticed?" Bethoc asked sarcastically. "They all are, including this girl."

"Good women are so boring. My third wife was a positive miracle of dullness. The most exciting thing she ever did was die in her sleep."

Rohan wondered if they thought him so dull-witted that he was unable to hear his aunt's name spoken right in front of him. So Sioned was admired, was she? He felt at once smug and jealous, and suspected he'd be feeling only the former if she was his acknowledged lady.

Prince Lleyn of Dorval, who sat to his right, caught his attention and asked, "I don't suppose I can convince you to persuade Lord Chaynal not to ride tomorrow? The very least you could do is limit him to entering only half the races. He takes away all the sport, for he invariably wins."

Rohan laughed. He liked the old man, whose son Chadric had been a squire at Stronghold when Rohan was little. "You'll take away all *his* sport if you forbid him to race. He likes to terrify my sister, then laugh at her when she blisters his ears for not being more careful of his precious carcass."

Lleyn's blue eyes, faded with age but merry as a boy's, twinkled with pleasure. "I take leave to doubt that, Rohan. I don't believe your sister has ever been frightened in her life, and I'm positive that even a scold from her would be purest music to any man's ears."

Rohan leaned over and tapped Chay's shoulder. "Did you hear that? He thinks Tobin's rages ought to be set to music!"

"War drums," Chay agreed. "She smiles at *you*, Lleyn, because you dandled her on your knee when she was a child and gave her sweets to make her fat. And you still flirt with her until I ought to run you through! But being her husband isn't all it's rumored to be!"

"Then to escape her wrath, you'll not race tomorrow?" Lleyn asked with a sly grin.

"Not a chance! My Akkal is more than ready, and he'll

win unless somebody has something hidden away with four good legs on it."

"If I were thirty years younger—" Lleyn chuckled.

"But I thought you were!" Rohan said. "You're certainly about to drink everyone right under the table."

"When you're old, the only pleasures left are food and drink—and winking at pretty girls like Tobin. But if I could ride anything capable of more than a trot, I'd give Chay a run for that prize money."

"Hadn't you heard?" Chay asked. "We're racing for jewels this year, not money. Pity I learned that only after my wife spent half my fortune at the Fair yesterday. Still, the race will get me a big handful of rubies, and no stone suits my Tobin better."

Rohan turned to the High Prince, who was seated two places down from him on the other side of the table. Roelstra had obviously been listening to the conversation, and smiled as Rohan said, "That's an interesting change of tradition—the crafters will have a lot of business to keep them happy."

"That was the idea. They've been complaining that ladies don't wear enough jewelry anymore and it's hurting their trade. I'm counting on creating a demand again—and Princess Tobin will be the one to set the standard, as always," he added with a slight bow to Chay. "But it wasn't really my idea. Ianthe is responsible for it."

"She's a clever girl," Rohan said. And meant it.

Wispy lavender clouds washed deep blue beneath like dragon wings vanished into blackness as the sun descended, and the dinner party came to an end. Rohan left with Chay after thanking their hosts, and the sweep of night air down by the river made him catch his breath. "Oh, but that feels good! Let's go walk off some of this food or Akkal will refuse to carry you tomorrow."

"Let's try to sober up, too. I must've had enough tonight to float that damned barge of Roelstra's."

Chaynal slung a companionable arm across Rohan's shoulders as they walked along the shore, where moonlight threw silver across the river.

"If only we had just a little of this water in the Desert," Rohan mused.

"Then it wouldn't be the Desert, would it?" Chay responded reasonably.

"Are you always so brilliant when you're drunk?"

"Are you always so stupid about women?"

"What?"

Chay sank down onto the grass and stretched out long legs. Leaning back on his elbows, he squinted up at Rohan. "This Sioned of yours. I heard what that lecher Ajit said tonight. Your face froze up like Snowcoves in midwinter."

"You've never been that far north in your life."

"Don't try to evade the issue," Chay said severely. "Be more careful with your eyes, Rohan. I saw it because I know you so well, but if Roelstra catches on, your plan won't work."

"And what do you think you know about my plan?"

Chay snorted. "Sit down. I'm getting a neckache." As Rohan crouched down nearby and began pulling grass up by its roots, he went on, "And don't rip up the landscape, either. I watched you simper around the princesses, and I've also watched you watching while Roelstra agrees to sign. You're dangling a marriage in front of him, aren't you? I don't know why it took me so long to see it," he added in aggrieved tones. "You're smarter than I would've guessed."

"What a glowing compliment to your prince," Rohan said irritably.

"If it's taken *me* this long to figure it out, then I'd say it was an excellent compliment. Lord Narat asked me this afternoon if you were capable of ruling a princedom—not in so many words, of course, but that's what he meant. And Lord Reze nearly said flat out that you're a fool this morning in the *Athr'im* Council. You don't need to worry about any of them, but if I were you I'd keep a careful eye on those princesses."

"What could they possibly do to harm me?" He laughed.

"Marry somebody nearly as powerful as you and make your life hell."

"The only prince who'll come close to me in power will be Roelstra—and not for long."

"Ambitious, aren't you? But more to the immediate

point, those daughters of his could make Sioned's life hell."

"They wouldn't dare."

"Oh, no? Tobin mentioned that she and Sioned and Camigwen had run into Ianthe and the other pretty one—Pandsala? Yes, that's her name. They tried to stick their knives into Sioned—and right now they think she's a *rejected* bride! What d'you think they'll be like when you present her as your wife?"

"Who says I'm going to?"

"Damn it, Rohan, stop it! I can't help you if you won't be honest with me!"

"If you're telling me I should fear for Sioned, don't bother. She's being watched. I'm not that stupid."

"Who'd suspect a woman, and a princess at that? Roelstra's daughters want you, Rohan. Not for your charming self, but as an escape from Castle Crag and into power. It doesn't hurt that you're not a pockmarked, cross-eyed hunchback, of course. There's lust in their eyes for you as a man, too. But once you reject them, you've made fools of them—and they'll go after Sioned. She's where you're vulnerable."

"There are other princes—other lords with as much money and power as I have. Why does it have to be me?"

Chay shook his head. "You don't see it. I owe you an apology for all the years I thought you a nice, over-learned little boy. I've watched you since Zehava died. You're as ruthless as Andrade and much more dangerous than your father ever was. His armies were in the field. Yours are invisible. Those ideas of yours are your soldiers, and your schemes are your armies going to battle. Nobody expects it. You play the fool of a prince, but there's something about you that you'll never be able to hide, not after killing that dragon. It's power—and it's very personal. That makes you worth a lot to any woman, especially one who has a taste for power herself."

Rohan stared. He had never heard Chay talk this way before and had no notion of how to react.

"You don't think Roelstra gives those girls anything useful to occupy their time, do you?" Chay went on.

"Zehava always kept Tobin busy—he gave her enough work so that she knew her own strengths. She was her own woman before she became mine. Sioned's the same kind. She has the look about her. She knows who she is and she has worth in her own eyes. But those princesses— you're their chance to become somebody other than just another of seventeen daughters. They've been stewing in that castle their whole lives, looking for the day when they'll marry some man who'll let them play with his power. And once they find you've played them all for fools—"

Rohan's fingers clenched around handfuls of moist grass. "You're right, Chay. I'm stupid about women."

"You've only known Tobin and your mother, Maeta, a few others. None of them has a vicious bone in her body. Rohan, anything spoils when it's not allowed to live. A few more years and I would've started being afraid for *you*. But you've felt your own power now. The princesses see it. They want it."

"I should have listened to Sioned," he murmured. "She tried to tell me the same thing."

"I thought you never even *spoke* to the poor girl!"

"Remember how I used to arrange meetings between you and Tobin? Walvis used the tricks I taught him."

"Corrupting innocent youth. You should be ashamed of yourself."

"Me? Who taught me in the first place?"

"I know a few more, and I'll have my people use them to keep watch on her."

"Just as you've set watch over me," Rohan guessed.

Chay grinned in the darkness and got to his feet. "I don't have to." He gestured to the rise above the river. Rohan peered into the trees and after a moment made out the shape of a tall man. "Her fellow Sunrunners take turns," Chay informed him dryly.

Rohan stood, speechless with fury. Then, very slowly, drawing out each syllable, "Why that sly, conniving, secretive, cunning little—"

Chay laughed and clapped him on the shoulder. "All of which makes her just like you!"

Rohan managed a very sour smile and started up the

bank, his eyes on the shadow next to a tree. As branches shifted and moonlight seeped down in new patterns, he saw the outlines of a frame much broader than his own, and made a guess. "Meath!" he called out, and the shadow moved abruptly. Rohan snorted. "I've seen you, so you might as well come explain this."

The *faradhi* stepped out of his hiding place and bowed formally before straightening to his full height. "Your pardon, my lord. The Lady Andrade—"

"I quite understand," Rohan interrupted. He knew very well the Sunrunner was about to tell him a convenient lie on Sioned's orders, and did not wish to hear it. "I appreciate your concern, but I have a favor to ask of you, Meath—something my aunt apparently hasn't thought about."

"Yes, my lord?"

"You know the rumors about Sioned. Roelstra's daughters aren't likely to take those rumors of her presence very kindly."

"I heard them with her and Princess Tobin at the Fair, my lord," Meath remarked calmly.

"Just so." Rohan knew he had no need to speak further, and smiled to himself. Sioned would now be guarded not only by his people and Chay's, but by her own kind—and without her knowledge. It was a neat trick to play on her for guarding *him*, and one that would solve the problem of her protection. "My thanks, Meath. And now I think we'd all best retire so we'll be fresh for the races tomorrow. I hope you're placing a bet on Lord Chaynal's horses—"

Suddenly Meath gave him a powerful shove and he staggered down to hands and knees in the grass. Chay swore sharply and as Rohan glanced up he saw Meath running headlong for the river.

"What the hell—?" Chay exclaimed, helping Rohan to his feet. "Are you all right?"

"Fine." He brushed off his clothes. "But what was all that about?"

Meath soon came striding back, carrying a limp figure over his shoulder. "Your pardon, my lord," he said again to Rohan, and dumped his burden on the ground. "I hope you're not injured."

"Not at all. Who's this?"

Meath casually conjured a small flame above the man's form, and Rohan gave a muffled exclamation. Chay bent down and touched the man's face, turning it from side to side as if unable to believe what he saw. But the dark hair and ritual chin scar of the Merida royal house were unmistakable, even in the dim light.

"You don't appear all that surprised, my lord," the *faradhi* observed.

Rohan glanced up, startled by the man's perceptiveness, and only then saw the dark stain on Meath's left arm. "I wasn't aware Lady Andrade allowed her Sunrunners to walk around the holes in their clothing," he said mildly, though his whole body had clenched with fury. It was one thing for his own people to be wounded in his defense; it was quite another for a Sunrunner's blood to be spilled.

"Nothing but a scratch, my lord." Meath produced a wicked throwing knife, its glass blade twinkling in the conjured flame. "There's enough of me so no harm was done," he added.

Rohan cleared his throat. "Come to my tent and my squire will look after you, then, if it's not serious. I'd rather Andrade didn't hear about this." He turned to Clay. "And not a word to Tobin or anyone else, please. Meath is right—I'm not especially surprised, except for the fact that it's a son of the Merida Blood responsible."

"What are you talking about?" Chay demanded.

"Come with me, and I'll show you. And leave that here," he said, nodding to the Merida. "It'd be too much bother to keep him captive, and I want him alive to tell his brethren he failed."

The three men made their way by a roundabout route to Rohan's tent, where Walvis wakened instantly from a light doze. His eyes went wide as Meath shrugged out of his shirt to reveal the knife wound, and he scrutinized Rohan intently to make sure there were no similiar holes in his lord's hide. While the boy cleaned and bandaged the wound as all Stronghold squires learned to do from

Princess Milar, Rohan dug into his saddlebags for the other knife and presented it silently to Chay.

"When?" the older man asked.

"On the way here. Both knives missed me. I think the other one went into the river, but this one stuck in the mud near the bank. Merida," he added unnecessarily.

"I can see that!" Chay growled. "Why didn't you tell anyone?"

Rohan shrugged.

"Sometimes you are the most damnably stupid—"

"Well, what would you have me do? I didn't want Andrade and Tobin fussing over me—or you either!"

"What about the Merida?"

"I'd rather see what their game is than try to stop it at this point."

Chay drew breath for an explosion of temper, but Meath, his wound now invisible beneath a bandage, spoke first. "You're well-guarded, my lord, as you now know. I think your decision to do nothing about them is wise."

Walvis had turned a look of pure reproach on Rohan. "Why didn't you *say* something, my lord?"

"Never mind, Walvis," Chaynal said. "You and I both know he does as he pleases, with no thought to anyone else. Well then, Rohan, with so many eyes watching you, I suppose you're safe enough. Is it any use asking if you've any idea about what caused this?"

"A few."

"But you're not telling." Chay sighed with exasperation.

Rohan smiled. "Meath, if you can part with your souvenir, I'd like to keep it for a while."

The *faradhi* handed it over, and Rohan fingered the hilt. "They're advertising their presence, all right," he mused. "This is a knife fit for a prince—look at the jewels in it. Even if it wasn't made of glass. . . ."

Meath hesitated, then said, "A good thing it is, my lord. It's only a rumor, and nobody I know has ever tested it out—but it's said that Sunrunners pierced with steel can't control their powers."

Chay frowned. "I can understand why it's only a rumor. There are quite a few people who'd be interested—if it's true."

Meath shrugged, wincing slightly as his injured shoulder protested. Rohan gestured to the doorway. "Go back to your tent and get some rest. And thank you for my life, Meath."

"They weren't serious about trying to take it away from you, my lord, not tonight or the other time. If they had been, you'd be dead." He bowed and left them.

"He's right, you know," Chay said thoughtfully. "Three Merida knives are three warnings. But of what?"

"To make me nervous, I suppose, so I'll make mistakes. I wonder whose tents they sleep in?"

"High Prince Roelstra's," Walvis muttered as he put away his medical supplies.

"No proof," Rohan told him.

"Only evidence," Chay added, toying with the glass knife in his hand. "And speculation about what they'd gain with your death."

"A five-year-old child on the Desert throne. Oh, with a very capable fighting commander and a princess to rule during his minority, but a child just the same." Rohan sat down and stared at his boots. "I never realized that before, Chay—about Maarken and Jahni, I mean, being in danger because they're my heirs. Thank the Goddess they're safe at Stronghold."

"It hadn't occurred to me, either," Chay said slowly. "But your own son will be a Merida target from the moment he's born."

"I know."

"Does Sioned?"

Rohan had no answer for him. Chay gave Walvis the knife and silently took his leave. The squire fingered the blade for a time, his young face dark with worry. At last he said, "My lord, they wouldn't really try to kill you, would they?"

"Do I need to answer that, Walvis? But stop looking so grim. There are plenty of people watching me. And I'll be in a crowd all day tomorrow at the races. Nothing can happen to me there."

"In a crowd of princesses? It's then that I'll fear the most for you, my lord!"

Rohan laughed. "Oh, I'll have a very effective guardian against the princesses. My sister." Who would also take good care of Sioned, he told himself. He wondered suddenly if part of Andrade's motive in providing him with a Sunrunner wife was to weave a network of their protection around him—but to defend him against the Merida, or Roelstra, or both?

Chapter Thirteen

Trees had been planted generations ago between the princes' camp and the racetrack, as much to provide the horses with peace and quiet as to protect the tents from the dust and smell. Paddock and pasture had been laid out long ago, too, and the track pounded by innumerable hooves, *Rialla* after *Rialla*. The racing oval was a full measure around and wide enough to allow twenty horses between its multicolored rails. Each third was presided over by a judge who watched for violations from a little wooden tower—although anything that happened out of their line of sight went unpunished.

The stands faced south. Seats reserved for the nobility were protected this year by a leaf-green silk canopy that had cost Prince Clutha half a year's revenues; it would have cost more, but Prince Lleyn had given him a discount on the material, for he disliked getting sunburned while he watched the races. The common folk milled around the perimeter of the track, sampling food and drink from the booths set up there—race day being the only one of the *Rialla* when merchants were allowed to bring their wares across the river. But highborn or commoner, everyone bet on the races; only the sums wagered were different.

Rohan had always liked race days. This year's added attraction was that he would not have to bite his tongue and pretend ignorance. As the son of his father he was expected to know horseflesh, and it was a relief to be able to show off his knowledge as he walked the paddock for a time, sizing up Chay's competition before joining his brother-by-marriage.

Chay finished inspecting Akkal and swung up into his

saddle. "I look like a damned rainbow," he complained, plucking at one red silk sleeve. White elk-hide trousers and boots completed his own colors, and he wore a blue sash about his waist in honor of his prince.

"Tobin thinks you look wonderful, so shut up about it. Watch out for Lord Reze's big gray over there. He's the one horse in the field with legs on him."

"Going to bet on him?" Chay grinned as he patted Akkal's neck.

"He doesn't look *that* fast!" Rohan turned his head as the trumpet sounded for the first race. "There's the call. The track's fast, but I thought I saw a rough section in the second third."

"Thanks. Go hold Tobin's hand and remind her that I've never fallen off a horse in my life."

"Blesandin sent you over backward two years ago."

"That beast had the very devil in him, and I was drunk at the time."

Rohan laughed and watched Chay guide Akkal into line, knowing he had some time before the start of the race to inspect his own horses. Chaynal raced his stock for business purposes, but Rohan had decided to participate purely for the fun of it. He called his grooms around him and began giving out final riding assignments, then saw Ostvel hovering around the edge of the group, looking wistful.

Rohan gestured him over. "You have an easy face to read," he observed with a smile.

"I know," the young man said mournfully. "My lord, I didn't want to ask but—"

"See that dappled mare? Her name's Eliziel and she's a handful on her best days, so be careful. You'll be riding my colors in the fourth race."

Ostvel's eyes shone and for a moment he looked as if he'd drop to one knee in gratitude. Sense got the better of emotion, much to Rohan's relief. "Thank you, my lord! She's a beauty! I'll win the race for you, I promise!"

"You'd better," Rohan threatened playfully. He gave out the other assignments and went to the royal stands. Being a ruling prince could be fun when one could make other people's pleasure, as he just done with Ostvel. He looked for Andrade's blonde head, then climbed up to where she was seated with Camigwen.

"Good morning, ladies," he said as he took a place beside his aunt. "Where's Tobin?"

"With Sioned and the High Prince's charming children," Andrade replied.

"Oh." He didn't want to be reminded that the princesses existed, and he especially didn't want to worry about what poison would ooze from their remarks to Sioned. "Tell me, Aunt, is Tobin intending to have a good time with them?"

"I wouldn't put it past her, my lord," Camigwen said, her eyes dancing. "She's an education."

"I agree—but the lessons were rather painful until I grew taller than she."

"Do you still have the scar where she bit you?" Andrade asked, amused.

"To the end of my days. But don't reveal my secret, Camigwen—my squire thinks I took it in battle and spreads word of how brave I am."

"Now that I know your sister, I think your squire is right!" she laughed.

Andrade pointed to the track. "There's Chay. He'd better win this race—I bet Lleyn a hundredweight of wine against half a measure of his best silk."

"Start planning your new wardrobe," Rohan told her.

Jervis, city lord of Waes, had delegated starter's honors to his eldest son, Lyell. The boy was a gangly sixteen, but stood tall and proud on the platform as he held up the bright yellow flag. The horses lined up and even amid the riot of colored silks it was easy to pick out Chay's red-and-white, especially when the flag swept down and Akkal surged to the lead.

The first race was a distance trial of three measures that tested heart, lung, and leg. Its matching race would be the last one of the day; the same horses and riders would go the same distance, providing prospective buyers with an excellent idea of the merits of the different studs. Akkal was passed at the measure-mark by Lord Reze's gray, and the crowd gasped. Chay was always a popular favorite, both for his personal charm and his habit of winning, and the spectators held their breath as Akkal narrowed the gap. The two horses matched each other stride for stride over two-thirds of a measure. Suddenly an arm wearing white striped with russet and Ossetia's dark green lifted once, twice, and a whip landed with ruthless force across the gray's hindquarters. Chay's hands never left the reins, but Akkal's strides lengthened until it seemed he was flying. When the yellow flag swept down at last, a roar went up all around the track—for nearly everyone had bet on Chay, and won.

"Well," Andrade said, pleased. "My silk was in doubt for a time, there."

"If you ladies will excuse me, I'll go take a look at that gray and see if he's going to be in any shape for his revenge this afternoon."

He met Chay on the path back to the paddock, where Akkal would be walked and rested for the final race. Radzyn's lord had dismounted and was indulging himself in a few creative descriptions of his opponent.

"Did you see what that whoreson did?" He asked Rohan furiously. "Flicked Akkal with his whip, right in the middle of the third where no one would see him! I've never even put a *spur* to Akkal, and he had the nerve—!" He stroked the stallion's sleek neck protectively.

"I didn't see it," Rohan confessed. "But I had a look at the gray just now. You'll be able to take him in the last race, Chay. No trouble."

"Take him?" Chay's eyes flashed. "He'll choke on our dust!" A groom came up and Chay handed him Akkal's reins, giving precise instructions for the horse's care that obviously insulted the boy. As they walked along the row of paddocks, the trumpet sounded for the second race and Chay smiled tightly at the sight of one of his favorite mares prancing eagerly to the track. "Reze has a mare entered in this one, too," he said. "I hope he can get used to losing. But isn't that Ostvel over there with Eliziel?"

"I'm letting him ride the fourth. He wanted to impress Camigwen." Rohan winked. "It's not uncommon for a man in love."

"Next thing, *you'll* be riding."

"You know, that's not a bad idea."

"Don't be an idiot! Princes don't ride in these races!"

"No?" He called out to one of his grooms. "How's Pashta feeling today?"

"Ready, my lord. What race do you fancy?" The man grinned.

"Brochwell Bay for emeralds," he replied casually, and waited for Chay to explode. He was not disappointed.

"You're crazy!"

"I'll see to it at once, my lord," the groom said. "And may I say I'm glad you've decided to enter?"

"You may not," Chay snapped, then rounded on his brother-by-marriage. "Impress the girl if you must, but not at the risk of your neck! There's not a woman alive who'd thank you for bringing a pair of broken legs or worse to your wedding night!"

"What I bring to my wedding night will be in perfect working condition," Rohan answered.

"Oh, wonderful," Chay said in a voice that dripped sarcasm. "I'll be sure to tell that to everyone while you're galloping out to Brochwell Bay and back, with whole measures between where nobody will have an eye out for you—Rohan, didn't you hear a word we said last night?"

"I'm riding, and that's an end to it," he stated, turned, and came face to face with Princess Ianthe. Cool and lovely in lavender with silver jewelry, she had not come to the paddocks to admire the horseflesh, and they both knew it.

"It was an exciting race, Lord Chaynal," she said gracefully. "Your wife will look magnificent in her rubies."

"I hear you're responsible for the idea," Rohan said.

"Excuse me," Chay interrupted. "I see one of my grooms signaling to me."

Rohan looked, saw nothing of the kind, and shot a murderous look at Chay. The older man grinned and left him alone with the princess.

"Are you enjoying yourself, cousin?" she asked him.

"More so than last time, before I became an eligible prince," he answered forthrightly, and they started back to the stands.

She blushed, with fascinating results. "It must be tiresome for you."

"I'm sure you go through the same thing, being an unmarried princess."

"Mostly I see ambassadors," she said, looking down at her hands. "But I won't consider any man who can't be bothered to meet me himself." She was shorter than Sioned, and when she glanced up at him her heavy dark lashes were thick veils over her eyes. "It's a little like being offered at the Fair."

"A little," he agreed. "May I escort you up to your sisters? I have an entry in the next race that I'd like to watch."

Thus it was that Sioned's first view of him all day came as he guided Ianthe to a seat, her fingertips resting elegantly on his wrist. Rohan saw at once that he had done something both smart and stupid. There was advantage in being seen publicly with Roelstra's daughters, dividing his attentions among them. But he had made a personal error by placing himself in a position where he could compare them directly with Sioned. She was less beautiful, less regal, less elegant—and she was also the only woman he wanted.

"Here you are at last!" Tobin said brightly as he sat down. "Is Chay all in one piece? I suppose he'll spend all day with Akkal instead of with me. It's easy to see which of us he values more! But I'm having a wonderful time with our cousins, and it's so nice to be out of the hot sun. How sweet it was of Prince Lleyn to see to our comfort!"

There was more in a similar vein, and Rohan blessed her for turning into a scattershell for his benefit. Sioned sat in cool silence, her back stiff and her expression set in stone. She wore a russet linen gown and no jewelry but her Sunrunner's rings and his emerald. Aware that noticing the ring had brought a smile to his lips, he looked from her to Pandsala.

She met him stare for stare, and unlike her sister Ianthe did not blush. He offered a pleasantry about the weather; she responded with a polite nod. He asked if she was enjoying the races; she nodded again and stared down at the track. Rohan began to feel irked. He deserved better than this and had nearly decided to go about getting it when he realized that he was reacting precisely as Pandsala wished. The notion that his clever self had nearly been outsmarted by this girl both amused and irritated him. Pandsala with her ploy of indifference and Ianthe with her obvious interest were a potent pair. All at once he wondered if Andrade had foreseen his reaction, and provided Sioned to counter any attractions he might feel toward the princesses. Certainly he had twice today come close to forgetting his probable lifespan if he wed either. But the thought of Sioned kept him from any serious danger.

His mare came in second in the race. Through the next interval and the race following he divided his attention between his sister and the two princesses, ignoring Sioned completely. She did not appear to notice.

To Ianthe he said, "I have great hopes for my entry in the fourth. There she is now—her name's Eliziel, which means 'cloudfoot' in the old language."

"She's a beauty," Ianthe responded warmly. "Do you take an interest in the old tongue, cousin?"

"After a fashion. Mostly to name my horses."

Sioned's brows shot up. "We're taught at Goddess Keep that the old words have great power and should not be used lightly, my lord."

"How quaint," Pandsala murmured.

"Who's that up on Eliziel?" Tobin asked quickly.

"Ostvel," Sioned supplied in a colorless voice. "I marvel, my lord, that you allow someone from Goddess Keep on one of your precious horses."

"He more than earned the privilege on the way here, so I rewarded him with the honor of riding her."

His own reward was a frigid silence. Tobin giggled and pointed to their right. "Oh, look—there's Camigwen with Andrade. She looks as if she doesn't know whether to be proud or terrified!"

Ostvel on a mere horse was an excellent rider; Ostvel mounted on a mare of Eliziel's quality inevitably won the race. Rohan grinned smugly.

"Camigwen will look lovely in carnelians," Tobin observed.

"Is that to be the prize for this race?" Pandsala asked her sister, then turned to Rohan without waiting for an answer. "Will you really give the rider gems won by your horse?"

"He needs a wedding gift for his lady." He delighted in having made not only Ostvel's pleasure but Cami's as well. Being a prince was *wonderful* fun.

"How generous of you," Ianthe said, smiling. "And how lucky that carnelians will suit his lady so well, according to your sister. But surely such jewels are a little grand for a *faradhi*."

"A beautiful woman deserves beautiful things," Tobin said sweetly. "All the better if the man has the taste to match her bridal necklet to her coloring."

"No two women are alike," Rohan agreed blithely, and won a blank stare from Sioned for this idiotic statement. "For Pandsala, for instance, nothing would do but diamonds to match the sparkle in her eyes. And for Ianthe—the darkest of garnets, though they would be poor rivals to the color of her lips."

"And Lady Sioned?" Ianthe purred.

"Emeralds, of course," Pandsala said before Rohan could open his mouth. "You do have the most remarkable eyes," she added to the Sunrunner.

Sioned nodded civil thanks for the compliment. "I would settle for common river stones from a man I truly loved."

"A man who truly loved you would provide emeralds," Rohan shot back. "Whoever he may turn out to be, I hope *I* provided him an example in that ring."

"*You* gave it to her?" Pandsala was shocked into an honest reaction, and Rohan struggled bravely not to laugh.

"He did," Tobin affirmed. "She saved my sons' lives on the Hatching Hunt."

"Not I, your highness," Sioned protested. "It was Prince Rohan who chased the dragon away."

"A dragon!" Ianthe exclaimed. "Cousin, you must tell us all the details!"

"I will, at some other time," he said, rising to his feet. "You ladies must excuse me—I need to talk with Prince Lleyn. We have bet on the next race, and I want to see his face when he loses." He distributed smiles all around and left the silken battlefield with relief.

After the fifth race—which Rohan lost to Prince Lleyn, much to the old man's delight—there came a break for refreshments and the paying off of debts. Rohan declined Lleyn's offer of lunch and went down to the track; there jumps were being set for the next few races. Two fences, two hedges, and two "stone" walls made of painted wood—he measured them with his eyes and nodded to himself. They were nothing Pashta couldn't handle with ease.

He watched the sixth and seventh races from railside, making mental notes about the number of strides necessary between jumps. No one paid much attention to the slight, plainly dressed young man who cheered on Lord Chaynal's horses. Prince Haldor of Syr's entry took the sixth, and a stallion from Radzyn Keep won the seventh. As the eighth was called, Rohan felt a tug on his sleeve.

"It's time, my lord," his groom said. "I've brought your shirt." He held up a sky-blue silk blouse, and Rohan stripped off his tunic before sliding his arms into his colors. The men and women around him, having heard the honorific and seen him change clothes, gaped. Then someone gave a mighty guffaw and clapped Rohan on the back.

"I'll be wagering on you, my lord!"

"The odds should be very good against me!" Rohan answered, grinning. "Enjoy your profits!"

On the way to the paddocks, the groom provided him with a wealth of information. The course was easy enough until the climb to the sea cliffs began. There the trail turned rocky and dangerous; many horses would founder on the way up, still more on the way down. Pashta's training in the Desert would serve him well here. As for the other entries, all were considered inferior, but Rohan was to keep an eye on Prince Haldor's stallion. The Syrene horse had been battle-bred to sink his teeth into anything that got in range.

"I'd slow Pashta a bit during the two measures back from the Bay, my lord," the groom finished. "He won't save much for the jumps on his own—you know he'll run his heart out for you, so you'll have to make him spare himself."

"I'll remember." He entered the paddock and approached the stallion, who was in fine trim and seemed to know that all the attention meant he would be racing today. He butted Rohan's shoulder playfully with his nose, and the prince laughed.

"No plain river stones for our Sioned, eh, my lad?" he whispered, rubbing the white blaze down the stallion's face. "We'll beat them all in a walk."

Pashta's huge dark eyes closed lazily, almost a wink. Rohan laughed again, then mounted and gathered the reins.

"I've had to slip in weights, my lord," the groom said. "Rules say all the horses carry the same. You haven't enough flesh to cover your own bones, let alone make up the legal weight—so remember he's carrying extra today."

The blue silk clung to him in the afternoon heat, and he shifted his shoulders against the trickle of sweat down his spine. As the trumpet sounded he stood in the stirrups to signal his readiness and told himself he was *not* nervous. He'd never ridden in a *Rialla* race before—no prince had—and as he walked Pashta decorously to the starting line the prize jewels became secondary to not making a fool of himself. He glanced up at the stands only once, but could not see Sioned's red-gold hair in the crowd. Perhaps it was better so.

Nothing prevented her from seeing him, however, and her careful composure nearly cracked. What did that madman think he was doing? She shared a horrified glance with Tobin.

"Ianthe, look!" Pandsala exclaimed. "There's Rohan!"

"I didn't know he would enter the races himself!" Ianthe said.

"Neither did I," Sioned muttered. "I didn't think he was that foolish."

A section of the railing had been shifted so the horses could exit the track before the first jump. Excited spectators strained against the fences as the yellow flag dropped. Sioned held her breath as thirty horses thundered past, jostling for the best position through the gap. It was surely too narrow for all to get through safely, but somehow they made it. Everyone squinted for a last look as the horses topped a rise before vanishing.

Sioned listened to the shouted wagers and wished she had the courage to ride the sunlight and follow the progress of the race. She cared nothing about Rohan's winning; she simply prayed he wouldn't break his neck. She intended to perform that service herself to repay him for this insanity.

"Will you not wager on Prince Rohan's success, like the rest of us?" Ianthe's' voice was smooth as warm honey.

"I have nothing of value," Sioned began, spreading her hands to indicate her poverty—then caught sight of the emerald. "What will you wager against this emerald, your grace?"

"You'd bet *against* the prince?"

She smiled, wondering if some of Rohan's recklessness had infected her as well. "I doubt him as a man, not as a rider. I had another wager in mind."

"Yes?" The dark eyes were wary, and the lips Rohan had complimented were stretched into a false smile.

"My emerald against whatever you like that neither you nor your sister will win *him*."

"How dare you!" Ianthe hissed.

Sioned laughed. "Your grace! Never tell me you doubt yourself as a woman!"

"I doubt your manners, Sunrunner! But I cannot lose, for there is no one else worthy of Rohan—as you of all people must know. Do you want him for yourself?"

"I haven't yet decided," she lied easily. "But if you're unsure of yourself in the matter . . ."

"Done!" the princess snarled. "Your emerald against all the silver I wear!"

"Done," Sioned nodded, and insulted the princess further by taking visual inventory of the necklet, earrings, bracelets, and belt. Ianthe crimsoned with rage and turned her back on Sioned.

She gazed down at her emerald, not believing for an instant that she might lose it, but knowing all at once how much it meant to her. Biting her lip, she glanced quickly around at her companions. They followed Ianthe's lead in ignoring her. Sioned made her decision, rose, and edged her way to the outer stands where the sunlight was unshaded by the green silk awning.

She felt the sweet warmth on her skin, permeating her bones and blood. Lacing her fingers together, she felt the rings grow warm—even the emerald—and she was reminded of the night in the Great Hall at Stronghold, and Tobin's assurance that this ring had a magic all its own. She faced in the direction Rohan had gone and her gaze darted down the sunlight until she saw him clinging close to Pashta's neck as they neared the wood. Her breathing quickened in response to his; she winced along with him as, entering the trees, branches whipped at his shirt and hair. The cliff trail ahead of him was murderous, and Sioned's heart began to beat very fast.

Rohan cursed as a sharp branch tore his shoulder. Cries of alarm came from all around him and set his palms sweating inside his riding gloves. He wrenched his horse around a fallen rider, thanking the Goddess for Pashta's years in the Desert which had made him swifter of wit and hoof than most of the other horses. Out of the wood now, they made the turn up the steep slope that culminated in a green pylon near the cliff edge. Behind him, Rohan heard an anguished scream and there was a crunch that sounded like cracking bones. But he had no time to look back, for the pylon loomed up—and the horse beside him, its rider wearing Lord Reze's colors, had left him almost no room to make the turn. Pashta's ears were laid back threateningly; the other horse faltered slightly on a slippery patch and Rohan took the chance presented, urging Pashta through the narrow gap and closer to the pylon. He rounded it in a tight curve— and an instant later heard a terrible cry followed by a heavy splash in the surf below. Rohan winced; it could have been him and Pashta. His sole ambition now was to emerge from this wild ride alive.

The field was down to twenty. Nineteen too many in Rohan's opinion, and in Pashta's, too; the stallion, never one to allow another horse precedence, made for those ahead with single-minded fury. Rohan pressed his cheek to Pashta's neck, branches slashing his shirt to ribbons, and simply hung on.

A dun-colored horse came out of nowhere and plowed into them from the right. Rohan nearly toppled from his

saddle. The other rider wore the pink and crimson of
Lord Tibayan of Pyrme—but the face that grinned viciously at him had the brown eyes, dark hair, and ritual
chin scar of Merida Blood. Rohan swore luridly in recognition, and the Merida laughed.

Sioned had lost sight of him in the forest, but as the
horses raced onto the flat plain, she stiffened in shock as
a dun stallion slammed into Pashta. Yet Rohan had been
prepared for the attack—his fist lashed out in a backhanded blow that swayed the other rider in his saddle.
Sioned caught her breath as a whip came up in the man's
hand. It came down across Rohan's already lacerated
back and his blond head jerked in pain. Sioned's fingers
clenched into numbed, bloodless claws. The Fire in her
rings spread up through her whole body as if she was
suddenly sheathed in flames then leaped forward on the
woven sunlight. Her lips moved as she gathered herself
to activate an ancient technique Urival had taught her
at Stronghold.

Rohan's back was afire with pain. He turned his head
just in time to see the Merida lift a hand, glass knife
winking in the sunlight. Rohan couldn't believe that the
man would attempt a throw from horseback at a moving
target—then revised his opinion as the knife whizzed a
finger's span past his shoulder.

Pashta picked up speed, not shying in the slightest
from the glittering blade that shattered on the stones
ahead of him. Rohan, thighs aching with the force of his
grip on his horse, let the stallion have his head. Distance
between himself and the Merida was what he wanted
now, before the next knife could reach its target. This
desire coincided precisely with his horse's passion to con-
quer the four stallions ahead. They were nearing the
track now, and they overtook one horse on the gallop
through the opening in the rails. Rohan remembered his
groom's warnings and took the reins in a tighter grip.
Pashta responded to minute signals of hands and knees,
and cleared the first jump with smooth precision—unlike
the horse directly ahead, whose rider had been sloppy.
Losing rhythm, the dappled stallion faltered and the rider's whip could not compel him to speed. Rohan passed

him between jumps and flinched as he saw the blood-flecked lather on the animal's flanks.

Again he dared a look behind him. The Merida was catching up fast. Rohan turned to face the next obstacle, guided Pashta over it. But as the stallion's hooves plowed into the dirt, Rohan felt dizzy, disoriented. He shook his head, his throat and nostrils clogged with dust, thinking that what he needed was air. But he could not help another glance back over his shoulder.

He saw nothing—but the Merida's thin lips parted in a high-pitched scream, body straining backward as if to escape some hideous vision, dark eyes stark with terror as his mount crashed into the rails.

Between a hedge jump and a stone wall Rohan passed a tiring horse whose rider wore Syrene turquoise. Sure enough, the stallion's head whipped around to try for a bite out of Rohan's thigh. Pashta's ears flattened and it took all Rohan's skill to keep the two horses from turning to battle it out. Pashta submitted to Rohan's orders, stuck his neck out, and ran.

There was only one horse ahead now, clearing the fifth obstacle easily, and as Rohan measured the distance he said into Pashta's ear, "It's all right if we don't catch this one, you know. I can well afford a few emeralds on my own."

But the stallion had been bred from Chay's finest studs and mares and he saw only one horse and one jump between himself and victory. Rohan let the reins go slack on the sweating neck after the last fence was cleared. There was only space and the bright hues of the railings and the yellow flag sweeping down like a dragon's wing— and the other horse half a length behind him.

Sioned unwound her fingers and chafed them against her thighs. The conjuring had been both more and less difficult than she'd feared. Urival had taught her well, but sustaining the fearsome Fire-image of a dragon for only those few essential seconds—and for only one man's eyes—had drained her of energy. She felt only fierce joy as the enemy toppled from his horse—yet an instant later she cried out with the rest of the crowd as the dun stallion went down.

"No, I didn't mean—" she whispered, stricken by what she had done. "Oh no, please!" But though the stallion struggled to his feet from the dirt, the rider, flung half-way across the track, did not move.

She heard Tobin cry out and forced herself to return to the others. The three princesses were hurrying down the steps. Sioned waited until she could breathe without gasping, then followed, careful to keep her distance.

They were waiting for Rohan in the paddock by the time she joined them. He rode up slowly, dismounted, and ignored everyone as he walked the lathered stallion, crooning to him and rubbing his neck and flanks tenderly. A groom came up and flung his arms first around the prince and then around the horse before leading the latter away for a much-needed rest. Rohan wobbled a bit on his feet, winced, and gratefully accepted a large winecup from another groom.

Worry competed with pride as Sioned saw the slashed shirt and the bloody scrapes on his back, face, and arms, much worse than she had thought. She wanted to go to him, scold him for his foolhardiness, and then hug the breath out of him before resuming her verbal abuse. Forbidden these things, she watched enviously as his sister did them all.

"Your clothes are shreds, you're scratched raw, and I'm positive you're limping, you idiot," Tobin said sharply. "Take off those rags and go wash this minute. There's no telling how many of those cuts will fester if you don't."

"Yes, Tobin," he replied with teasing meekness. "Just don't hug me again, please!" He seemed to notice the other women for the first time. "Don't look so appalled," he said, smiling slightly. "It was only a race."

Ianthe's delicate fingers plucked at his sleeve. "You took a very great risk, cousin," she said. "The horse behind you was not so lucky."

Rohan's expression tightened, and Sioned glanced away.

"We heard on the way here that the rider is dead of a broken neck," Pandsala said. "The horse will survive, although he'll never race again. As for what actually happened—no one seems to know, or to have ever seen anything like it. They're investigating now."

Sioned looked anywhere but at Rohan. She had killed a man for him. Moreover, she had done it using her *faradhi* gifts—a thing absolutely forbidden, the worst thing a Sunrunner could do. She could hear herself confessing to Andrade that she had not meant to cause a death, she hadn't—but as she looked at Rohan again, she learned a bitter truth: he was her price.

"He was a Merida," the prince said.

"What?" Tobin's cheeks went white.

"He tried to unseat me during the race. Oh, stop it, Tobin, I'm fine," he added irritably, shrugging off her concern. "Pity he's dead. I wanted to talk with him."

Sioned saw a warning glance pass between brother and sister, and rallied to provide the necessary distraction. In as sharp a tone as she could muster, she said, "It's a risk that might have been very expensive for your highness."

"No word of congratulation on my victory, Lady Sioned?"

She could have strangled him for the look in his eyes. Tobin came to her rescue by saying, "Go dunk yourself in the river. I swear I was able to smell you all the way from the stands."

He smiled down at her. "Sister dear, you're so soothing to my conceit."

"Well, you're not soothing my nose! Chay!" she called out as her lord came toward them. "Take Rohan to the river and throw him in."

"No time," Chay responded, and paused to lift Rohan off his feet in a hug that made the prince's face screw up with the pain of his cuts and bruises. Setting him down, Chay went on, "Wonderful ride, you daredevil! I've got to get ready for the last race, but tell me all about it over dinner tonight!" He leaned down to kiss his wife and strode off.

"Perhaps we should return to the stands and watch Lord Chaynal's race," Sioned suggested coolly.

"You still haven't congratulated me," Rohan said with his sweetest smile and a wicked gleam in his eyes. "But perhaps you bet against me and lost?"

"Oh, I have a wager going, my lord," she replied with equal sweetness and a glance at Ianthe. "But on another race entirely."

Chay won his race by a handy third of a measure, leaving Lord Reze's horse breathing dust as promised. After this the highborns left for their tents to rest before making ready for the evening's banquet. The commoners returned to the Fair, the servants to their duties within their masters' camps. Sioned knew she could have attended the feasting if she'd wished, for Tobin had firmly established her as a friend, but she also knew she was incapable of spending another instant in the princesses' vicinity—especially if they were in Rohan's company. So she went down to the river, sat beneath a tree, and tried not to think about him—and what she had done for him today.

Full of himself he'd been, flushed with triumph, attention, and a safe escape from mortal danger. Flirting with that insufferable pair, using those eyes and that smile to an effect he was only too happy to exploit. Speaking to Sioned only in hopes of igniting her temper. Damn him, anyway.

A cheer went up from the direction of High Prince Roelstra's tents and she made a sour face. The awarding of prizes had begun. Tobin would have her rubies, Cami her sultry carnelians. Sioned hoped Rohan choked on his emeralds.

"Congratulations, my lord prince," she muttered, and lay back flat in the damp grass to watch the clouds drifting over the rising moons. She knew what her trouble was—one of her troubles, anyway. She was jealous. Sickeningly, foolishly jealous of the jewels and silks and beauty of the two princesses, jealous that they could flirt with him and she could not, jealous of his compliments and attention. "But you're mine, you conniving blue-eyed son of a dragon," she whispered. "And by the Goddess, I'm going to prove it to you."

But did she want a man who could make her do what she had done today? She argued with herself for a long time, one part of her reasoning that she had probably saved Rohan's life by setting up the conjuring of a dragon to terrify the Merida. Yet that conjure had killed. Against all her intentions she had broken the most binding of *faradhi* vows. It was the culmination of what Urival had warned against—using her powers for Rohan alone, not caring a damn for anyone but him. Her feelings had betrayed her into murder. Could there be any justification for that? Was it possible to merge *faradhi* and princess into someone new? How could they ask her to serve so many loyalties? Her training at Goddess Keep, her love for Rohan, her duty to the Desert—what about her duty to herself, to Sioned? She was not even sure she had a choice.

She could marry Rohan and forswear her gifts, become only a princess and reject all temptation to use them to his benefit. But part of his reason for wanting her and Andrade's in proposing her was the power she possessed. She was *expected* to be both *faradhi* and princess. If she stopped being the former, then what example would her children have in the wise use of gifts they would almost certainly inherit? They would have princely powers from Rohan—but they would be *faradh'im* as well. A Sunrunner's loyalty was to Goddess Keep, not to any single princedom. She was being asked to split herself—and her children—between Andrade and Rohan, and the choice was tearing her apart.

No. That was a lie. She put her hands over her face and turned onto her stomach, unable to bear the touch of soft, cool moonlight on her cheeks. She had made her choice today. She had used her powers to kill.

It was not the first such death, either. She remembered the wine steward at Stronghold, how he had been caught between her and Roelstra's *faradhi*, how he had died. She had made her choice then and not even realized it.

But, knowing what she now knew, she could refuse to marry Rohan. She could stay Sunrunner only and not become a princess, remove all temptation. She could see him wed to another woman.

Never.

She lay there a long time, breathing deeply of the moist, pungent scent of crushed grass beneath her cheek. The night chill made her shiver. She had no choice, and she knew it. She had set the trap herself with her own feelings, her pride, her needs. She would marry Rohan, be Sunrunner and princess. If they expected it of her, it was no less than she expected of herself.

Sioned sat up, raked her fingers back through her untidy hair, and stared moodily out at the river for a time. Then, rising, she went down to the sandy shore and searched by moonlight for a few smooth river stones. She rolled them between her hands, a grim smile crossing her face. She had faced up to the truth. Rohan was her price, and she had been well and truly bought. There was a strange peace to the knowledge. But now it was time he paid up, too.

Pocketing the stones, she thought of her purchases at the Fair and a slow excitement began to build inside her. She nurtured the feelings carefully, conjuring details in her thoughts: smooth golden skin, sunsilk hair, lean body pressing close, flesh warm and lips opening. . . . She would have victory tonight to match his, and the princesses could rage at leisure. The thought of their fury made her laugh aloud. Rohan was hers; she had paid for him.

Her senses abruptly warned her that she was not alone. She turned as a deep, resonant voice said, "Your laughter is as lovely as your name, Lady Sioned. And your face is lovelier still."

"Your royal highness!" she managed, and bent her knees to the High Prince, her mind whirling.

"I didn't mean to startle you," he continued. "I've just returned from seeing Lady Palila to the barge. She sleeps better there than in the tent."

"Has the banqueting ended, then, your grace?"

"Only just. It began early, and I'm thankful it didn't end late. There's much work to be done tomorrow. But I found myself wakeful, and decided to walk along the river. Beautiful, isn't it? Especially in the moonlight."

He was neither speaking of nor looking at the river; he referred to Sioned herself, and they both knew it. She felt his masculinity deep in her bones, her already sensitized body responding to Roelstra's undeniable attractions. "Very beautiful, your grace," she stammered, mortified by her awkwardness.

"Would you do me the honor of sharing the moonlight with me, Lady Sioned?"

One did not refuse a request from the High Prince, especially not when one planned to be the wife of his chief rival. She could use this time to glean information for Rohan—and, if she was clever and lucky, perhaps learn something about Roelstra's Sunrunner as well. She smiled, recovered some of her poise, and nodded agreement.

"Did you enjoy the racing today?" he asked as they began their leisurely stroll. "I saw you in the crowd, seated with my daughters and Princess Tobin."

"It was very exciting. Lord Chaynal rode well, didn't he? I'm told he always does." She paused as he lifted a branch out of her way. "Was the princess pleased with her rubies?"

"Naturally. It's the nature of a beautiful woman to covet those things that enhance her beauty. That's why I'm surprised to find you dressed plainly—although charmingly—and without jewels. You ought to be covered in silks and emeralds, my lady." He smiled.

Just you wait, she wanted to tell him. "Perhaps I'm not pretty enough to be covetous, or perhaps Lady Andrade breeds it out of us *faradh'im*."

"I'm sure some generous man is waiting to indulge you as you deserve."

She had a moment of panic that he might have seen through the game she and Rohan were playing. But as she slanted a glance at him through her lashes, she saw that he had another man in mind—and the realization nearly made her stumble on the smooth sand.

"But—but I'm a very unimportant person, your highness. I would bring a man very little."

"Your lovely self would be more than enough, even if you were not a Sunrunner. You set too low a value on yourself, my dear."

"And what value would you set on me, Prince Roelstra?" she asked boldly.

"I believe you know the answer to that, my lady."

This was a dangerous man. The price of discovering this frightening piece of information was rising rapidly. "It's very late," she began nervously.

"Not any later than it was a few moments ago, before certain things were said." He touched her shoulder.

His eyes were a paler green than hers, and avid as they traced the lines of her face and body. Sioned was astounded. His mistress was the most beautiful woman she had ever seen. He could have any female he wanted, just for the asking. She was out of her depth and utterly confused.

"But I see I'm upsetting you," Roelstra said, and took his hand from her shoulder. Her flesh felt cold after the heat of his fingers. "As many times as I've observed you in the last days, you haven't looked at me at all. I'm a stranger to you, I know. But I hope you'll allow me to change that." His voice was low, caressing, seductive, and her reaction to it scared her. "I am a patient man, Sioned, and a powerful one. When you've decided that the little prince isn't man enough, I'll be waiting."

"What are you offering me?" she whispered, knowing full well what he meant.

"Whatever you would have of me. In return I would expect certain things—nothing you would not gladly give."

"Such as?"

"I find you beautiful and desirable, Sioned. I believe you know what it means when a woman captures the eye of the High Prince. I would honor you above all others, and we would give to each other as pleased us both."

"And you would take what you wanted—especially my honor." She knew now what he was truly after, and was terrified.

"My daughter Ianthe described you as proud, but I believe I could change your mind." He moved closer to her, fingertips on her shoulders, sliding up to her neck and jaw.

A trembling invaded her body, born of both fear and desire, and she wondered wildly if Rohan felt the same thing around Ianthe. To accept would mean death—yet there was a fascination in this man's touch. Was it there in his daughter's? She backed away and shook her head. "I am no man's whore, not even when the man is you."

He laughed. "If you wanted to intrigue me, you couldn't have chosen a better way to do it. But if you mean to reject me—I suggest you reconsider, Sioned." He look down at her, still smiling, and without warning took the

step that separated them. Before she could move or
protest, he had taken her shoulders once more and bent
to capture her mouth. Just as suddenly he released her,
bowed as deeply as if she had been born royal, and
strode up the slope to his tents.

Sioned was frozen, shivering, terror and lust at war
within her. The High Prince wanted her—and as a woman,
she could not be immune to the compliment of this
powerful, alluring man's desire. But she was also a
Sunrunner, like the one already corrupted into betraying
their kind. Roelstra wanted her *faradhi* skills for himself.

And didn't Rohan want the same thing?

She wrapped her arms around herself, shaking convulsively. Rohan loved her. She repeated that to herself
over and over again. It did no good. He would use her
gifts just as Roelstra would, only Rohan had the blessing
of Lady Andrade who had arranged it all. She took the
river stones out of her pocket and gripped them until she
thought her bones would crack around them. Who was
she to judge which prince would be more worthy of using
her? She laughed bitterly. She had no choice. And how
she hated them all for it.

Rohan was half-asleep by the time he slid between the
sheets of his bed, fuzzy-headed with wine, gloating still
over his victory. He mumbled a dismissal to Walvis, who
left the tent, and shifted around to find a position that
wouldn't chafe the cuts on his shoulders and back. But
wine had dulled the aches and as sleep crept up on him
he turned his thoughts to dreams of Sioned.

It crossed his drowsy mind that he must be picking up
some of her conjuring abilities, for she was almost real in
his arms, her soft lips caressing his forehead and her slim
fingers stroking his cheek. He smiled and reached for
her, finding it entirely natural that there were indeed
smooth shoulders beneath his palms, the skin warm velvet. She sat on the bed beside him and began a greedy
exploration of his body. As she pushed aside the blanket
for access he gasped aloud, eyes wide as her hand cradled
his stirring flesh.

"Shhh," she whispered, placing her fingers on his lips. He kissed them, wishing the lamp was closer to the bed so he could see her face. The soft light from the glass-shaded candle on the far table combined with the glow of the watchfire filtering through the tent walls to backlight her night-darkened hair. She continued her caresses, sensations he'd never known existed ripping through his body.

"Stop," he said at last. "My turn, damn it, girl—" He was surprised to hear his voice so thick and throaty. He slid his hands down her arms, back up to her shoulders, along her breasts that were covered by silk warmed with the heat of her body. He clasped her waist in his hands and pulled her closer.

And froze.

Slender enough, but not as firm as he remembered. Pliant now, the way her shoulders and arms had been, with a slight covering of soft flesh between bones and skin. But he knew Sioned to be firmly muscled, very strong, not sleek-fleshed like this. A scent of rich perfume came from her body, not the clean fragrance of wind and wild things he had come to associate with her.

This was not Sioned.

A sudden flare of fire outside in the brazier reshaped and sharpened the shadows within the tent. The woman turned her head in alarm, and Rohan got a good look at her profile. The violence of his reaction made him shove her completely off the bed and she sprawled on the carpet, sobbing for breath.

"Ianthe," he whispered at the same time the guards outside shouted that there was fire.

"Hide me!" she pleaded frantically. "If anyone finds me here—"

"Get out! I don't give a damn what happens to you!" He rose and tore the blanket from the bed to cover his nakedness, feeling sick. "I'll distract them, but you'll have to run fast. Go on!"

"Rohan, please—"

Her face was eerily lit in blue by the flames through the silken tent. "You *want* to be found in here with me!"

"Yes!"

He hauled her up by an elbow and shook her. "Did

you think you'd force me into marriage by tricking me into dishonoring you? You fool! Get out!''

"You wanted me!" she flung at him.

"Shut up." He pulled her over to the entrance and drew one of the flaps aside. The guards were trying to stamp out the small fire that had leaped from the brazier onto the grass. "If you're here when I come back, I'll see to it everyone knows you for the whore you are. Wait until I've got their attention, then run!"

He pushed through the flaps and tightened the blanket around his waist, feeling a total fool. He ordered the guards to run and get water buckets; they obeyed. Only he glimpsed Ianthe's flight. Other people emerged sleepy-eyed from their tents, and Rohan sent them back with calming words. The fire was out, and there was no more danger.

When all was quiet, he returned to the brazier. The green grass should not have caught fire. He inspected the patch that was now soaked with water, expecting to find it charred. It was not. There had been no fire—not of the usual kind.

Rohan looked around him, and in the far shadows thought he saw a slim shape in a dark dress. He started for her, but one of the guards approached him with apologies.

"My lord, I don't know how it happened! The fire leaped right up out of the brazier!"

"Never mind. No damage done." He went back inside his tent, for the shadow had vanished. Just inside the doorway he stopped as his bare feet contacted a few small, hard objects on the carpet. He bent, picked them up, and slowly smiled. How had she gotten them in here? he wondered. While Ianthe was leaving and he was speaking to the others? It seemed probable.

"So you yourself were watching over me tonight," he whispered. "May I always defend you as effectively, love."

He held the stones a little while longer, then placed them in his jewel coffer next to the emeralds he'd won that day.

Chapter Fourteen

Against every evidence of the night's wispy clouds, the next dawn saw a prodigious downpour that kept everyone in their tents until at least noon. Most of the highborns woke at the first thunder, heard the rain, shrugged, and rolled over to go back to sleep. Their suites did much the same, except for a few luckless souls who had to get fires started in anticipation of the inevitable morning calls for steaming hot taze later on.

Lady Palila's servants on board the barge were fortunate. They had no need to rig up protection for cookfires, and could provide her and her early guest with a full breakfast prepared in the galley. If they were astounded that it was Princess Pandsala who shared their mistress' meal, they spoke of it only in whispers, and only among themselves.

"So Ianthe tried to make a whore of herself last night," Palila said, her eyes mirroring the satisfaction in Pandsala's. "From what I've seen of our golden-haired hero, he's not the type to appreciate it."

"You should have seen her, coming back to the tent with her hair in tangles and her feet covered in dirt." Pandsala laughed. "She's still there, pretending she went for a walk and took a chill so she won't have to face anyone. I wish her much joy of Naydra's remedies."

"And Lenala's scintillating conversation! It was good of you to come tell me about it and keep me company this morning. I do believe I've done you an injustice all these years, Sala. We work well together."

"We have much to gain and we both hate Ianthe. That makes us natural allies."

"Well, she's ruined herself this time. Even if Roelstra

doesn't hear of this, our noble Prince Rohan will never have her now. I would say your cause has been won, my dear."

"Not quite." Pandsala stirred her taze with a golden spoon tipped by an amethyst. "There's something about that Sunrunner girl that bothers me. He never has a soft word for her, and she's barely polite to him. But Tobin and Andrade are both pushing for her. Rohan seems just pliable enough to give in if the two of them try hard enough."

"I don't think Rohan's that stupid," Palila mused. "And they're reckoning without your determination to have him, of course. Besides, the girl's *faradhi*, without family to speak of—no matter what Tobin says about her connections to Syr and Kierst. She can't offer anything approaching what you can."

"I still wish she was out of the way." She poured fresh cups of taze and gave one to Palila. "It wasn't wise of you to come all the way from Castle Crag with your time so near, you know. We don't want you delivering early in a place where we can't control events."

"Why do you think I insisted on bringing those other women along? It took me hours to convince your father that I needed their care and company as well as that of my own maids. A pity one of *them* didn't get pregnant when I did."

"You're not due for another thirty days or so," Pandsala said, looking her over with a critical eye. "Although I must say you're big enough to be at least that long overdue."

Palila hid her annoyance at this reminder of her bulk. "Goddess forbid I should have to carry a child past the usual term!"

"Even a son?" Pandsala asked archly. "I've found all the drugs we'll need, by the way. It wasn't difficult. There are merchants enough here so I could buy one thing here, another there. A swallow or two of drugged wine, and they'll start labor pains almost at once. We've thought of everything."

"Unless all four of us produce daughters." Palila picked at her nails, frowning. "To be really safe, we should have brought the other two with us."

"Impossible. Even Father would find that suspicious, even though he hardly knows a woman is alive when she's pregnant."

Neither did Palila appreciate this reference to Roelstra's distaste for child-heavy women. "I told him I wanted their company—and deathly dull it is, too. If I didn't need them, I'd have them all deprived of their tongues now instead of later. Listening to them is sheer torment. But I have to have them with me a few hours every day for appearances' sake. I depend on you for rational conversation."

"And news of what goes on at the *Rialla*. It's a pity you can't be up and about more."

This, too, was a sore point, and Palila did not bother hiding her irritation this time. Roelstra insisted she attend the important functions—the banqueting, the Lastday ceremonies—but she had no energy and her feet had swollen right out of every pair of shoes she owned. At previous *Riall'im* she had been constantly at his side, admired, coveted, envied. But last night there had been many women who had dared to flirt with Roelstra—and in Palila's presence, too. It was infuriating to be so huge and indolent and sickly. Her son would have much to answer for once he was born.

"Sioned worries me," Pandsala said, returning to her former theme. "She isn't anything special in looks or wits, but there's something about her—"

"So you've said," Palila responded impatiently. "I tell you, Sala, don't bother about her. Now that Ianthe's own foolishness has ruined her, you need have no concerns. On the Lastday feast I see you standing with Prince Rohan as his bride."

The picture enchanted the princess, who laughed gleefully. "Did I tell you what he said yesterday about my eyes? My bridal necklet will be of diamonds!"

"Delightful," Palila said, trying to sound enthusiastic. "But now that your new position is assured, we ought to make some plans. I'll get your father to give you Feruche as a wedding present, and through the pass there we'll be able to control much trade—to our mutual profit, as we planned, with no one the wiser. Our sons will be very rich men."

"Very rich princes," Pandsala corrected silkily. "And the firmest of friends."

Palila smiled her sweetest smile. "Naturally, my dear! Now, we really ought to be planning what you'll wear on the Lastday ceremonies."

They spent the rest of the morning discussing Pandsala's wedding gown, these two strange and dangerous allies.

Sioned was less fortunate in her physical circumstances. Instead of a snug, dry cabin on board Roelstra's barge—something a Sunrunner would not have appreciated anyway—she was stuck inside a leaky tent. No sooner did she and Camigwen and Hildreth stop one drip than another began. The beds were damp and the wet wool carpet smelled awful. But there was nowhere to go for escape, and when Cami suggested a game of chess to take their minds off their misery, Sioned gladly agreed.

But her mind was not on the game. She could not stop thinking about what she had seen the previous night. Had Rohan welcomed Ianthe? Had the Fire interrupted the first caresses of their lovemaking? Sioned's response to Roelstra's advances had educated her most painfully in the fascinations of his deadly breed. Had Rohan felt the same?

She lost to Cami in less than fifteen moves. Rising, she grabbed up a cloak and pulled the hood up over her hair. "I'm going for a walk."

"You'll catch a chill," Hildreth warned.

"This is the cloak Tobin lent me—see?" She spread its folds to show the fur lining. "I'll be warm enough." As Cami began her own protest, Sioned exclaimed, "I have to get out of here!"

She pushed aside the sopping tent flaps and started walking. The cloak, made for the much shorter Tobin, reached only to Sioned's knees. She knew she must look absurd, but there was nobody to notice her in her rich crimson cloak over plain riding clothes. A few guards huddled beneath the slight shelter of entry overhangs; a servant or two hurried through the rain on errands. Sioned left the maze of tents for the river and crossed the bridge to the Fair. The booths were shut down and deserted, bright hangings drenched, wood dark with rain. The merchants had taken their wares back to the tent village over the hill for safety and protection from the storm, and undoubtedly sat cursing the weather that deprived them of a day's sales. Deserted, silent, the place looked like a battlefield, lacking only corpses and black-winged birds to pick the bones clean.

Sioned gave an annoyed shrug at the grim turn of her thoughts, and kept walking up the crest of a hill, where a small wood provided welcome if inadequate shelter. Damn Rohan's leaky tents. Damn Rohan.

Hunkering down beside dripping ferns, she forced herself to think things through once again. It wasn't even last night's scene that was bothering her, she admitted privately; she could understand if Rohan had desired Ianthe for a time. She had felt the same around Ianthe's father. The trouble lay deeper, and she looked down at her rings with a bitter smile twisting her lips.

What would Andrade say if she knew what Sioned had done to that Merida? Meaning only to frighten, her conjuring had killed. Worse, she felt no real remorse over the man's death. He had tried to kill Rohan; that was reason enough for him to die.

She tried to believe she hated Rohan for doing this to her. The truth was she hated herself for allowing it to happen. She hadn't meant for the wine steward at Stronghold to die either, but he had, his mind pulled apart by two Sunrunners warring for control. Sioned was partly responsible. But she could not feel much remorse over him, either.

She had killed for Rohan and she did not even have the excuse yet of being his princess. What would happen in the future, when she could hide behind that convenient obligation? Rohan's power over her was terrifying, but it was power she had given him along with her heart and her mind. She could be his princess only—and feel like only half a person if she gave up being a *faradhi*.

It must be possible to balance them, be both Sunrunner and princess. Andrade would never have done this if it was impossible to be both. No prince or princess had ever been an active Sunrunner as well; it was too dangerous. She huddled more deeply into her cloak and closed her eyes, wondering why Andrade should think her strong enough to resist using her power if her husband or her lands were in need. Sioned had not intended to kill, but that was no excuse. She had shattered a *faradhi*'s most binding vow in Rohan's defense.

All at once it occurred to her that perhaps Andrade had counted on exactly that.

The concept stunned her. The Lady was wily, manipulative, ambitious, and arrogant, yet she could not intend for Sioned to ignore all traditional restraints on the use of *faradhi* power. Surely she could not be that cruel, to make Sioned responsible.

But maybe she was. Maybe in making a princess of a trained Sunrunner, she had calculated that the gifts would become partisan ones, that Sioned would break the vows for the sake of her prince. Andrade could not have ordered such a thing, nor said outright that she expected it of Sioned. But, abruptly, it made sense. Andrade had said nothing, but Sioned suddenly realized what was being asked of her. Not merely to create a son who would be prince and Sunrunner as well—but to create the new rules by which her son would live.

And Rohan—what would he ask of her? Could she trust his wisdom to keep her from having to make the choice again and again? She trembled inside the heavy fur, knowing that she had made her choice: Rohan. And for him she would do whatever she had to, as *faradhi* and princess.

As she sat under rainy branches there was yet one thing that puzzled her until the obvious answer occurred to her. The princes would be livid when they found out Andrade intended to marry one of her Sunrunners to a prince. But they did not yet know, thanks to Rohan's little scheme with Roelstra's daughters. Wiping rain from her face, she smiled with grim anticipation of the uproar. If they disliked *that* event, they'd have fits when the children were born.

Sioned was unaware of those who watched her from the meager shelter of other trees. Walvis was nearly invisible, shivering in a cloak wrapping him from nose to boots. Meath *was* invisible to both squire and Sunrunner,

whom he had been following since Hildreth warned him
of Sioned's restlessness. He told himself that if she wanted
to be alone to think, she could at least have picked a
nice, dry tent instead of wandering all over the country-
side. Muttering a curse under his breath, he huddled
closer to his tree.

Rohan was at that moment cursing himself for inflict-
ing his more radical ideas on unsuspecting princes. Despite the rain, the conference continued—if one could
dignify the current argument by that polite term. Rohan
had made a serious error, inexcusable even by his weariness. He had not slept after Ianthe had left him, and had
come very close to seeking out Sioned for satisfaction of
desires the princess had aroused. The very idea had disgusted him. Still, he had not closed his eyes until dawn,
for as he considered Ianthe's actions, he worried more
about their implications. To put the finish to his discomfort, rain made him nervous right down to his Desert-
bred bones. But a prince could make no excuses for his
mistakes, not even to himself. Rohan, listening to the
conflict that raged around him, wished he'd kept his
stupid mouth shut.

He had begun well enough. In innocent tones he had
put forth the suggestion that it would be useful for him to
know what his borders were. He really did need to know,
after all, exactly what he was prince of. His intention had
been obvious enough even for a dull-witted prince like
Saumer of Isel. The Merida attack had again prompted
the question of rights to certain Desert lands—with
Roelstra doing the prompting—and Rohan wanted to
define what belonged to him—and, more importantly,
what no longer belonged to his enemies. The princes did
not realize that his true goals were more subtle. With
everyone agreed on what he owned, failure of the Merida
to remove themselves from Desert land would give Rohan
the legal excuse he needed for invasion. No other prince
would dare aid the Merida while Rohan was engaged in
recovering what had been decided was his. But, more
far-reaching than this, he knew that stable government
required stable borders. He had intended to start by
proposing distinct boundaries for his own lands, and then

in future years encourage other princes to do the same. But they had leaped ahead to things Rohan had hoped to save for the next *Rialla*. He had not counted on the fierce rivalry between Princes Saumer and Volog. They shared their island in an uneasy truce that had never come within shouting distance of real peace, and their borders fluctuated yearly. When Rohan proposed precise definition of his own lands, they had seized on the concept like dragons discovering an unprotected deer.

"What shall set the precedent?" Roelstra had injected into the discussion, and the battle had begun.

Everyone had a precedent. Everyone's great-great-grandsire had had a precedent. That was what territorial wars were all about. Rohan condemned himself for a fool, because another war seemed ready to break out right now. But he had no one other than himself to blame for this.

Yet as he glanced toward the High Prince, wondering why Roelstra did not intervene to settle this, he learned something very interesting. Roelstra actually wanted them at each other's throats. The conflict between Saumer and Volog had ignited the same kind of argument between the princes of Firon and Fessenden. And though Roelstra's face was composed into serious lines, his eyes were laughing. Their disunity was his goal and his delight. Divisiveness was the key to his personal power.

Rohan sat back in his chair, chewing his lip. He had never realized before how Roelstra kept the princes doing pretty much what he wanted. Now he understood. They fought among themselves, encouraged by the High Prince, who waited until factions were ready to tear each other to shreds before proposing some compromise that would see both sides indebted to him for the settlement. And Roelstra would call it "peacemaking."

Rohan stared down at his hands to hide the disgust he knew must be in his eyes. He wanted only to claim what was his and nurture it in real peace. Care, caution, and cooperation coaxed the Desert into bloom; his vassals had to work in concert to survive, pushing aside their petty differences. It was not the same in richer lands. There was little work involved in bringing forth fruit and flowers from Princemarch or Ossetia or Kierst-Isel. The rulers of those lands had time for other things, and for many years Roelstra had seen to it that their energies had been wasted in quarrels. All that time, all those resources, all that power of mind and wealth—and it had been squandered. Rohan felt as angry at the waste as if he had caught someone purposely draining precious water from the cisterns at Stronghold.

Government was the fine art of coordination. Rule was the subtle and divisive art of power. What Rohan wanted most—peace by rule of laws understood by all—Roelstra would work to prevent with all his might. Rohan understood that now. More, he understood Ianthe's desperation which had driven her to him last night. She had seen the chance of gaining power through him, and it was the only thing she had ever learned how to want. She had only her father's example of waste and treachery to learn from.

Suddenly he thought of Sioned, and his heart ached. He himself had played at Roelstra's game of divisiveness without even knowing it, setting Sioned against the princesses the way Roelstra set the princes against each other while he sat back and enjoyed the show. Rohan had even pitted his own heart against what his mind had made him think was so very clever. But he could not live that way. He needed Sioned beside him—openly, honestly, freely. He saw himself now as an arrogant child who had played the wrong game and hurt not only her but himself in the process.

He became aware that Prince Lleyn was watching him. The faded blue eyes smiled knowingly for a moment, and then the old man got to his feet.

"My lords," he said; then, more loudly, "My lords!" They settled down. "I congratulate Prince Rohan on his excellent if revolutionary idea. But I suggest that without maps and documentation, we're wasting our time."

"Can you solve our problems, cousin?" Roelstra asked smoothly.

"I believe so. We must apply to Lady Andrade."

"For what?" Saumer asked, a world of suspicion in two syllables.

"Not for a ruling, certainly," Lleyn reassured him. "But before the next *Rialla* she might be persuaded to organize land claims so everyone will know where everyone else stands—literally. I suggest that we save the drawing of borders until three years hence, and search our archives for proper precedent."

"I approve," the High Prince said. "Your words are wise, as ever. In fact, I am inspired by them to suggest something else rather new. I propose that until we have all agreed on our borders, that things as they stand now be considered the legitimate boundaries of our lands, to be revised as necessary in three years' time. I further propose that any prince who attacks another be swiftly punished by the rest of us."

Saumer frowned. "Let me understand this, Roelstra. If, say, Haldor attacks Chale over a few square measures that are in dispute—"

"Then I would be there with all my armies as soon as I could to defend Prince Haldor's rights. And those of us on the border of Meadowlord or Syr—Prince Rohan, for instance—would come to Haldor's defense as well. It would take much of the profit out of war, and we could cease spending our substance on useless wars."

"I like it," Ajit of Firon declared.

"So do I," said Saumer, with an eye on Volog, who smiled.

"May I speak?" Rohan heard himself say.

"Please do, cousin," Roelstra replied graciously.

"I think that Prince Lleyn should be the ultimate arbiter of any serious disputes. These are not matters for Lady Andrade to decide, and on his island Lleyn has little interest in who owns what on the continent."

"Are you agreeable to this proposal, Lleyn?"

The old man bowed to the High Prince. "I shall do myself the honor of accepting the task."

Sanity at last, Rohan thought gratefully.

"I hope," Roelstra went on, "that we will be able to work out differences between ourselves without bothering Lleyn." The hint was not missed by a single man present, not even Saumer. "And now, my lords, we deserve a rest. Prince Vissarion has kindly provided refreshment in his tent. We meet back here this afternoon."

Rohan escaped from the close atmosphere of the violet tent and drew up the hood of his cloak against the rain. The morning had not been quite the disaster he'd feared at one point, but there were many things he had to think through. He needed privacy, and there was none to be found in his own camp. At Stronghold he could have disappeared for hours as he chose, but where could a prince hide at the *Rialla*?

He went down to the river, hoping no one else would venture out in the rain for a stroll, and from the corner of his eye caught sight of Meath slinking around the trees on the opposite shore. He supposed he ought to be reassured by the zeal of those who watched over him, but the constant surveillance annoyed him, too. Briefly he considered making a game of it, trying to outwit the *faradhi*, but the dutiful portion of him forbade it. He would be an idiot to go off alone without escort, what with the Merida possibly roaming around.

Rohan finally saw the perfect place for privacy: the steps leading up to the bridge. He felt a little foolish as he slid beneath them and hunkered down out of the rain, but Meath could think what he liked. He drew his cloak more tightly around him—like a dragon with wings folded against the rain, he told himself with a grin. The wooden planks above leaked a little, and he shifted around to find a spot where he wouldn't get dripped on, finally settling down snug and hidden from prying eyes.

The morning had not been so bad, he reflected, though Roelstra's suggestion about mutual aid and defense troubled him. The possibilities for mischief were endless. He set himself to thinking as the High Prince might—something far too easy for his peace of mind—and the scenes that played out in his head were far from reassuring. Any attack, no matter who arranged it, would compel the other princes into punitive action. Questions would come only later—*if* the fighting stopped. For there were factions among the princes that would not vanish in the face of any treaty. *Athr'im* picked fights with each other all the time, more often than not on the orders of their princes, who usually kept out of the actual battles. Rohan's own father had used the tactic often enough, though he had loved fighting and was always in the thick of any minor war. Rohan, however, had no intention of living that way.

But he could easily imagine a force of mercenaries laying siege to a keep and placing the blame on someone else. High Prince Roelstra could march through in the attacked prince's defense—and work whatever damage he cared to inflict. By the time everything had been sorted out, no one would be certain what had happened.

Still, perhaps everyone would think twice now about making war. Localized conflicts were one thing; major wars were to no one's profit. Rohan shrugged, knowing that all he could do was hope for the best.

He felt better about his own proposal of legal borders. Not for nothing had he gone over every document in Stronghold's archives. He already knew what was legally his—not only regarding the Merida, but along his borders with Syr, Princemarch, Meadowlord, and Cunaxa as well. He would have to give up a farm or two, but he would also gain substantial properties in return. In all his vast holdings, he could afford to cede a little in exchange for undisputed right to the rest of it. The vassals involved would have to be appeased, of course, now that they were going to own the land, but thanks to his father he had money enough to soothe the loss of a few square measures here and there.

What a dragon's egg he had cracked today, he thought with a smile. The princes would go mad rummaging around for old treaties and the surveys made by *faradh'im* long ago. In their searching they would, without even realizing it, come to value the precedent of law. With luck and a push here and there, he could persuade them to extend that belief to other things.

Footsteps sounded on the bridge above him, returning from the other bank, and for a moment he thought it must be Meath. But the steps were too light to belong to the big Sunrunner. As the person descended to the gravel shore, curiosity got the better of him. He peeked out from his shelter and with complete delight recognized the girl wrapped in a cloak much too short for her.

"Sioned!"

"Who's there?" She whirled around, fear in her voice.

"It's only me. Rohan. I'm under the steps. Come in out of the rain."

She approached, her riding boots muddy to the knees, and bent to peer in. "Whatever are you doing?"

"I could ask you the same. Come on." He held out a hand, which she ignored. "You're supposed to be safe and dry inside your tent," he scolded as she crouched down beside him.

"*Your* damned leaky tent," she corrected. "And you're supposed to be in a conference."

"I got bored." He shifted around to kneel behind her, careless of the mud, and began rubbing her arms and shoulders. She was shivering beneath the fur-lined cloak. "You're soaked through! How long have you been outside, woman? Here, let me warm you up." He tried to draw her back against him, intending to hold her while explaining his discoveries of the morning, but she shrugged him off angrily.

"Don't handle me as if I'm your property," she muttered. "You don't own me yet, my lord prince."

Bewildered, he kept his mouth shut. A few moments later he was rewarded for his self-control.

"I saw Ianthe last night, coming out of your tent! The only reason I'm even speaking to you is that she didn't look very happy."

Rohan was glad her back was to him so she missed his delighted grin. "I didn't give her much reason to be. You conjured Fire last night, didn't you?"

"What if I did?" she said sulkily. "She was there to seduce you or kill you, and I wasn't about to let her do either."

"I wonder which would have been worse?"

She twisted around and stared at him, her lashes all tangled with raindrops he longed to kiss. "How I'd love to be able to hate you," she whispered.

Rightly interpreting this as a declaration of emotions having nothing to do with hatred, Rohan took her in his arms. They sat there in the mud beneath the leaky bridge and kissed each other, hampered by the bulk of their clothing, the chill, and a total lack of adequate space. Rohan had never been happier in his life.

They might have stayed like that all afternoon and well into the evening, but gradually Rohan became aware that rain no longer dripped into his hair, the blue-gray dimness of their hideaway had brightened with sunlight. Reluctantly he eased his hold on her. She pressed her hands to his chest and nestled her head comfortably against his shoulder.

"There's so much to tell you, and there's never any time. Rohan, meeting in secret will be fun once we're married and don't have to in order to talk to each other, but for now it's getting ridiculous!"

"Just wait till I get you alone in Stronghold this winter," he promised.

"Saddle the horses and let's go home, then!" She laughed and moved away from him. "Only a little while longer, I know. Just remember that I don't really mean the things I say around other people."

"Not even about the river stones?" he teased. "I found them last night. Very romantic!"

She turned crimson and pushed at his shoulders. "Get out of here before they miss you. And go change clothes—you're caked in mud."

"So much for romance." He stole another kiss. "As for you, my lady, go dry off and get into something warm."

"I *was* warm until you let go," she complained, her arms sliding around him again.

"Stop that. Sioned, I absolutely forbid you to seduce me."

"Will I need to?" She giggled. "Oh, very well. I'll go. I suppose it wouldn't be very elegant of me to sneeze my way through our wedding. I'm going to look gorgeous in those emeralds, you know."

"Greedy witch," he accused. "Just for that, I'll have your necklet made of river stones after all."

"Oh, no, you won't!" She took his face between her hands and kissed him soundly. When she let him go, he said the only thing possible under the circumstances.

"I love you!"

The green eyes filled with tears. "You've never said that before."

"Of course I have!"

"No. That was the first time."

"But you knew, Sioned. You must've known."

"I like to hear it sometimes, Rohan. It makes things easier."

"What things, love? The princesses? Don't pay them any attention."

"*You* did," she reminded him tartly. "But it's not really them."

"Then what is it?"

She lifted the hand that wore his emerald. "I don't know how long I'm going to be able to wear these other rings honestly."

"I don't understand."

A small sigh escaped her. "I don't know anymore what I'm supposed to be. Sunrunner or princess or both? I feel—caught."

He finally understood her earlier words. "Sioned, no one can own you unless you allow it. Not me, not Andrade. Anyone who tries will want to use you. I promise I won't do that. I love you so much—I don't ever want to see you hurt. Don't be afraid of me, love. I won't trap you."

"You already have." She forestalled his protest with another kiss. "Just keep your other promise, Rohan. Always be honest with me. Please."

They crept out of the small space, shivering in the brisk wind that had blown the clouds away, and parted—she returning to her fellow Sunrunners, he to his fellow princes. Neither of them noticed their shadows: one a *faradhi*, one a squire, one an expert swordsman of Rohan's own guard. And none of these saw the figure in a dark violet cloak who stood concealed by a tree, hate seething in her dark eyes.

The next afternoon Lady Andrade stood in the conference tent, setting the seal of Goddess Keep on a score of documents. All the princes watched as she dripped hot black wax onto the white ribbons Urival had placed on each parchment and pressed her seal to leave an image of the great castle. Secretaries had been at work all day to make the requisite number of copies—and there were plenty to be made, Andrade reflected, with her nephew's name on quite a few of them. Privately she was amazed at what he had accomplished here. He had gained a good deal and given away just as little as Zehava ever had. Andrade suspected that the other princes were beginning to realize that behind the guileless smile and innocent blue eyes were a cunning brain and a driving ambition, but they were all eager to conclude treaties with the man they thought would soon be Roelstra's son-by-marriage. The High Prince had led them to believe it; Rohan had not had to say or do a thing. And all the princes were locked into these agreements for the next three years.

She nodded cordially to Roelstra when the last document bore her seal, and he turned to the assembled princes. "Cousins, I thank you for a peaceful and profitable *Rialla*. May we all reap our just rewards from our work here, and meet in even greater friendship three years hence."

As they bowed to Andrade and filed out of the tent, she drew her cloak a little closer against the sharp breeze coming through the entry. Urival replaced ribbons, seal, and wax in their case and stacked Goddess Keep's copies into a coffer for transport. The neat, graceful movements of his hands caught her attention, lulling her somehow, and she gave a start as Roelstra's voice came from behind her.

"A few moments of your time, Andrade, if I may."

"Of course. Urival, I'll expect the catalog to be done by tomorrow morning. Get Camigwen to help you. She has a clear hand."

"If I can pry her away from Ostvel," he murmured with a slight smile. He gathered up the two cases, bowed, and left her alone with the High Prince.

"Please sit down," he invited, and Andrade sank into a chair. Roelstra seated himself opposite her at the table. "You know my hopes regarding your nephew and one of my daughters."

"A blind man could see it," she replied pleasantly. "You can be subtle when it suits you. I wonder why you're so obvious now?"

"Without insult, may I venture the opinion that there was no other way to get the idea across to Rohan? He's been very intent on the business of the *Rialla*, and unresponsive to any but the most direct hints about my girls."

"I think he's received the impression you wished him to have," Andrade told him straight-faced.

"But I understand you have your own candidate for his hand."

She nodded. "In her own way, Sioned is as stubborn as Rohan."

"I have an offer to make you, Andrade. Lady Sioned doesn't really want him. He would do much better by way of wealth and prestige by taking one of my girls. A marriage bond with me would be a very good thing, and we all know it." He paused. "As you also know, I have been without a Sunrunner at Castle Crag for some years now."

"That was your doing, not mine. Johoda was highly skilled, but you rejected his service."

"An action I have come to regret. As you are aware, I have other sources of information. But now I need a *faradhi*."

"And you want Sioned." Her fingers beat a steady rhythm on the table. "You may not have her, Roelstra."

"And if she herself should request it?"

Andrade burst out laughing. "For the honor of being your whore? Don't fool yourself, Roelstra—not about this girl, nor about yourself. You're no longer young. You're thicker than you used to be, and the years are beginning to show. Scarcely the handsome youth who came riding into my father's keep nearly thirty years ago, looking for a wife!"

He gave her a narrow smile. "Thank the Goddess I chose neither you nor that witless twin of yours."

"Your memory is failing, I see," she taunted. "Milar loathed you on sight, and I had already seen what you'd become."

"I will have Sioned!"

"You will have nothing!" She leaned forward, no longer laughing. "Do you think I'd even consider entrusting that girl to a man who has already corrupted one *faradhi*? Oh, yes, I know all about it—and you knew that I knew. You have my permission to explain yourself."

He surged to his feet, towering over her. "Your *permission?* How dare you accuse me—"

"I ought to have accused you before the other princes!"

"And why didn't you?" he shot back. "Too proud to admit you can't control everyone and everything the way you control Rohan?"

"Whatever gave you the idea that I tell him what to do or say? You have a great deal to learn about him, Roelstra."

"I warn you, Andrade—"

She rose, pulling her cloak around her. "It was your face, the face you wear now, soiled by power, that I saw in the Fire while I was still a young girl. Live your own life as you will. But *I* warn *you,* Roelstra. Don't you ever touch one of my *faradh'im* again."

She swept out of the tent, racked by an inner shaking. Goddess, how she hated that man, wanted to ruin him— but without the renegade Sunrunner at hand, she had no proof. She surprised herself with the depth of her need to see Roelstra utterly broken. But she knew that only when he was would Rohan and Sioned be safe.

The High Prince ignored his servants as he strode onto his barge. He heard Palila's voice rise on his name, but had no time for her—bloated, useless Palila, who would never bear him a son. He entered his own cabin and locked the door against her, should she manage to lever her bulk from her couch, and thought of Sioned's slender body, Sioned's graceful movements, Sioned's fathomless green eyes—and Sioned's *faradhi* rings.

He opened a compartment concealed in the wood panels and pulled out a small velvet sack. Weighing it thoughtfully in his hand, he considered Crigo's needs. The man was valueless. He would receive no more than what he already had in his tent.

There was more than enough *dranath* here for Sioned.

Chapter Fifteen

Rohan left the High Prince's tent in great good humor, for he alone of the princes knew Andrade well enough to understand the little quirk of her brows as she read treaties with his signature on them. He had not done too badly for a putative idiot, he told himself—but he wondered if his aunt would catch the real intent behind certain otherwise innocent agreements with Princes Clutha and Volog.

No self-respecting cow lasted more than one season in the Desert, no matter how hearty the breed, and Meadowlord had produced too many cattle in the last few years. Rohan had offered to trade Clutha some of Chay's best horses and a tidy amount of cash for the hides of cattle that had been butchered to thin out the herds. This was his first step down a much longer road; the treaty with Volog was the second. From that prince—Sioned's cousin—he had gained the loan of two masters in the art of parchment making, in exchange for increased shipments of glass ingots to Kierst's crafters. His official reason was that he wished his nephews' education enhanced by copies of the books in Rohan's own extensive library. Thus was Chay's contribution explained.

But what he really wanted, someday in the future, was to set up a school. Rohan had had the advantage of an indulgent—if bewildered—father willing to spend any sum to keep his voracious scholar of a son supplied with books. But not every young highborn, and certainly none of the lower classes, were similarly fortunate. One of the things he wanted to work out was a means through which talented young men and women could be educated, their minds trained, their gifts explored. There were schools for some of the major crafts—the crystallers in Firon, the weavers in Cunaxa—but most people were locked into a family trade, no matter what their own natural inclinations. He knew his scheme would find an enthusiastic partner in Sioned, who was as mind-hungry as he. He was looking forward to a winter alone with her at Stronghold for more reasons than the obvious.

He stacked the parchments and leaned back to stretch, then heard footsteps on the other side of the partition separating his private quarters from the more public area of the tent. "Walvis?" he called out, and a moment later the squire appeared. Rohan stared and gave a low whistle. "Sweet Goddess, what happened to you?"

Walvis' freckled cheeks crimsoned, accenting the angry bruise over one eye. "Nothing, my lord," he muttered.

"Come over here and let me see." Rohan turned the boy so he faced the light coming in through the fine mesh screening of a window. "If that's 'nothing,' I'd hate to see your idea of 'something.' " He picked up the squire's right hand to inspect it. "From the looks of your knuckles, you gave something back."

"That I did, my lord," Walvis replied grimly.

"Would you care to tell me the trouble?"

"A matter of honor."

"Yours or mine?"

"Both." A man's stubborn jaw suddenly jutted out of the child-round face. "One of Prince Durriken's squires said that—he said you were—"

"Yes?" Rohan prompted, knowing that under no circumstances must he laugh.

"I don't like to repeat such things, my lord."

"Repeat them anyway."

The boy gulped and blushed again. "He said—that you were going to have trouble getting a son on any woman because—forgive me, my lord—because you're too stupid to find the pisspot, let alone—"

"I see." Rohan kept stern control over his facial muscles.

"I repaid him for the insult, my lord!"

"I can see that, too."

Walvis touched the bruise and shrugged. "I was really something to see a while ago," he admitted.

"Mmm." Rohan turned away, occupying himself with the arrangement of the parchments in his traveling desk. When he could keep a straight face, he said, "I trust you have use enough of your limbs to go see our jeweler at the Fair."

"Are my lady's emeralds ready?"

"I'd like you to find out. If they're finished, bring them back here. And if they're not—"

"I'll find out why!"

"Gently, please," Rohan cautioned with a smile. "After all, we've given the poor man hardly any time at all. Off you go, now." When the squire was at the partition he called softly, "Walvis?"

The boy turned. "Yes, my lord?"

"I'll wager Prince Durriken's man looks *much* worse than you do."

Walvis grinned proudly. "He won't be chewing anything harder than water for days—nor walking straight up, either!"

This time the laughter escaped. As Walvis bowed and left him, Rohan's amusement turned to a sigh. Oh, to be eleven years old again and able to take the direct route toward a goal—preferably with a solid right to Roelstra's jaw. He still smarted over the blocks the High Prince had tried to place in the way of his harmless trade of glass and horses for the craftmasters and cattle skins. It had been nearly impossible to keep his mouth shut and look bewildered while Volog and Clutha did his arguing for him.

A mild commotion outside the tent distracted him, and through the window opening he caught sight of Camigwen directing the placement of a dozen long tables. Rohan belatedly recalled that this evening he would be hosting an informal dinner. There would be dancing afterward, and a very late night—for all the work was done and it was time to enjoy the social life to the fullest before tomorrow's Lastday ceremonies.

"Camigwen? May I interrupt for a moment?"

She turned, squinted to see through the mesh, and said, "Of course, my lord." She hurried around to the entrance and ventured inside, her eyes darting around curiously at the furnishings of his private quarters. "Everything's going splendidly, my lord," she reported. "There's no more rain coming up from the south, so no danger of our outdoor feast turning soggy. The cooks are well in hand—they've finished the roasts and the ices and wines are chilling in the river, and I've timed the breads to be nice and hot just as dinner begins."

"You're a marvel," he said, smiling. "You've taken wonderful care of me here and on the journey—and I've been wondering if you'd like to make the arrangement permanent."

Camigwen frowned. "I can write down all the directions—"

"That's not what I meant, and you know it," he scolded gently. "Sit down, won't you?"

She sank onto a small upholstered stool, hands folded in her lap, and he spent a moment in silent admiration of her extraordinary dark eyes. It was as if one could see her heart and mind through them, so limpid and clear were they. For an instant he envied Ostvel the sight of those eyes smiling at him every morning of his life, then smiled. There would be another pair of eyes, green as summer leaves and just as extraordinary, to gaze at him.

"You've lived at Stronghold," he began, "so you know how complex life there can be. I need someone who won't drive me to distraction the way my present chamberlain does. He's really my mother's man, not mine. I also need someone to oversee the guards and all those other things my father used to do for himself, but that I've never been much interested in. Would you and Ostvel consider coming to live at Stronghold and taking on those duties? I know it's not very important work compared to what you could be doing at other courts as a Sunrunner. And I know Ostvel has the talent and ambition to become chief steward at Goddess Keep one day. But I wish you'd both think about it."

A flush rose into her dark skin. "You're kind to ask, my lord."

"No, I'm selfish. I need you both. I'd consider it an honor if you made Stronghold your home."

Walvis burst into the tent just as Camigwen started to

reply. The boy skidded to a stop on the carpet, nearly dropped the velvet pouch he carried, and gasped out, "My lord, they're finished—just look!"

He upended the pouch onto the desk. Eight emeralds as big as Rohan's thumbnail were set in a maze of delicate silver, as if moonlight had been *faradhi*-spun around the stones. Two more emeralds had been worked into matching earrings, and yet another surmounted a fantastic silver hairpin sprinkled with tiny diamonds. Rohan had neither specified those last two nor provided the diamonds; the jeweler had evidently been inspired.

"Lady Sioned will outshine the starlight," Walvis said proudly.

"Oh, yes," Rohan murmured. With an effort, he tore his eyes from the jewels and slid them back into the pouch. "Lock these up for now, please, Walvis. And thank you."

"You *do* mean to marry her!" Camigwen exclaimed.

"I thought you knew!" he answered, startled.

She sprang to her feet and threw her arms around him. "Of course we'll come to Stronghold, Ostvel and I! We thought you didn't *want* her!"

"Now, what ever gave you that idea?" he growled, hugging back.

"You did, my lord," Walvis contributed, grinning.

Cami stepped back, hands on hips, dark eyes dancing. "You're a dangerous man, my lord prince."

"I've been called a lot of things, but—dangerous? There's a condition for your coming to Stronghold, by the way." He tried for sternness, but neither voice nor face obeyed. "I have to set an example, you know, and I will *not* have you and Ostvel in my household unless you're properly married. Now, what do you say to that?"

She sank into a deep curtsy marred by shaking shoulders and a giggle. "Dragon-spawned you were, I'll take oath!"

"Actually, it's Sioned and I who'll follow *your* example, for I had tomorrow in mind for you and Ostvel and it'll take time to arrange a wedding for us. Will that suit?"

"Perfectly!"

Rohan got to his feet and impulsively kissed her. "Lucky man, our Ostvel," he said to make her blush.

"Lucky woman, our Sioned!" she retorted, and they laughed.

Palila sat alone in her cabin, colossally bored. One of her maids had just finished rubbing oils into her body to keep the pregnancy from marking her flesh, but even that sensuous pleasure no longer held any charms for her. She wanted to be out in the world, enjoying men's glances of admiration and women's glares of envy. By the Storm God, how she hated being pregnant.

Roelstra's entry into her cabin startled her nearly speechless. She gave rapid thanks that she was dressed in a lavish bedrobe and her hair was arranged as he liked it. But he did not appear to notice. To any other man she would have presented the very picture of ripening womanhood in which he would find smug pride. But Roelstra had seen more child-heavy females than any man except a physician.

"Crigo doesn't seem well," he said without preamble.

"Has he been taking too much, or too little?"

"Probably the former, after his deprivation during the journey here." He paced the cabin restlessly, fingers brushing over tables, chairs, brass fixtures, tapestry curtains shielding the windows. "I've forgotten what the usual dose is of *dranath* to wine. It's been a long time since we took him—useless fool," he added irritably.

Every instinct she possessed stood up and howled out a warning, but she managed a smile. "A profitable time, my lord. I believe it's half a handful to a large pitcher. But why not ask him? He's been preparing his own for years."

The High Prince shrugged. "Didn't you hear me? He's been taking too much. He's sitting in his tent now, barely coherent, unable even to tell me where he keeps it. We'll have to ration him, Palila. Where's the supply?"

"In the third drawer of my wardrobe." She watched as he retrieved the wooden box from among the array of her filmy silk underclothes—a sight that invariably turned his thoughts to making love with the woman who owned them. But he didn't even see her. "What shall I tell him when he wants more?"

"He won't. I don't want him bothering you, my pet." He traced the carvings on the box with one finger, then met her gaze, smiling. "Not a single thing should worry you, in case it might worry our son."

She cried out happily. "That's the first time you've said it will be a boy!"

"I hope it will be so," he corrected. "But then, I've been hoping for twenty-five years. Still, by the next *Rialla* I just may be presenting the rabble with their next High Prince."

"I hope he pisses on Andrade," she declared, dimpling.

"No son of mine would have such barbaric manners—but I like the idea!" He came to her, ran one finger down her cheek. "Rest well, my dear. I'll want you at your loveliest for the Lastday celebrations."

"As you command me, my lord," she said, smiling up at him.

"I wish my daughters were as careful of my pleasures as you are, Palila. Remind me to tell you about their maneuverings, especially regarding that Sunrunner girl." His eyes lit with amusement—and something more—as he smiled and left her.

She sank back into the cushions and shredded their fringe distractedly. Instinct continued to shriek at her while she reviewed every word of the conversation, cold to her marrow as the words became a single hideous sentence: her sentence of dismissal and Crigo's of death.

She had not lived with Roelstra for over fourteen years without coming to understand him. His gaze wandered each time she approached term, but each time she managed the affairs herself, making sure they were brief and unproductive. The girls vanished from Castle Crag once Palila was physically recovered from childbirth. It was part of her longevity as Roelstra's mistress that she saw to his pleasures even when she was unable to participate in them herself.

But this time was different. She sensed it along every nerve. She reviewed the princesses' descriptions of the *faradhi* girl, stripping them of jealousy and adding to them Roelstra's own words about Crigo's uselessness. This time his need for a new woman had coincided with his need for a new Sunrunner—and this Sioned was his choice for both.

Palila used the energy of panic to lever herself up from her couch. Her back ached as she went to the wardrobe and searched the lower shelves for a small packet always kept with her lesser jewels. *Dranath* was an herb that increased its potency over time, and this packet was very old indeed—one of the first given her by the old mountain witch. She grunted as she got to her feet with the drug clutched in her hand, returning to the couch out of breath after even this small exertion. Crigo would be brought to her here, and have a strong dose tonight; the barge could be in the worst storm off Goddess Keep and he would think himself on dry land. He would need all the false strength *dranath* could give him, for tonight he would do for her what he had not done in more than five winters. He would deliberately seek another *faradhi*'s colors on the moonlight.

Andrade sat in a comfortable chair, a plate of food on her lap and a wry smile on her lips. The atmosphere of Rohan's outdoor dinner party was romantic enough even for her fool of a nephew. Torches cast golden light over faces made rosy by wine, a breeze off the river stirred the huge buckets of flowers around the perimeter of the dancing area, and musicians played lilting tunes she recalled from her girlhood. Immune to the ambience, she watched the couples around her succumb to it—several young highborns and their Chosen ladies whom she herself would unite on the morrow, and various married couples who should have been long past such nonsense. Camigwen and Ostvel had eyes for no one but each other; Chay and Tobin were behaving as if they'd just fallen in love, standing over by Rohan's tent feeding each other wine-soaked berries and giggling like children. Andrade sighed. She would be hard-pressed to find some intelligent conversation tonight. Thank the Goddess she had never lost either heart or head to a man. Still, as she watched a young lord glide by with his intended wife on his arm, she wondered briefly what she might be missing.

Urival approached, slightly unsteady as he balanced a bowl of fruit and wine in one hand and a goblet in the other. He sank down at her feet, smiled happily up at her, and announced, "Wonderful evening!"

"Anything becomes bearable after enough wine. How many is that for you?" She nodded at his winecup.

"My lady," he said with mock regret, "Ive lost count." Then he grinned. "Rohan's being a bit obvious, isn't he?"

"Aren't they all? Still, it's good to see them happy. May the Goddess keep her blessing on them." Her gaze sought Roelstra automatically. He was seated beneath a tree with several of his daughters.

"Don't worry," Urival soothed. "He hasn't done a thing tonight except smile and eat. He doesn't even notice what a fool Rohan's making of himself."

"He's not being foolish. Sioned won't let him." Andrade chuckled. "Watch now—he's gone over to her again. She'll frown just a little, back off, and—there, she's away!"

"It's a good thing one of them is still sober. Were we ever that young, do you think?"

"Longer ago than I care to remember, my friend."

Urival laughed. "Have some more wine, and you might remember more than is good for your dignity."

Rohan, deprived of the object of his desires, went to his sister and appropriated her goblet right out of her hand. "I'm thirsty," he explained.

"Rohan! Give that back! And stop being such an idiot with Sioned. You're supposed to be a witless prince who hasn't yet made up his mind—not a truly witless one who can't hide the fact that he's in love, or drunk, or both!"

He grinned at her, holding the goblet high out of her reach. "Neither Ianthe nor Pandsala is here yet, and they're the only serious pretenders to my royal hand and arm and all the rest of me. Besides, I haven't said more than ten words to Sioned all evening." He paused. "I may dance with her, though."

"Don't you dare!"

"I suppose you're right," he sighed. "If I touched her, it wouldn't end with just a dance."

Chay, who had been listening with an indulgent smile, plucked his wife's winecup from Rohan's fingers. "All things are forgiven a drunken prince."

"Drunk on happiness," Rohan agreed.

Tobin giggled. "Rohan, you're beautiful!"

"So I am! And so are you!" he added generously. "Ah, here's Pandsala come to have her dinner at last. I'll go be sweet to her, shall I, and confound them all!"

He danced with Pandsala and with Roelstra's other daughters as well. He led his sister in a measure and made her laugh so hard she forgot the steps. He danced with the wives and daughters of other princes and lords, presenting them with what they expected to see: a young man excited by giving his first big party and more than a little drunk on his own wine. If anyone outside his immediate circle suspected the true source of his high spirits—well, they could suspect as they pleased until tomorrow night. He could hardly wait.

Music and wine flowed on late into the evening. The moons rose full and bright, and Rohan ordered most of the torches doused so that silver shadows could play more softly over fine silks and lovely faces. He was getting just drunk enough to risk asking Sioned to dance with him, but when he looked around there was no sign of her red-gold head. He sighed mournfully. She had probably gotten jealous again, watching him dance with every woman but her, and gone back to her tent.

Now, *there* was a thought.

He turned with a smile on his face and every intention of leaving his own party—to find Ianthe boldly inviting herself into his arms for the next dance. She was temptingly beautiful in a deep violet gown strewn with tiny silver beads that glistened in the moonlight. He accepted her hands on his shoulders, put his own about her waist, and they began the slow steps required by the music.

"Isn't it interesting that they've stopped playing those country dances?" she asked.

"How much did you pay them?"

She threw back her head and laughed. "Quite a bit!

You're not the fool you pretend to be, Rohan. I saw that days ago."

"You flatter me, cousin. I'm not wise enough to pretend anything."

"You're lying to me, cousin." Her body pressed more closely to his and her grip on his shoulders tightened. "Wouldn't it be nicer to lie *with* me rather than *to* me?"

"We settled that before, as I recall."

"Ah, no." Her fingers slid down his arms, back up to his neck, admiring him. "You need me, Rohan. There's passion in your eyes that I can match. I can help you with my father, too—no one knows him the way I do."

"You're a clever girl."

"I'm so glad you finally noticed." Their gazes locked, bright blue to deep brown. "You want me," she breathed. "You wanted me the other night, and you want me now."

"I wanted a woman, and you were convenient for a time," he said brutally. "Do you think your father would thank me for dishonoring his daughter?"

"Do you think he cares a damn for any of us?"

"Then he's the fool, not I. He should be watching you without blinking. You're a desperate lot, you princesses."

"Yes," she said softly. "Oh, yes."

The dance and the conversation ended there. He bowed and walked away from her, seeking another goblet of wine to cool his flesh where her fingers had touched him. The same kind of Fire sprang from Sioned's body to his own—yet it was so very different. He wondered why.

When he felt in better control of himself, he turned back to the party. But Ianthe was gone now, and so was Pandsala—and so was their father.

Sioned was not nearly as sober as her restraint in dealing with Rohan indicated. She watched from the shadow of a tent awning as he danced with any woman who caught his eye, amused until Ianthe showed up out of nowhere. The sight of them breast to breast ignited something reckless inside Sioned. The man was hers, and it was time he started acting like it. More, it was time those damned royal bitches understood just who was going to be his princess.

She giggled softly to herself when his dance with Ianthe ended and he went straight for the nearest goblet of wine, obviously in need of it. But her main attention was on Ianthe, who paused for a moment to watch Rohan with glittering dark eyes. All at once her gaze found Sioned, and hatred was scrawled all over the princess' proud face. Sioned smiled sweetly. Ianthe glared at her, picked up her long violet skirts, and strode off into the night, Sioned drained her winecup, set it on a table, and went after her.

"Your grace!" she called mockingly, and Ianthe whirled around. They were in the area just outside Rohan's camp, where only the moons illuminated the path. "I see you're not wearing your silver jewelry tonight. Does this mean I should expect to find it in my tent as a token of your defeat?"

Ianthe's brows arched delicately. "Do I look defeated to you? It's not a rejected woman who spends time in Prince Rohan's arms, Sunrunner."

"That's an odd thing for you to say, considering how little time you spent there the other night." Sioned knew this was a mistake. One did not humiliate a woman as potentially dangerous as Princess Ianthe. But she could not resist the chance to pay back a few insults.

Ianthe turned wordlessly away, rigid with fury, and started walking again. Sioned followed, laughing softly to taunt her. At last the princess swung around again.

"Leave me alone!"

"But I thought we were going to your tent so I could collect my winnings," Sioned responded innocently.

"You have won nothing!"

"And *you* don't even know what game's being played!"

"You're mistaken if you think it one of *your* choosing." Ianthe suddenly smiled, sleek and superior. Sioned ignored the warning and laughed again.

"I thought it had been established that the game is Rohan's."

"Not tonight." And with that the princess pulled a slim

silver knife from her belt, its jeweled haft winking purple and crimson.

Sioned was delighted. She lifted one hand almost casually and the blade began to glow. Sunrunner's Fire licked lazily along the knife, moving toward Ianthe's fingers as Sioned exerted exquisite control. She had to admit that the princess was no coward; the tiny flames were nearly touching her hand before she finally dropped the knife.

"You *faradhi* witch!" Ianthe spat. "I'll have him, one way or another—and when I'm his princess I'll see to it that no court anywhere will have you! You'll spend the rest of your life walled up in Goddess Keep!"

"And that's what *you're* most afraid of, isn't it? Being likewise walled up at Castle Crag!" She gave the princess a mocking bow. "Learn the rules of the game before you try to play it, your grace. Good night."

Sioned left Ianthe trembling with impotent fury. Exhilarated by the encounter, she nearly danced down to the river, envisioning similar scenes in the future when she would have the power of her position as princess as well as Sunrunner. The first and possibly the best would come tomorrow night when she appeared at Rohan's side as his Chosen. The prospect of Ianthe's rage and mortification enchanted her, and she laughed aloud.

"I had hoped to find you alone, my lady," a familiar voice said behind her.

Palila sat on the edge of her couch, staring at Crigo's prone body on her carpet. "Damn you, wake up!" she hissed. "You've had enough wine poured down you to float a merchantman!"

One of her maids stood by, wringing her hands. "My lady, he doesn't look at all well—"

"Of course he doesn't, you fool! Give him more wine!"

Application of another goblet of drugged wine, most of which spilled from the Sunrunner's slack lips onto the rug, brought a groan from him. Palila gestured impatiently, and the maid helped Crigo to sit up. His dazed eyes began to focus.

"Slap him," Palila ordered.

One blow, two—and Crigo's hand came up to grab the

woman's wrist. "No more," he said thickly. "Get away from me."

"Get out," Palila seconded. The maid fled and the door slammed closed behind her. "Can you think now, or do you need more?"

He ran a hand back through his limp hair. "I was asleep."

"Never mind that! Allow me to tell you what you've missed. Roelstra has his eye on a new mistress and a new Sunrunner—and they're the same woman!"

"Sioned?" he breathed.

"Neither you nor I can afford to let him trap her the way he trapped you with *dranath*."

"Why don't you warn her? Oh—of course. She would hardly believe you. And then there's your little understanding with Pandsala."

She gasped. "How did you—"

"Does it matter? Let's just say you don't want the girl rescued too soon. After Roelstra's had her, Rohan won't want her anymore and Pandsala will have a clear field. Isn't that how it's supposed to go, Palila?"

"You're thinking rather precisely, considering the condition you were in when I had you brought here."

"Amazing stuff, *dranath*." He got shakily to his feet, using a chair as leverage.

"The point is that we're both about to be replaced, and you can stop it."

Crigo slid bonelessly into the chair, closing his eyes. "Goddess! How much did you give me?"

"Would you rather have woken up dead?" she snapped.

"Too kind, as ever. So you want me to warn her."

"But, as you say, not too soon."

Crigo began to laugh. "Poor Palila! Why should I help you? Seeing you go down would be my revenge on you at last."

"Are you so deep in your drug that you don't even care if you—"

"*Your* drug, dear lady, that you gave me and gave me and—" He laughed again, ending in a fit of coughing.

"If Roelstra has her, he won't need you—and he can't let you live! Do you really want to die?"

Crigo shrugged. "I can't see anymore what difference it would make." He drew in a deep breath, shook his head. "I need moonlight," he finished curtly.

She nearly moaned with relief and gestured to the windows. "There for the taking."

"I can't walk that far. Help me." As her face twisted in disgust, he snarled, "If you want this, you'll have to help! You gave me enough to addict ten *faradh'im*! Damn it, Palila, help me!"

He leaned on her during the short steps to the windows. She struggled to draw aside the heavy tapestry as Crigo braced himself against the wall and caught his breath. Moonlight streamed in over his ashen cheeks, his eyes that were sunken into bruised hollows.

"Do something!" Palila ordered.

"Shut up," he said roughly, breathing hard. "You gave me too much. I can feel it. I don't know how soon I'll be dead, but I know damned well I'm going to die."

"But you can't! Not before you—"

"Before I've helped you? Sweet Goddess, Palila, do you think I'm going to do this thing for *you*?" He gave a feeble laugh. "There's a certain freedom to it, you know— the knowledge that you're about to die."

She shrank back from him. He hardly noticed. One last time he gathered his knowledge and his waning strength, one last time to weave the cool moonlight as Lady Andrade herself had taught him years ago, when he had been young and worthy of the rings he earned. He let his own colors form in his thoughts, marveling that the darkness that had dimmed them for so long now had fallen away, as if oncoming death had polished a renewed and youthful luster on gifts he had tarnished. So beautiful, he thought, fingering the strands of moonlight and weaving himself into them, this one last time as a true *faradhi*, a Sunrunner who could ride the light.

The sweet power rushed through him and the threads twined at his command into a single supple strand. His own colors merged into the moonlight, paled, washed away as he deliberately forgot the pattern of light that was his alone. He no longer cared. Shadow-lost would have been a terrifying death, but Crigo would die on the

light. He wove himself into cool moonfire and fled into
it, losing himself. The last time—but such sweet freedom
on the moonlight, such final fulfilling peace.

Andrade's rings glinted as she lifted a hand to brush
what she thought was a stray insect from her forehead.
Her fingers encountered nothing but a loose wisp of hair.
She walked faster toward her tent, shaking her head to
clear it of wine, and chided herself for succumbing to the
excellent Syrene vintage Rohan had provided with dinner. The sensation of something winged touching her
forehead came again, and again she wiped irritably at her
brow. Then she stumbled against Urival as a deep, flesh-
shrinking cry split the night sky.

Dragons. She looked up and saw their spread wings
black against the stars, across the moons. "Dragoncry
before dawn," she whispered, staring up at the fierce
shapes led by the single sire who again bellowed out his
mastery of the sky.

"Don't tell me you believe that legend," Urival said,
but his voice was not quite as casual as his words.

"Dragoncry before dawn," Andrade repeated in hushed
tones. "Death before dawn. Can't you feel it?" She shivered, rubbed her face with her hands. But the colors of
her rings lanced into her eyes, shattered colors deliberately broken, paling shards of glass lacerating her senses.
She cried out and clutched at Urival's arm. He called her
name, but she had no will or voice to reply. Her face
turned to the moons, cold white light shadowed by
dragonwings, merciless and beautiful. She felt a Sunrunner's touch, heard a voice both weary and ecstatic,
grasped for the fading colors. She knew who this man
was, remembered the elegant pattern from years ago—
but he eluded her, escaping on the thin unraveling moonlight even as she struggled to hold the weaving together.
He was gone—but not before he had told her what she
had to know.

"Sioned!" she screamed. "Goddess, no!"

Urival caught her up in his arms and ran headlong for
her tent. Safely within the blue silk walls, the moonlight
lost its hold on her. Urival placed her on the cot and

crouched beside her, chafing her hands. "Tell me," he rasped.

"Find Sioned! Tell Rohan—Roelstra has her, he'll—"

"How do you know?"

Above them in the night the dragonsire shrieked again, and Andrade shied away from the imagined feel of his wings against her face.

"Dragoncry before dawn—Urival, he's dead, the Sunrunner is dead—died telling me—don't let Sioned die, too!"

Chapter Sixteen

Rohan stared down at the shirt he had just dropped onto the carpet. No, too much effort to pick it up again—and dangerous besides, considering the condition of his head. It was a good thing Sioned had not been in her tent, for he would not have been much use to her tonight. He made a mental note to abstain from anything stronger than water during his wedding feast. He would have enough to worry about without *that* happening to him as well.

Yawning and stretching were risky ventures, too, and after the attempts he stood very still until his head stopped spinning. His lips were numb; so was his nose. He wondered if his mother had taught Walvis any cures for a morning winehead. Come to think of it, where was his squire? The one night Rohan actually needed someone to help him to bed, and the boy had vanished. He sighed, pitying the poor prince forced to take off his own boots, and collapsed on the bed to consider trying it.

The dragon's cry shuddered through him as if he had never heard the sound before in his life. What was a dragon doing over Waes at this time of year? The scream came again and he braced himself against it, the echo staying with him as he fell back against the pillows. In the profound silence he heard his gasping breaths and the rapid pounding of his heart that had little to do with the quantities of wine he'd consumed that night. The third piercing call was like a sword through his skull and he wrapped his arms around his head, his whole body flinching. A dragon, far from the usual flight paths, traveling at night when landmarks below were only dimly lit by the moons—

"You there! You can't go in now, my lord is—"

"Get out of my way!"

He recognized Urival's voice and struggled to sit up as the *faradhi* burst into the tent. "What—"

"Listen to me," the Sunrunner said in rough tones. "Roelstra has Sioned."

The effects of the wine vanished as if a searing wind off the Long Sand had swept through his body. He surged to his feet and pushed past Urival into the night, looking up involuntarily at the dragon shadows. Urival grabbed him from behind and spun him around.

"Think! As much as you may want to kill him, you can't! Rohan, *think*!"

The dragonsire shrieked again above them, and Rohan stiffened as his flesh cringed again with the terrible cry. Urival was shaking him, fingers digging into his shoulders. "Take your hands off me," he snarled.

"Listen! Andrade felt the renegade Sunrunner call to her on the moonlight. He died giving her the warning. But it may be a trap."

Did Urival believe him unaware of the way Roelstra's mind worked? "Damn you, I can think! Now let me go!"

The older man looked narrowly into his eyes, then relaxed his grip. "Good. I'm coming with you."

"Just don't get in my way."

He didn't run. His heart was pounding too fast, and he couldn't seem to breathe properly around the knot of rage in his chest. But he could not give in to it. Urival was right. He could not afford to kill the High Prince. But if Roelstra had put so much as a finger on Sioned—he rejected the image. He must not consider it. He must think.

Urival's status as a high-ranking Sunrunner got them past guards who would not have recognized Prince Rohan in the half-naked young man accompanying him. A flash of jeweled rings and they were bowed to without challenge until they were within Roelstra's silent camp.

"Lift your torch, man, and look at him," Urival growled to the sentry. "Don't you recognize his royal highness?"

"Your grace! But what business have you here at this hour? I wasn't told to expect visitors."

"Private business between princes," Urival snapped. "Let us pass."

Rohan's strides lengthened, the rhythm of walking having steadied his body somewhat. He squared his shoulders, felt his face settling into hard, grim lines. As he neared Roelstra's tent he heard Walvis' furious young voice, strained as if someone had him by the throat.

"Don't you dare touch my lady!"

A lamp had been lit within, and two figures threw shadows onto the silk. One was Roelstra. He towered over the boy, who was tied to a chair. Rohan heard Urival's haughty command to the guards who'd come to protect their prince's leisure, heard the renewed thudding of his own heart. At last he heard Sioned's voice, thick and slurred.

"Let the boy go."

Roelstra laughed.

Think, Rohan told himself. *It may mean their lives. Think, damn you!*

"What was in the wine?" Sioned asked.

"Something I've found to be very effective in taming your kind. But it won't spoil our pleasure, my dear."

"Leave her alone!" Walvis exclaimed.

"Scream all you like, child. There's no help nearby, only my men—and they are deaf with loyalty to me."

Rohan glanced over his shoulder. Urival stood with the watchfire between him and the four guards, the threat obvious. Deaf Roelstra's people might be, but they were not blind to the *faradhi*'s nine sparkling rings.

"What do you want from me, Roelstra?" Sioned asked. "My body, my abilities as a Sunrunner, or both?"

"If you touch her, you'll die for it," the squire said. "It's forbidden to harm a *faradhi*—and she's under my lord's protection as well!"

Rohan abruptly realized that the two were trading Roelstra's attention back and forth to gain time. Despite whatever had been given Sioned, despite the squire's helplessness, each retained the wits to toss cues to each other as if they'd practiced all their lives. Rohan gave thanks to the Goddess for people who could think, and followed their example. He had to know where Sioned was within the tent. The angle of the two visible shadows meant that the lamp was in the center of the tent, on a table perhaps; she must be on the other side of the light, away from Roelstra. Good, he told himself; that would give him room to maneuver.

"Andrade won't much like this, you know," Sioned murmured. "You took one *faradhi* to your own use. I don't think she'll appreciate it a second time."

"My lady," Walvis said, "there won't be enough of him left for Lady Andrade to deal with, once my lord is finished with him!"

"Enough!" Roelstra commanded. Rohan saw him turn, his back to the entry. Sliding the flaps apart, he stepped noiselessly inside.

Sioned was huddled on the huge bed, her knees drawn up to her chin. The lamp on a central table shone cruelly on her haggard face, and there was something strained and odd about her eyes, as if she could barely focus. But she saw him, and her long lashes closed as she bent her head wearily to her knees.

"You have her rather inconveniently placed for a rape, High Prince," Rohan said softly.

Roelstra whirled around. "How dare you enter my camp? You insolent young fool—"

"Don't bother to call your guards," Rohan advised. "Consider the witnesses. Would their loyalty survive such things as Lady Andrade is capable of?"

"Finding refuge in auntie's skirts," the High Prince sneered.

Rohan smiled. "Free the boy. Now."

Roelstra shrugged. Rohan took another step, angling toward the squire bound to the chair. But Roelstra, moving with surprising swiftness, grasped the boy's hair and jerked his head back, a knife held to his throat.

"Witnesses?" he inquired silkily. "Who said there would be any?"

"You really must think your stories through, Roelstra," Rohan said, glad that his voice was cool. "Now, if you were really being intelligent, you would already have hit on the idea of accusing me or the lady or the squire of an assassination attempt. That way you could kill us all with your own knife, shame Andrade and my family, and enhance your own reputation at the same time." He took another slow step into the tent.

"How clever of you to guess my thoughts, princeling. Which of you would like to be first? This talkative child, perhaps?"

"You have a problem," Rohan told him, moving another small pace forward. "You don't think with your brain, but with what's between your legs. What motive could any of us have for killing you? My squire, cast as assassin? The ropes will leave marks on him. There'd be questions about that, you know. As for the lady—why should a Sunrunner wish you harm? They are expressly forbidden to kill. And why would *I* want to murder you? I've been looking over your daughters—and a man doesn't do away with his prospective father-by-marriage, you know. Who would believe I'm smart enough to realize that with you dead and one of your daughters as my wife, I'd control Princemarch? No, Roelstra," he said, smiling. "I'd kill you *after* the wedding, not before." He was in the middle of the carpet now, next to the table, within decent range—if only he could get to his own knife before Roelstra slit Walvis' throat. The boy's head was wrenched painfully back on his neck, but he gazed at Rohan with absolute faith. It hurt.

"My daughters will have to live without your infantile charms," Roelstra answered. Releasing Walvis, he took a step away from the chair. "I think it'll be you first, little prince. I grow weary of the sound of your voice."

"You're not thinking again," Rohan said, shaking his head as if at a muddle-headed student. "I thought the idea was to marry me to one of your charming girls, wait until we had a son, and *then* kill me. What profit to murder me now?"

"Roelstra!" Sioned moved on the bed, making the wooden frame creak, attracting the High Prince's attention. "Let them go and I'll do as you like!"

Rohan blessed her for the distraction. As Roelstra's eyes flickered involuntarily to her, Rohan pulled the knife from his right boot. Its blade winked in the lamplight, as sinister as the sudden smile on Roelstra's face.

"Good," he approved, circling around behind Walvis' chair, gaze riveted on the young prince now. "That makes it more interesting. You're not as smart as you like to believe, princeling. Drawing your knife is treason against the person of the High Prince. I'm perfectly justified in carrying out the death sentence myself."

"Try," Rohan said pleasantly. "Your Merida allies failed—but then, you never really wanted them to succeed, did you? Oh, yes, it could only have been you behind them, I've known that all along. You wanted to frighten me into grabbing at a marriage bond with you as protection against them—and what could be more understandable than my eventual death at Merida hands?"

He moved warily away from Roelstra as he spoke, one part of his mind analyzing the man. The High Prince had height, weight, and reach on him, but to Rohan's advantage were youth, strength, and quickness, as well as a genuine affinity for this kind of combat. Though he was good with a sword, he had discovered early on that the cunning necessary to a knife-fight came naturally to him. He smiled as Roelstra lunged for him and he sidestepped neatly.

"Then again, if I refused your delightful girls, was I to find a glass knife in my guts on the way back to Stronghold? The Merida would rule the Desert—but only until you could arrive with your armies according to that mutual defense treaty." Again he rocked lightly out of the way of Roelstra's blade. "Is there no end to your absurdity? My vassals would never stand for your army on their soil. And it *is* theirs now, you know—hadn't you heard?" Another taunting avoidance of the gleaming knife. "A man will do battle at his prince's side, but he'll destroy anyone who marches across land lawfully his."

"Can you fight, or only talk?" Roelstra demanded, punctuating the words with a powerful thrust. Rohan had been waiting for the impatience as his father and Maeta had taught him to do. Now he grinned tightly and answered Roelstra's question with his knife.

He discovered that Roelstra's heavier movements had advantages, and was surprised when the High Prince continued a surge forward even after Rohan's own knife had torn into his shoulder. The hot slice of pain along his ribs was another surprise, and as he rolled down and away he heard Sioned gasp as if she had felt it, too. Roelstra's boot lashed out. Rohan's knife went flying into the shadows and he bit back a groan at the pain in his hand and wrist. As the High Prince stepped back, laughing down at him, Rohan came up onto one knee.

"Quickly, through the heart?" Roelstra asked solicitously. "Or slowly, across your throat, so I can watch your life bleed away?"

Rohan slid the second knife from his left boot. No one had taught him this trick, but he had learned it was effective. Roelstra hissed in annoyance and charged him, just as Rohan had hoped. Still balanced on one knee, he swayed to one side and thrust the blade up and around to catch Roelstra's knife hand. A stumble, a clumsy turn, a gasp of shock that he had been wounded—and Roelstra was suddenly faced with an adversary now on his feet and poised for combat, smiling at him.

"I have my own plans for you," Rohan said, "so I'll do myself the favor of ignoring this incident—officially. I wouldn't want to spoil the *Rialla* with a funeral for its finish."

Roelstra switched the knife from right hand to left. "I've been planning yours for a long time now, princeling. Whether it comes now, by my hand, or later with a Merida knife, matters not at all."

They circled each other again until Rohan feinted to the left and made a quick move to the right, sneaking in past Roelstra's guard to slice crosswise across the first wound. His other hand caught and twisted Roelstra's left hand.

"Drop it," Rohan said quietly. "Drop it or I'll break your wrist." He tightened his grip for emphasis and held his knife-point to the man's throat.

Roelstra's eyes flashed, his free hand moving toward Rohan's arm. The tip of his blade pricked Rohan's skin. "You wouldn't dare kill me," he grated.

"If you're so sure of that, then cut me."

The High Prince's knife glittered to the carpet.

Rohan let him go and plucked up the dagger. "If you

bind that well and wear long sleeves, no one will ask
awkward questions," he advised, hiding his regret that
Roelstra had not given him the excuse to kill him. He
glanced at the entryway of the tent, where Urival stood
guard with a satisfied smile on his face. "Untie the boy,"
he told the *faradhi*, and himself went to Sioned. "Can
you stand up?" he asked gently, and she lifted her hands,
hidden until now in the folds of her skirt. He sucked in
an angry breath as he saw the ropes, and slit them with
his knife. There were others around her ankles; he cut
those, too. Then he put both knives into his belt and
cupped her pale cheek in his palm for a moment. "It's all
right, Sioned."

She nodded. "I know."

He helped her to her feet, an arm around her waist.
Together they faced Roelstra, who was holding his bleeding arm.

"I'll keep your blade as a souvenir," Rohan said. "I
suggest you save mine, as well, when you find it. A
reminder that I could have killed you." He smiled.

"Should I be grateful that you did not?"

"As a matter of fact, yes. Walvis, are you all right?"

"Yes, my lord." The squire came to his side, straight-
backed and proud. Rohan felt new fury as he saw the
bruises swelling the boy's wrists and darkening his throat.
"I'm sorry I didn't protect my lady better."

"I know you did all you could."

"Get out of my tent," Roelstra ordered.

"Shut up," Rohan told him. "And listen to me very
carefully, High Prince. Officially, this never happened. I
am a prince first and a man second—a concept you could
never comprehend, so don't bother to try. But I swear to
you that though the prince may ignore this, the man will
never forget it."

Roelstra laughed, not very convincingly. "The princeling doesn't know *how* to be a man!"

Rohan continued as if he had not been interrupted.
"If, during the next three years covered by our treaties,
you renege on a single item or a single man of yours sets
foot uninvited on my lands, I'll know about it—and I'll
leave you to guess what action I'll take. If you so much as

think an incorrect thought in my direction, I'll know about that, too. As for the Merida—I'll deal with them myself. But if a single arrow or sword or morsel of bread in their possession is supplied by you, I'll not only know about it, but I'll make sure every other prince knows about it as well. Your own proposal will come back to haunt you, Roelstra. And *then* try to keep your throne for the son you'll never have."

"Large words for a little prince."

"Believe them. There's just one other thing." He held Sioned closer. "If you touch my wife again, I *will* kill you."

He waited just long enough to see shock and fury break like a storm over the High Prince's face, then drew Sioned gently outside into the clean night air.

Urival and Walvis followed. Guards, kept at bay until now by the high-ranking Sunrunner, rushed into Roelstra's tent, and moments later there were shouts for water, bandages, and the High Prince's personal physician. Sioned stumbled as Roelstra bellowed an order to be left alone, his voice making her flinch. Rohan moved as if to carry her, but she shook her head silently. They left Roelstra's camp behind, and no one said anything until they reached the first of the blue Desert tents.

At last Walvis could stand it no longer and burst out, "I'm sorry, my lord! I watched and followed, but they took me by surprise, as they did my lady—"

"You're not to blame for any of this," Rohan said. "And you did very well to keep him distracted for so long. Walvis, I'm proud of you for not crying out. It wouldn't have done any good and it might've gotten you killed. I can't afford to lose you." Aware that Sioned's steps were faltering, he went on, "Urival, please tell Andrade that we're all right. Sioned will stay with me. Walvis, if anyone asks for me, tell them anything you like. Just don't let them know I'm not inside my tent."

"Yes, my lord," the pair said together.

"Rohan," Sioned whispered. "I want out of here. *Now.*"

He took her down to the river, frightened as she leaned on him and gasped for breath. He wanted to stop, but she insisted they keep going across the soft gravel, far enough downriver so no one could find them. Rohan knew they were being watched; he felt eyes on his back, but knew they were *faradhi* eyes and that *faradhi* ways would deal with anyone else who attempted to follow.

At last Sioned directed him toward a tree. Thin, supple branches rose over their heads and then swept down to the ground, forming a small, private darkness within. It was here that they sheltered from even friendly eyes, screened from the night by silver-green leaves, with the tree arching over them and rustling softly in the quiet night breeze.

"My head hurts," Sioned murmured.

Rohan cradled her against him. "Forgive me, love, for not taking better care of you."

"It wasn't your fault. I should've known." She shifted in his arms. "Roelstra—said things to me, before."

"What? Why didn't you tell me?"

"You would have been angry. And probably said something you shouldn't and ruined your plans."

"To hell with my plans!"

"See? You're angry now." She rubbed her cheek to his bare shoulder. "Aren't you cold?"

"No."

"I keep wondering how he drugged my wine. And what with. I saw you dancing with Ianthe, and when she left I followed her. Do you think she meant me to, so her father could get me alone?"

"You don't have to talk about it, beloved," he said as he felt her tremble.

"I have to understand what happened," she said stubbornly, and massaged her temples with her fingertips, stretching her neck to ease the tension in her muscles. "Goddess, what a headache! He had two winecups and gave me one of them. I can be so stupid."

"How could you have known?"

"Well . . . I did something even more stupid by going to his tent. I wasn't really sure what was going on, I think. He gave me more wine." She paused. "I wish you'd killed him."

"So do I."

"Good thing you didn't, though. I had to hide the

ropes from you—I knew they'd only make you angrier."
She laughed softly. "Oh, beloved, did you see his face
when you called me your wife?"

"Shh. Just rest now. You're safe, and no one can find
us here. I've got you and I'm never going to let you go
again."

"It was horrible, being tied up like that. I couldn't
conjure so much as a flicker of Fire. Not at first, anyway.
I tried later—and the flame flared up and scared me half
to death. And then he caught Walvis, and I didn't dare
try anything. I wonder what was in the wine," she repeated fretfully.

"Hush. Don't think about it." He smoothed her tumbled hair.

"Mmm. . . ." She nestled to him, her hands running
lightly over his chest. "You're so warm, Rohan. All gold
and silk and beautiful muscles . . . did you know how
beautiful you are, my love?"

"You're drunk," he said, blushing.

"A little," she admitted. "But the headache's going
away, at least. I'm beginning to feel quite wonderful, as a
matter of fact." She laughed again. "I've never had a
man fight a rival for me, you know."

"Rival, hell," he murmured as her lips caressed the
hollow of his throat.

"Sure of yourself, aren't you, my prince?"

"Sioned—" It was impossible to think when her mouth
drifted soft kisses over his shoulder. The ache of his
bruises and the sting of the graze on his hip had gone the
way of her headache, it seemed, and for the same reason.

"Oh, yes, I feel much better now," she murmured, her
arms sliding around him, her fingers dancing over his
back. "And *you* feel wonderful. . . ."

"Sioned," he said again, and felt tremors invade his
bones. A new ache had centered in the pit of his stomach, and as he held her he wondered how he could ever
have mistaken another body for hers, another fire for this
blaze that ignited in his blood now. "I—there's something I should tell you—"

"Unless it's that you love me, I'm not interested." Her
hands moved down to slide the knives from his belt, and

she giggled softly. "I heard about the clause in Tobin's marriage contract. Do I have to make you agree to the same?"

"If you don't stop that—"

"Oh, Rohan! You really don't want me to stop."

"No," he conceded, smiling as she pushed him down onto the soft moss.

"We'll have to plant a tree like this at Stronghold so we can always remember the first time we ever made love."

"Do you think I could ever forget? Besides which," he added somewhat breathlessly, "is that what we're going to do?"

"Foolish prince."

He drew away from her, wanting to see her face: shadowed and mysterious, lips parted on a knowing smile, eyes nearly incandescent, and so beautiful that his heart caught painfully in his chest. "Sioned," he said thickly, "it *is* the first time for me."

"You're a sweet liar, my love," she said, and lay back on the moss, holding out her arms to him. "Mine, too, I think. Nothing else counts."

"Nothing," he agreed as he held her to his heart, and knew it was true.

Chapter Seventeen

Palila could not wake herself from the nightmare.

She was awash in white silk that billowed around her swollen body like a vast ocean of snow. Above her wailed a chorus of birds, bright creatures with frightened eyes and chill hands that made her flesh shrivel at their touch. Through it all was the pain, lancing through her until she screamed with it, writhing through the white silk sea to find dry land, sunlit land where she could be free of everything and rest.

But there was no rest, and no respite from the agony, and as it spasmed through her again she remembered. Palila shrieked, seeing again Crigo's open, lifeless eyes gaping at her from his moonlight-pale face.

"You idiots, let me by!" came a new voice, crisp and decisive. "Don't stand there like cattle! Make everything ready for her! Get out and don't come back until you've found Lady Andrade!"

"No!" Palila cried, struggling to sit up. But Ianthe bent over her, dark eyes wide and avid, relishing every twist of pain.

"Be still. Yes, it's me. Stop behaving as if you'd never had a baby before. Lie back and relax or you'll make it worse for yourself."

Palila cringed away from the hands that stroked her hair. She could not be in labor, it was impossible. Where were her comfortable, familiar rooms at Castle Crag, her personal physician, her minstrel to play soothing tunes? She could not be having this baby now. She was not due until well into autumn. But as another cramp tore through her body, arching her up from the white silk sheets, she remembered again Crigo's pale, dead stare and the horrible cry of the dragon.

Ianthe's hands, cool and surprisingly capable, supported her during the spasm. The princess wiped Palila's face, gave her a sip of water, all the while with that sleek, pleased smile on her lips. As the pain faded, Palila glared feebly up at her in sick loathing.

"Why don't you want Andrade here?" Ianthe murmured sweetly. "What happened tonight, Palila, that we found Crigo dead in here and you unconscious on the floor? Father's physician is busy sewing up a wound he says he got in a fall. Nobody believes him, of course. Why is Crigo dead and Father wounded, Palila?"

The mistress shuddered away from the ministering hands. "Clever Ianthe," she whispered. "Can't you guess?"

"If you don't admit the truth now, then certainly you'll tell Andrade when she arrives. Oh, don't worry, Crigo's body has been hidden. But unless you tell me how and why he died, I'll have the corpse thrown into her tent." She placed one hand on Palila's belly, still smiling. "The others are gone. You can talk. I can lie to Andrade very nicely. I don't think you're going to have breath soon to do anything but scream."

"All right—I'll tell you—" She shifted away from the princess' chill fingers. "Roelstra wanted the Sunrunner girl."

"I know that," Ianthe said impatiently. "It wasn't as difficult to get her away from the others as Father thought it might be."

"You *helped* him?"

"Of course. I don't like you, Palila. I never have. But I like this Sioned even less, and the idea of her as my father's mistress and Sunrunner is, quite frankly, more than I'm willing to put up with. Yes, he came to me and asked my help." She shrugged. "He trusts me, you know. As much as he trusts anyone. But you ruined it by having Crigo warn the girl, didn't you?"

"No—yes—I don't know! I wanted him to and he agreed, but I don't know what he did or what happened after he—he—" She squeezed her eyes shut against the memory, but the dead face followed her no matter where she fled in her own mind.

Ianthe's voice brought her back. "So instead of a new mistress and a new *faradhi*, Father will have only a scar or two to show for his night's work. I see. And that bitch of a girl is unsullied. Damn! I ought to be very angry with you, Palila." She paused to let that sink in, then asked, "Is one dose of *dranath* enough to addict?"

"A large enough dose might even kill—oh, Goddess," Palila moaned, clenching her teeth. "How did you know its name?"

"I know more than you ever gave me credit for. I hope the dose was huge—I hope she dies of it! But just think, Palila. I'm not going to have my revenge on you by betraying you to Father about this. Isn't that kind of me? In a few hours you'll present him with his first son." She grinned. "No matter that it won't be his own!"

Palila found strength enough to strike out at the princess' smug face. Ianthe laughed and caught her clawing fingers, stroked them almost gently.

"Keep wondering how I knew," she suggested. "It'll give you something to take your mind off the pain."

"Ianthe—don't betray me! I'll do anything—name it—don't ruin me!"

"Oh, you'll do anything I ask, believe me. That was the whole idea. I'm going down to see Pandsala now. Three other women are in the same state you're in, thanks to us. Think of it, Palila. Can you be sure I'll substitute your girl for a boy? Or will I take your son and put another useless daughter in his place?"

Palila howled with rage and terror and the renewed agonies of childbirth. Ianthe laughed at her and left the cabin, pausing in the narrow hallway to savor the sound. She imagined Sioned screaming in similar pain and fear as her body succumbed to a furious demand for *dranath*. If the dose Roelstra had given her did not kill her, perhaps withdrawal would. Or, what might be even better, she would survive addicted. Not that she'd allow herself to live for very long, enslaved to the drug. No, she was too proud to endure the shame. In any case, the

Sunrunner would not be marrying Rohan. And neither would Pandsala.

Ianthe climbed down the staircases to a room below the waterline. Cramped, windowless, and stuffy, the only light came from a candle set into a tarnished holder on the wall, and by its weak glow Ianthe surveyed the occupants thoughtfully. Three of the sweating faces were drawn into lines of agony, their labor coming too soon. The fourth woman was Pandsala, tense with waiting, fidgeting with anxiety. She rose from her chair as Ianthe entered the room.

"I thought I told you to keep them tied up," Ianthe said, gesturing to the three women who lay on straw mattresses on the floor.

"How could they escape now?" Pandsala retorted. "We've been ruthless about this, Ianthe. There's no need to be cruel as well."

The younger princess shrugged. "I'm told the blonde has already borne three boys. Watch her carefully."

The fair-haired woman propped herself on one elbow, hate gleaming dully in her brown eyes. "You'll have to kill us. Did you think I didn't know that?"

"Perhaps we'll only have your tongues yanked out." Ianthe smiled. "Can you write? I thought not. I don't need to tell you not to learn, now, do I?" She turned to her sister. "Palila's women will do what they can for her. But one of us must be there when Andrade arrives."

"Who sent for her? She can't witness the birth!"

"Of course not. But I sent for her because she'll be an impeccable witness to what we wish everyone to believe happened. I'll provide distraction enough, don't worry. Did you remember to bring the blankets?"

"Over there." Pandsala nodded to three large squares of folded velvet, gold thread winking on violet. "They're identical to the one made for Palila's brat. You do think of everything, Ianthe."

She smiled as the blonde woman groaned and clutched her belly. "Oh, yes. Everything—and more."

Andrade recovered from the shock of the Sunrunner's death because she had to. She was sitting in a chair when

Urival returned, and listened to his report impassively. She ordered someone to go out looking for Antoun, the Sunrunner assigned to watch over Sioned tonight, and summoned Camigwen to her tent, all with absolute calm. While they waited for the girl to arrive, Andrade questioned Urival thoroughly on everything Roelstra had said, and then considered it in silence.

Camigwen came in with Ostvel, and Andrade spared a raised brow for their rumpled clothes, obviously donned in some haste, before giving them a brief description of the night's events.

"I don't know if you remember Crigo. He was older than you by several years. He was a good man, a decent man. Exactly what Roelstra did to him is unclear right now, but with tomorrow morning's sunlight I want you to see that all *faradh'im* are warned. I believe we can keep this quiet and among ourselves, but every one of us must be made aware of this."

Camigwen exchanged worried glances with her Chosen. "How much of a danger is this drug? Do we know the name?"

"Roelstra didn't mention it," Urival replied.

"He'll tell me," Andrade said grimly.

"No doubt," her steward commented. "He said something about being able to control *faradh'im* with it. I don't think Sioned was in full possession of her powers, though," he added musingly. "And that makes me wonder how Crigo was able to do what he obviously had done for Roelstra for years."

"But how vulnerable are *faradh'im* to this drug?" Ostvel asked.

Andrade shrugged. "Once I've gotten the information from Roelstra and Sioned tells us how this drug feels, we should be fairly safe." She glanced up as her name was called from outside, expecting that someone had returned with information about her missing Sunrunner. But instead a man wearing the violet of service to the High Prince came into the tent, breathing hard. He dropped to one knee after a scathing look from Urival.

"My Lady, you must come at once."

Andrade drew herself upright in her chair, ready to

blister the man's ears with her views of rude interruptions. "Let Roelstra's own physician stitch him up!" she began, but the man shook his head.

"Not the High Prince, my Lady. I was sent by the Lady Palila's women to fetch you immediately."

"Palila? Whatever for?" She stared, then traded a swift glance with Urival. "Oh, Goddess! She's in labor, isn't she?"

"Yes, my Lady, evidently so. I'm told it's early. Her women are frantic, for the High Prince's physician is unavailable."

Considering what Urival had told her of Roelstra's wounds, Andrade could believe it. She got to her feet. "Very well. I'll come." To the protests of the others she replied, "Don't be ridiculous. I'll be perfectly safe, and Palila will need help. Urival, stay here and question Antoun when he's brought back—in one piece, I devoutly hope. Cami, you and Ostvel meet with the other Sunrunners and tell them what was said here tonight. They'll help you tomorrow morning. And no arguments!" She turned to Roelstra's man. "You, whatever your name is—"

"Gernius, my Lady."

"Well, Gernius, you will have the honor of carrying my bag of medicines and conducting me to the High Prince's barge. Let's get started."

The instant she set foot on the ship her stomach rebelled. Gritting her teeth against nausea and the fiery throb behind her eyes, she clung to her dignity and followed a maidservant into Palila's luxurious cabin. She saw at once that the mistress was in a bad way. Snapping out orders to the useless women around her, she was disgusted to find that they, like their lady, were pathetically glad to have someone take charge. She conducted a swift, thorough examination and gave orders that would ease Palila's suffering somewhat. Andrade had seen enough birthings to know that this one would take some time yet, but she did not mention this to Palila—who screamed loud enough to waken the Storm God for the winter.

"Oh, stop it," she advised, not unkindly, as she sat on the bed beside the thrashing figure. "Don't fight so hard.

You're using up all your strength in yelling." Palila's nails dug into Andrade's arms and she philosophically added this new pain to the grotesque hammering in her skull. "Quiet down now. You're doing just fine."

"My Lady?" The murmur at Andrade's shoulder made her turn, and she found Princess Ianthe, of all people. "Three more await you below," the girl said.

"Three more?" Andrade repeated blankly.

"Giving birth."

"Sweet Goddess!" she exclaimed. "Why didn't you tell me?"

"I am," Ianthe said, her lips quivering as she tried to suppress a smirk. "Besides, they're only servants."

"They're *women* like you and me!"

Palila moaned, "Don't leave me!" The terror in her eyes went beyond that of an essentially cowardly woman in labor. Her gaze was fixed on the princess, and Andrade surmised that hatred ran even deeper at Castle Crag than she'd previously thought.

"I'll be back as soon as I can," she told Palila. "Ianthe, stay with her."

"No!" Palila shrieked.

But Ianthe settled into a chair next to the bed and stroked Palila's hand soothingly—having to hang onto it hard to create the pretty picture of solicitude, Andrade noted sourly. She shrugged off her uneasiness and left the cabin.

Down a steep, dark staircase she went, swearing under her breath as the barge's gentle rocking made her stumble and threatened to deprive her of her dinner. She hung onto the rope rail, breathed with stern regularity, and refused to be sick. Following the sound of pain-weary groans, she arrived at a stifling little room where Princess Pandsala—of all people—had charge of the three women. One had brought her labors to a successful conclusion and held a newborn jealously to her breast. One was too deep in her pain to notice anything. But the third, a pale-haired woman with burning dark eyes, glared in silent loathing at the princess and held her swollen belly as if to keep the child safely within her.

Andrade knelt beside the new mother, fighting dizziness and renewed nausea at the stench of blood and sweat in the room. "Don't tell me *you* delivered this child," she said over her shoulder to Pandsala.

"Ianthe helped. It was very quick, really."

"Small wonder," the blonde woman hissed.

Pandsala shot her a vicious glance of warning. "She's had a baby before—and so have you. Fine sons, aren't they, back at Castle Crag?"

The woman turned her face away. Andrade, puzzled at the byplay, wondered if there was something she was missing. Her head hurt too much to chase down the idea right now. The new mother was doing nicely despite her inexpert assistants. Her infant girl was pink, healthy, and in possession of the correct number of limbs, fingers, and toes. Andrade had never been a mother herself, but there was a deep vein of maternal feeling in her that found its safest expression in admiration of babies in which she had no personal or political interest. She congratulated the new mother warmly, and moved to the woman beside her.

"Why does the Goddess make so many daughters?" Pandsala asked suddenly.

"There does seem to be an abundance of them at Castle Crag. Perhaps it's the air." Andrade eased the struggling woman into a more comfortable position, murmuring, "There, my dear, you'll do better now. Only a little while longer, I promise."

One born, three to go, Andrade told herself. It strained credulity that four women were giving birth on the same night at the same time, but what explanation was there other than bizarre coincidence? What matter if these servant women birthed their children the same night as Roelstra's mistress? Andrade rubbed the center of her forehead where the pain had settled, and tried to put her wits in proper order. Most Sunrunners on water lost their ability to think as well as their dinner. But not *this* Sunrunner, she vowed.

"They say it takes longer to have a boy than a girl," the princess went on. "Is that true?"

"I've no idea. Come here, Pandsala, and wipe her

down. She'll take a while yet. I'll send one of the women down to help you."

"Make it Ianthe," Pandsala said quickly. "Those others give me the fidgets."

"As you like. Though why a princess should be attending three servant women in their labors—"

The girl shrugged. "You saw upstairs how hopeless those others are. We have an obligation to our people, after all. Besides, somebody has to take care of them while we're waiting for Father's physician."

Urival's vivid description of the knife-fight came to mind. Roelstra would be twice as dangerous now—wounded animals always were—but Andrade savored the mental picture of Rohan's blade slicing the High Prince's flesh. A pity it hadn't been his heart that had been cut, but Andrade doubted that such a thing could be found in Roelstra.

She turned at last to the blonde woman, examined her carefully, and nodded her satisfaction. "You're doing excellently, my dear. Keep an eye on your friend, if you would. You can reassure her, since you've been through this before."

"Please the Goddess, make my baby a girl," the woman whispered.

Puzzled by the vehemence, Andrade replied, "Be easy, now. Boy or girl, you'll soon have another fine child in your arms."

"My Lady—please don't leave me alone with her!" The woman clutched at her arm.

"She has more important concerns than you!" Pandsala snapped.

"Everything will be all right," Andrade soothed, then gratefully escaped the strange, tense room and went up on deck, hoping the night air would cool and clear her head. The crew, unnerved as men always were by women's hurryings during childbirth, stood about in clumps and speculated about the mystery of babies. Andrade spared a tired smile as she thought of Rohan waiting for his child to be born. Chay would get him so drunk he wouldn't remember his own name, let alone how to worry about Sioned.

Chill river dampness began to seep into her bones, adding a new ache to those in her head and stomach. Roelstra would owe her for this, she promised herself, then staggered as a tiny wavelet rocked the barge out of the rhythm she had more or less grown used to. She clapped a hand over her mouth, horrified, and felt a strong arm supporting her.

"Nothing to be ashamed of, my Lady," said a gruff, kind voice. "It's expected of you *faradh'im*."

A moment later her dignity became irrelevant. The sailor Gernius skillfully held her head over the rails as she lost her battle with the river. She struggled not to faint as well, and after he had wiped her mouth and given her a swallow from his pocket flask, the stars stopped spinning.

"There, now, my Lady," Gernius said. "You'll do better now. I've sailed with *faradh'im* before, and it's always for the best to give in to it at once."

Andrade nodded curtly, thanking him for his care of her with a complete lack of graciousness that only made him smile. She expected her head to crack open like a dragon shell any instant as she made her way back to the hallway outside Palila's cabin. The door was blocked by women who were supposed to be inside assisting with the birth. Anger sent new strength rushing through her—and also set a whole new chorus of nerves screaming in her skull. "Why aren't you in there?" she demanded.

"She ordered us out, my Lady! All but the princess."

"Damn you, Ianthe!" Andrade swore under her breath. One princess attending servant women, the other helping the mistress they all loathed. She would understand this if it took all night. "Let me pass. Somebody send for the High Prince. Two of you, get down below and—"

A thin wail from within the cabin interrupted her, the unmistakable cry of a newborn. The women gasped and surged forward, jostling Andrade away from the door.

"It's locked!" one of them called.

"Ianthe! Open this door!" bellowed Andrade, and winced at the volume of her own voice. But she knew the princess would literally have her hands full, and ground her teeth with impatience. The servants shifted nervously, and one of them suggested calling a few sailors to break the door down. Andrade was about to order that very thing when the door was flung wide.

Ianthe stood there, holding a violet-wrapped bundle in her arms and wearing a sweet smile. Andrade spared her a searching glance, then went past her to the bed.

"You're all right?" she asked Palila.

"Hmm?" Dreamy eyes smiled at her. "Oh, yes. Yes! I have a son!" She began to laugh. "A son, Andrade! A son!"

"Goddess blessing," she responded automatically, although her thoughts whirled as she tried to project the implications of this birth down a dozen different paths. She called Palila's women, who came forward to make her comfortable and dress her to receive the High Prince. Roelstra triumphant, Andrade thought sourly as she watched. So he had a son at last. Damn him.

She turned, looking around for Ianthe. But the princess had disappeared—and with her, the child.

Ianthe gazed down at the murmuring bundle in her arms and laughed softly with excitement. Its sex made no difference to her. Boy or girl, she had won. Now it was merely a choice among advantages; she had thought them all through.

She paused in the hallway, listening, and laughed again as the ship's bell pealed a shrill announcement of the birth. It was the agreed-upon signal and Pandsala would be up here soon. Without a boy-child to hand, she would have to bring up a girl. A pity Roelstra had not yet arrived—but Andrade would do even better as a witness. She heard the fretful crying of another infant, quickly hushed, and caught her breath. Her own game was about to begin, the one for which *she* had devised the rules.

"Ianthe?" Andrade said behind her, and she hid her jubilation at the perfect timing. "What are you doing? The baby will catch a chill."

"Oh, no, it's a very thick blanket." She turned, smiling. "I thought all that chattering in there would scare the poor little darling. Such a beautiful child—I long for one of my own."

Andrade's expression clearly indicated her doubts that Ianthe was the motherly type. "Let's take a look at him," she said, pushing the blanket away from the baby's face. "A fine child. Look at all that hair!"

They had been speaking in normal tones, but the ringing bell and the chatter from within Palila's cabin obliterated their voices at a few paces. Thus Pandsala came with total innocence into the hall from the stairwell, calling out, "Ianthe, I brought another baby back up with me, but—" She stopped cold and gasped, "Lady Andrade!"

Ianthe knew her own face was the perfect picture of astonishment; she had practiced the expression in a mirror until she had it without a tremor of betraying amusement. "Pandsala! Why is that baby away from its mother?"

Pandsala turned sickly white. She staggered slightly against the wall, arms tightening convulsively around the violet-wrapped bundle. Ianthe paused a moment to enjoy the shock in her sister's eyes, then turned to Andrade.

"Yes," the Lady said smoothly. "Why have you brought that baby up here?"

Pandsala was still staring at Ianthe, horror congealing her face as she realized how she had been tricked. Her lips parted, moved, but no words came forth. Another peal of the bell signaled the arrival of the High Prince, and they all heard Roelstra's joyous shout.

"By the Goddess! Can you believe it? I have a son!"

Ianthe looked at Andrade. "Who told him *that*?" she whispered.

Light spat from the many rings as Andrade gripped her arm bruisingly. "Is it a girl? A *daughter*?"

"A very sweet little girl," Ianthe responded with just the right amount of bewilderment. "Father's used to them by now."

Roelstra's presence filled the narrow hallway. "Andrade! What brings you here? Surely you're not here to congratulate me on my son!"

"For lack of your own physician, I attended your lady. But I hardly think the corridor is the best place to greet your new child." She commanded Pandsala and Ianthe into the cabin with a cold glance. Roelstra followed, sensing something not quite right. Andrade ordered the servants to take the baby from Pandsala's frantic grasp and leave the room. Then she locked the door and faced the room's occupants with a frigid smile.

"Now," she said, "I will know the truth of this."

"What are you talking about?" Roelstra demanded. "I want to see my son!" He looked from one princess to the other, then at the closed door. The second child had been taken out by a maid. His eyes slowly darkened. "I do not believe there were twins," he added, his voice deadly.

"You have no son," Andrade told him, and Ianthe heard the grim satisfaction in her voice. "I'm wondering which of your daughters will explain this."

The High Prince swung around to spear Palila with his glance. "What do you know of this?" he shouted.

"Nothing!" she gasped, huddling back into pillows that were no whiter than her cheeks.

Roelstra turned on his daughters. "Whose child was just taken away?"

"Father—please!" Pandsala cried out, and Ianthe judged it a nicely inopportune moment to present her father with his eighteenth daughter.

"I'm sorry it's another girl, Father, but she's very pretty."

Roelstra ignored her. "Andrade, discover the truth of this. If I speak again, it will be to order them all executed." He strode to the windows, ripped back the tapestry, and clasped his hands behind his back. He was shaking.

Ianthe sat down, the baby in her lap. "I don't understand, my Lady. You saw me with this child, and then Pandsala came with another. What's going on?"

"Shall we find out?" Andrade asked calmly enough, but Ianthe had a moment of raw terror as piercing blue eyes searched her face. She had faced that same look from Rohan a few nights ago. She forced herself to relax, for even if Andrade figured out the whole plot, nothing could be proven against her.

"Those vipers!" Palila suddenly screamed. "They stole my son!"

"First you know nothing, and now you know whose fault this is," Andrade said. "How interesting. Pandsala, explain this little comedy."

"I—" She flung an anguished look at Ianthe. "It was her idea! She planned that we would exchange a girl for the boy—"

"What?" Ianthe exclaimed, wide-eyed.

"Be silent!" Andrade snapped. "Go on, Pandsala—from the beginning."

Ianthe listened as the story gushed from her sister's mouth, delighted by Pandsala's guilty incoherence. Andrade's expression slowly changed from cool composure to shock. Palila lay back against her pillows looking as if she wished herself dead. Roelstra turned and stared at Pandsala as if she had grown talons and a tail. Ianthe sat, cuddling the baby.

"If I understand you," Andrade said heavily when Pandsala had sobbed to a halt, "things progressed as follows. Ianthe suggested substituting girl for boy, should Palila have a son. To this end you arranged for those poor women to be brought along, and induced labor in them when Palila began her own. I've no doubt we'll find the appropriate herbs in your things, Pandsala, not Ianthe's.

"But then you struck a bargain with your father's mistress. In exchange for her help in winning Prince Rohan for you, you would substitute a boy for a girl, should Palila produce yet another daughter. Because the only woman who had given birth thus far had a daughter, you had no choice but to bring her up, just in case there was a son to be rid of. Palila would have been no use to you in such a case, so you reverted back to Ianthe's original plan. Is this the essence?"

Pandsala nodded, tears streaking her face. "Father—I'm so sorry—I only meant to give you the son you wanted—"

"Roelstra!" Andrade called out sharply as he took a threatening step toward his daughter, arm raised to strike her. Ianthe saw the white bandage as his sleeve fell away, and wondered if that bitch Sioned had given him the wound while defending her nonexistent honor. Her lip curled, and she bent her head to the child.

"We have yet to hear from you, Ianthe," Andrade said.

She looked up. "What can I say? I never heard so

ridiculous a scheme in my life! How could anyone be sure those women would have babies of the right sex for whatever exchange Pandsala seems to have planned? Quite frankly, I'm confused. Am I supposed to have plotted to *give* Father a son, or *deprive* him of one?"

"Go on," Andrade invited icily.

Ianthe shrugged. "What kind of monster would give over a royal prince—and her own brother!—to be raised by common servants? I'm not so base as that, Father, nor so stupid. Do you truly think me capable of so horrible a plot? And one which, moreover, is so incredibly impractical?"

"No," Roelstra said very softly, his green eyes glittering. "If it had been a boy, *you* would have arranged to have him killed. I know you, Ianthe."

"Father!" And for a moment she was terrified.

"Stop it, both of you!" Andrade surveyed them in disgust. "You're *all* vipers, every one of you. What do you plan to do about this, Roelstra?"

"I'm more interested at the moment in what was planned for the women down below." He kept on staring at Ianthe. "What would *you* do, my dear?"

"Nothing, because I have nothing to do with it," she replied promptly.

"But if you did?" he pressed.

"Father—do you seriously think I could have those women murdered?"

"I thought you'd see the necessity. You've always been clever, Ianthe." He turned to Pandsala then and asked, "Do you know the penalty for treason?" His gaze flickered to Palila, who gave a wordless cry.

"Father—no!" Pandsala slipped to her knees, shuddering.

"Treason," he repeated softly.

Andrade stepped between them. "Roelstra," she said in a low voice. "Don't do this."

"It's none of your concern, *faradhi*."

"Don't kill her. Give her to me."

"What? Why?"

"You owe me. The Sunrunner you corrupted died tonight."

"Crigo's dead?" Roelstra looked shaken.

"It was an accident," Palila said feverishly, leaning forward, hands outstretched and quivering like delicate leaves. "He took too much, and I—"

"Silence!" Roelstra shouted at her, and she cringed back again.

"I'll take Pandsala as payment," Andrade said, and Ianthe chortled inside. "And the new child as well. The last thing you need is yet another daughter. Give them to me."

"Living death in Goddess Keep," he mused, eyes shining with cruel humor, and Pandsala screamed. "Very well. They're yours."

"Father—no!"

"What about Palila?" Andrade asked.

"You won't deny she deserves death for killing your *faradhi*. I'm sure your precious Sioned has told you all about *dranath* by now, hasn't she? Pity I didn't kill her with it tonight."

The High Prince and the Lady of Goddess Keep confronted each other and Ianthe watched, bewildered. What had really happened tonight with Sioned?

"Don't interfere, Andrade. I warn you." He paused. "Ianthe."

She stood, wary in spite of the victory she was almost sure she'd won.

"Show her to me."

She came forward and held out the baby. He looked at it for a moment, then unwrapped the violet blanket to make sure the child was indeed female. "Chiana," he said. "Name her that, Andrade, so she'll always know."

Ianthe hid a flinch. The word meant "treason" in the old tongue. Andrade took the child from her and glanced down at the weeping Pandsala.

"Get up. The first thing you'll learn is that a Sunrunner kneels to no one. Not even a High Prince."

"Unless he is my Sunrunner, not yours," Roelstra said, and Andrade shot him a vicious glance.

Ianthe looked into Pandsala's eyes, eyes that were glazed with hopeless terror, unable to believe what had happened. All at once she seemed to recognize Ianthe and surged to her feet, hands closing around her sister's neck.

Roelstra dragged his daughters apart. Pandsala collapsed onto the carpet and Ianthe swallowed hard past the ache in her throat. The High Prince flung open the cabin door, shouting for guards to take Pandsala to Andrade's tent—bound and gagged if necessary. Ianthe heard her scream once in the passageway, a howl of hate and despair, and she shivered.

Then there was silence. Palila was too frightened to do more than lie mute with terror in her bed. Andrade held the baby close, staring at Roelstra.

"Where is Crigo?" she asked.

"I'll have him delivered to your tent, if you wish."

"Do that," she snapped.

Ianthe drew back from the fierceness of their emotions. This was an ancient loathing, far more powerful than any she had ever seen before. It had a bitter life all its own and writhed almost visibly in the space between them.

"I'll destroy him," Roelstra said suddenly. "His marriage will finish him."

"*You* wished a similar marriage long ago with another Sunrunner."

"So that's what gave you the idea. Did you take my anger into account when you arranged it?"

"Your anger is your own problem. I arranged nothing. The Goddess—"

"Usually does what you tell her to. Make what excuses you like. If you believe his sons will follow after him, you're mistaken."

"This from the man who still believes he can have a son of his own?" She laughed maliciously. "Find yourself another mistress, Roelstra! Get another dozen women with child! There will be no son for you!"

"Get out!" he roared.

Andrade's laughter seemed to echo in the cabin long after she had slammed the door behind her. Ianthe sank into a chair and closed her eyes. She had won. If Roelstra believed her—and even if he did not—she had won. He had not condemned her along with Pandsala.

"Roelstra—oh, no, my lord, please—for the sake of our children—"

Ianthe's head snapped up. Palila cowered back into white pillows, her eyes huge as she stared transfixed at the candle Roelstra had taken from a table.

"I remember the fire, Palila," he said almost tenderly, and she whimpered. "Did you hear the dragoncry tonight?"

Ianthe leaped to her feet. She had never heard that note in her father's voice before—and she wanted out. Now. He sensed the movement and, without turning, commanded, "Stay." Ianthe froze, barely breathing. Roelstra moved closer to Palila's bed, holding the naked candle. Its flame licked hungrily at the air.

"Do you know where Feruche is, Ianthe?" he asked.

"Yes, Father."

"It sits on the border between Princemarch and the Desert," he went on. "I've been thinking about Feruche for some time now, and whom I could place there. It must be someone I can trust." He glanced over his shoulder at her. "Do you still wish possession of the princeling?"

"Yes," she answered forthrightly.

"Your luck has run out for the night, my dear," he told her, grimly amused. "Feruche you may have for your own, but Rohan you may *not* have. It seems the Sunrunner has a prior claim."

"The Sunrunner," Ianthe whispered. All at once she understood the hatred that had lashed the air between her father and Andrade. Fury and wounded pride and the desire for vengeance swept through her, creating a hatred she embraced as if it was a lover. She had been empty all her life, waiting to be filled with this sweet, hot thing that grew inside her, singing of blood and revenge. And at last she had found her definition of power—not through a princely husband or her father or any other person—power stronger than the paltry gifts of a Sunrunner. This thing was what made her father so powerful a prince. He knew how to hate.

"I see you understand me," he said. "Return to the camp, Ianthe, and wait for me. We have much to discuss after I finish here."

As she closed the door she glimpsed the candle flame

hovering near Palila's stricken face. And as she stepped off the ship onto the dock, she heard the first of many, many screams.

Dawn's light filtered through pale silver-green leaves, light as velvety as new roses. Sioned, sensitive to color like all *faradh'im*, lay on her side and wondered if she had ever seen light this beautiful. She smiled at her own foolishness; it wasn't the color or even the softness that caught at her heart. It was the sleeping face that the light caressed.

He had been shy at first, trembling, uncertain—until the fastenings of her skirt had frustrated him into a muttered curse that brought a burst of laughter from her. And all at once they were both giggling like children, the knotted ties of her clothes and the tight fit of his boots ridiculous obstacles after the other things they'd endured for this moment.

Sioned smoothed the sunsilk hair from his forehead, knowing now that her vision of years ago had been true. She was the one who had made him a prince and a man. For a little while the two had been ensnared within each other. Sired by a dragonlord whose virile image lingered, the prince had wanted to live up to an imagined, impossible standard and the man had been unsure of his ability to do so. But in her arms he had found both identities. The prince and the man joined in becoming her lover.

His caresses had sighed along her skin and his whispers shone like sunlight in her mind, kisses glowing rich with his colors that she touched in all their power and purity: diamond, sapphire, topaz. All her senses awakened to him, knowing the Sunrunner blood within him would merge with hers and make their son a *faradhi* prince.

"Just so long as he has your eyes, beloved," she whispered, fingertip skimming along the silky curve of his lashes. She smiled as his eyelids slowly opened, almost too heavy to lift.

"Ohhh. . . ." he whispered, voice slurred. "What'd you *do* t'me?"

Sioned stroked his cheek, relishing the rough stubble of blond beard. "Would you like me to do it again?"

"Some other time, when I'm alive enough to enjoy it," he replied drowsily. Pulling her into his arms, he settled her head on his shoulder. "Damn. I forgot to undo your braids. I wanted to see your hair loose."

"Oh, save *something* for our marriage bed," she chuckled.

"But I did. Chay told me once about—"

"Rohan!"

"—something I've always wanted to try," he finished. "I'll let it be a surprise." He rubbed his cheek to her hair. "Mmm, but you smell good."

"Not me, the mossberries. I think we crushed them into wine." She rolled onto her stomach and pulled her skirt from under his head where it had been their pillow. "See?" She poked a finger under the moss where the plump green berries were hiding.

Rohan turned over with an inelegant grunt. "Are there any we didn't mash to a pulp? I'm starving." He pulled aside the moss and plucked a few of the plump spheres. "Here—open your mouth."

"Again?"

Rohan's eyes went wide with shock, but in the next instant they were both giggling again. They lay side by side and fed each other mossberries while the sunlight warmed the leafy canopy above them. At last she said, "That's enough, we'll get sick. We'd best sneak back to camp now, before they miss us."

"I swear to you, this is absolutely the last time I sneak anywhere with you because I have to. *Not* having to will be fun. But no more of this!" Rohan sat up and reached out lazily to part the curtain of branches. "It's awfully bright upriver, for it being only dawn. Take a look."

She moved closer, rested her chin on his shoulder, pressing herself to his muscular back. The light hurt her eyes a little and her head was beginning to throb again. But she kept silent, not wanting to spoil the peace of the morning. She squinted into the daylight and frowned. "Rohan, that's the wrong direction for the rising sun."

"Smell the wind," he said tightly.

"Fire," she breathed.

"Get dressed. Hurry."

They ran upriver hand in hand, the rising sun at their backs, the smoke thickening as the breeze shifted. "Is it the bridge?" she asked.

"No."

They emerged from the trees. Roelstra's barge was an inferno rocking gently on the water, its violet sails crimson wings of flame.

Chapter Eighteen

Rumors chased each other with frantic speed from camp to camp all during the Lastday of the *Rialla*. Roelstra had murdered all his daughters. They had murdered him. Lady Andrade had started the fire on board the barge and killed them *all*. Roelstra had been deposed by persons unknown, possibly the Merida. Prince Rohan had died in the fire. He had died in Roelstra's tent. He had called for his armies to march on Castle Crag. He would marry Princess Pandsala—no, Princess Ianthe—no, both, and take the other girls as concubines. Lady Andrade was on her way back to Goddess Keep with Princess Ianthe—Princess Pandsala—

The only thing anybody knew for certain was that the High Prince's barge wallowed on the Faolain, gutted, smoldering, its dispirited crewmen at a tavern in Waes getting drunk. One more interesting item of known fact: Lord Chaynal had hiked up the price of his horses, which would be in great demand now that whatever was left of the Castle Crag party had to find another means of going home.

Prince Clutha of Meadowlord and Lord Jervis of Waes did themselves the courtesy of ignoring the rumors. They ordered the ceremonies to progress as usual, and by midmorning a hilltop overlooking the camps had been made ready. The highborns gathered, whispering the latest, and waited for the procession of brides. When Lady Andrade arrived, there was a collective sigh of pure relief.

Frankly curious stares greeted Roelstra's daughters. They were lacking their father and one sibling, and were dressed as richly as brides themselves. Pandsala's absence

fueled speculation that she was the Chosen of Prince
Rohan; Ianthe's sullen face seemed to confirm this. But
when the wedding procession came up the flower-strewn
hillside, the missing princess was not among the brides.

One of the first to step forth and be married was young
Lord Eltanin of Tiglath, who still looked stunned at his
success in winning Jervis' middle daughter. She was a
small, delicate girl with golden-brown hair and the musi-
cal name Antalya, meaning "spring cup" in the old language, and with wildflowers plaited in her hair and in
bracelets around her arms, she was the embodiment of
youthful beauty. As she was presented by her father to
her new husband, she looked up at Eltanin with radiant
eyes. Rohan, as the young man's overlord, presented him
to his bride with an elegant flourish. Andrade called
Goddess blessing down on the pair, and Tobin was sure
her brother would start dancing with delight. An alliance
between his vassal and the powerful *athri* of Waes would
strengthen his ties with Meadowlord; Clutha's lands were
a buffer between the Desert and Princemarch, and Jervis
was Clutha's man. Yet Tobin also detected a more personal joy in her brother's smile. It was only natural that a
young man who had won his own lady would wish all
those around him equal happiness. Tobin had heard from
Camigwen that Sioned had not returned to their tent the
previous night, and wondered whimsically what kept Rohan
from calling out his delight to the whole world.

Younger sons had found brides, heiresses had found
husbands, and the parade of fathers and overlords leading young men and women to receive Andrade's blessing
went on and on. A sweet breeze from the east had blown
away the lingering smoke from the dawn fire on the
river, and the day shone with the last of late-summer
brilliance. The hilltop was the perfect setting in which to
begin a new life. Tobin smiled to herself and glanced up
at her lord, remembering their own marriage on the cliffs
near Radzyn Keep.

Andrade had ordered Camigwen and Ostvel to come
last. "Who desires to marry a Sunrunner, a *faradhi* who
rides on moonlight?" she called out, and Ostvel, with

Urival as his sponsor, walked forward across the carpet of flowers.

"I do, my Lady," the young man said proudly. "I am her Chosen and she is mine."

"Let her come to you, then." Andrade replied, smiling.

Camigwen stepped forward shyly, dark and exotic. But the dress she wore was very different from her everyday clothes; Tobin had seen to that. Her gown was the color of very old bronze, embroidered with gold flowers down the panels of the skirt. The small pouch at her waist bulged with Ostvel's wedding necklet. Sioned walked beside her, wearing a plain russet dress, her emerald ring sparkling where she had laced her fingers with her friend's. Tobin knew the murmurs through the crowd were not only for the rare public marriage of a *faradhi*, but for the rumor now current that Sioned was Rohan's Chosen wife. Stealing a glance at him where he stood with Eltanin and Antalya, Tobin was surprised to find a thin furrow of worry on his forehead. Searching Sioned's face, she understood why. Where Camigwen glowed, Sioned looked almost fragile, her flaming hair seeming to have drawn all the color from her cheeks and lips. Urival had not said much, but he had mentioned something about drugged wine. Tobin cursed the absent High Prince.

Andrade handfasted the two young people, and Sioned and Urival stepped back. The words that joined a Sunrunner and her Chosen were more elaborate than those for anyone but royalty, for there were vows other than those of marriage to consider. Tobin heard the echo of words Andrade would soon speak over Rohan and Sioned, and saw the girl's green eyes come to life even though the rest of her seemed frozen.

Ostvel drew the carnelian necklet from a pocket of his tunic and as he fumbled to fasten it around Cami's slender throat the stones gave off a sultry dark red fire. Not even Eltanin's sapphires, at which Antalya had gasped, had been as magnificent as this. Cami then stood on tiptoe and clasped a thin gold chain around Ostvel's neck. It was set with a single large piece of black coral carved in a sunburst pattern—the stone from Gilad,

Ostvel's home, and the symbol of the sun to represent her status as a *faradhi*.

"As the sun and the moons circle the world of waters," Andrade chanted, "as the waters circle the lands; as the lands circle the body of the world; so surround and sustain each other. Be as light to each other's eyes and life-giving water to each other's souls. Give of the richness of the earth, one to the other. Catch the wind within to sweep away all doubt, all pain, all fear. Be all things within your love."

She turned to Ostvel, holding up her left hand, palm out, rings sparkling in the morning sun. "In your keeping is a Sunrunner, one who calls Fire and weaves the light. Help her to keep her paths true and unshadowed, free of all hurtful things. You will be the sire of *faradh'im*. I judge you worthy, Ostvel of Gilad."

He bent his head and responded, "You honor me with your trust, Lady, as the *faradhi* does with her love."

Andrade smiled slightly, and nodded. To Camigwen she said, "You are a Sunrunner and know your work and your vows. To serve, to speak truly, to weave the light across the world in company with your brothers and sisters. To rightly use your knowledge, and never to kill. All these things are impressed on your heart. To you I give this man, to cherish with the Fire of your calling and guard with the strength of our ways. Repose in his heart, and listen to his soul." She took their clasped hands between hers. "Goddess blessing, all your lives."

They faced each other, smiling as first gazes met and then lips. Tobin sighed and sniffled a little, and felt Chay shake with silent laughter at her side. "Stop that," she whispered. "It was lovely."

"For a princess with a political head on your shoulders, you're a terrible sentimentalist."

"Oh, really? And who is it who always remembers to wear his own wedding necklet to these ceremonies?"

"Well. . . ." Caught out, he shrugged, his cheeks suddenly red beneath his tan. Tobin reached up and fingered the elegant silver chain she had given him years ago, each flat link set with a small diamond so it seemed that his strong throat was circled by stars.

"Sentimentalist," she accused fondly.

Andrade had decided that enough was enough. "Ostvel, let the girl breathe!"

The crowd dissolved into laughter. Musicians began to play as friends and families hurried forward to congratulate the newly wedded couples. Tobin and Chay found Eltanin and his bride, who seemed to be competing with each other in a blushing contest, then looked around for Rohan.

"They're all wondering why he wasn't first today with a bride of his own," Chay observed, grinning. "How did Ianthe ever get the nerve to show up?"

"I don't know and I don't care. Where *is* that miserable brother of mine? And for that matter, what happened to Sioned?"

"Andrade, too," Chay said, scanning the crowd with narrowed eyes, no longer smiling. "She has some explaining to do."

"Don't they all?"

They made their way to the outskirts of the crowd and Tobin caught sight of a blond head and a red-gold one. Sioned was moving like an old woman, Rohan supporting every faltering step. He glanced around when Tobin called his name. Fear had taken all the joy from his eyes. "It's that damned drug he gave her," he said. "I should have killed him."

Chaynal put an arm around Sioned's bent shoulders. "Rough night last night, hmm?" he asked lightly.

"You could say that. Goddess, what a headache! It comes and goes with as much warning as the fogs at Goddess Keep."

"What did he give you?" Tobin asked as they continued down the hill.

"I don't know. I felt all right, and then I felt terrible—" She managed a smile for Rohan. "And then I felt wonderful."

"I'll bet you did," Chay replied to keep the bracing banter going.

"Oh, shut up," Rohan muttered, crimson to his earlobes. But there was a smug gleam in his eyes that brought a muffled giggle to Tobin's lips.

"I can hardly wait to hear the whole story," Chay went on.

"Tobin, you didn't tell him?" Rohan asked.

"There wasn't time." She fell silent as they reached the camp, and went ahead to pull aside the flaps of Rohan's tent. The two men half-carried Sioned inside, and Walvis was there at once with pillows to put behind her head as she wilted onto Rohan's bed.

"I'll go find Lady Andrade," the squire said without being told, and vanished.

Rohan sat beside Sioned, smoothing the hair back from her forehead, holding her hand. A deadly anger competed with the aching tenderness in his eyes. Tobin exchanged a glance with Chay, and they both pulled up low stools and sat down.

"You and Roelstra aren't just on opposite sides anymore," Tobin said. "You're enemies."

"I should've killed him," Rohan said again.

"Come on, out with it," Chay said impatiently. "I want to hear it all."

Rohan was spare in the telling. Sioned said nothing, merely gazed up at him, until he reached the part about the two of them walking along the river. She smiled, saying, "I think he'll forgive you the details of what happened after that." Rohan blushed again, and Tobin grinned at her husband.

"This morning," Rohan went on, glowering at his brother-by-marriage as if daring him to tease, "we woke up and found Roelstra's barge on fire. That's the part I want to hear from Andrade. If anybody knows what happened, she will."

"Nobody told you?" Chay asked, all humor gone.

"I don't listen to rumors."

"Neither do I," Andrade said from behind them. She took a swift assessing look at Sioned, frowning. "The *dranath*?"

"If that's the name of the drug, then yes," the Sunrunner replied.

Andrade gestured peremptorily, and Chaynal brought her a chair. She sat down, folded her hands in her lap, and announced, "The royal mistress gave birth last night.

For reasons unconnected to the fact that it was another daughter, Roelstra burned Palila in her bed."

"Goddess!" Sioned breathed. "Rohan, I wish you *had* killed him!"

Andrade nodded. "So do I. What are the symptoms of this drug?"

"A grandsire dragon of a headache. It comes and goes."

"Was there any odd taste to the wine?"

"It was Giladan, but I don't know enough about the variety to say if there was anything wrong with the taste."

"Damn," Andrade muttered. "Will you be able to appear tonight?"

"Of course I will!" Sioned tried to sit up.

Rohan pushed her gently back down. "You're not well enough. Don't even think about—"

"I'll be there," she said stubbornly. "Try and stop me!"

"Sioned," he began warningly.

"Don't be a fool, Rohan!" Andrade exclaimed. "She must be there!"

Tobin judged it was time to change the subject before frayed tempers snapped. "Aunt, why wouldn't anybody let me in your tent this morning?"

The Lady looked grimly amused. "I have a guest who doesn't appreciate my hospitality. The Princess Pandsala."

Andrade showed none of her usual enjoyment for the shocked silence that followed such an incredible pronouncement. She made brief work of the story, residual horror and disgust in her eyes no matter how strictly she controlled her voice. When she had finished, she considered each of them in turn, focusing at last on her nephew. "We've badly underestimated Ianthe, it seems. I don't know what Roelstra believes, but I know Pandsala is telling the truth. The whole scheme was Ianthe's, and the implications sicken me. She sat there cool as a cloud, without a trace of guilt—and I'm sure she feels none, for she'll get at least part of what she wants."

"*Not* Rohan," Sioned stated flatly.

"She'll have other means to power, you can be sure.

We'll have to watch her carefully over these next years. It's said he's given her Feruche."

"No!" Rohan cried furiously. "Feruche is going to be mine! And I won't have that bitch within a hundred measures of my lands!"

"There's nothing you can do about it," Andrade told him roughly. "Put someone you trust completely in command of your garrison below the castle. That's your only move for the moment."

"I'll thank you not to decide the disposition of my troops for me," he snapped.

Sioned placed a gentle hand on his arm. "What about the others, my Lady? The crew and servants—and those other women and their children. Did they escape?"

"The crew, yes. The servants, mostly. As for the women and babies—I don't know. I've tried all morning to find trace of them, but. . . ." She shrugged, a casual gesture at odds with the cold fury in her eyes. "It'll be a long, hard trip back to Castle Crag for the High Prince and what remains of his suite. You'll make a tidy profit, Chay. I've heard you've upped your prices."

"That was before I'd heard all this!" Chay shot back. "He can damned well walk! What kind of man could murder a woman who'd borne his children?"

"Daughters," Tobin corrected softly. "That's the difference, Chay."

"No," Andrade told them. "Palila died because she was guilty of treason."

"So is Ianthe," Rohan pointed out. "Roelstra's arrogant, but he's not stupid. He has to know she was behind it. Pandsala's clever enough to think up the variation, but only Ianthe could conceive the original plan. The fact that Roelstra's rewarding her with Feruche confirms it, as far as I'm concerned." He held Sioned's fingers more tightly, looking down at her. "He'll want Ianthe's talents directed at us now. Especially you."

"That makes it even more important for me to appear tonight with you as we planned," she insisted. "It'll be a slap in her face and I've been looking forward to it." She gave him a tight smile. "I'm not afraid of her, Rohan. You aren't, either."

"Exactly," Tobin approved, winning a furious glance from her brother. "And aside from all that, she has to show up healthy and smiling tonight. There will be rumors all over the camps by now about—what did you call it, Aunt?"

"*Dranath*. Shut up, Rohan, they're both right."

Chay sat forward and interposed, "How can we help?"

Andrade scrutinized Sioned once more. "You look a fright. Tobin, you and Cami will have to do something about that."

"Then the first thing is for her to get some rest," Tobin decided. "Chay, Rohan—out."

"I'm not leaving her," Rohan said.

"Listen to me, beloved," Sioned murmured. "I can't rest when you're sitting here looking like an avenging dragon."

Chay took a handful of Rohan's collar and drew him to his feet. "Come on. We have to get you prettied up, too, you know. Walvis can bring your clothes and so forth to my tent. Let the girl sleep. Goddess knows you didn't let her get any rest last night!"

After a moment's sulky rebellion, Rohan allowed himself to be led away. Sioned met Tobin's gaze, whispering, "He was so happy. And now this."

"You'll be free soon enough," Andrade told her.

"And with all the time in the world to be happy," Tobin finished. "Close your eyes, Sioned. Camigwen and I will take care of everything."

At sundown Sioned was looking into the mirror at the face of a stranger. Her eyes had been outlined in dark green pencil, and a dusting of gold powder on her lids lent a hint of the usual sparkle to her eyes. Salves had been applied to her cheeks and lips to simulate healthy color. It had taken all Tobin's and Camigwen's combined skills to create the semblance of her normal face to which the makeup had then been applied. They had done her hair in a mass of thin braids that twisted around her head and looped down her neck like plaited fire. She supposed she was beautiful.

"Where did Walvis get to with the jewels?" Camigwen

fretted as Tobin lowered the gown's skirt over Sioned's hair and pulled it into place around her waist.

"You'd think my idiot brother would be dressed to his own satisfaction by now, and have the decency to remember Sioned's emeralds."

Sioned finished tying the skirt's laces and stared bemused at her image. The dress was everything she had hoped when she'd first seen the heavy silk in the merchant's booth. Was this what a princess looked like?

"Perfect," Cami announced, standing back from her.

"I think so, too," Rohan said softly.

Sioned turned. Resplendent himself in a solid black outfit like the one he'd worn at Stronghold, he had added a sleeveless black silk tunic slit in front from the waist to the knee-length hem, belted in silver. He and Sioned stared at each other until Tobin broke the spell with laughter.

"Put your eyes back in your heads!"

"Is that my Sioned under all that?" Rohan teased.

"Want proof?" She held up the hand wearing his emerald.

"Oh, something a little more substantial than that," Cami suggested, laughing.

Sioned cast her a sidelong glance, then went to Rohan and kissed his lips. The Fire blazed up between them. She didn't dare put her arms around him, knowing he held back for the same reason. They knew each other's bodies now, understood the reality of ecstasy. When she stepped away from him, they were both trembling.

"Oh, it's you, all right," he murmured, eyes dazed. Then he shook himself and reached into a pocket. "Tobin, you put these on her. I'd drop them."

Within moments Sioned saw herself alight with green fire. She could see nothing but the emeralds that pulsed with a life of their own. A black shadow crowned with golden hair moved to stand behind her, and as he placed his hands lightly on her shoulders their eyes met in the mirror.

"Only one thing missing," Tobin said, coming forward with two thin circlets of silver that twisted open at the back. She gave them both to Rohan, who blinked in surprise before he smiled and kissed her cheek.

"Two things," he corrected. "But one, in the end," he added cryptically. Sioned smiled.

"Now, don't either of you leave here until Chay and I can join you," Tobin warned. "And where is he, anyway?"

"Dressed and waiting for you," Rohan said absently, fingering the circlets. "Sioned, are you well? Truly?"

"Truly," she answered. "But let's make it an early night, shall we?" She winked at him in the mirror, and he grinned.

"Now I'm *positive* it's you!"

Careful of the elaborate braids, he placed one of the circlets across her brow. Then, with a shy smile, he handed her the second one. Sioned bit her lip; this was her vision come to life at last. She gave him the mark of royalty, pulling strands of golden hair into place so the circlet gleamed visible only across his forehead. Princess in every fact but the actual ceremony, she looked into her prince's eyes for a long, silent time without doubts or strivings, at peace.

Andrade left Urival to deal with Pandsala and the infant, secure in the knowledge that the former could not escape and the latter now had a wet nurse. Urival's dismay had been almost funny; Andrade pitied him the impossible evening, left alone with a frantic princess, a newborn, and a girl chosen not for her brains but her breasts. But there was no one else she could trust to keep Pandsala in line. The girl had twice tried to run, getting as far as the outer row of Rohan's tents before the *faradh'im* had caught up with her, the regular guards being wary of placing rough hands on a daughter of the High Prince. Urival had no such scruples. Andrade hoped he would spend the evening making a few realities clear to her. The girl was not inherently vicious, she thought—unlike Ianthe, who was so twisted it was a wonder her own guts didn't strangle her.

The lesser nobility would have their own feast, as would all the servants but Lord Jervis' own. As Andrade left her tent she sniffed appreciatively of the roasts and breads being readied for the two other banquets down near the river. But Jervis had chosen the marriage hilltop as the site of the princes' Lastday banquet, and by the time Andrade had climbed the slope she was in need of refreshment. She chose a cup of fruit juice—unfermented, for she was still fighting off the effects of a sojourn on water, and of Crigo's death. She remembered him: proud, ambitious, thrilled to be assigned an important post, a capable Sunrunner who had been perverted by Roelstra and his *dranath*.

"Greetings, my Lady," Prince Lleyn said at her shoulder, and she turned. "Will you do me the honor of sitting with me tonight, Andrade?" he went on less formally. "I've been hearing things I'd like to know the truth of, if you'd be so kind. We are, in a sense, joined in guardianship of the continent now."

"I don't envy you the task of sorting out border claims."

He gave a grimace of a smile, the lines on his face softened by mellow evening light. "I give thanks that my island *is* an island—and all mine."

"Kierst-Isel will be a problem," she agreed. "If you wish, I'll have my people go through the records at Goddess Keep and transmit anything of interest to your Sunrunner."

"My thanks. But I give Eolie enough to do, poor child, finding the best fishing waters and shell beds for me, warning of storms, and the like."

"And keeping track of what everyone else is up to," Andrade finished wryly. "I assume you're hinting for another *faradhi*. How about Meath? He's the big youngster in my party who looks as if he could throttle a plow-elk barehanded."

"I would be most grateful. Of course, he won't much like crossing water—but I'll provide him with a private cabin and his own bucket." Lleyn grinned wickedly.

"*Too* kind!" Andrade glanced around at the growing darkness. Torches, lit by Clutha's court Sunrunner, were a double row of Fire leading up to the gigantic tent at the crest of the hill. "By the looks of things, you princes are about to be trumpeted in to dinner. I'll save a chair for you."

Clutha and Jervis got more ambitious every year in the marvels that accompanied the Lastday banqueting. Andrade, as Lady of Goddess Keep, took precedence over everyone else and went inside the tent first to choose the best seat at the best table. The others would, in effect, be announced into her presence—an amusement she anticipated with more than the usual relish tonight.

A state banquet for fifty was never a simple event to arrange, especially as all of those present were accustomed to magnificence. At the *Rialla* they expected even greater splendor, which challenged the combined households of Meadowlord's prince and Waes' lord. From a simple outdoor meal to celebrate the successful conclusion of the *Rialla*, the Lastday feast had over the years become a showcase for culinary artisans and was now the full-time occupation of a suite of masters who commanded the resources of a princedom. Andrade, who had long since grown used to the display of riches, considered herself fairly inured to spectacles. But as she was bowed into the green tent, an exclamation of pure delight escaped her lips.

A dozen round tables were artfully placed around a deep green carpet so thick it felt like spring grass underfoot. At each corner of the tent waterfalls splashed down rock cairns designed not only with an eye to beauty but to cooling the diners once the torches had been lit. The perimeter was a grotto of ferns, flowers, and trees in great silver pots; greenery was strewn from the ceiling latticework and decorated with more blossoms. The whole place seemed alive.

But the real marvels were the enormous sculptures set around the tent. Each was a faithful reproduction in miniature of each prince's major seat: Rohan's Stronghold, Roelstra's Castle Crag, Vissarion's Summer River, Lleyn's Graypearl, and all the rest. Andrade was surprised and flattered to find a rendering of Goddess Keep as well. The images had been worked in spun sugar and colored with the essences of a rainbow of herbs and flowers; masters of the confectioner's art had reproduced the blue-gray waves below Andrade's keep, the fine golden sand around Stronghold, the extensive formal gardens of

Volog's New Raetia in all their brilliant colors. Clutha's
faradhi must have assisted in the making of these master-
works, for none but a Sunrunner could make such detailed observations of land and keep to be recreated thus.

Andrade chose a seat with the best view. The wives,
sons, and daughters of the princes—those who had chosen to make the sometimes dangerous journey from their
lands to Waes—filed in and exclaimed in wonder before
remembering to bow to her. Tobin and Chay came in
last, seated at this feast rather than the one for the
athr'im by virtue of her relationship to Rohan and his
importance in his own right. Andrade smiled as they
bowed to her. Any other man would have used his unique
position to establish his own princedom, but not Chay.
Rohan was luckier than he knew.

Soon places were left only for the princes themselves,
and after a pause three trumpets began a silvery fanfare.
Each prince was announced by a short blasting chord and
a bellow from Clutha's high chamberlain that the Most
Noble Prince So-and-so of Wherever graced the humble
soil of Meadowlord, all hail His Highness' Grace. A
ceremony Andrade always found pompous at best suddenly moved her, for soon she would see Rohan make
his entrance. A pity Sioned had evidently not been well
enough to come tonight; she would have enjoyed it, too.

*Whatever wind your soul rides now, Zehava, look on
your son and be proud. He's well worth the trouble he's
caused us all. And here's the dragon's son himself—oh,
Goddess! He's got Sioned with him!*

The breach of protocol might have been due to many
things. Rohan might be pretending to be so young and
inexperienced that he didn't know a prince was supposed
to enter alone; he might be so genuinely careless in his
joy that he'd simply forgotten; or he might want only to
show off his *faradhi* prize. But Andrade knew that he
was putting everyone on notice that his wife would share
his princely station and his power as well as his bed.

The high chamberlain was horrified. The trumpet chords
had faded into the stunned silence before he drew a
breath that nearly popped the laces of his tunic. "The

Most Noble Prince Rohan of the Desert, and—and his Chosen Wife, the Lady Sioned!''

Rohan's eyes snapped with glee at the shock he'd engineered. He was all in black and silver, the perfect foil for Sioned's white and emeralds. They came forward to make their bows, and Andrade held back a gasp; each wore circlets of royalty. Rohan escorted his lady to the table where his sister and her lord sat, and at last the applause began for them as for the other princes. But there was wariness in some faces, and shock in others. Andrade's gaze traveled around the tables, quelling all outward signs of rebellion. There would be no trouble, no protest at this marriage of prince and Sunrunner.

Roelstra's own entrance immediately after was a complete anticlimax. The High Prince's stony expression indicated his displeasure at being upstaged as well as outmaneuvered by the princeling. Lleyn, who had come in just before Rohan and Sioned, chuckled at Andrade's side.

"Oh, he's a crafty one, your Rohan. No shame to the boy at all. He's ruined Roelstra's digestion and the meal hasn't even started yet."

"If Zehava could see him now, he'd be laughing himself silly—or bursting with pride." Not even Tobin and Chay—in vivid red and white with rubies and diamonds that made them a matched set in dress as in all else— were so regal and elegant a couple as Rohan and Sioned. It took all her self-control not to laugh in Roelstra's face as he passed her table.

The first course was exhibited for due tribute by the amazed company before being passed around the tables. Lleyn sat back in his chair and gestured idly to the feast.

"Clutha told me this was to be a 'light repast,' '' he commented.

"I shudder to think what he considers a good, honest meal," Andrade replied. "Did you bring those monstrous lobsters with you from Dorval?"

"*My* lobsters are much nobler creatures than these puny things from Snowcoves," he retorted indignantly, while gesturing for the servant to heap more of the succulent golden shellfish onto his place. Andrade laughed.

During the first interval musicians assembled in the center of the tent to assist digestion with soothing melodies. Andrade was pleased and surprised to find Mardeem, one of her own *faradh'im*, singing to the accompaniment of strings and flutes. He honored each prince with a folk song from his lands. Andrade had heard him many times before and would listen to the wonder of his voice again, so she took the time to judge how Sioned was faring.

The girl looked magnificent, of course. But strain showed around her heavily made-up eyes, and beneath the artful pink salves her cheeks and lips were pale. Andrade prayed she would last the evening, and guessed that Rohan was thinking the same. His own looks were serene, but whenever he glanced at Sioned there was worry in his eyes and a tightness to his smile.

"An exquisite couple," Lleyn observed. "The girl outshines the stars."

Andrade sipped at a goblet of iced water and eyed him over its rim. "You're about to start your interrogation, aren't you?"

" 'Questioning' is so much more polite a word," he replied, unruffled. "They say many odd things about the fire on Roelstra's ship."

"Indeed."

"A pity he lost his fabulous mistress—and her child."

"The mistress," Andrade answered curtly, "is cinders. But the child lives."

"Ah." He did not inquire further, and she knew it was a deliberate ploy to irritate her. Tonight, however, he could not succeed. She smiled at him and took another swallow of water.

But Lleyn was older than she, just as autocratic, and interested in the politics of the continent only for its entertainment value. He waited her out. Andrade knew he was waiting her out, and finally relented, but with another smile.

"Very well. I've taken the baby—and Pandsala, too. You don't seem surprised."

"At my age, very little surprises me. Roelstra has given it out privately that his daughter wishes to become a *faradhi*, so I already knew about Pandsala, you see. I'm curious, though. *Can* she learn your ways?"

"I haven't tested her yet." Singing and applause covered their conversation nicely, not that anyone around them was interested in the dull chat of two old folks. "Sickness on water is only the most obvious sign. Not every *faradhi* experiences it."

"I thought only those who blanched at the very thought could become Sunrunners."

"I have a theory about that," she mused. "It might be a weakness that shows up so often because of inbreeding. We do tend to marry our own kind, you know."

"Has it always been that way? The sickness on water, I mean."

"For some, yes. But it seems to be getting more and more common since we left your island." Andrade chuckled as the old man's eyes widened. "Aha! I've caught you! *That's* something you didn't know, isn't it? Meddling old gossip," she accused teasingly.

"You fascinate me, my Lady," he murmured. "Please continue."

"You know the ruins on the other side of Dorval from Graypearl. A keep once stood there, even more imposing than the one I now rule. Its walls stood for a thousand years before the *faradh'im* themselves tore the castle down."

Lleyn nodded slowly. "My father and I did some poking around there when I was a lad. Wonderful old place. I still have a few coins and bits of tile I collected back then. Why did they leave?"

"They chose to go out into the world—or perhaps return to it from exile, I'm not all that sure. The records are incomplete. They'd wrapped themselves in ritual and mysticism, and then for some reason rejected that way of life."

"What about the circle of trees on the bluff near the ruins? Was that theirs as well?"

"Doubtless, although *I* didn't know about that."

Lleyn grinned. "I ought to follow up my advantage and gloat a bit that I knew something you didn't. You needn't ask—I'll have Meath and Eolie investigate. But right now I'd like to hear about your ancient *faradh'im*."

"Isolated on your island of silk and pearls and gold—who can say why they left? But there's no mention in the records of their being ill during the crossing, which leads me to believe it's a fairly recent trait. I've never discovered exactly how the gift is passed on, though. Urival and I have been trying to puzzle it out in the genealogies for years. It's not linked to either male or female. Whole generations can go by without its showing up. Sioned's family, for instance. You'll know about the connection with Syr through the father's line, but through the mother she's related to Volog of Kierst."

Lleyn sat up a little straighter. "The Sunrunner who was stolen away by Prince—what was his name?"

"Sinar. Yes—her grandmother. I've been waiting for Volog to make the connection. He'll consider it useful when dealing with Rohan."

"I don't wonder. But your Sioned—or perhaps I should say *Rohan's* Sioned—she's the first one to show the signs?"

She nodded. "But sometimes it appears in families with no history of it at all."

"You like things in a neat pattern," Lleyn observed. "Life does not often oblige."

"Life can be nudged here and there."

"As with Rohan and Sioned?"

The singing had stopped, and they were now being presented with a towering pastry, a fabulous concoction of crust and fruit and sauce shaped like a fanciful hilltop castle. Lleyn and Andrade nodded their approval and it was taken to the next table.

"What do you plan for them, Andrade?" the old prince went on. "A line of *faradhi* princes? The others aren't going to like that."

"I do as the Goddess bids me," she replied coldly.

"I have never believed in revealed truth," he commented slyly. "It takes work and experimentation and confirmation to produce knowledge. Are Rohan and Sioned your experiment, Andrade?"

"You presume too much, Lleyn."

"So do you." He poured himself more wine. "I'm too

old to be concerned for my own position. My son Chadric will come after me, and his sons after him—because you *faradh'im* left Dorval behind and will never return."

"Now *you're* the one looking for a pattern. Why do you think we won't return to the places of our past?"

"For the simple reason that it *is* the past—and because, quite frankly, I would never allow it." He regarded her thoughtfully. "That's why I like young Rohan. He wants to change things for the better, and he refuses to look back to the past. But his plans may not coincide with yours, Andrade."

"My plans aren't something I care to make common knowledge," she muttered.

"Ah, but it's the knowledge that counts, isn't it? You Sunrunners rejected the isolation of selfish knowledge and chose to live on the continent, to disperse yourselves in service to the princedoms. Knowledge is useless unless it's shared. And *that* should be the basis for desiring *faradhi* children of this marriage. The ancient Sunrunners seemed to know that one cannot stand apart from life, and became the living link between the lands. Now you would link them to royal blood. You want things dangerous to the other princes, Andrade."

She knew from long experience that she could not stare him down the way she did nearly everyone else. That made him valuable. "Has age made you a philosopher then, my lord?" she asked sharply.

"One of its few advantages." He paused. "There's another rumor I'd like clarified, if you would. It's said that Roelstra made use of one of your own. I won't ask how. But I can see that it frightens you. It means you Sunrunners are vulnerable."

"And you know all about vulnerability, sitting there on your impregnable island!"

"Peace, Andrade. I'm vulnerable, too, you know. I seek change. Old as I am, I'm yet young enough to relish upheaval when it leads to betterment. That's a dangerous thing in any person, but in a prince it's unforgivable." He smiled. "I'll support Rohan, never fear. Aside from the fact that I'm fond of him, I happen to agree with him."

"Then why are we discussing this?"

"Because of that vulnerability I spoke of before. It's an important thing, for it prevents tyranny. You and I know that you Sunrunners have your weak places. The other princes do not. Both of those things are your strength. Because you know yourselves to be vulnerable, you don't overreach—which might possibly expose your weaknesses, and shatter the power you have with the princedoms. Consider Roelstra in the present case. He did not know his plans for Rohan were vulnerable to one fire-haired girl. Thus he's attempted tyranny, and failed—and is now very dangerous. Consider also yourself. You didn't know your people were vulnerable to whatever Roelstra did to your *faradhi*—and that's failure, too."

"Are you calling me a tyrant?"

"You have the potential," he replied equably. "Let me annoy you a moment longer, and then we will do nothing but gossip about our neighbors. I describe to you a circle, Andrade. At the bottom, you Sunrunners were isolated and impotent. You are climbing the arc now until you approach the highest point of the circle. But there is another half to it—the fall from power."

"I don't want power," she protested.

"Not for yourself, perhaps. But for your kind. I'm glad you *faradh'im* are in the world, giving of your skills and knowledge. But do not attempt to *become* the world, Andrade."

"The rest of you have made a proper mess of it."

"Do you think you will do any better?"

Andrade pondered this as a section of the pastry tower was set before her, a spire with a spun-sugar flag flying from a candy pole. "I don't know," she said to Lleyn in all honesty. "But I intend to try."

Roelstra endured the feasting sustained by his hate, and spent the dinner counting up those he intended to destroy. It was an interesting list, worthy of a High Prince. Andrade was at the top, followed by that Sunrunner witch in her white-and-silver dress and emeralds who sat next to Rohan looking like a living flame. The princeling was next, and for good measure his sister and her insufferable lord as well. He would obliterate the entire family—

leaf, branch, and root. Ianthe would help him do it, for she had learned life's most important lesson: how to hate. He would teach her its real power; how it could be fostered in others; how to create suspicion and division through skillful use of half-truths and insinuations, the manner in which he had presided over the princedoms for years. She would be an apt pupil, for of all his daughters she was the most like him. But because of this, he would never fully trust her.

As soon as he could decently do so, he left Clutha's absurd silken grotto. No one would expect him to stay. There had been lifted brows at his appearance here to-night, for all knew of the "tragedy" on board his ship. On the walk back to his tent he consoled himself with the memory of Palila's screams as he set fire first to the hangings of the bed and then to her lovely hair. It had burned like fine dry grass across a prairie. Roelstra found it a great pity smoke had so quickly filled the room, forcing him to leave; he would have enjoyed watching her flesh crisp.

After dismissing his servants, he gave orders that the single male visitor who would come to his tent that night be admitted without challenge. Then he reclined in a silken chair, his head resting against a cushion. When he closed his eyes he could see Sioned. Last night she had been within his grasp. No woman had ever refused him before, and she would live to regret it—live a very long time in the most exquisite torments he could devise, after he had possessed her in all the ways imagination could suggest.

Roelstra could wait for his vengeance, however. This was the essential aspect of hate that Ianthe had yet to learn. Rohan would be expecting a move against his lands, and with every season that passed, every year without a blow struck back, the princeling's nerves would tighten another notch. Clever as he was, not even Rohan would be able to guess the direction from which Roelstra's vengeance would come.

The candles had burned low behind their colored crystal screens by the time he heard quiet footsteps outside. He lifted his head and assumed the pose of a prince

granting favors, determined that the man he had summoned would not consider himself in a position to bargain. But the expected visitor did not enter his tent.
Rohan did.

They stared at each other for some time in silence,
taking measure not as princes but as sworn enemies.
Roelstra noted that the youth had taken off his fine
clothes and jewels, and was clad in a simple dark outfit
and scuffed black boots. He did not want to remember
the strength of Rohan's grip, the lithe muscular body.
Bred to the harsh Desert, this man took wealth for granted
but would never be softened by luxury. The High Prince
realized that he no longer thought of Rohan as a boy. A
man had been created during the days of the *Rialla*—
mature, confident, and powerful.

"Tell me about the *dranath*," Rohan said at last.

"Still feeling it, is she?" Roelstra shrugged. "She'll
survive."

"Tell me."

"It's grown only in the Veresch. There's nothing to
counteract it, if that's what you're after. She'll suffer
until it's cleaned out of her blood." Roelstra smiled.
"There's more over in the desk—second drawer at the
back. I didn't give her quite enough to addict on a first
dose, but she may relish another taste."

"What does it do?"

"Haven't you been listening? It addicts, worse than
wine to a man or woman with that weakness. Because
once it has strong hold, stopping the dose kills."

"You used it on the other *faradhi* to control him."

"Of course."

Never relinquishing Roelstra's gaze, Rohan moved to
the desk, opened it, and felt around for the small packet.
He slipped it into his tunic pocket. "I'll take this."

"There's more where it came from, but only I know
where to get it and how to refine it. It was Palila's gift to
me, the knowledge of *dranath*—poor darling."

The blue eyes regarded him coldly. "Butcher."

"She deserved to die. So do you, but much more
slowly than she. Now that you have what you came for,
get out."

"I wanted this, yes," Rohan said slowly. "But I also wanted to look at you one last time."

"And which of us will die before the next *Rialla*, do you think?" Roelstra chuckled.

"I don't have to kill you. Much as you need killing, Roelstra, all I have to do is break you." The finely shaped lips curved into an unpleasant smile. "And I *will* break you."

"Try," Roelstra invited.

"My word on it." Rohan gave him a mocking little bow and disappeared.

Roelstra folded his arms and leaned back to wait. After a time he heard more footsteps that announced the arrival of his originally intended guest. He called to the guard, who entered and stood at attention.

"Bring my daughter Ianthe here at once."

"Yes, your grace."

The man who stood just inside the tent flaps was thin, intense, with a ritual scar on his chin like all his noble Merida relations. He frowned at Roelstra. "A woman? Here? What help could she be to us?"

The High Prince smiled. "Beliaev, my dear scion of a dead dynasty—you have yet to meet my daughter."

INTERLUDE

The journey back to Castle Crag was as long and difficult as any of his enemies could have wished on High Prince Roelstra. Denied Radzyn's strong, fleet horses, he had to make do with lesser animals. Without baggage carts of his own, he had to wait while Prince Clutha rounded up wains sturdy enough for the hard roads through the mountains. The delay meant that Roelstra was caught in the first torrents of autumn while negotiating a pass treacherous enough even in summer. Rain tumbled mud and rock down the cliffsides to block the trail, drench everyone, and make a journey of twelve days in good weather into one lasting over thirty. When at last the exhausted party reached Castle Crag, Roelstra locked himself in his chambers with Beliaev and Princess Ianthe in attendance, and emerged several days later in a temper only slightly less foul than the one he'd taken in with him.

The journey back to Stronghold was of an entirely different nature. Lady Andrade accompanied Rohan to a remote hilltop just inside the Desert border where, surrounded by family and friends and with the Faolain River singing below them in the sunshine, the Lady of Goddess Keep celebrated her nephew's marriage to his red-haired Sunrunner witch. Afterward she returned to the great castle on the western shore of Ossetia with her *faradh'im* while the prince and new princess made a leisurely trip back to their fortress. Rohan then locked himself in his chambers with Sioned and emerged several days later looking sunnily pleased with himself and all the world.

By the following spring, Ianthe was established in Feruche Castle. There was no proof—not that anyone expected to discover any—that she was behind the Merida attack on Tiglath that season. Young Lord Eltanin, flushed with pride in his beautiful wife and their expectations of an heir, fought off the Merida with assistance from Rohan's armies and his father-by-marriage's money. Faced with three hundred troops and the knowledge that Jervis of Waes would provide endless supplies to keep his daughter's new home safe, the Merida withdrew. They marched back to their northern wastes and seethed, making occasional forays into Rohan's territory and trusting that time, Roelstra, and Ianthe would work in their favor.

Rohan and Sioned rejoiced when Eltanin's gentle Antalya was delivered safely of a strong son. It was a year for childbearing, it seemed; only a few days after news came from Tiglath, Tobin gave birth to twin boys and at the beginning of summer Camigwen presented the astounded Ostvel with a son. But for the prince and princess, there was no similar happy event.

The next year brought rumors that Ianthe had borne one son and was carrying another. The garrison below Feruche confirmed the rumors, and the procession of handsome young noblemen through Ianthe's bed made it impossible for anyone to determine exactly who had fathered the children. Rohan made a sour comment that nothing less could be expected of Roelstra's favorite daughter. Everyone wondered if the High Prince would name one of her sons as his heir. None of the other daughters had married, nor were they likely to.

Word came often on the sunlight from Goddess Keep, where Chiana thrived and Pandsala gradually accepted her lot, though sullenly, to be sure. Andrade reported the startling fact of *faradhi* potential in the princess and theorized that Roelstra's long-dead wife Lallante had carried the talent. Roelstra's own line was as barren of the gift as he was of sons.

And then it was another *Rialla* Year, a dragon year. The princes packed up their ancient maps and treaties in preparation for showing precedent for the lands they held—or wished to hold; Clutha and Jervis rejected a score of schemes for a Lastday banquet even more spectacular than that of the previous *Rialla*; Rohan and Sioned waited for the dragons to appear in the sky and nurtured the secret hope that this time she would carry their recently conceived child to term. The Merida were quiet; nothing was heard of Ianthe at Feruche; the High Prince was silent at Castle Crag.

But with the coming of the dragons, there also came a plague. It swept across the continent, ravaging the human population, making the summer of 701 a season of death from the Long Sand to the Dark Water.

And the dragons died by the hundreds.

PART THREE

Vengeance

Chapter Nineteen

To His Highness Prince Rohan, Lord of All the Desert and Ruler of the Long Sand, loyal greetings; and to His Lady the Princess Sioned, the same.

May it please Your Highness to know that the survey and census ordered six years ago at Your Highness' accession has now been completed. Detailed statistics are appended for Your Grace's further study, but presented on these pages is a brief analysis prepared in secret by my own hand and after long discussion with Lord Farid of Skybowl.

The dragons are in danger. Normal attrition due to disease, old age, accident, and mating battle kept the population fairly constant, even considering the decimations of the Hatching Hunts. The killing of mating sires was more seriously detrimental, but the dragons managed to survive.

But then three years ago the Plague came, and the results to the dragon population have been catastrophic.

In the year 698, the year of Your Grace's accession, 309 dragons were counted in flight from their Desert caves to various wintering grounds, as reported by persons assigned to count them throughout the other princedoms. There were 6 mating sires, 80 mature females, and 220 immature dragons, including the first-flight hatchlings of that year. The summer before the Plague, 234 dragons were in flight over the Veresch. But this spring, the most reliable reports place the number of dragons at 37: 5 mating sires and 32 mature females.

The potential for disaster is obvious. Your Grace can readily deduce that neither the hunt for mating sires nor the Hatching Hunt must take place this year. The 2 or 3 sires who survive mating battle must be allowed to mate with their females, and every dragon emerging from the caves must be allowed to fly. Otherwise, Your Grace's children, may they be born strong and wise, will never know what a dragon is.

A regional analysis of the dragon population is appended. It is the only copy, the original compilation of information having been burned, with Lord Farid as witness. His Lordship and I are the only ones who share knowledge of the impending disaster.

I would add one thing further, a thought that has occurred to me but for which I have no real proof. It is only a feeling, but it is a strong one. I believe that after the Plague losses at Rivenrock Canyon three years ago, the dragons will shun that place this year and seek others without the terrible memories. Dragons avoid mountaintops where one of their number fell to his death; there are tales in the high country of such things. If they are as intelligent as I believe them to be, and as sensitive, they will also avoid the place where so many of them died of Plague. Again, it is only a feeling, but I think that very soon we shall see the truth of it.

Therefore, as they will not mate in Rivenrock this year, they will find some other place—perhaps far from Your Grace's careful guardianship. May I humbly suggest that Your Grace issue an edict banning the slaying of dragons for this year—and for all years to come. The alternative is to see dragons no more in the Desert.

Lord Farid and I respectfully submit our conclusions to Your Highness' notice, with every faith that your wisdom will find a solution and that dragons will once again fill Desert skies.

All homage and wishes for the continued health and happiness of Your Royal Highnesses.

                                        Feylin of Skybowl

Rohan leaned back in his chair and sighed deeply. His gaze strayed from the parchments on the desk to the tall, wide-open windows of his private study. Stronghold was secure and serene in the spring twilight, its stone gentled

by a rosy-gold light from the setting sun. The scents of
new flowers and fresh grass drifted up from the gardens;
he could even smell the grotto waterfall, swollen by spring
runoff from the distant hills. The annual renewal of beauty
here was justification of the peace he had worked so hard
to create, and its seduction was nearly overwhelming. In
the last six years there had been so few times when he
could truly enjoy his home.

Delivery of Feylin's troublesome message had come
with another stack of parchments, and Rohan eyed the
pile with a grimace. The *Rialla* would happen this year,
the first since his portrayal of imbecile prince—an option no longer available to him—and his vassals had presented
their requests with almost indecent haste. He could not
in good conscience "forget" about them until late summer, and he certainly could not ignore the news from
Skybowl. But Goddess, how he wanted to, just for a little
while.

A wry smile crossed his face as he reflected on the
truth that a prince with too much leisure was a prince
who was not doing his job. Even in the good years there
were a million things to be done and decided and over-
seen. And in the bad years, like the year of the Plague—

So many dead. So much lost. Crushing the Merida in
the plains outside Tiglath that first spring of his rule had
demonstrated his strength, but there had been no fighting
the silent, stealthy disease. The power of a prince with an
army at his back had been impotent against the enemy
that invaded the body and took away breath, sanity, and
life in hopeless progression.

It had come with the flight of dragons three years ago,
and at first had been blamed on the great beasts themselves. As Plague and panic spread throughout the princedoms, demands had come for Rohan to eradicate the
dragons once and for all. But then the dragons had
started dying, too.

By the time the first huge, stinking corpse had been
discovered in the sand without a battle wound on it,
Rohan had been too desperate to worry about dragon
deaths. His mother had been one of the first at Stronghold to contract the Plague, and the first to die. The

disease swelled the lungs and burned the flesh from agonized bones; fever raged unchecked no matter what cures
were tried. Violent purging, coma, and death followed.
Princess Milar's struggles had lasted for twelve horrible
days. Others had survived a little longer, but of every ten
persons at Stronghold, four fell sick—and all of these
died.

Word filtered in from other courts and holdings, communicated by *faradh'im* who often used their last strength
to weave the terrible news through the sunlight. Princes
Seldeen, Durriken, and Vissarion; Lords Daar, Kuteyn,
Dalinor, Bethoc, and Reze; wives and sons and daughters and countless retainers—all dead. Andrade herself
sent the sorrowful news that Mardeem of the pure golden
voice had succumbed at Goddess Keep along with scores
of others. No castle, manor, or cottage was immune, with
the exceptions of the isolated Merida in their wilderness
and the islands of Dorval and Kierst-Isel. Prince Lleyn
had forbidden his harbors to all ships, and Volog and
Saumer had wisely followed his example. Indeed, in the
latter case the Plague proved a perverse sort of blessing.
Deprived of outside sustenance, the two antagonists were
forced to cooperate with each other so their people did
not starve.

Then the miracle happened. In midsummer, word
flashed on the sunlight that a cure had been found. An
infusion of a little-known herb, combined with more standard remedies, reduced the fever and stopped the purging, which gave the victims a chance at life.

Rohan's fingers clenched around the arms of his chair
and he consciously relaxed them. Memory of that time
could still send fury pounding through his blood. The
herb had been *dranath*. Roelstra, controlling its source in
the Veresch, controlled its dispersal. Not openly, of course,
for that would have brought all the other princes raging
across his borders, High Prince or no High Prince. He
had doled out the precious herb through his merchants,
and made a colossal profit trading on desperation.

Rohan's gaze went to the tapestry map hanging from
gold rods on the far wall. A bitter smile lifted the corner
of his mouth. Roelstra's slowness in providing the drug

had rid the High Prince of several opponents and weakened many princedoms. The map was a chilling reminder of how many rulers had died and how vulnerable their lands now were. Rohan knew in his bones that Roelstra had purposely held back shipments of *dranath* to Gilad, which had lost its most powerful *athri* as well as its ruling prince. In the cities of Einar and Waes, the holdings of Snowcoves, Kadar Water, and Catha Heights, death had claimed lords who had not been sympathetic to the High Prince.

Weakening the structure of power had been an unexpected bonus for Roelstra; all he needed to do was delay providing *dranath* until word came that those he wanted dead *were* dead. To the obscene amounts of money in his treasury he had added opportunities for mischief in too many places. It afforded Rohan little pleasure that the scheme had not worked in the Desert—but only through the Goddess' gracious blessing.

Rohan had emptied his coffers and the drug had seeped through to Radzyn port, where Chaynal had sent out riders on his swiftest horses to distribute the life-saving *dranath*. Too late to keep death from claiming Milar, Camigwen, and Chay's son Jahni, still it had come in time to spare countless others.

And then the dragons had started dying, and there was no more money left to buy *dranath*, and who would be fool enough to want to save the dragons?

Lord Farid had sent word from Skybowl that healthy dragons had been sighted in his hills. Rohan journeyed there. Together he and Farid had come up with the idea of lacing the bittersweet plants on the cliffs with *dranath* as a preventative. It was the only hope they had. Yet there was no drug to spare, and large amounts were necessary if even these few dragons were to be saved. Rohan had faced the unsavory choice of either demanding every coin his vassals possessed or striking a bargain with Roelstra.

A soft knock at the door turned the prince's head. "Yes, come in," he called, and a moment later was looking at Walvis' disapproving face. "I know, I know," Rohan said before his former squire could speak. "I missed the noon meal and I'm about to be late for dinner, and my lady wife will have me roasted with her own Fire." He smiled and pushed himself to his feet, gathering up the loose pages of Feylin's report.

"She wouldn't waste her energy, my lord," Walvis said severely. "There's not enough flesh on you to interest even a starving dragon."

Rohan shrugged and locked the report away in a coffer. Replacing the key on a long chain around his neck, he stretched widely and went over to the windows. Walvis joined him. At the age of seventeen, Walvis' freckles now competed for notice with a proud stubble of beard. Elevated last winter from squire to knight, he had begged to be allowed to stay on at Stronghold and serve Rohan in whatever capacity the prince desired. Rohan had been more than glad to keep him. Walvis was learning the ins and outs of stewardship from Ostvel these days, and the routine duties of squire had been delegated to another boy, Sioned's nephew Tilal. Lord Davvi had been only too happy to claim blood-bond with the powerful prince his sister had so unexpectedly married, and several times his wife had attempted to invite herself to Stronghold. Sioned had resisted the invasion, knowing Lady Wisla would ask favors that Rohan, loving and honoring Sioned, would not refuse. At last she had come up with the perfect solution: she would take her youngest nephew into her household. It was part of a squire's training to be completely separated from his family until he was knighted, and Sioned was thus neatly freed from any further importunities. Her sister-by-marriage had been faint with the honor of having her son educated in a prince's suite, and stayed happily at River Run, boasting to everyone she knew.

Shouts came from the gardens below, and Rohan saw Tilal come running along a path, tripping over a cloak much too large for him. Racing after him with a wooden sword in his hand was Ostvel's boy, Riyan. Tilal went down with a realistic flutter of wings as Riyan wielded his sword against the "dragon." Both boys rolled on the grass, laughing uproariously.

Rohan smiled, but his heart was aching as he recalled

other boys, just five years old like Riyan, who'd crowed with delight while slaying another dragon. Maarken alone had gone last year to Prince Lleyn for his training as a squire, for Jahni had died of the Plague.

"Tilal's turning into a fine lad," Walvis observed. "When I think of what a beast he was when he came here—! I never would have believed that one of my lady's blood could be so awful!"

It had taken time, and the back of Walvis' hand on more than one occasion, to cure Tilal of a tendency to lord it over the other squires. By now he knew his duties and his place, and no longer traded on his relationship to Sioned. That they were close kin was obvious; they had the same green eyes and fair skin, though Tilal had his mother's dark hair. The combination was striking, and even at ten winters old he had been well on the way to an obnoxious conceit. Walvis had cured him of that, too, over the last two years.

"Getting him away from his mother was the making of him," Walvis continued. "Is it true she'll be at the *Rialla* this year?"

"To catch sight of her precious darling? I've heard it rumored."

"My lady isn't going to be happy about that."

Rohan hid sudden laughter. Much of Walvis' conversation for the last six years had revolved around Sioned, and it had never been very difficult to discern why. Rohan could appreciate the feeling. He himself had loved her from the first moment he saw her. The squire-turned-knight fondly believed his worship of her to be a secret, and Sioned was perfection in her dealings with him. She was playful at times in the manner of a woman with a younger brother, and in public treated him with grave courtesy as a full-grown man, never as a little boy. When Rohan teased her about her adoring young champion, she replied serenely that she was only making sure that the woman Walvis truly fell in love with had a wonderful husband. Had she made mock of his feelings or tried to change them, he might have come to resent women. He was entirely content to adore and serve his prince's lady. "He'll grow out of it the minute he sees some pretty girl his own age," she had told Rohan. "I must confess I'll miss my squire, but—what do you want to bet the girl will be a redhead? *And* that he'll name his first daughter after me?"

Rohan was wise enough not to take the bet.

Tilal and Riyan had picked themselves up by now, still giggling. Sensing that they were being watched, they waved up at Rohan and Walvis. Riyan, dark like his mother and with her remarkable eyes, jumped up and down and called excitedly, "Play dragons again, prince!"

"Again? I was your dragon the other day all afternoon long, and you killed me at least ten times! Even a dragon needs some rest. And you seem to have found another who's much better at it than I am."

"Prince!" the child demanded, certain of indulgence. "Come down and play dragons!"

Walvis drew breath to call down a reprimand, but Rohan placed a restraining hand on his arm. "I'd much rather play dragons than read all those reports," he murmured wistfully.

"You haven't had your dinner yet, my lord. And my lady won't thank me for letting you exhaust yourself with those two whirlwinds again."

"Walvis," he said in exasperation, "if you and my wife don't stop behaving like she-dragons with a single egg—do I *look* sickly and delicate to you? Or do you think I'm getting old? Decrepit and drooling at twenty-seven?" He snorted. Leaning out the window, he told the boys, "I have to play prince tonight. We'll save dragons for tomorrow!"

Another voice came from down below, and Rohan grinned as Ostvel hurried into the gardens. "Riyan! Tilal! You know better than to make so much noise and trouble for your prince!" He shaded his eyes against the setting sun with one hand, squinting up at the window where Rohan stood. "I'm sorry, my lord. If there aren't fifty eyes on them both, they disappear." Ostvel clamped a hand on Tilal's shoulder as the boy began edging toward the gates.

"It's all right," Rohan said, careless of paternal discipline. "It's good to see them having fun."

"Well, no more dragons today, at any rate," Ostvel ordered, and scooped his son into one arm. "Come along, Tilal. You'll want to spend some time getting the grass stains out of my cloak, I'm sure."

"But I have to serve at the high table tonight," the boy began with a hopeful glance up at Rohan.

"And so you shall," Ostvel agreed. "The cloak will be waiting for you."

Rohan turned from the windows, keeping his smile in place to hide the child-hunger that rose in him. *His* sons should be down there, laughing and growing and playing dragons. His sons. . . . His eye lit on the reports and he made a quick decision. "I'm *not* going to play prince tonight, Walvis. I want a bath, my dinner, and my wife—in that order."

The young man grinned at him. "So now my lady takes third place to being clean and fed?"

"Unless she wants a dirty, bad-tempered husband, she does!"

Walvis went downstairs with the orders, and the household system Camigwen had created went smoothly into action. By the time Rohan was soaking in a tub, a copious supper for two was being prepared for delivery to their graces' airy chambers. Like most persons for whom such establishments are formed, Rohan was unaware of its workings. He only knew that the few orders he ever had to give were carried out promptly, quietly, and with a minimum of fuss—and none of the former chamberlain's hand-wringing.

Alone in the blue-and-white tiled bathroom, Rohan's thoughts returned to his interrupted musings on the past. Acquiring the *dranath* had afforded him a sight of someone he had not thought to encounter again: Princess Ianthe. Roelstra had been unable to resist the price Rohan had offered for the drug, and a detachment of troops had been dispatched to Feruche from the Veresch. Rohan and Farid had met the group halfway between Ianthe's castle and Skybowl, and bags of gold had been exchanged for bags of *dranath*. Ianthe had watched from the saddle of a splendid white mare, lovelier than ever and unashamedly—even triumphantly—pregnant. She still had no legal husband, but Rohan suspected that the beautiful young man riding at her side was the baby's father. Certainly his charms were sufficient to send lust raging through chaster hearts than Ianthe's. Rohan said nothing to her and met her gaze only once—and what he saw in her eyes had chilled him to his marrow.

How had he paid for this treasure of *dranath* that had saved dragon lives? How had he insured their survival and distributed even more of the drug to other princedoms without asking payment? Rohan luxuriated in cool bath water and shook his head in wry amusement, remembering his stark astonishment when Farid had casually shown him the gold.

For fifteen years, the *athri* of Skybowl had been melting dragon shells collected from long-abandoned caves in the hills. He had done it in secret and under Zehava's orders, his people loyal to their last breath as they brought forth the gold that had enabled Zehava to consolidate his power in the Desert. Everyone had always marveled at Skybowl's prosperity, that rough holding without decent farmland or grazing, and Rohan had finally discovered the source of Farid's complacency during good harvests and bad. Dragon gold. Zehava had forbidden the *athri* to tell Rohan of its existence, for he had wanted his son to become strong in his own right without having the prop of unlimited wealth from the very start of his reign.

"But *why*?" Rohan fumed as Farid told him this. "I, myself, found gold dust in a dragon's cave years ago. I never had the time to pursue this discovery before now. Why keep it from me?"

Farid shrugged. "Do you remember when he tossed you into the lake when you were a little boy?"

"And now you're pulling me out—just like before!"

"I would have told you eventually, once you'd found your feet as a prince. Your father didn't want things to be easy for you."

"Easy?" Rohan echoed in amazement. "With the Merida and Roelstra and the dragons—not to mention all those damned princesses—*easy*?"

Farid had laughed, and after a moment Rohan's sense of humor triumphed over his outrage. Part of his mirth

had been caused by the wonderful joke he would play on
Roelstra, for instead of beggaring himself and his vassals
or making odious concessions to the High Prince, there
was unlimited gold to fill his coffers even after the grotesque sum paid for the *dranath*. But there had been
bitterness in his laughter as well, for Zehava, even knowing how necessary the dragons were, had gone on killing
them. Rohan surmised that his father considered his warrior's reputation to be of more importance than the survival of the dragons and that he had further assumed
Rohan would, when he became prince, devise a way to
preserve their numbers and therefore their output of
gold.

A clever and ruthless man, Zehava—but he had reck-
oned without the Plague. Rohan shook his head again
and got out of his bath. He let the air dry him and,
wrapped in a thin silk robe, went into the bedchamber.
The serenity of the rooms his mother had created for him
and Sioned soothed him as always. Nothing that had
been his parents' remained but for the huge bed in which
generations of princes had been conceived, had given
their first cries, and had breathed their last. The rich,
bright colors of Zehava's day had been replaced by deep
greens and blues that complimented Sioned's fire-gold
looks and Rohan's blondness. Tables, chairs, and wardrobes of heavy dark wood had given way to lighter, more
casually elegant furniture. He had rarely been comfortable in these rooms when his parents had inhabited them,
and had been surprised at how quickly they had become
his refuge. Here he and Sioned had loved each other
through nights without end, shared secrets and plans and
dreams for the future. And here, too, he had wept with
her over the loss of their children.

The first time had been the winter after their marriage;
the second, that next autumn. She carried each child just
long enough to thicken her waist a little. Pregnant again
the summer of the Plague, the disease had not robbed
her of the child; the *dranath* had. The heavy dosage
necessary to save her life had devastated her *faradhi*
senses and come close to addicting her to the drug. Even
in the ungifted, the required amount brought hallucina-

tions as Rohan remembered only too well from his own brief illness. He and Sioned had both survived; their child had not, and there had been no sign of another since.

Rohan sat down at a table spread with silk and silver and the Fironese crystal goblets Sioned had bought at the Fair six years ago. Ianthe had spoiled that night for them, and Rohan's brows knotted at thought of the princess. She had three fine sons by three different lovers, and had protected them and her castle against Plague by having anyone who showed signs of any illness thrown down the cliffs. Rohan could not entirely condemn her for that. He knew he would have done the same if there had been any chance of saving his mother or Camigwen or Jahni, sparing Sioned an instant's suffering, or keeping their child alive within her body. He had himself executed seven people with his own sword when they were caught hoarding *dranath* to sell at staggering prices. But the law would say he had done justice where Ianthe had done deliberate murder. Yet he could not condemn her. He understood.

A small whirlwind blew in through the outer door and forgot to close it behind him. Rohan gasped at the impact of Riyan's small body against his chest and hugged back.

"Papa says for me to say I'm sorry," the boy explained. "I'm sorry!"

"Apology accepted—if you'll let me breathe!" Rohan laughed and settled Riyan onto one knee. Camigwen's beautiful eyes looked at him from her son's impish face, and Rohan hid another ache of loss behind a smile as Ostvel appeared in the doorway. "Don't scold him. He only came to tell me he's sorry."

"And well he should be. *Now* he's interrupted your dinner!" Ostvel lifted his hands in a gesture of surrender, grinning. "Sioned says start without her."

"I already have." He held Riyan out from him. "And if it's time for my dinner, then it's certainly time for you to be in bed, young sir. Take it as a royal command from your prince."

The child sighed. "You're much more fun as my dragon," he complained.

"I've heard little boys say that before. It didn't work

then and it won't work now. Off to bed with you." He
set the boy on his feet and Riyan went to his father.
Rohan had to glance away as the small fingers disappeared into Ostvel's hand.

"My lord?"

He met his friend's gaze, wearing another careful smile.
Ostvel wasn't fooled, but only his eyes spoke of his
compassion. What he said aloud was, "Sioned also mentioned something about sneaking around in the dark."

A genuine smile curved Rohan's mouth. "Oh, did she,
now?"

"Is it another game?" Riyan asked eagerly. "Can I
play, too?"

Ostvel winked at Rohan. "When you're older! Say
good night to your prince."

"Good night," Riyan echoed dutifully. "Don't forget
about playing dragons."

"I won't forget. Sleep well."

When the door had closed behind them, he resumed
his dinner with an appetite that would have pleased Walvis,
who, along with Sioned, waged a constant battle against
Rohan's tendency to work too much and eat too little.
When the food was gone he lazed back in his chair,
wineglass in hand. Obedient to the teasing promise they'd
made, he and Sioned met every so often in the gardens
late at night. Their household grinned, pretended not to
notice, and strictly observed the rule that whenever the
prince and princess disappeared, nothing short of the
impending arrival of Roelstra's armies was to disturb
them. Such delicious foolishness was exactly what Rohan
needed tonight, and when it was dark he took a full
bottle of wine and the glasses with him from the chamber.

Barefoot, clad only in a thin silk robe, he went down
the privy stairs and made his way through the empty
gardens to the grotto. Sioned was a whispering excitement all along his body, a cool breeze through his heart
and mind. He stood before the waterfall and closed his
eyes, sensing her presence an instant before her arms slid
around his waist and her body pressed to his back. He
savored the enchantment as her lips brushed his nape.

Her first words melted the spell of contentment. "You

were shut away with those reports all afternoon. We're in trouble, aren't we?"

"It's nothing that can't wait."

She let him go and he faced her. "Tell me, Rohan."

He lifted the bottle and glasses ruefully. "And here I thought we were going to—"

"Oh, we will," she assured him, and bound the promise with a kiss. "But I haven't seen you all day. Come talk to me, beloved."

They sat together on the soft moss, her head resting on his shoulder, the wine set aside for later. In her arms he had found joy, and in her love, strength. But perhaps the gift he cherished most was the solace of her mind. Most princes merely had wives; he had found in Sioned a princess worthy of the royal circlet he had given her.

He told her about the dragons, and as he held her he felt her reactions in her body. She could keep her expression as cool and neutral as Andrade, but just as his aunt's drumming fingers could give away her mood, Rohan had only to touch Sioned's hand to sense her real feelings. She was tense now, lithe muscles tightening.

"We'll have to cancel the vassals this year," she said when he'd finished. "Then there won't be anyone to demand a Hatching Hunt."

"I was thinking the same thing. Feylin is right about the dragons not coming here to Rivenrock, so there wouldn't be any sport for them anyway. But we have to summon the vassals. This is the first *Rialla* in six years. We all need to have a good long talk, and the ones who've inherited since the Plague must pledge to us in front of the others."

"Are you going to tell them about the dragon gold? They've been wondering where the *dranath* money came from, you know. When Farid was here last year he said that his people know where the gold comes from—"

"And haven't breathed a word about it for twenty years," he reminded her.

"Of course not. But those who don't actually work the caves think it's a mine like any other, without any connection to dragons. Maybe we should tell the vassals that."

"I'm not concerned with them as much as I am with Roelstra." Mention of the High Prince brought even greater tension, and he stroked her back soothingly. "Watchers have been sent to Skybowl—merchants, travelers, and so forth. They come away none the wiser. Farid's a crafty old liar, bless him. But Roelstra's had three years to puzzle out where I got so much gold so quickly. And I don't believe that *he* believes I wanted the dragons saved only because I'm a sentimental idiot."

"He can believe what he likes! As long as no one ever finds proof, what does it matter? Your father had the right idea. Let people think your wealth comes from the spoils of war."

"Ah, but where *does* it come from? The Merida didn't have two coins to make their purses jingle when we drove them north. And we had to spend a lot to replace the animals that died of the Plague."

"We've been careful," she protested. "We're not extravagant people. We can say that regular trade has filled our coffers again."

"And that I'm a miser!" He chuckled. "No, love. Trade *isn't* regular again yet, that's the point. We haven't had time enough to get rich on that. Trade will be the focus this year, more than ever before. With so many princes and *athr'im* dead and so many youngsters in their places, power has shifted. I'm afraid it's gone in Roelstra's direction, not mine. I have to counter that, and my best weapon is dragon gold."

"Buy them?" She said as if the words had a sour taste. "How can they lean toward him when *you* were the one who gave them *dranath*?"

"I could say that they see the deaths, not the lives spared, and it would be true. I could say they suspect me of having hoarded the drug at the very beginning, and that, too, would be accurate from their point of view. But the real reason—"

"Is that Roelstra has influence with these young lordlings who understand only one kind of power. His kind. We'll have to educate them."

"We shall. But I don't plan to buy them."

"Well, you'll have to think up a reason why you won't

be out there killing a mating sire, you know. The vassals expect it."

"I know," he sighed. "People have such absurd notions about proof of a prince's virility, thanks to my father."

Her shoulders flinched and he cursed himself. "They certainly can't prove it by me," she whispered.

"Sioned—my father was forty years old before I was born. There's time."

She pulled out of his arms and faced him. "I've never carried a child very long. I haven't been pregnant since the Plague. I'm not going to give you any children, Rohan, and we both know it."

"Stop that. We're both young and strong—"

"You need an heir."

He drew in a deep breath. "If it comes to it, and it won't, then Maarken is my choice. But you shouldn't fret about it, Sioned."

"How can I not? Rohan, I've studied the law. There's nothing that says your heir must be the son of your wife—only the acknowledged son of your body."

"Sioned!" He grasped her shoulders roughly. "What are you talking about?"

"I won't give up my place as your wife and your princess, but you need an heir."

He stared at her. "So you'd send some girl to my bed and then watch her swell with my child? Could you do that, Sioned?"

"I have your heart and your mind."

"And my body. Always. Only you. Tell me you could never do that, Sioned."

"I could," she insisted, though tears sprang to her eyes.

"And after the child is born, what then? Would you send its mother away? Or keep her here and watch her take precedence over you as the mother of my son? Have you thought about this at all, you little fool? You'd make me into another Roelstra!"

"I *have* thought about it! Rohan, I can't give you—"

"There's nothing I want that you can't give me. And one day we'll give each other a son. Sioned, I wouldn't

want a child by any other woman. I couldn't look at a son
that didn't have you in his face and his eyes." He looked
into those beautiful, doubting green eyes. "But can't you
see that it doesn't matter to me? You're enough. You're
more than I ever thought I'd have. Sioned, you are my
life."

And to prove it to her the only way he knew, he
coaxed her down onto the moss and made love to her as
the waterfall sang nearby. She wept a little, bittersweet
tears tasting of her love for him and her despair that she
was unable to bear a child. Afterward he rocked her
against his chest, her hair a silken curtain over their
bodies. When she lay quiet at last, he loosened his hold
and raised himself on one elbow to look at her. Years of
living in the Desert had burnished her fair skin to light
gold and paled her hair a little, streaking it with blonde
glints to make a finer setting for those eyes. Pride, surety
of his love, and confidence in herself as a princess showed
in every line of her face, as royal now as if she'd been
born to it. Sioned had been a lovely girl, but maturity
had transformed her into the most beautiful woman he
had ever seen. He traced the elegant curve of her shoulder with one finger and smiled tenderly.

"Besides which, woman, what makes you think I'd
even be capable with someone else? I have an exclusive
taste for long-legged redheads with green eyes."

"Fool," she accused.

"I know," he agreed, pleased that she was willing to
smile again. "That first summer—do you remember? I
tried and tried to find a girl to go to bed with—stop
laughing at me!" he chided as she giggled. "You were
awful to me and you know it. Would you put me through
that kind of humiliation again?"

"I just might. You've grown entirely too arrogant, my
lord dragon prince."

"Sioned, don't you dare tickle me! Sioned!"

They ended up laughing, and Rohan was relieved that
her moodiness had vanished. He opened the wine bottle
and they drank from the Fironese goblets, listening to the
waterfall and watching the stars. Yet part of him continued to worry. A son's legitimacy was secondary to his

existence—and his fitness to rule. It was entirely possible that a prince's legitimate son would turn out a fool and his illegitimate one suited to inherit the responsibilities of a princedom. But Rohan could not imagine touching any woman other than his wife, much less begetting a bastard son.

Maarken would be his heir, if the need arose. If Chay and Tobin decided that their firstborn would be happier with only Radzyn as his share, then there were the two younger boys, Sorin and Andry. In any case, a prince of Zehava's blood would rule over the Desert when Rohan was gone.

It was not until much later, when he and Sioned had gone upstairs at last, that he realized he had tacitly admitted he might not have any sons at all.

Chapter Twenty

Princess Ianthe ripped open her father's seal and unfolded the parchment, scowling as she noted the date of the letter. She reminded herself of dear, dead Palila's warning about wrinkles and smoothed her face into more pleasant lines. But her irritation was not so easily banished; it had taken fully ten days for this letter to arrive from Castle Crag. Through winter snows, spring runoff, summer heat, autumn rain—not to mention rockslides, bandits, or plain bad luck—the couriers never moved fast enough to suit her. Andrade's interdict on Castle Crag and Feruche was a vast inconvenience. But the messages that passed between father and daughter could not have been entrusted to a Sunrunner in any case, she reminded herself, not even one seduced by *dranath* as Crigo had been.

As usual, Roelstra wasted no time on family news. Neither he nor Ianthe cared about her sisters. Besides, she had her spies in his household just as he had watchers in hers who reported anything of interest. It was part of the cynical, amusing game they played in pretending to trust one another. His opening "Dearest Daughter" was in the same vein.

Plague deaths have opened up many excellent possibilities, most notably Einar for me and Tiglath for you. Kuteyn of Einar's surviving son is now a lad of ten winters, and his widow is a simpering nonentity incapable of governing her own maids, let alone the city and its lands. Additionally, certain documents have come to light suggesting that those lands once belonged to Princemarch. Pimantal of Fessenden will be irked by this, as he has eyes

*on the same territory. Saumer of Isel will support my
claim on this, you will be happy to know, for we recently
concluded a secret agreement based on my controlling
Einar. You may so inform his agents in your court—and
in Volog's halls as well, so he may decide whether his
profit lies in supporting me or Fessenden. He grew used to
working with Saumer when the Plague forced them to it.
This may continue.*

*Insofar as Tiglath is concerned, you know of course that
Eltanin lost his fair-haired darling bride in childbed and
their first son to the Plague. The second boy thrives, but
Eltanin himself is reported much aged, the result of his
personal losses and his own slow recovery from the Plague.
Others are similarly weakened, but more of this at another
time.*

*Our Merida allies tell me they are preparing an assault
against Tiglath as soon as Rohan is at the* Rialla. *THIS
MUST NOT HAPPEN. We must adhere to our original
plan. And I warn you, dearest daughter, that self-indulgence
at this time would be fatal.*

The princess' lips curved in a sarcastic smile. The pointed
reference to her many lovers was unnecessary. She had
not been touched since the beginning of winter, and
made very sure that her household knew she slept alone.
There were visitors enough to Feruche that would attest
to her chastity during this period, persons who could
have no stake in the game she and her father would soon
play in earnest.

*Speak to your Merida cub at the earliest opportunity.
Do not let their hot blood ruin our plans for Rohan and
his Sunrunner witch. Let the Merida know in the strongest
terms that if they spoil this, they will find themselves
positively yearning for their wastelands from the smallest,
darkest cells in the lowest depths of Castle Crag.*

*Regarding your unsubtle hints about the future of your
sons—if they are like you and me, and I suspect that they
are, then telling them what they will have when they are
grown will do no good. Currently Rusalka and Kiele are
battling for position over young Lord Lyell of Waes, who*

*needs a bride. I find this as amusing as the days when you
and your sisters were at it over Rohan. Daughters vie with
each other over men—but sons fight over castles and power.
Let us see how your boys turn out before we promise them
anything.*

*In any case, Ianthe, with any luck they will be ruling the
Desert when they are grown men. They can wait, and take
what they like at that time.*

She sighed ruefully. She had anticipated this reply and
had not really expected her suggestions to find any favor
with him. It would have been useful to have in writing
gifts of land and castle for her sons, but Roelstra was
correct in many ways: they would only grow up trying to
outmaneuver each other. Ianthe intended they should
work together as much as their ambitious natures would
allow. She had no illusions about their acquisitive instincts. Ruval at four and Marron at barely three already
fought over almost everything, and year-old Segev watched
his brothers' battles with great interest.

Their fathers were highborn men of excellent lineage
and spectacular beauty. Ianthe sighed again at the thought
of them: Chelan with his smoldering eyes and perfect
body, Evais' incredible imagination in bed, Athil's erotic
games. Poor Athil. He had not been content with clothes
and jewels and fine horses as the others had been. He
had wanted marriage to the favorite daughter of the High
Prince. His sunlight fairness had reminded her of Rohan,
and it had been surprisingly difficult to order his death,
annoying as his demands had become. At least Chelan
and Evais had had the sense to leave when told. It
amused her to reflect that she would have jumped at the
chance to marry any of them while she still lived at Castle
Crag. Years of exercising absolute authority in her own
keep had taught her that marriage was not for her.

Yet memories of nights with her lovers stirred her
vitals, and she damned the scheme that dictated her
continued abstinence. Her spies at Castle Crag told her
that her father disported himself with anything in skirts
these days, but there had been no more children—not
even daughters. Ianthe chuckled, for reports also fea-

tured rumors that Roelstra was impotent. Served him right.

His letter ended with a caution that this was to be their last communication for a long time. Ianthe felt no regret. She burned the parchment and left her private chamber, glad she would not have the trouble of composing a reply. She was compelled to restrain her temper with her father, a discipline she found more and more irksome as the years went on.

Her women were hard at work in the weaving room. The great tapestry with its matching pillows and bed hangings was nearly complete, and Ianthe inspected the work with growing excitement. The tapestry depicted various stages of the dragons' mating ritual, fascinating scenes woven in brilliant, clashing colors chosen by the princess herself. One panel showed males battling in the sand, their talons picked out in crimson and orange, blood dripping from their gaping jaws and from rents in their hides. The violence continued into the next panel, where ten females heavy with eggs circled above a cliff where a male displayed himself in ritual dance, his virility almost obscene.

The third panel depicted male and female in the act, dagger-teeth bared, tongues lashing out, bodies almost visibly writhing. Golden sand spewed up around them in the hot darkness of the cave. There was a terrible fascination in the rutting that made Ianthe smile.

The last panel was near completion, about half of it still only sketched in thread and not yet filled in. It was a scene of young hatchlings battling each other, white shells contrasting with blue, dark scarlet, bronze, and coppery hides. A strong young dragon dug his talons into a dead sibling, about to devour him. But in the shadows another hatchling waited, his eyes picked out in livid red as he watched the carnage and sought his chance.

The pillows were small vignettes of mating dragons and fighting sires, hatchlings feeding off each other, flames searing into cavern shadows. They had been her rejected designs for the larger tapestry. The bed hangings showed more scenes of savage mating, and when closed around a bed the thickly stitched curtains would produce a small cave of erotic violence.

Ianthe smiled her approval of the work and left the room, thinking of the lover for whom she had planned the weavings as she went up to the battlements to enjoy the dry breeze that lifted her hair from her nape and fluttered the hem of her gown. Below her was the border where Rohan's garrison sheltered in barracks carved into the cliffs. Three times in the last years Ianthe had sent for their captain when the Merida attacked trade caravans, attacks she planned most carefully for times when she wished the prince to know she had been delivered of a son. She laughed lightly and leaned against the pink stone wall, remembering the pleasure of flaunting her sons—sons his *faradhi* bitch would never bear him. But the fourth summons had gone down to the captain only fifteen days ago, and the attack had been arranged for a different reason. When the garrison captain had arrived, Ianthe had invited him to dinner as was customary by now—and had talked of dragons. There were ancient caves in the higher mountains where the great beasts might go this year to mate. Rohan was interested in anything concerning dragons, and by now had undoubtedly been told about these caves. But even if he did not investigate on his own, Ianthe had other plans. She had learned in a hard school that one must always have other plans.

She turned as her eldest son called out imperiously, and saw the nurse bringing all three boys for an evening hour with their mother. She kissed them all and dandled the youngest on her knee, gloating. Strong, healthy boys they were, long-limbed and handsome like their fathers, clever and quick-witted like her. Ruval and Marron chattered of the day's doings, fighting as usual over who had thrown a ball farther and run faster. She had produced sons, where the Sunrunner could not even carry a child halfway to term. She knew all about Sioned's failure to produce an heir, rejoicing that the difficulty was natural and she had not been put to the trouble of arranging miscarriages for the *faradhi*.

She wondered what the Desert had done to the woman

these last six years. Scrawny and withered, Ianthe told herself scornfully, her skin lined and rough, for she was not the type to pay strict attention to her looks. Motherhood had ripened Ianthe's beauty, turned girlish slimness to lush curves of breast and hip and thigh, though she had been careful to keep her waist trim. She had been just as careful to guard her skin and hair from the ravages of hot sun and wind, and had used Palila's tricks to prevent her pregnancies from marking her flesh. She would require all her perfections for this game, and knew herself to be flawlessly beautiful.

Marron climbed up onto her lap, nearly dislodging Segev, who screamed and clung to her with one hand while battering at Marron with the other. Ianthe hugged them to her breast, cherishing her triumph in their existence. When they were grown, they would hold the Desert and rule over Princemarch besides. The path to power for a woman lay in the men she controlled, and she laughed aloud as she played with her sons. The lands and castles might become theirs, but *they* were forever *hers*.

Tobin folded her hands in her lap and looked up at her husband. The morning sunlight that shone off his dark hair showed the faintest traces of silver. He wore supple riding leathers that clung to the long muscles of his thighs, and his open-throated shirt revealed an expanse of strong chest, sun-browned from long days outside. He stood before her, boots planted firmly on the sandy beach, scowling.

"You're giving me that look again," she observed.

"You were far away from me again," he countered.

"I'm always right here, love."

"Your body, yes." He dropped down beside her and rested his elbows on his drawn-up knees, staring out at the Sunrise Water. "I can't say I understand where the rest of you goes." He shrugged. "Just so you always come back, Tobin. I keep thinking about what happened the night of Zehava's ritual. I almost lost you."

Tobin looked down at her hands. On the middle finger of the left was the first Sunrunner's ring, sent by Andrade two years ago, set with a small chunk of rough amber.

Talisman against danger, she reminded herself, and sighed. She felt the need of protection now.

She and Chaynal had gone out riding early, trying the paces of two newly broken mares along the beach below Radzyn Keep. The sea was laced with white foam as it reached greedily onto the sand. A measure to the north along the bay was their port district where ships of all sizes folded their sails to become a winter-bare forest of masts as cargoes were off-loaded. It was good to see ships in the harbor again; their presence meant trade was at last resuming its usual pattern after the desperate years of the Plague and its aftermath. Radzyn was the only safe anchorage along the Desert coast, and Chay's forebears had grown rich on trade long before they had started breeding the finest horses on the continent.

Tobin had brought an impromptu breakfast along, and after tethering the horses to a driftwood log had spread out a feast of flaky pastries stuffed with fruit and meat. But the morning had been interrupted in a fashion she had grown more or less accustomed to over the years, for a gentle whisper had touched her mind, and with it the feel of Sioned's colors. Once again she had been caught up in this strange and wondrous thing Sioned had taught her how to do. As many times as they had communicated this way, she was always enchanted by the sweet clarity of her sister-by-marriage's light. Though at times there were darker accents when Sioned was troubled or unhappy, the colors were always fresh and shone with the beauty of her spirit. Tobin treasured her touch.

Her gaze returned to Chay and another smile crossed her features. He was made of ruby and emerald and sapphire, all the deep strong hues that were the perfect foil for her own amber and amethyst and diamond. It had impressed Sioned that Tobin thought exclusively in gem colors, for the *faradh'im* of old had symbolized their patterns of light with precious stones and considered them representative of certain powers and qualities of spirit. It had pleased Tobin that Andrade's gift of a first Sunrunner's ring had been set with amber. And the thought of protection against danger returned her thoughts to where they had begun.

"Rohan's going dragon-hunting up around Skybowl, perhaps even as far north as Feruche," she said.

Chay stared at her. "You're joking! I've *told* that idiot he shouldn't ride within fifty measures of Feruche!"

"When have any of us ever been able to tell him anything?" she asked rhetorically. Digging her fingers into the warm sand, she felt the gritty coolness beneath, the pressure that trapped her hands. "Sioned doesn't seem worried about it."

"But there's something else, isn't there? And it's not hard to guess what." Chay shook his head. "She's bound to have heard the rumors. There are several vassals who want Rohan to put her aside for another wife, or at least take a mistress who'll give him an heir."

"And she's just fool enough to listen. Chay, she'd never give him up—and he'd never let her go."

"Sweet wife, everybody knows that. But you know who the heir presumptive is, don't you? And that means I can't say a word. If I defend Sioned, they'll think I want Maarken to be the next prince. And I'm damned if I'll *encourage* the idea of a new wife or a mistress!"

"There has to be something we can do. I'm not sure Maarken would want the burden of a princedom. He's been so fragile since Jahni died." She could still see him wandering around Radzyn, searching for his brother, or waking up in the middle of the night crying out for him.

Chay drew patterns in the sand with one finger. "He doesn't need the Desert crown hanging over his head. In many ways he's like me, Tobin. We're good at things on a Radzyn scale, but we'd be hopeless at running a whole princedom."

"I don't agree with you, but I understand what you're trying to say. You'd both be unhappy living anywhere but here by the sea. It's taken Maarken quite a while to adjust to Lleyn's court, much as he's fond of the old prince. Meath has told me on the sunlight that he did better once they gave him a room overlooking the bay."

"Where else could we have sent him? There's no safer place. Whether we like it or not, he's Rohan's heir."

"No one would dare attempt Maarken's life!"

"Not while he's in Lleyn's care, no. But where do you

think Roelstra would stop? And, failing him, the Merida? They don't have any tender feelings toward me, you know. Graypearl is the only place for Maarken until he's old enough to defend himself." He smiled slightly. "Even if he does get sick crossing water. Should we have expected that?"

"Andrade seemed to. And he's working with Meath and Eolie." Her hands clenched around the sand. "Damn Roelstra!"

"And Rohan wants to get within spitting distance of Ianthe." Chay shook his head. "My love, have I ever told you that your brother is a fool?"

"I've known him longer than you have. He's fool enough to go for the throat of anyone who suggests anything about Sioned. Are you sure there's nothing we can do or say to keep the vassals quiet? They're bound to mention it."

"They can try," he answered grimly. "We'll just have to trust what little sense Rohan has to keep Sioned from acting on any insane ideas." He squinted into the morning sunlight and got to his feet. "Sails coming in, and a turquoise banner. The Syrene ship finally made it."

"From Prince Jastri? What does he want? And why come in a ship?"

"He wants horses. What else? And the ship means he wants them fast. I'm only a minor *athri*, love. I trade in what I understand, and leave the fancy politics to others." He helped her to her feet. "I'll send Jastri's emissary around to you after we've finished haggling over horseflesh. You hear things in people's words that I never do."

"Minor *athri*," she scoffed. "Warlord bred of ten generations of pirates—and legalized thief into the bargain."

"Makes me the perfect mate for dragon's spawn like you, doesn't it?"

Sioned stood at her windows, watching the sand and sky. She had never seen so many colors as there were here in the Desert. She had not expected this bounty when she married Rohan, had not dreamed that her *faradhi* senses would find shades of light here that she had never seen anywhere else.

Her childhood home of River Run had been painted in blue and green, lush with flowers and the brilliant plumage of birds. Goddess Keep's sunsets were the amazement of all who saw them. She had traveled through sunny farmland and shadowed forest, absorbing the colors of abundant life. But after six years of watching the seasons change, she was still caught by the colors unique to this harsh land. Each sunrise over the Long Sand brought subtle variations on blue and red and yellow; clouds sometimes streaked the dawn sky like wind-blown wheat sheaves tinted a thousand different colors. The blazing noon sun showed her frail silvers and palest golds across the sands, ruddy darknesses stealing along the rocks, and white so pure it hurt her eyes. Evening, especially in spring and autumn, created a rosy glow and strange greenish shadows that faded to purple along the dunes and wrapped Stronghold in mysterious warmth as night fell. And the stars—she had always thought them mere pinpricks of shining in the sky, but in the Desert she felt their colors, scarlets and blues and fiery oranges that sparked her senses. Most of all she loved the colors she sensed in the stars.

Most would say the Desert was lifeless. Except for small, isolated places, there were no trees, no grass, no flowers; no creatures singing to each other in the wastes; no rivers glinting with fish; no crops, no fruit ripening amid broad leaves. It was unlike any place Sioned had ever lived, yet she knew there was life here. She could touch it with her *faradhi* senses. The life of the Desert was in its millions of colors.

She turned as someone entered the antechamber, and smiled to see the vivid colors worn by her nephew Tilal. She went to him and set a cloth cap on his dark curls. "There—that finishes your outfit. Come look in the mirror."

He did, eyes widening. "Oh! You put in River Run's colors with my lord's!"

"One day your knight's tunic will be in the same

combination—Rohan's blue and silver, your own black and green. If it's all right with your father, that is."

"Mama will be thrilled," Tilal answered with a mischievous grin.

Sioned tried unsuccessfully to restrain a smile. To cover the lack of respect due her sister-by-marriage, she returned to the windows and gazed down into the courtyard. The horses were saddled and ready. Soldiers filled their waterskins at the well, and Ostvel strode among them checking off things on his list. The sight of him reminded Sioned of something else, and she beckoned the boy over.

"Did Ostvel give you the purse your mother sent? You'll find plenty of things to spend your money on, but remember to save some for the *Rialla*."

"I only took half, but I hope it's enough to buy new strings for Ostvel's lute."

Sioned's brows arched in surprise. Ostvel had not touched the lute in a long time—and not because the strings were old, she told herself sorrowfully. It was impossible to persuade him to make music when Camigwen was no longer here to listen.

"I made him promise to teach Riyan," Tilal finished smugly.

"That was very clever of you! I wish I'd thought of it myself." She took a few coins from a bowl atop a large chest and tossed them one by one at the boy, who laughed as he caught them. "Use these to buy the strings, and spend your own money on yourself."

"Thank you, my lady! Now I know I can afford the other things I want!"

"Such as?"

"They're a secret."

"Even from me?" she coaxed.

He hesitated. "Well . . . yes. Is that all right?"

"Of course. But do find something *you* want, Tilal. Riyan has quite enough toys." She laughed as the squire's green eyes went wide with amazement that she had guessed correctly. It had not been so difficult; the self-centered child who had arrived at Stronghold had undergone a great many changes, all of them for the better. "Your

mother sent that money so you could have a few luxuries
for yourself," she reminded him. "And there's nothing
wrong with buying yourself a present now and then."

"Thank you, Aunt Sioned," he said as he pocketed the
coins. Walvis bellowed his name from the courtyard below and he leaned out the window to yell down, "I'm
coming!" Then he went back to the mirror to inspect
himself once more.

"You look very grand," Sioned teased. "And in a few
more years you'll be spending all your money to impress
the ladies." She adjusted the fall of his light cloak. "You
won't let my lord ride too far or fast in this heat, will
you? And make sure he eats a good dinner, whether in
the halls or up in his own rooms. You know how he is."

"Yes," Rohan said from the doorway. "We all know
how he is. Tilal will make sure I come back pampered
and fat, without so much as a broken fingernail. Woman,
you worry too much." He tugged the cap playfully down
around Tilal's ears. "Let that be a lesson to you. Choose
a wife who's convinced you're older than ten winters and
can take care of yourself."

The boy resettled his cap and grinned up at Rohan.
"I've never seen you lesson *her* on the matter, my lord!"

Rohan snorted. "Run downstairs and tell Ostvel I'll be
along soon."

Tilal bowed formally to them both and left the room,
remembering to close both inner and outer doors behind
him. Alone with her husband, Sioned suddenly found she
had nothing to say, could not even look into his eyes.
Her gaze traced the silver embroidery on his gold silk
outer robe, thinking he would glisten in the sunlight from
the top of his blond head to the toes of his polished
boots. Beneath the sleeveless knee-length robe he wore
blue trousers and a white shirt, with a topaz set in silver
resting below the hollow of his throat.

"I know you want to come with me," he said quietly.
"But if the rumors are true and the Merida are readying
another attack against Tiglath, I want you safe in the
south."

She nodded. The progress had been her idea, after all.
Visiting each keep would spare them the bother of a

vassals' meeting at Stronghold before the *Rialla*. Sioned would go to the southern holdings while Rohan toured the north. The tactic was satisfactory on many counts. Each *athri* would be honored by the presence of one of his rulers, which would emphasize his personal relationship with them and underline Sioned's status as a working princess—as well as prevent the vassals from coming together to indulge in their usual squabbles. Besides all that, Rohan and Sioned would be able to see for themselves the state of each holding, and not be dependent on other sources of information regarding crops and herds. The convocation of vassals would be held *after* their return from Waes this year, when Rohan would present them with the terms he had won from the other princes on their behalf.

"I'll miss you," he said, stroking her braid with one finger.

"You'll have a care to yourself won't you?" she asked wistfully.

"Walvis and Tilal will see it to. I'm sure you gave each of them a list a measure long." He took her face between his hands. "Smile for me, beloved. When you don't smile, the whole world is dark."

She rubbed her cheek to his palm and closed her eyes.

"Sometimes I wish I was a Sunrunner, too, or had inherited at least a little of what Tobin did. Then I could talk to you when we're apart." He embraced her, rocking gently back and forth. "You take care as well, my lady."

"Ostvel says if you give him one more lecture on the subject he'll tear his hair out."

"I haven't been *that* bad, have I?"

"Worse." She drew away and smiled. "Remember to give Eltanin's little boy the present I sent along. Walvis has it, and gifts for the others as well."

"Hadaan will be furious that I didn't bring you along to Remagev so he can flirt with you."

"Your kinsman is a sweet old devil who flirts better with his one eye than most men do with both! Give him this for me." She kissed Rohan's lips soundly.

When she drew back he said, "I'll *tell* him about it. Most of it."

"Well, *don't* tell him about this one."

When she finally let him up for air, Rohan reflected dazedly that it would be nothing less than kindness to omit a description; Hadaan was an old man. Rohan was a young one and wasn't sure *he'd* survive.

He kept and arm around her waist as they walked through to the hall. "Come downstairs with me?"

"Certainly not. There'll be a stormcloud of dust and I'll be coughing for days. I'm going to be a properly forlorn wife and stand on the battlements waving my scarf."

Rohan made a face at her. "And people call *me* a fool!" He paused at the top of the stairs. "One of Andrade's itinerant *faradhi* is supposed to be at Tiglath soon. If there's any news, send to me there."

"I will." Sioned smoothed back his hair and smiled. "Goddess watch over you and bring you home safe, love."

After kissing both her palms in homage, he hurried down to the courtyard. A short while later he was at the head of the seventeen riders wending their way through the tunnel into the Desert. Tilal was just behind him, Rohan's standard proudly secured in his right stirrup. Walvis came next as knight-commander of the squadron. Emerging from the tunnel into glaring daylight, Rohan waited until he was sure he could see the keep, then turned in his saddle. He nearly burst out laughing, for there was the promised slender figure—waving a piece of silk the size of a battle flag. He called a halt and Walvis, understanding his wink, had the riders wheel smartly about to salute their princess.

Rohan saw the smiles on even the craggiest warrior faces. His people loved Sioned nearly as much as he did. They were proud of her beauty and her status as a Sunrunner; they approved of her care of him and his obvious happiness with her; and they loved her for herself. She tended their wounds and sicknesses, helped their wives in childbed, and had established a school for their children. From her household monies she dowered their marriageable daughters and sons. That she was utterly useless when it came to the everyday running of the keep was a matter for affectionate laughter, a foible that endeared her to them. Rohan knew that if he was ever so far out of his senses that he attempted to take a mistress, his own retainers would make sure he returned to his right mind in a hurry.

But sooner or later his vassals would start hinting about his childless state. He was fertile; it was Sioned's inability to carry a child that was the problem. The *athr'im* honored and respected her; half the letters from Stronghold bore her signature alone, and by now her authority was firmly established. She had studied Desert laws and customs thoroughly; her decisions were wise and fair when she sat in justice alone during Rohan's absences from Stronghold. But the vassals would want the assurance that only a male heir could give. Rohan shrugged in sudden annoyance that verged on anger. It was as if they considered a woman to be worth no more than the sons she produced, no matter what else she accomplished and how much she gave.

But at least he would not have to deal with any of that for some days yet. His first destination was Remagev Keep, the last of a series of castles that had once reached across the Long Sand all the way to the sea. Through the years the fortresses had been abandoned one by one as the land became impossible to live on, even for the hardiest sheep and goats. Remagev was the only one not in ruins, and from it Rohan's great-grandsire had begun his reconquest of the Desert and driven the Merida north. His distant cousin Lord Hadaan now held the keep. Childless, the last of his branch of the royal line, he had asked Rohan some time ago to find a worthy *athri* for Remagev—and part of the reason Ostvel had yielded his usual position to Walvis on this journey was that Rohan intended Hadaan to notice the young man.

After Remagev they would visit Skybowl, then several small manor holdings nestled in the hills, and then Tiglath. Rumor had the Merida poised in the rocky plains for yet another attack. Rohan wondered sourly if they would ever learn. Sioned had discovered a spy this past winter at Stronghold, a wayfarer craving a few nights' shelter, who had been caught trying to break into Rohan's private study. She had been all for sending the man back to his people in a large number of small boxes. Gentle as his lady could be, she had a streak of ruthlessness when it came to protecting what was hers—especially Rohan himself. He had ordered that the spy be given a horse but no water, and set him free in the Desert with a few trenchant words of warning for his Merida masters.

But they would never give up. Rohan knew that only too well, and it saddened him. War was such a waste of lives and substance and time. Yet he had no choice. The Merida had sworn to take Stronghold and butcher every member of Rohan's family. So he must keep fighting, keep pushing them back, keep them penned up where they could work no serious mischief. He cursed the lack of alternatives, but it seemed he would have to live by the sword for some years yet so that his sons could live in peace.

Sons. The forbidden subject again. He called Walvis forward, brows arching as the young man made him a formal bow from his saddle.

"I'm practicing my manners." Walvis explained. "Lord Hadaan is a real stickler for proper etiquette."

"When it amuses him—or when he's got his second eye in! Father used to tell me Hadaan kept the eye he'd lost to a dragon in his pocket and sometimes changed it with the real one when he wanted to scare people. I used to stare at him until my head ached, trying to figure out which was the real one! But I'd like you to keep *both* your eyes open, Walvis, and take a good look at Remagev for me. I'm considering some changes there. It could turn into a real asset if we put some effort into it. Hadaan is more warrior than *athri*, and the last time we visited the place was a mess. I'd hate to have to abandon it."

"I'm no expert yet, though Ostvel's been teaching me. But I'll survey the place as best I can, my lord, and tell you what I think."

Rohan turned the conversation to other things, satisfied with his ploy. Walvis would come away from Remagev excited about plans for renovating it and remain unaware of who might be in charge of the work until Hadaan made his decision. If all was agreed, then Sioned could start looking for a bride for the boy—*a redhead?* came the whimsical thought. Rohan would elevate Walvis to *athri* of Remagev Keep, Hadaan could live out his remaining years untroubled by duties he had never liked anyway while giving Walvis the benefit of his experiences in the Desert—and Rohan would end up with a revitalized keep, a loyal vassal, and the satisfaction of having rewarded the landless youth for his many years of service.

Yes, he reflected with a smile, sometimes being a prince was an excellent thing indeed.

With Rohan gone, attention turned to preparations for Sioned's departure for the south. She and Ostvel would head straight for Radzyn and spend several days there before following the line of holdings along the coast to the Faolain. Sioned's brother, Lord Davvi, would cross the river and meet her for a private visit at Rohan's suggestion for the twin purposes of family duty and political soundings. Prince Jastri, kin to the *athr'im* of River Run, had succeeded to his father Haldor's princedom, and Rohan had a few ideas about expanding the small port at the river's mouth in a joint venture that could prove profitable. From there, Sioned would travel northward and visit the rich lands bordering Syr and Meadowlord, whence most of the Desert's substance in foodstuffs came, and wait there for Rohan before they journeyed together to Waes.

She looked forward to the progress. Although she wished Rohan could be with her, she was eager to confirm her standing with those she now thought of as her vassals as well as her husband's. She sat up late at night to review everything about each lord and holding, choosing gifts for wives and children, discussing possibilities with Ostvel. But toward midnight on the day before she was due to leave, the moonlight called her outside to the gardens.

She stood before Princess Milar's fountain, watching the water turn to a shower of silver light. There was no breeze; drops fell in a perfect rippling circle out to the blue and white tiles that had been brought all the way from Kierst. Sioned sat on the edge of the pool and dipped her fingers into the water, her rings glittering.

What had *she* brought to Stronghold? she wondered. Milar had made the rough keep into a miracle of comfort and beauty. Her touch was everywhere. What would Sioned leave behind?

She knew her own worth both in private and in politics; six years as wife and princess had challenged her and not found her lacking. Except for a child. But if a wife was expected to give her husband sons, even more were they expected of a princess.

Tobin had sons. One of them would continue Zehava's line if Sioned could not. Ianthe had sons, she reminded herself bitterly—three of them, where her own father had produced none. It seemed Sioned had something in common with Roelstra after all. But Rohan would never be like him, would never seek sons in other women's bodies. She shook her head, knowing that she should have consulted the Mothertree back at Goddess Keep before she had left. But if she had, and had been shown herself with empty arms, she would never have come to the Desert. The girl she had been would not have known that a princess was worth more than her production of male heirs.

But whatever else she was to Rohan, she knew she would not be the mother of his children. She splayed her fingers in the water and counted off her rings—this for calling Fire, that for conjuring with moonlight, another declaring her to be a Master Sunrunner. She would give them all for a son—all except the great emerald on her left hand. The stone was a symbol of hope and renewal, the springtime jewel of fertility. Her lips curved thinly. How the gem mocked her.

And how its green fire suddenly blazed, catching her with a lash of color. The fountain of water drops became a fountain of fiery sparks falling in a perfect circle just beyond her fingertips. And within that green-gold-silver light she saw herself, and a child in her arms.

The newborn boy cuddled naked against her naked breasts, Rohan's golden hair a silken cap framing his small face in light. The Fire put greenish shadows into his blue eyes as he reached a tiny fist for her unbound hair. Sioned saw herself hold the baby closer, guide him to her breast to suckle. She caught her breath in wonder. A child, a son—but then she saw her own face lift, and recoiled from the sight of the fierce, angry green eyes. There were welts across her brow and one bared shoulder, burned into her skin by her own Fire.

The vision faded, and the fountain was only water again. The spray struck her face with a sudden wind through the garden. She shivered, drew her hands from the water and dried them absently on her skirt. Closing her eyes, she rewove the water circle and its vision in her mind. A son, held jealously to her breast; Sunrunner's Fire scarring her face and her body. A sudden trembling shook her, but whether of joy or fear she did not want to know.

Chapter Twenty-one

Five days later, riding up the steep path to Skybowl, Rohan still chuckled over Lord Hadaan's send-off. "Make sure that boy retains full use of his limbs and wits," the old man had ordered gruffly. "He'll need them if he's to make something out of this old wreck." Nothing else had been said of the matter, but a slap on the shoulder and the growled caution indicated Hadaan's approval of Rohan's choice for the next *athri* of Remagev. It was most gratifying, even if his shoulder had twinged all day afterward with the enthusiasm of his kinsman's farewell salute.

As the riders reached the lip of the ancient crater, Rohan drew rein to appreciate the vast blue lake. Skybowl Keep crouched on the shore like a bad-tempered gray dragon, wings folded at odd angles and claws dug deep into the stony soil. A road wide enough for three horses circled the lake, and a narrower path wound upward on the far side to disappear over the cliff. This led to the dragon caves.

"It's beautiful!" Tilal said at Rohan's side. "All that water!"

"You're starting to sound Desert-bred. Perhaps while we're here the dragons will come for a drink."

"Do you think so, my lord? I've never seen one up close, only flying over River Run. Are they really as big as people say?"

"Bigger." Rohan's attention was caught by a small group of riders leaving the keep, and he squinted into the afternoon sunlight. Lord Farid was easily distinguished by his loose white robes and heavy beard, but the other four were unknown to Rohan. He touched his heels to Pashta's ribs and rode forward.

386

"My lord prince!" Farid hailed him. "If it's dragons you're seeking, we've just had word they're on the high cliffs!"

"Then let's go watch!" He beckoned Walvis forward and said, "Take the others in and see to the horses. Tilal, how would you like to come with me?"

"May I, my lord?" The boy bounced in his saddle and his horse gave an irritated snort. "I won't get in the way, I promise." This with a sidelong glance at Walvis, who smiled and held out a hand to take the prince's standard.

Rohan and Farid exchanged news as they headed for the cliff path. After a time the old man called one of his escort forward for an introduction that made Rohan forget his manners and simply stare as Feylin of Skybowl was presented to him. It seemed that his counter of dragons was a woman—and a young and pretty one at that.

She acknowledged his surprise with a wry smile that lit up her deeply tanned face. "It's an honor to meet you at last, my lord," she said. "And to be chasing dragons with you!"

"The honor is mine," he said, recovering himself. "Forgive me for staring, but you're very young to know so much and be so good at what you do for me."

"Nineteen last autumn," she replied cheerfully. "Full young, I'll admit, but sharp-eyed and able to count—and to make sense of what I've counted."

"So I've discovered." He smiled, liking her easy manners. "Have you always watched dragons?"

"Ever since I was a little girl. Where we lived up by the Cunaxan border, the grounds were so near that we felt the wind of their wings and made knives of their teeth." She pulled a dagger from her belt and passed it to him, haft-first.

The knife was suitable for stabbing, not slicing, but the point was needle fine and would go through a man's belly all the way to his backbone. "Did you have to argue much with the dragon who used to own this?" Rohan asked as he handed it back.

Feylin laughed and thrust the dagger back into its sheath. "Not me, my lord! I never went near their homes until they'd flown back south. Get near those rows of teeth, most of them twice the size of this one? Not me!"

They reached the narrow path that led up the side of the crater, and it became necessary to ride single file. Rohan found it frustrating not to continue his talk with this gray-eyed girl who counted his dragons and probably knew as much about them as he did. But he promised himself a good long discussion with Feylin in private once they returned to the keep.

It was slow going along the ledge, and as Rohan guided Pashta close behind Farid's dappled gray, he imagined what it must be like to traverse this path with heavy dragon gold off-balancing rider and horse. A better road would have alerted outsiders to strange happenings at Skybowl, though. From the cliffs they rode down a slippery trail into a canyon where the wind had carved sculptures both beautiful and grotesque. Lumpish castles boasted graceful spires; hideous creatures sprouted multiple limbs; huge rocks seemed balanced on fragile spikes no wider than a swordblade. The rock shaded from garnet to amber to onyx, colors slicing through each other at strange, dizzying angles. The Court of the Storm God it was called, and Rohan's active imagination created a variety of impossible monsters lurking among the shadows. He had seen the canyon in most of its moods, from blazing morning to weird sunset to skin-chilling moonlight, when the shadows blurred and sometimes tripled depending on the position of the moons in the sky.

A full five measures of precipitous trail wound through the Court, and the riders maintained a respectful silence. Then Farid led them in the opposite direction from the caves, explaining to Rohan over his shoulder that the valley nearby was the perfect place for the dragons to perform their dances, and beyond this were more cliffs where even now the bittersweet plants were being devoured. Rohan knew the trail well; the crop of bittersweet was the one he and Farid had laced with *dranath*.

He glanced around at Tilal, whose eyes were circles of astonished curiosity. A pity he was the younger son and would not inherit River Run; the education and experience he was gaining in the Desert would have made him a fine *athri*. Perhaps when he reached Walvis' age and was knighted, Rohan could find a place for him that would utilize the talents being nurtured now.

After a steep climb out of the Court they halted on a crest to look out over a sandy valley. She-dragons rested in the sun, wallowing in warmth. Pale bronze and dark scarlet and deep silver-gray hides soaked up afternoon sun; here and there a wing slowly unfolded to gather up as much heat as possible, and great heads turned with snapping jaws when a neighbor crowded too close. They were huge, deadly, the most beautiful things Rohan had ever seen—but so few. He counted rapidly, and found that of the thirty-two females Feylin had reported, only nineteen lounged here on the sand. Gesturing her to his side, he asked, "Where are the others?"

She shrugged, tossing her untidy dark red braid back over her shoulder. "I don't know, my lord. They may have flown off looking for caves. They won't go near the ones at Skybowl. Lord Farid ordered them cleared out twenty days ago, hoping the dragons would use them this year, but I'm sure they sense that people have been there. Dragons are more intelligent than anybody thinks."

Farid guided his horse over and said, "I'm worried about the sires, too. Perhaps they're with their other ladies, but where?"

"The North Vere is too cold," Feylin mused. "The eggs would take too long to hatch. Down south it's hot enough, but except for Rivenrock most of the caves have collapsed. I made a survey last year, my lord," she explained as Rohan questioned her with a lifted brow. "The only suitable caves are here and at a place just this side of Feruche Castle. Hot enough, big enough, sturdy enough, and with bittersweet growing nearby to get those old sires ready." she grinned. "That's what the plant's for, you know."

Rohan choked on sudden laughter. "Is it really? I'll have to wrap some up and make a present of it to Roelstra."

Farid, straight-faced but with a gleeful, malicious sparkle in his eyes, said, "It's rumored that the production of daughters is down because certain things have trouble coming up."

Tilal, whose gaze had never left the dragons, called out softly, "My lord! I think they've seen us!"

Rohan's attention turned to the valley, where several females had raised their heads to stare up at the ridge. "We'd best be off, then. I wouldn't want to disturb these ladies from their naps. But I'd like a look at the sires. Farid, do you think they might be up on the cliffs? It won't be dark for some time yet."

Once out of sight of the she-dragons, they were able to pick up the pace without fear of attracting unwanted attention. The going was easier, too, as they followed an ancient riverbed down from the hillcrest and then went up another slope. They heard the dragons long before they reached the summit that overlooked a boulder-strewn gorge. On the far cliffs three massive sires were busy tearing up bittersweet by the roots. Occasionally one would roar at the others, and the echoes set off clattering rockslides.

Tilal's jaw had descended to his chest. "My lord, is it true you killed one of *those*?" he whispered.

"Yes," Rohan answered curtly, not wanting to remember. "Let's go closer, Farid." Slanting an amused glance at Feylin, he added, "I'll hold you excused from joining us."

"Thank you, my lord," she said fervently, wide and wary eyes on the three sires.

Scrub grew along the summit, dry bushes barely green in which a few birds perched on their way elsewhere. The shadows were deepening as the sun slowly fell, but Rohan had no thought for the time. He wanted to see those dragons up close—strong, healthy, proud creatures, not corpses rotting in the sand.

"Up there, my lord!" Tilal gasped, pointing to the sky.

A dozen more dragons sailed through the air on powerful wings, the missing females in northward flight. They paid no attention to the sires who screamed to attract them. Coppery and black and green-brown, the she-dragons flew in their arrogant strength, and Rohan suddenly laughed aloud with the joy of their freedom. He gave in to impulse and pressed his stallion into a gallop. Farid called out a caution that he ignored. He urged Pashta to greater speed along the hills and they soared over the rocky ground, his golden robe billowing out behind him like wings. He, too, was a dragon in free flight.

The way descended for half a measure, than banked steeply up. He could see the dragons above him and knew they would soon outdistance him and disappear into the mountains around Feruche—and damn Ianthe, who would probably send out her latest lover to slaughter a dragon for her whims. The wind swirled around him, blew Pashta's mane back into his eyes, whipped at his face and half-bared chest. Leaping a huge boulder, for just an instant he felt the surge of muscle and wing that would take him skyward along with the dragons—

A searing pain struck his right shoulder and he thought a rock had flown up from the stallion's hooves. But something dragged at the wound. He groped around with his left hand, drawing rein with the right that was beginning to go slightly numb, and his fingers snagged at the hilt of a knife.

A stand of thin, dry shrubs was ahead of him, and from it ran six men on foot, some with bows, others with swords. Pashta skidded on the loose stones, shrieking a battle challenge as his blood and training dictated, and reared up with hooves lashing out. Rohan hung on, grasping his sword with his left hand and one of his boot-knives with his right. The men came for him, one of them grabbing the stallion's bridle as he came down; a powerful yank jerked the horse's head around and the man lost a chunk of sleeve and flesh for his pains. But balance was lost. Even as Rohan hacked through upraised arms and stabbed into chests, Pashta foundered and Rohan toppled to the ground.

His vision exploded in black rainbows as a hand pulled at the knife in his shoulder, tearing down through muscle. His sword was wrested from his grip. He tried to roll away, but the man still had a grip on the blade and twisted it once again. Instinct alone drove his elbow back into the man's belly. Momentarily freed, he wrenched the knife from his flesh. The pain sent him reeling.

He heard Farid's shout of his name, Tilal's frantic call. He spun, crying out an order for them to leave him. He

could see nothing, feel nothing but the incredible fire in
his shoulder and a new stabbing pain along his thigh. He
fumbled at it, and the pain of removing the arrow somehow cleared his vision. A half-sensed movement made
him turn and thrust with the knife that still had his blood
on it. But his eyes betrayed him then, gaze flickering
down at the arrow's fletching, expecting to confirm suspicion by the sight of Merida colors. The glance was an
unforgivable mistake, for it left him open to the blow
that felled him. As he crumpled into the dirt, the colors
that chased him into unconsciousness were not Merida
brown and green, but violet edged in gold. Roelstra's
colors—and Ianthe's.

Feylin watched shadows fill the valley like an onrush-
ing tide, indigo and deep brown and a strange greenish
black. On the cliffs the dragonsires seemed to have melted
into the stone. She shook her head, asking herself why
men were so stupidly reckless. Dragons were marvels to
behold—but at a nice, safe distance. Prince Rohan, Lord
Farid, and the young squire ought to have returned by
now from their foolish dragon-chasing, and she said as
much to the man beside her.

Darfir shrugged and cast an uneasy look across the
gorge to the invisible dragons. "His lordship knows his
way home."

Though his words were casual enough, his hands constantly slid up and down the reins and his eyes constantly
scanned the trail. Feylin bit her lip. "We'll wait for
them," she said, and peered into the dying light.

A short time later Darfir gave a muffled curse and
pointed to the cliffs. A great winged shadow appeared
against the dusky sky and launched itself into flight.
Feylin's blood congealed as the dragon bellowed a hunting-
cry familiar to her from childhood.

"Sweet Goddess," Darfir whispered. "Is he coming
after us?"

"No," another of the men said. "Look."

The dragon swooped into the gorge and was swallowed
in darkness. A horse's thin scream rose and abruptly
died. Moments later the sire lifted into the sky once

more, flying to a remote perch with a large, limp shape
dangling from his talons. Even at a distance, the piebald
hide showed that this was the squire's mount.

"Oh, no," Feylin breathed, and in the next instant dug
her heels into her horse's flanks. The others followed
her, the arrhythmic pattern of hoofbeats in perfect keeping with the uncertain pounding of her heart.

Suddenly she drew rein, for ahead of her trotted Lord
Farid's dappled gelding, heading home. Darfir rode forward and grabbed the horse's reins. A quick inspection
showed the nicks in his hide and blood on the reins
where Farid's hand would have held them.

"He knows his way home, unlike the one the dragon
caught," Darfir said grimly. "As for the prince's stallion—
he could be anywhere by now."

"They didn't fall from their horses," Feylin said softly.

The oldest of the men, Lhoys, growled through his
beard, "Whatever lost them their mounts walked on two
legs and drew steel against them."

"Or glass," Feylin added. "And they won't have waited
around, either. Can you find the tracks, Lhoys?"

The old man nodded and dismounted to scrutinize the
ground. "Bring the gelding. We may have need of him."

Feylin glanced at Darfir. "What do you think happened?"

"How could the Merida have come so far south without our knowing?"

"They wouldn't dare." But it was a feeble protest.

Lhoys had gone some distance from them, and now
turned to call out success. After half a measure they
found the place where the squire's horse had turned into
the gorge, prints indicating a panicky gallop. They rode
on in silence as the light worsened and every shape
became a threat. At last Feylin stopped, seeing a stand of
brush and a dark shape on the ground. She cried out and
leaped down from her saddle.

Farid sprawled in a dirt-thickened puddle of his own
blood, a gaping wound in his side, sword still in his hand,
the blade dark with blood. Death had not gentled his
face, and as she crouched beside him she almost expected
him to sit up and bellow out his rage before slashing into
his attackers again. Smoothing his features tenderly, she
closed his sightless eyes and bent her head.

"Look here," Lhoys called out, and she glanced up, tears blurring her eyes. The old man was a few strides away, pointing at the ground. "There's blood all over. Our lord and his grace gave good accounts of themselves. Signs of bodies being dragged—see the marks of bootheels in the dirt? Three men were unable to walk by the time this was over."

"Or two of them and Prince Rohan," Feylin said, shivering.

"Did he wear spurs? These three did."

"I don't know. I can't remember."

"Trained by his father and mounted by Lord Chaynal on a horse like that? No spur ever touched that stallion— nor any other Prince Rohan ever rode."

She knuckled her eyes and said, "Darfir, put our lord on his horse. We'll take him back home."

"We follow the tracks as far as we can," Lhoys growled.

"There's no more light," Darfir protested.

Lhoys cursed and spat, and set off anyway. Feylin caught up with him. "What if we find them? Four of us against however many of them? And with a sword at the prince's throat? And what about the boy?"

"Small enough to carry, of course. I thought you were careful about observing things."

"And I thought you were a goldsmith."

Lhoys snorted. "Only after I had my bellyful of guiding other people's riches through the mountains, girl. There are less dangerous livings."

Twilight guided them to a rocky outcropping. Lhoys shook her head in defeat. "Six horses, by the scars on the bushes where they tied the reins. They took the harder path from here. Not even I could find them now."

"Lhoys, look over here." Feylin picked up a small, shiny object that had caught her eye. "It's a coin—no, a medallion."

He took it from her, ran a finger over both surfaces. "Minted back when the Merida held Stronghold. They had a legendary goldsmith then. I recognize the work." He spat again. "Merida—damn them!" As they went back to the others, he asked, "Did you ever see his princess?"

"No. All the times they've visited, I've been out chasing dragons."

"Fire in her hair and called to her hand when she pleases—but nothing compared to the Fire that will kindle around the Merida when she learns of this. She'll lead whole armies to get him back."

"They'll kill him if she tries!"

Lhoys' eyes glittered in the dimness. "You've never seen the princess," he said.

Beliaev rubbed at the ritual scar on his chin and glared at the shy slivers of the moons just visible between the jagged mountains. In only a few days they would rise full and provide light enough to ride by. As it was, he was in constant danger of slipping on treacherous rock or missing an essential landmark. The timing had been all wrong, he complained to himself as he rode, and the bitch princess was not going to be pleased. Well, that was her problem, Beliaev thought, and cursed as his gelding's forelegs skidded on loose stones. How could he have known that fool of a prince would go out sightseeing dragons so soon? How could he have anticipated that Rohan would ride through the very hills where Beliaev and his men were scouting suitable ambush?

They had arrived only yesterday. That meager stand of brush would not have been Beliaev's choice for cover, but he supposed things had worked out profitably despite the haste of the arrangements. He tugged the lead rein and indulged himself by spitting on the prince's blond head. Rohan was slung across the saddle like a sack of grain. Rope tying his wrists and ankles passed tight beneath the horse's belly. Beside him was one of Beliaev's dead, with a heavy cloth wrapped around his nearly severed arm so dripping blood would not provide a trail. The royal sword responsible for that death and yet another was now in Beliaev's possession, along with the prince's knives—he'd been warned about those—and the sleeveless golden robe. He rubbed his cheek to his shoulder, smooth silk and prickly silver embroidery luxurious against his skin. A pity the garment had been ruined by rips and blood, but perhaps the princess' women could mend and clean it. Now that they'd finished their hellish dragon tapestries, they had nothing better to do.

His mount's hooves skittered again, and Beliaev yelped a warning to the men behind him. Two of them were wounded, two of them dead and tied across saddles, and one was holding the bound and gagged squire in front of him. It had cost precious time to secure the casualties, and the going was slow with three horses on leading reins. But leaving the men behind was unthinkable. They were Ianthe's and identifiable as such by their clothes— and that damned arrow it had taken so long to find in the dirt. The prince's people must believe that the Merida alone were responsible for Rohan's capture; thus the medallion left where someone would surely find it. Beliaev grinned at the thought of Lord Chaynal riding north at the head of the Desert armies to the plains outside Tiglath— right past Feruche where Rohan would be kept until Ianthe had done whatever it was she planned to do to him. For his own part, Beliaev would just as soon have carved the prince up into interesting shapes to be sent back to his Sunrunner witch of a wife, but Ianthe had forbidden it. She had assured him that the eventual outcome would be much more satisfying, and there had been a feral glow in her eyes that made doubt impossible.

Not that he trusted her, he mused as he leaned slightly back in his saddle, trying to ease the ache in his back. Lord Farid had gotten in a powerful kick while still on horseback, and it had been a real pleasure to shove his sword into the old man's side. There were bruises elsewhere, too, that riding did nothing to soothe. Thirty more measures to Feruche, and then he would bask in the attentions of the princess' women while Rohan was given over to Ianthe. Beliaev trusted her not at all, but any change in plan would not profit him at this time. Possibilities teased him about her plans for the prince, but ended in a shrug. She could keep Rohan for a pet or throw him from the cliffs for all Beliaev cared.

He stretched, unable to spare a hand from reins or lead rope to rub his spine, and thought about the speediest way to get word to his brothers in the north that preparations would have to be hastened. The attack on Tiglath—

bold stroke, that—would have to begin earlier than
planned. Ianthe and Roelstra had warned against it, but
there would never be a better time for the obliteration of
the city. The High Prince, in collusion with young Prince
Jastri of Syr, would soon be conducting military maneuvers on the Syrene side of the Faolain River. It was
Roelstra's plan to use these armies to annihilate in one
swift battle all the troops the Desert could muster. Thus
he had ordered the Merida to make no move against
Tiglath which would compel Lord Chaynal to split his
forces to north and south. But Tiglath lay there ripe and
waiting, and if the High Prince thought the Merida would
pass up this chance, he was very much mistaken. If the
horse-thieving Lord of Radzyn's army divided to defend
Tiglath as well as the Faolain border, too bad for Roelstra.
Actually, Beliaev told himself, he'd be doing Roelstra a
favor by taking care of half the Desert for him. And, too,
with Tiglath in Merida hands, Roelstra would have no
way to renege on his promise that the northern Desert
would return to its rightful owners. Beliaev did not trust
the High Prince, either.

He glanced down as Rohan's fair head moved and a
strangled groan escaped his throat. Sliding his foot from
the stirrup, he delivered a careful kick just above Rohan's
ear. No further damage could be risked for fear of Ianthe's
wrath. The prince subsided back into senselessness. Feeble
moonlight shone off the bloodstain on his shoulder, and
Beliaev smiled. Rotten timing or no, he had Rohan secure
and would deliver him as promised. By winter the Merida
would rule from Stronghold once more.

This happy thought sustained him through the next few
measures of winding mountain tails. At last the sun began to finger tentatively at the eastern sky, and Beliaev
picked up the pace a little. He cursed the necessity of
swinging wide around the Desert garrison below Feruche,
for the back route added another ten measures to an
already interminable journey. But it would all be for
nothing if Rohan's men spotted this strange party riding
into Feruche.

The sun was summer-hot overhead all day, and by
dusk was still brutal. At long last Beliaev led the group

through the narrow back pass. Startled guards at lonely posts called down challenges he answered with a snarl. The castle spires rose beyond the rocks, tantalizing him for a full three measures before he finally reached the gates. Inside the courtyard he swung down off his horse, aching in every muscle, and seized the waterskin off the first servant who approached. After emptying it down his throat, he heaved a vast sigh and turned as Ianthe called imperiously from the staircase.

"What are you doing here so soon?"

"Be happy I'm here at all," he snapped back. Goddess, but the woman was beautiful, he thought. His gaze ran over the perfect body barely concealed by a yellow silk bedrobe. Her hair was in tangles and her feet were bare, and it was obvious that she had been aroused from a nap by his arrival with her prize. As her face suddenly lit with an inner fire, he knew she had spotted Rohan.

"He's not hurt, is he?" she asked, anxious as any mother, though there was nothing tender in her sharp dark eyes.

"Not much. A nick in his shoulder and a sore head. He's all yours, princess. Do what you want with him."

"I intend to," she said, and gestured to her hovering women. They maneuvered the prince to the ground and two men came forward with a litter. As Rohan was carried into the keep, Ianthe caught sight of the boy. "What's that?"

"His squire, I should think. Farid died in the skirmish. I didn't think you'd mind about that, but I do draw the line at killing children."

"So you do have limits. How interesting. Untie the gag. I want to hear what he has to say."

Stiff from a long night and longer day spent slung across a saddle, the boy's blood quickly warmed with the chance to vent his fury. He spat on the ground as the cloth was removed from his mouth, then spat once more, this time at Ianthe.

She backed off a pace, scowling. "Don't try that again, brat! What's your name?"

He set his jaw stubbornly and glared at her.

"Speak while you've still the tongue to do so!"

Green eyes widened, but he said nothing.

"Those aren't just Rohan's colors you're wearing," Ianthe mused. "The blue and silver are his, but the black and green—" Tapping a finger against one flawless cheek, she began to laugh. "Oh, I should have known it by the eyes! You're related to the Sunrunner witch, a kinsman from River Run!" Turning to Beliaev, she said, "How wise of you not to kill him. He'll be my messenger back to Sioned. Do you know what you'll be telling her, boy?" she directed at the squire with a viciously sweet smile. "That an army of Sunrunners won't get her precious prince back for her, not even with Andrade at its head and down on her knees before my father the High Prince. Rohan is all mine now, little one, as he should have been from the start. I'll let you keep your tongue after all, so you can tell Sioned exactly what you'll see while you're here."

"She'll kill you!" the boy burst out.

"A *faradhi*, kill? Never! She hasn't the courage. None of them do. But I'm a different sort, as your prince will find out soon enough. Beliaev, see that the brat is cleaned and fed. I want him in good condition for his journey back to Stronghold."

"What are you going to do to my lord?" the boy cried out.

"Things you won't be interested in until you're older," she laughed. "But I may let you watch so you can be educated—and so you can tell that green-eyed bitch exactly what sort of care I gave her beloved."

She swept away up the stairs, calling for her women to minister to the prince's wounds. Beliaev, understanding at last when she really wanted from Rohan, remembered the dragon tapestries and was very glad they had not been stitched with himself in mind.

Chapter Twenty-two

Kleve had spent fourteen of his forty-four years traversing the northern princedoms, accompanied only by two sturdy mountain ponies. The solitary life of an itinerant *faradhi* suited him; he avoided any place larger than a village with the same zeal that he avoided crossing water. But each spring he spent a little time in Tiglath, enjoying the company of a certain innkeeper's widow and congratulating himself on a life spent away from walls and cities.

Kleve presented himself as usual at Lord Eltanin's small palace of sun-yellow stone—a sad court since the death of lovely young Lady Antalya. Kleve expected that his lordship would as usual require him to contact Princess Sioned with reports too sensitive to be entrusted to parchment and which *faradhi* oaths kept secret. But Eltanin, whose face was scored by lines that made him look nearly Kleve's age, had only two messages for the princess: the Merida threatened, and Prince Rohan was many days overdue.

Thus it was that Kleve saw only one sunrise in Tiglath before setting off into the Desert again. The princess had told him on the sunlight to head for Skybowl with the twin purposes of finding out where her husband was and to give warning about the Merida. Her colors had been strictly controlled as befitted a ranking *faradhi* and a princess, but beneath them Kleve had felt a black terror that had given urgent depth to her orders.

Eltanin had provided a horse half again as large as Kleve's own faithful pony, and the gelding's strong, smooth gait proclaimed him one of Lord Chaynal's blooded stock. Kleve had never bestrode an animal as fine and fast as this one, and made silent apology to his abandoned old friend for his disloyal enjoyment of the gelding's speed.

But swiftness alone could not have saved him from the threat that appeared on the first afternoon of his journey. Four riders came toward him out of the sun. Kleve tightened his fingers on the reins to feel the comforting pressure of his rings. Only five, but enough to defend himself with Fire and a judicious bit of conjuring if necessary. In his years as a roving Sunrunner he had encountered his share of bandits and thieves who had scant respect for his calling. He had always obeyed the injunction against killing, but he had never scrupled to leave his attackers much the worse for their foolishness.

He reined in the gelding and began his preparations as the four riders bore down on him. When they were near enough to see him clearly, he held up his right hand, fingers spread and angled to catch the light on his rings.

"Thank the Goddess!" a young voice shouted. "Sunrunner, we're in need!"

Kleve stayed where he was as they rode up—a youth, a girl of about the same age, a man older than Kleve, and a boy with green eyes blazing in a bruised, angry face. He noted swords, knives, and telltale colors at a glance as well as the quality of clothing beneath the dirt. A young knight, a man-at-arms retired to more peaceful pursuits, a squire, and a girl whose position was not immediately clear. The *faradhi* nodded to himself, relieved. The only threat they posed was to the health of their horses, which bore all the signs of having been ridden too hard and too fast.

"How may I help?" Kleve asked politely.

"Where do I begin?" the girl asked bitterly, raking her hair from her face.

"Names might help," he suggested. "Mine is Kleve, and I think I'm the person you rode out from Skybowl to find."

"Exactly," the young man said. "We have news for Princess Sioned that can't be entrusted to couriers—and she's far from Stronghold in any case." Then he paused, blue eyes narrowing. "How did you know we're from Skybowl?"

Kleve smiled, accepting the belated tribute to powers of observation and deduction drilled into him at Goddess Keep, and declined to answer the question. After all, Lady Andrade never did. He cast a look at the sun, which barely topped the western hills. "Tell me quickly what message you wish to send, before the light fails and it becomes impossible for me to reach her before moonrise."

"They've taken him!" the boy burst out. "Princess Ianthe has stolen my lord to Feruche!"

The young knight hushed him with a glance and began the tale. Their names were Walvis, Tilal, Feylin, and Lhoys, the latter two of Skybowl, the former from the prince's own suite at Stronghold. Only Lhoys contributed nothing to the telling, and sat glowering on his horse as the other three traded the story quickly back and forth. Kleve readied himself as he listened, boiling all down to essentials even as he began the lightweave that he would ride to Faolain Lowland where the princess was. Along the ribbons of fading sun he flew, his second such journey today. He was grateful for her instantaneous response and her strong, steadying touch on the light.

Goddess blessing, my lady. Hear me quickly, for the sun dies and I have but five rings. Your prince, seeking dragons, found ambush instead and is now held at Feruche. His squire was released unhurt and found others who were crossing the Desert to me at Tiglath. Your garrison below Feruche is slaughtered. Skybowl has no troops for storming the castle. Lord Farid is dead. Tiglath cannot help, for the squire learned that the Merida will attack within days. Give me your orders, and I will relay them to Walvis.

ROHAN! Her anguished cry nearly shattered the sunlight itself and Kleve marveled that the other four could not hear it. She then disciplined herself to calm, but the colors of fury seething in her made Kleve wince.

Goddess blessing, Sunrunner. Send Walvis to Tiglath with news of the Merida. In my name he will summon the north for battle there. Accompany him, and send to me at noontimes when the sun is strongest. I will gather up the southern armies and—and by the Goddess, I will raze Feruche to the dead sands!

And then the sun left the high ridges in darkness, and

Kleve gathered himself back into himself. He took several deep breaths to calm his racing heart, for it had been a near thing. Another few moments and the dusk would have claimed him, shadow-lost.

When he could speak, he detailed the princess' orders. As might be expected of so young a knight, Walvis was torn between the intense desire to battle his prince's enemies and the equally deep need to rescue him from Princess Ianthe.

"Lord Eltanin can lead the north," he said at last. "My duty lies with my lord."

Feylin glared at him and snapped, "We argued this all the way from Skybowl! It was *not your fault* that the prince was taken! How could you have known? How could anyone? Your duty is to obey the princess and lead the north to victory against the Merida!"

Kleve bit back an untimely smile as the pair faced off. Both of them just under twenty winters, by his estimate, full of prickly pride and youthful impatience. He caught Lhoys' eye and saw the same amusement there before the older man's expression smoothed and he spoke.

"Go," he told Walvis. "She orders it. Tilal will return to Skybowl with us. He'll be needed to tell her about Feruche."

Walvis cast a stern glance at the squire, who had jerked upright in outraged protest. "Be silent," he commanded. "You'll go back with them. But I should be there, too."

"Goddess above in glory!" Feylin exclaimed. "Why are men so stupid? Princess Sioned ordered you to go. So go!" She turned to the boy. "There are pens and parchment in my workroom. Lhoys can show you. Draw as much as you can remember of the castle and the cliffs around it, and write down all that goes on inside, how many troops you saw, everything. Goddess keep you, and give my respect to the princess." She looked a challenge at Walvis. "Are you coming, or are you going to waste more time debating pretty points of duty when the Merida are poised for attack?"

She spared him the necessity of an answer by kicking her horse into a gallop—in the direction of Tiglath. Only then did the others realize she meant to accompany Walvis

and Kleve to the city. The young knight swore; Tilal and
Kleve simply stared. But Lhoys slapped his thigh and let
out a roar of laughter.

"Northern women! Speak the name Merida and they
go for the nearest sword! Best catch up with her, lad, or
she'll take command of the troops herself!"

Personal command of troops was precisely what Sioned
was thinking about taking unto herself when she recovered from Kleve's message. Lord Baisal, whose petition
for a new stone keep had included a sunset walk over its
proposed site, had gibbered with astonishment when Sioned
broke off what she was saying and acquired the distant
expression of Sunrunner conversing on the light. He had
witnessed her performance six years ago in the Great
Hall of Stronghold, of course, when she had used the
moonlight to grasp at Roelstra's renegade Sunrunner, but
to stand within touching distance of a *faradhi* at work
who was also one's liege lady was something else again.

His spluttering silenced with her first words to him.
Baisal, most placid and easy going of men, drew back
from the grim-faced fury who ordered him to call up his
levies for her inspection on the morrow and to send
riders to nearby manors and keeps for the same purpose.
The impossibility of these things robbed him of speech
for a few moments. By the time he was coherent again,
she was striding long-legged back to the holding's walls,
and he ran hard to catch up with her.

"But—my lady—provisions, horses, arms!" he puffed.
"They cannot be readied in a single day!"

"You'll be repaid for any provisions beyond those you
usually supply in times of war. I am not a thief. Horses
graze your fields. Catch them tonight and have them
saddled and ready tomorrow morning! As for arms—what
kind of *athri* are you not to have them to hand at all
times?"

"A peaceful one!" he exclaimed, quivering with insult.
"My lady, why are you speaking of war? What's happened?"

"Roelstra." The name hissed from her lips. "Roelstra
and his daughter Ianthe. Lord Baisal, I formally require
your duty as my liege man to recover your prince from

the High Prince's daughter at Feruche Castle. Is that specific enough for you?"

Baisal stopped dead at that. She went on without him. Sioned knew that if she paused to explain fully or even long enough to feel her own emotions, she would begin screaming. Rohan, held prisoner by Ianthe—who had no doubt released Tilal to provide details Sioned's own imagination could readily supply. The commotion in the central courtyard provided welcome distraction, and she concentrated on finding Ostvel in the midst of it.

Instead, she found her brother.

"Sioned!" he cried on seeing her. Tossing his reins to a groom, he hurried to seize her in an embrace scented with sweat and horse and leather. Stunned, she looked over his shoulder and finally registered the meaning of the crowded courtyard.

"Davvi!" Pushing herself out of his arms, she gaped at her brother. It was the first time she had seen him since he had brought Tilal to Stronghold two years ago. "What are you doing here? And with all these troops in full armor—Davvi, explain this to me!"

Their mother's green eyes regarded her from his half-a-head height advantage. He was twelve years her senior, but dirt caked in the fine lines around his eyes made him seem twice that. There were grooves cut into his cheeks, too, framing his tightly drawn lips.

"I've brought all the troops I safely could—not all in one group, of course, or Jastri would have suspected something. Two more detachments of twelve men each are following me, but I took the direct route. The others should be here in a day or so."

"What are you talking about? What would Jastri suspect?"

"Come into the hall and we'll talk. I'm exhausted. I've been riding for two days without sleep—or is it three?"

Mystified, she accompanied him into the stone-and-timber building that served Baisal as dining hall, seat of justice, and servants' sleeping quarters. There was a wooden staircase at the far end, leading up to a small addition that was the family's private chambers. Sioned led Davvi upstairs to the room Baisal's daughters had vacated for her use, talking all the while and receiving no answers.

"Damn it, tell me why you're here!" she demanded, digging her nails into his arm. "You were supposed to meet me in five days at the southern bridge!"

"It's a long way from River Run," he said irrelevantly.

"I know that!" Hearing the edge of hysteria in her voice, she slammed the door shut behind them and pressed her palms against the wood, taking several long, slow breaths to calm herself. When she turned, her brother was seated on a stool with a winecup in his hand. Sioned put her fists on her hips and after drawing another deep breath said, "Tell me."

Davvi drained half the wine at a swallow. "Is it beneath the dignity of a princess to pour out more wine? And you'd better have some too, Sioned."

"If you don't tell me at once why you're here with half an army, I'll pour this over your head!" She refilled his cup, then followed his advice and took some for herself.

"If only it *was* half an army." He sighed, clasping his hands around the cup, elbows on his knees and shoulders bent. "Roelstra's got our young prince right where he wants him."

For an instant she thought he spoke of Rohan, and wondered wildly how he could know. But then she realized he referred to Prince Jastri, sixteen-year-old son of their kinsman Prince Haldor who had died in the Plague. "What do you mean?" she asked.

"I was there at court, at High Kirat, when Roelstra's man came. None of us thought much about it. Jastri's not a bad sort, only very young. And ambitious. He and Roelstra are conducting military maneuvers around the Catha River plains. 'Military maneuvers,'" he repeated bleakly, glancing up at her. "I was supposed to join them. I came here instead. He's only my distant cousin. You're my *sister*."

Sioned paled as she reached the obvious conclusion. "Sweet Goddess," she breathed, seeing the tapestry map in Rohan's study as if it was flung out before her now. The Merida at work in the north; Roelstra and Jastri with troops in the south. No sane prince—or princess—could ignore either threat.

"You know what the High Prince is after, of course," Davvi went on. "Jastri will do his work for him. Under the guise of teaching the boy how to be a general—every prince must be that, and Haldor didn't live long enough to tutor his son in the arts of war—Roelstra will have troops positioned to invade the Desert. Sioned, he's only a day's march from the Faolain. You have my people if you need them. I don't give a damn about breaking my oath to Jastri. He's broken his to me and every other *athri* in Syr by throwing in with Roelstra."

"But—"

"You wanted to hear it, so let me get through to the end." He swallowed more wine and straightened his back. "If I were you, I'd send to Lord Chaynal at once and tell him to make ready for war. Roelstra will find some excuse to cross the Faolain. Maybe your Rohan can use that dragon-clever tongue of his to talk his way out of it, but I don't think so. I'm convinced that by the *Rialla*, Roelstra wants Rohan out of the way so the Desert can be his own—or the Merida's, which amounts to the same thing."

"Rohan—" She choked on his name, and steadied herself by staring fiercely at the emerald on her left hand. "The Merida will attack soon in the north. I just had word on the sunlight. Our forces will be cut in half, Davvi. I was going to call the summons and send them all—"

"By the Storm God—Sioned, that's Roelstra's excuse! The Merida attack—it will put those damned mutual defense treaties into play! That's how he'll do it, cross the Faolain pretending to go to Rohan's aid against the Merida! It's a damned long march to Tiglath, and anything could happen on the way!"

"What does the excuse matter?" she cried. "You don't understand! Ianthe has Rohan! She's holding him at Feruche!"

Davvi's eyes went wide and he dropped the cup on the floor, rising to put his arms around her. "Oh, Sioned," he whispered.

It would have been so good to cry. During childhood, before Lady Wisla had come to River Run as Davvi's bride, brother and sister had been close. Sioned wanted to hand everything over to him and trust him to mend what was wrong. But that feeling belonged to the little girl she had not been for a long time. She could not even weep in his arms; his embrace was not *home* to her, and it was impossible to find comfort when being held by a man who was not her husband.

She pulled away and found she was still clutching her winecup. Taking a large swallow, she raked the hair from her face. "You're right, I must send to Radzyn. There'll be moonlight enough tonight."

Davvi gave a start, then shook his head. "I keep forgetting what you are. It's funny—I can accept you as a princess, but—"

"But not as a *faradhi* witch?" she finished for him with a tiny smile. "When the moons rise, brother, you'll believe."

"Until they do, sit down and rest. Don't argue. Princess and Sunrunner or not, I'm still your older brother, girl." He pushed her gently onto the bed and sat down beside her. "Now, tell me how this happened."

She told him as much as she knew, cursing herself as he paled at mention of his son. "He's safe, don't worry," she added hastily. "Ianthe let him go, probably to come back to tell me exactly how she plans to kill Rohan." Sioned gazed unseeing down into her wine. "I'll kill her, Davvi. I swear I will."

"Lady Andrade—"

"Can take it up the Goddess at her leisure! I'll see Ianthe dead by my own hand! *Faradh'im* may be forbidden to kill, but princes are not. Hadn't you heard? Killing is one of a ruler's privileges." She saw her hand tremble and put the cup down. She had already killed; how many more times before she accepted that she was no longer a Sunrunner ruled by vows impossible for a princess to keep? Vows broken for Rohan's sake. "Oh, Goddess, my Rohan—" Wrapping her arms around herself, tight against the stabbing ache in her breast, she rocked back and forth in a vain attempt to escape the pain.

"She won't kill him." Davvi rubbed at her back.

"Not until she's finished toying with him! They'll pay for this with their lives. They want the Desert, do they? Well, then, the Long Sand will swallow them up!"

"With Jastri's troops added to Roelstra's, there are nine hundred across the Faolain," he warned.

Sioned forced herself to straighten up. She held out both hands, *faradhi* rings glinting, the emerald nearly on fire. "Look at them, Davvi. Does Roelstra have a single ally who wears them? This is what Andrade wanted all along. Not this way, I know, but *faradhi* princes are her goal. I have Fire itself at my call. They're worth at least those nine hundred."

"Sioned, I don't know much about Sunrunners, but I do know that your oaths forbid you to kill."

"And my oaths as a princess? As a wife? Andrade knew what she was doing when she put me forward as Rohan's bride. I think she counted on our breeding up *faradhi* children—but I'm barren, Davvi. The Plague ended my last hope of having a child. So it falls to me to use what I know and what I am." She gave him a small, feral smile. "I don't think Andrade counted on that. But she's saddled with it, and if I know her, she'll ride where she's reined. She's no fool."

Davvi's forehead creased even more deeply with worry. "Don't fly so high, Sioned," he cautioned.

"Ah, but I'm married to the dragon prince, brother."

Princess Tobin, splendid in a wine-red silk gown, entered her sons' rooms to bid them goodnight. She was in a hurry, for her hair was yet undone and she was giving a small farewell dinner for the Syrene ambassador that evening. Tossing the heavy braid over her shoulder, she went into the bedchamber prepared to do battle with the rambunctious twins. Rare were the nights when they slid meekly into their beds, and any night when they did meant either illness or scheming.

Sure enough, they were engaged in a pillow fight with their tutor and the hapless pair of squires assigned to them. The latter had barricaded themselves behind over-turned chairs. Tobin sighed, knowing that the time required to calm the skirmish would make her late for dinner.

"Enough!" she exclaimed into the uproar. The tutor, about to grab a royal ankle and initiate an assault with an embroidered cushion, looked up, flushed scarlet, lost his balance, and toppled into an undignified heap. The squires leaped from behind the furniture and fled. Deprived of their quarry, the twins armed themselves with bed-pillows nearly as big as they were and stalked the tutor. Tobin marched forward and, gathering a handful of nightrobe at the scruff of each neck, shook her sons playfully.

"Two against one—is that the behavior of a knight?" she scolded. "Leave poor Gervyn alone!"

Dark-haired, blue-eyed, as alike as dragons hatched from the same egg, Sorin and Andry showed no signs of repentance. Cheated of their victim, who had wisely picked himself up and hurried after the squires, they pelted each other instead, squealing with laughter when a seam split and feathers flew.

"By the Storm Devil, what am I going to do with you?" Tobin growled, her gown now liberally dusted with feather-snow. Scooping up a twin in either arm, she deposited them in their beds and stood over them with what she hoped was a stern glare. But the absurdity of the attempt when covered in white feathers was compounded by the mischievous grins decorating her offspring's faces. Tobin gave it up as useless, and laughed. "You're pests and I don't know what I ever did to merit you," she said, hugging each of them in turn. "I ought to blister your bottoms."

"With Sunrunner's Fire, the way Sioned said she would?" Sorin asked pertly.

"We didn't believe *her*, either," Andry put in with a smug smile, bouncing from his bed to his brother's for his share of maternal affection.

Tobin kissed them both and snuggled them. "Let me explain it to you this way. If you come up with any more pranks, jokes, or smart ideas, then you won't be allowed to go to Stronghold this year while your father and I are at Waes."

"But Sioned promised we could see dragons!" Sorin wailed.

"And it'd be a shame if your behavior prevented her from keeping her promise, wouldn't it? Now, to sleep with you. After riding all afternoon and that minor war you two just staged, don't you dare tell me you're not sleepy!"

Andry's small frame suddenly tensed in her embrace. The boy's dark head turned to the windows where the moons' silvery light shone through the casement onto the bed. His blue eyes were wide and shadowy, his cheeks pallid, lips moving in soundless whispers.

"Andry? What is it, love?" Tobin asked, though she was afraid she knew very well.

Sorin squirmed around and touched his brother's arm, smooth forehead wrinkling with concern. But what one twin sensed, the other could not. Tobin shifted into the moonlight and gasped at the touch.

Goddess blessing, my sister. Forgive me for startling Andry. Tobin—oh, Tobin, she's taken Rohan, Ianthe holds him inside Feruche! Roelstra camps near the Faolain ready for attack, and the Merida may already be at war with us in the north. Chay must summon the southern vassals and take the field against Roelstra soon—Ianthe has Rohan— the northern army must defend Tiglath—there's no one to go to Feruche—tell Chay to come quickly, please! He must!

Tobin swayed, clutching her sons to her breast as twin anchors to reality. She cursed her lack of training that prevented her from sending questions back over the moonrays to Sioned. There was a sharp wrench, utterly unlike the usual gentle leavetaking, and Tobin cried out softly.

"Mama?" Sorin breathed, frightened, and plucked at her sleeve. She looked down with what she hoped was a reassuring smile, then turned to Andry. Dazed and confused by what he had been inadvertently caught up in, when his eyes lifted they were swirling with moonlight.

"It's all right, darling," she soothed. "Just the moons,

nothing more. Here, let's get you both tucked up into bed now."

"But, Mama—"

"Hush, Sorin. It was only the moons." She busied herself with the comfortingly familiar task of arranging the sheets around them, kissing their foreheads, smiling a good night. Sorin was willing to believe that nothing unusual had happened, and settled down for sleep. But Andry, her second Sunrunner child, was still troubled. But not afraid, Tobin noted with pride, just as Maarken had not been afraid when he realized what gifts he had inherited. She stroked Andry's cheek and whispered, "Sleep now, my own. It's all right, I promise."

He bit his lip, then nodded and curled onto his side. She made herself wait until they were both asleep before hurrying to her rooms to change clothes. She brushed out her hair and left it loose, a breach of etiquette, for married women did not wear their hair unbound in company, but she cared nothing for that. Descending the stairs swiftly, she saw that Chay was just beginning to usher their guests into the private dining chamber. Tobin joined him, smiled, and hid her fretting impatience until the two of them were alone just outside the door.

"Make excuses," she said quickly. "I must speak to you. Now."

"Tobin, they're all waiting." He took a closer look at her face and the muscles of his cheeks tightened. "All right. Stay here."

She heard him make charming, wry apologies to the Syrene guests and order that dinner begin at once. Then he returned to her, closing the door behind him. "Tell me."

She did.

"Ianthe!" he spat. "By the devil who sired her—Tobin, are you sure?"

"Sioned is. I don't know how or why, but Ianthe has Rohan." She reached suddenly for the solid strength of him, terrified for her brother, for them all. "Chay, she'll kill him—"

"No. That's not her way." His lean body quivered with controlled fury and he drew away, grasping her shoulders. "Go in to dinner. Tell them anything you like about why I've gone. Just don't tell them the truth." She looked up into his eyes, saw the quicksilver grown storm-cloud gray, his rage feeding warrior's instincts and turning his face into a fierce mask. "Now I know why the Syrene court came to buy more horses in advance of the *Rialla*. Roelstra's troops threatening the Desert—I'll slaughter him myself!"

"How many other princes will be with him against us?"

"We'll worry about that later. I have work to do."

"I'll make sure dinner is brief, then come help. Hurry, Chay." She leaned up to kiss him, then settled her royal demeanor firmly around her and went into the dining room to tell lies.

Chapter Twenty-three

On first waking, he thought he had sickened with the Plague again. The grinding pain in his head, the fever, the swelling of eyes and tongue, the taste of *dranath*—all were the same. But as he struggled out of the murky darkness of illness and drugs, he felt the fire in his right shoulder and smelled the acrid medicine from dressings there. The same stench had permeated the room where his father had died. Rohan faced the memory and the possibility that he, too, might be dying. Light-headed, he groped to feel the extent of the injury. His wrists were caught in a firm grip and a voice he did not recognize told him to be still.

Panic lurched through his weakened body. Thick of tongue and wits, he was trapped within muscles that would not respond. "Sioned—" he tried to say.

"Hush. Sleep now, and you'll soon be better."

Something about the voice pinched at his memory, and he fought the hands that grasped his own. "Sioned!"

"You must sleep now."

Heavy wine laced with *dranath* and something else was poured down him, and he gagged. Another voice, a masculine one, swore. A second pair of hands held his face and more wine went down him. A fit of coughing nearly took the top of his head off, and contractions of muscles knotted his belly and shoulders and back.

"Lie down," the man ordered, and as the drugged wine seeped through him he had no choice but to obey. "I agreed to bring him here, not to nurse him," the man went on irritably.

"Shut up," the woman said, sounding slightly bored. "If you'd been more careful in the first place—"

"You'll note he calls out for her," the man jeered. "Did you expect him to call for you? I didn't kick him that hard in the head."

"Your jibes are as predictable as your rotten timing," the woman responded acidly.

"He should be all right by tomorrow. The fever's close to breaking."

"You don't understand the risk."

"All you need is for him to be capable. I should think you wouldn't *want* him to be coherent."

"Your delicacy of phrasing also astounds me."

Rohan almost had it, almost knew where he had heard that voice before. Yet even as he fumbled for the memory, the drugs swirled up, and he slept.

Sioned flexed her fingers inside dragonhide riding gloves, waiting in the coolness of the manor porch for her horse to be brought around. Aware of the crowd in Lord Baisal's courtyard and their furtive glances at her, she neither paced nor fidgeted. A princess' icy calm was a useful and strangely comforting refuge; by refusing to show emotions, she could also refuse to feel them.

Her brother approached as her gray stallion was led from the stables, and Sioned bit back impatience at the confrontation imminent in his eyes. She had no time.

"You're still determined to do this crazy thing," he accused, taking the stallion's reins from the groom. "At least take a more substantial guard with you! You can't know what's out there—or whom."

"Which is why my guard *is* so small, and my rather distinctive hair hidden, and my royal trappings gone," she countered. "Goddess! A princess riding disguised through her own lands!" She grabbed the reins from him and swung up onto the gray's back, wishing she could have left her head bare to the slight breeze. The sun was only two fingers up in the sky, and already it was hot. Six years of living in the Desert had not entirely accustomed her to its brutal climate, and this was only late spring. By summer she would be limp with exhaustion.

"I wish you'd wait until Lord Chaynal arrives," Davvi said.

"You know what to tell him when he does." She glanced around for Ostvel. "I know what I'm doing."

"I doubt it. Be careful, Sioned. For Goddess' sake, please be careful."

"For my husband's sake." Then, leaning down to pat his shoulder, she said more gently, "Don't worry so much."

He snorted his opinion of this caution. "Ostvel's on my side in this, you know. We had a long talk last night."

"I expected nothing less from either of you. He'll be your eyes watching over me, I'm sure." She spied Ostvel through the milling horses and troops and servants, and said, "I must go. Stay safe, Davvi."

Turning her mount, she rode to the gates where Ostvel and two men-at-arms waited for her. But she was waylaid by Lord Baisal, who came running from the encampment outside the walls, where Davvi's men and those gathered overnight from the outer farms were established. In a few days the lower pastures and hills would be covered in tents, and Chay would make efficient sense of the chaos. But Sioned could not stay to see the armed power she commanded.

"My lady," Lord Baisal pleaded. "I beg you not to leave so soon! What am I to do before Lord Chaynal arrives?"

"Feed the men, equip the horses, and prepare yourself for war. If you have any spare moments, you might begin the design of your new keep. Farewell, my lord."

She left him standing slack-jawed and staring, his expression a comic mixture of apprehension and delight. Ostvel, riding at her side, cast her a sidelong glance.

"He'll hold you to that, you know."

"If he manages to keep his wits and do what's needed, he'll have earned his stone castle."

They rode through the confused camp outside the manor walls, north along the Faolain. Sioned knew how insane her actions must seem to everyone, and was determined to implement her plan before Chay and Tobin could arrive with new objections. Not that anything they might propose could sway her. There was no one else to do what she knew she must, and it was something of a relief that her personal desires coincided with her duty as wife and princess.

Lord Eltanin's forces were locked into the defense of Tiglath; there would be no help for Rohan there. With Roelstra in the south, Chay could not lead an assault against Feruche. The castle was not susceptible to attack in any case, perched as it was on the cliffs with only two approaches, both well-guarded in peace and sure to be even more strictly watched in war. Rohan's only hope was Sioned, his Sunrunner princess. She wondered if Ianthe thought her incapable of violating her oath not to kill. She hoped so; it would make things easier when the killing time came.

Darkness blew at him, alternately warm and chill on the sweat that drenched his body. Eyes wide, heart racing, he shook his head and tried to find anchor in the reality of his own flesh. But the wind hit him again and the darkness billowed, and the dragons reached for him with acid claws.

He scrambled into a huddle against the cavern wall, hard stones at his back, and stared in horror at the scenes around him. Dragons fighting, mating, killing; jaws dripping blood and eyes flaring like exploding jewels; bodies weaving, thrusting, wings beating, tails lashing. The huge eggs cracked open, split with a terrible sound to reveal furious hatchlings who tore at each other tooth and talon, fire spewing from their throats to sear bright and hot as sunlight through the swirling darkness of the cave.

He cried out as dragonfire charred the skin of his face and arms, the stench of burning skin overpowering even the stink of dragon blood and dragon mating. They had not yet seen him, and he tried to melt into the cavern wall. They fought on, rutted on, exhaled fire and butchered each other, driven by the need to mate and the need to survive. The wind hissed like shaken silk through the cave and he cringed back, sweat and blood drying cold and then springing up hot and salty on his blackened skin. Violence swept around him and he shook with terror that those jewel eyes would find him, those bloody claws rip the remaining flesh from his bones. A rampaging sire loomed up over him, brought by a gust of wind, and he screamed, choking on a gush of bitter fluid in his throat that tasted of *dranath*.

"Rohan—!"

He reached for her blindly, clung shaking to her cool body. "Sioned—"

"Hush, darling, it's all right now. I'm here." There was a slick metallic sound like a sword being unsheathed, and he squeezed his dazzled eyes shut as sunlight streamed into the cave. Sioned, his Sunrunner princess, bringing with her the sun. "We're safe, love."

He could no longer smell the dragons or his own oozing blood, nor feel the fiery breath on his skin. The soft breeze touching him now was scented with starbriar, tender as her caresses on his back and nape. He shuddered, turning his face to her shoulder. He had forgotten what *dranath* could do to the mind.

There had been no cave, no dragons, no fire. Only the drug and his fever, the hold of both broken now. He rested against Sioned, ashamed of his panic. She curled up beside him on the bed and whispered gentle things until he slept.

Hard riding through the day and night brought Sioned to Stronghold just before noon. She wanted nothing more than to collapse, but kept herself alert, pacing the main courtyard where the stones' heat radiated up like a searing fountain. When the sun was at its highest she felt the tentative touch of his colors, gathered in the strands of light, and heard him speak.

Goddess blessing, my lady. We have reached Tiglath and warned Lord Eltanin. As yet there is no attack, but the signs of it rise with the sand on the horizon. Walvis plans and prepares, and we wait for your orders.

Sioned nodded, pleased. *Goddess blessing, Sunrunner. Continue preparing for war, as is being done in the south where Roelstra's armies are camped across the Faolain. There will be no help. You must do all on your own. Tell Walvis he is not to attempt an attack on Feruche. He must defend Tiglath. The prince will soon be freed, I promise. Now open yourself to me, Kleve, and I will show you*

*Princess Tobin's colors. Send to her from now on. She is
not faradhi-trained, and will not be able to reply to you,
but give her any information you would give to me.*

My lady—what of you? What will you do?

*I don't matter. Watch now, and feel, so you'll be able to
find her on the sunlight.*

She concentrated on relaying the bright and lovely
pattern that was Tobin to the faraway Sunrunner. When
she was sure he could recognize and contact the princess,
she unraveled their connecting ribbons of light before he
could ask further questions.

"I trust you're finished, and can come in out of this
glare," Ostvel said.

She glanced at him, surprised by his presence. "Yes.
Walvis will know soon that help cannot come from the
south. He'll have to lead the defense of Tiglath himself."
She looked around the courtyard, a chaos of people and
noise and brightness that suddenly dizzied her. "Ostvel—
take me inside before I fall over," she breathed.

He was careful to make it appear as if his hand at her
elbow was only a courtesy offered a princess, for it would
not do for her to seem weak. The steps were endless, but
at last she was in her chambers, sinking into a soft chair
by the windows. Ostvel brought her water and a wet
cloth as she unwound the heavy scarf from her head and
let her hair fall free.

"Seventeen winters old," she whispered. "Walvis is
too young to lead an army, Ostvel. Goddess help me,
what am I doing to him."

"Nothing he wouldn't be insulted if you hadn't asked
him to do. Here, let me get your boots."

"I have women to serve me," she protested.

"But none you'd want to see you in this condition," he
said unanswerably. He mopped her face and neck with
the damp cloth, then helped her with the hot dragonhide
boots. "Now, you're going to rest until sunset."

"If I do, will you send Maeta up to me then?"

He eyed her suspiciously. "What do you want the
guards commander for?"

"I'm responsible for Stronghold's defenses," she said,
ready with the diversionary answer.

"No," he corrected. "*I* am. But I'll send her up at sunset, and not an instant before."

When he was gone she did not go into the next chamber to rest, unwilling even to look at the bed she shared with Rohan. Instead she stretched out in a lounge chair that had been a gift from Princess Milar, closed her eyes, and systematically relaxed her body from toes to fingertips. But she did not really rest. She planned her attack on Feruche.

When Maeta arrived, Sioned was ready. The commander had inherited her position from her mother, the redoubtable Myrdal, who still held considerable sway over the troops even in her retirement. Myrdal might or might not have been Prince Zehava's half-sister; the respect accorded her and her daughter was due not so much to their possible kinship with their rulers, but to their own reputations as warriors. Sioned offered Maeta a comfortable seat and refreshment, wondering how much the woman knew of what was happening.

Everything, it seemed. Her first words were, "With the Merida on one front and the High Prince on the other, we'll have much to do in freeing Rohan."

Relieved that she would not have to make long explanations, Sioned told her, "I see Ostvel and the men have been talking. Good. Maeta, I need the strongest, fastest horse in the stables, a waterskin and food, and absolute secrecy. And I need them all tonight."

Maeta bit into a marsh apple, chewed, swallowed, and replied, "There's a gate near the grotto you can use. It lets out into the cliffs, with room enough for a single rider to pass safely and quietly."

Sioned blinked. "Rohan never told me about—"

"That's because he doesn't know. One day my mother and I will have to show you all Zehava's improvements. Milar wasn't the only one to leave her mark on Stronghold."

Sioned marveled at the effort and secrecy it had taken to carve such a path from the keep, but put nothing beyond the old prince. "I'll look forward to it."

"As for the timing—before dawn. We'll need deep sleep and no one stirring early."

"I'll leave the arrangements to you."

Maeta nodded. "My lady, I've been thinking. We have the chance for action against the Merida, and not just at Tiglath."

"Yes?" Sioned asked, bewildered but intrigued.

"Empty Stronghold of all but the best archers, and send everyone else to Remagev by night. The Merida will think them off to Feruche or down south with Lord Chaynal." She grinned as if she was a dragon spotting easy prey. "We'll leave ourselves vulnerable to attack. They won't be able to resist."

Sioned laughed. "They'll split up to take advantage, and we'll pick them off from the cliffs! And when they pause to regroup, we'll hit them from the east with the troops sent to Remagev!"

"Very good, my lady," Maeta approved. "We'll make a warrior of you yet. Shall I order it, then?"

"Please! Present the plan to Ostvel tomorrow. I know he'll like it." She thought with satisfaction that this scheme would also help Walvis and Eltanin—and keep Ostvel too busy to come after her. Then something occurred to her. "Maeta, you've made no objection to my leaving."

"You're sovereign lady here, and may do as you please when it pleases you to do it." The black eyes danced as the pious words were spoken, and Sioned knew that she and Maeta understood each other perfectly. "And no one is counting on a *faradhi*," Maeta added.

"Rohan must."

"But Ianthe is not. That's why I'm letting you do this thing that will have Ostvel ready to skin me alive. I know Sunrunners—and I know you, my lady." She paused, then smiled again. "I also know a little something about Feruche."

Sioned stared, then nodded slowly. "I see."

All at once the outer door was flung open and Riyan hurtled through to bury his face against Sioned's shoulder. She hugged him close, trying to make sense of his babbled words, and Maeta unobtrusively departed before Ostvel could catch up with his offspring and ask questions Maeta did not want to answer.

"Here now, a little slower!" Sioned held Riyan on her knees and looked into his eyes that were so much like

Camigwen's that it hurt sometimes to see them. She brushed the soft hair from his forehead, wishing her friend was here now. Cami would understand. "Tell me what's wrong."

"Tilal's home!" He bounded off her knees and raced from the room, returning a few moments later, dragging Tilal by the hand. "Hurry, hurry," Riyan urged.

The squire looked as exhausted as Sioned felt. She rose, embraced him tenderly, then stood back to inspect him. A young man looked out of his eyes, not a boy. Sioned drew him over to a chair, bade him sit, and gestured Riyan to quiet.

At first Tilal spoke in measured sentences that sounded as if he'd rehearsed them all the way from Skybowl. He was a soldier giving a report, not a boy made fearful and furious by what he'd seen. Yet as he talked on, his sunburned cheeks flushed a deeper red and his green eyes began to flash, and the words tumbled over each other.

"—and we got back to Skybowl and I made a map just as Feylin told me to do." He pulled a creased bit of parchment from his filthy tunic. "It's of the castle, as much as I saw of it. It's a horrible place, my lady, you can feel *her* all over it! Feylin told me to draw this so you'd know where things are." He handed it over and she unfolded it, seeing instantly that her original idea would not work. Tilal saw her frown, and went on, "With enough troops—you're a Sunrunner and we could—"

"The only thing you're going to do is take a bath and get some sleep," Ostvel said from the doorway. All three glanced around, startled that he had been there all this time.

"But Papa, I haven't heard everything yet!" Riyan protested.

"There'll be plenty of time tomorrow. It's time for boys to be asleep."

Tilal's whole body went rigid. Sioned shook her head fractionally at Ostvel in warning and said, "There's more I must hear, and more I must tell him. Riyan, you may ask your questions tomorrow. Go with your father now, please."

A stern glance from Ostvel silenced the boy, and he trudged out of the room. His father shut the door, and when she was alone with Tilal, Sioned took sorrowful inventory again of her nephew's face. He bore the marks of bad treatment, exhaustion, and worries far too heavy for a child of his years.

"I saw your father in the south," Sioned began. "The High Prince is encamped with young Prince Jastri of Syr. They say it's for training purposes, but your father is wise and knew it's really for war against the Desert. He came to Lord Baisal's holding to warn us and join us."

The green eyes went wide. "But—what about Mother and everyone at home?"

"No one has ever succeeded in taking the keep, Tilal. Besides, River Run is far from where the fighting will be."

He thought this over and nodded. "Lord Chaynal will lead, and my father will help. But what about Prince Rohan? *She* has him!"

"Not for long," Sioned told him grimly. "This map is precisely what I need, Tilal. You've done very well.'

"When do we leave for Feruche?"

"*We* do not." She instantly regretted the sharp answer as he drew himself up indignantly at the perceived slur on his manhood. "Tilal, you must trust me and obey me in this. Please promise me."

Rebellion flickered in his eyes, but after a moment he nodded and bent his head. "Yes, my lady," he whispered. "But hurry. She'll kill him."

"No. If she had wanted his death, the Merida would have killed him when you were captured."

The boy looked up with renewed hope; this logic had not occurred to him before. "That's true! And they were careful on the journey to keep him alive, even if he was tied up and unconscious."

She hid a wince at the image this brought to mind, and said, "Tomorrow I want you to present yourself to Maeta and tell her that I bade you to be her squire and do everything she tells you."

"I will. But what's going to happen?"

"She'll explain. She has a very interesting plan for

repaying the Merida for those bruises you wear and for
their complicity in Princess Ianthe's plan. Be sure to tell
Maeta that I also designate you Walvis' deputy when it
comes to all things regarding Remagev.''

Tilal frowned, trying to work it out, then sat up straighter
and smiled. ''You're going to give him the keep, aren't
you? That's why you want to take special care of it!''

''Yes, and you'll be partly responsible for making sure
it gets through this in decent shape. So when you're
there, be sure to see everything you can and stay to
supervise things, for it's your sharp eyes that will give the
best warning of any Merida mischief.'' There, she thought,
she had soothed the boy's pride, given him something
useful to do, and made sure he would stay safe in
Remagev, forbidden to join the battle. ''Tilal, I'd like to
talk further, but it was a long ride from Faolain Lowland.''

''You ought to sleep,'' he said, and stood up, every bit
the young nobleman worried for his liege lady's comfort.
But a breath later he came to put his arms around her
and be held for a moment, a little boy again. ''I'm sorry,''
he whispered miserably. ''I should have helped him more,
and I didn't—''

''You did all you could. And you gave me the information I need to get him back.'' Sioned stroked his hair.
''Would I have entrusted Walvis' future holding to a
coward—or a fool?''

Tilal recovered himself and stepped back. ''I won't fail
you, my lady. Good night.''

Alone once more, Sioned went to the two chairs placed
before the garden windows and sank wearily into one of
them. There was an emptiness beside her in Rohan's
usual chair that matched the void within her. They had
spent so much time here, planning their dreams into
reality. Ianthe would not kill him, but there were other
deaths besides those of the body.

Sioned waited while the moons rose and spread their
cool light across her face and hands. She gathered the
strands together, knowing she could go anywhere, see
anything, speak to any *faradhi* she chose. But there was
one she would not touch on the moonlight, for if Andrade
had any notion of her plans, she would forbid them on

pain of being cast out forever. While Sioned would risk anything for her husband, she still had need of other *faradh'im*.

Skillfully knotting the moonlight into a secure pathway, she flung it northward, past the great basin of Skybowl gleaming in the moonlight. She cast further until she saw the proud towers of Feruche. The garrison below was dark and deserted, but the castle windows shone with light.

Both approaches were indeed closely guarded. There were no weaknesses. She should have known better than to hope arrogance had made Ianthe careless. She had thought to use her skills to slide into this place somehow, divert guards and servants with the Fire and Air she could summon, frighten them into mistakes that would leave her free to enter unnoticed. But as she counted people and observed their actions, she knew that such subterfuge was impossible.

Which window? she wondered, hovering within the moonlight. Or was there any window at all where Rohan slept? Was he high in a tower, or down in a stone cell without light? Anger surged up and her control wavered, and she took some moments to steady herself.

She peeked into rooms at random, noting which held sleeping servants, which were empty, making mental adjustments to her memory of Tilal's map. She could only go as far as the moonlight reached into each chamber, but that was enough. One room contained three ornate beds, each occupied by a sleeping child. Ianthe's sons, Sioned thought, and just like her, for even in sleep the faces were willful and sly. How Roelstra must treasure them; thwarted of sons of his body, he had grandsons now that Ianthe would train up in his image.

She searched all the windows facing the moonlight, more and more afraid that Rohan was indeed in some belowstairs cell or a room on the other side of the towers where she could not go. But at last she found him. *Rohan!* she cried. But no one heard.

His sleeping face had been ravaged by pain and fever that had left deep bruises around his closed eyes. The fine, strong bones of brow and cheeks and chin were too

sharp, his mouth a line of tense exhaustion. A dark silk
sheet was pushed down around his waist and as he turned
restlessly onto his side she saw the dressing wrapped to
the wound in his shoulder. Moisture shone dully on his
skin, blond hair dark with sweat. He was out of reach of
the moonlight that pooled on the carpet beside the bed
but did not touch his body or face. If it had, she might
have touched him, that part of him that held some trace
of the *faradhi* gift. But she could not.

Someone moved into the light, a curving shape, nakedness half-hidden by a cascade of dark hair reaching to her
hips. Sioned trembled, felt her rings bite into her clenched
fingers back where her body sat in Stronghold. Ianthe
slowly insinuated herself beneath the sheet, sliding close
to Rohan's body. She placed one hand on either side of
him, shook her hair down so it covered his bare chest and
belly, then lowered her head to his.

"No!"

The raw howl of her own voice snapped Sioned too
abruptly back into her body. Colors whirled around her,
confused, chaotic, refusing to form their familiar pattern.
Her rings spat emerald and sapphire and amber and onyx
fire into her aching eyes, became burning circles that
ignited her flesh to the bone. The great emerald pulsed
as if it would fill to bursting with light. It swelled and
became the only thing she saw, plunging her into its
glittering green depths as she sobbed aloud in terror.

Yet in the brilliant stone she saw again herself, burned
by her own Fire, holding a newborn boy-child with Rohan's
golden hair.

Rohan's son. And Ianthe's.

A long time later, when she remembered who and
what she was again, she lifted her hands. There were no
charred circles of skin beneath her rings. Cool silver and
gold they clasped her fingers, mocking her. Sunrunner
enough to watch, but not to prevent by any arts what
Ianthe was about to do.

Sioned covered her face with her hands and wept.

Coaxing, knowing fingers brought him to life. He could
barely see her, backlit as she was by the moons, but he

felt the familiar sweetness of her in his arms, the silk of her skin and hair.

"Sioned," he breathed against her mouth.

"Love me! Rohan, love me—now!"

Fire blazed up between them. Her thighs parted and her breasts strained up against him, and he lost himself in the taste and scent and warmth of her, startled by her desperate urgency. But there would be time later to caress her, renew the magical joining he had known only with her and wanted only with her. Filling her body, filling himself with his need of her, filling the night with the singing soaring dragonflight of loving her.

"Yes—oh, yes—now!" she cried out, arching power-fully—and it made no difference to him that the flesh beneath his hands was too full, breasts too heavy, waist too thick and hips too sleek. He sought blindly between her soft thighs, drank from a mouth that tried to suck the life from him. Her thick perfumed hair was a living thing that twisted around him, chaining him to her. He wrenched his head away and cried out Sioned's name in agony.

"No, little prince," Ianthe laughed, gleeful, breathless, wrapped around him like a snake. "You know who I am and what I want—what *you* want! Give it to me! Give me your son!"

Even as his flesh withered away from her, he felt it happening, knew she had won. She let him go. He stag-gered to his feet, clutching the bedpost, flung back the hangings on their metal rings—tapestries of dragons in all their violence and lust.

Ianthe moved languidly on the bed. Her legs were spread wide, her head thrown back, but her arms cradled her breasts as if a child already nursed there. The eager-ness of her fertility would welcome the mindless gift of his—meeting, matching, fusing together inside her belly, creating a life that would be partly his and partly Ianthe's. He understood now why time had been so important to her, why she needed him "capable."

Long lashes lifted from eyes the color of dead leaves. "Sometimes it takes only once," she purred. "But I won't risk that. Come here to me, princeling. Be sure we've made a son."

A son. "I'll kill you," he whispered.

"No, I don't think so." She laughed up at him. "Come, Rohan. You've already betrayed her. What would once more matter? I make sons, and she can't even carry a child!"

Thighs splayed for him, arms held out, triumphant laughter. Something hideous lurched inside him, feeding on his hate, capable of killing. Ianthe laughed again as he dug his fingers into her throat. She writhed beneath him, hands grasping, guiding, greedy. Rage snarled through him and he loomed over her, tightening his grip. He drove himself into her in mindless fury, lifted one hand to strike her, laughing madly at the blood that streamed from her lip. She screamed then, a sound hoarse and frightened and shrill with lust. And he laughed again.

"You wanted me, Ianthe? Let's see how much you want *this*!"

He wallowed in her, spent himself in a vengeance that was her victory over him. He knew it, could not stop himself. He let it go on and on, setting the marks of his hate onto her flesh. When he was finished he fell to one side, nauseated by his own body, hating himself for not having the strength to kill her where she lay. But she had said something that made killing her impossible. She had spoken of a son.

It was a long time before she roused, bruised and bloodied, and slid out of bed. Rohan saw her fingers spread over the curve of her belly. She smiled down at him, raking her tangled hair back from her face, and licked the blood from her lips.

"My father makes only girls," she said scornfully, her voice rough and throaty. "Your Sunrunner witch can't even make those. Oh, she'll get you back, Rohan, safe and sound—I need you alive to confirm that this child is yours." She laughed again, enjoying his flinch. "You wanted me—all these years, ever since that night I came to you at the *Rialla*, you've wanted me. Don't bother denying it. We both know it's true. But you Chose Sioned. Tell me Rohan—could you touch her, after being with *me*?"

"No," he whispered, though not in the manner she

heard it. He could never touch Sioned again, not having befouled himself with Ianthe. He could still feel her on his skin, feel himself in her flesh.

The door locked heavily behind her. She had won—for now. When she returned, he would kill her. He must.

Chapter Twenty-four

Most of the winter had seen Goddess Keep washed by torrential rains. Unpredictable cloud cover made *faradhi* communication sporadic at best. Andrade, irked at having to rely on more conventional means of learning the news, subjected visitors to questioning so intense they came away terrified. With the coming of spring, thick fog walled up the keep and the Sunrunners grew as restless as hawks denied flight. Thoroughly sick of reading, chess, lessons, cleaning, and each other's company, they were united in avoiding Andrade with what amounted to religious devotion.

But at last the fog lifted and the sun shone, and the castle emptied of nearly every living creature—including the denizens of field and forest who had wintered in the castle and now went home. *Faradh'im* and apprentices and the keep's ordinary folk roamed the hillsides, half-drunk on sunlight. Andrade, watching from the battlements, waited until they were all out of sight in the woods or along cliff paths before she undid her silver-gold braids and ran her fingers back through her hair, luxuriating in the warmth of spring sunshine. Her last walk here, some days ago, had been a depressing affair; the castle had been wrapped in the fog that was the Storm God's last little joke after a long and unamusing winter. But now the Goddess had reclaimed the sky for her own.

Replaiting her hair, she grimaced at the streaks of white in it, swearing to herself that they had been caused by Roelstra's impossible daughters. The impulse that had made her claim them six years ago was one she regretted daily.

Pandsala at twenty-three had been, for all her royal upbringing, abysmally ignorant. She had a certain cleverness that kept her from complete mental stagnation, but her formal learning was almost nil. She had not appreciated being sent to the schoolroom with the younger students, but the tactic had the double benefit of pounding a basic education into her skull while curing her of some of her more objectionable arrogances.

Pandsala at twenty-nine was a vast improvement. Discouraged in her attempts to dramatize her chosen role of captive princess, she had abandoned the effort and was now almost tolerable. But it was the shocking discovery of her potential as a Sunrunner that had supplied a needed sense of self-worth. Last summer she had earned her third ring.

Chiana was a different problem entirely. Adopted by the women at the keep, pitied her sorry lot, spoiled by almost everyone, she was quick of body, mind, and spirit. No one knew what she would get into next. To Roelstra's fine aristocratic features and Palila's wealth of auburn hair Chiana added her own winsome charm and a pair of green-brown eyes that could brim with slyness or tears at a moment's notice. Andrade and Urival kept close watch on her, suspecting that her beguiling ways could turn to low cunning if she was not carefully guided.

Pandsala provided discipline. Seeing her sister as the cause of her own exile, she remained uncharmed and unbeguiled. Oddly enough, Chiana behaved, wishing for her elder sister's good opinion, and a bond of sorts had grown between the two. This winter Pandsala had busied herself with teaching Chiana to read, and seemed more content with her lot.

Andrade wondered how long she would have to keep the pair with her. Despite the circumstances of her birth, Chiana would eventually be sought in marriage, and when Roelstra finally obliged everyone by dying, Pandsala would be free to do as she liked.

Thought of the High Prince reminded Andrade of why she had come up here today—not to breathe in the spring but to take a look at what was going on around her. She shook back her loosened hair and closed her eyes, the instinctive mental loom absorbing her thoughts, and she sighed with the pleasure of the weaving denied her every winter. Across the green downs of Ossetia she roamed, eastward to Gilad where flooded manors were being repaired; a glance for the Catha Hills where herds were being coaxed to rich grazing on the coast; an approving nod for the white sails of Lleyn's ships plying regular trade routes again now that the danger of storm was gone. All was fine and fair in the south, and Andrade smiled her satisfaction.

For the sheer pleasure of it she followed the bright ribboning rivers to the north, sensing the sunlight cool as it danced across the water. Up to the lower hills of the Great Veresch Mountains she flew, pausing to admire the snow-capped peaks. Pleasure faded as she looked down at Castle Crag, and annoyance set in, quickly superceded by curiosity at the quiet of the place. Was Roelstra on progress somewhere? Off to one of his hunting lodges? She could see only a few daughters arranged languidly around the gardens, only a few servants, and barely enough troops to secure the gatehouse.

Andrade sped across the mountains, dazzled by the brilliance of white snow beneath her, then flung her skeins westward to Fessenden. A hard winter for them, too, she saw; snow still heavy on the ground, fishing boats huddled in the harbors, the port city of Einar shivering in the chill sunlight. She would gather reports soon from the Sunrunner assigned to the court there, and find out what help Lord Kuteyn's widow needed to replenish her winter-ravaged lands.

A quick glance over Kierst-Isel heartened her; garrisons along the borders were at ease this spring where they normally bristled for the usual skirmishes. Memory of Rohan's proposal of legally set boundaries made her smile; perhaps Volog and Saumer had at long last decided who owned what. A leap across the wide bay between the island and the mainland, and she was over a Meadowlord soggy with spring runoff. As often as she wondered why the ancient *faradh'im* had built Goddess Keep on this fog-bound coast, she gave thanks that they had not chosen the marshy lowland with their muggy summers and never-ending supply of insects.

Farther, to Syr that lay between rivers, rich land and fertile, the soil dark with new turning and planting—and a nostalgic glance at her own childhood home of Catha Freehold that had never belonged to any but her own family who had never bent the knee to any prince. On her father's death it had reverted to Syr, for she had given up all claim to it and it was too far from the Desert for Zehava to rule effectively. The plain stone tower rose proud and white in a hollow between low hills, within sighting distance—for a *faradhi* on the wing—of Sioned's family's River Run. She paused to survey the huge holding, and frowned as she discovered that it, too, was nearly empty.

One place left to go today; snowbound Firon and Cunaxa could wait for another time. She wanted to see the Desert, look in on Stronghold and the Long Sand, possibly glimpse the two who ruled there as wisely and well as she had always known they would. But as she glided once more over Syrene fields, she saw tents. Horses. Archers and sword-soldiers drilling in strict formation. And on a rise overlooking the whole were two huge pavilions: one turquoise, one violet. Syr and Princemarch, camped not a day's march from the Desert border.

Andrade hurried to Faolain Lowland, Lord Baisal's holding that seethed with activity under Chaynal's red-and-white battle flag. Fury stung her. Why had no one told her of this? And why were Rohan's own colors not flying? And who belonged to that black and green flag set up in the fields outside the manor, where troops organized for war?

Though powerfully motivated to find Sioned and demand an explanation, Andrade returned instead to Goddess Keep. She would have to inform the other princes through her *faradh'im* at their courts. Yet as she passed over Lake Kadar, she gasped aloud in shock. Along the main road there marched a considerable force of men-at-arms, with officers on horseback and red-and-yellow pennants proclaiming them soldiers of young Lord Lyell of Waes. They were headed directly for Goddess Keep.

By nightfall Andrade's anger had steadied into a slow, fierce hate. She called everyone into the hall and waited in an awful silence for all of them to assume their seats at the long tables, Urival and the senior *faradh'im* to one side of her, the others in descending order of rank all around.

"Troops belonging to Lord Lyell of Waes, betrothed now to the High Prince's daughter Kiele, have set up his banner in a camp outside our gates. We are told it is for our protection. We are told Lord Lyell is concerned for our safety in these troubled times, with High Prince Roelstra and Prince Jastri of Syr camped near the Desert border and the Merida besieging Tiglath. We are told Lord Lyell takes on himself the duty of defending us. We are told he does this because he knows *faradh'im* are forbidden to kill, even in their own defense." She paused and smiled grimly. "We are told many things—most of which are lies.

"Many of you have ridden the sunlight today, seeking information. Sometimes you have sought other *faradh'im* in vain, for they have been locked away out of the light by lords and princes allied to Roelstra. They are as captive as we are—and as Prince Rohan is at Feruche Castle."

Most had not known of this, and a startled murmuring went through the assembly. Andrade held up both hands for silence.

"Of Princess Sioned, one of us, there is no word. I sought her myself and she is not to be found. But we know from the Sunrunner Kleve in Tiglath that the High Prince's daughter Ianthe holds Prince Rohan."

Urival, seated just beside her, muttered, "Not for long, if I know Sioned."

Andrade tried to ignore the panic this remark brought to her heart. "Though we are free to weave the sunlight, we are pent in this keep. Urival and I have been discussing ways to free some of us in secret while the rest remain here, soothing Lord Lyell's troops into thinking we are all still caged. We have—"

"I can do it."

Andrade stared down the hall to where Pandsala had risen from her chair.

"I can free some of us," the princess said. "Lyell's men

will not detain my father's daughter in her escape from the keep."

Urival sucked in a breath and Andrade cursed herself for not having thought of Pandsala earlier. Suspicions darted through her mind, but she let Urival voice them.

"Is this escape to be for our benefit—or yours?" he asked coldly.

"I understand your hesitation," Pandsala replied. "It is true I would rather be out in the world. But I have had chances before and not taken them. Do you think I would give aid to my father, who sent me here against my will? He cast me out. You took me in. I wear three *faradhi* rings. If you do not trust me, do not use me."

Urival would have questioned her further, but the dignity of her reply had impressed Andrade. She gestured her chief steward to silence, and said, "Tell me what you propose."

The princess clasped her hands before her, not quite tightly enough to hide their excited tremors. "At dusk, when the light is uncertain and torches are needed, I and whomever you choose will leave by the postern gate. When we are within range of Lord Lyell's camp, make an outcry here to encourage the idea that I have escaped with my friends."

"And then?" Urival prompted, suspicion still in his voice.

"I am a frightened princess," Pandsala said with a hint of a smile. "I will require guards to take me to my father's camp in Syr. To deplete Lord Lyell's troops by ten or twelve would not be much, but it would help a little. And there would also be at least one man, possibly two, who would have to ride to Waes and inform his lordship of my action. If we are fortunate, we can rid Goddess Keep of fifteen men."

"Fifteen of fifty," Urival mused.

"And I will insist that the very best fighters accompany me," Pandsala added slyly. "It is my right, after all."

Andrade nodded slowly. "Very well. Urival, Pandsala, attend me in my chambers. The rest of you—sleep soundly tonight, for there will be much to keep you busy tomorrow."

As she walked down the long aisle between the tables

to the door, Urival and Pandsala joined her. Andrade's gaze shifted to Chiana—who suddenly looked too much like her father for Andrade's peace of mind.

"If Rohan wants some use out of this place once this is over, we can't continue to camp here." Chay turned from the window and faced his wife, who was changing out of dusty riding clothes into fresh ones. He frowned at her. "Tobin, I need you to set things straight here at the manor. You're not coming out into the field with me."

"Stop me," she invited, and pulled on her boots. "You're the military commander, but I'm my father's daughter. And until Rohan and Sioned arrive—"

"Whatever possessed that foolish woman to leave?" he growled, pacing the chamber with an agitation he would never have shown to anyone else. "Of all the stupid—"

"Oh, don't you understand?" she exclaimed. "There's no help for Rohan but Sioned!"

"I gathered that much, thank you," he snapped. "But I still say that with a small troop—"

"You're forgetting what Feruche is like. And what Sioned is like, too." Tobin rose and stamped her feet to secure the fit of her boots. "Did you expect her to sit here and wait for us to arrive and try to talk her out of it? Goddess, how I wish I was a real Sunrunner! We've nobody to use in contacting her or Andrade or anyone!" She tucked her shirt into her trousers and went on, "Let's go, Chay. I want to look at the provisions in the field camp. And you're right about having to move. Lord Baisal can't go on feeding them all."

Down in the courtyard, the arrival of Chay's levies had added to the chaos. Horses, foot soldiers, archers, swordsmen—and all of Lord Baisal's frantic servants—milled about in no discernible order. Chay had every confidence that by nightfall his captain would have everything sorted out, so he and Tobin mounted up and joined Lord Davvi at the gates.

"I've done all I could," Sioned's brother told them. "But I've no real authority here except over my own people. I'm glad you're here, my lord."

"Titles are fine in public—but please call me Chay. We're brothers after a fashion, you know."

Tobin hid a smile of her own as her husband's smile worked its usual magic. In two sentences he had made Davvi his, a man who would follow him unquestioningly into whatever battle Chay cared to fight.

"Thank you," Davvi said simply. "We'll tour the camp now, and I'll—"

He was interrupted by a shrill cry from behind them. Parental instinct had Tobin and Chay off their horses in an instant, neither mistaking the urgency in Sorin's voice. Chay pushed a path for them through to where the twins had been currying their ponies in a corner of the stableyard. Sorin ran to his father and clutched at his arm, frightened. Andry stood in a well of sunlight, rigid and trembling, blue eyes huge.

Tobin knelt beside Andry. Sharing sunlight with him, she felt, as she had known she would, the dizzying touch of a powerful *faradhi*. But it was not Sioned she felt on the sunlight. It was Andrade.

Tobin? Sweet Goddess, girl, why didn't you tell me the boy was so gifted? But never mind that now. That young idiot Lyell of Waes is trying to feast from both ends of the loaf—giving aid to his dead sister's lord in Tiglath and marching his troops here to pen me in while Roelstra and Jastri work mischief in the south. Urival and I are working on that, but I'm not sure yet how we'll manage it. I've sent word to every court where my Sunrunners aren't locked away from the light—Roelstra's orders, I'm sure, to those he's got beneath his boot heels. Count among them Syr and Cunaxa—hoping to win portions of the Desert from the Merida war. Saumer of Isel in secret—Volog of Kierst says there are rumors of trade agreements. Waes plays a double game and I'm sure Clutha is having fits and may bring Lyell into line. Of those to trust—only Lleyn, and perhaps Pimantal of Fessenden, for Roelstra has eyes on his city of Einar. Tell this to Sioned if you can find her, which I cannot. I know about Feruche. Get Andry to Stronghold and Sorin with him for safety, for Roelstra will attack as soon as he decides to notice Lord Davvi's desertion. Have a care to yourself and Chay—I'll come as soon as I can.

Tobin felt strong arms lift her up and carry her out of

the hot sunlight into the cool dark manor house. The relief nearly made her cry out. It was a long while before she recovered from the length and ruthless power of Andrade's weaving, and when she was fully aware again she found herself lying in bed, limp with exhaustion and unable even to consider arguing with Chay as he stripped off her clothes and tucked her beneath a sheet.

"Andry?" she murmured.

"He's all right. Sorin got him into the shade, and he's resting now in his room." Chay sat beside her and pressed her palm to his cheek. "Damn it, Tobin," he muttered hoarsely. "I hate this!"

"I'll be all right, sweet," she soothed. "It's just that Andrade isn't as gentle as Sioned." She relayed the gist of the news and his shoulder muscles worked with renewed tension.

"Perfect," he rasped. "Wonderful! Help from Lleyn and Pimantal and Volog! Islands on either side of the world, and a princedom that might as well be! Where's the help in that?"

"The rest are either in league with Roelstra or terrified of him. With no *Rialla* in six years, and so much at stake now—"

There was grim determination in his gray eyes and the set of his long jaw. "Roelstra will not be attending the *Rialla* this year, or any other year," he said quietly.

Tobin watched him leave, and only when he was gone did she allow the shiver to claim her. She had never seen death in his eyes before.

Davvi was not encouraged by the report of Chay's captain the next morning, and said so. "One hundred sixty-three horse, one hundred five archers—and of trained regulars, not nearly enough." He turned worried green eyes on Chay. "If we count the ones who can use a scythe but not a sword—"

"Have you ever had a man come at you with a scythe, Davvi? A man with reaper's muscles who has every intention of lopping your head off as easily as he'd take care of a stalk of grain?" Chay smiled tightly. "We'll do just fine. Two hundred and thirty-six with swords and scythes. Of the horse, your people are the best trained—"

"Excepting your own," Davvi interrupted wryly, and Chay shrugged. "Of those brought in by Lord Baisal—"

"Ah, but there's a look in their eyes. It's their own fields they'll be defending. If you'd do me the favor, please help with the plans for the move. We'll recamp tomorrow. Battling *for* one's own land is an admirable spur, but battling *on* it makes people nervous."

Chay had learned that from Zehava. As he went upstairs to his wife, he experienced a fleeting wish that the old prince was here to direct this battle. Or, better yet, that there would be no battle at all. Fine thoughts for a seasoned warrior, he told himself acidly. Rohan had indeed infected him with peace, and Chay suspected that it was a thing which, once in the blood and the brain, was something from which one did not recover. Nor wanted to.

Tobin had spent the morning working within the manor, organizing Baisal's capable but confused servants into an efficient war machine. But by midmorning she voluntarily sought her bed for a rest, more exhausted than she'd thought by her contact with Andrade. Chay stood watching her for some time, relieved to see that color had come back into her cheeks and her sleep was deep and quiet. She was more beautiful now than the day he'd married her—richer in spirit, more regal of bearing, the dragon's daughter calmed but never tamed. He smoothed the black hair from her shoulders and placed a kiss on her forehead, then left to wash the morning's stink off him.

By the time she woke he was clean, redressed, and seated at a small table with a meal spread out before him. "Come and eat," he invited.

She stretched widely, yawned, and joined him—naked as a baby. "Oh, who's to see me but you?" she said with a shrug in response to his lifted brows. "And you're used to me. It's too hot for clothes, Chay."

"My shameless darling, the day I'm used to the sight of you is the day I've gone blind—and even then my fingers would do the looking. Here, have some cheese. It's pretty good. I wonder what they feed their goats?"

"Has Roelstra made a move yet?" she asked as she sat down.

"The wine's not bad, either. I think we're raiding Baisal's private reserve."

"Are more troops coming? How many do we have now?"

"Save your tongue to lick your spoon."

She made a face at him, but hunger was stronger than curiosity just now. When she had made substantial inroads on the food, Chay began to share his observations of the day and ask her opinions. He would miss her, he reflected, when she was gone away to Stronghold. But her safety and that of their sons was more important.

Their hellions had flatly refused to stay at Radzyn Keep, arguing that if Mama got to go to war then they should be allowed to do the same—and if they weren't taken along now, they'd find a way to sneak out. Chay knew his sons too well to doubt that they would do just that, and reasoned that having them under his eye was better than not knowing what they were up to. Tomorrow, however, they would be sent to Stronghold, but Tobin did not yet know she would be going with them. When he finally mentioned it—casually, around a bite of apple—her reaction reminded him why he prohibited knives in their bedchamber.

"I won't go! You need me here!"

"I need you to be safe."

"No one else can act as *faradhi*, and even the little I can do will keep you informed. Damn you, Chay, I won't go!"

"Will you be sensible, please? We have to send Sorin and Andry to safety—especially Andry! I'll tie them to their horses and have their squires slug them unconscious if I have to. Don't make me use the same tactic on you."

"You wouldn't *dare!*"

It was amazing how much she looked like Zehava when she was angry. "Listen to me. You're useful to me here, yes. But I won't spend my time worrying about your safety. Do you think the boys would leave without you? At Stronghold you'll be able to help Sioned. Do I have to list the reasons you already know, Tobin."

She glared at him. "You're loathsome when you make sense."

He thanked the Goddess for a woman with brains as well as spirit. Reaching across the table, intending to take her hand and express his gratitude for the towering virtues that sometimes drove him to distraction, he smiled wryly as she snatched her fingers away. Pride forbade her to be gracious right now. So Chay leaned back to appreciate her where she sat with one leg tucked beneath her, clad only in the black glory of her hair.

His silent admiration was ended by a frantic pounding on the door. As he rose to answer it he threw his discarded shirt at his wife and told her to put it on. It came to her knees and decently covered everything else, but when Chay opened the door Baisal's eyes popped and his cheeks turned scarlt. Just behind him, looking pallid and ill, was Maarken. Chay stared in astonishment at the son he had not seen in two years; the abrupt change from child to tall, self-possessed young squire was more than he could take in at a glance. Father and son gazed at each other for some moments before Chay pulled Maarken into his arms for a hard embrace.

"Goddess, but it's good to see you! What are you doing here?"

Tobin gave a glad cry and rushed toward them. "Maarken—oh, Maarken, you've grown so tall!" Her eyes filled as she hugged her son.

The boy smiled tiredly. "I kept telling everyone at Graypearl how beautiful you are, Mother. Now they'll get a look for themselves and find I didn't exaggerate."

Chay looked to Baisal for explanation. The older *athri* cleared his throat, embarrassed at witnessing the family reunion and the princess' unconventional state of dress. It was Maarken who answered his father's unspoken question.

"I've come with archers, Father—fifty of them, sent by Prince Lleyn. We set sail early yesterday and came up the Faolain as far as we could." He gave a slight shudder. "And then we finally got to *walk*."

"No wonder you're green," Chay commented. To Baisal he went on, "Please ask my captain to find places for the new arrivals. You and I and Lord Davvi will have to talk to whomever's leading the archers."

"As you wish, my lord." With a last furtive glance at Tobin, he left.

The princess was trying to persuade her·son to eat something, and Chay grinned as the boy's complexion paled further at the sight of food. "Leave him be, Tobin. He'll eat as soon as he's recovered from crossing water. I'm surprised he's upright, frankly. What's Lleyn up to, Maarken?"

"Exactly what you'd expect. He only regrets that he couldn't provide more troops on short notice. But more will be coming soon, and ships with them."

Chay sank into a chair and thought this over. He had never fought a war utilizing ships, but the possibilities enchanted him.

"Meath—that's Lleyn's second Sunrunner—was contacted day before yesterday by the *faradhi* up in Tiglath," Maarken continued. "The sunlight's been thick with messages, Father. When Urival contacted Meath yesterday at dawn, Lleyn had already put everything together so we could leave as fast as we could." He paused, then turned haunted eyes on this father. "Is it true about Ianthe?"

"Yes," Chay told him. "I'm glad Lleyn acted so quickly—not only in the matter of archers, but in sending you to me." He glanced at Tobin. "There's no excuse now for you not to go to Stronghold. Maarken can be squire and Sunrunner both."

"Meath and Eolie have taught me enough for a first ring, Mother," Maarken said as Tobin's brows knotted. "They're going to ask Lady Andrade for permission to give me the token and further training. I can do what you can do—really I can."

Chay watched emotions battle on his wife's face: irritation that she had been deprived of her reason for staying here, pride in her son, sadness that she would have so little time with him before she left tomorrow. But all she said was, "If Meath has had the foresight to make your colors known—"

"The *faradhi* in Tiglath knows. He can tell others. You can go to Stronghold with a clear conscience, Mother."

Chay coughed to cover laughter. Conscience had not been keeping Tobin here, but it would certainly take her to Stronghold.

"So. Your father has managed to get his own way. As usual."

Her capitulation was enough; Chay had learned long since not to gloat about his rare victories over her. It was the surest way to ignite her considerable temper and her incredible stubbornness. So he changed the subject. "I'd like you to talk with Andry before tomorrow, Maarken. Twice now he's been caught in a *faradhi* weaving and he doesn't understand it. You've learned enough from Meath and Eolie to explain it to him."

"It *is* kind of scary the first few times," Maarken said with all the wisdom of one earned but unworn Sunrunner's ring. Chay reflected that from now on he would have to treat his son not as a little boy, but as a man, and had a moment of poignant regret for the child Maarken had been. He could have asked for no better companion than the youth he saw before him now—scarcely eleven winters old yet behaving exactly as a princess' son ought. Still. . . .

"I'll get some clothes on," Tobin said, "and we'll go find the boys." She disappeared behind a tall screen in a corner of the room.

Maarken regarded his father thoughtfully. "Shall I really to be your squire?"

"I assume Lleyn and his son Chadric have trained you adequately."

The boy nodded. "But does it mean I can go to war at your side? Not just sit in your tent?"

Chay heard Tobin make a soft sound. *Goddess help me,* he thought. *I don't want my boys to grow up and go to battle so young. Rohan is right—and this must be the last war. If only Sioned can free him so he can fight it, and never fight another—*

"Father?"

"Yes, Maarken. I doubt you'll do much sitting around in my tent."

Night again, hot and close. The sixth night since Ianthe. Rohan turned away from the dinner laid out for him. Food, wine, even water were suspect. He trusted neither his tongue nor his nose, for everything tasted and smelled of *dranath* to him. He was over the worst of it, having eaten in the last few days only those things he considered least dangerous—unsliced fruit from which he peeled the skin, dragontail cactus root washed clean of its sauces, a few other things. His stomach growled at times with emptiness, but he had no other way of ensuring that he ingested no more of the drug. He found it ironic that the *dranath* that had saved his dragons was so great a danger to him.

Yet he could not attribute his actions solely to the confusion of the drug and the fever from his wound. His glance went to the corner where he had piled the obscene bed-hangings and the tapestry. He had yanked them down after Ianthe had left him, shamed and furious at the memories they evoked, wishing he was a *faradhi* so he could set them afire. But he was not allowed so much as a single candle, let alone the means to light one. The weavings were useless to him in any escape attempt, for his chamber overlooked the courtyard from seven floors up. He intended to die only if he could take Ianthe with him.

She had been careful and clever. There was nothing sharp in the room, not even knife or fork to use in eating. Neither was there anything heavy enough to fell her or thin enough to twist into an effective garotte. All he had were his hands—his guilty, betraying hands that should have throttled the life from her six nights ago. He should have killed her then.

He wondered when she would come to him again, or if. He had seen no one but the brawny guard who brought his food, a man who made two of Rohan. He occupied himself in keeping track of the movements outside his windows, the timing of meals, changes of the guard, numbers of troops and servants. He had worked on the lock for two days to no avail. His guard had taken away the heavy bronze curtain rods; there was no furniture but the bed to break into a weapon; nothing in the entire chamber he could use. Escape was not one of his options.

Surely someone should have come for him by now. An attempt to parley, an attack on the castle, anything. He despised himself for looking to others for help, but there was no other hope. He began to be filled with a distracting horror that his own capture was only a small piece of a more elaborate plan, that everyone else was either prisoner or dead. Caged and restless, he paced the bare stone floor night after night, conjuring in his head not only the destruction of Feruche but of Castle Crag and all Princemarch. Himself at the head of the Desert armies, he laid waste to the land, exacting his vengeance. And the High Prince he executed with his own sword while the other princes and lords looked on and trembled at this demonstration of Rohan's power.

Pretty thoughts, he told himself bitterly. A life lived by the sword, dealing out death. Land scorched and dead, thousands killed, more thousands homeless. So much for his ideals. All the splendid childish conceits of his youth sifted away like windblown sand, and he watched them disappear without any emotion but shame.

Not at their passing, or at letting them go. Shame that he had ever deluded himself in the first place. Life was not civilized. People were not disposed to follow the rule of law. They were all barbarians, and Rohan knew himself for the worst of the lot. He was a prince with the power of Desert courage and dragon wealth at his command. He had fooled himself that he was better than the others, him with his noble aims and high ambitions. At least the others had always known themselves for what they were. At least they were honest about life, looked it in the face, and did their killing without illusions.

Roelstra had the truth of it. Pit everyone against each other and collect the spoils. Rule through divisiveness and cunning. Work for dissension, not cooperation. Prey on and play on the baser emotions—greed, jealousy, cowardice—and laugh at the foolish princeling who wanted to inspire minds to honor and hearts to peace.

And of the woman who had believed with Rohan, whose steady intelligence and faith in him had reinforced his belief in himself, he dared not think at all. In betraying her he had betrayed all, for Roelstra's daughter had the truth of *him*. He was the same as the High Prince, the same as every man who wished to see himself reborn. He craved a son. That first time with Ianthe, that might be excused. But the second, when he had known who she was and what she wanted of him—there could be no pardon for that.

Oh, yes, he was just like all the rest, all the self-centered barbarian princes who killed first and gloated later. But even as his mind supplied satisfying scenes of the High Prince dead beneath his sword, Rohan never conjured up Ianthe. He knew very well why. He would not kill her. Could not.

The clattering of hooves and swords in the courtyard took him to the window. Shouts echoed up the castle walls to his aerie. The massive gates, stone hinged by ancient bronze, swung outward with a sickening groan. He could not see who or what caused the commotion, only the knot of guards moving into the main yard.

"The rings!" someone shouted. "They're helpless without them!" The knot untied itself with the struggle, and then one of the soldiers gave a crow of triumph. "I've got 'em! *Faradhi* rings!"

"Oh, sweet Goddess, no," Rohan whispered.

Ianthe strode down the steps in a swirl of pale gown and streaming dark hair. "You idiots!" she spat. "Believing in that old tale! Give those rings to me at once! And keep an eye on her!"

The guard lost his swagger and approached his lady, bowing humbly as he placed the rings in her hand. Torchlight caught the sparkle of gold and silver and a great emerald before Ianthe gripped the rings tightly in her fist. She gestured and the guards fell back to reveal a straight, slender woman in riding clothes, her red-gold hair tumbled around her face.

"So you've come to claim your princeling," Ianthe said sweetly. "How devoted. How loving. I'd expected half an army—but you were all that could be spared, I daresay. Your Desert armies are busy elsewhere, aren't they?"

She half turned, lifting her face to Rohan's window. He ducked back into the shadows, unwilling to give her the satisfaction of seeing his stricken face. "Do you hear me, Rohan? With the Merida attacking in the north and my father in the south, this is all they can spare to come for you! And you their prince!"

Instead of shocking him into frozen horror, the information burned his soul. He understood now, and the fury sent tremors through his very bones. Only Sioned, only his Sunrunner princess—who would not have made this journey in order to die with him. He knew her too well. Hope stirred for the first time, and the old confidence welled up, sweet water to a man half-dead of thirst. He and she together could do anything.

But there was Ianthe. Rohan stared down at Sioned from the shadows, saw her weary face uplifted, eyes seeking but not finding him.

"Ianthe!" she called out, and the princess turned from the castle steps. "I *have* come for my lord and husband—but I've also come for *you.*" And all at once a great gout of Sunrunner's Fire sprang up in front of her, a twisting column of flame half the height of Feruche itself. And in the fire there appeared a dragon, gleaming crimson and gold.

No one screamed; throats contracted in terror as the *faradhi* worked her arcane magic, her long fingers naked of rings. But whatever else Ianthe was, she was no coward. She faced down the towering Fire and cried out, "Stop—or I'll have him killed now, tonight, with his own sword!"

The flames wavered, died. Ianthe laughed. "Take her to an inner room where no sunlight or moonlight reaches! Don't fear, Sunrunner—I'll give him back to you soon!"

Rohan closed his eyes and pressed his forehead to the rough wall. Soon—when she was certain she carried his child, and could flaunt the fact to Sioned. Son or not, he would kill her. And the child, too.

Barbarian.

Chapter Twenty-five

Andrade knew it had to be a dream. Roelstra and Ianthe and Pandsala, dressed in dark violet cloaks, held her hands to a Fire of her own conjuring. When they pulled her away from the flames, her arms ended in blackened stumps at the wrists. The High Prince and Ianthe then reached into the Fire and salvaged the hands. Pandsala gathered up rings and bracelets, thin chains shivering. With ritual solemnity they circled around the blaze, gave the hands to a shadowy figure beyond the light. And within the depths of a voluminous cloak Andrade saw her own wrists and palms and fingers merge into those of someone unknown. Pandsala slid the jeweled rings onto the fingers, clasped the bracelets around the wrists, attached the delicate chains. A gesture of those hands, and the Fire rose powerfully, flung itself around Ianthe, who vanished into nothingness. The white-gold flames then formed a gleaming sword that pierced Roelstra's flesh; he, too, was taken by Fire, gone forever. But Pandsala remained, head bowed in submission to the unknown who wore Andrade's *faradhi* rings, had mastered all the power they symbolized—and was unafraid to use that power to kill.

There the dream ended, and she woke to the sounds of the forest shifting around her. Sitting up, she gulped in the clean morning air, knowing it was foolish to inspect her hands—and inspecting them anyway. She believed in prophetic dreams only when it suited her. This one was best forgotten as quickly as she could.

She attempted to distract herself with the details of her surroundings. Urival slept uneasily nearby, wrapped in his cloak on the hard ground. Two other forms curled on

the other side of the dead fire. Trees screened the first
sunlight, hazy through the blue-green mists rising from
the river. Andrade rubbed her back that ached from
having to sit her horse like a sack of grain in aid of her
disguise as Pandsala's servant. Five days of it had left her
sore in self-image as well as in body, and both gave her
the source of her dream. Her hands were stiff, the joints
laced with hot needles; she still smarted with the indig-
nity of having to pocket her rings and bracelets until
Lord Lyell's men were taken care of; fury seethed within
at Roelstra, Ianthe, and especially Pandsala for putting
her in this humiliating position. But that shadowy figure,
unidentifiable even as male or female, still troubled her.

There were simple cures for morning aches and dream
phantoms. Andrade pushed herself to her feet, wincing
as her bones protested the morning damp and chill, and
walked down to the river. Exercise gradually warmed her
muscles as she sought convenient shallows for washing,
and the cold water cleared her head. She shook droplets
from her face and hands, rebraided her hair, and felt
more equal to dealing with an intransigent world.

Or at least to learning what new inconveniences it had
in store for her today. Goddess knew, the last five days
had been bad enough. In addition to Pandsala, she had
had to endure Chiana's presence on the road from Goddess Keep, for the girl had somehow managed to secure a
horse and ride out with them. Discovery had come too
late. Taking seriously Chiana's whispered threat to expose the whole scheme to Lord Lyell's men, Andrade
had gritted her teeth and rebuked herself silently for
having taken the brat in to begin with. But it had been
too late for self-recrimination, as well.

Urival, knowing they would need help crossing the
rivers between Goddess Keep and Syr, had delayed the
application of sleeping herbs and Sunrunner magic on the
detachment sent along to escort Pandsala to her father.
Andrade had been all for trussing them up the first night
out. But this afternoon on a rest stop she had done the
necessary, and now they were free. Pandsala couldn't
have been happier, and Chiana bounced along on a horse
too large for her, singing. Neither sight was calculated to
improve Andrade's temper.

The news on the sunlight had been terrible. The Merida assaulted the walls of Tiglath with infuriating regularity. Their arrows found a few targets, they lost a few men, and they retreated until the next skirmish. Andrade understood the tactic: constant harassment to wear down the city's spirit. Open battle exhilarated, but a slow, steady siege exhausted morale. Young Walvis had plans to raid Merida supply lines, both to gain provisions for the city and to give his troops the reassurance of action. But a pitched battle on the plain was denied him.

Tobin and the younger twins had arrived safely at Stronghold, but Andrade's view of the castle had shown it to be nearly deserted. A glimpse of the area around Tiglath showed a force had broken off from the main Merida army to head south. And at Feruche life went on as if all was usual and normal, as if the garrison below the keep was still full of Rohan's soldiers. Of Rohan and Sioned, there was no news and no sign.

Andrade dried her face and hands on a relatively clean section of her skirt and started back. Urival's sudden shout of alarm came just as she topped the rise. He stood before the cold fire, rumpled and furious, holding Pandsala's empty cloak.

"Gone!" he bellowed. "Damn that bitch—she's gone!"

Chiana sat with her feet tucked under her, unimpressed by Urival's rage. Andrade saw the artful arrangement of saddles that had simulated two sleeping forms where there had been only one, endured Chiana's smug smile for five long breaths, then hauled the girl to her feet and shook her.

"You knew!"

"Yes, my Lady," Chiana affirmed with a nod. "My sister has gone to our father, of course," she went on as if Andrade was too old and addled in her wits to grasp the obvious. "She ought to be with him by now. And she took all the horses with her."

Andrade let her go, turning away, not wanting Urival to see the murder she knew was in her eyes. Pandsala's weeping, hand-wringing performance to Lyell's captain had renewed suspicions, but she had behaved herself perfectly on the journey when she could at any time have

denounced the two Sunrunners. But now this—with Chiana
as gleeful accomplice. Andrade had saved their lives and
they would ruin her, for Pandsala wore *faradhi* rings now
and her talents would be put to the service of the High
Prince.

Slowly, she faced Chiana again. She saw her own hand
draw back. But she did not strike. Chiana let out a soft
whimper of fear.

"You are old enough to understand events—and old
enough to betray," Andrade told her in a deathly quiet
voice. "I should have expected this from someone whose
name means 'treason.' "

Chiana stood her ground unflinching, defiance blazing
in her eyes. "My father—" she began proudly.

"Is a walking dead man." Andrade turned to Urival.
"Thus far for tradition's sake I have hesitated. But today
the sunlight will tremble. The *faradh'im* choose the Desert, her prince, and her armies."

"Please consider, my Lady," he replied in formal tones
that spoke his misgivings more clearly than if he had
cried out a hundred reasons against her decision.

"I am within my rights. Roelstra has shut the *faradh'im*
away from all light. For this alone he deserves what we'll
do to him."

"His death?" Urival asked.

"We are not murderers."

"Nor executioners?" he pressed.

"No," Andrade said, and for the first time in her life
regretted the ten rings on her fingers, the bracelets and
chains linking them and her to ancient vows. "No," she
repeated. "Never."

Sioned had grown used to the dark. Not a thread of
light was permitted, not even a candle. She had no way
of knowing how much time had passed, how many days
and nights and days again. Meals came at irregular
intervals—as did men who were a darkness she could
taste and smell as well as feel.

She had been unable to test out Maeta's information
about the hidden entry to Feruche; though she had anticipated most of the guards and the time they changed

duty, one had caught her just the same. Her own fault, she knew, for being careless in her urgency. And now she was here in this black cell, alone.

It was the lack of colors that disturbed her most. A Sunrunner shut away from the light was an unnatural thing, yet panic had not lasted long. The suffocating heat did not trouble her after what must have been a day or so. But she missed the colors. She spent her time tracing the shape of each one in memory: not the faces and landscapes and sky they formed, but wanting only to feel them, wrap them around her in the blackness. They were life to her, the gorgeous spectrum that made up the world she touched as a *faradhi*. But without light, she could not feel them. They had no substance.

She did not waste her energy by conjuring Fire very often. It hurt her eyes, and the colors of flame raged with her inner turmoil, her fear. And what was the use, in any case? She knew she would not be here forever.

A squeal of hinges alerted her a few moments before a torch spewed red-gold into her cell. She covered her face and turned away to spare her eyes that teared and stung with the pain of light.

"Goddess blessing, Sunrunner," Ianthe greeted mockingly.

Sioned took her hands from her cheeks and slitted her eyes open, wiped away tears. But she was not yet equal to meeting Ianthe's gaze.

"Here," Ianthe went on, "cover yourself. You're looking rather awful, my dear. Like Rohan—too afraid of the *dranath* to eat much. It shows, princess." She laughed. Sioned held herself from a flinch as clothes were flung at her.

She could open her eyes now without too much pain, and after brushing away the last of the tears she faced the princess. Ianthe's smile sickened her.

"You'd enjoy killing me, wouldn't you, Sioned? Almost as much as Rohan would. But you're both too cowardly to dare it here in my castle. Tell me, Sunrunner, do you love your life so much you'd willingly endure this? Or do you love life even more than you hate me?" She laughed again. "There's a subtlety here that has escaped you, I think. Hate is everything. My father understands that, and so do I, thanks to you and Rohan. Yes, I really ought to express my gratitude! Hate is the only thing that endures. It's kept you alive thus far, hasn't it?"

Ianthe took another step into the cell, firelight playing off her unbound hair, her jewels, her dark crimson gown. "But neither of you will risk your own lives to fulfill your hate for me and my father. Very practical of you, and very satisfying for me. There's another life in question now. When a woman has borne three sons, she knows the signs of another in her body."

Sioned stared at the torch Ianthe held. She could do it—conjure the Fire higher and hotter, send it writhing down the princess' body, do to her what Roelstra had done to his mistress—

Ianthe cursed and threw the torch onto the stones. But Sioned had already doused the small flare her thoughts had given the flames. She would not kill Ianthe. Yet. There were no burns on her own flesh, no child in her arms.

The light fluttered up in strange patterns of shadows that both burnished and blackened Ianthe's face. "I knew seven days after my youngest son was conceived," she said. "But I wanted to make especially sure this time. Perhaps you think I won't be believed. Put your mind at rest, Sioned. There will be no doubt that this child is Rohan's. With my father victorious on his battlefield and I on mine, who will dare to doubt? Rohan will live long enough to acknowledge his son—and I want you alive to hear him do it. After that. . . ." She shrugged. "You're free to go now, and your princeling with you. Enjoy your life while you may, for it lasts only until midwinter when my son is born."

Sioned waited until the princess had turned to the door in a sweep of crimson, then said, "Enjoy your hate while you may, Ianthe, if hate is life to you. It ends when Rohan's son is born."

The princess' spine stiffened and for an instant she froze. Sioned smiled to herself. Then Ianthe was gone, the door wide open behind her.

Sioned took her time, gathering her strength. Slowly she put on the riding clothes given her to cover her nakedness, then made her way from the torchlit dark along an empty corridor. There were many stairs, and several times she had to stop and lean against the wall while dizziness shook her. At last she emerged into a chamber washed with feeble dawn, where Rohan waited for her.

The pale light spared nothing of the hollows gouged out around his ribs, the stark bones of his face. They had given him rags to wear, the proud dragon prince—trousers, boots, a cloak he held awkwardly over one arm. The blond hair was dark and lank with sweat, the eyes bruised, and in those eyes was a despair that tore at her soul.

She knew what he must be seeing as he looked at her. The clothes hung from her shoulders, and the light would be equally merciless on her own gray skin, her features still drawn tight against screams she had refused to give. She saw him staring at her and hurt more for his hurt than for any of her own.

"I was with her," he said abruptly.

"I know. And now she carries your son, as I cannot."

"I should have killed her."

"No." But she could not explain, not yet.

He came forward, placed the cloak around her shoulders, careful not to touch her. "We're free to go."

"Rohan—you're mine," Sioned told him. "Mine."

He shook his head, moved away from her to the door.

"She could never take you from me. The only one who could do that is you—and I will never give you up or let you go."

"I won't let you claim soiled goods," he rasped.

"Is that why you won't touch *me?*"

He swung around, fresh agony crying out from his eyes. "Sioned—*no*—"

She waited until her meaning was completely clear to him, calculating the balance of his love for her against his hatred of himself. "I lost track of how many used me," she said at last, words chosen for their cruelty, words that were a terrible risk. But she knew this man—stricken, stripped of pride, whom she had just hurt again. The shock would either break him or bring him back to her.

She knew him. He held her gently, as if she would shatter in his arms. Sioned rested her head on his shoulder and let the tears fall, cleansing her eyes, washing his skin.

The courtyard outside was empty, but Sioned could feel hundreds of eyes in the shadows. There were two horses tied just inside the gates, a waterskin strapped to each saddle. Ianthe evidently meant them to survive the Desert. As Sioned and Rohan mounted and rode out of Feruche, neither missed and neither commented on the sight of Ianthe, high on the battlements, watching them.

Rohan was as tense as if he expected an arrow in his back at any instant. Sioned knew there would not be. Midwinter, she repeated to herself. Midwinter. She had until then to decide the manner of Ianthe's death.

"Just a skirmish," Prince Jastri begged. "The men are restless. They know we have the superior force and want to prove it! Just one small skirmish—"

Roelstra's lips twisted and he pushed his breakfast away. There was no sense continuing the meal with Jastri nagging at him and destroying his appetite.

"One small skirmish," he mused. "Something Lord Chaynal will know very well how to turn into a major battle. Haven't you listened to anything that's said of him? He knows war, Jastri. He had a most competent teacher in Zehava, and plenty of experience with the Merida. There will be no skirmish. Not yet. Now, be a good boy and leave me to finish my breakfast in peace, won't you?"

Jastri, usually flushed with the delight of commanding his own troops in their drills, now flushed with rage. A handsome boy of sixteen winters, he had all the high spirits and impatience of youth released from the onerous supervision of tutors and advisers. But he had found that Roelstra's rule was even more confining. The leather battle-armor decorated here and there with garnets fit him most attractively now that life in a soldier's camp had run the baby fat from him, but he had not yet learned a soldier's discipline. Roelstra, inspecting the scarlet cheeks and flashing gray-green eyes, considered it was time to teach a lesson.

"I am a prince," Jastri informed him hotly. "I am no man's boy!"

"You are and will remain a boy until you've blooded yourself with a virgin girl and a battle," Roelstra snapped back.

"And you're the one to instruct me in both!" the young prince scoffed. "You, whose wife and five luckless mistresses have made no sons for you! You who sit here in this tent stuffing yourself on breakfast when we could be feeding our swords with Desert blood!"

Roelstra sighed, comforting himself with the thought of how pleasant it was going to be to have this irritating child killed. He said, "When you have sons of your own and scars of battle on your skin, then you may gloat. *Boy*. But until that time, you will do as I say."

Jastri flung himself out of the tent, shouting furiously for his horse and escort. Roelstra ignored the commotion and attempted to interest himself in breakfast once again, but could not. He hoped Lord Chaynal was equally incapable of enjoying his meals, his sleep, and his every waking moment.

Yet he smiled as he considered what must be going through the Desert commander's mind. Roelstra's troops outnumbered Chaynal's, a weakness that could be exploited at any time—yet Roelstra did not attack. The excuse for battle had been handed to him by Lord Davvi, who was with the Desert armies rather than supporting his rightful overlord—yet Roelstra did not attack. The High Prince picked up his goblet and spoke to his reflection in its polished silver surface.

"Do I wait for Lord Chaynal to attack first? No, I'm too clever to think he'd put himself in the wrong. Do I wait for Rohan to arrive so I can destroy him and his armies in a single battle? No, for I know the princeling will be surrounded by a wall of swords and shields. Then why do I wait on my side of the river like a sandstorm brewing in the Desert?"

He chuckled and drank, conceding that if Jastri had a virtue, it was his ability to provide the finest of Syrene wines. Probably his only virtue, Roelstra added with a sigh as he heard a renewed commotion outside his tent.

A squire slunk in and bowed, a convenient target for the High Prince's temper.

"Am I to have no peace at all? What is it now?"

"Forgive me, your g-grace, I—"

The tent flaps parted to reveal a woman he had thought never to see again. She made a cursory obeisance, her dark eyes insolent and cool, and said, "Welcome me back, Father." She held up her hands, and he saw the three Sunrunner's rings on her fingers.

Guards stood behind her, wary and uncertain. Roelstra waved them and the squire out of the tent. "Do you think my daughter is here to kill me? Get out, all of you! I'll speak alone with the princess."

Pandsala seated herself without permission and folded her hands in her lap. "Thank you for my title, Father. With that and my rings, I should have no more trouble making these people obey me."

"Why should they obey you, and to what purpose?"

She laughed. "Lord of Storms, what do you think these last six years have been like, walled up with Lady Andrade? Even if you'd turned me out—which you're too smart to do, having seen these rings—and even if you'd had me killed, it'd be preferable to what I've endured."

He regarded her silently, allowing his suspicions to show on his face. At last, he said, "You've not aged well, my dear. Andrade and her pious household have not agreed with you any more than they would with me. I don't trust you, Pandsala. But you don't expect me to, I take it. What do you want?"

"My freedom. And my position as your daughter, and a princess. I can be of use to you, Father, and you know it." She smiled. "You're showing your age, too, you know. White hairs here, more flesh there, lines and wrinkles. Are you still wasting your time and energy trying to beget a son, or have you decided Ianthe's brats will make princes after you're dead?" Laughing, she went on, "Princes! Goddess, that's funny! They'll rip your lands apart from one end to the other! Anything Ianthe gave birth and suck to would turn out vile."

"She and I have that in common," Roelstra observed

coldly. "I gave your little sister the name I should have given you—having betrayed first me, and now Andrade."

"You're right, I don't expect you to trust me. But I can be useful, Father. And you were never stupid."

They watched each other for some time—Roelstra calculating, Pandsala confident with the assurance of one who had nothing to lose.

"Very well," he said abruptly. "Serve me. But trust in one thing. If you betray me again, your years with Andrade will seem a carnival of delight compared to what will happen to you."

"How could I doubt it, Father?" She smiled again, stretched languidly. "May I share your breakfast? It was a longer trip than I thought from where I left Andrade and Urival and Chiana."

He gave a start and saw her satisfaction at his reaction. But before he could ask his questions, a guard burst into the tent, barely remembered to salute, and gasped out, "Your pardon, your grace—there's a rider here who demands audience at once!"

Roelstra half-rose to his feet, then sank back into his chair, slanting a look at his daughter. "Leave me. I'll call for you again shortly."

She arched her brows, but left the tent without comment. Roelstra gestured and the rider was brought in. When the man had given his news, he summoned Pandsala again and met her outside in the sunlight.

"I do intend to use you, my dear," he told her. "And it seems I must trust you a little in order to do so. Show me now that you're worth those rings you wear. Find Rohan."

"I'm an apprentice, not a fully trained *faradhi*!"

He relished the apprehension in her eyes. "Then train yourself, and quickly. I want to know where Rohan is. Do it, Pandsala—or find out what happens when your father is angry." He smiled, menace in his eyes.

She swallowed hard, then faced the sunlight and closed her eyes. He watched her tremble and wondered why of all his daughters by Lallante this was the one with the gift. Then again, had it been Ianthe—

Pandsala gasped and her eyes flew open. "I saw them!

Rohan and the *faradhi* princess—and dragons, out in the Desert—I saw them!"

Roelstra nodded, pleased that she had passed the test. "Excellent."

"But I don't understand!" she cried. "Why did Ianthe let them go?"

"For reasons of her own."

"You knew about this?"

"The courier who just arrived told me." He took her back into the tent and poured wine for them both. "The night before she released him, the signal fires were lit. All across the Veresch to Castle Crag, where a boat waited to sail down the Faolain more swiftly than a rider could go."

"But Lord Chaynal is upriver—"

"Precisely. Horses were waiting. And now I know what Lord Chaynal does not." He smiled, thinking that only he and Ianthe shared another interesting piece of information, which would remain secret until the time was right. He, Ianthe—and Rohan.

Pandsala took a swallow of wine—and suddenly turned white, staring into the cup in horror. Roelstra choked laughing.

"Oh, that's rich! What did you expect—*dranath*? Don't be an idiot, Pandsala! When did I have the chance to drug the wine?" He took the cup from her and drank, mocking her.

She calmed down, but the fear was still in her eyes. He enjoyed it, knowing she would not eat or drink without first having to overcome terror of the drug. The constant uncertainty would keep her honest, though he would never really trust her.

"So we've each passed the first test," he told her. I've restrained myself from binding you to me with *dranath*, and you've confirmed on the sunlight something I already knew." He lifted his cup to her. "Shall we drink to mutual trust, my dear?"

The noon sun beat down on Rohan's unprotected head and back. He knew they had to stop soon and find shelter from the worst of the day's heat. The morning had passed in absolute silence as they rode past the empty garrison below Feruche and out into the Desert, keeping close to the hills where they could find a little shade. He led the way, shamed by his gratitude that he did not have to look at his wife.

Usually when he was confused or troubled, a ride through the stark beauty of his lands soothed him. Where others saw only arid emptiness, he saw freedom. The vast golden sands and endless sky reassured him that there were answers to be found if only he searched, the way one had to search for water in the Desert. There were no limits here, not to the land or to his dreams. A man could find liberty here to think, to feel, to live.

The Desert threatened him now. The Long Sand was too great, the skies too huge, all of it looming around him, over him, alternating cries to preserve their freedom with shrieks that he was alone, alone, with no hope of answers. The dreams were gone like water into the sand. He could find no strength here and he had no right to seek strength in Sioned.

Rohan turned the horse to the hills, eyes scouring them for cool shelter. He heard the soft shussh of hooves behind him, the muted jingle of the bridle as the horse tossed its head. He could not look around, could not look at his wife. He squinted up at the sky instead, where a dark shape had taken wing.

Dragon.

He caught his breath, heard Sioned's small murmur of surprise behind him. One dragon, wings beating against the blue, flying toward the near dunes. Sweet Goddess, Rohan thought, how could anything be so beautiful?

But when another dragon soared into view and screamed out a challenge to the first, he realized what was about to happen. "Sioned! Hurry!"

He kicked the mare forward, heading for a shallow cave made by an overhang of streaked brownish rock. Once inside, they stayed on their horses, trying to calm the terrified animals as dragon shrieks split the air. Sioned huddled low on her horse's neck, reins drawn so tight that the gelding's chin was against its chest. Rohan struggled to control his own horse, turning it around and around in the narrow space with the reins gripped nearly at the bridle bit.

Sioned cried out as her gelding reared and she hit her head against the low ceiling. Rohan made a wild grab and missed, nearly toppling from his own horse. Sioned fell, one booted foot twisting as it caught in the stirrup, then slid to the ground and lay still. The gelding, free now of any restraints, galloped headlong from the shelter.

Rohan leaped down, reins wound around his hand as his own horse plunged, wanting to follow the frantic flight of the gelding. "Sioned—" He bent down, touched her face with his free hand, battling the mare all the while. "Sioned!" Screams of dragons and horse echoed off the rock and the mare nearly broke his wrist in her desperation to be free. He groaned in pain and let her bolt.

Sioned's eyes opened as his arms went around her, glassy with pain. "Hush," he told her. "You've got a bump on the head and a wrenched ankle. Don't move."

She took his hand, inspecting the leather burns, then glanced out at the sand. Very softly, she said, "It doesn't matter."

The words enraged him for reasons he did not comprehend. He sprang to his feet, glaring at her. "It doesn't matter!" he shouted, shaking with fury. "Nothing matters, does it? Not a damned thing! Look at us!" he roared, lost to all control for the first time in his life. "Do *we* matter?"

She gazed up at him with a terrible calm, and said nothing. He swung around, braced his trembling body against the rocks, and stared out at the Desert where the dragons stood, wings spread, bellowing with a fury to match his own. They lunged for each other and the battle began.

Rohan stood transfixed. It was his hellish dream again, only this time the dragons were outside. The scenes stitched into the tapestries came alive. One dragon greenish-bronze, the other brown with patches of iridescent black on his head and flanks, both with jaws wide and dripping blood. The undersides of their spread wings shimmered in the heat. They came at each other again and again, drawing more blood, the stink of it and their maleness thick on the sand-heavy air. They reared up, slashed at each other, aroused and obscene and primal—and beautiful. The violence of their screams and thrusts quivered through him, spread down his arms and thighs, heated his blood. He made a guttural sound low in his throat and dug his fingers into the rocks, eyes slitted.

The touch on his arm went through him like a sword-stroke. He stared into her green eyes, so quiet and cool, but as a tremor shot through him it found its answer in her and she stepped back, afraid.

"Rohan—"

He crushed her to his chest. For an instant she sobbed and clung to him, and the savagery ran like wildfire through them both. He bent her backward, curving her spine, forcing her head back, and took her lips as he intended to take her body.

She wrenched away from him panting. "No!" she spat, eyes blazing, and he slapped her so hard her head snapped around and blood trickled from her lip.

"You will not rut with me the way you did with her!" she screamed.

A dragon's death howl poured into his brain and he staggered. There was hate in Sioned's eyes, her fingers curling into claws that would rip his eyes out if he touched her again. Rohan choked and stumbled away from her, out onto the sand, to his knees. Nearby the victorious dragonsire beat his great, bloodied wings and soared away, leaving a broken corpse in the sand.

I am worse than a barbarian. I am a savage. All his pretenses of civilization, rationality, honor—they were nothing. He had spared Ianthe when he should have killed her, when everything demanded that he kill her—and why? For the son Sioned would never give him. He was a savage with a taste for rape, lusting to reclaim what was his, what others had taken. Lust, possession, jealousy, rape. What had he become? Only what he had been all along but had never had the courage to admit.

The hill shadows gradually stole over him, cooled the sunburned skin of his back and shoulders. He sat up, dully noting that it was only a little while after noon, with a long time to wait before starting across the Desert again. On foot. At night. When they would have a chance to survive.

He laughed then, a harsh and grating sound that snagged in his throat. Survival. What a splendid joke. He could think these things, feel these things, do these things, and still his stubborn fool of a brain told him what was necessary in order to survive. It really was hilarious. He clasped his knees to his chest and laughed, rocked back and forth, threw his head back and shouted his mirth to the sky.

Sioned huddled in the mouth of the cave, hands over her ears to shut out the horrible laughter. She ought to go to him, knew she should, but could not. He terrified her.

When she heard silence again, she forced her aching body to rise, steadying herself against the rock walls. He was pulled in around himself, head on his knees, the wound at his shoulder weeping blood in a thin trickle down his back. Shadows pooled around him, lengthened as she watched for she knew not how long.

Finally she moved, limped across the sand. He was shaking, muscles rippling in spasms beneath his skin. She knelt, unable to speak or touch, and his head lifted. His eyes had gone dark and blank.

"We're not going to die, you know."

She nodded wordlessly, not understanding.

"I wanted to. But I'm too much of a coward." A long breath shuddered out of him. "I have to live, so I can kill. *There's* irony for you."

Tears slid slowly down her cheeks. He caught one on his fingertip, stared at it for a moment. When he met her gaze, his eyes had kindled with anguish.

"I'm not worth this," he whispered. "Oh, Sioned. What have I done?"

Chapter Twenty-six

Prince Jastri got the battle he so ardently desired on the morning after Princess Pandsala's arrival. The High Prince's troops engaged Lord Chaynal's just after dawn, having crossed the river during the night at one bridge on the main road to the north and a second bridge hastily constructed much closer to the encamped armies. Chay, alerted before daybreak, nodded his satisfaction at the prospect of a fight, ordered his troops to ready themselves as silently as possible, and was waiting for the attack. His captains were frantic to assault and burn the bridges, but Chay had his own plans for them.

Prince Jastri's horse forded the river to the south, and came north in a flanking maneuver designed to distract from Roelstra's main thrust. Design and execution were two entirely different things. Jastri and his unseasoned troop of young highborns proved unequal to the hail of arrows and spears that greeted them a full measure before they had expected to encounter resistance. Shocked and furious, the young prince was forced into a confused retreat. He lost thirty-nine of his one hundred horse to Desert archers and the river. Lord Davvi, to whom Chay had entrusted the ambush, returned from it with only slight losses and in good time to give support to the main defenses.

But by late afternoon Roelstra's troops had gained a swath of shoreline to which they clung ferociously. Chay withdrew, willing to let them have their landhold for now, unwilling to spend any more lives trying to retake it. He left enough archers behind to discourage further advances, and repaired to his tent with his captains, his son, and Lord Davvi.

"Losses of eighteen horse, thirty-seven foot, and fourteen archers," he summarized after they had given their reports. "Scouts estimate enemy casualties of about twice that, but they have twice our numbers to begin with. I'm not interested in a war of attrition." He toyed with a jeweled eating knife that had been a present from Tobin, watching the candlelight play off its rubies and steel. "But we have an advantage now."

Lord Davvi expressed the surprise of the others in a single word. "How?"

Chay smiled tightly. "I make their numbers at upward of seven hundred, and by tomorrow morning about half that should be on this side of the river. I want regular reports on the numbers of men and horses and supplies brought over during the night."

"What we ought to do is fire those bridges, my lord."

"No, Gryden," he told Radzyn's guard commander. "Not yet. When half their forces are here within our grasp, *then* we will burn their bridges behind them." He drew a line on the parchment map with his knife, making a deep scar. "I want to show Roelstra something really spectacular."

"Why not now, when there are fewer of them to rise against us?" Davvi asked.

"Because I'm going to crush the High Prince in two battles. Two are all we can afford. Once we've butchered half his army, we'll cross the Faolain and do the same to the other half."

"But if the bridges are burned—"

"I have my ideas on that as well. No, Gryden, you will *not* call a meeting of the engineers and start tearing down trees. Our bridges will be quite different from Roelstra's. Questions?" He eyed each in turn, noting they were puzzled, exactly as he had intended. Zehava had taught him long ago to keep his battle plans secret as long as possible; it had nothing to do with trust, only prudence. "Very well. Dismissed."

Maarken stayed, taking up his father's battle gear for cleaning. Chay watched the boy seat himself on the carpet near a lamp encased in clear glass. The careful fingers began their work, rubbing at the dull film of dirt on steel.

"You should be in bed," he said.

"A squire doesn't sleep until his lord does—or *unless*," Maarken responded.

Chay smiled. "Nice try. Now you can tell me what's really bothering you."

The boy glanced up, then back down at his work. "Father, you don't need archers and arrows to fire the bridges. You have *me*."

His mind spun. He had never paid much attention to the various levels of *faradhi* training, not until Sioned had begun tutoring his wife. Ten rings for a Lord or Lady of Goddess Keep, seven for Master Sunrunners—

"My kind of Fire won't damage the bridges as much if I'm careful, because I can put it out with a thought."

—five for a trained Sunrunner, three for an apprentice—

"I don't even have to be that close, just so I can see where you want me to place the Fire."

—and one for the ability to call Fire. Chay stared at his son's ringless hands that still rubbed assiduously at an imagined stain on the sword.

"No one will be in danger, Father. Roelstra won't be alerted by any movement of troops. I can do it."

"When those bridges go, there'll be people on them. People who will die." He waited until Maarken glanced up, held the bright blue gaze with his own. "I won't have you responsible for that."

"Andrade has sided with the Desert against Roelstra," Maarken reminded him.

"But not to kill."

"*You* have," was the flat reply. "Your weapon is this." He lifted the sword. "Mine, for now, can be Fire."

"No!" he shouted at his son, afraid. "If you don't see the difference, then you'll never use either while I'm around to stop you! I want you to grow up to be Radzyn's lord someday, not an outlaw condemned for misuse of *faradhi* powers you shouldn't have in the first place!"

The sword slipped from Maarken's fingers and brushed a silvery note from the shield on its way to the carpet. "Do you feel that way?" he whispered, his cheeks white. "Do you?"

"Yes. And it took this to make me realize it." He

shook his head wearily. "Do you have any idea what Andrade did by marrying her sister to your grandfather?"

"I've thought about it. Meath and Eolie and Prince Lleyn make sure I think about it. I was born as I am, and I couldn't change it even if I wanted to. But it's not just me, is it? It's Sioned's children, when she has them. Prince and Sunrunner both. How do you think we'll all turn out, Father? Power-mad and ready to slaughter everyone who gets in our way? Is that what you think?" he accused bitterly.

Chay bit his lip, then said, "I think that I have a son I'm proud to call mine. Maarken, the world is changing and people like you will change it further. Born to one kind of power—but born *with* quite another."

"We're not one thing or another, Andry and I. Will we grow up to rule the lands you give us, or will we be ruled by Andrade?" His eyes were haunted now. "What am I to be, Father?"

Rohan would understand, Chay thought suddenly. He loved dragons and had been forced to kill one; he wanted desperately to live by rule of law, not by the sword. Rohan would understand the division in Maarken's soul. But Sioned would understand even better, for it was the choice she lived with every day of her life.

Chay could and did take that choice from his son now. "I'm your father and your commander, and you're doubly bound to obey me. You will not call Fire, Maarken. I forbid it."

Rebellion and relief warred on the boy's face for a moment. But he bent his head in submission. "Yes, my lord."

Yet they both knew this was only a postponement of the inevitable choices Maarken would one day have to make on his own.

"Come," Chay said, "time for bed, whether we sleep or not. One of the first rules of war is that the commander must always *appear* to be resting easily in his tent at night."

The Flametower at Stronghold was an excellent vantage from which to observe the arrival of the Merida host. Tobin and Maeta stood at the windows, watching the hundred armed soldiers on horseback, their battle harness gleaming in the last evening light. The two women exchanged a glance.

"Will they try tonight or wait for morning?" Tobin asked.

"First light," the warrior replied. "Look at them down there, setting up camp right in the shadow of Stronghold! Arrogant idiots. They act as if we're already beneath their swords." Her smile turned feral. "I'll enjoy this."

They started downstairs and Tobin said, "Chay would, too. As it happens, Maeta, I'm not a bad shot myself. And there's a nice little niche left of the gates that would fit me like a glove."

"I'm not afraid of your great roaring stallion of a husband, if that's what you're hinting. He can shout all he wants at me for putting you into the fight. The place is yours, along with as many Merida as you care to bring down." She chuckled. "I remember when my mother gave you archery lessons."

Instruction by Myrdal herself was recommendation enough, it seemed. "I'll find a bow of the right weight, then, and be ready before dawn."

"What about your boys? Locking them in their rooms won't work, you know. Would you permit them to run arrows for us? If I give them the first section of the relay, they'll be safe in the inner court the whole time."

"Thank you. I really had no idea how to keep them out of this, and your way, they'll be useful without being in danger."

Well before dawn, Stronghold was ready—and absolutely silent. Tobin, dressed in riding clothes that blended with the stones around her, wedged herself into a narrow stone shelf cut exactly for this purpose in the outer walls of the gatehouse. Slung at her back and in a second quiver at her feet were arrows she had spent the night repainting in her husband's red and white. There was nothing to be done about the blue fletching, but she wanted the Merida to know that Radzyn was represented here. When her fifty ran out, she would use those stock-piled in Rohan's armory. But with a hundred Merida out

there and twenty archers trained by Myrdal defending
Stronghold, Tobin had the feeling she would run out of
targets long before she ran out of red-and-white arrows.

It began when a helmeted Merida rode up the canyon
toward the tunnel's mouth. He reined in and lifted a
hand in a pompous gesture that made Tobin want to
giggle. The desire increased as he shouted in a ringing
voice that had undoubtedly procured him this mission:

"Usurpers of Stronghold! Surrender to us now, and live!
You cannot hope to survive against us, and there is no
hope from north or south! Open the gates to the rightful
rulers of the Desert!"

Because she was listening for it, Tobin heard the soft
hiss of an arrow and was able to follow its flight. It sank
into the man's saddle a finger's breadth from his thigh,
and trembled there delicately. To his credit, he did not
flinch. But he did ride back down with something akin to
haste.

There followed a short wait while the sun climbed the
eastern sky over the Long Sand and the shadows shifted,
grew sharper. Tobin began to wish for the cool sea breezes
of Radzyn. The sound of horses up the road made her
forget the sweat that stuck her tunic to her skin, and she
readied herself to draw her bowstring.

Unhappily, the Merida were not the fools Maeta had
hoped. Not only the soldiers but their mounts were well
protected by leather harness studded with bronze. Don-
ning it had caused the delay. Tobin reflected sourly that
this was unquestionably where Rohan's gold had gone,
and the artisans of Cunaxa had been hard at work to
their great profit. She promised herself the Merida would
not profit today.

She counted six rows of six each, horses riding shoulder-
to-shoulder from one wall of the canyon to the other.
When the first went down, close quarters would confuse
and hamper the rest. Yet the signal for the first flight did
not come, and Tobin began to fret. The riders were
within range. She could almost discern eye-color behind
the helmets with their long nose-pieces and cheek-guards.

At last a long, thin wail split the heat, a horn made of
dragon bone, the ascending notes startling the horses

below. Arrows spewed from the canyon and the gatehouse. It was all as Maeta had planned—the high shrieks
of pain from the horses as they bucked and reared to
escape the arrows pricking their flesh, the shouts and
curses from the riders as steel found its way between and
through leather. Tobin nocked, pulled and let fly with
cool regularity, and twenty others just like her did the
same.

Eight down, nine, ten—she saw why Maeta had waited
until the last row of horses was in range, for the injured
at the back pushed the others forward, and fallen horses
would block part of the road if the Merida decided to
retreat.

But they did not retreat, and all at once a tan-clad
body fell screaming from Stronghold's gatehouse and thud-
ded to the hard-packed sand below. Above and opposite
Tobin were a dozen archers, perched precariously on a
ledge rising above the canyon. She had no time to wonder how they had gotten there, for she heard the hissing
of an arrow and the clink of its steel head in the rock at
her shoulder. She changed her stance and let fly, hearing
Maeta shout orders that all on Tobin's side of the gate do
the same. The others were not in position to respond to
this new attack.

Another of Stronghold's archers was lost, plummeting
down like a fallen dragon with an arrow in her chest. The
riders assaulted the first gates, opened one of them,
gained access to the long tunnel. Maeta commanded a
regrouping above the outer courtyard, where they would
be out of range of Merida bows and could pick off the
horsemen when they breached the inner gates.

Tobin plucked up her second quiver with a muffled
curse that was half-annoyance, half-pain. An arrow had
scored her thigh though she only noticed it now that she
had to move. Struggling to climb down from her niche,
she stumbled into the gatehouse, still cursing.

She followed the others through a narrow passage to
the crenellations above the inner gates. The archers arranged themselves, grim-faced now, the atmosphere of
easy victory gone. Old Myrdal was down in the courtyard
yelling at servants who had armed themselves with sword,

spear, and shield—anything not taken to Remagev with
Ostvel and the rest of the Stronghold guard.

Maeta gave Tobin's leg a rough inspection and an even
rougher bandage that stank of herbs. "Clever me," the
commander said bitterly. "But don't worry—we'll get
them on this side. I've ordered your boys to the back
passage by the grotto, just in case."

"*What* back passage by the grotto?" Tobin demanded,
but Maeta was already gone.

Whatever salve had been on the bandage, it soothed
away the pain and Tobin no longer limped as she found
position near a man who had a similar bandage wrapped
around the broken haft of an arrow in his hip. Blood
seeped through and he could put no weight on his leg,
but he was balanced and ready just the same as they
waited for the Merida to come through the gates directly
underneath. At that point the Stronghold archers would
shoot the Merida in the back.

Tobin traded a smile with the man—but the daughter
of a warrior prince abruptly became the mother of twin
sons whose shouts of defiance echoed up from the courtyard below. As the Merida battered at the gates, Sorin
and Andry battered long kitchen knives against small
shields used for training, shields nearly as tall as they
were.

"No!" Tobin screamed. "Andry! Sorin! Run!"

But the gates toppled and the horses clattered into the
courtyard. And she had only the slender red-and-white
arrows with which to defend her sons.

"It's this way," Sioned told Rohan, leading him to a
passage through the rock hitherto unknown to him. He
followed her through the cleft that was just large enough
for a single horse to pass. Two people on foot negotiated
the stone corridor swiftly and easily, and before Rohan
knew it they were beside the grotto, panting for breath.

"Come on," he managed when he had caught enough
air to speak. "Goddess, I hope we aren't too late—"

They ran to the deserted inner courtyard, but beyond
the walls were sounds unmistakable even to Sioned, who
had never heard real war: clashes of steel on steel, horses'

screams, cries of the wounded and dying. Rohan gave her a boost and then took her hands to haul himself up onto the walls. He gave the chaos a single glance, then leaped down and sprinted for the nearest fallen sword.

Sioned stayed where she was. The Merida horse had spread out in groups of three and four, tight little knots bristling with hooves and swords on all sides. She chose the nearest of them, lifted her ringless hands, and encased the group in Fire.

She did the same to a second knot and a third, creating small infernos of screaming, burning flesh. A rider broke from another trio and hurtled toward her, determined to slay this wild-eyed, fire-haired witch who called down Sunrunner's Fire on them. She wove a net of flames around him, too, with a casual gesture of her hand. His sword clanged to the ground from burned fingers and he shrieked in pain. Sioned smiled very sweetly and wrapped another group of horses in flames.

Rohan saw the Fire spring up four times, five, six. He plunged his borrowed sword into a nearby blaze, killing men and women he could barely see. When the rest of the Merida turned and took flight back through the tunnel, he bellowed Sioned's name. She was still on her knees on the narrow wall, rocking lightly back and forth, her hands spread out before her and her hair streaming down like a river of her own Fire.

"Sioned!" he cried again. "Enough!"

Her hands fell. Her gaze found his and her smile died. She swayed, nearly toppling. Myrdal limped over and held up her arms, helping her down from the wall. Fire had vanished; it had not burned long enough to kill, but the stench of seared flesh and hide was nauseating in the heat.

Rohan found a horse whose rider had fallen to a red-and-white arrow—and what was Tobin doing here, anyway? he asked himself as he caught sight of his sister's slight figure in the confusion. Leaping up, he reined the terrified animal around and kicked it through the gates.

Tobin snatched her sons into her arms. They were mercifully whole, though Sorin's tunic was ripped and Andry had a long, shallow cut on one arm. She embraced the pair fiercely, then let them go and dealt each a resounding blow on the backside that put tears into their eyes.

"How dare you disobey me!" she raved. "Don't you ever do such a thing again! Get out of my sight before I have you horsewhipped!" She pulled them close for another breathless hug, then pushed them toward the keep. "Move!"

They did. Tobin straightened up, near to fainting with anger and relief. And then she caught sight of Sioned. Myrdal was supporting her, for Sioned was only half-conscious. Tobin forgot her own dizziness and hurried over, wedging her shoulder beneath Sioned's other arm.

"Get her inside," Myrdal said. "Can you manage by yourself?"

"I can walk," Sioned whispered with no voice at all.

Tobin looked her over. Sioned's face, neck, and bare arms were blistered and bloodied. Even her hands, ringless now and without even white circles where those rings should have been, were sun-ravaged. And the body Tobin circled with her arm was nothing but bones.

"I can manage," she told Myrdal. "She can't weigh any more than I do. Sioned, come with me now, dearest. It's all right. You're home."

"Tobin?"

"Yes, it's me. You're safe. You're at Stronghold. Hang on to me." She kept up the soothing words as they made their slow way into the castle. The coolness within revived Sioned a little, and she was able to support herself as Tobin helped her up the stairs.

"Where's Rohan?"

"Gone to join Ostvel and the other troops come from Remagev." She hoped so, at any rate, but there was no use worrying about that now.

Sioned nodded slowly. "I told him Maeta's plan. Fool. He'll want to lead the battle."

"We're almost there. Just down this hallway and then you can rest."

Tobin got her onto the great bed and stripped the torn clothes from her. The shirt had once been a beautiful garment, made of fine material and laced through with tiny violet ribbons. The color made Tobin's jaw clench. Drawing a basin of water from the next room, she took up a soft towel and began washing Sioned's feet.

"We had to walk, you see," the younger woman said, her voice clear and colorless. "The dragons bolted the horses that first day. We couldn't stop at Skybowl. The Merida left men there to watch for us. Oh, Tobin, that feels so good. Thank you."

She ripped a pillowcase into strips and bound Sioned's blistered feet. "Hush now. You just rest."

"I wonder if I killed any of them with Fire," Sioned went on in that strange voice. "Andrade would not approve. But it wouldn't be the first time—or the last." She stared up at Tobin, her green eyes hazy. "I'm a *faradhi* and a princess. What else did she expect of me?"

"She's ordered the Sunrunners to support us against Roelstra."

A thin smile curved the cracked lips. "Tobin, she did that the instant she ordered me to come to Stronghold."

Tobin finished washing her. Later she would salve that burned, parched skin, wrap her in sheets soaked with herbs. But at this moment sleep was more important. She stroked back tangled red hair and placed a tender kiss on Sioned's forehead. "Sleep now, my dear. You're home."

"Tobin. . . ." Her voice was dreamy, her eyelids drifting closed. "You must tell everyone . . . there's going to be a son."

The Merida, galloping back down the canyon, ran smack into the middle of another battle. Ostvel's forces had come from Remagev, marching all night after riders hidden in the hills around Stronghold had reported the Merida arrival. Ostvel's force fanned out into a half-circle and was engaged in closing it tight when Rohan and a few others who'd jumped on Merida horses rode into view. The sight of the prince brought two groups from either side of the arc to join in a rear assault. By noonday it was over.

The ten who were still in their saddles were relieved of their horses and armor, but not their lives. Rohan sat his horse with his borrowed sword across his thighs, watching the ten Merida haul their dead and wounded into the sand. He was sick with exhaustion and the battle just concluded, and he had no idea what was keeping him upright. But upright he stayed, with Ostvel silently at his side. When all the Merida had been accounted for, Rohan had the survivors line up before him.

"I will spare your lives," he told them. "For I have a message for you to deliver. It requires that you sever the right hand of each of your comrades—dead or not."

Ostvel caught his breath. Rohan cared not at all. When the grisly task was accomplished and the dying had been given a swift knife to the heart, he ordered the hands placed in saddlebags, one for each soldier still alive.

"These you will carry north to your masters. You—" He pointed his sword at the man wearing the finest clothing. "A captain of some sort? I thought so. *You* will have the privilege of going south, not north. You will deliver that as a gift from me to High Prince Roelstra and inform him of what occurred here. Be sure to impress upon him that it will not be his hand I will deprive him of when next we meet, but his head." He paused, then finished mildly. "I suggest you leave Skybowl alone, incidentally. Before you reach it on foot, my troops will have slaughtered your compatriots there."

"On foot!" the captain burst out. "But we've no water!"

Rohan gave him a quiet smile. "Neither had I and my lady wife during the days we walked here from Feruche. You have the longer path to tread, my friend. Start now, before I change my mind and have all of you killed where you stand."

He turned his horse and rode back up to Stronghold, dismounting in the inner courtyard. No one dared approach him. As he climbed slowly to his chambers, he met his sister hurrying down. She was limping, and there was a bandage wrapped around her thigh, and through his monumental fatigue he felt a pang of concern.

"Rohan! Is it true?" She grasped his bare arm, the coolness of her fingers on his sun-blistered skin acutely painful.

"Not now, Tobin." He pulled away from her and continued climbing.

"Answer me! Is it true you're to have a child?"

He stopped dead.

"Rohan! She told me you were going to have a son! Is it true?"

"She told you that, did she?" He turned and looked into his sister's black eyes, heard the bitter hollowness of his voice as he replied, "Yes. It's true. I'm going to have a son."

He walked away from her bewilderment and closed the door of his chambers behind him. He stood for a long time beside the bed, gazing down at his wife. They lived, as he had promised. He had not been raised in the Desert for nothing. Such food and moisture as the sand and cliffs provided, they had partaken of, and survived.

He traced the fine lines of her gaunt face that was so oddly at peace. Suffering aged most people, but Sioned's face was a miracle of childlike purity as she slept, lips curved in a tiny smile, the fine sweet bones in sharp relief.

He had promised her life. She had promised him a son. Could she hold Ianthe's bastard to her breast, even considering that she could wrest him from his mother in the first place? And could he ever look at the child and not see the woman who had borne him?

If Sioned could, then he must. Goddess help him.

He lay beside her, staring at the high ceiling painted blue to match Desert skies. It was a vague surprise to find there was still water enough in his body for tears.

Tobin and Ostvel found them like that at dusk, sleeping. She had come to tend their hurts, he to bring them food. They exchanged glances and the princess spoke.

"She said nothing about a child to you before she left?"

"Nothing. Do you think I would have let her go?" He shook his head. "And do I really think anyone could have stopped her? But why did Ianthe release them?"

"Perhaps they escaped."

"From Feruche? The only way to leave is to be allowed to leave."

They watched the pair for a time: Sioned peaceful in

sleep, Rohan haggard. Tobin saw that youth had fled her brother's face, and mourned its loss.

"Doubtless we'll learn as much of it as they care to tell," she said.

"Doubtless," Ostvel agreed. "We'd better let them sleep."

Chapter Twenty-seven

Late in the day the cool scents of water and trees around the Faolain gave way to the warm smells of food cooking in the great firepits of the Desert camp. A sentry could be forgiven a certain drowsiness after a long, uneventful watch, especially if her duty was nearly over and dinner enticed on the breeze. In the ten days since the battle, nothing had happened and nothing was likely to before sunset; she shrugged to herself and found a more comfortable position with her back against a tree, eyes closed.

"Were I the High Prince, you'd be dead right now."

The clear incisive voice snapped her upright, arrow nocked and bow drawn with admirable speed. But she lowered her arms at once and bent her head. "My l-lord prince!" she gasped.

Eyes of wintry blue gazed down at her when she dared lift her face again. She had seen the old prince once or twice on his visits to the small coastal holding she called home, and this young man was suddenly very like him— not in coloring or size, but in the expression that chilled his thin face.

"Now that you're awake," he went on, "perhaps you'd be so good as to inform me of Lord Chaynal's whereabouts."

"In his tent, your grace, with young Lord Maarken and Lord Davvi of River Run."

He nodded, his blond hair catching every ray of fading sunlight. "Having just come down the northern road, I can assure you it is free of enemies. But had it not been. . . ." He raised a brow. "Do I make myself understood?"

"Yes, your grace."

"Good. You have my permission to inform Lord Chaynal that I am here."

She bowed again and fled.

Rohan heard the sound begin as he rode forward, a murmuring that swelled to cheers when they caught sight of him. He had heard soldiers greet his father this way, seen them emerge from their tents and leave off work to line his path with shouts of welcome, swords and bows lifted with pride in the victory Zehava always brought with him. But the accolade and the tumultuous welcome were not for his father this time. They were for him. Rohan. Their dragon prince. The knowledge made him a little sick.

He had brought with him twenty archers and thirty horse, and his squire Tilal. The one pleasure he had was knowing the boy would be reunited with his father. The prospect of explaining events to Chay was not something to be anticipated with anything other than dread. He cursed his cowardice and kept all emotion from his face as he rode to the plain dark war tent, distinguished from the others by the Radzyn standard hanging from a silver pole. Desert colors would soon take its place, and Chay's flag would shift to the other side of the entrance. As if, Rohan told himself, *he* would be in command of this war.

Chay was waiting for him along with the captains and a man bearing a superficial likeness to Sioned and a much stronger one to Tilal. And could that possibly be Maarken? He returned their bows with a crisp nod, grateful for rituals a prince could hide behind. Thank the Goddess for ceremony, no matter how false. No, he corrected, there was no falseness here but him.

"My prince," Chay greeted him, sending an urgent message with his eyes. Rohan understood. His people pressed close for a word from their prince, and he would have to give it. He dug his heels into his stallion's sides and pulled back on the reins. His beloved Pashta, restored to him from Skybowl, rose impressively on his haunches and swerved around. Rohan held up his fisted right hand, and all was silence. He smiled tightly.

"Tonight the High Prince rests across the river in his camp. But, by the Goddess, soon he will find *eternal* rest."

A roar went up and Rohan gave himself acid congratulations for the stupid speech—brief enough to be repeated verbatim throughout the camp tonight. He noted Chay's approval as he swung down off his horse. Tossing the reins to Tilal, he drew off his riding gauntlets and approached Lord Davvi, whom he had met only once, and very briefly, at Stronghold two years ago.

"My lady wife has told me of your goodness in coming to us," he said formally, aware of being watched. He wished he could let down even a little of his guard, but that would have to come later, in private. "I thank you for your help, my lord, and will talk longer with you later. But for now I think there's someone else here with a prior claim on your attention." He nodded to Tilal, who was practically dancing with excitement.

Davvi had scarcely been able to take his eyes off his son. Now he gave Rohan a slightly abashed smile. "Your grace, I'm honored by your friendship and your indulgence. I would indeed like to speak with my son."

The curve of his lips felt strange; it was the first genuine smile that had come to him in a long time. "Until later then, my lord." As Davvi want to embrace Tilal, Rohan saw that Chay had dismissed the captains and sent them to give orders that should have dispersed the troops.

But one of them shouted Rohan's name, and the cry was taken up, turned into a chant, bellowed out loud enough to be heard by Roelstra all the way across the river. Rohan paused on his way to the tent, his people's excitement and faith catching painfully at his heart. He lifted a hand to accept the tribute, then sought refuge in the cool, dim interior of the tent.

Maarken, acting as Chay's squire, presented chairs and goblets of wine to his princely uncle and his father, then stood waiting for further orders. Both men sat, drank, and stared at each other for a time. Chay roused himself first.

"That will be all, Maarken," he told his son. "Come back later to remove my things from here and—"

"No!" Rohan exclaimed. Then, more calmly as he saw their startlement. "No, I don't fancy being alone in this great wind-tunnel you call a tent, Chay. Maarken, you and Tilal set up a bed for me in here, please."

"I'm honored to serve you, my prince." The boy bowed to him.

Again Rohan felt himself smile, and it felt more natural this time. "You've grown up, I see. Lleyn has taught you very well. But I think here in private we may be as we always were to each other."

The stiffness went out of the young body and Maarken gave him a smile. "I could hardly believe it when I felt Sioned's colors on the sun and she told me you were both safe! Did you hear the soldiers shouting for you? They say your dragons protect you—and their strength and cunning come with you."

"Is that what they say?"

The edge in his voice darkened Chay's quicksilver eyes. "You can go now, son. I'll call when you're needed."

"Yes, my lord." Maarken bowed, formal again, and left them.

"*Very* grown up," Rohan observed. "You must be proud."

"I am," Chay said simply. "Tell me what Sioned didn't tell Maarken."

Rohan shrugged. "I don't know that she left anything out."

Chay leaned back with a snort of derision. "This is *me*, Rohan. I've known you practically from a hatchling, my lord dragon prince. What happened at Feruche?"

"What you really mean is why did Ianthe let us go." He took a long swallow of wine. "Swear to me that this goes no further. On your sword and the lives of your sons, Chay—swear."

The older man froze for a moment. Then, slowly, he said, "You know me better, so you must be trying to impress me with how serious this is. Very well. I so swear."

"I meant no insult." He rolled the goblet between his hands, staring down into the swirling dark wine. "Sioned—" The catch in his voice humiliated him. "She's emptied Stronghold again. Those not with me went to Skybowl to take care of the Merida there, and will go on to Walvis at Tiglath. She says—and Tobin agrees with her—that if anyone gets close enough to threaten Stronghold again, there won't be anyone left to save it for anyway."

"Logical," Chay grunted. "Why are women always so logical?"

"Most of the servants went to Remagev with the twins. Only a few stayed behind at Stronghold—those loyal enough to lie."

"About what?"

"Ah. Then she *didn't* tell Maarken." He took another swallow of wine. "There's to be a child in midwinter. Ianthe got what she wanted of me."

Chay's expressive face was immobile with shock. Rohan shrugged.

"Aren't you going to ask how she managed it? The first time I thought she was Sioned. The second time—I raped her. I should have killed her. I didn't. She timed it perfectly and now she's carrying my child. Sioned says it will be a boy. Beyond that she doesn't say much at all. She won't talk to me, Chay, and I *can't* talk to her, I can't—"

"No more," Chay whispered. "This can wait."

"I have to talk to someone!"

Chay set his winecup down and rose, deliberately looming over Rohan. "You *have* an army awaiting your commands. You *have* an enemy across the river who wants you dead. Feel sorry for yourself some other time—when you *have* the time!"

Rohan knew he was being manipulated and part of him hated Chay for it. But this brother in all but blood was right—damn him. He saw the hard eyes watching for telltale changes in his face, and turned away. But even that movement was enough.

"That's better," Chay said, resuming his seat. "Now that you're capable of thinking again, turn that mental maze of yours to this. I've given Roelstra ten days to get half his army across the bridges, and he hasn't moved more than fifty men. We can withstand two more battles if we're lucky—but that's all. I wanted half his troops on this side to wipe them out and then I was going to cross and take care of the other half. But he's not obliging me. If you have any suggestions, I'd like to hear them."

Rohan nearly laughed. In camp only long enough to wet his throat, and Chay was asking him to make the kind of tactical decision he'd never been much good at anyway. He drank down the remains of the wine, got to his feet, and said, "I'm going for a walk. When I get back, I expect to see a bed waiting."

"Have some dinner while you're at it. The way you look now, you could hide behind your swordblade."

"Is that what you think? That I want to hide?" he demanded.

A slight smile played around Chay's mouth. "*Much* better. Now you're a prince again."

Urival watched long fingers drum impatiently on the table where a meal lay untouched. Candlelight picked out each gem in each ring as Andrade's fingers lifted and fell in angry rhythm: ruby-agate-amethyst-sapphire on the left hand, emerald-topaz-garnet-diamond on the right. Both thumbs were flat on the polished wood, amber on one and moonstone on the other. On Andrade's fingers were symbolized formidable attributes: luck in war, persuasiveness, nobility, truth, hope, intelligence, constancy, and cunning. But somehow Urival was more concerned with the two other stones, the ones that promised protection against danger and wisdom. They were sorely in need of both.

"Well? Is it merely the inactivity, or the inability to give them all orders?" he asked, deliberately provoking her.

"Would any of them listen? At least we'll be spared the fine Lady Wisla from now on. Thoughtful of her to remove to River View."

Urival nodded. The chamber in which they sat was Lord Davvi's own at River Run, a tidy room unencumbered by his wife's notions of elegance that burdened much of the rest of the keep. Lady Wisla had been faint with shock at receiving such august visitors, horrified by the revelation of Chiana's identify, and only too glad to accept Urival's private suggestion that she would find life much easier and safer at her late father's keep of River View, five measures distant. Her absence freed them from her nervous whining and gave them a comfortable base of operations. The question, of course, was what sort of operations were possible. The *faradh'im* all knew where Andrade was—those not shut away from the light—and were constant in their reports. Andrade and Urival were close enough to observe both armies without strain, and far enough away to be undetected by Roelstra. If he decided to take Lord Davvi's family hostage, they might find themselves in difficulties. But Roelstra had made no move toward River Run, probably surmising that Lady Wisla had long since departed. Urival, with the best charity in the world, could not discover a reason why any man would want to ransom such a wife.

Still, her household was efficient and she had left enough servants behind to cater to her guests' needs. But lack of worry about ordinary matters here left too much time to think about the extraordinary events elsewhere.

"Still nothing from Sioned," Urival said to himself.

"I can't force her, thanks to the training *you* gave her," Andrade snapped, fingers drumming faster now. "I need a Sunrunner at Stronghold, one I can trust to tell me what's happening there."

"And you no longer trust Sioned. That's what you're really saying. Andrade, *you* placed her where she is! Trained her, took her to Rohan already half in love with him, showed her to him so he was just as in love with her. You planned it, Andrade, and now you're going to have to live with it."

"You never let up, do you?" She paced in front of the windows, rings flashing as her fingers clenched and opened, clenched and opened. "How was I to know? What I foresaw and what's turned out to be are so different. What should I have done?"

He shrugged. "Probably nothing at all."

"Damn you, Urival, let me be!" she cried. "Don't you know why I matched them in the first place? *Faradhi* princes would have ended all the petty quarrels—"

"You still don't see it, do you?" He went to her, took her shoulders in his hands. "You always forget *people*. That's what your new manner of princes will be. People with all the honor and vices and feelings the rest of us have. But you've never been very concerned with feelings, have you? Except when you can use them." He frowned at the stubborn denial in her pale blue eyes. "Did you think you could use the children the way you used the parents?"

"Stop making me sound evil! I would have taught them, shaped them—"

"Made them tools for your ambition. What gives you the right, Andrade?"

"You want me to admit it?" she shouted, wrenching away from him. "Yes, I used them all, starting with my own sister and Zehava! I took the chance, hoping they'd produce a prince with the gifts. When they didn't, I tried again with Sioned and Rohan."

"Who next? Tobin's sons? Andrade, you can't *use* people that way—not and stay human yourself!"

"I loved them! I love Rohan and Sioned as if they were my own—and Tobin, and Chay, and their sons—" She leaned her shoulder against the smooth stone walls, arms wrapped tightly around herself. "I loved them too much. I wanted too much for them. And I hated Roelstra even more than I loved the others. Does that make me human enough, Urival?"

"I think there's something you haven't learned yet," he responded softly. "There's nothing you can do now. Whatever you've set in motion, whatever your reasons, you'll have to wait it through—just like everyone else."

He was astounded when tears glittered in her eyes. "Drive in the knife a little deeper, why don't you? Am I bleeding enough yet?"

He was even more astounded when he put his arms around her. "It's not like you to be helpless," he whispered against her silvering blonde hair. "It's not like my Lady at all."

The gardens Princess Milar had planned and cared for so lovingly wilted as summer dragged on. The grotto waterfall dwindled to a thin ribbon and the pond below it was nearly dry, thirsty plants and mosses drinking up what little moisture the spring provided. But it remained a haven of cool shade in the oppressive heat and silence of Stronghold, and it was to the grotto that Sioned often went in the long days of her waiting.

She did not go there to be alone. The keep was empty; she, Tobin, and Ostvel remained, along with Myrdal and three servants. The rest had gone with Rohan or north to Tiglath or to escort Sorin and Andry to Remagev. Solitude was a fact of life in Stronghold.

Neither did she seek the grotto to indulge herself in memories. The paradox was that empty as the keep always seemed to her when her husband was gone, his presence filled the place. The delicate balance between the ache of missing him and the ache of sensing him everywhere perfectly matched her equally precarious juggling of serenity and rage. Most of the time she preserved her equilibrium. When she could not, she went to the grotto and counted off each day of Ianthe's bearing, numbering the days left until midwinter when she would return to Feruche.

She had lost count of how many times she had felt the touch of Andrade's colors on the sunlight. She had rejected each assault with defenses Urival had taught her— not because she feared Andrade would sway her, but because of her jealous guardianship of hard-won balance. The Lady's arguments and prohibitions would have loosed Sioned's rage, and she could not afford it. Not until midwinter, when she could face its object.

It was after yet another attempted contact one day, an insidious weaving of great skill that very nearly worked, that Sioned left the sunlit inner court where she had been currying her horse and made her way through the half-dead gardens to the grotto. A few paces from its sheltering trees she stopped, transfixed by sudden music. Ostvel's lute sang so rarely that its notes brought tears to her eyes. It was said that the Storm God rarely gifted Sunrunners with the music that was his voice in the wind and water; Mardeem's talent had been an anomaly. But Ostvel, for all that he had served most of his life at Goddess Keep and was now steward to a *faradhi* princess, had been gifted with the sensitive fingers and soul of a bard.

It was Camigwen's favorite song he played. A sprightly ballad when she had been alive, since her death it had slowed to a stately tune that slipped every so often into a minor key. Sioned was filled with tender, painful memories of her friend's dark face and lustrous eyes, her scolding and smiles, the warmth of her colors. Though Sioned had walled herself off to all other *faradh'im* and Tobin was the one who received messages on the sunlight, at this moment she was filled with recollections of that first joyous weaving of sunlight, lessons learned and practiced with Cami. How young they had been, how eager to discover their gifts, how excited by the wonders to be seen and felt on the light, how entranced by this incredible thing they could do. Sioned remembered what it had been like, and instinct opened her mind and heart to the sunlight around her.

She felt the colors of the music—sapphire and diamond and topaz and amethyst, all shot through with pulsing silvery shadows. Tilting her head back, she presented her face to the sun, eyes closed, watching her own colors form the distinctive pattern she used to weave the thread of light. Yet the lute colors were strangely insistent, swirling in momentary chaos before resolving into a coherent pattern—as if they belonged to a living being instead of wire and wood.

Help me!

Sioned could not help but respond to that cry. Master Sunrunner's training took over and swiftly she meshed the hues together, perceiving the unique design of a clever, even devious mind, unfamiliar to her but carrying something oddly familiar in its undertones.

Goddess blessing, Sunrunner—I've been trying for days to find you. Your colors are well-known, but you haven't wanted to be found—and I can well understand why. Please—don't withdraw from me—please!

Sioned did not withdraw, but neither did she venture down the sunlight to discover who had called to her thus. Tense and wary, she examined the pattern and found little to reassure her. There were shadows here, and flickers of diamond-white that was the color of cunning.

I've only three rings—I'm no danger to you! Listen to me, please! I know things your prince will need if he's to defeat Roelstra. Prince Jastri is angry and hot-headed, and instead of being chastened by his losses in battle he chafes for vengeance. He commands over three hundred. He will not obey Roelstra if temptation enough is provided him. Give him a reason!

The deeper colors burned, outlined in Fire now, hatred clear. Sioned drew back, uncertain where that hate was directed.

Believe me! Would I dare this if I was not sincere? I want to help you!

"Sioned?"

Startled, she lost the pattern, and a faint cry echoed away into the sunlight. She opened her eyes and saw Ostvel, lute in one hand, staring at her.

"I was just thinking," she managed in a fairly natural voice. "Forgive me, Ostvel, I didn't mean to intrude on your music."

"You didn't. I'd finished." He glanced away. "Sioned, I have to talk to you. Tobin heard from Kleve in Tiglath this morning."

"What does he say?"

"No change. Minor skirmishes, but the siege continues. Walvis is worried and impatient, and that's a dangerous combination. They need a battle to lift their spirits." He smiled ruefully at the irony.

"Death to make them more hopeful of life." She shook her head. "What are we doing to these children, Ostvel? Walvis should still be practicing with his sword, not using it in earnest. And Maarken—he should be learning the arts of a gentleman, not a warrior."

"At least they're *doing* something." Ostvel shrugged irritably. "I feel like one of Roelstra's daughters caged up in Castle Crag."

Sioned gaped at him for a moment, then threw her arms around him, laughing. "Roelstra's daughters! Ostvel, you're brilliant!" Not giving him the chance to voice any of his bewilderment, she ran for the keep, shouting for Tobin.

Rohan knew very well that the option of playing idiot was no longer open to him. Between his first *Rialla* and this campaign to save his princedom had come six years of capable government and ample demonstration that he was no fool. Yet his experts at war were taken aback when, on the twentieth morning after his arrival, he ordered them to break camp and move back from the Faolain. He smiled slightly, glad that the notion of retreat was abhorrent to them, and waited for them to understand.

Chay's captain, Gryden, saw it first. "Draw them into the Long Sand, your grace?"

"Exactly. I want the troops spread out as thinly as we dare, always keeping some in sight of the sea. You'll all leave at different times and by different routes. Confusion is the idea here, with the hint that some of you are thinking about going home. Three days from now I want this area clean, and by this I mean that Roelstra's troops will find nothing to live on here. Strip the trees and fields bare." Shock widened their eyes, and Rohan shrugged. "Lord Baisal's unhappiness would be the greater if the High Prince ended by ruling the Desert. We'll lead them as far from his holding as we can. He's had orders to stuff and garnish his own keep, so he'll survive. Besides, it's not him they want. It's me. Any questions?"

If there were, the captains were wise enough not to voice them. When they had gone, Chay met Rohan's gaze levelly. "Are you sure you trust this information? Sioned didn't even tell Maarken who gave it to her."

"I trust the information and Sioned implicitly. As to the identity—we all know that *faradh'im* are capable of using eyes and ears other than their own. I don't really care how she gets the news. You'll admit that the analysis of Jastri's mood is probably accurate."

"I still don't like it."

Davvi cleared his throat. "Roelstra has ruled the boy thus far. Can we count on his losing his hold?"

"What else can we do? Even if they can resist coming after us, then surely they won't be able to ignore a riverbank left open to them."

Green eyes, so like Sioned's, danced with sudden anticipation. "We'll see how far they're willing to swallow the bait. After all, we can turn and attack them at any time. Chay's made sure of that."

In carefully planned bad order the various companies

of archers, horse, and foot soldiers packed up and marched in what appeared to be any direction their captains felt like taking them. It took Roelstra several days to investigate this, and ten more to commit himself. Though he had not followed Chay's enticing lead, he was now unable to resist Rohan's, and it was the presence of the young prince that made the bait irresistible.

Thus things continued through high summer. Rohan ordered retreats of a few measures at a time, his forces spread in a dangerously thin line as they pulled back to the edge of the Long Sand, with some always in sight of the sea. The green hills of the Faolain Lowlands gave way to brown scrub, with golden dunes not far beyond. Yet Roelstra was cautious about extending his lines of supply and communications. Sioned reported to Maarken that Roelstra's own men had stayed pretty much on the other side of the river, leaving Jastri's men to explore. And Jastri was fit to be tied.

When Rohan received word that his troops were exactly where Chay wanted them, he hesitated. Desertbred, his people knew how to live here. Jastri's did not. Nightly he debated with Chay and Davvi the wisdom of an attack now or further waiting while the heat debilitated Jastri's troops. He knew his own people were puzzled by his indecision. His actions at Stronghold were common knowledge by now, and they could not help but wonder why a prince who had calmly ordered his enemies butchered should now be reluctant to perform the same service for an even greater enemy.

Yet he waited. If he could save a few lives by waiting for summer to weaken the enemy, he was willing to wait. He did not fear the battle or his own death; he feared the loss of lives held in his hands, lives for which he was responsible as their prince.

It was worst at night. During the day there were reports to be heard and ploys to be discussed and the searing heat to be lived through. But at night, after the maps had been rolled up and he lay in his cot, knowing the coolness ought to soothe him into badly needed sleep, he stayed awake. He dared not rise and pace the camp, not wishing to awaken Chay, Maarken, or Tilal, not wanting the soldiers to see his restlessness. So while his body lay quiet, his mind roamed endlessly.

Thoughts of Sioned were the most painful. She had given him cool lips and a serene smile at their farewell, but had he not held her night after night during her terrible dreaming? The woman who wept and clung to him was a stranger, as alien as the one who held out chafed, ringless hands to be kissed. Yet neither was as troubling as the Sunrunner who had conjured for him in a candleflame the night before he left Stronghold.

He flinched still when he remembered the image of herself and the boy-child, the sound of her voice, deep and redolent of Fire and shadows. "What Andrade wanted from me, Ianthe will give her. But they'll both lose, Rohan. This prince will be yours and mine. What do I care what you did with her or to her? You tell me there was rape. Didn't she and Andrade do the same to us? Andrade used me, Ianthe used you. But they will not use our son. Believe that, Rohan."

Yes, he believed. He saw Ianthe's death in Sioned's eyes, and believed. Sioned would wait out the child as if the pregnancy was her own, while Rohan destroyed the High Prince like any other barbarian.

His child. Sioned's child. Goddess help the boy, what sort of world would he be born into? One in which his father's wife had killed his mother, and his father had killed his grandfather. Goddess help him.

The waiting ended eight days later for Rohan. Maarken, caught very suddenly on the sunlight, recovered from Sioned's weaving and hurried to his father's tent, brushing past the Desert standard on its golden staff, interrupting a conference between prince and *athri*.

"Jastri's on the move south! Sixty horse, seventy archers, and two hundred foot! He's broken with the High Prince and will attack tomorrow."

Rohan grabbed for a map. "Now we find out how good you are at strategy, Chay. All captains here at once, Maarken. Get Tilal to help you, then make it known among the troops that tomorrow we fight at last."

Prince Jastri's three hundred and thirty arrived from the south, unhindered by the horse Chay directed there.

These merely shadowed the host, unseen. When Jastri turned east for the attack on what his scouts had reported as Rohan's weakest position, he found three hundred facing him with the prince himself at their head.

This time there was no Faolain River to wash away the blood. It soaked into the gritty sand for hours, then was left behind as Rohan's forces pushed Jastri's back measure after measure toward the Faolain. But there was no escape across the river, for between Jastri and the bridges were another hundred Desert soldiers, led by Lord Davvi.

The young prince fled south whence he had come. Rohan, riding with Tilal and Davvi at his side, topped a small rise in time to see Chay's red-and-white standard flash into view from the trees. Jastri was caught in the middle, the reserve horse thundering at him from the south, Rohan and Davvi's troops marching inexorably at him from the north and west.

Rohan sent a man forward with his battle flag to signal Jastri an offer of his life if he surrendered at once. But Sioned and her informant had been correct; the young man was hot-tempered and very proud. He led his remnant of an army against Rohan, bellowing out his fury.

Feeling Davvi's gaze on him, he knew his brother-by-marriage was wondering if mercy was a part of his character. He hesitated, knowing that he could order Jastri sectioned off from his troops and spared. But as he glanced at the older man he saw Sioned's green eyes, remembered her ravaged face. Rohan lifted his sword.

Jastri's force broke utterly. Some soldiers laid down their arms; others fought to preserve their own lives without thought of winning a larger battle already lost. Rohan had to admire the courage of these latter people, as he admired Jastri's, even though such bravery in these circumstances was folly. He tried to fight through to the young prince, deciding that he would offer honorable treatment as befitted princes. But he was too busy defending himself and Tilal from ambitious stripling lords who wanted his head. He never saw who killed Prince Jastri.

The banks of the Faolain had long since been secured

by Davvi's contingent, so when the battle cooled at last
Rohan led the way back there, Pashta snorting at the
stench of death as he picked his way delicately around
the corpses. Rohan's gaze fastened on the empty bridges.
Roelstra was too smart to have committed more than a
handful of his own troops; he had probably ordered them
back across the Faolain this morning. Neither had he
risked his own precious person. Pity. Rohan would have
liked to end it all here.

Chay rode up with Jastri's ripped and bloodied turquoise standard furled across his saddle. Rohan held out
his hand and Chay dropped into his palm two rings, one
gold and one silver, both set with deep garnets, the gem
of Syrene princes.

"I had them take him from the field," Chay murmured.

"Thank you." Rohan turned, called a group of archers
forward, and bid them ready their arrows.

"What are you doing?" Chay hissed as flint was struck
and a small fire made in the sand. "We need those
bridges!"

"If we cross them now, we'll be slaughtered. Roelstra's
troops are fresh, and we're exhausted. If we leave the
bridges, he'll either use them or burn them himself to
keep us from crossing. I would rather they went up with
our fire, not his. Do you agree?"

The question was for form's sake only, but Chay's
reaction surprised him. A small, hard smile touched his
sweat-streaked face as he said, "It's something Zehava
would have done, you know. The grand gesture—and the
warning."

Clenching his fist around the two rings, Rohan glanced
over at the archers. But before he could give the order, a
cry went up from across the river, soon taken up by his
own troops. Fire had spouted up from the bridges in
fountains of flame.

Maarken, cheeks white beneath the dirt and sweat of
battle, stood at the water's edge, his arms held up and his
hands balled into trembling fists. He called down Fire
and it fed on the wooden bridges, sent dancing sparks
into the reflecting water. As the sun dipped lower and
shadows touched the river, the Fire blazed higher and the
Desert cheered its young Sunrunner lord.

Chay whispered his son's name, anguished. Rohan sat his horse in silence, feeling the heat of battle drain out of him, making him aware of his sore shoulder and weary muscles. There were other small hurts, shallow slices of sword and knife, insignificant in themselves. But they merged into the whole, augmented by a real grief for another foolish young princeling, and as the Fire flared he winced.

Maarken finished his work and with visible effort climbed the rise to where his prince and his father waited. "I killed no one, my lord," he told Chay.

Seeing that the father was incapable of speech, the prince said, "You have our gratitude, and you've gained us Roelstra's fear. Look." He pointed to the opposite shore, where atop the embankment the enemy had gathered to watch as Sunrunner's Fire licked hungrily through the wood, glowing red-gold to create two blazing rivers of light across the cool one of dark water. He could easily pick out the figures he wished most to see: Roelstra in a deep violet robe, his head bare, black hair ruffling in the Fire-born breeze, and Pandsala, her eyes dark hollows.

"Archer," he said softly, and a girl ran up. He gave her the gold-and-garnet ring. "For the High Prince, with my compliments."

She grinned up at him, and beneath the bruises and the dirt he recognized the sentry he had scolded here along this same riverbank. "I'll plant it right at his feet, your grace!"

She very nearly did. Rohan admired the consummate skill that adjusted the arrow's flight for the weight attached to it and calculated to a nicety the desired distance. Blue-and-white fletching came to rest ten paces away from Roelstra. Pandsala darted forward. Drawing the arrow from the ground, she handed her father the ring.

Rohan held up the other one. "As I presented Princess Sioned with a token of my gratitude before she became my princess, thus I now give recognition to my beloved nephew of Radzyn." Maarken's eyes went wide before he bent his head and extended his left hand. "No," Rohan said clearly. "The other hand, and the middle finger. This is the first of your *faradhi* rings."

Filthy and exhausted as he was, yet Maarken's face was shining as he raised his eyes to Rohan, man's pride competing with boy's excitement. Radzyn troops cheered their lord, and Maarken suddenly turned scarlet.

Rohan smiled, but as he counted up the survivors he knew how much this victory had cost him. A quarter and more of their strength had been spent in taking what they had owned to begin with. In doing so they had halved Roelstra's forces, but they were essentially back where they had started. Chay had specified two battles, and the first was over.

A sudden instinct made him tense as a strange, familiar sensation fluttered in his chest. He looked up, breath strangling in his throat. Soaring through the sky were dragons, more than a hundred of them. The sires and she-dragons Feylin had so carefully counted had produced hatchlings, none of which had been slaughtered by a hunt. No bigger than young children, they beat their wings powerfully, keeping up with their watchful elders on the journey from the caves around Skybowl and Feruche to the cool heights of the Catha Hills in the south.

Rohan felt his throat tighten, his eyes sting. His dragons, more than he had ever seen before in his life, free and proud and alive. His dragons.

As they flew from the Desert across the Faolain, the chant began again. But it was not his name that rumbled along the riverbank, growing louder, following the dragons over Roelstra's camp as hundreds of wings cast shadows on the violet tents. Someone knowing the old tongue had renamed Rohan, given him the single powerful word that would be his for the rest of his life.

Azhei. Dragon Prince.

Chapter Twenty-eight

Pandsala stood on a hillock, staring moodily at the storm clouds to the north. They were a distant threat for now, both to encamped troops and Sunrunners, but soon they would shadow and then drench the pastures of Meadowlord before slinking to Syr. She simultaneously dreaded and welcomed the anticipated downpour, first of autumn. Six winters at Goddess Keep had taught her to loathe overcast skies, but here in her comparative freedom, storms would keep the armies mired down and all *faradh'im* effectively caged—not just those ordered so by her father.

He paced beside her, still raging—though in merciful silence now—about the note that had flown in on an arrow from Rohan's camp that morning. Prince Jastri was dead without a son or brother to assume his title, and only a sister, Gemma, left of his branch of the Syrene royal house. Rohan had proposed, and Andrade had agreed, that subject to the approval of the other princes, Lord Davvi of River Run was to be elevated to the princedom. His lineage was of the princely house; he was the heir. Young Gemma, at barely ten winters old, could not inherit without treaties stipulating that her assumption of the princedom had been agreed to by all the other princes and the *athr'im* of Syr. Of course, if Roelstra had had a son, he could have had him marry the girl at once, no matter her tender years. Of course, if Roelstra had had a son, he would not be in his present pass. The thought gave Pandsala grim amusement.

"Smiling?" her father sneered. "Is it the beautiful day that pleases you, daughter mine? Or the fact that that whore's brother has been named Prince of Syr? I'll have

Rohan spitted and roasted over a Sunrunner's Fire—and his witch with him!"

Pandsala stayed wisely silent.

"Declaring him prince and putting him in High Kirat are two different things! The Syrene lords will defend their princess—just as I intend to do! And as for her dear uncle of Ossetia—Chale will send troops. Yes. He'll want to see Gemma as ruler of Syr."

"But will he want to make war against Rohan?" she murmured.

"He will if I tell him to!" Roelstra bellowed. "And he'll raze Goddess Keep as well, with Andrade in it!"

Pandsala felt she ought to say something soothing. "Surely the other princes will realize how powerful this action will make Rohan. If they don't, you can point it out to them. They can't acclaim Davvi until they're all met in one place, and we're past time for the *Rialla* this year. Between now and whenever Rohan is able to call a convocation—"

"He won't be alive past midwinter!" he roared.

"Of course not, Father. Forgive me."

His glare softened. "You have your mother's temperament. She always spoke softly, no matter what threatened. I loved her well, you know. Goddess, if only one of you had been a son!" He frowned, then shrugged. "Another three hundred troops should be here before the worst rains begin."

"Who has such strength on short notice?"

"My greedy friend Prince Saumer of Isel, for one. And Lyell of Waes, your sister Kiele's Chosen, will allow him to land his soldiers in Waes. He's decided that his interests lie with his future wife, not his dead sister's husband in Tiglath."

She nodded. "There was a courier yesterday."

"Yes." Roelstra looked grim. "It seems the Cunaxans want more money. The courtiers who've ruled since Prince Durriken's death find the current jingle of my gold too soft a sound, and wish to hear it ring louder. If only those stupid Merida had attacked when I planned it! They were to wait until Tiglath had emptied of troops gone to rescue the princeling. They could have walked right into the city and used it as a base when Rohan was forced to split his armies to go to Tiglath's aid. It would have worked, too."

"The results have been livable," she remarked.

"Barely. But now the Cunaxans want more money to supply the Merida, who should have taken their supplies from Tiglath itself." He flicked an imaginary spot of dirt off his cloak. "They could have moved south, captured Stronghold, and attacked the Desert army from behind."

"Rohan will have to come to this side of the river to establish Davvi in High Kirat. And then you can kill him."

"Oh, no. Not yet. He still has his uses." Roelstra's expression turned thoughtful. "You've been useful, too, Pandsala. You deserve a reward for warning me not to cross the Faolain with Jastri, and alerting me to Rohan's maneuvers. I know now how his mind works in war. How would you like a castle of your own, the same as your sister Ianthe?"

"Like Feruche?" She laughed. "Thank you, no. I've been at Goddess Keep for six years, and I've no desire to trade a foggy prison for a Desert one."

"I'm told River Run is a pretty place. It was the Sunrunner witch's childhood home, you know. It might amuse you to live there with some fine young lord as your husband." His eyes held a gleam of cunning. "And yourself as Princess of Syr."

She was surprised to feel eagerness compete with her suspicions. "I'd expected you'd set up one of Ianthe's sons as prince."

"Let them earn their positions when they've grown," he replied gruffly. "Do you want Syr or not?"

"I do," she replied. "But not to be princess at River Run. I want High Kirat itself. And there's another small condition."

"Condition? I give you a princedom and you—"

"Just a little one." She smiled. "I choose my own husband."

Roelstra chose to laugh, and Pandsala relaxed. "*You* should have been the son," he told her. "I'll have you established by midwinter, my pet. But you'll have to allow me the fun of removing Andrade from River Run first."

The repeated reference to midwinter puzzled her, but she hid it and smiled again. "Thank you, Father," she said demurely, bending her head to him as a sign of her submission.

Prince Lleyn had been sorely vexed that his ships had not arrived in time to assist in the battle. He made his feelings known through Meath, who kept Maarken quite busy on the sunlight one morning. Afterward, the squire made his way to the command tent, bowed, and presented his information with a wide grin on his face, shared by Tilal, to whom he had already told the news.

"He sent them to Tiglath!" Tilal cried before Maarken could speak. "Loaded down and wallowing in the water when they passed back by Graypearl!"

"Ha!" Chay clapped his hands together and rubbed the palms gleefully. "Lleyn's never had any use for the Cunaxans since he caught them stealing from his pearl-beds. Has there been any fighting in Tiglath?"

Maarken elbowed Tilal to silence. "The Merida tried to ambush the party sent to escort the new troops—and lost." He chuckled. "Tiglath is set for now. Lleyn's ships will sail again to resupply at Dorval and then come here."

Rohan shook his head. "Goddess, the concessions Lleyn will demand in the silk trade to pay for this!" But his eyes were dancing.

"We'll let Davvi contribute," Chay said slyly.

The new Prince of Syr bowed. "I promise faithfully to suspend any and all horse-thieving along the borders, and to make sure that all the Syrene wine that reaches the Desert is at least of the second-best quality, rather than the third."

"Decent of you," Rohan drawled. "What else does Meath say, Maarken?"

"Kleve is on a mission for Walvis. He's not in Tiglath at all." The boy shrugged. "Meath says they had to rely on a scout sloop that came down from Tiglath to inform the prince."

"Wonderful," Davvi muttered. "Now we have no way of knowing what happens in Tiglath."

"Walvis must have good reasons," Tilal said in defense of his idol.

"I wish I knew what they were," Rohan said.

"*I* wish we knew what passes on the sunlight between Stronghold and Tiglath," Chay remarked.

"You think my sister has something to do with this?"

"Davvi, I think Sioned has something to do with nearly everything. And I thank the Goddess who made her that my Tobin can only listen on the sunlight, not ride it." He took the sting out of his words with a smile at his son.

"But Father, you always say Mother's more closely related to the Storm God," Maarken replied pertly.

"That she is. And so are you." He rose, stretched and ruffled the boy's hair. "I've a tour to make of the lines, squire."

"Yes, my lord. But when Lleyn's ships arrive, may I please be excused from inspecting them with you?"

"More likely I'll dump you in one and send you on a grand tour of all the princedoms to complete your education!"

"Father! How would it look for the next Lord of Radzyn to be seen puking from one end of the continent to the other?"

Chay growled affectionately at him and pushed him out of the tent. Rohan watched them go, smiling, then leaned back in his chair and addressed Davvi in all seriousness.

"This is your part of the world. When will the heavy rains come and how long will they last?"

"Soon—and perhaps until spring." He traced the storms' usual route on the map spread before them. "We'll know when the river begins to rise that the bad ones have come to the Veresch and Meadowlord. Are you equipped for winter quarters?"

"Well enough." He got to his feet, paced, caught himself at it, and scowled. "What will Roelstra do? Will he withdraw for the winter? If he does, should we? We could take ship when Lleyn's people arrive and go to the relief of Tiglath. Or we could stay and wait, and take the first chance to march and establish you at High Kirat."

Davvi shifted uneasily. "I would rather not be be-holden to you there, my lord, if you'll take no offense. I'd like to fight that battle myself."

Rohan smiled, pleased by the answer. "I thought you might. And I doubt you'll get much resistance. Another season of Roelstra and the *athr'im* of Syr will be only too glad to have you."

"I realize you have first claim, Rohan, but leave me just a little piece of him, won't you? Although I think I may have to fight Chay for a place at the front of the line."

"Ah, no. He and I have a good understanding. He's going to hold my cloak. I'm afraid there won't be any-thing left of the High Prince. I hope you're not too disappointed," he finished dryly. Sitting back down at the desk, he stared at the map unrolled before him. "Rain," he murmured. "We see very little of it at Strong-hold, you know. We're on the wrong side of the Vere Hills for it. Radzyn and the other coastal holdings get a sea-squall now and then, and it's been known to flood and even snow in the far north."

"You'll get more rain here than you ever wanted to see." Davvi gave his son a playful nudge. "And you'll have to get used to it again after the Desert."

"Can we go hunting? And take my lord with us?"

"We'll show him the delights of getting soaked to the bone in pursuit of a single skinny elk!"

They laughed, obviously sharing memories. Rohan forced a smile, wondering if he would always be sur-rounded by loving fathers and their adoring sons, and hated himself for the petulance. He traced one finger along the map from the Faolain to Feruche, where Ianthe's son was growing within her body. *His* son, whom Sioned had seen in *faradhi* vision.

Tobin and Ostvel stop her? He had fooled himself with that only for as long as it had taken to ride here from Stronghold. But since then he had made plans. He would end the war as quickly as he could and then raze Feruche. Ianthe would die and the child with her.

Could he kill his own unborn son?

Rohan sank into moody silence, and did not notice that Davvi and Tilal had left him alone.

Andrade, caged with a sly little girl, a sharp-tongued Sunrunner, and a passel of witless servants, counted off the dismal days of autumn with even less patience than she had numbered those of summer. The Storm God was having a good laugh, amusing himself with sheeting rain and endless clouds that frustrated all *faradhi* communication.

But at least she had accomplished one thing before the storms, she told herself one gray afternoon in Lady Wisla's solar. Davvi was Prince of Syr in all but formal acclaim. That Roelstra controlled High Kirat and Princess Gemma within it, and that the full roster of princes had not yet affirmed Davvi, only made her shrug. She could call a convocation of princes anytime she pleased. Her predecessor had done it to ratify the Treaty of Linse that had given the Desert to Zehava's line "for as long as the sands spawn fire." She toyed with the notion of calling such a meeting now, at River Run, but decided that the risk of Roelstra's armies at the gates was not worth the amusement it would give her to see the princes arrive, soaked and irritable, at her whim.

Chafing her hands together, she stood before the hearth and scowled. One small accomplishment, acknowledging Davvi as Prince of Syr, did not weigh equally against interminable days of nothing. Boredom was the worst—that, and her bitter aversion to Chiana. The girl had grown this summer in one of those startling bursts some children experience. At barely six, she looked and behaved more like a child of ten. Each sight of her reminded Andrade of her sister, and how Pandsala was serving Roelstra with all the cunning of her breed and all the skills of her three *faradhi* rings.

As if called up by her thoughts, Chiana came dancing into the solar, bright and blooming. She swept Andrade a mocking curtsy and sang out, "My father's come to fetch me! Look over the walls and you'll see hundreds of his soldiers, all of them come to rescue me!"

Andrade pressed her lips closed and left the room for

the hallway, where wide windows opened onto the courtyard. Urival was down below, and as he raised his head
on sensing her presence, she saw the truth written in his
face. Chiana was giggling and pirouetting beside her, and
it was all Andrade could do not to slap her.

"How many are there?" the child cried out eagerly.
"Two hundred? Three?"

"Be silent!" Andrade hissed, and went down to meet
Urival in the foyer. Chiana scampered along behind her,
still laughing.

The steward's face was bitter as he reported, "Sixty of
the High Prince's troops seem intent on setting up camp
outside in the mud."

"A little late, isn't he? Why didn't he try this during
summer?"

"You know him better than I," Urival snapped.

"I know him better than I want to. Sixty, you say?"

"They'll attack and kill you and I'll be free!" Chiana
crowed. "I'll never have to go back to that horrid keep
again!"

"Silence!"

"You've lost! You're nothing, and I'm a princess!"

Urival took a step toward her, eyes like thunder, but
Andrade was closer and swifter. She grabbed the child's
arm roughly. "Listen to me! I helped birth you, and
watched while your precious father nearly ordered your
death! You want to go to him, Chiana? All he lacks is yet
another daughter! Would you like to be shut up at Castle
Crag with all the rest?"

"Ianthe is free—and she has her own castle! Pandsala—"

"Used you," Andrade told her. "It's the thing your
family does best. Ianthe is valuable to him for her cunning, and Pandsala for her rings. But you? Of useless
daughters he has more than enough! He has no use for
you!"

"He's come for me!" Chiana screamed, breaking loose
to flee out into the courtyard, masses of auburn hair
streaming out behind her.

Andrade and Urival followed much more slowly. Neither spoke; there was nothing to say until they had heard
what the troop's captain demanded. He had evidently

been waiting for Andrade's appearance on the walls; riding confidently forward, he saluted her with all due ceremony. His words were polite and precise: he had been ordered by the High Prince to secure River Run from possible attack by the traitorous Lord Davvi, who had forfeited all rights to this holding by his actions.

"I assume you refer to Prince Davvi of Syr," Andrade replied pleasantly.

"The High Prince does not recognize that title. He does, however, offer you his protection. Should you wish to leave River Run, we have orders to provide escort back to Goddess Keep."

Urival whispered, "Now, why does Roelstra want us gone from here?"

Andrade called down from the battlements, "I find one cage very like another. And I am *not* partial to them."

The captain smiled winningly. "And where else would you go, my Lady? Between you and the Desert lies the High Prince—and a rather substantial river you'd rather not cross, I'm sure. There's nothing for you in the north, and the Catha Hills to the south are hard traveling in any weather. Your only choice is Goddess Keep, and I'm quite willing to provide escort."

"Too kind," Andrade sneered. "But perhaps you've not seen Sunrunner's Fire kindled."

"Should you attempt it, I will take River Run, along with River View." He was no longer smiling. "And leave *you* alive."

His meaning was clear enough, and she ground her teeth. She had only her powers to defend this place, and if she used them Lady Wisla and the people of two keeps would die. "There is the sunlight," she bluffed.

"Of course," he agreed readily. "And ride it as you will, my Lady, there is also me." He bowed an end to the conversation and rode back to his camp.

"I hope he drowns in mud," Andrade muttered.

"We could escape," Urival said. "A circle of Fire around the keep—"

"For how long? Would he see it and ride off in terror?

Here we are and here we stay. I won't go back to Goddess Keep and be even farther away from things."

"Assuming, of course, you'd live long enough to get there."

"Precisely. There has to be some way out of this."

Urival shook his head. "All summer you've been able to ride away if and when you pleased. Now that there are troops outside to prevent us, you want to leave at once. My Lady, I will never understand the workings of your mind." He paused. "But I believe Roelstra does."

Andrade gave him a sharp look. "Do you mean he intends for me—"

"—to give him an excuse." Urival nodded. "But there *is* the sunlight."

"And to whom? Maarken, who would tell Rohan and Chay and give them one more worry? Sioned, who won't listen? Tobin, who sits in Stronghold as helpless as we? Or maybe you had Pandsala in mind! Now, *that's* a brilliant notion!"

He took her elbow and escorted her back down the stairs. "I *was* thinking of someone, actually. Meath."

Andrade gaped at him. "Sweet Goddess! Of course!" So enchanted was she by the idea that she didn't even mind the lecture he gave her about thinking everyone but herself a fool when she was the biggest fool of them all.

Rohan fought the impulse to pace as he watched Maarken. The boy sat on a folding stool, thin winter sunlight woven all around him. His eyes were closed, brow furrowed in concentration. Chay stood nearby, his back turned to the sight of his son in communication with another *faradhi*. Rohan had little patience for Chay's uneasiness with his son's abilities, though he understood its cause. But what had happened to Tobin six years ago had occurred only because she was untrained. Maarken would become an accomplished *faradhi*—as would Andry. Chay had better get used to the idea.

Six years, he thought, since he had watched Sunrunners call the wind to disperse the ashes of his father and the dragon out over the Desert. Would Zehava approve of what he was doing now? Probably. Zehava had never had any illusions about the world or the people who lived in it, unlike his son, who was only now discovering that all his pretty plans and notions were useless. Yet some impulse toward them stirred again as he watched Maarken. New generations should not have to fight the same battles their fathers had. There should be something more for the children, he told himself, something better for Maarken and Sorin and Andry—and his own son.

Hiding a wince, he turned as Tilal and Davvi approached calling his name. He held up a hand for quiet and went to them.

"My lord—wonderful news! The ships are here!"

Davvi hushed his son with a glance. "They've sailed as far as they can up the Faolain, and are now off-loading troops and supplies. They sent a rider ahead to inform you, my lord."

Chay turned, a broad smile on his face. "Not ships—bridges!"

"Huh?" Rohan stared at him.

"Think about it," he advised. Putting a hand on Tilal's shoulder, he went on, "Take me there. We have plans to make."

Davvi looked to Rohan for an explanation the prince was rapidly reasoning out. Bridges? Roelstra had drawn his troops back across the river in obvious mimicry of Rohan's summer tactic, and was camped on a large plain suitable for pitched battle. Rohan might have succumbed to the temptation but for one thing: Maarken had left the two bridges usable, after a few repairs, and Roelstra would be expecting the Desert host to cross in exactly those places. If Rohan had learned nothing else about war from Zehava and Chay, he knew that behaving as the enemy expected was the surest path to defeat. Thus he had declined to accept Roelstra's invitation to cross the Faolain and be slaughtered.

But now Lleyn's ships had arrived, and Chay seemed to have ideas for them. In Davvi's face he saw the same conclusion appear, and shrugged. "I very much doubt that the masters of those ships are going to appreciate demotion to captains of ferryboats."

Davvi snorted. "They'll live."

Rohan smiled slightly and began another comment, but from behind him he heard the squelch of something falling into the mud. He turned quickly to find Maarken pushing himself up from the ground, dazed of expression and glazed of eye. Rohan and Davvi helped the young man up.

"What happened?" Maarken stammered.

"You fell over, of course. Here, sit down and drink this." Rohan pressed a winecup to his lips.

Maarken sipped, coughed, and shook his head to clear it. "Oh, Goddess," he breathed. "I can hardly wait until I'm a real Sunrunner—"

"You're doing just fine," Davvi assured him.

"I can't control anything," the squire complained. "It just happens to me and I don't have any say in the matter. It's like—like being a field somebody marches over." He pulled a wry face and brushed ineffectually at the mud on his clothes.

Rohan bit his lips together over impatient questions. As color returned to Maarken's cheeks and a smile began on his face, Rohan stopped worrying, an instinct confirmed by the boy's first words.

"Walvis beat the Merida!"

Davvi whispered rapid thanks to the Goddess as Maarken went on with his report. It seemed that Cunaxan supplies had been mysteriously delayed for some time—no one knew why—and with the diminishing of their food the Merida had turned to the only source of sustenance available to them: Tiglath itself. The battle had raged for two solid days, but by its end the Merida were destroyed and Tiglath more or less intact.

"The wall between the Sea Gate and the Sand Gate collapsed after the Merida spent a whole night undermining it," Maarken explained, "but Lord Eltanin isn't worried about that. He even wants to leave it as it is. What was it Kleve told me he said?" he frowned. "Something about making it a reminder and a warning, and that the walls built by his prince will be better defense than mere stone ever could be." He looked up at Rohan, puzzled. "Do you know what he means, my lord?"

"I do," Davvi said. "And he's quite right. Go on, Maarken."

"Well, there was lots more. The Merida were strung around Tiglath like jewels on a necklace, Walvis said, but Kleve said they were more like insects caught in a spider-web, with lines of archers between. The wall collapsed and then they invaded, but Walvis was ready for them. Our people came out of the gates and took the battle out to the plain, and—" He paused for breath. "Walvis killed the leader and at least fifty more. Kleve and Feylin were watching but they lost count!"

"Is Walvis hurt?" Rohan asked.

"Just a scratch or two. He's too good a warrior to be wounded. The fires to burn the Merida dead went on for three days. Walvis wants to march south now to defend Stronghold or come to us here."

Davvi gave a muffled exclamation. "Lleyn's ships!"

"Exactly." Rohan nodded.

"What ships?" Maarken asked.

"Later," Rohan ordered. "Davvi, would you see him to his tent for some rest, please? I'll be with Chay."

As he mounted Pashta and rode slowly along the river-bank, he thought over Eltanin's words. Walls stronger than stone, built by Rohan. The *athri*'s faith galled him. He would have to topple fortresses more formidable than castles if his dream was to come alive again within him. *We hide behind our savagery,* he thought bitterly. *All of us. I have to destroy those walls before I can build others.* And, more to the immediate point, he would have to demolish the very real fortress of Feruche, and quickly. Midwinter was approaching. He must finish things here, play the barbarian warrior prince with Roelstra, before doing the same thing at Feruche. But after that— *Never again, I swear it,* he told himself. Barbarian he might be, but he could put down his sword. He must. He could not live this way.

Rohan had been correct about the masters' reaction to Chay's proposed use of their ships. But the transfer of troops, horses, and supplies to the Syrene bank of the Faolain was completed in two days, well south of the bridges where Roelstra had expected Rohan to cross.

The High Prince had no opportunity to deploy his army for serious harassment of the move; there were brief skirmishes but Desert archers kept the losses minimal. A measure was marched off and a new camp established, and all was ready just before the next storm blew in from the north. Once more both sides settled in for the duration, polishing swords and keeping bowstrings dry.

Lleyn's ships had to wait in the mouth of the Faolain for a break in the weather. It was a long time coming, ten days before the fleet commander considered it safe to put out to sea again. Rohan and Chay watched the sails rise and fill with brisk wind, and knew that with the ships went any possibility of escape back across the river. They were in Syr for good or ill. Whatever the outcome of the battle, whenever it was fought, Rohan was oddly pleased to have his actions forced this way. Diminishing choices diminished interior conflict.

He and Chay and Davvi formulated endless plans, fighting battles on maps to explore tactics, arguing placement and timing. It was all they could do until their scouts reported back, and when they did, the news was bad. In the brief two-day stretch of sun that had allowed the ships to set sail, Roelstra's army had moved back yet again and in doing so seemed to have multiplied twofold.

The morning brought a freezing mist as the trio rode out with their squires and captains to investigate for themselves. Rohan shivered beneath a heavy cloak, cursing the clouds that hung rain-heavy in the north. But what he saw from the top of a hill chilled him more thoroughly than the wind.

The whole of the pastureland that had lately been the High Prince's camp was awash in thigh-deep water. Trenches had been dug from tributaries of the Faolain. When added to the already saturated earth, the river water had turned a two-measure-wide plain into a lake. Crossing was impossible; the bottom was thick, viscous mud like that around the lake's edges. Drainage ditches and a whole summer's heat would be required to bake the land dry again. But there was something more, something only Roelstra in his cunning would have thought of, something that had ruined this rich land forever.

"Do you smell it?" Rohan asked softly. "Salt." He
heard Davvi's despairing curse, Chay's sharp intake of
breath. Rohan breathed deeply of the distinctive bite on
the wind. "I suppose the trees were too wet for burning,
or he would have done that, too," he commented. Then
he turned Pashta and rode back to his tent, and did not
admit anyone until nightfall.

When Chay was at last told that Prince Rohan wished
to speak with him, he entered the tent in the liveliest
apprehension of what he would find. Rohan sat on his
cot, round-shouldered, an empty bottle overturned on
the carpet and a half-empty one between his boots. There
was a goblet in his hands and he turned it around and
around in some private ritual before each swallow, five
times before drinking. Chay watched this for a while,
wondering if the remedy of liquor applied to Rohan's
wounds would dull them for at least a little while. But
when the blue eyes finally lifted to his, he knew the pain
was as piercing as ever.

"Sit down," Rohan said, and it was not an invitation.
"This time I have to talk. And this time you'll listen to
me."

Chay sat. He was not offered a cup and would not
have accepted one. Rohan stared at him for the time it
took to rotate the goblet again, five times before taking
another sip. His voice and his eyes were stone cold sober.

"I've told myself I'm clever and civilized. I've said that
my goal is the rule of law, not that of the sword. And
look what I've done. I was raised a prince to protect and
nurture the land and my people." Another sip, sensitive
fingers turning the goblet round and round. "I'm no
better than any man who's gone before me. I've told
myself I'm only doing what I have to do. But I've got a
real talent for this, Chay. I'm proficient in all the barbarian arts—war, rape—"

Rohan drank and leaned over to refill the goblet with
alarmingly steady hands. "*Azhrei.* They've never called
anyone that before, not even my father. Eltanin is going
to leave the wall in rubble—and do you know why? He
thinks the walls I'll build to protect the Desert will be
better than any stone. I'm not worthy of that kind of

trust. I'm not worthy of anything except to die with a sword in my guts, the way I've killed others. The way I'll kill again."

Not analytical by nature, still Chay could discern the vast difference between these weary, nearly emotionless musings and the anger of Rohan's arrival that summer. Then he had seethed with fury and guilt, seeking refuge in words and begging Chay for the negation of them that would signal forgiveness. But now he was merely resigned, a man looking at himself from outside himself, knowing there was no excuse—and not seeking any.

"I enjoyed slaughtering Jastri's army. I enjoyed raping Ianthe. I'm going to *love* destroying Roelstra. Look what that makes of me."

"It makes you a man like all the rest of us," Chay said quietly.

A tiny smile touched Rohan's lips. "Do you know how galling that is for someone like me?"

"You don't understand," Chay said, struggling to find the words. It was so important that they be the right ones. "You're like us, but unlike. Rohan, you've *tried*. You have the courage of your dreams—when most of us don't even know *how* to dream. You know this isn't the way to live, always at each other's throats. Your people trust you because they know the sword goes against your nature. It takes greater courage to—"

"To live by it when it's not of my choosing? Oh, but I chose it, you know. I'm doing a very good job of living with my sword in hand."

"But when this is over, there's something more for you—and for everyone else."

"Yes, of course. I can force everyone to do things my way, and that will make me into another Roelstra. Nothing better than he, in spite of my pretensions. I'd do anything to butcher him and his army, and I've done everything to secure myself a son. But there's one thing I have that he tried to get and failed. I have my very own Sunrunner, and I can use her without first binding her to me with *dranath*. She's all mine, Chay, just as Andrade planned she'd be." He lifted the goblet again, but this time did not drink. "What gives me the *right*?"

Chay heard emotions battling to break through the calm facade, and sent up a small whisper of thanks. A Rohan pretending detachment from himself was a Rohan who had nearly lost himself. "Power frightens you," Chay murmured. "You use it, but you don't feed off it the way Roelstra always has."

"And *that* gives me the right? The fact that I'm a coward?"

"You're not listening to me." Chay leaned forward in his chair, speaking quickly so Rohan would not be able to withdraw again into the unfeeling shell. "With you, we've got a chance for life. You're our only hope. Do you think I enjoy seeing my son at war? Gentle Goddess, he just turned twelve! What makes you different is that you hate all this! You fear power and you're scared you won't use it wisely—Sioned's power, too, and she's just like you! That makes you the prince and princess we need! Do you think she's not frightened by her power?"

Rohan flinched. "I saw my son in her Fire. I can't deny him—no matter who his mother is."

"If Sioned has courage enough to take him, can't you find enough to accept him as yours and hers, and not Ianthe's?"

"Make believe he wasn't born of rape?" Rohan shook his head bitterly, blond hair lank and dull in the lamplight. "It's not just Ianthe. I'd be raising the grandson of the High Prince."

"Rohan, it's a *baby*! What fault can there be in an innocent child?"

"His birth!" Rohan threw the goblet across the tent and the wine made a crimson splash against the fabric, dripping down onto the carpet. "He should have been Sioned's!"

"What makes you think he won't be? Maarken is as much Lleyn's now as he is Tobin's and mine. Rohan, there's no two people in the world who are solely responsible for what a child becomes. Ianthe may have the bearing of him, but he'll be yours and Sioned's to raise."

Rohan lay back on the cot and stared up at the tent roof, silent for a long time. At last he sighed quietly and said, "You're right about power. It terrifies me. Not the everyday kind princes have—deciding who has the better claim to grazing lands, ordering a new keep built or an old one replenished. It's *this* kind of power, Chay—an army around me, power at my disposal just because I'm a prince and I decide who's going to die. I'll accept it as a responsibility, but I won't believe that there's anything about me that gives me the *right*. I'm not wise. I'm not clever." He put an arm across his forehead. "All I am is scared."

For the first time since Zehava's death, Chay stopped comparing father and son to Rohan's lack. Zehava would have chosen a path and marched down it without any further thought. But the son differed from the father in constant examination for the right of things. Rohan questioned and doubted, sought deeper truths and hidden motivations. It would be the same when the High Prince's death opened paths of even greater power to him. Rohan would never stride arrogantly down them, blind to all else, never questioning his right to do as he pleased. He would always question—and this was what would make him wise. At that moment Chay ceased regretting that the son was not more like the father. He would have followed either wherever they cared to lead, but with Rohan, he knew that the path would always be the right one.

Chapter Twenty-nine

This time Sioned did not go to Feruche alone.

As Ianthe's time neared, Tobin and Maeta made quiet plans which they discussed with the reluctant Ostvel only when all was arranged and he could make no real objection. If he had hoped for an ending different from the one understood and unspoken all this time, that hope was now gone. Rohan and Chay were bogged down in the south, and though Tiglath's fighters were now free to make an assault on Feruche, Sioned had ordered Walvis to stay in the city. The child must be taken in secret if she was to have any chance of presenting him as her own.

That Ianthe would die was something equally understood, equally unspoken. One night in early winter, Tobin and Maeta described to Sioned plans for the infiltration of the castle. She merely nodded. No one mentioned Ianthe's name.

During the clearer days of autumn Ianthe had often strolled the battlements of Feruche, almost as if she knew Sioned would be watching. Her sons were usually with her and Sioned wondered bitterly why the Goddess had seen fit to give such wealth to such a woman. As Ianthe's pregnancy advanced, the envy was sometimes more than Sioned could stand. But now Ianthe's burden was too heavy to permit much walking. She slept uneasily in the huge bed with its dragon tapestries, for Rohan's son rode restlessly in her womb. Envy turned to hate when Sioned caught sight of the great emerald sparkling from her finger. Ianthe was in possession of things not rightfully her own, and Sioned's need to claim what was hers became a demand that threatened to destroy her hard-won balance.

For some days after plans were confirmed for the journey to Feruche, Sioned lapsed into a strange, waiting silence. Tobin understood; as her own birthing-times had neared, she had grown detached, all thoughts and feelings directed inward. Sioned's womb might be empty, but she was going through pregnancy as surely as Ianthe.

One early winter night at moonrise, as clouds brushed the northern horizon, the alarm Sioned had been waiting for flushed servants out of bed at Feruche. Lingering long enough on moonlight to be sure this was no false labor, she smiled with an odd mixture of envy and satisfaction as Ianthe's body arched in agonized spasms. Then she returned to Stronghold and sent for Tobin and Ostvel.

"She's early by forty days," Sioned told them when they came to her rooms, sleep-rumpled and apprehensive. "I felt she might be. We leave tonight."

Soon thereafter three riders on Chay's best horses were galloping north. Pale figures on pale horses, they rode in silence and made swift progress through the night made dazzling by three full moons. Sioned alone showed no fear. Tobin, schooled over the summer and autumn by Sioned in certain *faradhi* techniques, kept her mind busy reviewing what she had been taught but could not banish the intermittent quivers that ran through her body. Ostvel clenched and unclenched his fingers around his sword hilt, unable to protest and unable to stay behind. Neither of them dared speak to the woman who rode between them with her body straining eagerly forward, her green eyes blazing.

Sioned took the lead during the day through hills where, earlier in the year, dragons had basked and battled and mated. She had used this back approach to Feruche before, but this time was sure of the path. In spring she had mistaken the way. The dark nightmare of that lonely journey had merged into the horror of Feruche and the return to Stronghold. But though this trip also had something dreamlike about it; everything seemed outlined in bright Fire like a conjure, with all the singing colors of her gifts making her lightheaded.

Ten measures from Feruche they stopped, just beyond the first sentries, to rest for a little while after the long day's fast ride. After dismounting and securing the horses, they walked the last of the road as night gathered behind them. The castle came within sight above the rocky hills, bathed in winter sun, its towers crowned by a golden glow that seeped down the walls like honey. Sioned paused for a moment to contemplate the beauty of Feruche, recalling that Rohan had promised it would be hers one day. And so it would, she told herself. *This* day.

Sounds of revelry came from within the keep, drunken celebration of the princess' safe delivery of her son. Sioned listened, a tiny smile touching her mouth from time to time. She was aware of Tobin and Ostvel standing behind her, waiting nervously. In her own mind she conjured up Maeta's instructions of that spring, seeing her as surely as if the warrior was with her now.

"There's not a castle in the Desert I don't know inside and out—and more to the point, how to *get* inside from out. There are more secrets here at Stronghold than just this grotto passage, but we'll talk about them another time. Let me tell you about Feruche."

Sioned closed her eyes, visualizing the hidden entry, the corridors carved out of the rock, the twists and turns she had memorized but had not yet used. At their end was the upper hallway leading to Ianthe's chamber. A shudder ran through her, but she was not afraid. She felt nothing.

"Sioned. . . ."

Tobin's whisper turned her head, and she nodded slowly. "Yes. It's time I finished my work here."

She led them forward in the shadows below the sunlight, out of sight of the guardpost where she had been captured before. She had no worries about that this time; all of Feruche celebrated Ianthe's fourth son, and the stones outside the castle were silent. She moved around the curtain wall to the place where castle and cliff joined. A chink in the stone. A thin knife blade inserted to work the invisible catch. A moment when Ostvel's breath quickened with fear that the mechanism was too old and too long unused to function.

The slab of rough-hewn rock slid soundlessly aside. Sioned slipped through first, concentrated for an instant,

and produced a finger of Fire to see by. As Tobin and
Ostvel moved into the narrow passage beside her, she
inspected the workings of the entry. They had not been
touched in Goddess alone knew how long, but the builders' skill had been such that the system of weights and
catches still functioned perfectly.

The miniscule flame lit their way through the shoulder-
wide passage, glanced off long-empty sconces rusting on
the walls. The floor sloped up, turned sharply, then descended, and in places rotting planks had been set over
water seeping in from the underground spring that allowed Feruche to live. But there were no rats, no webs,
not the slightest sign or whisper of life here.

At last there was another weighted stone door, and
they emerged cautiously into a place Sioned recognized
only too well. She had been held in a cell here, away
from the light. A quiver chased down her backbone as
the nightmare of colorlessness flickered through her memory, and she coaxed the fingerflame a little higher, a little
brighter.

"Who's there?"

Tobin caught back a gasp and exchanged a wild glance
with Ostvel, who drew his sword with a sharp hiss of
steel. Sioned seemed not to notice. She walked forward
as the guard appeared from around a corner.

He choked and blanched in the glow of Sunrunner's
Fire. "You!"

"Yes," she murmured. "I remember you, too." She
pointed one long, ringless finger at him, and a new Fire
sprouted a handspan from his chest. He flattened himself
against the wall, eyes huge and staring, mouth open in a
soundless scream.

"Sioned—" Ostvel put a hand on her arm. She shrugged
him off, smiling; there was that in her eyes that made
him swallow hard. But he stepped forward and sunk his
blade into the man's throat. The guard slid down the
wall, still staring, dead.

Sioned whirled on Ostvel, fury in her face. He wiped
his blade and met her gaze without flinching. "No one
can know we've been here—not if this is to work. Any-

one who sees us must die—and I won't let you do the killing, *faradhi*."

The look in her eyes frightened Tobin. She had seen it in Chay's eyes this spring, that dark glitter that meant death. She gripped Sioned's hand and would not let her pull free. "Ostvel is right. Sioned, we must hurry."

The fire-gold head nodded once. She said nothing as she drew her fingers from Tobin's, let the Fire flicker out, and started for the stairs. Tobin traded another worried glance with Ostvel—who had not put up his sword.

Feruche's reputation as a castle that could not be taken had made its guards careless. The few not partaking of the wine-soaked celebrations were easy to avoid; Tobin created soft breaths of Air that distracted attention by ruffling a tapestry or rattling a window. Sioned paid no attention, confident that the guards Tobin did not distract, Ostvel would silence permanently. But the sword tasted no new blood on the way to Ianthe's chambers.

Sioned paused at a high window overlooking the courtyard, light from the central bonfire down below blazing across her face. Tobin grabbed Ostvel's arm as Sioned's hands lifted slightly.

"Sioned—no!" Tobin exclaimed.

An unnatural light appeared beyond the windows, the gold and crimson of Sunrunner's Fire. Tobin stared in horror at the outbuilding directly below, its wooden roof alight. Sparks blew onto the next roof and the next, leaping with terrible hunger. Ordinary fire would not have caught so swiftly, but Sunrunner's Fire flared and grew. The screams of alarm began, the panic. Sioned smiled slightly.

"Damn you!" Ostvel cried. "The balconies will catch! Sioned, you fool!"

"There has to be Fire," she said softly, and turned from the conflagration and the screams of drunken panic in the courtyard, heading unerringly for Ianthe's chambers.

Roelstra's daughter lay in her dragon-tapestried bed, weak from the birthing, sobbing for help. A cradle rocked silently in a corner, but the woman who tended the child was gone—and with reason, for the flames were clearly visible at the windows now, even so high in the tower. Stairs leading up the inner walls had caught, and a wooden balcony three floors below was now afire. As smoke filtered into the chamber, the baby began to cry.

Ianthe's pleas for help became screams of rage. Sioned ignored her. She went to the cradle where the infant lay, blond as sunlight. "Sweet Goddess," she breathed, almost afraid to touch him. One finger, hesitant and shy, across his cheek. "Shh," she whispered. "I'm here now, little one."

Ianthe pushed herself upright and shrieked, "Get away from my son!"

"*My* son," Sioned answered softly. She lifted the boy and held him to her heart, lips caressing the golden down covering his head. He stopped whimpering and snuggled close. "My son, now and forever."

"You wouldn't dare!" Ianthe struggled to rise, moaned, fell back onto her pillows. "Take your hands off him! You wouldn't dare steal him from me!"

"It was you who stole this child from my husband's body." Sioned faced the princess, holding the baby closer, tucking the blanket around him. "I'm returning to him what's his—and mine."

"I'll have you burned in your own Fire! Guards!" she screamed in a voice already hoarse from earlier cries. "*Guards!*"

"Be quiet," Sioned murmured absently, stroking the child's plump cheek with one finger.

Tobin came to her side, staring at the boy as if not quite able to comprehend his reality. "Oh, Sioned," she whispered. "He's *beautiful.* . . ."

"And mine." Sioned held him so Ostvel could see.

"Give him to me," Ostvel said.

"You bitch!" Ianthe howled. "I'll kill you myself, with my own hands—"

Sioned backed away as Ostvel reached for the child. "No! He's mine!"

"Did you think I'd give him back to *her*?" he snapped, taking the baby. Firmly and quickly he stripped off the velvet blanket. It fell to the carpet in a splash of gold-shot violet. "No son of Rohan's wears Roelstra's colors."

The smoke was thicker now. Ianthe found strength in panic, rising naked from the bed. Her fingers dug into the curtains, features contorted into a mask of fury as she clung to a post for support. "You'll die for this, all of you!"

Sioned walked slowly to her, pried the clawing fingers from the hangings. "You have something else that belongs to me, Ianthe." The princess tried to slap her, but Sioned was swifter and stronger. She caught a wrist and twisted it. Ianthe groaned and collapsed onto the bed, cursing as Sioned wrenched the emerald from her finger and returned it to its rightful place on her own hand.

Ianthe surged up again, her eyes slits of rage. "You dare take my son? You whore! I'll butcher him while you and Rohan watch!"

"A mother's love," Ostvel said.

Ianthe swayed to her feet. "Did Rohan tell you how it was?" she shouted at Sioned. "Did he tell you how he made love to me here in this bed? He's mine now, and his son with him! The way it should have been from the first!"

Sioned suddenly backhanded her, and the emerald tore a gash across the perfect cheek. Ianthe fell back onto the pillows, fear in her eyes now. Sioned spent a moment enjoying it, then turned. Tobin had taken the baby and wrapped him in her tunic. The child whimpered fretfully, smoke stinging his nose.

"Hush, little one," Tobin soothed, rocking him. "Little prince."

"Sioned, we've got to hurry," Ostvel warned. "The Fire—"

"Yes," she said, looking at Ianthe again. "The Fire."

The princess spat defiantly, "You couldn't kill me before, Sunrunner, and you won't now! You're—"

"I am what I have to be. Did you stay to watch your father ignite his mistress' bed, Ianthe?" Sioned slapped her again as she lurched up from the bed. "My Fire is of a different kind."

She held her hands out so Ianthe could watch them, the emerald a seething reflection of the flames outside the windows. Sioned smiled at the terror in Ianthe's dark eyes. Hate was a wonderful, living thing in her guts, giving her power beyond anything she had ever felt. Sweet and hot and potent, the hate wove its magic through her with threads of blackened sunlight, stitching together her need to kill and her delight in Ianthe's mortal fear.

But all at once the princess drew herself straight and looked to the child Tobin held. Sioned saw triumph in her face, laughter in her eyes. Sioned longed to strike her again, but there were better ways of killing her and the emerald blazed in response as Sioned sought the Fire within it. She gathered herself to wrap flames around the smirking, victorious princess.

A lean flash of fire-shrouded steel suddenly quenched itself in Ianthe's breast. She grasped it with a cry that was more surprise than pain. A flicker of comprehension lit her eyes before all light fled them forever, and she sank back, taking the sword with her, hands clasped feebly around its hilt.

Ostvel slid his sword from the dead woman and wiped the blade on a fistful of bed hangings. He met Sioned's rage without apology, his face set in stone.

"It's over, Sunrunner," he said.

She wanted to claw his face until the blood ran. "She was mine to kill, *mine*!"

"No. Not to kill." He sheathed the sword. "You have what you came here for, Sioned. Do you want to stay and watch the Fire take her? It's over!"

She made a harsh, animal sound and whirled, setting the bed ablaze with a single thought. Ianthe's long hair caught, and the hangings, and the tapestry dragons writhed in obscene mating dances with Fire spewing from their teeth and talons. Sioned hauled at one of the bedposts and it split apart at its joining, the burning weave cascading down onto Ianthe's corpse. Curtain rods fell and Sioned screamed as one of them cracked across her shoulder, spat flames across her face, seared her cheekbone a finger-width from her eye.

Ostvel hauled her away and she shrieked at him, tears streaming down her face. "Sioned! Stop it! Do you hear me? Stop it!" His open palm cracked across her injured cheek, snapping her head around. Through the haze of smoke she saw the empty doorway and screamed.

"My son! Where is he? *Where?*"

"Tobin took him downstairs, and if we don't follow we're going to die here! Sioned, it's over! Ianthe's dead!"

She gasped for breath, struggling against his grip. Sanity was returning and she dreaded the loss of the hate that had given her such power. "Let me go! Damn you for killing her, Ostvel—she was *mine* to kill!"

"And how did you plan to tell *him* that when he grows up?" he asked bitterly, pulling her from the room where the stench of Ianthe's burning flesh swirled up into the thickening smoke.

They ran down the hallway, coughing and stumbling down the stairs. Fire had invaded the lower hall, taken hold; tapestries in flaming tatters flung sparks on the fireborne wind. They could not leave Feruche the way they had come in; the whole castle was on fire.

Outside on the steps Sioned searched frantically for Tobin's small, white-shirted figure, saw her running through the crowd toward the gates. The child was bundled close and safe against her breast. The courtyard was ablaze, outbuildings collapsing. Smoke billowed from the lower windows of the keep. By morning Feruche would be nothing but stark, blackened stone.

Someone reeled into Sioned, his clothes on fire. Her Fire. She would have killed Ianthe with it, laughing, but this man was not her enemy. The inferno would take Feruche, and she could do nothing about those who might be trapped within, but this man she could save from death. Save herself from having killed him. She knocked him to the cobbles, flung herself atop him to stifle the flames. Boot heels crushed her leg, smashed the tip of one finger, and she sobbed her pain into the man's nape, begging his forgiveness, smelling his burnt flesh and her own singed hair. But he stirred beneath her, moaned, tried feebly to push her off his back. Strong hands helped her up, steadied her.

"Sioned! Hurry! He'll be all right. I promise you he'll be all right."

She couldn't seem to stop crying. Even as she hauled

the man to his feet and gave him a push in the direction
of the gates, saw him stagger his way to and through
them, the breath sobbed in her lungs and she kept repeating, "I'm sorry—I'm so sorry—"

"I know," came Ostvel's deep, sorrowing voice. His
arms were around her in a hard embrace for just an
instant. Then he said, "Come on, or we'll lose Tobin and
the baby."

She clung to him as he shoved a path for them through
this furnace of her making. The main gates were a hollow
ring of Fire through which terrified people leaped for
their lives. Sioned sucked in a shallow breath of smoke-
heavy air and followed Ostvel, then looked over her
shoulder. Flames fountained from the castle now, fierce
and deadly. Feruche was dying because of her; perhaps
people would die because of her.

She dragged a sleeve across her sweaty forehead, her
tearing eyes, and whimpered as the material scraped her
burned cheek. But it wasn't supposed to be like this, she
thought, panic tightening her chest. The mark of her own
Fire set into her shoulder—that she had known would
happen. But in the vision she had seen scars across her
brow. Not one on her cheek.

"Ostvel, it wasn't supposed to happen this way! Not
like this!"

"What in the name of the Goddess did you *think*
would happen?" he rasped, pulling her along with him
away from the burning castle walls.

"Not like this!" She flung away from him and stared
wide-eyed at the flames, one hand to her cheek to feel
the salt sting that brought fresh tears to her eyes. "There
was supposed to be Fire—but not this way! Ostvel, how
many did I kill?"

He turned her around by the shoulders and then gripped
her head between his hands. "Don't start," he ordered
roughly. "I won't let you take any of these deaths onto
yourself. Do you hear me, Sioned?"

"It was my Fire! Mine! Goddess, what have I done?"

"Ask yourself that once we're safe! Sioned, I'll knock
you out and carry you if I have to! Now *move*!"

It was a long way to where they had tethered the

horses. Someone had stolen them. Tobin waited for them there, walking back and forth in the shadows, trying to quiet the fretful baby. Sioned took her son into her arms, shaking with silent tears.

It was Tobin who suggested the empty garrison below Feruche as shelter. Most of the other refugees continued along the main road, through the Veresch into Princemarch. The blazing castle lit up the night and the people around her, showing Sioned injuries more serious than her own. Ostvel asked a servant if anyone had been caught in the flames, and received a dull shrug in reply.

"Not that I'm knowing. Most everybody was out in the court, drinking to the princess and her new little one." The woman's face suddenly crumpled. "And now she's gone, and the baby, and the three other boys with her—"

A man walking beside her said, "When the High Prince hears of this, I wouldn't put the price of a day on the life of anyone who was there. I don't recognize you, so you must be with the Cunaxan lord that rode in a few days ago. Give my advice to your master—disappear. That's what I'm going to do."

Sioned, who had hung back slightly, listening, reached for Ostvel's arm. "Leave it be," she whispered. "I'll never know for certain." She trod along in silence for a moment, then added bitterly, "With Ianthe, at least I would've known I'd killed deliberately, and taken the consequences." She held the child tighter. "I wouldn't have the luxury of pretending it was an accident."

They separated from the crowd soon after that, melting into the rocks at the side of the road. When the last stragglers had gone past, they emerged again and headed down the stony trail to the garrison. It was nearly dawn before they reached it. Sheltering alone within, they stood at the empty windows and watched as Feruche burned high on the cliff. Sioned rocked the frightened baby close and would not give him up to Tobin or Ostvel, not even when the princess would have tended the wounds on her shoulder and cheek.

"No. It doesn't hurt. Let me alone."

Tobin was wise enough not to press her. Sioned sat cross-legged in the doorway, holding her son in her arms as he slept at last, and watched the castle burn. She could not think past the holding of her child. Let Tobin and Ostvel worry about getting back to Stronghold. She could not.

She glanced down at the emerald, back where it belonged on her hand. The clifftop flames plunged into its depths, gave it a life and fire of its own. Andrade had told her long ago that she could work to make a vision real if she wanted it enough. Well, she had wanted, and had worked, and now the child was here in her arms and there was a welt across her shoulder that would leave a deep, wide scar.

But there was another on her cheek that should not have been there, and it throbbed a stinging reminder that the power to make visions real did not necessarily include the wisdom to make them just.

Dawn was nearly as soft as spring over River Run, and as Urival wove its strands together he paused to let its gentleness caress his senses. There were tender colors to the morning, rose-gray and muted greenish gold, the blue of sky as fragile as Fironese crystal. He traveled across Syr and Meadowlord and the Vere Hills, the colors intensifying with the stronger light of day. Yet there was still a misted, almost tentative quality about them, beautiful and shy.

But the colors rising from a Desert cliffside were harsh: stark spirals of gray-black smoke stained the sky. He saw the smoldering ruin that had been the castle and his delicate weave of winter dawn nearly snapped with the violence of his shock. Casting about for signs of life, he found none. Here and there small flames fingered a few remaining timbers, but all else was charred and dead. Ranging outside the keep, he saw groups of hollow-eyed people trudging into the western mountains. Ahead of them by some measures were others on horseback. Three of those horses caught his eye, for there was no mistaking the points of Lord Chaynal's breed. How would Ianthe come upon such animals? he asked himself—and then saw the distinctive blue saddle blankets of the Desert. Shock again threatened his control and he calmed himself, only to give a silent exclamation as he looked closer and found that the three horses were ridden by large, muscular guards, each one holding a sleeping child across his saddle.

Urival drew back, hovering in the morning stillness to quiet the turmoil of his mind. Then he returned to Feruche. He knew who those children must be, and was equally certain that their mother must be dead. Ianthe would never give over possession of her sons to anyone while she lived.

Urival again surveyed the blackened husk of the keep, circling around it. A flicker of movement caught his attention. Pale figures against pale golden sand, the trio walked in the direction of the road to Skybowl. The man was tall, broad-shouldered, his dark head left bare to the morning sun. One of the women was coiling her heavy black hair at her nape. The other woman was taller, her hooded cloak drawn close, arms crooked to carry something against her chest. Urival did not need to see her hair to know who she was. And he was afraid he knew what she had done.

He wove the sunlight south, over the Faolain and the salt marsh of Roelstra's cruel making, and saw Rohan's encampment well into its day's work for all that it was only a little after dawn. He was tempted to find young Maarken and tell him about Feruche, but restrained himself. Andrade would have to know first, and she was busy at the moment observing Roelstra's arrangements for the battle that everyone knew must come soon. The skies had cleared over the Veresch where the Father of Storms usually did his work, and for many measures out over the South Water the air was free of clouds. Pandsala would be reporting the same thing to her father that Andrade would soon tell Maarken: days of good weather lay ahead, and it was time to attack.

Returning to River Run, he opened his eyes to the silent walled garden and rested for a time before walking slowly to the bench where he had left Andrade. She sat with eyes closed and hands tightly clasped in intense concentration, the spun sunlight glowing very faintly around her as sometimes happened with powerful Master Sun-

runners. Urival kept a respectful silence, considering how
he would phrase the news about Feruche, remembering
the cant of Sioned's body around the small burden she
carried.

All at once Andrade's eyes opened, sparkling with
mirth, and she laughed. "Urival! Come with me quickly
or you'll miss it!"

He obeyed, bewildered by her merriment that spilled
over into her colors and danced around his own threads
of light as she guided him. Some forty measures from
River Run, well south of Roelstra's main camp, about
two hundred of his soldiers had established an outpost.
But strict military discipline had utterly collapsed, for the
fools had chosen a dragon hunting-ground, and the infuriated hatchlings were on the attack.

Horses stampeded in every direction as they fled sharp
talons; men and women raced about with frantic speed or
huddled on the ground with their cloaks pulled over them
while the small dragons soared, wheeled, and darted
down to chase the invaders from their territory. The
plummeting green-bronze and dark gold and russet shapes
were considerably grown since summer, but most of them
retained the ability to spew fire enough to singe a few
backsides.

It was absolute chaos, a total rout. A little gray dragon
with blue underwings flailed angrily above a huge caul-
dron, and when the cook fled he perched daintily on its
rim and helped himself to a free breakfast. After slurping
up most of the stew, he lifted his head and let out a great
fire-tinged belch. Two hatchlings, one nearly black and
the other a dappled brown, were fighting over a violet
cloak; it evidently retained enough scent from the sheep
that had originally worn the wool to be of interest to
dragons. Some of the little beasts had latched onto horses
in the wildest rides of their lives; the horses seemed to
have sprouted wings, about to fly. One dragon came up
with a saddle, girth straps dangling, and let out a happy
shriek, but when he craned his head down to take a bite
of the cured leather, he spat in distaste and dropped the
saddle right on the head of a soldier who staggered,
clutched at her skull, and went over like a felled tree.

The detachment's commander, wearing a violet cloak with a huge rent in its embroidered back, lunged desperately for a fleeing horse and scrambled up to rally his troops. He waved a hand high in the air—and nearly lost several fingers to a fierce little blue-green hatchling. Giving it up as useless, the man let the horse have its head and streaked away from the battlefield in frantic retreat, leaving the dragons in firm possession.

Back again at River Run, Urival and Andrade laughed themselves completely out of breath. "Perfect!" Andrade chortled. "Oh, the little darlings! Did you see the greenish one go for that man in his underwear?"

Urival sat on the bench beside her and wiped his streaming eyes. "That's the best laugh I've had in years!"

"It'll get better," Andrade assured him. "We have to get word to Rohan about this. It's an omen he can't afford to pass up! I'll send to Maarken and describe the whole thing while you get us ready to move. It seems our Dragon Prince has allies he never even dreamed of!"

It was only when Urival was nearing the gates that he remembered he had not told her about Feruche. After a moment's hesitation, he shrugged and decided not to ruin her mood. She would find out soon enough. He pushed the gates open and walked across the field to where men wearing Roelstra's regimentals lolled about in the sunshine. One of them rose to greet him, smiling.

"A fine day, my lord!"

"That it is, Cahl. And we'll be on the move at last."

"Out to sea?" he asked eagerly, then laughed when Urival shuddered. "Ah, I forgot—you Sunrunners! Well, it'll be a relief to get out of the High Prince's clothes, anyway." Cahl plucked at the gold-embroidered tunic, freckled face screwed up in comical disgust.

"How's our good friend the captain? Recovered yet from all those lies he's told Roelstra's messengers?"

"Oh, he's become very philosophical, even about his losses at dice. Will you want him locked up with the rest of his men before we leave?"

"Yes. Lady Wisla will get a shock when she comes home." Urival grinned. "We'll take all the horses with us, so even if they do manage to escape, they won't be able to warn Roelstra in time."

Urival gave his instructions and returned to the courtyard, chuckling at the memory that teased his thoughts. Roelstra's captain had received quite a shock one winter morning when the gates of River Run had opened to him and Lady Andrade had signaled her readiness to be escorted back to Goddess Keep. Lleyn's sailors, their agility in climbing ship's riggings put to good use in scaling the back walls of the keep one night, had deprived the captain and ten of his men of their weapons, their clothes, and their ability to warn their fellows. Others had come to investigate and been treated in like fashion. A minimum of blood had been shed before Roelstra's men had been incarcerated with fine thoughtfulness in River Run's wine cellar. Andrade had reasoned that Davvi wouldn't begrudge the loss of a few casks, and she hadn't wanted Roelstra's men to complain of mistreatment, after all. Only the captain had been allowed back outside with several sharp-eyed sailors watching him at all times. When Roelstra's couriers came, he had said all the right things— motivated by a knife held unobtrusively to his spine.

Thus Andrade had waited on *her* terms, not Roelstra's. One cage was indeed very like another, except when the guards were on one's own side and one could walk out whenever one pleased.

There had been only one sour thing about the whole satisfying proceeding: Chiana. She had been locked in her room to keep her quiet during the maneuver, but had subsided only when tied to a chair with a towel stuffed halfway down her throat. It had not been a pleasant experience for anyone, and daily Urival had expected some act of revenge. If the girl did not behave herself today, he was quite willing to tie her to her saddle with the gag back in her mouth.

But he forgot about her as he directed the preparations for departure. By midmorning all was ready—and Chiana had not been seen. Urival had the keep searched, and emerged puzzled and impatient into the courtyard to report his lack of success to Andrade.

She was stalking across the cobbles, practically spitting

fire. "Do you know what Chiana's done? Cozened one of those fool grooms into giving her a horse early! And now she's gone!"

"Good riddance," Urival muttered. "I hope she gets lost and falls in the river." And then, because Andrade's excellent humor had already been spoiled, he told her the bad news about Feruche.

High Prince Roelstra received three increasingly nasty shocks that day, and his daughter Pandsala was in a position to observe them all.

The first came when he had finished his breakfast and was taking a morning stroll through his camp. He had risen late, and Pandsala was kept waiting for some time outside his tent, for he liked to have her accompany him so the soldiers could see that they had their very own Sunrunner. Father and daughter had begun the rounds, exchanging remarks about the clear weather and the possibility of a battle soon, when a rider crested the low hill to the south and thundered down into camp. Stragglers followed in bad order behind him. He leaped from his horse, made frantic obeisance to his prince, and started babbling about dragons.

"More than ever before in the world—all of them after us! We fought them but it was no use, your grace. That wizard Prince Rohan has them under his spell, him or his Sunrunner witch of a wife! There were hundreds of them, your grace—with claws like swords and breathing fire—we had to retreat or all would have been lost! It's surely Prince Rohan's work!"

Pandsala watched her father gape speechlessly at the commander, who was now sucking on three bleeding fingers, having completed his story. The rest of the rag-tag group that had once been the High Price's finest mounted detachment galloped up in the interval and shouted out the same tale to their appalled compatriots. From them it was learned that most of the horses had fled beyond hope of recovery, and the other troops were walking back to camp. Pandsala made a quick count of the survivors, keeping stern control of her expression.

Her father, not having had hard training at Goddess Keep, turned all the colors of the rainbow.

"Thirty-five!" he roared. "Out of two hundred, you bring me back thirty-five, and praise your own wisdom in the loss! You credulous idiot! Dragons! As if Rohan could order them into battle!"

The commander flung himself to his knees. "I beg forgiveness, your grace—but the others will tell you—the fierceness of the attack—had we stayed, there would not even be thirty-five left—"

"Moron!" Roelstra swung around and pointed a finger at Pandsala. "You! This is your doing!"

"Mine?" She countered, incensed. "Is it my fault he's a fool? I advised you to send a detachment of horse against those Rohan is hiding in the woods to the south. I didn't advise this imbecile to camp in a dragon feeding-ground, which is what it seems he did! How can this be my fault?"

The High Prince lashed out a booted foot and caught the prostrate commander in the ribs. "Get out of my sight," he snarled. "And be grateful that I need everyone who can sit a horse!" He stormed off and Pandsala hurried along after him, keeping her distance but curious to see what he would do next.

He circled the perimeter of the camp, much more quickly than at his usual regal pace. He slowed as he reached the horse pickets, but she did not catch up, wisely assuming that he was counting the mounts available to him, an exercise that could only renew his fury.

Then he received his second shock of the morning.

It came in the form of a small, auburn-haired girl clinging to the neck of a sweating gray pony whose lungs were heaving like bellows. Soldiers tried to snatch the girl down, but she kicked and spat in a rage no less impressive for the fact that she was so young. A real royal tantrum, Pandsala told herself, a sick feeling in her stomach, for she knew her half-sister's rampages of old.

"I want to see my father!" Chiana shrieked. "You don't dare touch me! I'm the daughter of the High Prince!"

Roelstra turned on his heel and swore. Pandsala hurried to his side and he turned a killing look on her, green eyes like a frozen sea.

"Father," she began.

"Where did that brat come from?" he grated.

"She was with me and Andrade and Urival—"

"What is that whore's spawn doing here?" he shouted.

Chiana turned, gaze unerringly finding the sire she had never before seen. She leaped from the pony, eluded the soldiers, and flung her arms around Roelstra's legs, lifting a pale, dirt-streaked face.

"You have to listen to me, Father, please! Andrade is coming, with soldiers—she can't be very far behind me! I came to warn you!"

Roelstra stared down at this replica of himself and his dead mistress. Then he pried Chiana from his legs, took her by the shoulders, and raised her so he could inspect her face. She flinched slightly with pain but did not cry out.

"You've the look of your mother," he said softly, dangerously. "My daughter, Treason—who's spent her whole life in Andrade's keeping."

"I hate her! I hate her even more than Pandsala does!"

"Come, Treason, tell me how much." Abruptly he loosened his grip and Chiana tumbled to the ground. She was up instantly, proud and straight.

"I've always hated her! And now I'm going to get back at her! She tricked your soldiers, Father, she's coming here with Prince Lleyn's troops and—"

"Lleyn?"

"They climbed the wall at night and Urival tied me up so I couldn't scream and warn—"

"His ships were reported off the coast," Roelstra mused. "I wouldn't put it past Andrade, even to the reports that came back from River Run saying all was well." He looked down at his youngest daughter and a thin smile curved his lips. "Very well, Treason. I'll choose to believe you, but only because it doesn't matter. Our dear Lady Andrade is helpless and powerless, even in her freedom. She can do nothing against me, but it's interesting to know she's loose. You were right to come to me, Treason."

The child stared him directly in the eye. "My name is Chiana," she said flatly. "And I am a princess."

Roelstra's eyes narrowed for an instant, and then he burst out laughing. "By the Father of Storms—so it is, and so you are! You must have given Andrade a time! I always knew Palila and I should have produced a wildcat instead of those mewling kittens at Castle Crag! Very well, Princess Chiana, go with your sister and make yourself presentable." He pinched the girl's chin. "My daughters do not appear in rags and dirt."

Pandsala concealed her chagrin at hearing the child so openly acknowledged. She took Chiana away to her own small tent and gave the girl water, soap, and orders to scrub herself head to heels. A servant was dispatched to find something Chiana could put on in place of her filthy dress. Then Pandsala set off in search of her father again, needing to be at his side to hear his revised plans.

She had just glimpsed him leaving his tent when the third—but not the final—shock of the day appeared. A scout, arrow still in his shoulder and blood staining his tunic, fell to his knees in the grass and looked up at the High Prince.

"Your grace, the Desert attacks! Now!"

Chapter Thirty

Rohan gathered the reins more tightly in his gauntleted hands and shifted his shoulders against the restricting battle harness. The stiff leather tunic was dyed dark blue and decorated across chest and back with brass plating that shone as if made of gold. Chay was similarly attired in dark red leather, and Davvi wore the turquoise of Syrene princes. They were as gaudy as whill-birds and that was precisely the idea, for their soldiers would be able to see them a measure distant. So would the enemy, but Rohan only shrugged. The armor was for their protection, of course, but it was more ceremonial than anything else. They would not be in the thick of the battle today. This would be no swift fight, but a pitched battle according to all the traditional rules of war. They were to act as princes and battle commanders, not as warriors on the field.

Rohan quieted the restive Pashta, knowing the stallion was eager for a fight he would not be allowed to join—unless Chay was utterly wrong and they started to lose. Even then a wall of swords and shields would spring up around Rohan, protecting him. Others would die, he told himself, but not him. Not their Dragon Prince.

Davvi was still grinning at the news Maarken had supplied a little while ago; Andrade had told him about Roelstra's troops and the dragons. "What I don't understand is why they were in the south at all," he remarked as they waited for Chay's signal to begin the battle.

"Some sort of flanking action, I suppose. Although why he thought we'd send soldiers there and give them a hard ride uphill to the fight, I have no idea." He chuckled in spite of himself. "A dragon feeding-ground! I wish I could've seen it!"

"Maybe we ought to drive them down that way so your dragons can finish them off," Davvi mused.

"I'll settle for a nice, clean fight on an open plain, thanks, without hatchlings biting my nose. There's no guarantee the little fiends would recognize their prince!"

The dragons had done Rohan a prodigious favor, weakening Roelstra's host both in numbers and in morale. When the story had been spread through the Desert forces, the warriors had cheered their prince, completely certain now of victory. Rohan himself felt a strange excitement throbbing in his veins, not the anticipation of battle or even of winning the battle, though those things were part of it. He felt almost as Sioned had described her emotions when she rode the sunlight: swift, free, touched by the Goddess' own colors.

With the army behind them, at Chay's signal, he and Davvi crested a low rise overlooking Roelstra's camp. Troops were spread out all over the plain, about five measures square of prime battleground. While no advantages would come to either side on it, neither did it present any difficulties. The routing of nearly two hundred by dragons that morning had made the numbers just about equal, still tilted in Roelstra's favor but acceptable to Chay. For Rohan had the invaluable impact of surprise on his side. The alarm had just gone up in the camp below, and people scurried about in desperate haste.

Rohan caught the nod from Chay, and lifted his fist. The dragon horn sounded. Suddenly it was as if the battle maps had come alive before him. Seventy riders swept down from his right, while on his left foot soldiers marched forward in orderly ranks, framed by fifty archers on either side. The remaining eighty horse, one hundred foot, and one hundred archers fanned out on either side of Rohan, forming the arc of the half-circle he would tighten around Roelstra. He paused while his forces moved into position, watching the gleam of harness and sword and scythe, the bright fletching clumped in shoulder-slung quivers.

"This ends it," he murmured in a voice only Chay heard, as Chay had been the only one to hear his promise never to kill another dragon. "My sword will rust, and I'll be glad of it."

"Mine with it, my prince," Chay responded quietly.

Rohan glanced at him, surprised at such words from his warrior friend. "Truly?"

A slight, almost wistful smile curved Chay's lips. "Truly. Lord Eltanin was right, you know, about the walls."

"But no one recognized us!" Tobin exclaimed again. "And even if some die, who'll take the word of those who deserted their mistress and forfeited their honor thereby? Especially when their stories are pitted against the word of two princesses!"

Sioned bent her head to the baby's and tried not to listen to the argument being waged behind her. She concentrated on moving, her exhausted body crying out for rest, water, food.

Ostvel's voice was harsh, raspy with weariness. "You'd base the boy's life on a lie? What about when he's older and people whisper about what happened at Feruche?"

"Who would dare?"

"So no one's going to tell him at all? Ever?"

"Who'd be the one to tell him? You?" Tobin challenged.

Sioned stopped, swung around. "The child is mine," she said very clearly. "I waited for his coming, I'm the one who'll raise him, and I'm the one who will give him his name. Only a mother may Name her child. This baby is *mine*." She looked at both of them in turn, then resumed walking.

There were no more arguments.

As they passed through the rock sculptures of the Court of the Storm God, Sioned saw nothing of its stark majesty. There were only weird, frightening shadows cast by the winter sun. The climb out of the canyon was slow work, and when she could go no farther she sank down in the shade, closing her eyes. The infant nuzzled feebly at her breast, but she had no milk to give him. Old Myrdal knew of herbs the helped bring a new mother's milk and they had both reasoned that these might help Sioned. She had grasped eagerly at the possibility of feeding the child with her own substance, of being the source of life for him. But the birth had come too soon, and she was unprepared. They would have to reach Skybowl soon, or he might die.

"Poor little one," Tobin murmured, sitting beside Sioned, one finger stroking the baby's downy golden hair. "If only we hadn't lost the horses."

Sioned nodded. "He'll feed tonight at Skybowl. And then I'll Name him. I need you to be there with me, Tobin."

"Shouldn't you wait? Rohan—"

"Will just have to forgive me one thing more," she answered quietly. Then she looked up at Ostvel. "Sooner than I'll forgive you for stealing Ianthe's death from me."

He shrugged, his voice cold as he said, "Easier to never forgive me than to never forgive yourself." He glanced at the sun. "If you're rested, we should start off again."

She walked beside Tobin as Ostvel took the lead, and tried not to think. Her mind did not oblige.

She had killed. Intentionally or not, she had used her power and people had died—at the *Rialla* years ago, at Feruche. But it was not Andrade whose forgiveness she needed, or Ostvel's, or Rohan's, or even her own. She gazed down at her sleeping son and pleaded with the Goddess that she would never find condemnation in his eyes.

"Davvi! Behind you!" Rohan wheeled his horse around to defend his brother-by-marriage, and in doing so left his back unguarded. He hacked off a wrist and the spear it carried fell just before it would have pierced Davvi's spine. A quick-eyed soldier wearing Roelstra's violet lunged up and sliced through Rohan's leather tunic, reopening the old wound in his right shoulder. He cursed and twisted around in his saddle, signaling Pashta with his heels. Rear hooves lashed out and caught the swordsman in the belly.

Tilal, blood streaming down his cheek from a slice above his eye, cried out in alarm as Rohan swayed, Davvi yelled at him to get the prince out of the line. Rohan wobbled, unable to defend himself with a right arm growing numb, and Tilal leaned precariously over to grab Pashta's reins. He kicked his own horse into a gallop and ignored Rohan's luridly phrased opinion of the retreat.

When they were safe on the hill beneath some trees, Tilal flung himself down from his horse and shouted for a physician. Rohan glared down at him, and the boy stammered, "My lord, you're injured—it's my duty—"

"Damn your duty!"

"Shut up," came a familiar growl, and Chay, his forearm bound with white cloth, reached with his good hand and hauled Rohan out of the saddle. "You'll have that tended or I'll tie you up myself."

A large goblet of strong wine and some rough ministrations later, Rohan grudgingly admitted that Tilal and Chay had been right. His surly tone made Chay grin tightly.

"Our gracious, generous prince," he told the young squire. "Don't worry about that cut, Tilal. There won't be any scar, and you'll not lose a whit of those good looks."

The boy blushed and picked at the bandage across his forehead. "It doesn't even hurt."

"Well, mine does," Chay said, flicking a finger at his arm. "Serves me right for not anticipating Roelstra's move north. Let that be a lesson to you, Tilal." He stretched and shook his head. "I'm getting too old for this sort of thing. But it's a good fight just the same. A pity you'll miss the rest of it, Rohan."

"The hell I will!" He flexed his shoulder and held back a flinch. "Once the salve gets to work and I can hold my sword again—"

"Oh, really? Here—catch!" Chay threw an empty goblet at him and blinked in surprise as Rohan caught it neatly. "All right, you win," he muttered.

"Not yet, but it won't be long now." Rohan hid the pain the catch had cost him and went on, "We're doing well to the north, in spite of Roelstra's charge. Davvi's got the regrouping in hand, and we'll close around them like dragon claws. But they're not falling back through the center as fast as I'd like. What now, tactician?"

"I'll order the south to pull back a little at a time, and that should confuse them some. We'll swing around and attack from the rear." He glanced around, picked up a long stick, and sketched the action in the dirt. "Like this. See?"

Rohan committed the plan to memory and nodded. "Right. Tilal, my horse."

"But your wound, my lord—"

"Can't feel a thing," Rohan lied cheerfully. "Let's go. It's late afternoon and I still haven't had sight of Roelstra."

"Signal me when you find him," Chay remind him.

"I will. Goddess knows, you're easy enough to spot."

"Tobin finds me irresistible in this," Chay informed him, eyes dancing.

"She'd better find you in one piece at the end of the day!" He rose and gripped Chay's hand briefly. "Luck to you, and Goddess blessing."

"And to you, my prince."

As the light began to fail, Roelstra's defenses failed with it. Maarken had set Sunrunner's Fire atop a hill that lit the near portion of the battlefield like an arena. By the eerie light Rohan fought and killed and was fiercely glad that circumstances had compelled him into battle himself. Had he been forced to sit watching much longer, he would have gone mad. But now his fever was of use to his soldiers, and their cheers welcoming him into the fray still rang in his ears. If this was to be the last time his sword tasted blood, then let it drink deep.

Every free instant he swept his gaze in a furious search for Roelstra. Had the coward quit the field early? Was he hiding? Where in all hells was he? And Pandsala—what of her? Did she scan the fight on the waning sun, directing her father's armies? He would find them if it took all night and morning.

All at once Tilal cried out. Rohan saw a cluster of riders thundering up from the south, about fifty of them, skirting Desert lines. Too far away in the twilight for him to identify, he hacked his way clear of troops wearing Saumer of Isel's colors and snarled as his sword caught in a leather strap. Yanking it free, he bellowed Tilal's name.

"Find Chay! That might be Roelstra!"

"At once, my lord!"

The salve had long since ceased to numb his wound, and his shoulder ached abominably. He could feel sticky warmth on his back, could even smell his own blood over the stench of death around him. Rohan fought with one eye on the approaching riders, frantic lest someone else kill the High Prince before he could do it himself.

And then he was free of enemy swords and spears, and Chay was at his side, and they kicked their tired horses to speed across the heaped and mangled bodies. But it was not Roelstra who rode to meet them in the growing gloom. It was Andrade.

Her silver-blonde hair had come loose, blowing out behind her and tangling around her shoulders. She drew rein only when she was almost upon him, her eyes wild.

"You've lost him!" she screamed. "He escaped past us, to the south! Damn you, Rohan, you've lost him!"

"Not yet, by the Goddess!" he shouted back. "Chay!"

"At once, my prince."

"I ride with you," Andrade stated grimly.

Rohan laughed in her face. "Can't miss out on your vengeance, can you, Andrade? If you think you can keep up with me, then come. But don't interfere!" He turned to Tilal. "Go to your father—don't argue with me! Tell him where I've gone, and that he has the honor of cleaning up this battle on his home soil, just as he wanted. You and Maarken stay with him. That's an order, squire!"

Tilal unhappily obeyed. Chay had assembled thirty riders, men and women with new determination in their battle-weary faces. The Lord of Radzyn narrowed his eyes as he scanned Andrade's escort.

"Lleyn's sailors. Go claim a piece of Roelstra's armies for your prince!"

Their leader glowed with eagerness, then glanced guiltily at Andrade. She nodded. "Stay and fight, Cahl," she told him.

He bowed his gratitude for the release from her service, then addressed Rohan. "One favor, my lord. If it comes to it, burn our ships before Roelstra can board them."

"He won't get that far, I promise you."

Urival said quietly, "I'll ride with you, my lord. You'll need Sunrunner's Fire to see by." He was staring at Andrade as if daring her to object. Rohan laughed again.

"Scruples? You cast your lot with me the moment you brought me Sioned. Come along, Aunt. Come savor the outcome of your work."

* * *

Sioned knelt on the rim of Skybowl's crater as the last shadows faded into night unlit by moons. The baby lay quiet and sleepy-eyed on a blue-and-gold blanket, his stomach full of goat's milk, blissfully unaware of the commotion he had caused.

Skybowl was nearly as empty as Stronghold. Those who had gone to fight at Tiglath had not yet returned, and those few who remained accepted without murmur that the child was Sioned's own. Tobin had expected nothing less. Having kept silent about the gold for so long, they were not likely to reveal this new secret.

Tobin knelt to Sioned's left, Ostvel to her right. The fourth position that should have been Rohan's was left open to the Desert below the cliff. The child murmured drowsily, his body pale and perfect in the dimness, so small compared to the vastness of the Desert and the infinity of the emerging stars.

"Child," Sioned whispered at last, beginning the ritual, "you are a part of this world. Water will quench your thirst, Air will fill your lungs. Earth will guide your steps, and Fire will warm you in winter's chill. All these are yours by right of birth, the right of every son and daughter born."

As Sioned paused, Tobin remembered other Namings, when the gentle ritual had been spoken over Maarken and Jahni, Andry and Sorin. Ostvel's fingers were clenched on his knees, and she knew he was remembering, too, the night when Sioned had presided and Rohan had been with them as Camigwen Named young Riyan.

"But you are a prince," Sioned continued softly, and Ostvel looked up, as startled as Tobin at this departure from the time-honored formula. "Born of a long line of princes, sire to generations more. For you this world holds more—and will demand more."

Sioned lifted her hands, emerald ring glittering, and a soft breeze swept up from the lake behind her. With the Air came a mist of Water and tiny motes of Earth. Tobin sensed, as Ostvel could not, the careful gathering of delicate threads of starlight, fine and thin as spider-spinnings, the weaving of its pale Fire into the breeze.

The slow swirl surrounded them, gradually centering at arm's length above the baby in a tight, glistening spiral.

Tobin was torn between amazement and fear. The *faradh'im* used the glow of sun and moons, but never that of the stars. Yet Sioned did exactly that now, pulling down skeins of almost invisible brilliance to create this unique Naming for her son.

"Child, by the name of your kinswoman Tobin, daughter of Zehava and Milar, wife to Chaynal, mother of sons, I give you Air that is the sigh of the Father of Storms in the Goddess' arms. May it rise and give flight to your wings, as strong as the woman in whose name it is given."

The starglow was directed toward Tobin and the baby's head turned, eyes huge as he stared up at his aunt. Tobin saw her own colors sparkle in the whirling mist, amber and amethyst and sapphire, and caught her breath.

Sioned spoke again. "Child, by the name of this man Ostvel, son of Ostlach and Avina, husband to Camigwen, father of a son, I give you Water to cleanse your soul—for his soul is the purest I have ever known."

Again she gestured the spinning light, this time to shine on Ostvel's tense features, and more colors were added—deep garnet, bright ruby, black onyx he could not see. Or perhaps he could, for he met Sioned's gaze, awed, caught in the spell she had woven of forbidden starlight.

"Child, by the name of your father Rohan, son of Zehava and Milar, I give you Earth—this sand and stone around you, this Desert you will rule as wisely as he who gave it to you. This is his flesh, as it is your own." And colors Tobin had never before sensed spun into the light— the pure white of diamonds, the intense sapphire of Rohan's eyes, the golden amber of his sunlit hair. This was her brother, she told herself, these colors dancing and gleaming in the night.

"Child. . . ." Sioned drew all the soft spinning starlight into her hands and held it above the infant. "My child, I give you Fire to light your way. Sunrunner's Fire from the mother who also gives you your name."

The baby's hands groped up toward the threaded colors and Sioned allowed him to touch it for an instant. Then she lifted the Air and Water and Earth all spun together with Fire from the stars, and flung it out to the Desert below. The weave spread out like an unfurled tapestry, strands of color augmented now by Sioned's own, and she spoke her child's name for the first time.

"Pol," she whispered. "Born of starfire. That is your name, my son, and it is your mother who gives you all these things."

Lifting him in her arms, she turned him to face the expanding fabric of light over the Desert, vibrating now like sparks from a windswept hearth or a carpet of multicolored flowers shimmering in the breeze. It slid along the curves and hollows of the dunes below, wrapped around the rocks, glowed blue and crimson and green and gold, all shot through with glittering points like diamonds. At last the weaving sank slowly into the sand, and all was starlit silence once more.

After a moment Sioned murmured the traditional ending of the Naming ritual. "It is the duty of a mother to Name her child. So I have done. His name is Pol."

The familiarity of the final words did not release Tobin from the enchantment. She knew she had witnessed something never before seen, never even dreamed of. Yet there was something else familiar here, the feeling that spread through her head and heart. She had felt it on the night of her father's ritual, when the *faradh'im* had ridden the moonlight and taken her with them. Yet no sun or moons shone, no light to weave into pathways through the sky—nothing except the stars and their delicate Fire. Fragile, almost transparent lanes of light trembled around her, routes opened by Sioned, who knelt beside her clutching the child, her eyes glazed over. Tobin knew she was no longer here, but traveling on those ribbons of starfire. And Tobin, closing her eyes, followed.

She had no consciousness of the flight, swift and sure as it took her to the battlefield. By the glow of Fire she saw the dead being gathered and the wounded being tended, and shivered. Where were her husband, her son, her brother? She could feel Sioned's colors ahead of her, searching as frantically as she. And then they were together, gliding down a single filament of starlight now, beyond the silent field and over small hills that cradled shadowy valleys between them like the slight hollows between the muscles of a powerful man's back.

She saw then, and knew the two groups of riders who faced each other in a broad valley. She saw her husband, tall and tense as he sat his horse in perfect stillness, more carving of warrior's beauty than living man. She saw her brother, golden hair turned to silver, poised, waiting, as motionless as Chay. She saw Andrade, pale hair streaming down her back, strangely helpless as she spoke urgent words that Rohan and Chay ignored. There were others, but Tobin did not look at them—for the star-thread drew her across the emptiness between to Roelstra.

The High Prince gestured sharply, and a slender young woman rode forward. Chay went to meet her. They exchanged words Tobin could not hear, wore expressions the shadows did not allow her to read. But she saw her husband nod slowly, and when the woman straightened from her slight bow of acceptance, Tobin saw that it was Pandsala. The pair returned to their princes, and Rohan and Roelstra each dismounted.

Confused and frightened, Tobin quivered in the grip of the starlight. Andrade held up both hands, rings shining, her mouth contorted as she cried out words that would forbid, her face terrible as she flung her head back. Roelstra shouted, Rohan shook his head. Not even Andrade could stop this now.

The two princes stripped off battle harness and clothes until they were down to trousers and boots, nothing more. There was a bandage wrapped around Rohan's right shoulder, blood seeping through in an ominous stain. Chay spoke with swift urgency, gesturing, warning; Rohan nodded absently and unsheathed his sword. Tobin heard in imagination its angry hiss from the scabbard, the blade a long gleam of steel in the night, lean and pale as its owner.

Andrade at last submitted, withdrawing in response to Urival's hand on her sleeve. The two *faradh'im* moved apart and dismounted. Urival walked to the other end of the line of Rohan's soldiers. Both Sunrunners paused a

moment before their lifted hands conjured two small
spheres of Fire. Rohan's people formed a loose arc on
one side, Roelstra's on the other. The *faradh'im* and the
Fire hovered between to complete the circle and give the
princes light to see by, light in which to kill each other.
Andrade stood with head bowed and shoulders bent like
an old woman's; Tobin saw, and grieved, but knew that
whatever the Lady had planned for Rohan and Roelstra,
this was the only possible conclusion.

They stalked each other warily, moving with elaborate
care. All advantages of youth, strength, and swiftness
that should have been Rohan's were negated by the
wound in his shoulder that would slow and weaken him
the longer the fight went on. Roelstra was heavier of
body and motion, and it had been a long time since he
had used his warrior's training. But that the muscles
beneath his flesh were strong and that his instincts were
intact became obvious with the first swing of his sword.

Tobin did not hear the clang of blades, nor the grunt
wrung from her brother's throat as the impact shuddered
up to his wounded shoulder. She did not hear whatever
taunting words Roelstra flung into the space between
them. But she could see—and there was a spark, a narrow gleam of steel far back among Roelstra's people.
They shifted. A pathway cleared. The starlight spun around
Tobin and her colors seethed with panic, twining, merg-
ing with Sioned's—and Urival's, and Andrade's—and
someone else, someone trained but not perfected in the
faradhi arts. Suddenly there was yet another, a tiny, raw
gift that surged up in answer to Sioned's need. Light and
shadow skittered around Tobin, through her, and she lost
her own colors to the greater whirl of power borne on
Fire from the stars.

Andrade was too stunned by the assault on her senses
to begin defending herself until it was too late. Caught up
in the threads of starlight, she saw in an instant the
treachery of the upraised knife—and for the first time
since the tenth ring had been placed on her finger she
found herself subordinate to the powers of another
Sunrunner.

Chill silvery flames sprang up around the two princes,

a circle of dangerous starlight that rose, met, created a
shining dome that enclosed Rohan and Roelstra in shivering Fire. Colors flashed as each *faradhi* pattern was
woven more deeply into the structure: her own colors,
Urival's, Tobin's, Sioned's—and those of two others whose
presence shocked Andrade to her soul. Realizing too late
that Sioned had trapped her, she fought panic and tried
to gain control of the starlight. But this weaving was
Sioned's, and Andrade could do nothing but feel her
strength given as Sioned demanded.

Rohan drew back, dazzled by the cold Fire that arched
up around him. Roelstra cursed frantically as a flare of
diamond-bright light hit the dome with a sound like a
great glass bell being rung, echoing deeply from curve to
curve of the dome. Rohan took advantage of his enemy's
distraction and lunged in, sword ready to take Roelstra's
head. But the High Prince moved just in time, escaping
with a only gash cut into his left arm.

"So Andrade has closed us in," he rasped. "That's too
bad—I wanted everyone to see you die."

Rohan wasted no breath on a reply. His shoulder had
not warmed to the exercise as he had hoped; there was
no battle fever to counter his weariness, and the anticipation that had burned along his veins during the ride was
gone. He had spent too much of himself this long day,
and his only hope was to finish Roelstra quickly—if he
could.

The High Prince laughed as if knowing Rohan's
thoughts. "Tired, princeling?" He drove in, without fi-
nesse but with a great deal of strength, and Rohan sidestepped out of his way.

Steel clashed again and again, resounding off the star-
spun dome until Rohan's ears rang. Neither man indulged in elegant swordplay; each was after blood. Cold
sweat ran into Rohan's eyes, sheathed his body in ice.
Lunge, parry, evade, thrust, dodge, lunge again. His
right arm was fast becoming incapable of hefting the
sword that was heavier each instant. He heard Roelstra's
harsh gasping breaths, smelled the sweat sheening the
fleshy body, saw the welts leaking blood where his blade
had cut the High Prince. But he would not have wagered

right then on his own victory. For all Roelstra's years and excesses, he seemed inexhaustible.

Angling his sword as Roelstra brought his own back for a powerful thrust, he tried to cut the man's legs from under him. The tip of his blade caught just behind the knee, and steel flawed in the day's battle snagged in the High Prince's soft leather boot. In the attempt to free himself, he drove the sharp tip into his flesh, growling with pain. Rohan wrenched the blade away and tried to follow up, but his arm chose that moment to falter. The sword slid from his hand. Balance lost, he fell hard to his knees, gasping at the impact.

"Excellent position," Roelstra taunted, "one you should have adopted long ago. I'll teach it to your Sunrunner princess before I teach her to forget you in my bed—the way you forgot her in my daughter's!"

Rohan dove for his sword and forced his two hands to close around it, good hand locked over the strengthless one. Roelstra sliced almost contemptuously into his back as Rohan rolled away and came up on one knee. He barely felt the new rent in his skin, but for the trickle of blood that mingled with the renewed flow from his right shoulder. Roelstra gave a short burst of breathless laughter and closed in. Twisting around, Rohan caught the hilt of his sword against Roelstra's, struggling to keep the blades locked even as the High Prince struggled to separate them. With a groan of agony as the effort tore his shoulder completely open, Rohan felt Roelstra finally give way. The suddenness of it flashed suspicion through his mind that it was deliberate—but the High Prince stumbled down onto the grass, cursing.

Rohan gasped, each breath a stab of fire. It was beyond him to use the sword now, its weight insupportable. He went for his boot knife and heaved himself onto the sweating body. Powerful fingers closed over his wrist, wrenched his arm back, nearly tearing it from the socket. He realized that in another moment he would black out, and writhed from Roelstra's grip.

The High Prince grunted with pain as he heaved to his feet, swaying, blood dripping from his knee. Rohan went for the other knife and had his ribs kicked for his trouble.

Body curling in anguish, breath sobbed in his throat and for the first time he was cold with the fear that he was going to die.

Roelstra stood over him, panting. Sword retrieved, he leaned on it, the tip imbedded in the soil. The jeweled hilt shone in the silvery surrounding Fire.

"I'll teach your son to kneel," Roelstra hissed.

There was a sudden roaring in his ears, salt bitterness on his lips. Fury came to him at long last, a killing rage that had nothing to do with clean battle or even with vengeance. *My son*. The words echoed over and over in time to the vicious pounding rhythm of his blood: *My son*—

"Kneel to me, princeling," Roelstra demanded, his voice thick with hate. "Kneel!"

Rohan moved very slowly. He pushed himself up, holding his ribs with his good hand, groped out with the other as though seeking support that would get him to his knees. *My son*. There was a burning in his flesh and something cold and dew-moist in his hand. One foot under him, leaning heavily on the other knee, he looked up through a stinging mist at the grandfather of his son.

Roelstra was smiling. He continued to smile even as Rohan surged upward and shoved a knife he could barely hold into the soft flesh of Roelstra's throat. The long blade stabbed through the underside of the chin and Rohan thrust it deeper, through tongue and mouth all the way to the base of the brain.

The High Prince toppled to one side. Rohan watched him fall, knowing Roelstra was dead. And then the wet grass slicked with blood came up to meet him, and he knew nothing more.

Only the frightened rasp of Chay's voice made Andrade recall that she had an existence apart from the raging cold starfire that by now had bled all color into its pallor. She heard him, and painfully gathered into coherence the splintered pattern that was herself. The others, less powerful than she, were still caught in the glowing dome. She labored with all her strength to separate them, to rebuild the shimmer of each distinctive mind.

Urival was first, his deep sapphire and pale moonstone and shining amber forming once more into the familiar design. Truth, wisdom, protection against danger—all these things were Urival, and she wept with relief that he was whole. He helped her with the others, unraveling the chaotic weave that was comprised of Sioned and Tobin and the two startling, shocking others. The two princesses, known to them, were swiftly separated and re-formed, cherished patterns not lost to shadows lurking in the night. The last pair—Andrade left the familiar one to Urival and explored the new and unexpected presence herself. Topaz for sharp intelligence; emerald for hope; iridescent pearl for purity; all lit by a diamond brightness that was beauty and cleverness. She knew who he was, this brilliant pattern of green and white and gold. The Sunrunner Prince. Rohan's son.

"Andrade!" Chay was almost sobbing now, and she opened her eyes to see his stricken face above her. She was vaguely curious about how she had come to be lying on the ground with her head cradled in his arm. When she moved, bruises told her of a hard fall. "Sweet merciful Goddess," Chay whispered. "I thought you shadow-lost."

"No," she said, and coughed. "It'd take more than this to kill me." She pushed herself up. "Urival?"

"Here," came his voice from nearby, where Pandsala lay senseless on the grass. "Do you know what happened, and what she did?" he asked softly, his eyes sunk into hollows. "And why?"

Andrade swallowed and nodded. "Yes. Is she—"

"I don't care about her or about what happened!" Chay snapped. "It's Rohan who needs you, damn it!"

He pulled her up and helped her to walk. They crossed the faint dark line where Fire had risen. No one had yet dared cross into the circle. Roelstra's people, seeing that the unthinkable had occurred and their prince had fallen, were too stunned to attempt either revenge or escape. Rohan's soldiers were equally silent and motionless. Andrade sank down beside the slight form curled in the starshine, light gleaming off his fair hair.

He lived. Blood covered him like a cloak, but he lived.

Andrade nodded at Chay, who lifted Rohan very gently
and carried him to where Urival had made a small,
warming fire. Rising to her feet, Andrade stood over
Roelstra and gazed down into his dead eyes. Rohan's
knife was sunk into his throat and he wore a half-smile
that chilled her. She bent stiffly and closed his eyes, but
the feeling of insects crawling on her skin did not fade.
For he smiled still; like her, he finally had what he
wanted, though not quite in the manner planned.

She ordered the corpse wrapped in its violet cloak,
then went to tend her nephew's wounds. She had no
salves, no ointments, no soothing draughts but a skinful
of wine taken from one of Rohan's men. This she poured
down his throat as Urival washed the blood away. Chay
sent riders back to the main battlefield for supplies. They
returned at top speed, led by the frantic Tilal and Maarken.

It was a long while before she was satisfied that Rohan
had taken no serious hurt. He had not opened his eyes,
but the blank unconsciousness had become reassuring
sleep, the signs unmistakable to Andrade's trained eye.
Two litters were prepared, one for the living prince and
one for the dead one. Tilal remembered to reverse
Roelstra's banner on its pole to signal his death so that
Rohan's people would not think it was their own prince
who had died.

Andrade glanced up as Chay touched her arm and
spoke her name. His face was rough with stubble, smeared
with dirt and sweat, his gray eyes dull and bloodshot as
he looked up at the sky. She was surprised to find the
stars nearly gone, blackness becoming deep blue washed
with rose-gold on the horizon.

"Dragons," he murmured.

They flew in small groups, hatchlings chased through
the air by watchful she-dragons and sires who called
down warnings against any threats to their precious brood.
Dark and graceful shapes against the misted dawn, they
flew in search of a feeding ground unspoiled by the blood
of humans. Andrade wanted to follow them on the new
light, soar with them on wings of her own, and began to
understand Rohan's love for the dragons. For them there
were no complexities of choice, motive, treachery, de-

ceit; no battling against their own natures. She looked down at his sleeping face, smoothed back lank fair hair.

"I wish you could see them," she whispered. "They belong to you, Dragon Prince."

"To the Desert," Chay corrected quietly. "Just like he does. Not the other way around, Andrade."

"I envy him—and them," she murmured. "I've never owned anything but my rings and my pride. And nothing's ever owned me."

"To claim anything you have to be willing to be claimed in return. That has to come first, Andrade. You have to give yourself, first." He paused, knelt beside Rohan, touched his shoulder "We're lucky that Rohan's known that all along."

"I gave him Sioned, didn't I?"

"Do you think she was yours to give?" Urival asked softly.

Andrade stiffened. Rising to her feet, she gestured for Rohan to be placed on the litter, and turned away from the others. Nothing but her rings and her pride—but they were all she had, and she would defend herself with them as long as she lived.

A dragon roared in the dawn, and she looked up again, wondering suddenly what it would be like to be both possessed and free.

Tobin opened her eyes.

Ostvel was clasping the shivering, crying infant to his chest. Pol's eyes were fixed on Sioned, the misty newborn blue gone in the flashing Fire. Tiny hands reached out, fists clenched exactly as Sioned's were clenched. She was on her knees, white cloak blowing back from her shoulders like dragon wings, arms outstretched and features strained into terrifying intensity. The stars had found focus in her eyes, seemed to flow into the very bones of her slender body as a cold silvery brilliance writhed around her, a white Fire from the stars striking rainbows from her whiteness. Tobin knew what Sioned had done, how she had woven every thread of light from the sky into the patterns of power that were her framework: Urival, Andrade, Tobin herself—and the child.

Ostvel glanced up. "He started screaming. I couldn't quiet him."

Tobin nodded. There would be no protecting the child from his heritage. Sunrunner and Prince.

All at once Sioned trembled as if her bones would shatter. The infant's cries softened to whimpers and then he was silent, his small face relaxing at last into serenity. It was a long time before Sioned's features showed any hint of the same peace.

"The one with the knife—you could have killed him," Tobin whispered hoarsely.

Sioned nodded, and in her eyes were lingering traces of stars and power. "You understand about Pandsala now, don't you? She and I have the same regret—that Roelstra never knew she was betraying him all along."

Sensing Ostvel's bewilderment, Tobin turned to him and said slowly, "There was—combat between Rohan and Roelstra. One of the High Prince's men thought to end it with a knife. Sioned—she used the stars, Ostvel. There wasn't any other light."

Sioned touched Pol's cheek. "There's Fire in the stars," she murmured. "Sunrunner's Fire."

Ostvel held Pol closer. "He felt it. All of it, Sioned. You know what that makes him."

She nodded again, bright head bending low. "It begins too young for him. I hope one day he can forgive me."

Chapter Thirty-one

Dragon gold.

It bought the labors of a hundred master crafters, and by the beginning of spring the Great Hall of Stronghold was splendid with the results. The artisans would have worked for nothing, of course; the honor of boasting that they had had a hand in the making was worth more than any payment. But Rohan paid. Gold was simple coin and cost him very little, though only a few privileged people knew that. He stood surveying his stage, knowing it was exactly that, and nodded his satisfaction.

Three hundred lamps shaded by sparkling Fironese crystal were set high along the walls where torches had once been. Tiles made in Kierst formed a pattern of blue and green on the floor. A new suite of fruitwood banqueting tables and chairs from Syr were laden with a fabulous dinner service of Gribain porcelain and utensils of Fessenden silver. Flowers were arranged in low vases of blue Ossetian glass; on either side of each was a wine pitcher made from the giant seashells found off the coast of Isel. Dorval's silk provided the green napery folded into fanciful shapes atop the plates; pinewood boxes from Cunaxa held spices; fingerbowls of black deerhorn from Meadowlord and white elkhoof from Princemarch waited for noble hands that would be dried on small soft towels of blue Giladan wool. Beside each princely goblet was a delicate little cup, the only obvious use of the dragon gold that had bought all the rest.

The banners of Desert *athr'im* had been removed to the foyer, replaced by a single tapestry behind the high table: the new dragon symbol. Stylized into simple, elegant lines, the bold arch of outspread wings balanced the proud lift of the beast's head. Gold on blue, the dragon was crowned with a thin circlet and held a small ring surmounted by a real emerald set into the cloth. Zehava would have approved the grand gesture—and the warning.

Rohan finished his inspection of the Great Hall and complimented his household staff, then walked between the empty tables to the side aisle where Maeta stood in full battle harness over a new blue silk tunic, her black eyes snapping with pride.

Rohan gave her a smile. "Stand easy. You're making me nervous!"

She snorted. "You made me responsible for his safety, and here I stay." She nodded at Sioned, who sat at the high table with Pol in her lap.

"Did you hear that old fool Chale say that Pol has Sioned's eyes?"

"And *your* manners," Sioned called out as the baby gave a loud burp. "Let's get this started, Rohan. He's quiet for now, but there's no telling how long it will last. I don't want him shrieking at the guests who've come to admire him."

"And you," he added. She wore a green gown dark as a mountain forest. The emeralds were around her throat and a thin silver circlet crossed her brow to hold back her loosened hair. He mounted the dais to stand beside and just behind her, fingers resting on the ornate carving of a dragon in flight that decorated the back of her chair, knowing very well what picture they would present. He wore a dark blue tunic and trousers, a topaz winking deep gold from a chain around his throat, a band of plain silver around his head. Pol's clothes were green to match his mother's gown, and the blanket around him was blue stitched with tiny golden dragons. A more perfect portrait of regal domesticity could not be imagined—precisely what Rohan had intended.

He signaled to Ostvel and the main doors were opened. The chaos outside in the foyer abruptly hushed as the chief steward of Stronghold announced Her Royal Highness the Princess Tobin and Lord Chaynal of Radzyn Keep. Tobin still favored her injured leg a little, but not in public. She and Chay, dressed in his red and white accented by rubies and diamonds, crossed the shining glazed tiles, made their bows, and joined Rohan and Sioned at the high table.

Next came Rohan's vassals: Eltanin of Tiglath; Abidias of Tuath Castle, who guarded the far northern border of the Desert; old Hadaan of Remagev; and Baisal of Faolain Lowland. Less senior vassals followed, bowed, made new vows to the heir, and went to stand behind their chairs at various points throughout the great Hall—a strategic placement of approving voices worked out in advance by Rohan, Ostvel, and Sioned. Walvis was the last of the Desert highborns to enter, tall and handsome with his blue eyes sparkling above a neatly trimmed black beard. He took his place at the head of the knights' table. Rohan caught his eye and smiled.

The princes were next, with the exception of Miyon of Cunaxa. Sixteen winters old and forbidden to make a move on his own, he had sent word that he was too ill to make the long journey from Castle Pine. It had been decided to take no offense, as his presence was unnecessary in any case. There were princes enough to make this convocation valid.

Lleyn of Dorval came in first, and winked at Rohan. He placed a lingering kiss on Sioned's wrist and tickled Pol's chin until the infant crowed with laughter, then went to his place near the high table. Pimantal of Fessenden entered to express his gratitude that his city of Einar was safe—for no one doubted that had the late High Prince succeeded in Syr, Fessenden would have been next on his list. Saumer of Isel, Roelstra's erstwhile ally, came in wary and defiant, but polite. He was followed by his enemy, Volog of Kierst, looking smug as he greeted Sioned as her kinsman. Prince Ajit, who showed no ill effects from the long journey to Stronghold from Firon at his advanced age, said pretty things to Sioned and agreed with Chale that the baby had her eyes.

Clutha of Meadowlord was tight-lipped and contrite, having already given Rohan many speeches of apology for not keeping a closer watch on Lyell of Waes—whom he had in tow and who looked sick with apprehension. A poke in the ribs was sufficient to launch the young man

into a babbled speech to which Rohan listened without
any expression at all. He nodded briefly in dismissal,
wanting Lyell to sweat a little longer.

Chale of Ossetia walked in, radiating innocence regarding Lyell's work. Then came the younger princes
who, like Miyon, had lost their sires in the Plague but,
unlike him, controlled their own governments. Cabar of
Gilad and Velden of Grib were much the same age, and
much on their dignity at this first meeting of princes since
they had gained their lands. Yet they were still boys
enough to respond with blushes when Sioned bestowed
on each her most dazzling smile.

At last Davvi came in, accompanied by his wife. Wisla
was gaudy and overjeweled in Syrene turquoise and garnets, with a huge diamond nestled in her ample cleavage.
She beamed at all as if she were princess of Stronghold as
well as of Syr.

Then it was the turn of Roelstra's daughters. There
were twelve left now; five had died of the Plague, and the
circumstances of Ianthe's death in the fire that had destroyed Feruche were still the subject of intense speculation. Pandsala led her sister and half-sisters up to the
high table, and not one of them knew that the boy to
whom they bowed was their sister Ianthe's son.

As they rose, Sioned spoke clearly into the quiet. "A
moment, my ladies, if you would be so kind."

They all froze, clumped together, eyes wide with fear
or startlement or both. All except for Chiana and Pandsala.
The former glared defiantly at Rohan; the latter stared at
the floor.

"You have behaved with honor, and that is the truest
mark of nobility—caring first for the peace and well-
being of your land. By renouncing all claim for yourselves and your descendants to the properties, titles, and
wealth to which you were born, you have acted with
great wisdom that all here will acknowledge."

The sop to their lacerated pride, Rohan thought, composing himself to enjoy the rest of Sioned's speech. She
had insisted that she be the one to grant them this favor.

"Your lives are now your own," she told them. "Should
you wish to continue in quiet retirement at Castle Crag,

you may do so. If there is a manor you would like to live in, that place and all its revenues will be yours for as long as you desire."

"Your Highness!" gasped Naydra, the eldest of them.

"It was never our intention to leave you in nameless poverty," Sioned assured her, and Rohan heard astonished whispers in the Hall. "And if there is a man you wish to wed, you will be dowered as befits your royal blood."

A babble of voices greeted this announcement. Rohan let the noise play itself out, amused. He and Sioned had cast themselves in the role of generous prince, but there were reasons other than public show of magnanimity. Locking up Roelstra's daughters was not in Rohan's nature, not even for Pol's sake, and making silent, captive martyrs of them would have been more dangerous than setting them free to breed children who might one day become a threat. Most would probably sink into obscurity, either living in pleasant manors under close if benevolent watch—he was no fool—or married to some minor lord or other. He looked them over as they struggled to comprehend this total reversal of their fortunes and the prospect of more freedom than their father had ever given them. Eight nonentities, he told himself, but four who would bear observation: Kiele with her new husband Lyell of Waes; Cipris, who at eighteen was sharp and beautiful as a new morning; and sly-eyed little Chiana and her full sister Moswen.

He doubted, however, that many men would be willing to marry a daughter of the late High Prince, despite the rich dowries he intended to provide. He could afford to be generous—especially as he had claimed for the Desert a nice chunk of Princemarch, including the ruins of Feruche and the dragon caves nearby. All thought his reasons were due to some ancient claim of his family. Rohan was not about to enlighten them.

The procession into the Great Hall was nearly over. The daughters took their places, Kiele fuming at the prospect of married sisters as she joined Lyell. Then absolute silence descended as Andrade and Urival walked in. They were both in silver and white, she with moonstones binding her white-gold hair, he with the same gems in a belt around his waist. Knees and heads bent to them as they passed up the long aisle to the high table, and as Rohan bent his own head to his aunt he caught the glimmer of gleeful anticipation in her eyes. He had told her certain things about his plans for tonight that merited the malicious sparkle; he had not told her certain other things, which would probably give her apoplexy. Still—she loved a good show.

The feast began as soon as the wives, heirs, and important retainers of some of the princes present filed in and took their seats. The lowest tables were for the knights and squires, the latter freed from regular duties at table by Rohan's own servants. Their group was presided over by Maarken and Tilal, two boys who differed from their companions in the self-assurance that came of having known battle. Andry and Sorin were there as well, along with Ostvel's son Riyan. The trio would be allowed to stay up late so long as no infringement of decorum attracted parental attention.

As the first course was served, Maeta and a nurse came to take Pol up to bed. He was irritable after being subjected to inspection by so many strangers. Rohan sympathized; he had uncomfortable childhood memories of being similarly on display. But a prince was a prince. It was something Pol would get used to.

Walvis had charge of the knight's table, his poise shaken only when he happened to glance over at a slim, red-headed girl with gray eyes whom it had pleased Rohan and Ostvel to place at the next table, directly in his line of sight. The two men exchanged a meaningful glance and a grin.

It had also pleased Rohan to order special cups made for the high table. Souvenirs of this night they were, magnificently wrought. A goblet of red Fironese crystal footed in silver served his sister and her lord; plain silver set with moonstones was shared by Andrade and Urival. Beside Ostvel's plate was a golden cup studded by a single carnelian, and a pair of iridescent blue-green goblets for himself and Sioned had been etched with their new design and footed in dragon gold. He lifted his to her in silent tribute, and she smiled. But then she touched the small, empty golden cup between them, that matched those given to all the other princes. He knew her meaning; they were not Rohan and Sioned tonight, but the Dragon Prince and his Sunrunner princess.

With Lord Farid of Skybowl gone, Rohan's *athr'im* had chosen Baisal as their spokesman. Obedient to a signal from Ostvel when the last dishes had been taken away, Baisal got to his feet and waited for quiet. His joyous grin over the prospect of his fine new stone keep had not faded since midwinter, and probably would not disappear until he was dead and burned—and perhaps not even then. Davvi had informed Rohan privately that if payment for the stone was even mentioned, he would cheerfully break his beloved sister's beloved husband's neck. Baisal had performed a great service to Syr as well as to the Desert, and Davvi intended to reward him.

Voice rumbling from deep in a chest the size of a winecask, Baisal called for silence and beamed at everyone. "Your highnesses, my lords and ladies, knights, squires, and all here assembled!" he thundered. "Raise your cups and drink with me to the glorious peace won at Dragonfield!"

"Dragonfield!" some yelled, and Rohan's people turned it into "Dragon Prince!" He caught Sioned's amused glance as he had the bad manners to drink to himself, and chuckled.

"Through the past days we have all had the honor of private consultation with Prince Rohan, and he has listened to our hopes and plans for the future. This is his custom," he added blithely, and Rohan bit back a smile at this description of a technique used only once and that had made his vassals very nervous before his first *Rialla* as their prince. "We have also had the honor of speaking with Prince Lleyn, and this afternoon treaties were signed that define the borders of each princedom and holding for all eternity!" He raised his cup again, flushed with his own eloquence and Davvi's best Syrene wine. "To the wisdom of Prince Rohan, and the peace that will live forever!"

As the toast was drunk, Sioned whispered. "We'd better shut him up before he starts leading everyone in singing that fool ballad."

"Oh, I don't know, I'm rather enjoying this," he teased, and grinned as she made a discreet face at him. "Oh, very well. Two toasts are enough, I agree, for modesty's sake."

"Modest? You?"

Saumer of Isel solved the problem of silencing Baisal's oratory. "Your pardon, my lord, but we have yet to understand the exact nature of this peace!"

"Watch out," Chay whispered.

"He couldn't have given me a better opening if I'd told him what to say," Rohan answered softly, then stood up. "My thanks, Lord Baisal, for your tribute to the peace we all desire so much." As Baisal sat down, smug with the compliment from his prince, Rohan addressed Saumer. "Your grace is wise to seek clarification. With the permission of this gathering, I will answer our cousin of Isel's doubts."

"In your element, you damned show-off," Tobin muttered at her brother's elbow, and he kicked the leg of her chair.

He then spoke the name of each prince, who rose in his turn. Taking the small golden cup into his hand, he gestured for the princes to do likewise. When they had done so, he waited while servants poured thin, sweet Syrene wine. "All princes here present are confirmed in their possessions as stipulated in the treaties signed here today and witnessed by Lady Andrade." Their graces drank to their own lands and titles. "All *athr'im* are also confirmed," Rohan added.

Lyell of Waes stared at the high table with his eyes popping half out of his head. Clutha nudged him and he glanced up to find a stern gaze promising unthinkable consequences if he so much as set a foot wrong in future. Kiele sank back into her chair, faint with relief.

"There are several additions to the lists of *athr'im* and I am pleased to name them to you tonight." He heard Sioned give a satisfied sigh. "We present to you first of all Lord Walvis of Remagev."

It was some moments before the young man understood. Feylin leaned across her own table and hissed at him, "Stand up and bow to your prince who honors you so!" This brought a burst of laughter from the Hall and a flush to Walvis' cheeks. He shot a furious glance at the girl and took the long walk up to the high table, head high and knees shaking only a little.

When he had made his bow, Rohan murmured for his ears alone, "Hadaan insisted we give you Remagev to-night in front of everyone. He has a condition, though— that you let him stay on at the keep to spoil your children and flirt with your wife."

Walvis looked involuntarily over his shoulder, but not at Hadaan, who was grinning as proudly as if Walvis was his own son. Sioned quivered with silent laughter and whispered, "What did I tell you? A redhead!"

Crimson to his earlobes, Walvis stared at them and gulped. "I—my lord, my lady, it's too great an honor."

"Oh, nonsense," Sioned told him. As Rohan slipped a ring onto his finger, she continued, "Topaz for a long and happy life, dear Walvis. We love you even more than you love us, and in further token of that love—" She slowly drew a string of shimmering iridescence from a pocket of her green gown, a teasing smile on her face and mischief in her eyes. She was so lovely that Rohan wanted to kiss her in front of the whole Hall.

"My lady!" Walvis gasped as the rivulet of glowing silver-gray pearls trickled into his palm.

"Suitable for a wedding necklet, I'd say," Tobin contributed, and Chay aided and abetted by drawling, "Don't fuss the boy, Tobin. He's got the idea."

Walvis' wide blue eyes went helplessly from his prince to his princess. Sioned winked at him. "One day, Walvis, you must tell me *exactly* what happened at Tiglath. You may bow to us now, my lord," she prompted. He did so and started back to his seat in a daze. Ostvel rose and escorted him to a place made amid Rohan's other vassals. He sat with the pearls in both hands, stunned.

Rohan cleared his throat. "We present to you next Lord Tilal of River Run. Prince Davvi, the honor of confirming your son in his holding is yours."

This elevation was no surprise to any of those directly

involved. Tilal left the squires' table and went to where his parents sat with his older brother Kostas. A ring was given and Tilal bowed to his father before turning to bow again in the direction of the high table. Wisla, already dizzy with delight at five days of being addressed as her grace of Syr by other princes, burst into happy tears. Kostas, eighteen winters old and a prince now himself, grinned at his little brother and made room for him at the table. A servant brought a chair for the new Lord of River Run, who hardly dared breathe.

"Goddess, how I *love* being a prince!" Rohan whispered to Sioned, smiling down at her. She was alight with an even greater excitement now, for next would come the best of the night's surprises, known only to the two of them.

"We present to you now," he called out, "Lord Ostvel of Skybowl."

He froze at the far end of the high table, unable to move or speak. Chay pushed him up with a hand beneath his elbow and he managed to put one foot in front of the other until he stood facing Rohan and Sioned, his back to the assembly. His face was ashen and so bewildered that Rohan worried about his ability to stay upright.

From far down the Great Hall a small voice cried out, "Is Papa in trouble, prince?"

"Not in the least!" Rohan called back above the laughter. "You come up here too, Riyan."

The boy raced up and clung to his father's hand. Ostvel looked down at him, this irrepressible little boy with Camigwen's wonderful dark eyes. When he faced Rohan again, his own eyes shone with tears.

"You trust me with the caves?" he murmured.

Sioned answered for them. "We trust you with our lives."

"Forgiven?" he asked quietly.

Rohan did not understand the look that passed between them. Sioned bit her lip, then nodded solemnly. "If *I* am."

Ostvel bowed his head. "*She* would have understood much sooner than I did, Sioned. If you're determined to give this honor, do it for her, not me."

"For you both," she replied.

Rohan slipped onto Ostvel's finger a ring set with a topaz so dark a golden-brown that it was nearly the color of Riyan's eyes. To the child he said, "Your papa is a great lord now."

Riyan looked excited, then suddenly forlorn. "Does that mean I have to be good *all* the time? No more playing dragons?"

"Oh, *lots* of playing dragons," Rohan assured him. "You'll have to teach Pol how, you know." He reflected that there would be real dragons aplenty in the years ahead, seeking the caves around Skybowl now that they had forsaken Rivenrock for good. He envied Riyan the chance to see them so often.

The boy nodded his relief. "That's all right, then. And I'll be good, prince. I promise."

Father and son went to the end of the high table, Riyan snuggling comfortably onto Ostvel's lap. Rohan sought out the other fine young lords who would teach Pol: Maarken, Sorin, Andry, Tilal, who would be his friends and support in the future. Eltanin's boy Tallain would be another, and the children Walvis would have with Feylin—who loved dragons. He smiled, wondering if Sioned's other prediction would be right, too, and they would name a daughter after her.

Just as Rohan had arranged to have happen at this juncture, a loud, powerful voice boomed into the Great Hall. "Cousin," called out Prince Volog of Kierst, "I ask the indulgence of this assembly on a private matter."

"You have our attention, cousin," Rohan agreed affably.

Volog grinned, unable to contain his glee. But his voice turned to silk and Saumer's head jerked around, his eyes slits of suspicion. "My esteemed cousin of Isel and I have more in common than our island. We each have several charming daughters—and we each have an unmarried heir."

"Yes? That's intriguing," Rohan commented blandly, and barely kept a straight face as Andrade gave a complex snort. "Go on, cousin."

Volog turned to Saumer. "Need I say more?" he asked sweetly.

Saumer turned scarlet and tried not to choke. The audience tittered, appreciating that the price Saumer would pay for retaining his princedom after his support of Roelstra would be its eventual union with Kierst. His grace of Isel glared briefly at his grinning rival of Kierst, then swallowed and said, "How perceptive of you, my lord. and how elegant a suggestion it is."

Rohan smiled with benign good humor. "We are all certain that by the next *Rialla*, your island will be united in true affection and harmony." His eyes told Saumer it had better be. It was an excellent bargain, after all; they had managed to work together during and after the Plague, and with a little effort, the union of at least one pair of children would submerge the age-old enmity between the princedoms in the interests of family harmony. He felt a little guilty about dictating the lives of the young people involved. After all, he had not much liked the idea of being married off to some girl chosen by his parents. Looking down at the wife chosen for him by Andrade, he gave a rueful inner laugh. Leave it be, he decided; there was a good chance that duty would coincide with real affection, both heirs being pleasant young men and most of the daughters being as charming as Volog had asserted. The *faradhi* power ran in Kierstian royalty, too; Sioned's grandmother was Volog's grandmother as well, and it was possible that even if none of his offspring was fully gifted, a little of the magic would be there. The possibility of another prince with Sunrunner skills like Pol's troubled Rohan a little. But that, too, was for the future, when they would puzzle out just what kind of new prince Andrade's scheming had created.

Thought of his son brought Rohan back to the last and most serious shock of the evening. In pleasing himself through the elevations of Walvis, Ostvel, and Tilal, he had formed a future for Pol; in the maneuver with Saumer and Volog he had done the same while amusing his fellow princes mightily, if their dancing eyes were any indication. Now would come the final announcement. He glanced furtively at Andrade, who leaned back in her chair with every evidence of delight at the entertainment he had provided her. She read nothing in his eyes—but

Sioned did, and rose to stand beside him, taking his hand in hers. The breach of etiquette—a princess standing when only princes were allowed to do so—silenced the Hall.

"There is yet one land lacking a prince," Rohan said softly, a deceptively casual observation that no one had dared make out loud in the last five days, at least not in his hearing. "No male heir of the late High Prince's body lives. His daughters have renounced all claims for themselves and their children. We were the victor in the war waged by Roelstra in violation of the law, a victory gained with the invaluable assistance of their graces of Syr and Dorval." He paused and swept his gaze around the room, as if noting all those who had failed to give active support. "And by the rights of this victory in war we lay claim to Princemarch, all its lands, holdings, titles, trade, and wealth. We make this claim not for ourselves,, but for our beloved son, Prince Pol. Will your graces freely accept him?"

They could not do otherwise, but Rohan was a little startled by the volume of their assent. They must fear him more than he'd realized, or perhaps they were beginning to believe what Chay and Tobin and Lleyn and Davvi had been telling them for five days: Rohan was their only hope.

"We thank your graces," he said. Sioned's fingers tensed in his own, for she knew what was coming. His next move was her suggestion; Chay, Tobin, and Ostvel had been horrified at first, but had reluctantly come ·to see the wisdom of it. The cowed vassals of Princemarch could not be governed the way Rohan governed the Desert—yet. Pol was only a baby. And there was no one else who would guard his second princedom so well.

"It will be many years before our son is old enough to assume the full responsibilities of his position. Thus we have decided to appoint a regent to govern Princemarch until he comes of age."

Some of them looked at Chay; others at Maarken, young as he was. Rohan marveled that they could be so blind—even Andrade, who was sitting forward now so he could see her bright hair from the corner of his eye. Not even she looked to his real choice, who sat unnoticed, hands folded, waiting in silence.

"We name as Regent of Princemarch Her Royal Highness the Princess Pandsala, *faradhi* of three earned rings."

Pandemonium.

She rose in the midst of it and walked gracefully to the high table. Her sisters were limp with shock—except for Kiele, who was white with fury, and Chiana, who jumped up and fled the Hall.

The commotion died down. Pandsala stood before Rohan, calm and slender in a plain brown silk dress. Sioned gave her a ring set with a Desert topaz and an amethyst taken from Roelstra's sword; the ring Pol would wear one day as prince of both lands. Rohan took her clasped palms between his own, and Sioned placed her fingers atop theirs.

Pandsala looked up at them with a small, wry smile, murmuring, "I got Andrade out of Goddess Keep, spied on my father and warned you of his plans, misdirected his forces, and supported you on the starlight. I risked everything. And yet we all know you don't really trust me."

"We understand you, Pandsala," Sioned replied just as softly, and Rohan thought, *We understand your hatred for your father and sister. And you will never know about Pol. Never.* "I've touched your colors. You are *faradhi*."

"And that will do in place of trust?" Andrade hissed furiously.

"It will have to, won't it, my Lady?" Pandsala met her gaze levelly. Then, loud enough to be heard through the Hall, "By my mother Princess Lallante's Sunrunner blood, by my *faradhi* rings, by my faith and with my life, I pledge to guard and sustain Princemarch in safety and plenty until such time as Prince Pol claims it for his own."

Andrade's voice lashed out this time, cold and menacing as unsheathed steel. "By the rings I gave you, if you prove false to this trust I'll see you shadow-lost by my own arts as Lady of Goddess Keep!"

"She is our choice, Lady Andrade," Rohan warned.

For her ears alone he added, "Make your peace with
that, if not with her."

"Remember," was her only reply, delivered to Pandsala
in a threatening growl.

The princess went to the far end of the high table, next
to the horrified Urival. A servant came with a chair and
the last of the princely gold cups. Wine was poured again
in dead silence.

It was Lleyn who raised his cup and, in a tone that
fairly ordered the appropriate accolade, called out, "The
Princess-Regent Pandsala!"

Voices rose in affirmation and wine was drunk. It was
done.

Rohan took the small goblet from Sioned, who had
drained the last of it after he had sipped first, and set it
on the table. He noted that his hand shook just slightly,
and became aware of a sudden exhaustion. He wanted
nothing more than to order everyone out of his castle so
he could go to his chambers with his wife and son and not
emerge for days if he felt like it. But there remained one
last thing, and he resisted the impulse to compel Andrade
with a sharp command.

She finally rose and left the high table for the center of
the Great Hall. Urival followed, then Rohan and Sioned,
handfast. He sensed the strength of her Fire flow through
him, lending endurance enough to make it through this
ritual that would be performed by the woman who had
put him here, and who now stared at him with cold,
unforgiving eyes for what he had done.

Everyone was standing now, tense with expectation.
The Lady raised her arms, sleeves falling back from rings
and bracelets that sparked with silver and gold and gems.
Urival was at her side, holding a plain golden bowl filled
with water. Rohan and Sioned, facing her with their
backs to the wall of windows, where the moonlight shone
through pale and calm.

"Will you have them as High Prince and High Princess?" Andrade asked.

One by one, the princes and lords gave affirmation.
Rohan heard reluctance in some voices and kept himself
from a bitter shrug. Not even the sincere joy and even

relief in most of the responses could soothe the ache as
he met Andrade's gaze. *You wanted me here. They haven't
any choice, and perhaps it's better so. There's a son to
come after me, prince and Sunrunner both, just as you
planned. But though I understand, I will never forgive the
pain. Never.*

His fingers clenched convulsively around his wife's hand
and he glanced at her proud, quiet profile, saw the cres-
cent scar of Fire on her cheek. She refused to cover it
with makeup and wore it instead as a brand of honor—
and penance. The mark would always be there, just as he
would always move his right shoulder stiffly and Tobin
would always have a slight limp—and Andrade would
have to live with the fact of Pandsala as regent in
Princemarch.

And Rohan would have to live with power.

Andrade took the bowl made of dragon gold and held
it high, braced only by her fingertips—talons holding a
huge jewel. The bowl trembled and glowed. A breeze
through the open windows snuffed out most of the three
hundred lamps and rippled the dragon tapestry behind
the high table.

"By the Earth that cradles us and of which this bowl is
made; by the Water herein that gives us life; by the Fire
that lights our paths; by the Air that is our breath." She
held the bowl over the two bent heads. "In the name of
all who live in these lands, I charge this man and this
woman. Use your gifts for rightness. Abide by the law.
Strive for wisdom. Search your souls for truth. Humble
yourselves in the moments of greatest glory. Make no
battles for personal gain. Protect the lands and all who
live on them. Cherish them as you do each other. Will
you do these things?"

"We will," they answered.

She held out the bowl to Rohan, who drank and passed
it to Sioned. She sipped, keeping it in her hands as
Andrade spoke again.

"High Prince and High Princess, by the Goddess and
the Father of Storms I proclaim them."

The Lady held out her hands for the bowl, but violation of the ritual was something prince and princess had

agreed on. Sioned placed the bowl on the blue and green tiles. There was yet a little Water in it, a breath of Air swirling, a touch of Sunrunner's Fire dancing along its rim. Rohan saw Andrade's fleeting scowl before he turned to watch his princess extend her hands over the bowl. Sioned's emerald, the only ring she would ever again wear, spat green flames in the dimness; the cascade of her fire-gold hair shone.

The bowl caught Fire.

Rohan spoke into the stillness. "This is the first of the new laws. No one shall kill a dragon. Not for sport, for cruelty, for loss of property, not for any reason shall anyone kill a dragon. Whosoever breaks this law shall forfeit half his wealth in retribution for his attack against us, for we shall consider the killing of a dragon as a sword raised against ourselves."

He knew they were shocked and did not care. The wealth this law insured would be used on their behalf. If they never understood, so be it.

As he spoke, the vessel of dragon gold seethed. Flames rose in a powerful conjure and the air shimmered with vision. From the writhing orange and yellow and silver there coalesced a dragon nearly as tall as the rafters. Wings tipped in flame, talons trailing fire, eyes burning blue and green and blue again, the dragon's head lashed up toward the ceiling. The fiery apparition beat incandescent wings and leaped up, surged through the air and vanished into the tapestry. It melted into the stylized crowned dragon holding a *faradhi* ring set with an emerald.

Rohan never knew who began the chant—one of his own people, perhaps. But the cavern-dark Great Hall shuddered to the sound of it.

Azhei. Dragon Prince.

Sioned eased herself back onto soft pillows, the laces of her bedgown undone, smiling as Rohan placed their son to her breast. He sat beside them and stroked the baby's blond hair with one finger.

"Andrade won't soon recover from the way you upset her ceremony," he observed mildly.

"It was *our* ceremony, not hers. She didn't win us a princedom or gain us a son."

He shared her lingering resentment. "I don't see that she has anything to be unhappy about. We're making her new manner of prince, after all."

"Rohan. . . ." She hesitated, and he encouraged her with a caress to her shoulder. "If I'd been the one to carry Pol and give birth to him, then in a way he would have been Andrade's, too. But this way, he's ours. Do you understand? The things we did—they were for us, not to make a *faradhi* prince for her."

He nodded, because for Sioned it was true. But it was also true that they had done it for the future Pol would make, the new manner of prince he would become.

The things they had done. . . . Rohan had killed in battle, where every barbarian worthy of his sword was supposed to do his killing. Irony of ironies, he had even had the law on his side, law he had always wanted to use to create peace. As an excuse, it was convenient and tidy—but it did not justify the heated joy he'd taken in his bloodied sword, in burying his knife to the hilt in Roelstra's throat.

He had raped, too—but all good savages did that. Trapped into it, drugged, seduced? Perhaps the first time, but not the second. He wanted to believe that Ianthe had conceived Pol that first time, when he had thought she was Sioned. He wished he could believe that. But the fact that he did not was no excuse for allowing Sioned to claim the child for him. Circumstances had been against him—the war that dragged on, Ianthe's early delivery—but there was no excusing himself for not killing her when he'd had the chance. He should have, but he had not. Every barbarian prince desired a son who would rule after him.

He had used the power won by his sword to make himself High Prince and take what had been Roelstra's, establish his own people in positions of power, impose his will—all of it legal, all of it agreed to by the other princes. Was his excuse that he was more fit to rule than Roelstra had been? What right had he to do what he'd done, what he'd allowed Sioned to do, what Chay and

Tobin and Ostvel and Walvis and all the rest had done on his behalf?

During his early youth he had struggled to learn all that was good in the world, all that he would use to make life better, more peaceful and civilized. He had wanted a life rich in dreams and the striving toward those dreams, not replete with death, deceit, and divisiveness. He had chosen to learn what he considered to be good, and had turned his face from the foul—not only in the world around him, but in his own soul. He had told himself that once he was prince, the things of the past that had made men war on each other would be swept away by his own dedication to honorable law.

But this year of war and anguish had taught him that the past lived inside him—all the impulses toward killing rage and rape that had governed his world for so long. They were all within him, all the acts that marked him as a barbarian, all the things said and done that made his soul writhe with shame. He knew what he was, and admitted it.

Rohan had looked into his own heart and seen Roelstra's gleeful manipulation of one prince against another; he had seen Ianthe's scheming need for power; he had seen his father Zehava's warrior instincts victorious, the urges that had slain dragons even when he had known full well their importance to the Desert.

But had Rohan truly seen the worst of himself? Probably not—for all those things were nothing compared to what power could make of him.

Only Sioned knew how deeply he despised the princes and lords who had so cravenly handed such power to him, the ones who had bowed to him the way they had bowed to Roelstra without ever seeing the truth of power itself. Only Lleyn, Davvi, Chay, those who knew Rohan as a man, understood a little of what being High Prince would mean to him. He would use it to create new laws that, please the Goddess, would feel like old laws by the time he died. Chay had told him that he was their only chance; Rohan knew that his was the only risk. It was his heart that power might twist, his dreams it might warp.

Yet he would not have given up knowledge of what he

was. He had seen himself, recognized all the things he had feared as the enemies of the life he wanted to make—and he was no longer afraid of them. The only thing he feared was power. Taking it into his hands, making sure all accepted his authority, still he knew that it could become an enemy even more deadly than the barbarian within him. Yet for his son he would dare it, knowing that as both prince and Sunrunner, Pol's struggle with power would be even more fearsome.

Rohan watched his wife and son for a long time in silence, wondering how the boy had so quickly won him. There had been bad times after his return to Stronghold, times when he had deliberately hurt Sioned, seeking to ease his own pain and guilt by causing deeper pain in her; times when she had lashed out at him for the same reason. But always there was the child, and in many ways it was through him that they had found their way back to each other. Pol had a way of fastening his wide blue-green eyes on his father that seemed to see into his soul. Rohan had not wanted to acknowledge this son who was not of Sioned's blood or bearing, but Pol had been the one to claim *him* with those eyes. It was love for their child that linked Rohan and Sioned those first difficult days after his return—love that had reawakened the Fire between them.

Rohan stroked his son's downy head, smiling as the child wriggled contentedly to Sioned's breast. She might believe that what they had done had been for themselves, but Rohan knew it had been for Pol. He had forgotten for a long time something he had always known, something Roelstra's taunts in the circle of starfire had caused to rise up within him once more. He supposed Sioned's barrenness had made him forget on purpose; he had not dared think too much about children when there was so little hope. But, driven to his knees beneath that dome of silvery light, he had known again that all he dreamed and planned and did was for his child. Pol, innocent of the past, would have the best future he and Sioned could give. A life meant little if the world it had had the power to fashion was no better than the one it had been born into.

"I think our hatchling is finished for the moment," Sioned murmured. "Would you like to hold him?"

Rohan accepted Pol into his arms. Sleepy eyes blinked up at him and the child gave an inelegant burp. Rohan grinned. "He doesn't seem too impressed by the honor."

Sioned chuckled and tied up the laces of her bedgown. "You get quite enough bowing and praise from everyone else. The last place you'll find such things is in your own family."

"Would you believe me if I told you that's a relief?"

"Of course—and I can hardly wait to see the back of all these highborns so we can be just ourselves again."

"They'll be gone soon. But it can't be the way it was before, Sioned," he warned gently.

"I know. Too much has changed—especially us." She smoothed the hair from his forehead, where the silver circlet had left marks. "I understand what's happened, but understanding isn't the same as forgiving."

"I can't say I care whether Andrade forgives us or not."

"Nor I," Sioned admitted. "I love you, and that's stronger than any *faradhi* vow I ever made. It frightened me at first. It still does. But I think the one who'll have to do the forgiving is Pol."

They put the child to bed in the next room where his nurse waited in the soft lamplight. The carved wooden cradle had been a gift from Chay and Tobin at the New Year. Pale green silk was draped over half the cradle, gathered above the baby's head in the jaws of a benevolent ruby-eyed dragon whose carved wings spread out on either side to guard him. Rohan and Sioned stayed long enough to make sure Pol was asleep, then returned to their own chamber.

She sat down on the bed to brush out her hair. Rohan lay at her side to watch. Candlelight was soft on the graceful lines of her shoulders and arms, shone golden in her red hair. He was beginning to get used to the single emerald on her hand. Though Andrade had offered to replace the other rings, Sioned had refused. This had been a major point of contention between them, signifying as it did that Sioned, while a Sunrunner, was no longer to be ruled by those at Goddess Keep.

"Lleyn told me something the other day," Rohan mused. "Andrade may have thought she was mating the powers of a prince to those of a *faradhi*—but he said that what she really did was join those powers in love. I think that makes us dangerous people, Sioned."

"More dangerous than Roelstra and Ianthe?"

"Much. They found their power in hate. What if they'd won? There'd be nothing left for them to take their vengeance on. But for us, love—there's nothing we can't do, and nothing Pol won't be able to do. And that makes us very dangerous indeed."

"No wonder Andrade's not speaking to me," she said lightly. Then, setting the brush aside, she smiled and went on, "Now that you mention it, there *is* someone who'd give full appreciation to being held by the High Prince—dangerous or not. And with the hatchling asleep, there's a Fire to be rekindled here."

"My lady, it never went out—and it never will."